WITHDRAWN

A
WEST
QUARTET

A WEST QUARTET

*Four Novels of
Intrigue and High Adventure*
by
MORRIS WEST

The Naked Country

Gallows on the Sand

The Concubine

Kundu

WILLIAM MORROW AND COMPANY, INC.
New York   1981

Library of Congress Cataloging in Publication Data

West, Morris L., 1916-
  A West quartet.

  Contents: The naked country—Gallows on the
sand—The concubine—Kundu.
  1. Adventure stories, Australian.
PR9619.3.W4A15   1981   823   81-4871
ISBN 0-688-00637-X   AACR2

Printed in the United States of America

First Edition
1 2 3 4 5 6 7 8 9 10

BOOK DESIGN BY MICHAEL MAUCERI

About the Novels

The Naked Country was based on my own experiences in the Northern Territory of Australia, where I made more than one trek with the aboriginal tribes and learned a little of their age-old lore of survival in a harsh land.

Gallows on the Sand was the result of my first visit to the islands of the Great Barrier Reef, the onetime haunt of black-birders and pirates and—so say the legends—of castaways from the Spanish fleet that plied between the Philippines and South America.

As for McCreary, the hero of *The Concubine*, I still have a great fondness for the fellow. Long before I became a novelist, this pawky Irishman was a character on radio and later on television, and he kept us eating for quite a long time.

Kundu had its roots in the upland jungles of New Guinea where Australians and Americans had fought side by side during the Pacific war. The magical elements in the story came from an old French missionary who had spent many years in the uplands and who firmly believed in the cassowary-man who could be in two places at once and the tribal magician who killed by serpent bite.

—MORRIS WEST

Contents

THE
NAKED COUNTRY

Chapter One

HE HAD BEEN RIDING SINCE DAWN, away from the homestead, eastward towards the climbing sun. The river was at his left, a torpid snake, sliding noiselessly through the swamps and the lily ponds and the floodplains green with the flush of wild rice. On his right was the fringe of paperbark forest and, ahead, the gaunt heave of the escarpments, which were the beginning of the Stone Country.

He sat loose in the saddle, long in the stirrup, head bent forward against the glare, his rangy body rolling to the ambling gait of the pony. Dust rose about him in small, grey eddies. Heat beat down on him from a steel-blue sky, parching his lips, searing his eyes, bleaching the moisture out of his brown, leathery skin; but he rode on, tireless and patient, towards the red ridges where the spinifex grew out of the stones and the woolly butts thrust their roots into cracks and crannies of the sandstone.

His name was Lance Dillon, and he held title, along with a pastoral mortgage company, to Minardoo, newest and smallest station on the southern fringe of Arnhem Land. He was thirty-seven years of age, which is late enough for a man to come into the cattle business and set himself in competition with the big syndicates and the old families who are the kings of the Australian Northwest.

Twenty miles behind him the aboriginal stock boys were fanning out, north, south and west, to begin the muster, which is the yearly prelude to the long trek to the railhead. They would brand the new stock, cull out the scrub bulls, stringy cross-blooded sires who might taint the breeds—then begin herding back towards the homestead. Lance Dillon was the boss-man, staff-general of this wide-flung operation, but today he was riding away from it, intent on a private business of his own.

To the newcomer the cattle country promised little but debt and disillusion. The syndicates held most of the land, and the best of it. They had easiest access to port and railhead. They kept priorities over trucking and shipping space. They had first call on experience and manpower, and above all, they had capital—money for pasture improvement, water conservation, transport, slaughter yards and freezing plants. They could kill their own beef, chill it and fly it straight to the holds of waiting ships, while the small man must drive his steers a hundred and fifty miles and watch his profits decrease with every pound they lost on the trek.

It was a gambler's business and the winnings went to the man who could sit longest on his cards. Lance Dillon knew it as well as the next, yet he had spent his last shilling and mortgaged himself to the neck to buy into the game. He had reasoned long and logically that the only answer for the small man was better bloodlines: stock bred to the climate with its monsoon summer and its parching dry season, resistant to ticks and parasites, growing meat instead of sinew, and hardy enough to hold their poundage on the gruelling drive to the railhead yards.

And this was the reason for his ride to the ridge on the edge of the Stone Country. Behind the first escarpment was a valley, a landlocked basin, watered by a spring that gurgled up perennially from some underground source. There were shade trees and sweet grass, where a new and noble sire could breed his wives in comfort, free from the raids of scrub bulls and dingoes, untouched by the parasites that bred in the swamp pastures by the river. Behind the red-brick wall were three thousand pounds' worth of blood bull and fifty first-class cows ready to calve. If his judgment had been right, it was the first smell of success, and he could soon spit in the eye of the financiers who kept him close to strangling point when all he needed was two years without their thumbs on his throat.

He reined in the pony, dismounted and unhooked the canvas water bag from his saddle. He took off his hat, half filled it with water and held it under the animal's muzzle until the last drop was gone. Afterwards he held the bag to his own lips, threw back his head and took a long, grateful swallow. . . .

It was then that he saw the smoke, a thin high-rising column, over the saddle of the hill. He cursed quietly, jammed the stopper back into the water bag, hoisted himself into the saddle and set off at a smart canter.

The smoke had only one meaning: the myalls were in the valley, and he wanted them out of it as quickly as possible.

There was nothing singular or sinister in this presence of tribal aborigines on homestead property. All this land was blackfellow country and the myalls—the tribal nomads who lived resolutely apart from the white settlements—had ranged it for centuries. They were the most primitive people in the world, who had never built a house or made a wheel, or learned the use of clothing. Their weapons were spears and clubs and boomerangs and imple-

14

ments of stone. They slept on the ground, naked as Adam. They ate kangaroo and buffalo and reptiles and grubs and yams and lily roots and honey plundered from the wild bees. They ranged free as animals within their tribal areas, and the only signs of their passing were the ashes of their campfires or a windbreak of branches, or a body wrapped in bark and perched in the fork of a tree. Sometimes, if game were scarce, they might kill a steer or a scrub bull from the white man's herds, but this was a convention of existence with no hostility on either side.

Lance Dillon understood the primitive rights of the nomads and respected them; but the valley was his own domain, and he wanted it private to himself. His word had gone out to the tribal elders and, until this moment, they had respected it. The smoke, rising above the ridges, was a kind of defiance which puzzled him. More, it was a symbol of danger. A campfire might grow to a grass fire which would destroy his pasture in a night. The myalls saw no difference between bloodstock and bush buffalo, and this herd was for breeding—not for blackfellow meat.

The thought was painful to him, and he urged the pony into a lathering gallop which brought him swiftly to the foot of the sandstone escarpment where a narrow gorge marked the entrance to the valley.

Dillon's face clouded when he saw that the log barrier had been torn down and the thornbush palisade pushed to one side. Thoughtfully, he walked the pony past the logs and brushwood and inward towards the basin, where the gorge opened out into a small, grassy knoll, twenty feet above the valley floor. When he reached it, he reined in and looked across the green amphitheater, gape-mouthed with shock and fury.

There was a hunting party of eight or ten myalls, husky, naked bucks, armed with spears and clubs and throwing-sticks. Three of them had worked the cows and the calves away from the bull and into a blind corner of the valley. The others were circling the bull, who, well fed and satiated, was watching them with hostile eyes. Before Dillon had time to open his mouth, there were three spears in the great animal, and two men with clubs were battering at his hindquarters to bring him down.

For one suspended moment Dillon sat, paralyzed by the sight of the senseless slaughter. Then, with a wild howl of anger, he clapped spurs into the pony and went racing down the incline, towards the myalls. As he galloped, he wrenched the stockwhip from his saddle and whirled its long lash, trying to cut them down. They scattered at his approach, and his momentum carried him through and beyond them, while the dying bull bellowed and tried to raise itself on its forelegs. Dillon wheeled sharply and charged again, flailing at them with his whip, but before he had gone twenty yards a spear caught him in the right shoulder, so that he dropped the whip and almost toppled from the saddle. Another flew over his head, a third carried away his hat, and the three bucks came running in as reinforcements, so that he knew they would kill him if he stayed.

Gasping with pain, he wrenched the pony's head round and galloped him

15

back towards the defile, with the bellows of the dying bull in his ears and the spear haft dangling from the bloody wound in his left shoulder.

The myalls followed him, running, right to the mouth of the defile, then they turned back to the slaughter of the great bull for which Dillon had paid three thousand pounds.

For the first wild minutes of his flight Dillon was incapable of coherent thought. Anger, pain, and a blind animal urge to self-preservation, drove him headlong through the gorge and out towards the shelter of the paperbark trees. He was a mile away from the valley before he slackened rein and let the jaded pony's head droop, while he slumped wearily in the saddle and tried to take command of himself.

The wound in his shoulder forced itself first on his attention. It was deep and painful, and bleeding profusely. The barbed spear had torn through the shoulder muscles and the drag of the hanging haft was an intolerable agony. He could not hope to ride twenty miles like this under a noon sun. Yet to rid himself of the spear would call for a surgery more brutal than the wound itself. It could not be pulled out—the barbs would lacerate muscle and sinew. The haft must be broken off and the head forced clean through his body until it could be drawn out in front. The mere contemplation of the operation made him dizzy and sick. He closed his eyes and bent his head almost to the saddle pommel, until the faintness passed.

His thoughts leapt back to the valley and anger seemed to pump new strength into his body. The slaughter of the bull made a monstrous mockery of all his hopes and plans. He was finished, cleaned out, ready for the bailiffs . . . because a bunch of meat-hungry myalls wanted to show their maleness by cutting down the master of the herd.

Then a new thought struck him. They weren't meat-hungry at all. The grass flats were full of game, kangaroo and wallaby and stray steers. There were geese on the billabongs and fish in the river reaches. No need for the largest tribal unit to go hungry.

There was more, much more to the killing of the king beast and the attack on his own person. There was deliberate trespass—against the elders and against himself. He remembered that all the bucks had been young ones, sleek-skinned, fast on their feet, aggressive. The old ones understood the conventions of coexistence with the whites. They knew the power of the Northwest police—solitary, relentless men who would follow a man for months to exact the penalty of rebellion. Tribal killings were one thing, but violence against the white man was quite another, and the old men wanted no part in it.

The young ones thought differently. They resented the authority of the elders. They resented still more the presence of the strangers on their tribal preserves. The sap ran strongly under their dark skins, and they must prove to themselves and to their women that they were men who would one day rule in the councils of the tribe. They were not fools. When the first blood heat had subsided, they would see how far they had fallen under the displeasure of the

16

old ones, and how the vengeance of the white man would fall on the whole tribe. So they would become cunning and try to conceal their trespass.

Then, Dillon knew, they would try to kill him and hide his body, so that no one would know for certain how he had died.

Fear took hold of him again, a cramp in the belly, a cold constriction round his heart. Instinctively, he looked back towards the ridge, to see, silhouetted against the skyline, a solitary figure, trailing a bundle of throwing-spears in one hand, and with the other shading his eyes as he scanned the spreading plain below. Dillon urged the pony deeper into the shadows of the paperbarks and halted again to consider the situation.

Soon they would begin to follow him, tracking him like a bush animal by hoofpad and chipped stone and broken twig and the ants clustered over his blooddrops. They would circle between him and the homestead, cutting off his retreat, and if he tried to outdistance them they would find him the sooner, because a fresh bushman could last longer than a jaded horse and a rider wounded and rocking in the saddle.

The river was his one hope. It would break his tracks and water his pony and cleanse his wound. Its tropical shore growth would shelter him while he rested and, with luck and a care for his strength, he might work his way downstream back to the homestead. It was a slim chance; but the strength was draining out of him with the slow seep of blood under his shirt. Now, or never, he must make the move, heading southward in a wide arc so that the trees would shelter him as long as possible. The course would take him five miles farther upstream, but he dared not risk a break across open country to the nearer reaches.

He took a long drink from the water bag, tightened the reins in his left hand and, with the spear still jolting pitilessly in his back, set off through the grey trees towards the distant water.

Mundaru, the Anaburu man, squatted on a flat limestone ledge and watched the white man ride away. He could not see him, but his progress was plainly marked by the shift of a shadow among the tree boles, the rise of a flock of parrots, the panic leap of a grey wallaby out of the timberline. The progress was slow, and would get slower yet, but the direction of it was clear. He was heading towards the river.

Mundaru noted these things calmly, without rancour or jubilation, as he would have noted the movements of a kangaroo or a bush turkey. He calculated how long it would take his quarry to reach the water, and how long more it would take him to work his way downstream to the point where Mundaru planned to intercept and kill him. There was no malice in the equation. It was part of the mathematics of survival, like the slaying of the newborn in time of drought, like the killing of a woman who dared to look upon the dreamtime symbols that only a man must see. Dillon had been a little right and more than half wrong in his judgment of Mundaru and his associates. Their entry into the valley had not been a trespass but a ritual

17

return to an old and sacred place where the spirit people lived. An order to stay away from it was meaningless. It was a place to which they belonged—a question not of possession, but of identity. The ridges which Dillon saw simply as a pen for his stud were a honeycomb of caves whose walls were covered with totem drawings, the great snake, the kangaroo, the turtle, the crocodile and the giant buffalo, Anaburu, which was Mundaru's own totem, the source of his existence, the symbol of his personal and tribal relationship.

The slaughter of the bull was no wanton act, but an act of religious significance. In some tribes a man must refrain from killing or eating his totem animal. In Mundaru's tribe the people of the dreamtime had set a different pattern. The totem must be killed and eaten, for from this mystical merging flowed strength, virility and a promise of fertility. Mundaru had prepared himself for the moment by taking red and yellow ochre and charcoal and the blood of a kangaroo, and drawing his own buffalo figure on the wall of one of the caves. The intrusion of the white man was, therefore, a violent and dangerous interruption of a life-giving ritual, which must be avenged if Mundaru and his brothers of the buffalo totem were not to suffer in their own bodies.

Dillon had been right when he guessed at other motives—resentment of white intruders, fear of the elders and of the inexorable vengeance of the policeman. But these considerations were secondary and sophisticated, the pragmatic reasoning of men who lived in two times, with one foot in the twentieth century and the other in a tribal continuum of magic, sorcery and spirit symbols.

So Mundaru, the buffalo man, sat on his high rock in the sun and planned his pursuit and his killing.

First he would go down into the valley and eat the flesh of the big bull, which the others were now roasting over the fire. When he had eaten, he would sit down and have them paint his body with totemic patterns, in ochre and charcoal and the blood of the bull. The others would go with him to flush the quarry and cut off his lines of retreat. But, because Mundaru had drawn the picture in the cave, and Mundaru had thrown the first spear into the side of the great bull, Mundaru must be the one to kill him. When he was dead, they would hide the body in a spirit place, where the policeman would never find it.

To this point everything was simple and consequential for Mundaru, but beyond it there was doubt and a small darkness of fear.

By attacking the white man, he had taken the first step outside the tribe and into a pattern of existence he did not understand. He had killed before, in a tribal blood feud. But in this he had been directed and supported by the elders. They had taken him to a secret place and shown him the stone with the symbol of the victim on it. They had given him the feathered boots and the spear made potent by a special magic and sent him off on his mission. When he returned they had welcomed him with honour.

But this was a matter of totem and not of tribe. The elders would be divided. There would be no magic to help him, because Willinja, the sorcerer,

18

was a kangaroo man, and, moreover, he hated Mundaru, because he knew Mundaru coveted his latest wife. In the council he would speak against him, and if he swayed them, a magic might be made which was terrible to contemplate. But he was committed now and he could not turn back. The spear does not return to the hand of the thrower, or the blown seed to the pod. He could only drink the blood of the bull and trust to it for strength and security.

Far away to the south he saw a white egret rise, flapping and screaming, and knew that the white man had left the trees and entered the high grass of the swamplands. He stood up and, carrying his spears and club, walked back to the campfire to eat the flesh of the bull.

Lance Dillon groped his way through darkness and a fiery, enveloping pain. His head was full of thunder and a high, cacophonous screaming. There was dust in his mouth and bonds around his chest, and his body was stuffed with sawdust like a doll's. He tried to move and brush aside the darkness, but the pain rose in a high wave and his limbs refused to obey him. He felt himself slipping down the long trough of the wave into blackness.

After a while he opened his eyes, a man waking from eternity into space and time. Above him was the dazzling blue of the sky, about him a forest of grass stalks filled with the scream of cicadas and the crepitant bustle of insects. The thunder in his head had subsided to a low, persistent throbbing, but the dust was still in his mouth and the pain was only an inch away, so that when he moved it stabbed through him like a knife blade. He lay still again, closing his eyes and trying to remember.

He had cleared the timber and the pony was thrusting carefully through the six-foot grasses towards the river flats. Suddenly, scared by a snake or a flying-stick insect, it had reared and thrown him. He recalled the high, parabolic fall, the sickening impact. After that, nothing. He opened his eyes again and saw the flattened grasses where he had fallen and the broken stalks where the animal had trampled through them.

Cautiously, he stretched one leg, then the other. The cramped muscles obeyed him, slowly. There was no pain; the bones were still unbroken. His left hand was outflung on the dusty grass. He watched it, curiously, from a long way off, trying to make it obey him. He saw the fingers flex, the wrist bend, the elbow flex and then the whole arm move slowly back, lift itself and lie across his belly.

Encouraged by this small success, he set the hand groping again, upwards to the diaphragm, across the rib cage and towards the right shoulder. The fingers encountered a sticky mass of blood, the minute scurrying mass of ants, and then the serrated edge of the spearhead. He understood that the fall had snapped off the spear haft and driven the head out over his breast.

The small pressure of his fingers sent a sharp agony through him, and the disturbed ants pumped their poisons into his skin. He closed his eyes and lay back sweating until the pain subsided. Then he groped blindly among the grass roots until he felt the haft of the spear and drew it towards him.

19

Inch by painful inch, he rolled himself over on his stomach, worked himself up to his knees and, using the spear haft as a stave, tried to hoist himself to his feet. Twice he collapsed, gasping and retching, with his face among the grass roots, but the third time, he made it, and stood, dizzy but triumphant, steadying himself on the haft. After a while he raised his head and, leaning on the staff like an old, decrepit man, began to stumble through the high grasses towards the river.

By normal measurement it was no more than half a mile away, but it took him more than two hours to reach it. A dozen paces and he had to rest, head swimming and heart pumping, his body bathed in sweat, a slow blood seeping out round the spear blade in his shoulder. Each step must be measured, each foot planted firmly, before the other was moved. If he fell again, he might never get up. He was parched from loss of body fluids—blood and lymph and perspiration—and the first torments of thirst were beginning to nag him. The ants were still clustered on his skin, and from the low ground insects rose in clouds about his face, but he dared not let go the staff to brush them away.

When he reached the river, he saw that it was twenty feet below him, screened by a tangle of bushes and the long, tuberous roots of pandanus palms. He had to grope his way fifty yards upstream before he found a small, sandy slope that ran down clear to the beach. With infinite pain, he eased himself into a sitting position till his legs hung over the bank, then pushed himself off with the staff and slid down on the seat of his trousers to the water's edge.

He drank, greedily, lifting the water in his cupped hand and lapping it from the palm like a dog. When he felt a small strength seeping back to him, he worked his way out of his shirt, rinsed it in the stream and then tore it with his teeth and his left hand into strips and tampons, which he laid carefully on a rock shelf beside him. This done, he rested and drank a little more, trying to steel himself to the brutal surgery of extracting the spearhead.

It must be done swiftly or not at all, but his body was weak and his will reluctant to invite a new pain. Finally he came to it. Summoning all his strength, he closed his fingers round the barbed wood and wrenched it forward. To his surprise, it came free, with a small rush of blood and a pain that made him cry out. His impulse was to fling it from him, far into the water, but he checked it swiftly, remembering that he was a hunted man, with no weapon but the broken haft. He laid the jagged head on the rock beside him, and, using the strips of torn shirt, began to bathe and cleanse the wound. It was long, slow work, because the spear had entered high up in his back and every movement sent a leaping pain through the torn shoulder muscles. He thought of bathing himself in the river, but remembered in time that this was crocodile water and that the blood might bring them swimming, in search of him. Suddenly there was a new fear: blood poisoning. A native weapon must be crawling with infection. Sick and hunted, he was days away from medical attention—if, indeed, he would ever come to it.

He sat a long time, chewing on the bitter thought, until he remembered a thing out of a lost time. He had seen the homestead aborigines plastering cuts

with spider web, and someone had remarked that there was a relation between the glutinous web and penicillin. He looked around and saw, strung
between the roots of a pandanus, a big web with a huge black spider in the
center of it.

With the spear haft in his hand, he inched his way up the bank and struck
at the web. The spider swung away, hanging on a single filament; Dillon
wound the wrecked strands around the top of his staff and drew them towards
him. He rolled the sticky threads into a ball and packed them into the wound
with a tampon of shirt. Finally, after many failures, he succeeded in fixing a
bandage over his shoulder and under his right armpit and tightening it with a
tourniquet. It might hold long enough to stanch the bleeding and let the blood
congeal.

When it was all done, he felt weary and hungry and desperately alone. He
was faced with the simplest problem of all—survival—yet he had only the
sketchiest idea of how to solve it. First he must eat, to restore his ravaged
strength. If he wanted to sleep he must go, like an animal, to a safe earth. He
must pit his twentieth-century mind against the primitive strategy of the
nomad hunters. Elementary propositions all of them, until he came to apply
them.

Where did the fish run? What bait would attract them to a line? And failing
a line and bait, how did one catch them? How did one stalk game, while men
were stalking him? What plants were edible and what poisonous? Where to
hide from men who read signs in the dust and in the chipped bark of a tree
trunk?

As he sat, sick and light-headed with concussion, ruffling the water with his
hand, the nature of his dilemma became vividly clear. All this land belonged
to him, but he knew almost nothing about it. He was in it but not of it. Its
secrets were lost to him and he walked it as a stranger. All its influences
seemed malign, and he knew that he could starve amid its primal plenty.

So he tried desperately to reassemble the scraps and shards of knowledge he
had picked up from the aboriginal stock boys and the old bushmen who had
lived blackfellow-fashion for months on end in the outback country. There
were edible grubs in the tree boles, lily roots in the lagoons, yams and
groundnuts on the river flats. A man could make a meal of the screeching
cicadas, provided his civilized stomach did not revolt at the strangeness. The
flesh of a snake was white and sweet-tasting, but a lizard was oily and hard to
digest. The aborigine did not hunt at night. He was afraid of the spirit men
who haunted the rocks and the trees and every dip and hollow of the ancient
earth.

Dillon's vagrant mind caught and held this last scrap of memory. Here, at
last, was hope—a pointer to possible salvation. If he could gather a little food
and find himself a hole for the daytime hours, he might build enough strength
to move at night, while the myalls were huddled over their campfires. The
river could be his road, the darkness his friend. But time was running against
him. He must act quickly. Any moment now, the hunters might come: black,

21

naked men, with flat faces and knotted hair and tireless feet and killing spears wrapped in bundles of paperbark.

When Mundaru and his myalls came out of the valley, the first thing they saw was Dillon's horse, riderless and cropping contentedly in the wild rice that bordered the swamp.

Two of the bucks began moving towards it with spears at the ready, but Mundaru called them back. It was a good thing, he told them. The white man was wounded and now had been thrown. There was no need to split up. They would find him quickly and dispatch him. The horse would make his way back to the homestead, or be picked up by one of the stock boys. Its discovery would lend the colour of an accident to the white man's death.

They grinned, acknowledging his cleverness, and followed him as he walked in a wide arc until they found the point where the pony had emerged from the grass flats. It was a simple matter to backtrack his movements until they came to the tiny clearing where Dillon had lain after his fall.

Mundaru knelt to examine the signs. There was the bruised and flattened grass, the blood, congealed now and covered with crawling ants; but the size and spread of it showed how long the white man had lain there, and how badly hurt he must be. There was a splinter of wood from the broken spear, and a scrap of cotton from his shirt. Under the tangle of grass were deep heel prints in the earth and rounded hollows made by his knees as he struggled to his feet. As Mundaru pointed out all these things, the others nodded and talked in low voices.

He had stood here a long time. There he had begun to walk, leaning on a stick. The intervals between his prints were irregular, showing him weak and uncertain on his feet. As they followed them through the parted grasses, they saw where he had rested and where a drop of blood had spilt on the stalks and how deeply his staff had dug into a soft patch of ground. The track was as plain as that of a wounded animal, and they followed it swiftly to the sandy slide which led down to the water's edge.

Here they halted, momentarily puzzled, until Mundaru's quick eyes saw the broken spider web and the patch of sand whose surface was still soft and friable, while the surrounding area was set in a thin, dry crust. He frowned with displeasure. The white man knew he was being hunted. He had begun to cover his tracks.

He stood up and, while the others watched him, walked a few yards upstream and then down again, scanning the bushes on either side of the water, then the shallows themselves, where the stream slid quietly over white sand and rocky outcrops and pockets of rounded stones. Twenty feet from the spot where Dillon had entered the water, he found what he was looking for: a flat stone, kicked out of its mooring, so that the underside of it was exposed through the clear water. All the other pebbles in the pocket were rounded and smoothed by the rush of water and sand, but this one was rough and reddish where it had lain protected in the riverbed.

Mundaru called to the bucks and showed them the sign. Their quarry was heading downstream. They had only to follow him, beating the banks as they went. He was weak and moving slowly. In the water he must move slower still. It was still a long time to sunset and they could not fail to find him.

He waited until three of the bucks had waded across to the opposite bank; then they set off, walking fast, heads bowed and eyes alert, like hounds closing in for the kill.

Chapter Two

WHEN SUNSET CAME, Mary Dillon stood on the veranda of the homestead, watching the shadows lengthen across the brown land, the ridges turn from ochre to deep purple, the sun lapse slowly behind them out of a dust-red sky. It was the hour when she came nearest to peace, nearest to comfort in this alien, primeval country.

The days were a blistering heat when the thermometer on the doorpost read a hundred and fifteen of shade temperature and the willy-willies raced across the home paddocks—whirling pillars of wind and sandstone grit. The nights were a chill loneliness, with the dingoes howling from the timber and the myalls chanting down by the river, and Lance snoring happily, oblivious of her terror. But in this short hour, which was neither dusk nor twilight, but simply a pause between the day and first stride of the dark, the land became gentle, the sky softened, and the bleached, neighbourless buildings took on the illusory aspect of home.

It would never be truly home to her. After three years of marriage to Lance Dillon and two visits to her family in Sydney, she knew it for a certainty. She was a city girl, born and bred to tiled roofs and trim lawns and the propinquity of people like herself. She needed a husband home at seven, pulling out of the driveway at eight-thirty in the morning, and a comforting domestic presence in between—not this brown man with the leathery strength and the distant eyes, gone for days at a time, then ambling homeward, dusty and saddle weary, to demand her interest and her comfort and her encouragement in this bleak ambition of his.

Other women, she knew, made a life and a happiness for themselves in the outback country. They lived a hundred miles from the nearest neighbour, their only company the homestead lubras and the pickaninnies, their only visitors the policeman, the pilot of the mail plane and the flying doctor. Yet when she heard them talking in the daily gossip session over the pedal-radio network, she read the contentment in their voices and wondered why she had never been able to attain it. "Give it time," Lance had told her, in his calm, positive fashion. "Give it time and patience and you'll grow to love it. It's an old land, sweetheart—not old and used up like Europe, but old because the centuries have passed it by and the seas have cut it off from change. We've got birds and animals and plants you'll find nowhere else in the world. The myalls—even the homestead blacks—are our last link with prehistory. But it's new too. The soil has never seen a plough, the waters have never been dammed, and nobody's even guessed at what's under the surface. All we need is oil and we could explode into growth, like America, overnight. Isn't it worth a little waiting and a little courage?"

When he talked like that, so strangely out of character for a hard-driving cattleman, she had never been able to resist him. So she smiled ruefully and submitted. But now, after three years, the land was still a stranger, and Lance, it seemed, was becoming a stranger too. He was gentle as ever, considerate in his casual fashion; but he seemed not to need her anymore, because she had failed him as she had failed herself.

Soon she must face the question: what to do about it? This land demanded a wholeness. One could not love it with a divided heart, nor fight it with a defective relationship. A rifted rock split swiftly under the daylong heat and the bitter cold of the inland nights. A rifted marriage had as little chance of survival. A man with a discontented wife was beaten before he began. Her choice, therefore, was simple and brutal: make good the marriage promise of submission and surrender, or make an honest admission of defeat and go away, leaving the man and the land to work out their own harsh harmony.

Yet, for all the apparent simplicity of the equation, there was a subtler corollary. Given the submission and the surrender, was there love enough in her and understanding enough in him, to guarantee a permanence and an ultimate contentment?

Three years ago, when Lance Dillon had come striding into her life, bronzed, smiling, confident, a country giant in suburbia, she had had no doubts at all. This was a land tamer, a man to walk deserts and watch them blossom under his boot soles; a woman tamer too, strong as a tree for shelter and support. Now, in another time and in a far country, he looked disappointingly different. The immensity of the land dwarfed him. Its harshness honed the humour out of him, as the winds scored the sandstone rocks and twisted the trees, so that roots must thrust deeper into the hungry soil for nourishment and anchorage. But if the soil were dry and the roothold shallow, the tree would die, as a man would die if there were not love or strength enough to support him against the storm.

She had loved him once. She still loved him. But enough . . . ? That was a hard question and she could not wait too long to answer it.

She shivered as the first chill of evening stirred in the wind, and walked into the house where the soft-footed lubras were bustling about the kitchen and laying the table for dinner. Tonight was an occasion—whether for cheerfulness or irony, depended on her. It was their wedding anniversary and Lance had promised to be home by sunset.

Normally he paid little attention to wifely demands for punctuality, explaining patiently at first, and later with irritation, that in the Territory no one could possibly live by the clock. It was big country, the herds were scattered. A man could travel only as fast as a tired horse; and horses fell lame, wandered in their hobbles or were taken with colic from cropping too long in the rank river grasses. She must expect him when he came and learn to be neither scared nor impatient and, above all, not to nag. A nagging woman was worse than saddle galls to a bushman. More importantly, the stock boys had scant respect for a hen-pecked boss. They reasoned, accurately enough, that a man who could not control his woman could hardly control his cattle or his men either.

But tonight—his eyes had brightened as he said it—yes, tonight was different. He would not go to the muster, but out to the valley, where the breeders were. He would be home by dark—give an hour, take an hour, in the fashion of the bush. Then he had kissed her and ridden off and the memory of the kiss was the one small light in the gathering darkness of doubt and disillusion. Perhaps tonight it would flare up into a renewal of passion, of hope for both of them.

In the dining room, Big Sally, queen of all the housewomen, was laying the last of the silver. She was married to one of the stock boys and her heavy body was swollen and shapeless with continued childbearing. She was dressed in a black cotton frock with a starched apron over it, but her feet were bare and her broad, flat face incongruous under the white maid's cap. She looked up, grinning, as Mary Dillon entered and said in her thick, husky voice: "All right, missus. Boss come soon, eh? Catch 'im bath, clean clothes. Eat good, drink good. Maybe this time make 'im pickaninny longa you?" Her big body quivered as she went off into long gurgles of laughter and, in spite of herself, Mary laughed too.

"Maybe, Sal. Who knows?"

The big lubra chuckled wheezily.

"Boss know. Missus know. You dream 'im right, he come . . ."

She bustled out, with a slap of bare feet and a rustle of starched linen, while Mary Dillon stood looking down at the white napery and the bright silver so incongruous here in the middle of nowhere.

"You dream 'im right, he come . . ." The aborigines believed that, in the making of a child, the act of union was only the beginning, but that an enlivening spirit must be dreamed into the womb. Perhaps this was the lack between Lance and herself—the dreaming. They wanted a child, wanted it desperately, each for a different reason; she, because of the hunger for completion, the need to fill the loneliness in which she lived; he, for the promise of

26

continuity, a son to carry on the conquest of the land, push out the frontiers and hold them against time and nature. But so far, it seemed, they had not dreamed right, and soon there might be no dreams left.

For want of anything better to do, she walked to the sideboard and began refilling the whisky decanter from Lance's last bottle of Scotch. Then, almost without thinking, she poured a glass for herself, laced it with water and drank it slowly. It was cocktail time in the city and this was her ritual commemoration of the life she had left behind. But there was defiance in it too—a small symbol of rebellion.

Once, in their first year of marriage, Lance had come home late to find her sitting by the fire with a drink at her elbow. He had frowned and then chided her, smiling:

"Never drink with the flies, sweetheart. This is the wrong country for it. I've seen too many station wives hit the bottle because they'd slipped into the habit when they were lonely and bored. It's not pretty to watch, believe me. If you want to drink, let's drink together—and if we hang one on, there's not much harm done."

The insinuation angered her and she blazed out at him.

"What do you expect me to do? Hang around for forty-eight hours waiting for you to come home for a cocktail? If you can't trust me in a little thing like this, how can you trust me in the big ones?"

He was instantly contrite.

"Mary, I didn't mean it like that! I know this country better than you do. I understand how it can take people unaware. It's—it's like a half-tamed animal, strong, compelling, but dangerous too, if you don't handle yourself carefully. That goes for men as well as women. The territory's full of fellows who've gone native, or hit the bottle, or just simply surrendered themselves to the madness of solitude. We call 'em 'hatters'—like the Mad Hatter at Alice's tea party. At first meeting, they're normal enough, but at bottom, crazy as coots."

His voice softened and he laid his gentle work-roughened hands on her shoulders.

"I love you, Mary. I know these first years aren't going to be easy for you. So, I try to warn you. That's all."

The touch of him and gentleness of him charmed the anger out of her, as it always did. But this time she could not bring herself to surrender; and, each night, at the same time, she took one drink—no more, no less—in futile affirmation of her right to be herself.

Still carrying the drink, she walked into the living room, sat down, picked up a month-old newspaper and began leafing through it idly. The news was as dead as if it had happened on another planet, but the gossip columns and the fashion plates piqued her to jealousy of the women who lived a walk away from stores and boutiques and the daily novelties of a city. Society in the Territory was limited to a clatter of voices on the pedal radio, a picnic race meeting and a yearly dance afterwards on one of the larger properties, where the women wore frocks that had been in mothballs for a year and the men got

27

cheerfully drunk round the drink table, or danced stumbling and tongue-tied to an out-of-tune piano.

It was enough, perhaps, for the others—the weathered matrons, the leggy adolescents who had never seen a city; but for her, Mary Dillon, all too little.

Memories flooded back, soft, insidious, cajoling. The drink warmed her. The paper slipped unnoticed to the floor. She dozed fitfully in the chair.

Suddenly she was awake. Big Sally was shaking her gently and the clock on the mantel read 9:45. Big Sally looked at her with questioning eyes.

"You eat now, Missus. Boss no come. Dinner all burn up, finish!"

Anger took hold of her and she stood up, knocking over the glass so that it shattered on the floor. Her eyes blazed, her voice rasped hysterically.

"Put the boss's dinner in the oven. Give the rest to the girls. I'm going to bed!"

The dark woman watched her go with soft, pitying eyes, then shrugged philosophically and began to pick up the fragments of glass from the floor.

Mary Dillon hurried into the bedroom, slammed the door and threw herself on the bed, sobbing in bitterness and defeat. Lance had failed her, the country had defeated her. It was time to be quit of it all.

From his hide among the pandanus roots, Lance Dillon looked out across thirty yards of moonlit water to the myalls' campfires on the beach. They were squatting on their haunches, roasting a quarter of meat from the slain bull, and the smell of burnt hair drifted across the water. Each man had built a small fire at his back, and the flames leapt up, highlighting the corded muscles and the sleek skin of their shoulders and breasts.

Their weapons were laid on the sand and they seemed absorbed in their meal and their talk, but at every sound—the cry of a night bird, the leap of a fish—they became tense and watchful; their eyes searched the river and their teeth shone like new ivory out of their shadowy faces. Dillon huddled back against the wall of the bank and cautiously daubed more mud on his face, lest a chance gleam of fire or moonlight should betray his presence.

He had found this place no more than five minutes before the hunters had come stalking him down the banks, and he had been here six hours already. It was at a point where the river swung out into an elbow, with a wide beach on one side, and on the other a steep bank plunging down into deep, still water. The bank was thickly grown with bush and the searching roots of the pandanus palms reached down, ten feet or more, like a fish cage into the stream, so that the driftwood piled about them in a kind of barricade.

He was in a dangerous spot—"croc water" the bushmen called it—but he had to choose between the certainty of a myall spear and the chance of a big saurian, sleeping in the mud. Cautiously, he parted the driftwood and eased himself in behind the roots. His feet plunged deep into the muddy bottom and braced themselves on a buried tree trunk. The water was waist-deep and he had to bend his shoulders painfully to find headroom under the tangled roots. But the spot was in shadow, the driftwood was thick, and on their first downstream cast the myalls had passed within a yard of him.

28

When he saw their retreating backs, he had to fight against the panic temptation to break out and head for open country; but he knew that they would soon understand that they had missed him, and then they would come back. So he stayed, the water bleaching his skin, the leeches battening on him, a black spider dangling within an inch of his eyes, a cloud of insects buzzing frantically about him. As the cold crept into his blood, his wound began to throb painfully and he forced a thick twig between his teeth to stop their chattering.

He experimented cautiously, trying to find an easier position, but the dangers in movement were only too apparent. A piece of driftwood, dislodged and floating downstream, an eddy of mud in the current, would betray him in a moment to the practiced eyes of the pursuers. Nothing to do but wait it out and hope they gave up at nightfall.

They came back sooner than he expected. He saw them, fifty yards off, beating the banks more carefully, probing shadowy overhangs and the hollows under the bushes. One big buck was working his way swiftly towards his hiding place. Dillon eased himself slowly down into the water until it was lapping at his chin. Then when he could see only the buttocks and knees of the pursuer, he took a deep breath and immersed himself completely in the dark water. The myall came abreast of the pile of driftwood, jerked some of it away and thrust his spear into the hollow behind. His feet churned up the muddy bottom, and Dillon, an inch below the surface, held his breath until it seemed his heart must burst and the top of his head blow off. Then the myall moved away, splashing upstream, and Dillon surfaced and gulped in great draughts of air. When he had recovered sufficiently to look about him, he saw that the screen of driftwood was breached, dangerously, and he set himself to repair it, piece by careful piece, while the myalls worked their way upstream again, calling to each other in husky musical voices.

The ducking and the exertion dislodged the bandage and started the wound bleeding, and he had to battle against the old fear of the crocodiles, while he struggled to adjust the tourniquet and the sodden dressing. Suddenly he was desperately weary, from hunger, exertion and loss of blood, and he knew that he could not stay conscious much longer. Yet, if he let himself lapse into sleep, he would slide into the water and stifle.

Painfully, he turned his head, searching in the half-light for a root or a projection that might hold him. Finding none, he undid the buckle of his belt and slid the strap out from the loops of his trouser top. The sodden trousers sank slowly down to his ankles, but he did not care. He looped the belt high round his chest and buckled himself to one of the slim, tuberous palm roots, so that when he leaned back, his body hung, suspended under the armpits. The friction of the belt on the rough cortex might hold him while he dozed. He tested it, once, twice and again, then let his body go limp, while his mind surrendered itself to the illusion of rest.

It was no more than an illusion, pain-haunted and full of feverish terrors. Black grinning faces swelled and exploded close to his own. Bull horns gored at his ribs like spears. Mary's face, cold and withdrawn, mocked his appeal and, when his hands groped out to her, she retreated from him, hostile and pitiless. He was burning in a dark sea, drowning in a cold fire. He was swinging, a fleshless skeleton, from a twisted tree.

Then, mercifully, he woke, to moonlight and silver water, the gleam of campfires and the torturing smell of cooked meat. The upper part of his body was cramped and constricted, and from the waist down, there was no sensation at all. With infinite care he began to move, easing himself out of the belt, flexing himself to reach the fallen trousers and drew them up again to his waist, biting his lips to stifle a cry as pain started in every nerve. Finally he was standing again, his feet firm on the sunken log, his back flat against the muddy bank.

A night in this place would kill him for a certainty. Before dawn he must break out of it, find food and warmth and set the sluggish blood moving again. Soon, when the myalls had gorged themselves with meat, they would lie down like animals on the sand and sleep till sunrise. Then he must move; but how and where? There was the river in front and a wall of mud at his back and over all, the cold and treacherous radiance of the hunter's moon.

Mundaru, the buffalo man, was puzzled. Squatting on the sand, with fire at his belly and his back, and the meat of the totem making another warmth inside him, he thought back over each step of the trail from its beginning in the high grasses to its end in the river shallows. He timed it again; how many paces a fit man might run and walk while the shadows extended by a spear's length. He added more distance and more time to the calculation to allow for some unexpected reserve of strength in the white man—and was still convinced that he could not have outdistanced them.

Therefore, he must have left the river and struck out to open country. But at what point? Mundaru himself had scouted every inch of one bank and he was confident that he had missed nothing. The bucks from the other bank had sworn with equal conviction that they had overlooked nothing. But Mundaru was not so sure. This was the difference between one hunter and another, the reason for the old tribal law that the weak must share with the strong, the keen of eye must hunt for those who failed to read the signs. In the morning he himself would cross the river and look again.

He sat a little apart from the others, a painted man, his jaws champing rhythmically on the tough meat, his eyes now scanning the water, now staring into the last leaping flames of the cook fire. He did not speak to them, nor they to him; but their thought was clear. He was diminished in their sight by his failure to come up with the white man. They were asking themselves whether they had made a mistake by committing themselves to his leadership; whether there was not some defect in his totem relationship; whether the white man had not some malignant magic working against them and against Mundaru in particular. If their doubts persisted, they might well leave him in the morning and carry back the news of his failure to the tribe, and to Willinja, the maker of magic.

30

Mundaru himself could not go back—not without shame, not without fear of the uncompleted ritual cycle. He must follow to the kill or to his own death, as he had when he wore the feathered boots and looked on the stone which was the secret name of a man.

Now he had walked all round the thought and come back to the starting point. He had seen all there was to see, good and bad. He was ready for sleep. He yawned, scratched himself and stretched his body on the sand, working a hollow for himself between the two fires. Then he drew his spears to within a hand's reach and, without a word to his companions, closed his eyes. But sleep would not come. His thoughts flew back, like a green parrot, to the camp, where Menyan would be sleeping by the side of her husband, Willinja, the sorcerer.

She was named for the moon, the new moon, slim and young. When she was still a child, her father had promised her to Willinja, because he needed the favour of a man who understood the secrets of the dream people, who could make rain and call death into the body of an enemy. From the moment of this promise, she was wedded to Willinja. She slept at his fire. His women taught her. She learned all that a wife should know to be valuable to her husband. But he did not take her until she had become a woman and had sat in the secret place, covered with leaves and eating none but the foods permitted to a woman at the time of blood.

From this moment she was lost to Mundaru. But he still desired her. He sought occasions to meet her alone, to speak with her, out of sight of the other women. He was young, while her husband was old. He was pleasing to her. Her eyes told him that; but she was afraid of her husband—as Mundaru was afraid. Because Willinja's cold eyes could look into the marrow of a man's brain and his spirit travelled abroad out of his body, seeing what was done in the most secret places.

Even now, on the edge of sleep, Mundaru could feel his hostile presence, shepherding his thoughts away from Menyan. He must not fight him—yet. But with the white man dead, and the white man's strength absorbed into himself, then, he might be ready to enter into open conflict. A small, cold tremor of anticipation shook him, then burrowing deeper into the warmth of the sand, he composed himself for sleep.

The bucks watched him, with sidelong, speculative eyes. They talked a little in low voices, then they too stretched themselves on the sand, and before the flames had died to a dull red glow, they were snoring like tired animals.

To Lance Dillon, penned in the small, liquid darkness under the pandanus roots, had come a small ray of hope. It was a moonbeam, slanting down from a point above his head and falling on the black, still water in front of him. Inch by inch, he slewed himself round in the confined space until, looking up, he could see a narrow opening between the upper roots and the mudbank. It was, perhaps, three feet above his head, and he judged it almost large enough to take his head and shoulders. If he could reach it and pass through it, he might scale the high bank under the shadows of the bushes and head across the grass flats away from the sleeping myalls.

It was a big "if." He was very weak. One arm and shoulder were useless and this gymnastic effort might well prove too much for him. The slightest noise would bring the myalls leaping to their feet and splashing across the river. The first problem was the bank itself. The black soil was damp and slippery and its contours were clotted into large projections, any one of which might break away and fall noisily into the water.

With infinite care he began to scoop out with his hands a foothold just above the waterline. As each handful was dug, he laid it gently in the water, letting it float soundlessly away from his palm. He dug deep, so that his feet would not slide; he groped around the mouth of the hole, feeling for friable pieces that might fall away under pressure. Then, when the two lower holes were dug, he reached up and hollowed two more above his head.

It was a child's labour, but before it was done, he was trembling as if in ague and the sweat was running down his face. Then new risks presented themselves. His clothing was full of water. The moment he climbed upwards, it would spill out, noisily, into the pool. The roots above his head were matted and rough. They might tangle themselves in his belt or in the loose, flapping fabric.

Bracing himself against one of the log roots, he bent down into the water and took off his boots. The simple operation took a long time. The laces were leather, tight-drawn and slippery. He had to rest many times before he was free of them. Trousers and shirt came next, and, as he worked his way out of them, he could feel the leeches, squamous and bloated, clinging to his flesh. He tried to pull them off, but they clung all the tighter. He must endure them a while longer while they drained him of blood he could ill afford to lose. He crouched mother-naked in the pool, debating whether to try to salvage his clothing against the heat of the coming day. Finally he decided against it and let the sodden garments sink to the bottom of the pool.

He was ready now—ready to make the attempt on which his life depended. He looked up towards the narrow opening where the moonlight gleamed, then, with a wracking effort, hoisted himself into the first foothold. Behind him, in the water, floated the spearhead and the broken haft which had slipped, unnoticed, from his grasp while he was preparing himself for sleep.

Chapter Three

For Sergeant Neil Adams, Northern Territory Mounted Police, the dog days were coming. He knew the symptoms: the daylong depression, the restless nights, the itch in the blood for whisky or a woman or an honest-to-God brawl—anything to break the crushing monotony of life in the outback emptiness. The disease itself was endemic and recurrent—regular as the lunar periods. It had a name in all languages: *Weltschmerz*, *cafard*, and, here in the Territory, they called it simply "gone troppo."

It began as a languor, a distaste for the repetitive elements of living: food, work, company and confinement. It built to a brooding moroseness, which lasted sometimes for days, sometimes for weeks, and in chronic cases, became permanent.

Its climax was a feverish melancholy which broke usually in a catharsis of violence or drunkenness but ended, sometimes, in suicide or murder.

No one who lived long in the Territory escaped it utterly. All, in one fashion or another, were marked by it, as folks are marked by the yellow tinge of latent malaria. The "hatters" surrendered themselves to solitude and crazy contemplations. The cattlemen and the drovers hit the outback settlements and launched themselves into a week of drinking and fighting. The stock boys and the station aborigines grew sullen and disobedient and finally went walkabout into the bush. Women became tearful and shrewish. Some of them lapsed into brief heartbreaking love affairs with the nearest available man; so that one more item of gossip was bruited in the bars from Darwin to Alice Springs, from Broome to Mataranka. Only the intelligent, the disciplined, the responsible managed to suppress it, as malaria is suppressed, by therapeutic treatment.

For Sergeant Neil Adams, the treatment was simple—work, and more work.

His headquarters were at Ochre Bluffs, a small huddle of clapboard buildings under the lee of a range of red hills. His territory extended a hundred miles in every direction and included a mixed population of cattlemen, publicans, storekeepers, two doctors, four bush nurses, transient pilots, stock inspectors, well sinkers, drifters and whites "gone native." His duties were legion. He took the census, sobered drunks, tracked down tribal killers, settled disputes on brands and boundaries, registered births, marriages and deaths, leprosy and syphilis.

Much of it was paper work in the dusty office of his bungalow at Ochre Bluffs. The rest of it meant days in the saddle, nights by a campfire, with Billy-Jo, the aboriginal tracker, for company. Yet in the sprawling, inchoate life of the Territory, he was a symbol of security, of ultimate order. He could not afford to be a drunk or a lecher or a chaser of tribal women. At the first lapse, his authority would be destroyed completely.

So, when the black mood began to grow on him, he would saddle and ride away from Ochre Bluffs, into the myall country. Billy-Jo would pick up the tracks of a nomad group and follow them—for days sometimes—to a water hole or a riverbed. He would talk with the elders, look to the sick, note the newborn and the dead, pick up hints of feuds and medicine killings. At night he would sit by their fires, listening to their songs, watching the dances of the men, piecing out, step by step, the intimate progression of their lives, adding a new word or a new symbol to his knowledge. Practice had made him proficient in the exercise, and after a while his old identity would fall away; he would find himself absorbed in an ancient, complex life, from which he would emerge relaxed, renewed and ready for a new effort.

He had one inflexible rule. At such times he never went near a homestead unless called to an emergency. He was thirty-five years of age, six feet tall, handsome in a rugged fashion and full of the sap of manhood. He knew himself too well to trust himself to the company of a lonely woman whose husband might be absent for days at a time. He had learnt his lesson early, at the cost of one near-tragedy. He liked his job. He had the taste for dependence and authority. He knew the price he had to pay to keep them. For the rest, there was a month's leave every year; and what he did with it was his own affair.

So, a few minutes before nine on this raw, hot morning, he sat in his office, smoking the first cigarette of the day and waiting for the radio circuit to open. Soon the monitor station at Jamieson's Creek would come on the air, calling in, one by one, the homesteads and the mission stations and the police offices over three thousand square miles of territory. They would report their needs and their problems. They would pinpoint the locations of the flying doctor and the bush nurses and the mail plane. Adams would detail his own movements and tell where he could be found on each day of his trip. Telegrams would be passed, news and gossip exchanged. When it was over, he would be free to go and purge his own devils in the privacy of the emptiest continent on the planet.

He walked across to the set, switched on and waited. Dead on the hour, the voice of the monitor came crackling in:

"LXR . . . Jamieson's Creek calling in Network One. Check in everybody, please. . . . LXR, Jamieson's Creek. . . . Nine o'clock call-in. No traffic until everyone has reported. Come in, Coolangi . . ."

And then roll call began.

"This is Coolangi. We're in."

"This is Boolala . . ."

"Hilda Springs in and waiting . . ."

Behind each distorted voice was a face, a family, a community, and Neil Adams knew them all. Knew them by name and habit, by bankroll and taste in liquor. They were, in a very real sense, his people. The monitor went on calling steadily through the checklist and each station answered briskly and briefly. But when he called Minardoo homestead, there was a change. A woman's voice, high and urgent, answered.

"Hold it, please! Hold it! This is an emergency. I'm Mary Dillon."

The monitor reassured her, calmly.

"O.K., Mrs. Dillon. We've got you. Let's have it slow and clear. What's the trouble?"

Neil Adams turned up his amplifier and listened attentively. Mary Dillon's voice filled his small room.

"It's my husband. He was due home last night. He didn't come. The stock boys found his horse wandering near the homestead this morning. There was blood on the saddle. I've sent them out to look for him, but I'm worried, dreadfully worried."

Fifty listeners heard her, and felt for her, but only the monitor answered.

"Hold it, Mrs. Dillon. . . . Did you get that, Sergeant Adams?"

"Adams here. I've got it. Let me talk, please. Mrs. Dillon, can you hear me?"

"I hear you, yes."

"I want you to answer my questions clearly and simply. First, where did your husband go yesterday?"

"He went to a breeding pen we've got, just behind red ridge. Twenty miles more or less from the homestead."

"Anyone go with him?"

"No. All the stockmen were out mustering."

"When the pony came in, was he lathered?"

"No. Jimmy, the head stockman, said he must have just ambled home during the night. He was reasonably fresh."

"Has anyone gone out to look for your husband?"

"Yes. Jimmy and four boys."

"What did Jimmy say about the blood on the saddle?"

"He—he said he didn't like it. But he wouldn't add anything."

"All right, Mrs. Dillon, just sit tight a moment. I'll talk to you again. . . . Does anybody know if there's a plane near Ochre Bluffs? Over."

Out of the crackle of static, a new voice answered, a thick Scots burr with an edge of humour under it.

"This is Jock Campbell, laddie. Gilligan's due in with the mail in twenty minutes. He's flying the Auster. Do you want me to send him over for you?"

"Yes, please, Jock. Tell him two passengers with packs. Me and Billy-Jo."

"Will do, laddie. I'll tell him the score. Expect him in about an hour and a half. Over."

"Mrs. Dillon? Sergeant Adams again. I'm coming over with Tommy Gilligan. With luck I'll be there in three hours. I'm bringing a tracker. I want two saddle horses and a pack pony. Also, make me up a medical kit. Bandages, antiseptic, sulfa powder and whisky. Is that clear?"

"Quite clear. I'll be waiting."

"Jamieson's Creek? Pass the word to the doctor. Keep a check on his movements. I may have to get in touch with him in a hurry. Is there anything more for me?"

"No. . . . All clear, Neil. We'll hold the routine stuff. If anything urgent crops up, we'll know where to get you. Good luck. Good luck, Mrs. Dillon, and we'll be waiting for news. Don't worry too much. Over to you, Neil."

"Thanks, man. Ochre Bluffs, over and out."

Neil Adams flipped off the power and began to pace thoughtfully up and down the narrow office.

Mary Dillon's report troubled him—for more reasons than one. At first blush, it was a commonplace bush accident: a man thrown from his horse and sweating it out with a broken arm or leg until the stock boys came to find him. Some survived it, some didn't. But, normally, the policeman simply took the reports and waited until the station staff had made their own search, by which time it was a case either for a doctor or an undertaker. But blood on a man's saddle meant trouble—blackfellow trouble—and this was always police business.

Tribal violence against the white had died out long ago. Single incidents were now so rare as to be sensational; and they were generally connected with women, smuggled liquor or the intrusion of shady characters into tribal preserves. But, whatever their cause, they were a headache to the local police authority. Native affairs were a tender political issue in the Federal Capital as in the Territory itself. The Government needed to make a good showing in the United Nations, to bolster its Trusteeship claims in New Guinea. It fostered education, social betterment, ultimate integration. The cattle interests were less enthusiastic. They depended on aboriginal and half-caste labour to run their holdings cheaply. They were committed to the status quo—and they opposed anything that looked like soft handling of the natives. The unwary policeman was apt to find himself caught between the upper and the nether millstones.

36

All this was only part of Adams's problem. The other half of it was Mary Dillon herself.

Of all the women in his territory, this was the one to whom he felt himself the most vulnerable. He had seen her first at a dance on Coolangi Station, a slim, dark woman in a modish bouffant frock, strangely out of place among the local matrons and their suntanned daughters. He remembered the smile she gave him when he asked her to dance, the feel of her body as she relaxed in his arms, her relief when he was able to talk about things that interested her, the hint of fear and discontent when she talked of her own life in the Territory. He understood how she felt. Lance Dillon was a man ploughing a rough furrow, a driving, persistent man, with little understanding of women. He had neither the time nor the wit to give this one what she needed.

But Neil Adams understood. Neil Adams had time, passion and a practiced bachelor's way with the ladies. While Dillon was swapping stories at the bar, he squired Mary through the introductions, charmed her with tales of his roving life and made her laugh with the spicier gossip of the outback.

They had warmed to each other, but a mutual caution had made them withdraw from intimacy of voice or gesture. When the evening was over, she had thanked him without coquetry and let him hand her back to her husband. Three or four times since then, he had met her at the homestead with Dillon and they had welcomed him with the offhand friendliness of the bush. But the memory of that first night still clung to him: the sound of her voice, the heady drift of her perfume, an itch in his blood when the dark moods took him.

Now they must meet again, alone with the unspoken attraction between them and her husband hurt or dead on the fringe of the Stone Country.

He frowned and ran his fingers through his hair in a gesture of impatience and indecision; then he walked to the door and shouted for Billy-Jo, the blacktracker.

Willinja, the sorcerer, sat in the shadow of a high rock and waited for the men of the tribe to come to him.

The rock was shaped like Willinja's own totem, the kangaroo—broad base, which was the rump of the animal, tapering upwards to a small head, on which two projections stood up like the pricked ears of the marsupial. When the sun was climbing, as it was now, the shadow fell upon Willinja, and the small head lay forward of him, the ears pressed to the dust, listening.

Behind the rock, in the full blaze of sun, was a water hole which, even in the drought time, never quite dried up. There were thus the sun, the water hole, the rock, the man, and the shadow covering the man and extending beyond him. Their positions, their relationship to one another had ritual significance.

The pool took knowledge from the sun, which saw everything. The rock drank knowledge from the pool, but sheltered the sorcerer from the malignant reflection of his own magic. Through the shadow, it passed on power and protection, and the listening ears searched out secrets even in the dust.

Willinja himself sat cross-legged on the ground, his face turned towards the encampment from which the men would come to him. In the dry dust, he had drawn, with a sharpened stick, the totems of the tribe: the great snake, the buffalo, the crocodile and the fish which is called barramundi. Each drawing showed the outline of the animal, and the framework of bones inside it, as if an all-seeing eye had stripped off the meat and muscle to come to the core of the being.

Behind the drawings were laid out the instruments of Willinja's magic: a round river stone, marked with ochre; a long sliver of quartzite pointed at one end, and at the other, coated with gum and trailing long strands of human hair; a small bark dilly bag containing human bones.

The sorcerer was a tall man, strong but aging, so that the skin of his body puckered and wrinkled over the long, decorative scars on his chest and belly. His mouth was wide and full of yellow teeth. His broad, flat nose receded into the craggy brows, from which quick eyes stared out across the sunlit plain. His hair and his beard were grey, but powdered with ochre dust, so that against the dark skin of his face they stood out like fire.

To the ignorant and to the stranger, Willinja was a nothing—a primitive squatting in the dust, toying with childish trifles. To his own people, he was a man of power, a keeper of ancient knowledge, an initiate of the spirit folk who, at the time of his induction, had killed him, dismembered him and then made him whole again, gluing his parts together with magical substances. When personal or tribal life was disturbed by malignant influences, he alone had the formulas and the power to use them for the restoration of order and well-being. He was not a charlatan. He believed in himself. The spirits had made him what he was and their potency worked in him and through him.

Now the men were coming towards him from the direction of the camp. They came in three groups, the first carrying spears and clubs, the second, bearing sticks and the long, deep-voiced instrument of music which is called the didjeridoo. Behind them, unarmed, lagging and shamefaced, walked the men of the buffalo totem who had been Mundaru's companions at the killing and who, two hours after sunrise, had returned to the tribe without him.

Questioned by Willinja and the elders, they had told of the killing of the bull, the wounding of the white man and Mundaru's pursuit of him. They did not think to lie. They knew that Willinja saw the truth with spirit eyes. On this level they were afraid of him. On the lower one they understood his jealousy of Mundaru and hoped to make it work in their favour.

Willinja watched them through narrowed eyes, feeling the power rise in him, collecting himself for the ritual which must follow.

When the first group came, they settled themselves in two files, facing each other to the right and the left of Willinja, the musicians on one side, the spearmen on the other. When the buffalo men arrived, they sat in a line facing Willinja, so that between them all was a hollow square of sacred ground. There were no women, no children. They had gone off in the opposite direc-

38

tion, gathering food, for to look on what was done in the secret place meant terrible and sudden death.

They were seated now and waiting. Willinja closed his eyes and sat rock-rigid under the mantling shadow. He could feel all his vitality being sucked upwards and concentrated inside his skull case. After a long while he began to speak in the spirit voice, which issued more like a chant than normal speech.

"There is earth and there is water. The wind blows over the earth, but does not shake it. The leaf floats on the river, but does not harm it. We are the river and the earth. The white man is the leaf and the wind. . . ."

The buffalo men sat silent, but the spearmen and the music men gave a long-drawn cry of approval. . . .

"Ai—eee—ah!"

"We have lived in peace. We have slept safe with full bellies. Our spirit places are untouched because the white man and his people pass by like wind and the blown leaf."

His voice rose to a high, wailing pitch.

"Until now . . . ! Until Mundaru and his friends raise the anger of the spirit people—so that the wind is now an angry voice and the leaf grows into a tree and the tree becomes a club and a spear to destroy us."

"Ai—eee!" cried the spearmen. And the music men cried louder. . . .

"Ai—ee—ah!"

Willinja leaned forward, pointing at the drawing of the buffalo in the dust.

"This is Anaburu, the buffalo, which is the sign of Mundaru. This he may kill and eat, and no one would refuse him. But this . . ."

He scrawled swiftly in the dust a new outline representing the big Brahman bull.

"This is not Anaburu. This is another thing, a white man's animal. There is no life in it for Mundaru. But he kills it—and now he tries to kill the white man. If he does that, there is death for all of us. The other white men will come and move us away, to a strange country, where our spirits will forget us and we will wither and die. We will be the wind. We will be the leaf, lost and drifting nowhere. Where then shall we put our dead? Who will sing them into peace? This has happened before. Now it can happen to us, the men of Gimbi."

He broke off. The buffalo men sat, bowed in guilt; but this time there was no answering chant from the others. They held themselves erect and silent, touched with fear at this imminent threat of expatriation—of exile from the earth which was their only source of life and tribal identity.

Willinja watched them and knew that he held them in the hollow of his hand. He waited, so that they might suffer their fear a little longer. Then he dropped his voice to a low, soft key.

"I have talked with the spirit men. I have heard their voices answering. They say there is a hope for us, if the death that threatens us is sung into the body of Mundaru!"

Immediately, the fear went out of them, in a long, audible exhalation. There was no protest, only relief. The victim had been named. With the spilling of his blood, the land and the tribe would settle back to peace and security.

Willinja, the sorcerer, stood up. From the row of objects in front of him, he picked up the stone with its ochre markings and laid it in the center of the square where all could see it. They knew what it was—the symbol of a man, whose name was Mundaru. What was sung into the stone would be sung into the man. He could no more move to escape it than the stone could walk away across the dust.

Willinja walked back to his place, knelt on one knee and picked up the long quartzite blade, with its haft of gum and its trailing pennon of hair. Then he flung out his arm and pointed it, straight at the stone which bore the name of Mundaru. The others watched, tense and silent. The blade was a spirit spear, pointed at the victim. The gum was fuel to burn his entrails. The hair would make it fly straight and true towards its target.

Then, abruptly, the singing began—a low, heavily accented chant, its rhythm beaten out on the hollow sticks, its melody counterpointed by the deep, throbbing notes of the didjeridoo. Every line of it was a death wish, directed against the man-stone in the dust.

"May the spear strike straight to his heart. . . ."

"May the fire burn his entrails. . . ."

"May the Great Serpent eat his liver. . . ."

On and on it went, a projective sorcery directed against an absent man, an accumulation of malignities, sung over and over again while the sun climbed in the sky and the shadow of the kangaroo rock grew shorter and shorter, until it reached the feet of Willinja.

When it did so, the chanting stopped. Willinja put down the spirit spear, and with a gesture of finality, obliterated the drawings he had made in the dust. The spearmen and the musicians stood up, walked slowly round the death stone, then, by common accord, headed back to the camp. Only the buffalo men remained. They had been partners in crime. Now they must be the instruments of punishment.

They waited, submissive and patient, until Willinja showed them how and when and with what sacred ritual they must kill Mundaru.

Naked as Adam in his primal Eden, Lance Dillon lay on a patch of warm mud and looked up at the sky through a meshwork of reeds and swamp grass. He had slept a long time, and he was still lapped in the languor of rest and warmth and ebbing fever. He felt no pain, no fear, only the genial detachment of a ghost sitting on a fence and looking down on its own discarded body.

It wasn't much of a body anymore—a poor caricature of Lance Dillon, the land tamer. It was streaked all over with mud, from the midnight climb up the

40

riverbank, scored into weals by brambles and thornbushes and the bites of swamp insects. One shoulder was a pulpy red mass, from which the tracks of infection spread out like ganglia. Leeches clung to it, gnats swarmed about it, ants tracked over it with impunity. Its mouth was twisted in a rictus of unfelt pain, its eyes, inflamed and bloodshot, stared up at the morning sky. But it still belonged to him. Life was still pulsing sluggishly under the welted skin, and, somewhere inside his skull, pain and panic and hunger pangs were beginning to wake again. However unwillingly, the ghost must step down from the fence and enter again into his battered habitation.

But not yet, not just yet. This small suspension of pain was too precious to surrender. He must use it to take hold of reason before it slipped away forever.

He had left the river. He remembered that. He had climbed the bank from the dark pool to the bright moonlight, while the myalls slept by the embers of their fires. He had lain a long time under a bramblebush, husbanding his strength and trying to plot himself a course across the grass country. Beyond the bush was swamp grass, and beyond the grass, a billabong—a long, narrow lagoon, fringed with reeds, covered with lily pads, whose bulbous roots would give him food.

Again, his problem was to reach it without leaving tracks. When he crawled out from the bush across a small, clear patch, towards the grasses, he dragged after him a small dead branch, like a broom, to sweep away the marks of hands and knees. When morning came, there would be dew on the ground, and, with luck, the myall trackers might miss him. Reaching the fringe of grass, he parted the tall stems carefully and stepped over them so that they swung back, an unbroken wall of greenery. He heaved the thorn branch away and began to crawl towards the swamp.

He reached it sooner than he expected and, anchoring himself to a small reed-covered bank, began to scrabble for the roots under the broad lily leaves and the sleeping flowers. They were watery and bitter, and at the first mouthfuls he retched, painfully. But, after a time, he managed to hold some down; then he lay down on the wet mud and, in spite of the insects and the swamp noises, slept till the sun was high.

Now the sleep was over, the last drugged languor gone. He was no longer free but burdened with a body, cramped in every muscle, bitten on every inch of skin, with poison spreading out from the festering wound in his shoulder. Painfully he worked himself to a sitting position and scooped up mouthfuls of the still, swamp water. He crammed a lily root into his mouth and chewed on it slowly until he was able to swallow.

Before him the water lay bright in the sun. The lily flowers were open. The green slime in the shallows shone with a sickly brilliance, and the ripples spread out from a brood of cruising ducklings. Against the farther reeds, a pair of egrets stood, contemplating the flat water and waiting for an unwary fish. The lagoon was full of life and full of food; but he was too weak to hunt it, and

41

he dared not raise his head above the high grasses, for fear the myalls might be watching.

This was his chief terror now: that he could not surrender himself to the simplest instinctive gesture. He must think with two minds—the mind of the hunter and that of the fugitive. Every move must be planned and measured to his small strength. He could not think of combat—only of flight and concealment. This discipline of terror made him shut out of his mind every other thought—of Mary, of the homestead, even of ultimate rescue. He could count on nothing and nobody but himself.

Suddenly, out of the blank sky, he heard the aircraft . . .

Mundaru, the buffalo man, heard it too. He leaned on his spear and looked up, searching the air for the big bird which carried the white men in its belly; but the bird was flying in the track of the sun and for a long while he could not see it. Of the bird itself he had no fear. He had seen it many times and wondered at the magic which could command such a messenger. But the men inside it were another matter. These he had good reason to fear.

Earlier in the morning, before his companions had left him, they had warned him of just such a coming. There was a power the white men had to call each other over great distances, and when they called, the big bird always came, sometimes with the policeman, Adamidji, sometimes with the other, who carried a powerful magic in a little black bag. For this reason they would not stay with Mundaru any longer. They would go back to the camp and—they did not say this, though Mundaru understood it very well—they would seek counsel and protection from the evil that had already been done.

Mundaru had not argued. He had shrugged and let them go. He had expected no better. Once a man stepped outside the tribal framework, he was naked and alone, with only his totem to help. But he was still afraid of the displeasure of the tribe and of the potent magic of Willinja.

But he was committed and he could not turn back. When the others had gone, he set himself to search every inch of the farther bank, along the water and the high ground above. So far he had found nothing. The dew was still fresh in the sheltered places; in the open, the ground was crusted and brittle. There was no depression in the grasses, where a wounded man might have lain. The only thing that puzzled him was a thorn branch, dried and broken, lying fifty paces from its parent tree.

The big bird was closer now. He heard its pulsing roar filling the air. Then, as it dived out of the sun track, he saw it, banking in a high, wide turn over the swamplands.

As he followed it, his eye was caught by a movement far away near the edge of the lagoon. The movement was repeated, and when he turned to it, he saw, diminished by the distance, the head and shoulders of a man and one arm waving frantically at the droning bird.

Mundaru stood, stock-still, waiting to see what the bird would do. It swung

42

round slowly, completing its turn, and headed away towards the homestead. The head and the waving arm disappeared, but a gaggle of geese and swamp duck was rising and clattering above the lagoon. Before the last sound of the plane had died out of the sky, Mundaru stooped and, silent as a snake, began thrusting through the waving grasses towards the lily pond.

Chapter Four

IT IS ONE OF THE IRONIES OF EXISTENCE that a man's life may hang on the humour of his surgeon's wife, or the state of a taxi driver's liver, or the angle of sight from a bucketing aircraft. At the precise moment when Adams might have seen Dillon waving from the grass, his attention was caught by Billy-Jo, shouting in his ear and pointing out through the Perspex window.

"Look, boss! Kirrkie come up! Bird belong dead thing."

Sighting along the blacktracker's hand, Adams saw, high above a sandstone saddle, the wheeling flight of hundreds of kite hawks, sure sign to the bushman of a carrion kill.

He leaned forward, tapped Gilligan, the pilot, on the shoulder and shouted in his ear: "Over to the right—behind the ridges!"

Gilligan gave him the thumbs-up sign, banked and headed for the red hills. As the aircraft came in, low and lurching through the air, the kites rose, screaming, and Adams looked down to see the green valley, the brood cows cropping contentedly with their calves at heel, and, in the center, the mangled carcass on which the kites had been feeding.

The next moment he was flung violently back in his seat, as the plane climbed steeply to clear the saddle. When he levelled off, Adams tapped him again.

"Any chance of putting her down in there?"

Gilligan shook his head and shouted, "Not a hope. It looks flat enough because of the grass, but we'd probably tear the undercart off!"

"Can you make another circuit?"

44

"Sure!"

As he banked and turned again, Billy-Jo turned to Adams.

"Boss! I know this place! Spirit caves for Gimbi tribe!"

"You sure of that, Billy-Jo?"

"Sure, boss! White man's cows in spirit place. Maybe Gimbi men make trouble, eh?"

Adams nodded thoughtfully, staring out at the red scoriated rocks and the rich pastures between them. It was, at least, a working hypothesis. Half the trouble in the Territory began with the clash between the pragmatic philosophy of the whites and the dreamtime thinking of the aborigines. The small aircraft rocked again as Gilligan lifted it over the ridge.

Gilligan turned back and shouted, "Where to now?"

"Head for the homestead. See what we can pick up on the way."

"Roger!"

The Auster lurched and shuddered in the air currents that rose from the hot earth, and Adams sweated and battled against the nausea that threatened him at every moment.

Billy-Jo called to him again: "Stock boys, boss!"

They were riding in line abreast, strung out across half a mile of grassland and sparse timber. When they saw the aircraft, they reined in and waved their hats in greeting. Adams counted them—five in all. They would be the riders from Minardoo, and they had still not found Lance Dillon. Again he questioned Gilligan.

"I'd like to talk to 'em. Any hope at all of a landing?"

"Look for yourself! Rocks and anthills! I daren't risk it—unless you want to walk home. . . ."

Adams grinned and shook his head.

"No, thanks. Cruise around for a bit. Let's see if we can spot any myalls."

He was not sure what he was looking for; he was simply going through a routine—assembling the sparse human elements in this big country, setting them in their geographic location, in the hope that the geographic relationship might develop into a human one. A man, black or white, was in a given place for a specific reason. His reason and his attitudes were, normally, predictable. There was no place for strollers and vagabonds in the outback. The country was too harsh, the loneliness too oppressive, to coax them outside the familiar circuits of water hole and game land and grazing areas and sacred places.

In the next fifteen minutes he saw nothing that deviated from a workaday pattern of primitive life: a dozen women, waist-deep in a lily pond, another group digging for yams on a river flat, three bucks flushing an old-man kangaroo out of the paperbark trees, a lone man squatting in the lee of a conical rock, a deserted camp, with lean-to shelters made of bark, and thin smoke rising from the sand-covered fires.

The things he needed to see were hidden from him: Lance Dillon, crouching in the swamp reed, Mundaru, working his way through the six-foot grasses, the buffalo men in a limestone cave, burning their small toes with a hot stone, then dislocating them, and, afterwards, putting on the feathered kadaitja boots which are always worn in a ritual killing.

Adams leaned forward and tapped Gilligan on the shoulder.

"That's the best we can do from up here. Make for the homestead."

Five minutes later they were bumping across the runway to where Mary Dillon was waiting for them.

She came to him, running, a slim, dark woman in a mannish shirt and jodhpurs, her face flushed from the sun, her hair windblown from the slipstream of the aircraft. At the last step she stumbled and almost fell into his arms. He held her for a moment longer than was necessary, feeling her need and her relief and her unconscious clinging to him. Then, reluctantly, he released her. With Gilligan and Billy-Jo looking on, his greeting was studiously formal.

"Hope you haven't been too worried, Mrs. Dillon. We made a circuit of the property before we came in."

"Did you see anything?"

The eagerness in her voice gave him an odd pang of regret. He shook his head.

"Only your stockmen. They haven't found anything yet."

Her face crumpled into fear and disappointment.

"We flew over the valley behind the sandstone bluffs. That's where your husband was going, wasn't it?"

"Yes. That's where the breeding herd was. You didn't see him there?"

"No. . . . But one of the animals was dead. It looked like the bull."

"Oh no!"

The terror in her voice seemed disproportionate to the occasion. Adams questioned her gently.

"Is it so important, Mrs. Dillon?"

Her voice rose on a high, hysterical note.

"Important! Everything we had was there! We paid three thousand pounds for that bull. Mortgaged ourselves to the neck to buy it. Lance said it was our only hope of holding out and making a success."

"I'm sorry." What else was there to say? He shot a quick glance at Billy-Jo. The blacktracker's eyes flickered in agreement with his unspoken thought. Dillon would not kill his own animal. If the myalls had done it and he had come upon them in the act . . .

Mary's voice challenged him sharply.

"What does it mean, Neil?"

"We don't know yet, Mary, and there's no point in making nightmares for ourselves. As soon as we're ready, we'll ride out and see. Can you give us a quick lunch? It's a half-day ride."

"Of course. It's ready for you now. The horses are saddled and the packs are made up."

"Good girl!" He turned to the pilot. "You'd better eat with us, Gilligan. I'll want you to look out for a few things on the way back."

"Suits me, Neil. I'm hungry, anyway."

"Let's go, Mary."

They turned and walked towards the homestead, with Gilligan and the blacktracker walking behind them.

Luncheon was a hurried meal and a dismal one. Mary Dillon was full of questions which Adams parried carefully, because he did not want to be drawn into speculation on the fate of her husband. Gilligan's attempts to brighten the conversation with Territory gossip fell flat, and after a while they ate in silence. When they had finished, Adams sent Mary outside to check the supplies on the pack ponies, while he had a swift, private conference with the pilot.

"This looks bad, Gilligan."

The pilot nodded.

"Time's running against us. We've got a twenty-mile ride before we even reach the Stone Country. Dillon could be dead already."

"What do you want me to do, Neil?"

"Can you make another flight out this way tomorrow morning?"

"If it's a police matter, sure."

"How much runway do you need to land?"

"Three hundred yards'll do me. Provided it's clear."

"I'll try to find you one. When we catch up with the stock boys, I'll set them clearing a strip. Billy-Jo and I will try to pick up Dillon's tracks. Better we don't have a whole mob milling about and messing up the signs."

"How will I know where you are?"

"We'll build a smoke fire. If we want you to land, we'll lay the word in stones on the ground."

"If not?"

"Make the same flight the following day. After that, I don't think it will matter."

"Blackfellow trouble?"

"I think so."

Gilligan whistled softly and jerked a significant thumb towards the door.

"Are you going to tell her?"

Adams frowned and shook his head.

"Not before I have to. When you get back, pass the word round, but keep it general. I'm not sure of anything myself yet."

"Will do, Neil. And good luck."

They shook hands and walked out into the sunlight, where Mary was fixing the last straps on the saddlebags and Billy-Jo was examining the shoe prints of Lance Dillon's pony. Gilligan made his farewells to Mary, and Adams went with him to watch the takeoff. When he came back, he saw for the first time that there were three saddle horses instead of two, and that the pack ponies also carried blanket rolls and groundsheets and water bags for three.

47

Before he had time to comment, Mary told him in a rush of words, "I'm coming with you, Neil. Lance is my husband and—and I think I'd go mad if I had to wait here for news."

For a moment he was tempted to refuse violently. All his experience—of the country, of women and of himself—told him that this was a dangerous folly.

Instead, he grinned and said simply, "Better bring something warm. The nights are damned chill. Pack some liniment too—you'll have saddle sores before you're much older."

"Thank you, Neil."

She gave him a small, grateful smile and hurried inside. Neil Adams shrugged and began to check the saddle girths and the set of the packs, while his private devils grinned sardonically at so easy a surrender.

Lance Dillon was very near to despair. The moment he had leapt up from his hiding place and tried to signal the aircraft, he knew that he had made a fatal mistake. Even had the pilot seen him, he would have understood little of his situation, and even had he understood, there was little he could have done about it. The nearest safe landing strip was at the homestead, twenty miles away, and no pilot on earth would have attempted a landing in the swamp-lands. In one futile gesture he had expended his strength and the advantage he had gained during the night.

Now, for a certainty, his pursuers would be on his track. He had not seen them, but he had no doubt at all that they had seen him. Soon, very soon, they would come to beat him out of his hiding place. He was trapped between the grass and the lily water, a pale frog on a mud patch waiting for the urchins to scoop him up in a bottle.

A sob of weariness shook him, and the first tears since childhood forced themselves from his eyes. Self-pity swamped him, and every instinct urged him to lie down and wait for the merciful release of a spear thrust. He buried his face in his muddy arms and wept like a baby.

After a while the weeping calmed him and he began to take note of the swamp noises: the shrilling of the cicadas, the low buzz of the insects, the susurration of the grass, the occasional boom of a frog and the chitter of a pecking reed hen. There was a rhythm to it, he found, a comforting regularity, as if the giant land were snoring and wheezing in its noonday doze.

Suddenly the rhythm was broken. Far away to his left there was a shrill squawking, and a few seconds later a big jabiru flapped its ungainly way over his head. He knew what it meant, and the knowledge jerked him back to reality. The hunters had flushed the bird as, soon, they must flush the man. Desperately, he tried to discipline his thoughts. There was no way of escape, and there was no weapon to his hand but the swaying reeds.

"The reeds . . . !"

From somewhere out of a forgotten storybook, a picture presented itself, vivid as a vision: a prisoner, hunted by his jailers, hiding in a stream and breathing through a reed. His reaction was immediate. He grasped a handful of reeds and tried to tear them out, but the tough fibers resisted him and the stalks frayed in his hands. A few seconds of reasoning showed him a simpler way. He knelt and bit off a pair of stalks close to the root. Then he bit off the tops, tested them by suction and found that the air flowed freely.

With infinite care he slid himself into the water, feet first, at a spot where the green scum had parted. When he found it deep enough, he exhaled, so that his body sank to the bottom, and then, anchoring himself to the mud, he worked his way slowly under the lily roots, feeling blindly for a snag or a sunken tree that might hold his buoyant body submerged. His rib cage was almost bursting before he found it, but he hooked his toes under it and let his body lie diagonally under the surface, face upwards, so that the reed projected up through the lily pads. He had to blow desperately to clear it of mud and scum, but finally he was able to breathe in short, regular gasps through his mouth.

His body tended to drift upwards against the anchoring feet, and the stretch of his muscles was a painful strain, but after a few moments, he began to hold himself in equilibrium, breathing the while through the slim reed. He could see nothing but the dull underside of the lily pads and the vague bulbous shapes of their roots; but he wondered desperately whether the myalls had come and seen his first blundering passage through the water and whether they might not be coming, even now, to gaff him like a fish, a man-fish, helpless under the pink lily blooms.

Mundaru, the buffalo man, was puzzled. He had moved fast and straight through the grasses, and now he was standing on the very spot where his quarry had lain. The marks of him were everywhere: the shape of his body in the mud, the crushed and torn reed stalks, the place where he had slid into the lagoon. Yet there was no sign of him.

The surface of the pond was clear and unbroken. The green scum in the shallows was neither torn nor disturbed. The blue ducks were swimming placidly, the ripples fanning out in their wake. The egrets stood in elderly contemplation round the verge. A blue kingfisher dipped like a flash of lightning over the pink flowers.

Mundaru squatted on his heels and waited, his eyes darting hither and yon across the shining water and the broad, gleaming stretches of lily leaves. He waited a long time, but no alien sound disturbed the familiar harmony. The swamp birds fed unruffled and the grasses swayed in unbroken rhythm to the warm wind blowing off the Stone Country. The white man had disappeared completely, as if he were one of those spirit beings who could hide themselves in the crevice of a rock, or the trunk of a tree, or the hollow of a grass stalk.

A small chill fear began to creep in on the buffalo man as the leaven of unacknowledged guilt began to work in his subconscious. Perhaps, after all, it was a spirit man. Perhaps the white man was already dead, drowned in the river, and his restless emanation was walking abroad, mocking Mundaru and leading him on to ultimate destruction. Perhaps he was still alive, but using a more potent magic than Mundaru had known or expected. Perhaps this was not white man's magic at all, but the malignant working of Willinja, who had already begun to sing evil against him.

As the fear grew, the guilt thrust itself further and further into his consciousness, until, finally, it was staring him in the face. Like all his people, Mundaru was a believer in the supernatural; and, though he lacked the words to define it, he was facing the dilemma of all believers: the dichotomy between belief and practice, the conflict between tribal discipline and personal desire. By his own act, he had set himself outside the tribe, made himself an outlaw. The channels of strength and sustenance were closed to him forever. His choice therefore was predetermined. He must go on to complete the killing cycle—be the victim ghost or man. He must survive by his own efforts, live on his own fat, and on the protection of his own totem.

Abruptly, but with a curious, inverted logic, his thoughts turned to Menyan, who was the wife of Willinja. Inside the tribe, she was denied to him, but now, an outlaw, he might take her, if he could, and whether she consented or refused. Afterwards, they could not stay in the tribal lands. But they could flee to the fringe of the white settlement, where other detribalized men and women lived a new kind of life, incomplete, but free at least from the threat of ancient sanctions. The thought pleased him. It gave him a new goal, a new, if temporary, courage against the influences working on him from hour to hour.

But first he must find the white man. . . .

The water was still unbroken. The reed bed still whispered in the breeze. Wherever the white man was, he would be heading roughly in the direction of the homestead. His track must lie along the inner bank of the lagoon, nearest to the river and pointing downstream. Mundaru picked up his spears and his killing club and headed off through the reed fringes.

When, a long time later, Dillon broke despairingly out from the lily beds, the myall had disappeared and there was nothing to show which way he had gone.

Mary Dillon and Sergeant Neil Adams were riding stirrup to stirrup across the red plain, with Billy-Jo a few paces behind them, leading the pack pony. The heat and the glare and the steady jogging of the horses had reduced them to a drowsy harmony, a laconic familiarity, as if they and their dusky attendant were the only folk left in an empty world. For long stretches Adams rode in silence, staring straight ahead, absorbed in himself; but, just when it seemed to Mary that he had forgotten or was deliberately ignoring her, he would turn and point out a new thing to interest her—a strange bird, a distorted bottle tree, a pile of fertility stones raised by the aborigines. He had a care for her, an unspoken understanding, and she was grateful to him.

But there was still something that needed to be said, and she put it to him calmly.

"Neil, there's something I want to say to you."

"Go ahead and say it."

"You mustn't try to hide anything from me—anything at all."

He shot her a quick, shrewd glance from under his hat brim, but his face was in shadow so that she could not see whether he smiled or frowned. Only his voice held a hint of humour.

"I'm not hiding anything, Mary. I don't know anything yet."

"But you think it's serious, don't you?"

"Any accident is serious in this country, Mary."

"But you don't believe this is an accident. You think it's blackfellow trouble, don't you?"

"I told you, I'm guessing. I don't know anything."

"But Lance could be dead . . . killed."

"He could be. He probably isn't."

"It might be better if he were."

The bleakness of the statement staggered him, but he had been long drilled to composure. His eyes never wavered from the vista before him and the ponies continued their steady amble over the plain.

After a moment he said quietly, "Do you want to explain that?"

"There's not much to explain, Neil. We're head over heels in debt to the pastoral company, and they told us last month they wouldn't advance us any more. If the bull is dead, as you think, we're finished—ruined. I don't think Lance could stand that. I'm sure I couldn't."

"Aren't you underrating yourself—and him?"

"No. It's the truth."

They rode on a while in silence, then Adams reined in and said casually, "Let's rest awhile and cool off."

He dismounted and came to help her out of the saddle. She was stiff and cramped and she had to hold to him a moment for support.

He grinned and said lightly, "That's nothing to the way you'll feel to-morrow."

"I'm tougher than you think, Neil."

"I believe it," he told her soberly, and moved off to water the horses while she drank greedily from the water bottle.

Later, when they were sitting in the shade and smoking a cigarette before remounting, Adams picked up the thread of their talk. He asked her, "Do you really think Lance would crack?"

She nodded emphatically.

"Yes. I think it's quite possible. I know him very well, you see. He has great courage, great endurance. But he's too single-minded—too dedicated, if you like. Everything in his life has been subordinated to this ambition of his—even me. He's gambled everything on this breeding project, and he's told me more than once it was his last throw. I believed him. I still do. There are people like that, you know, Neil. So long as the goal is clear and possible, they can take anything. But when the goal is unclear or beyond them—they snap. Lance is a man like that."

51

"And you?"

His eyes were hooded, but she caught the undertone of irony in the question. Her answer was blunt.

"I'm one of those who survive by walking away and cutting their losses."

"You'd walk away from Lance?"

"From the country first. But from Lance too, if he insisted on staying. I'd already made up my mind to do it before this happened."

If the answer shocked him, he gave no sign, but looked at her with level eyes and said, "Don't you love him, Mary?"

"Enough to be honest with him—yes. But not enough to stay and let this blasted country wear out everything that was good between us. Does that shock you, Neil?"

He shrugged and gave her a sardonic, sidelong grin.

"Nothing ever shocks a policeman. Besides, it's a pleasure to meet an honest witness. If you've finished your cigarette, we'd better move. I want to get to the ridges before sunset."

He turned and began walking away towards the horses, but her voice stayed him.

"Neil?"

"Yes?"

She moved to face him, her eyes cool and challenging.

"One question, Neil. What odds will you give me on Lance being alive?"

He chewed on the question a moment, then answered it flatly, "At this moment, even money. But the odds might be better on the course. . . . Come on, let's ride."

But the longer they rode, the more the question nagged at him: which way did she want the odds—longer or shorter? And which way did he want them himself?

Willinja, the sorcerer, was waiting for the buffalo men to complete their ritual preparations and present themselves to him, ready for the kill. He too had his own dilemmas of time, circumstance and responsibility.

Like all the initiates of the animistic cults, he was a man of singular intelligence and imagination. In any society he would have risen to eminence and the exercise of power. The whole history and tradition of his tribe was stored and tabulated in his memory. He knew all its chants and all its rituals, many of them hours long and all of them intricate.

The complex relationships of tribe and totem, of marriage and generation—the whole codex of human and animal relationships was as clear to him as the legal canons to a twentieth-century jurist. He was pharmacist, physician, psychologist—and within the limits of his knowledge and experience, good in each capacity. He was priest and augur, diplomat and judge in equity. Behind his broad, receding forehead he carried relatively more knowledge than any four men in a twentieth-century society. More than most men, he understood

52

social responsibility. He, and others like him, held the tribal life together and maintained it in a workable pattern against the constant tendency to disintegration.

This, in effect, was his problem now. He had ordered a killing—in the tribal code, a legal killing. But the legal process would fail of its effect if Mundaru killed the white man first. Adamidji, the white policeman, would see two crimes instead of one, and the punishment would be all the greater. Even tribal killings were forbidden by the white man's law, and so he could not explain, in any intelligible fashion, his effort at prevention and punishment. There were things the white man would never understand, like the exchange of wives to satisfy a quarrel, or to show hospitality, like the payment of blood for blood, and the need to keep certain things secret under penalty of death.

When a man stole another's wife, or took to himself a woman of the wrong totem, the white man gave him sanctuary and protected him against the spears of the avengers. He impeded the course of age-old justice. When, in the old days, he drove a tribe out of its own preserves into a new territory—even a better one—he did not understand that he was signing the death warrant of the social unit. There was no bridge between these two worlds—no concordance between their ethics and philosophies.

So, in this moment of crisis, Willinja must work alone, according to his own knowledge and tradition, a Stone Age Atlas, carrying the weight of his world on his own aging shoulders.

From the shadowy recesses of a cave in the kangaroo rock the buffalo men came out, limping from the recent ordeal. Their feet were shod with the kadaitja boots—made of emu feathers and the fur of kangaroos and daubed with blood drawn from their own arms. When they walked, they would not leave footprints like ordinary men—because until the act was done, they were not ordinary men anymore. Even the spears they carried were special to the occasion.

When they came to Willinja, they stood before him, heads bowed, eyes downcast, waiting his commands. They were crisp and clear, but ritually careful. Time was important. If possible, Mandaru must be killed before he killed the white man.

The manner of the killing was equally important. He must be speared from behind—in the middle of the back. The spear must be withdrawn and a flake of sharp quartz, representing the spirit snake, must be inserted to eat the liver fat. The wound must be sealed and cauterized with a hot stone, and Mundaru, bleeding internally, with the spirit snake eating his entrails, must be driven forward until he died in his tracks. No woman or child must see the act or the death. The man who threw the spear must never be named, because this was a communal act, absolved from all revenge or the penalty of blood.

Did they understand it all? Did they understand that if they failed they too lay under threat of death? Yes.

He dismissed them curtly and stood a long time, watching their swift, limping run towards the river. Then he picked up his instruments of magic, wrapped them carefully in a bundle of paperbark and strode back to the encampment.

The women were beginning to straggle back, loaded with yams and lily bulbs and wooden dishes full of wild honey, but Menyan was not among them, and Willinja waited, puzzled at first and then uneasy, for the arrival of his youngest wife.

Chapter Five

It was late afternoon when they reached the sandstone escarpment and pushed their tired horses through the gorge into the valley. The kites were still wheeling round the carcass of the bull and they rose in screaming, flapping clouds as the riders approached. The air was heavy with carrion smell, and Mary Dillon gagged desperately and reined in while Adams and Billy-Jo rode forward to examine the kill.

She saw them dismount, examine the kill and then begin casting the ground for tracks. They were like figures in a lunar landscape of raw colours, harsh contours and long, distorted shadows; but they moved her to sudden and vivid resentment. The males were in council. The woman must wait their pleasure, no matter how deeply she might be involved in the outcome.

Then she noticed a curious thing: the whole emphasis and balance of the tableau seemed to have changed. Although Billy-Jo was kneeling in the dust and Adams standing above him, it was the black man who was suddenly in command.

All the way from the homestead, she had hardly noticed him. He had that attitude of effacement which the aborigine affects in the presence of the white man—a kind of grey, faintly smiling acquiescence in whatever the white boss chose to do. He was no longer young. His hair was grey and his face deeply lined. He wore riding boots, denims and patched shirt of checked cotton. His shoulders stooped as if he were ashamed of being seen in the white man's castoffs. But here, in this wild landscape, he seemed to take on new stature and authority. His gestures were ample and expressive. When he spoke, Adams listened attentively; and when he stood up, his shadow fell giant-like along the dust.

In spite of her fatigue and ill humour, she edged her horse closer to follow their talk. Before she had gone a dozen paces, Adams looked up and yelled at her:

"Stay where you are! We've having enough trouble. The stock boys have walked all over the ground."

She was parched, dusty and aching in every muscle. This male brusqueness was the last straw. She propped the pony hard on his hindquarters and yelled back:

"It's my husband you're looking for! Just remember I'm interested!"

He did not answer but threw her an ironic salute and bent again to talk to Billy-Jo, who, crouched like a scenting dog, was moving away towards the far end of the valley.

As quickly as it had risen, her irritation subsided and she felt small, foolish and regretful. Loneliness invaded her—a sense of failure and inadequacy, as though she were built to breathe a grosser air, to demand a sicklier nurture than these sturdy, inland people. She felt like an exotic fish in a glass bowl, envious of the free life of the river reaches. It was the old problem in a new shape; but this time there was no Lance to blame for it. There was only Mary Dillon, cross-grained and saddlesore, a nuisance to others and a singular disappointment to herself.

Twenty minutes later Adams and Billy-Jo finished their circuit of the valley, remounted and rode back to join her. Adams's face was clouded with concern and his voice was oddly gentle.

"Sorry to keep you standing about, Mary. We had some trouble picking up the tracks."

Billy-Jo grinned at her in deprecation.

"Stockmen stupid, missus. Walkabout all over. Kick up ground alla same cattle muster."

"But you did find what you wanted, Neil?"

He nodded gravely.

"It's clear enough, Mary. The myalls were in the valley. Five, six, maybe more. They speared the bull, then broke his hind legs with clubs. They made a fire over there and cooked some of the meat."

"And Lance?"

"Lance was here too. His pony has a worn hind shoe. He came in at a gallop, and there are two spots where the pony reared. He must have caught the myalls in the act."

"And they wounded him—is that it?"

"It looks like it. The tracks show that he galloped through the valley, then out again. It looks as though he was wounded by a spear, because he wasn't thrown or pulled out of the saddle."

Shame and a sharp, cold fear took hold of her. Her voice trembled as she asked, "What happened then?"

"We don't know. We'll pick up his tracks at the mouth of the gorge and just

56

follow from there. The stock boys may have found something, but from the way they've been blundering round in here, I doubt it."

They rode on in silence for a few moments while she digested this proposition, then she said in a small voice, "Neil, I'm sorry I was a nuisance. I'm scared and edgy."

He turned and grinned at her in his quirky, sardonic fashion.

"It's a woman's privilege, Mary. You're doing fine. Just try to relax a little. Billy-Jo's the best tracker from Broome to Normanton. We'll know something soon. There's still an hour and a half of daylight."

"Neil?"

"Yes, Mary?"

"What are the odds now?"

He frowned, considering the question, then he answered frankly, "They've shortened a bit, Mary. All this happened twenty-four hours ago. We don't know how badly Lance was wounded, or how much he was hurt by the fall. There's only one thing that tips the odds in our favour. He can't be very far away."

The answer seemed to satisfy her, and he was content to leave it incomplete. There was no point in telling her the other things that he and Billy-Jo had found: the ochre dust and the charcoal sticks and the animal fur, with which one of the myalls had been daubed, in preparation for a new killing.

When Lance Dillon crawled out of the water and back into the reeds, he was in an extremity of weakness. He was chattering with cold; his skin was crinkled and pulpy; one shoulder and breast were throbbing with pain, and his limbs were shaken with uncontrollable, spastic tremors. He lay face downward on the ground, gasping for breath and fighting desperately to clear his mind of the fever mists which were the prelude to helpless delirium.

He knew now, with absolute conviction, that unaided he could never reach the homestead alive. The infection in his shoulder was spreading, and his strength was running out much faster than he could maintain it with the meager vegetable diet available to him. The least effort was a dangerous expense, which soon would become fatal.

He closed his eyes and tried to direct his vagrant mind to an assessment of his situation. The appearance of the aircraft meant only one thing: Mary had understood that he was in trouble and had summoned help. Even now they would be out looking for him. He tried to add the hours he had been wandering, the hours it would take mounted men to reach the area. But even this simple calculation was beyond him, and he slipped off in a dozing daydream of Mary, of faceless horsemen, of aircraft turning into birds and circling above his own dead body.

The dream faded back to reality, and brief reason told him that he must get out of the high grasses and head back to the river, where at least he might have a chance of meeting the searchers. Here in the swamp reaches he was buried, as if in a green tomb, and if the myalls had missed him, the chances of being found by his friends were reduced to nothing. The waving stalks would cover him until he rotted into their roots.

The thought gave him a deceptive consolation. He need not run anymore, need not fear anymore. He had simply to sink down and let the grass swallow him like the sea. As if in confirmation of the thought, a schoolboy tag floated up into memory . . .

> Where the green swell is in the havens dumb,
> And out of the swing of the sea.

The rhythm of it rocked him soothingly. The voices of the cicadas sank to an undulating drone. He felt himself slipping into a warm deep, like a water-logged leaf, until a sharp spasm of pain jerked him back to consciousness.

This was the way death would come—an insidious luxury, robbing him of will. This was more dangerous than the myall spears. He must summon his strength and fight it. He looked up, trying to gauge the direction of the sun from the tangled shadows of the grass. It was afternoon. The sun was on his right, so the river must lie straight ahead of him. Now or never, he must begin to move.

Slowly, foot by painful foot, he began to drag himself slug-like along the ground, among the green-white stalks, whose crowns waved infinitely high above his head.

Menyan, who was named for the moon, and who was the youngest wife of Willinja, the sorcerer, was digging yams on the river flat. She was alone, which was unusual, because usually the women worked in groups or under the care of an old man, to keep them safe from the wandering bucks who some-times tried to seduce them from their husbands. Except for a small pubic tassel of kangaroo fur, she was completely naked, and she squatted on her haunches prizing up the long brown tubers with a pointed stick. It was an easy labour. The ground was soft and the ripe yams grew close to the surface; so her thoughts wandered and she was able to enjoy the rare privacy and the warmth of the westering sun on her skin.

By the white man's measure, she was fifteen years of age, and she had been married to Willinja from the time of her first period, but so far she was childless. Her breasts were still small, her belly flat, and there was no sign of the pain or the swelling, which the older women told her were the signs that a child had been dreamed into her.

This was the reason for her working alone. The older women had made fun of her. Willinja's other wives had mocked her as barren and useless, until she had quarrelled with them and wandered off to escape their taunts. She knew as well as they did that it was not her fault, that old men did not make so many children as young ones; but the stigma was still there and she resented it deeply.

Tribally and personally, she was incomplete. Just as a man was not fully

58

initiated until he had been circumcised and had passed through fire and taken a woman to wife, so the woman was not fully admitted to the secret life until she had given birth to a child.

Some women, she knew, had made a quick progress to this last initiation. They had lovers who dreamed children into them in secret or after the last dances of a big corroboree. Some were lent as wives to a relative or in payment of a debt, and from these unions a child came sometimes more quickly than from an old husband. But so far Willinja had kept her exclusively to himself, and she was afraid of the far sight with which the spirit men had endowed him.

Yet, all in all, she was not too unhappy. She was still child enough to throw off cares quickly and still woman enough to hope that one day a young man might come to buy her from Willinja, or "pull" her from him in the conventional elopement which might be absolved later by the payment of a suitable price. If she could choose—and choice was limited for a tribal woman—she would prefer Mundaru, the buffalo man.

There was a vitality about him, an urgent strength, that set him apart from the other bucks. He wanted her badly. Given the opportunity, he would try to take her. But now she knew she could not surrender to him. What the men did or said in their secret places was a forbidden mystery; but the women understood well enough that Mundaru had been named an outcast to be cut off forever from the tribal communion. A woman might dare her husband's anger to join herself with a younger man; but few would dare the interdict of the tribe. To mate with Mundaru now would be like mating with a dead man.

The thought chilled her and she turned away from it. There were other men who desired her and who might yet be bold enough to take her. She began to sing softly the song which the women used to call their lovers to them. Suddenly, there was a rustle in the grasses behind her. A shadow fell across her naked back and on the warm soil under her hands. She looked up. Her eyes dilated, her mouth opened in a soundless scream as Mundaru, painted and armed for the kill, advanced towards her.

When they reached the mouth of the gorge, Billy-Jo dismounted and walked ahead, casting about for the tracks of Dillon's pony among the newer prints made by the stock boys. Adams and Mary Dillon sat watching him while the ponies dropped their heads and began cropping the sparse tussocks at their feet. Adams mopped his face, took a couple of sips from the water bottle and handed it across to Mary.

"A thing to notice, Mary . . ." He pointed across to Billy-Jo. "Billy-Jo has kept his primitive skills. The stock boys have lost theirs. They don't have to depend on them anymore to stay alive. They're halfway into our world, but they've lost foothold in their own."

She looked at him sharply.

"Are you stating a fact, Neil, or pointing a moral?"

"Read it any way you like." He shrugged off the challenge. "It's still true.

59

It's the secret of living in a country like this. Make the earth your ally and you can survive. Make it an enemy and you're fighting a running battle that you must lose in the end."

"I've lost mine, if that's what you mean."

"I wasn't thinking of you, Mary." His voice grew grave. "I was thinking of Lance. Back in the valley he was wounded—how badly we don't know. Somewhere out there between the river and the trees, he dismounted or was thrown . . ."

"Or finished off by the myalls."

"That too." He nodded a sober agreement. "But if he escaped, then his survival depends in part on his own physical condition and in part on knowledge and his sympathy with the country. It's a good area hereabouts. There's the river and the grassland and the timber. Lots of game, lots of food, if you know where to find it."

"Lance used to say the same thing. I—I think he knows."

A hundred yards away, Billy-Jo raised his hand in signal, then pointed away towards the paperbarks. Adams waved an acknowledgment and they trotted over towards the blacktracker.

Adams frowned in puzzlement and asked, more of himself than of Mary, "I wonder why he headed that way, away from the homestead?"

It was Billy-Jo who supplied the first, tentative answer.

"Wounded man, tired horse, both need water. Maybe made for river, maybe for shade under trees."

Still walking, he led them step by step towards the paperbark fringe, but before they reached it they saw the stock boys ride out, churning up the dust in a hand gallop. Adams swore softly when he saw that they had not yet found Dillon, then he reined in and waited for them.

Mary gave a small gasp of fear when she saw that Jimmy, the head boy, had Dillon's hat hung on his pommel. He handed it to Adams and then made his report in tumbling, liquid pidgin.

"Catchim tracks in timber. Horse belong boss Dillon, tired, walkim slow. Hat he come off, boss Dillon maybe sick. Catchim more tracks by river grass. Man lie there long time, bleed much. More tracks go down to river. We leave. Come back longa Adamidji."

Adams listened until he had finished, then explained it quickly to Mary.

"They picked up your husband's hat in the timber, where they found his tracks. They followed them into the grasses and came to the spot where he must have been thrown, then they came back to meet us."

"Didn't he say something about blood?"

Adams dismissed it curtly. "He must have lain there some time. We know he was wounded. That would explain the blood."

"What are you going to do now?"

"Get Jimmy to take us there. We'll set the other boys working to clear a landing strip on the open ground. Gilligan's flying back this way tomorrow morning. Wait here a while."

60

He began a swift explanation to the stock boys, and after a few moments he rode off with them towards the open plain at the foot of the ridges, leaving her alone with Billy-Jo.

The old man watched her a moment with shrewd, sidelong eyes, then said tentatively, "Sergeant good man, missus. See much, say little, trustim sure."

"I know, Billy-Jo. But I'm worried about my husband."

The old man shrugged and scuffed his feet in the dust.

"Missus young. Catchim new husband, makim pickaninny long time yet."

She flushed and threw him a quick look, but his head was bowed and his dusky face hidden under his hat brim. It was no new thought to her, but uttered by a stranger in bastard tongue, it had a new and shocking impact. She turned and stared away across the red plain where Adams was pacing off the rough strip and showing the stock boys how to clear it with their bare hands and with branches broken from the scrub timber.

She was drawn to him. So much was easy to admit, but what drew her harder to name. An ease, perhaps? A confidence in the way he wore the world—as if it were a sprigged waistcoat instead of a hair shirt. He was a man in equilibrium, stable and content; whereas Lance, for all his strength and driving power, seemed always in conflict. Neil Adams made no demands on life, and yet life seemed to pattern itself in order about him. Lance was always restless, prescient, as if building, all too slowly, a rampart against chaos.

Was this, perhaps, the nub of the matter? That she was dissatisfied with the man she had and wanted another; that the land had taken on the colour of her own wintry discontent? Would it look more like Eden, if she were travelling it with Neil Adams?

When she saw him galloping back with Jimmy, the stockman, she dismissed the thought abruptly, lest he read it in her eyes. If Lance were dead, she would have the right to nourish it, but if not . . . She had a vision of him, spread-eagled in the sun, the life bleeding out of him; and once again she was bitterly ashamed of herself.

The shadows were lengthening as they rode into the timber, with the stockman leading and Billy-Jo following, intent on the signs. When they broke out on the paperbarks and came to the grass patch where Dillon had been thrown, they dismounted. The stockman held the horses, while Billy-Jo and Adams made their examination, with Mary a pace behind them, watching intently.

This time, Adams was more careful of her. As the tracker read the signs, he translated them crisply.

"This is where he was thrown. You see how the grass was broken and the ground hollowed a little by the impact. He lay some time, bleeding . . . then apparently got up and walked away, using a stick. . . . There are no trees hereabouts, so it looks as though it might be a spear he's using. From here he headed down to the river. . . . That's natural, because he'd be thirsty from loss of blood and body fluids. It's a good sign, because it shows he's thinking straight and seeing straight. . . ."

He broke off as Billy-Jo called his attention to new signs—a wisp of fur, a

61

faint smear on a grass stalk, a depression in the swampy earth. She saw him frown and then mutter something to the tracker. Then she questioned him sharply:

"Something new, Neil? What is it?"

He straightened and faced her. His eyes were hard, but his voice was carefully controlled.

"The myalls came this way too, Mary. It must have been afterwards, because there's no sign of a struggle. But they were very close on his tracks."

"How long ago?"

"At a guess, this time yesterday."

"That makes it twenty-four hours."

"Near enough."

"You can say all that, just from looking at the ground?"

"I can't. But Billy-Jo can. The little I know confirms it."

"That means Lance is dead, doesn't it?"

For the life of him, he could not tell whether a wish or a fear prompted the question. He shook his head.

"Not yet. It just means that the odds on his survival have shortened again."

He turned to the stockman. "Jimmy, you head back and join the others. Keep 'em working until dark, then make camp and start on the strip again at sunrise. We'll push on and I'll get word to you before Gilligan arrives. Is that clear?"

"All clear, boss." He touched his hat to Mary and rode off, as casually as if he were going to a muster. Adams watched him go, then handed Mary the bridles of the ponies.

"You lead 'em, Mary. I want to stay close to Billy-Jo. We'll go on tracking as long as the light lasts."

"And after that?"

But Adams was already three paces ahead, following Billy-Jo through the long grasses towards the river.

Five miles away, the kadaitja men, limping in their feather boots, had reached the river and were fanning out over the flats to begin the hunt for Mundaru. They were in pain, but the pain was an ever-present reminder of the sacred character of their mission. It was more than this, for the burnt and dislocated toes had now become magical eyes to guide their steps towards their quarry. They walked in two worlds, infused with supernatural power, but still applying the simple, pragmatic rules of the hunter: stealth, concealment, calculation.

Their calculation was simple but sound. If the white man were still alive, it was because he was using the abundant cover of the swamplands. If he were dead, Mundaru would first hide the body and then use the same swamplands to provide himself with food. He would not risk a break into open country during the daylight hours.

There was no doubt in their minds that Mundaru knew of the sentence promulgated against him. This was the whole virtue of projective magic—that the victim sensed it, felt it in his body long before the moment of execution. The knowledge would weaken and confuse him, so that he would become an easier prey. More than this, they knew that the white men were out. They had seen the plane and the dust clouds kicked up by the horses. They gauged, accurately, that the white men would follow the tracks from the valley to the river, so that they would end by driving Mundaru downstream towards the sacred spears.

The spearmen were hidden from each other and spread over a mile of country, but they moved in perfect coordination. Their communication was a cryptic mimicry of animal noises: the raucous cry of a cockatoo, the honk of a swamp goose, the thudding resonant beat which a kangaroo makes with his tail on the ground, the high-rising whistle of a whipbird. The sounds were never repeated in the same sequence or from the same location, so that even the wariest listener would hardly suspect their origin.

Towards the end, Mundaru would hear and understand, but then it would be too late. The kadaitja men would be circling and closing in on him. There would be a silence, long and terrible; and out of the silence would come the throbbing note of the bull-roarer—the tjuringa, the sacred wood or stone, which is pierced with holes so that when it is twirled in the air, it roars deeply in the voice of the dreamtime people. To Mundaru it would be a death chant, and before its last echoes died, he would fall to the sacred spear thrust.

But all this was still far ahead of them. It was ordained, but it was not inevitable. It still depended on their own skill and on the use each man made of the magic with which he had been endowed. So they moved silently, every sense prickling, upstream towards their victim.

Chapter Six

THE RIVER SLEPT, shade-dappled under the late sun. The sound of it was a whispered counterpoint to the creak of palm leaves and the crepitant buzz of insects.

They came to it on foot, leaving the horses tethered on the high bank, and while Billy-Jo began scouting the sandy verge, Neil Adams and Mary Dillon waited together, watching the play of shadows and the jewelled flight of a kingfisher across the water.

The weariness of the long ride was in their bones, and Mary felt her courage thinning out with the decline of the day. Her face was drawn and dust-marked. Her eyes burned with the glare. Every muscle was aching from unaccustomed hours in the saddle. Adams, too, was tired; she saw it in the deep lines about his mouth, the droop of his shoulders and the slackness of his strong, hard hands. Yet his attitude was one of relaxation and not of tension. He was alert and watchful as ever, and she envied him his leathery strength while she resented his seeming indifference to her own condition. The resentment put an edge on her voice as she questioned him.

"What have you found, Neil? What are you thinking? You've hardly spoken a word for the last half hour."

To her surprise, he was instantly apologetic.

"I'm sorry, Mary. I'm not used to company on the job—certainly not women's company. Billy-Jo and I don't need many words, we think in harmony."

"And I'm an intruder, is that it?"

He grinned at her disarmingly.

"No. Just a figure in the landscape that I haven't had time to notice. Besides, there's not much to tell that you don't know already. Your husband reached the river at this point. The myalls were on his tracks. We still don't know how far they were behind him. All this happened twenty-four hours ago, you see, and the ground dries quickly in the sunlight. The two sets of tracks look as though they were made at the same time—although we know they weren't."

"You're trying to tell me they caught Lance?"

"It's possible—yes."

A cold finger of fear probed at her heartstrings, but her voice was steady as she questioned him again.

"He could be dead by now—is that it?"

"He could . . . but he may not be. If I were you I'd prepare myself for the worst—and still hope for the best."

Once again the calm containment of her shocked him. She said simply, "I'm prepared. You needn't be afraid of me."

He gave her a shrewd, sidelong look and said dryly, "You have a lot of courage, Mary."

"More than you expected?"

The question was barbed, but he shrugged it off.

"Maybe. But I'm glad, anyway. Whatever happens, you're going to need it."

Swift anger took hold of her and she blazed at him, "You're very practiced in brutality, aren't you? I suppose that's what makes you a good policeman."

Before he had time to frame a reply, Billy-Jo came hurrying towards them along the sandy bank, his dark, weathered face set in a frown of puzzlement.

Adams questioned him sharply: "Find anything?"

The tracker pointed along the bank, upstream and down from the point where they stood.

"Blackfellow tracks all about. Walkim up and down. Makim fire, eat and sleep. No tracks for white boss. No clothes, no blood, nothing."

A gleam of admiration brightened in Adams's eyes. More to himself than to Mary, he muttered, "Clever boy. He used the river to break his tracks. Must have been far enough ahead to throw them completely off the scent. I wonder which way he was heading?"

His eyes searched the farther bank, where the steep, muddy incline was tufted with thornbush and creeper and the tangled, water-hungry roots of the pandanus palms. Mary Dillon watched him intently, not daring to intrude again on the patient privacy of his thoughts. It was Billy-Jo who spoke the first word, quietly but with the authority of complete understanding.

"Loseim light fast, boss. Maybe we cross river and look around, eh?"

Adams pondered a moment, then nodded gravely and turned to Mary.

"We'll have to leave you for a while, Mary. There's swampland on the other side and we'd like to make a quick survey before dark. Bring the horses down here, water them and then tether them. Then you could start collecting wood for a fire. There's a rifle in my saddle bucket. There's no danger, but if you want us in a hurry fire two shots. We'll be back by dark."

The words were already on her tongue to tell him that she knew nothing about handling horses, that she had never fired a rifle in her life, that whenever they had camped, it was Lance or the stock boys who had gathered the firewood, that her flesh crept at the sight of an insect and that the terror of emptiness haunted her like the beginning of madness. The words were there, but she choked them back and said only:

"You go ahead. Don't worry about me. I'll have a meal ready when you come back."

For the first time in their daylong company, Adams's lean face relaxed into a smile of genuine approval. He patted her shoulder and said gently, "Good girl! We won't be long. We may have better news for you when we come back."

He turned away and, with Billy-Jo at his heels, walked downstream to where the river narrowed and the water ran swiftly over a stony outcrop where they could cross without fear of crocodiles. Mary Dillon watched them until they scrambled into the bushes of the farther bank; then, alone, scared yet oddly elated, she walked back to untether the horses and bring them down to drink at the river.

As the tired animals drooped their muzzles into the water, she unsaddled them, awkwardly, yet with a curious satisfaction in the simple labour. Always before she had avoided it, as if it were some kind of concession to the hated country. Now she was happy to do it, at the casual behest of a man who challenged her with mockery instead of love. It was a bleak commentary on her relation with Lance, a terse query on her attitude to Neil Adams. She resented him, but she was eager to please him. She wanted to hurt him, but when she found him beyond the reach of her ill temper she did violence to herself to earn his offhand praise.

Not once in three years of marriage had she conceded half so much to her husband, who might even now be lying dead and staring with blind eyes at the peach-bloom sky. In this last hour of the day, with perception heightened to feverish clarity by fatigue and resentment, she understood how far she had failed him and how much he, in his own fashion, had failed her. He had loved her, but love was not enough. He had set her too high, conceded her too much, handled her too gently. He lacked the perceptive brutality of Neil Adams, the egotism, the cool certainty of ultimate conquest. Even now, fear for him as she might, she could weigh his death for profit and loss as if he were alien from her life.

Strange that here in the narrow solitude of the river valley she could face the thought without shame—if not without regret.

When the horses had drunk their fill, she hitched them to a palm bole near the embankment and began to walk slowly along the bank, gathering driftwood and branches for the fire. Each armful she gathered took her a little farther from the horses and the rifle. Each return took a little longer in the paling light. At first she was nervous; her eyes searched this way and that among the shadows of the undergrowth, her head full of nameless terrors. Then the tension in her relaxed slowly, so that a moment came when she thought suddenly: I am not afraid; I am alone, but not afraid. There is water and sand and rock and trees ruffling in the wind, but I walk as if in a familiar place. The terrors are elsewhere—with Lance, with Billy-Jo, with Adams, but not with me.

By the time she had finished, the driftwood was piled high on the sand, and she was hot, filthy and uncomfortable. She looked about for a spot to wash herself and found, twenty yards upstream, a small rock pool. It was deep, ringed by scored sandstone, clear as crystal over a sandy bottom where small speckled fish swam in a low slant of sunlight. She felt it with her hand. It still held the warmth of the day. Without a second thought she stripped off her clothes, spread them carefully on the rock shelf and stepped into the water, sliding down into it until it covered her breasts and lapped the hollow of her throat.

The touch of it was like silk on her parched skin. The weariness and the saddle ache drifted off her like the dust of the red plains, so that she seemed to float, a new creature, slack, content, invulnerable, in a strange new element. The tree shadows lengthened and lay weightless across her body, the peach-bloom sky darkened slowly to crimson, the chorus of cicadas ragged and scattered, the first spasmodic cool of the evening came ruffling along the river reaches, but she still lay there, lapped in the waters of this illusory baptism, until from far across the river she heard Billy-Jo hailing:

". . . Dillon. . . . Boss Dillon . . . !"

And then, more distant, the long, despairing ululation of Adams's voice: "Dillon! . . . Answer me! Where are you? Dillon!"

Mundaru, the buffalo man, heard it too—so close that he could see, through the stalks of the grass, the trunk of the shouting man. A single leap and a single spear thrust would silence the shout forever; but Mundaru squatted, motionless as a rabbit, in the depths of the grass until the man and the voice had passed far beyond him. This was not his victim. To kill him would profit nothing. Besides, he was tired now from the day's stalking, from hunger, and from the long, violent ravishing of Menyan.

It was a thing he had not counted on: her terror, her cowering rejection of him, as if he were unclean or a threatening spirit man. Withdrawal, yes—a token flight, an ultimate surrender—this was the ritual of a tribal abduction when a young wife was "pulled" from an aging husband. The woman must prove fidelity before she could be unfaithful. The man must prove strength before he could possess another man's woman.

But Menyan's reaction had been quite different: a panic horror, the desperate bone-breaking struggles of a trapped bird; so that in the end he had to stifle her and beat her savagely before he took her. Only afterwards, in the hour of staleness and disgust, did he understand the reason: Menyan knew what he himself had only suspected. The tribe had ranged itself against him. They had pointed the bone at him and sung him to death. Already the executioners were on his traces.

So now he sat crouched in the six-foot grasses, listening to the retreating voices of the white man, listening for the sounds that would herald the coming of the kadaitja men and clinging to his last tenuous hope: that he might find his own victim, eat his liver fat and arm himself against the magic of the tribal avengers. If he failed in this, he was lost and he might as well lie down and die in his tracks.

He had not much time. Night was coming down on the land. He must spend it alone, without fire or company, in a last desperate search for his victim. He clasped his hands round his knees and let his head drop forward, lapsing like an animal into fitful sleep, while far voices rang above the clatter of the evening insects.

"Dillon! . . . Where are you? Dillon . . . !"

The kadaitja men heard it too and they froze, their painted faces pointing like the muzzles of hounds towards the sound. They did not understand the words, but their import was clear: the white men were out looking for their lost brother. The white man might be dead or alive—it made small matter. But those who were seeking him were a danger, a possible impediment to a ritual act necessary for the safety of the tribe. If they came upon Mundaru first, they would take him away, beyond the reach of the sacred spears. But since they were still shouting, they had not found him yet. Somewhere in the long, undulant stretches of grass, higher than the head of the tallest man, he was hiding. He could not break out now. He must spend the night in the swamp. In the darkness he would be blind and beset by spirits. They themselves had no fear of the dark, because of the potent magic with which they were armed and because of the all-seeing eye planted in their small toes under the feathered boots.

So they waited, rigid and alert for the signal from their leader which would tell them what to do. Ahead of them the cries continued awhile, then stopped. Out of the silence they heard the signal—the cry of a whipbird, once, twice and again. They moved forward slowly, parting the grasses as the wind might part them, rhythmically, without damage to leaf or stalk fiber.

Distant but clear, the shouting began again, but this time on a new note, sharp and urgent:

"Billy-Jo! Over here! Hurry, man, hurry!"

Lance Dillon heard it, as he had heard all the others, through the whirling confusion of fever. Like the rest, it meant nothing to him but a new, shapeless nightmare against which the tired mechanism of his brain struggled continuously as he made his sluggish, reptilian progress through the grass roots.

In these last dragging hours he had learned many lessons: that time is relative, that there is a climax to pain and, after that, a numbness; that sick men see visions, that reason is a razor path, with darkness on one side and a howling madness on the other, that once a man topples off into darkness there is only the blind compulsion of the will urging him forward to a goal once clearly seen but now lost, like a beacon quenched in the storm wind.

It was the will that drove the tired heart and kept the sick blood pumping round the circuit of arteries and veins and capillaries. It was the will that kept the hands clawing, one after the other, trailing the body after them like a bloated bladder. The will gave sight to eyes puffed and glued with suppuration; it stifled the screaming agony of sunburn and insect poison; it fought off nightmares and shouted down the siren voices that urged him to lie down and sleep, to stand up and dare the spears, to weep for pity in this pitiless land.

Yet there was a limit to what the will could do. One by one, the instruments at its command were wearing out . . . flesh and muscle and blood and the marrow that kept the bones alive. One by one, they would refuse their functions until the driving dynamo which is the core of a man seized up and shuddered to a standstill.

Lance Dillon was beyond reason, but the final syllogism of his last logical thinking was etched deep in the cortex of his brain. He must keep moving. All else was illusion—a swamp fire luring him to destruction. So he paid no heed to the voices calling his name and kept dragging himself forward. But being part blind, he did not see that the sun was standing in the wrong position and that every movement was taking him farther from the river and his rescuers.

Darkness came down at a single stride, and Mary Dillon piled more wood on the fire, so that the flames leapt up to make a small island of light on the sand. She could not begin to cook until the blaze had died into coals, but she needed the warmth and the radiance to hold at bay the new terrors of the night. For a long time now there had been no shouting, no human sound at all—only the whisper of the water, the spasmodic clamour of birds settling themselves to roost, the clump of a leaping wallaby, the squeak and chitter of bats dipping out of the shadows across the star-spotted water.

Never in her life had she felt so lonely. She wanted to scream at the top of her voice for Adams and Billy-Jo, but she feared the echo that might come mocking out of the wilderness. Tags from old bushmen's tales distorted themselves into nightmares that lurked just outside the ring of firelight: the bunyip monster who lived in dark pools, the headless stockman of the Stone Country, the totem crocodile who picked his teeth with a hairpin and ate a white woman every birthday, the mad Duke of Kilparinga, heir to an English title,

69

who ran crazy with an ax because he caught leprosy from a native girl. In another time she had laughed them off as follies told by simple men in outback bars, but here on the river verge they were suddenly monstrous and real.

To divert herself, she began unstrapping the packs and laying out the food and the utensils. The tin plates fell from her hands with a clatter. The startled horses whinnied, and from the leaves over her head a bird squawked and flapped away into the night. She threw herself on the sand and covered her face with her hands.

Then away downstream she heard the sound of men splashing through the water and the merciful echo of Adams's voice. Sick with relief and shame, she gathered up the fallen plates and began to make a brave show of preparing the meal. But when Adams and Billy-Jo stepped into the light, she had a new shock. Billy-Jo was carrying, slung over his shoulders, the limp body of a native girl.

Adams's face was drawn, his mouth tight as a trap; he said curtly, "We found her over by the swamp, she's in a bad way. Put her down, Billy-Jo."

The tracker laid the dark, childish body down on the sand, and Mary gasped when she saw the extent of the injuries. The face had been battered to a bloody pulp. The breasts were torn, as if by animal claws, and the narrow flanks were covered with blood. She was alive, but her breathing was shallow and irregular. Mary looked at Adams with startled eyes.

"Who is she? What happened to her?"

"Beaten and raped. She's married, the pubic covering shows that. She was gathering food away from the other women. Whoever did it must have surprised her. She fought and this happened. That's all we know."

"She's only a child."

"They marry young in these parts."

"It's horrible . . . horrible." Mary turned away as the nausea gripped her.

Adams bent over the small broken body, examining it with clinical care. Without turning, he called sharply, "Mary! Bring me a water bottle and the whisky."

When they were brought, he raised the girl's head and forced a few drops of raw spirit into her broken mouth, then he laid her back on the sand and stood up, shaking his head.

"She'll die tonight. I'd like to get a word or two out of her before she goes. See if you can clean her up a little, then cover her with blankets and start bathing her face."

Mary hesitated a moment, then without a word turned away to get blankets and a towel from the saddle packs.

Adams followed her and laid a tentative hand on her shoulder. He said wearily, "I'm sorry, Mary, I haven't anything to tell you about your husband. It might take us half a day to pick up his tracks in the grass over there."

He ran his hand through his thick hair in a gesture of puzzlement.

"The girl's tied in with this somewhere, but I can't see how just yet. It's

70

possible that the man who raped her is the man who is hunting your husband."

"Man? I thought there were a number of them?"

Adams nodded.

"At the beginning, yes. There were a lot of them searching the river yesterday. They camped for the night. But when we scouted the ground on the other side, we found only the tracks of one man. Billy-Jo seems to think the others went back to their camp and left the one to hunt your husband. At this stage, it's just a guess. If we could bring the girl round . . ." He grinned and patted her shoulder encouragingly. "It's a messy business, I know, but see what you can do for her."

Once again she felt the small surge of pride in his reliance on her and was glad he had not seen her in her moments of fear and humiliation. She said simply:

"Give me ten minutes and then I'll get your supper ready."

"Thanks. We could all use it, I think." He stretched himself out on the sand, leaned his head on one of the saddles, lit a cigarette and lay staring up at the velvet sky in which the stars hung low as lanterns.

He too had his own pride and part of it was to preserve his credit for strength, experience and laconic wisdom with this woman who was another man's wife. By all his reckoning Lance Dillon was dead, but until he could prove it, he could not say it because the saying might open a proposition he was not yet ready to discuss, even with himself.

The rape of the child-wife puzzled him. It was out of character with what he knew of aboriginal custom. Infidelity was less important in tribal code than the preservation of public order and the saving of face for the husband. A girl of this age would probably be married to an old man. Sooner or later, a young one would be expected either to seduce her privately or abduct her and pay the penalty. In either case, the presumption was that the girl would be willing and reasonably cooperative. Most natives set great store on their virility and claimed that their wives were insatiable. Inside the tribe, rape was an uncommon crime, because there was generally no need to resort to it.

There were other contradictions too. As a Territory policeman, he knew something of forensic medicine and more of the sexual habits of the primitives. He had seen more than one case of sadistic mutilation. But the girl lying on the sand did not fit into this category. She had simply fought with her attacker and then been battered into submission. Again the question arose: why? She had been alone. She had neither reputation nor honour to defend. The man must have been known to her. Why was she prepared to risk violence and death rather than satisfy him?

Then a new thought came to him, half-formed at first but growing quickly into shape and solidity. He got stiffly to his feet and walked over to watch Mary bathing the girl's face with a damp towel, while Billy-Jo still squatted on his heels staring into emptiness.

71

After a while her body began to be shaken with rigors, her eyelids fluttered and her head began to roll from side to side. A babbling, incoherent mutter issued from her swollen lips. Adams took the towel from Mary and handed it to Billy-Jo.

"Keep bathing her. If she makes any kind of sense, talk to her."

The tracker nodded and bent over the girl, crooning softly in his tribal language. Adams took Mary's hand and walked her out of the firelight down to the edge of the river. She looked at him curiously.

"Why did you do that?"

"Just tactics, Mary. If she woke and saw you, she would be afraid. She would probably say nothing at all. Besides, Billy-Jo understands her language. He's the only one to handle her."

"You really know your job, don't you, Neil?" Admiration coloured her voice.

"I know the country, Mary. I like my job . . . most of the time."

"What do you mean by that?"

He made a small, eloquent gesture of deprecation.

"Nothing of importance. Except that the work is easier if you can do it without personal involvement."

She turned to look at him sharply, but he was staring down the dark reaches of the river.

"Meaning you're involved now?"

"In a way, yes."

"D'you want to talk about it, Neil?"

"No. Not yet, anyway."

As if on a common impulse, they turned and walked down the beach, hearing as they went the low babble of voices behind them. For the first time since they had met, they seemed to be in harmony, thought and emotion pulsing slowly in a matching rhythm with their steps. Their silence came placid and inconsequent as their talk, while the low current of communication ran uninterrupted between them.

"Neil?"

"Yes, Mary?"

"The girl back there . . . the thing that happened to her . . . how can people—even primitive people—live such brutal lives?"

"The answer is, my dear, that they don't. They live differently, but not brutally. They love their children. They love their wives. They are tender to them, though they never kiss as we do. Walk through a camp and you'll see a man tending a sick woman, stroking her hair, fanning her with a leaf, crooning to her. The same man, on a long, waterless trek, might have killed her new-born child. But the two acts are not incompatible. They belong in different categories, that's all. Survival comes first. Survival for the group. A suckling child might hold back the mother, drain her strength so that she could not bear her part as a member of the trek. The fellow who raped that girl is as

72

much a criminal inside the tribe as he is to us. In many things our attitudes are common, in others they differ, because the circumstances of our lives are so different."

"Lance used to try to tell me the same thing. I was never interested before."

"You never had to be interested. Your husband was prepared to think for you."

There was no malice in his tone. He was stating a simple fact, baldly.

"Do you think that was a mistake?"

"I'm a policeman, not a judge, Mary."

They walked on until they came to a large flat rock that thrust itself out into the river. They sat on top of it. Adams lit cigarettes for both of them and they smoked a few moments, watching the eddies swirling around the base of the rock.

After a long while she asked him, hesitantly, "Neil, can you explain something to me?"

"Depends what it is," he told her with rueful irony. "There are lots of things I can't explain to myself just now. What's bothering you?"

"Myself . . . Lance too. How does it happen? How can two people like us begin in love, live together for a few years and end . . . the way we are?"

"Just what is . . . 'the way you are'?"

Her hands fluttered helplessly, as if trying to pluck the answer out of the air.

"For Lance, I can only say that he loves me, that he's hurt and disappointed and beginning to resent me. For myself . . ." She flicked her cigarette stub into the water and watched it float away into blackness. "For myself . . . I'm shocked. Somewhere out there, Lance is lying, wounded or dead. I'm going through all the motions of a good and faithful wife, but deep down inside me I don't care." Her voice rose to a sharp, hysterical pitch. "Do you understand that? I don't care at all!"

"You've had a rough day," said Neil Adams with cool good humour. "You're in no condition to care about anything. For that matter, neither am I."

"Is that all you can say, Neil?"

"It's all I'm going to say, Mary." He gave her a sardonic, sidelong grin. "Neither of us wants to eat our indiscretions for breakfast. You're tired and so am I. Let's get back and start supper."

When they reached the campfire, they found the tracker squatting beside the coals, smoking placidly. The black girl had lapsed again into unconsciousness and a small mucous foam had formed at the corners of her mouth. Adams stood for a moment, looking at her, then shrugged and turned away to talk to Billy-Jo. Mary busied herself with the meal, listening all the while to the rapid, low-toned parley.

"Did you get anything out of her, Billy-Jo?"

The tracker nodded, his old eyes bright with triumph.

"Name Menyan, boss. Wife of Willinja, man of big magic. Man who beat her want her long time."

"Why didn't she take him?"

"Willinja pointim bone, singim dead. Send kadaitja men killim. Woman no want dead man."

"Why did they point the bone?"

"Killum bull. Try killum white man. Blackfella want no trouble with you, boss."

"What's the name of this fellow?"

"Mundaru, buffalo man."

"So that's it!" Adams's face brightened as understanding dawned. Then abruptly it clouded again, as the full import of the situation struck him. "They're all out there—kadaitja men, Mundaru, Dillon."

The tracker shook his head and shot a swift, significant glance at Mary. His voice dropped to a whisper.

"Dillon dead, boss."

"Why do you say that?"

"Easy, boss. Blackfellow way. Make killing first, eat liver fat, make strong. Take woman after."

Adams frowned, pondering this simple pragmatic logic of the dark people. It was easy to accept. It fitted perfectly, the cyclic psychology of the primitive. But there was a flaw in it, and the flaw was Dillon himself—the twentieth-century man, whose liberation from ancient codes had thrust him into an area of unpredictability.

A sudden sound cut across the path of his thoughts, a scraping and slithering, a long splash and a gurgle of water.

"Crocodile, boss!" said Billy-Jo quickly.

But Adams already had the rifle in his hands and the bolt cocked, while he stared at the pool of shadow on the farther side of the river. Mary Dillon watched, admiring the swift, automatic reaction.

"Over there, boss, by driftwood."

The tracker's sharp eyes had caught the sheen of moonlight on squamous skin.

"I've got him. He's a big fellow."

Three seconds later Adams fired, and the next instant the big saurian was thrashing and heaving in the water, his tail clouting the piled debris and sending it flying in all directions. After a while the thrashing ceased, the crocodile rolled over, exposing the pale underbelly, and drifted into a backwater under the pandanus roots.

Without waiting to be told, Billy-Jo plunged into the shallows and began wading across the stream. Crocodile skins were worth money, and since a policeman could not engage in private trade, this was the tracker's perquisite. Before he reached the backwater he halted, waist-deep in the water, and they saw him fish something out of it. Then he headed away from the dead beast

74

and back to the pile of driftwood. They saw him tear it away with his hands, scrabble among the debris and then stand a long time probing in the dark recesses behind it.

Five minutes later he was back at the campfire, sodden but triumphant, holding Lance Dillon's shirt and trousers and the long, serrated head of Mundaru's spear.

Chapter Seven

MARY STARED AT THE TATTERED GARMENTS IN HORROR, but Adams spread them on the sand and examined them with professional care. After a few moments he gave a low whistle and a gleam of admiration showed in his pale eyes.

"Your husband's quite a man, Mary."

"I—I don't understand."

Item by item, he pieced out the deductions for her.

"We lost his tracks just here, remember? He must have crossed the river and hidden himself behind that driftwood over there. He was wounded in the shoulder . . ." Mary gave a small gasp of fear as he showed her the rent in Dillon's shirt and the brown bloodstains around it. "He got the spearhead out and dropped it in the pool. He probably tore strips of the shirt to bandage himself. . . ."

"And then?" There was tension in her voice. "What happened then? Why did he leave his clothes?"

Adams laid a restraining hand on her arm.

"Take it easy, Mary. Let's think it out in sequence. He would have reached the river in daylight, yesterday afternoon. He would be wounded and weak. He would know that he had no hope in open country by day. What did he do? Settled himself into this place and waited for darkness. We know the myalls looked for him. They didn't find him, so they slept on the riverbank and waited till sunrise. Lance probably made a break during the middle of the night."

"But why without his clothes?"

Adams rubbed a reflective hand over his stubbled chin.

"I don't know. It puzzles me. What would you say, Billy-Jo?"

The tracker shrugged.

"Boss Dillon cut holes in bank. Climb up. Maybe clothes snag on roots. Maybe wet and heavy for sick man. I dunno. Anyway, big mistake."

"Why?"

"Nighttime, no clothes, fine. Daytime, hot sun, white man burn up, finish."

Adams frowned. The thought had occurred to him, but he would have preferred to leave it unspoken.

"Maybe. Maybe he hoped to work his way downstream and take to the river again. We'll know better when we try to pick up his tracks in the morning. At least we know two things—he was alive when he hit the river. He was alive when he left it." He turned to Mary with a grin. "Now, can we eat, please? I'm hungry."

His casualness was disarming, even though she knew he was using it only as a gambit to gain thinking time. But that was his right and she was too tired to dispute it. She began ladling out the meal: tinned stew, thick slices of damper—the bushman's bread—pannikins of coffee laced with condensed milk. While they ate, Menyan stirred and muttered in delirium. Adams got up to force more water and whisky into her mouth and draw the blankets closer around her. He hoped she would last till daybreak. A death in the night would add the final macabre touch to the complex little drama—and Adams, a good policeman, had no taste for theater.

When the meal was over, they washed the dishes in the river, spread out the blanket rolls and lay back, heads pillowed on their saddles, smoking a last cigarette. Mary noticed that Adams chose the place between herself and Menyan and that he was lying without a blanket, on his groundsheet. She offered him one of her own, but he refused it, smiling.

"I've slept colder than this. Hang on to it. You'll need it before morning."

"Let's share it then."

"Bundling's a risky pastime. I wouldn't trust myself."

To which blunt answer she had no adequate reply. So she lay back against the smooth, cool leather of the saddle and watched the smoke of her cigarette drift upward towards the pendant stars.

After a while Adams said quietly, "You're probably asking yourself why we're not doing anything about your husband at this moment. I'm asking myself the same question, but I don't see that there's anything we can do. There's a couple of square miles of swampland over there. The grass is higher than a man's head. We could blunder about all night and find nothing. We could cross and recross your husband's tracks a dozen times without seeing them. Besides, there's Mundaru and the kadaitja men—they'd scent us like dogs in the dark. . . ."

"You don't have to justify yourself to me, Neil. I trust you."

"Thanks, Mary."

Her face was shadowed, so that he could not read it, but when she spoke again, her voice was shaky.

"I—I've learnt a lot today. Don't judge me too harshly. I'm mixed up, lost. But I'm still trying to go through the right motions. It's the best I can do."

"You're doing fine, Mary." His voice was gruff but oddly gentle. "Go to sleep now. Everything will look different in the morning. Good night."

"Good night, Neil."

He saw her roll over on her side, draw the blanket up around her shoulders, and before his cigarette was finished, the steady rhythm of her breathing told him she was asleep.

Now that he was free of the problem and the provocation of her presence, free too of the need for constant movement and action, he could begin to pick up the jigsaw pieces and try to fit them into a coherent pattern. . . .

Lance Dillon first. A dour, driving man, tackling a problem bigger than his expectations, gambling beyond his collateral. A man not built for sympathy, who would either tame his land or break himself—but who had not yet learnt the elementary lesson of taming a woman. This was the tally up till twelve hours ago.

Now. . . ? A man cool enough to take a twelve-inch barb out of his own body, quick-thinking enough to find himself a lair in crocodile water, bold enough—or fool enough—to pit himself naked against the naked land and the naked primitives who lived in it. Where was he now? Halfway home, down the river valley? Impaled on a killer's spear, like a moth on a pin? Or crouched out there in the swamp flats, dumb with weakness or terror? The betting was all in favour of the last possibility.

If he were dead, the kites would be circling over his remains, but in the last hour of sunlight they had seen no carrion birds. Alive then. . . . But how long could he stay alive? And where could he hide from Mundaru? If he were thinking straight, the swamp was still the best place. But leave him there till daybreak—what would be his condition after twelve hours naked in the sun, two nights of wounds and possible poison?

Let him survive that too. Then ask: could he survive the shock of financial ruin and the loss of his wife? Or perhaps he had already faced them and found them both bearable. But if you, Neil Adams, had bundled with his wife to-night, could you face him alive—or, worse, could you face him dead?

Leave him then, a moment, and think about his wife, resentful, discontented, afraid—hungry too, perhaps—yet with a core of honesty and courage that keeps her going through the motions of loyalty if not of love. She attracts you, galls you like a pebble in your shoe. She is frank about her unhappiness— a common symptom of the spring itch. But she is equally frank in blaming herself for it—and how does that weigh in the cynical balance of experience?

You've never asked more of a woman than a happy tumble in the hay and a good-bye without any tears. Why should you care what goes on behind the brooding eyes of this one? She offered you a blanket. Was she promising more? When you refused it, were you afraid of yourself or of her? If Dillon is dead, will you want to take over his wife? Or do you want to see first what is the truth of her? When you find Dillon with his eyes pecked out—or babbling on the edge of the last delirium—will you be brutal enough to stand and watch how she reacts?

An untimely thought, perhaps. An uncomfortable indication of what years of solitary living can make of a passionate man. Push this one away too. Turn a policeman's eye on the drama which is even now being played out on the grass flats. There is a rapist-killer out there. By law he belongs to you and you must take him. If you fail and the kadaitja men kill him, you must visit vengeance on them and the tribe—even though you know this will be a legality and not justice.

That's where Dillon complicates the issue. A tribal rape, a tribal murder, you can treat at your own discretion. Your report can say as little or as much as you choose and few will be any the wiser. But with a white man murdered, it is a matter for Headquarters, for ministerial reports, for questions on the floor of Parliament. Your career is at stake. Are you prepared to jeopardize it for the sake of an abstract justice? Twenty-four hours ago life was very simple. But now there's a woman in it, and you can't read this one from a book of rules. . . .

Suddenly, out of the darkness, he heard the cry of a whipbird, twice repeated. He sat up, every sense alert. It was nighttime and the bush birds were roosting. The blacktracker sat up too, and Adams stepped over Mary's body to squat beside him.

Billy-Jo's dark eyes rolled in his head. He pointed out across the water.

"Kadaitja men, boss."

Adams nodded.

"I wonder if they've found him yet?"

The tracker shook his head emphatically.

"Not yet. When find him, hear Tjuringa—bull-roarer."

"But they know we're here. Will they still use it?"

"Sure, boss. Kadaitja magic stronger than white man. Tjuringa make spirit song for death."

"We'll move in when we hear it. We sleep in turns, an hour at a time. You sleep first. I'll wake you."

"Good night, boss."

He tipped his hat over his eyes, stretched himself under the blankets and was asleep in two minutes.

The whipbird called again, and this time it was answered by the squawk of a cockatoo and the honk of a swamp goose. The cockatoo cry seemed to be the closest of all—downstream and near the riverbank. Adams picked up the rifle, loaded it and, hugging the shadows, began to work his way down towards the ford where he and Billy-Jo had crossed the river earlier in the afternoon.

When he reached it, he stepped in, planting his feet delicately one before the other, so that no splash disturbed the whispered rhythm of the current. It

79

took him ten minutes to cross, and when he reached the other side he wormed his way up the bank and squatted in the shelter of a big thornbush. The bird cries were on his left, more frequent now. The man making the cockatoo call was very near the river fringe.

Adams waited, his heart thumping, holding the rifle so that the barrel was covered by his arm, lest the glint of moonlight on the metal betray him to the hunter. Time passed with agonizing slowness—five minutes, ten—then the kadaitja man came into view. He was a tall buck, daubed from forehead to knee with ceremonial patterns, between which the sweaty sheen of skin gleamed in the pale light. He moved with a swift, shuffling gait, favouring the right foot, and when he came closer, Adams saw that his shins and his feet were covered with parrot feathers and kangaroo fur. In his right hand he carried three spears and a throwing-stick, in his left a short club, carved in totem patterns.

Adams was not a superstitious man. He had lived a long time in the outback. But the sight of the painted man woke in him the old atavistic terror of the unknown. Death had many faces and this was one of them. He held his breath as the kadaitja man came abreast of him and passed on, his feathered feet soundless in the powdery dust. Twenty yards ahead he halted at the sound of the whipbird call. Then he turned aside, parted the tall grass stalks and disappeared. Adams waited a few moments longer, then eased himself out of his cramped position and slid down the bank to the ford.

Halfway across it, he heard Mary's cry, a long, hysterical scream of pure terror. Heedless now of the noise, he splashed through the last twenty yards of water and went running to her along the sand.

Mundaru, restless on the border of sleep, heard the scream, and the marrow clotted in his bones. He knew what it was: the spirit essence of Menyan, haunting the place where he had killed her, because there was no one to perform the ceremonies of singing her to rest. She would be looking for him now, eyeless in the night, ranging over the swamp. She would not be alone. The "wingmalung" would be with her—the malignant ones who strike illness into the bodies of those who neglect their debts to the departed.

He was lost now, without recourse. He had heard the calls of the kadaitja men, but he had counted on time to find the white man before they came to kill him at sunrise. Now he knew that even this hope was gone. There was no escape from the dead, no remedy against the malice of the "wingmalung" except the tribal magic and from this he was forever cut off.

The terror grew on him like a palsy. Death was all around him. But even against the terrors of the spirit world, the primal instinct of self-preservation asserted itself. Menyan's spirit voice had come from the river. The kadaitja men were at his back. But all of them were still a distance away. If he ran, he might gain a little time—even though everything he knew told him he could not escape them utterly.

He picked up his spears and, bending double, began to work cautiously through the grass, away from the river, away from the kadaitja men. His limbs were cramped, his belly knotted, his entrails full of water. He moved slowly and with great effort as though he were hauling against a heavy load. He knew what it meant. Magical influences were at work on him, draining his life fluid, dragging him back.

He fought against them savagely, and after a while they seemed to grow less, although he knew this was an illusion. They were still there, still potent.

Eastward the moon rose higher in the sky and its radiance filtered through the mesh of fibers, lighting up his course. But even this held no joy for Mundaru. Menyan was named for the moon. The moon was an eye spying out his movements, reading them back to the spirit essence and the "wingmalung."

He dropped to his knees and began to crawl, close to the ground, as Lance Dillon had done before him. He was a primitive without understanding of irony. He was doomed and beyond the temptation of triumph. But a faint hope sprang up inside him when, after an hour's progress, he found that he was crawling in a set of tracks made by another man—a man bleeding, vomiting sometimes and leaving scraps and snippets of himself on the razor edges of the grass leaves.

Billy-Jo was piling a small mound of sand over the body of Menyan, the moon-girl. Neil Adams was sitting on a blanket, cradling Mary in his arms, soothing her like a child after a nightmare. Her shirt was stained with blood, her eyes stared, her whole body was shaken with rigors. The words tumbled out of her in disjointed narrative.

"... Asleep and dreaming ... I seemed to hear a cry. When I woke up, she was lying across me ... her face on mine. She ... she must have died just at that moment. ... It was terrible. ..."

She clung to him, hiding her face against his breast as if to blot out the memory.

"Easy, girl ... easy. It's over now."

"Don't leave me again, Neil! Please don't leave me!"

"I won't."

"... Billy-Jo was down by the river. I thought you'd both left me. ... I screamed and ..."

"I know ... I know. Now forget it, like a good girl. Did you bring any clean clothes?"

"There's a shirt in my saddlebag, but this cardigan's the only one I have."

He laid her down on the blanket, found the shirt and then peeled off his own cardigan and handed it to her.

"Get out of those things. I'll rinse them in the river."

But when she tried to take them off her hands would not obey and her fingers fumbled helplessly at the fastenings. Adams knelt beside her and undressed her to the waist. She shivered as the cold air struck her and he drew her white body against him for warmth, while he buttoned on the clean shirt and drew the heavy cardigan over her head. She surrendered herself like a child to the small, intimate service, and Adams was glad of the dark that hid his own face from her. If love were anything but a fiction of the marriage brokers, he was close to it now in this rare moment of tenderness and pity.

Billy-Jo came ambling back from the crude obsequies, and Adams tossed him the bloodstained clothes to wash. He tried to get Mary to lie down and sleep again, but she held to him desperately, and after a while he lay down beside her on the blanket, with her head pillowed on his arm and her arm flung twitching across his chest. He stroked her hair and talked to her: soft tales of the island men, from Macassar and Koepang, who traded along the coast in the old days, quaint ribaldries from the miners' camps and the bullock trains, legends of the dream people.

Little by little the panic drained out of her, her body relaxed, her breathing settled into the easy rhythm of sleep. For a long time he lay wakeful, her hair brushing his lips, her breast rising and falling against his own. Then, finally, the cold crept into his bones; he huddled against her for warmth and they bundled like lovers under the same blanket, while Billy-Jo paced the river-bank and listened for the bull-roarers and the song of death.

During the night the last wind dropped. Moonlight lay placid on river and plain and the ramparts of the Stone Country. The glacial cold of the desert crept across the swampland.

The cold was a trial to the kadaitja men. They were accustomed to going naked, night and day, but at night they slept with fires at their bellies and their backs, with the camp dogs curled beside them and their womenfolk lending them the warmth of their bodies. This night of solitary, hungry walking was a ritual pain, another symbol of the sacred character of their mission. They must endure it until the cycle had been completed with the death of Mundaru.

The moonlight and the still air were other symbols—proof that the magic of Willinja was working in their favour. When the moon was high, the man with the whipbird voice called them together and they converged on him accurately, although he was hidden from their sight. When they were all assembled, he had them hoist him on their shoulders, so that he stood, dark and massive in the sky, like a man walking on a moonlit sea.

For a long time he stood there, the light playing on his daubed body, quartering the grassland with his sacred spear, scanning every quadrant with eyes made keener by the aura of power within which he moved.

The whole country was wrapped in a silver dream. The swamp was flat as ice; the tree boles were grey sentinels against the skyline; their foliage drooped motionless against the stars. The grass was an unbroken carpet from the river to the lagoon and away to the dark ridges.

No bird sang. No animal stirred. Only the frogs and the crickets made a mystic chorus, punctuated now and then by the distant howl of a dingo and the haunting cry of a mopoke. The kadaitja man waited and watched while his companions grunted and braced themselves under his feathered feet.

Finally he saw the thing he had been expecting. Half a mile away, the grass was stirring as if a little wind were running through it or an animal were nosing its way through the undergrowth. But the kadaitja man knew that the animal was a man and that his name was Mundaru. He knew more—that the magic of Willinja was working and drawing the buffalo man towards a sacred place, where the tjuringa stones were hidden in a deep cave at the roots of a bottle tree and where the painted poles stood weathering round the leaf-covered entrance.

Before he reached it, they would take him. And when the spirit snake had been planted in his body, they would drive him towards it, so that he would die in the shadow of the power he had flouted.

It was enough. It was time to go. They lowered him back into the pit of grasses, and he told them where they must walk and how quickly, to come up with Mundaru at the first light of the new sun.

Sometime in the small hours of the morning, Lance Dillon woke, cramped, chattering and agonized, but lucid for the first time in many hours. The place in which he found himself was strange to him. The ground was hard and pebbly and dotted with small tussocks of coarse grass. When he turned his head painfully from side to side, he could see the shapes of stunted mulga trees, white and skeletal, under the moon. Ahead lay a low, tufted ridge of limestone, at whose foot was a thick clump of trees. When he tried to look back to see how far he had travelled from the grassland a spasm of agony shot through his shoulder, and he lay flat on the harsh ground trying to recover himself.

He knew very well that the lucidity was only temporary, a trough in the wave-like pattern of the fever. He must hold to it as long as he could. In the bleak radiance of the moon he saw how far he had strayed from the river and how his last hope of rescue had dwindled to nothing. It surprised him that he was not more afraid—that he was even relieved to be absolved from further effort and agony. The most he need do was dispose himself to die as comfortably as possible.

Many times in the years of his maturity he had been troubled by the questions: "What would I do if I were to lose this and this—my hope, my ambition, my wife? How would I react, if tomorrow a doctor told me I had only six months, six weeks, a week to live?" Now, in this brief interval of reason, the answers were plain to him. The hardest thing to accept was the inevitability of pain and loss and death. Before one accepted, there were the haunted nights when one lay awake thinking of money and overdrafts, and bank managers and the wise faces of the barroom prophets who knew all about bankruptcy except what it did to the innocent victim.

There were the bitter days when one was too proud to ask for a kiss or a word of understanding, the silent evenings when a man and a woman sat together in a room, yet in heart a million miles apart. There were the hours when they lay a foot apart in bed, each waiting for the other to make the first gesture of reconciliation—and finally slide dumbly into sleep.

And when one day the seed of death was planted in the body, there was the wracking fight to dislodge it—the fight he had just endured and which had brought him to this place—waterless, barren, a hundred yards from the limestone ridges. One had to submit in the end, but once the submission was made there was calm, the calm of the silver age, the last quiet time before the lights flickered out altogether.

One more effort was demanded of him—to drag himself the final hundred yards into the shadow of the trees. Once there, he could compose himself decently in the shade and wait for death.

He raised his head again and sighted on his target—a large bottle tree whose bloated trunk stood out from all the others in the clump. This would be his lodestar, the last goal of the last journey in the life of Lance Dillon. Summoning all his strength, he began to drag himself over the shaly ground towards it.

Every few yards he had to stop and rest, feeling the fever wave rising to extinguish the fire of reason. He would lie flattened from face to foot on the pebbles, weak, gasping and waiting for the mists of weakness to subside; then he would go on, heedless of the sharp stones that raked his belly and his chest into running wounds. Each time he moved, he took a new sight on the bottle tree, and as he came closer he saw, ranged in a semicircle before it, painted poles, some flattened like palm leaves, some tall as maypoles, others hollow and thick as a small tree. Between them the ground was piled thick with fallen leaves.

Dillon had seen the like of them before many times. They indicated a sacred place: sometimes a burial ground, where the dead were stored in hollow palm trunks, after their flesh had rotted away on platforms in the bush; sometimes a repository of sacred objects. The sight of it reminded him of the myalls who were coming to kill him. It was a casual reminder, tinged with irony. It was well that they should approach him with respect, walking over holy ground. Perhaps the ground might be too holy and they would fear to come to him—but he would still die and they could squat and watch him, just outside the painted poles.

His last halt was only five yards from the edge of the ring. The bottle tree lay perhaps another five beyond it and the intervening space was a carpet of dry leaves. He wanted to reach the tree, because its knotted, bulbous trunk would give him a backrest, and he had the idea that he wanted to sit upright to watch the dawn and the coming of his killers. A bushman's caution told him that the carpet of leaves might well hide venomous snakes, but a second reflection urged him forward. A snakebite might finish him quickly—truncate the final agony to a manageable limit.

He crawled foot by foot over the last rough ground and into the dead leaves. There was a kind of pleasure in their touch on his scarred and naked skin. There was a dusty aromatic scent about them, as if an essence of life still lingered. He wondered whether anything of himself would linger after the final dissolution.

The tree was only ten feet away now, and he was pushing towards it through leaves as deep as his face, when, without warning, the ground gave way beneath him and he felt himself rolling over and over into blackness.

Mary Dillon woke to moonlight on her face and the warmth of Adams's body against her own. His breathing was deep and regular, and under the rough texture of his shirt she could hear the strong beating of his heart. Her head was still pillowed on his arm and she felt the stubble of his cheek on her forehead, just below the hairline. His free arm lay slack over her body and the dead weight of it held her to him like a bond.

The last mist of sleep still clung to her and she surrendered herself to the comfort of his presence. She had slept three years in the marriage bed with Lance Dillon, but it was longer than she cared to remember since they had lain like this, relaxed, content, with passion a whisper away, yet dormant and unprovoked. It was a sour comedy that a day's ride and ten minutes of terror had brought her to this point with Neil Adams, while three years of contract and companionship with her husband had taken her a lifetime away from it.

Whose fault was it—Lance's or her own? Whose fault was this moment of dangerous propinquity, when she shared the same blanket with a man who was not her husband? The love with which she had entered marriage had worn perilously thin under the chafing of time and circumstance. What drew her to Neil Adams was of new strong growth, hard still to define by name, harder still to deny, untested. Both situations carried a measure of guilt, but a greater one of accident and inevitability. In both the same question cried for an answer: where did she go from here?

Neil Adams stirred, muttering in his sleep, and his arm fell away from her. Carefully, so as not to waken him, she eased herself up to a sitting position and looked about her. The moonlit river flowed placidly through the night; where the shadows broke, the sand and rock ledges lay silver to the sky, and fifty yards away Billy-Jo stood, a black sentinel staring across the river towards the hidden chorus of the bullfrogs.

As if for the first time, she saw the other face of the hated land—not hostile, but passive, not harsh, but empty and hungry for the touch to transfigure it to fruitfulness. What she was seeing now was what Lance had seen, in one mutation or another, and what he had tried vainly to communicate to her. In the first flush of revelation, it seemed she could get up and walk alone through the vastness without fear of man or bird or beast.

Lance had urged it on her many times, telling her that there were no wild beasts in the Territory and that even the wild nomads lived in order and peace, so long as their beliefs and customs were respected.

Then hard on the heels of the flattering illusion came the realization that hardly a mile away was being enacted a drama of pursuit and killing, in which her own husband was one of the victims. As if to emphasize the pathetic fallacy, from far to the west there came the long, mourning howl of a dingo.

From the east another answered, then another and another, until the night was filled with a dreary graveyard chant, rising and falling like wind in the vacant air.

She shivered and slid back under the blanket. At the same moment Neil Adams opened his eyes. Their faces brushed. His arms went round her, and the wasteland howling was hushed by his first whispered words.

Chapter Eight

IT IS NOT GIVEN TO EVERY MAN to approve the interior of his own tomb before he occupies it, and Lance Dillon was vaguely grateful for the privilege. He saw it from the position he would finally occupy in it—flat on his back on the sandy floor with a cone of darkness above his head and a moonbeam slanting downward from the hole through which he had fallen.

The hole was high above him and he wondered, inconsequently, what he must have looked like, flailing through the air as he fell. Then, as his eyes grew accustomed to the dim twilight, he saw that he had rolled down a long sandy ramp onto the floor. Tentatively, he moved his limbs, his head and trunk. They were painful but articulating normally. He was whole in bone and still lucid—an uncommon triumph for a man lying in his own burial vault.

The air about him was dry, warm and clean, but tinged with a faint fusty odour which he could not identify, until his straining eyes caught the outline of the bats hanging from the fretted limestone above him. One or two of them, disturbed by his fall, were dipping about in the darkness with faint mouse-like squeaking. They were odd, timid creatures, well made for this graveyard dozing, but they were harmless and infinitely better company than the kites, who would have come wheeling about him at the first warmth of dawn aboveground.

He closed his eyes and let his fingers scrabble in the sand. It was fine and powdery, with no hint of moisture. Sluggish reason told him the rest of the story. He had stumbled into a cave, scored out by one of the underground rivers that had run, centuries ago, beneath the surface of the Stone Country. Beyond this cave would be others, large or small, linked by a tunnel which

87

was the course of the ancient river. If he wanted a deeper grave, it was here waiting for him, given the strength and the drive to find it.

But for the present he was content. The sand was soft. The warmth was grateful after the bitter cold aboveground, and after the moonlight there would be the sun, striking through the peephole of the vault. He might not be alive to see it, but it was pleasant to think of, a hope to hold, while reason remained with him.

Slowly the vague shapes of his surroundings solidified: the groining of the rock roof, the pendant points of stalactites, the narrowing gullet of darkness where a tunnel ran downward into the bowels of the earth, the niches in the walls, stacked with stones, and bundles wrapped in tree bark. These last he could not identify, but he guessed that they were the weapons and bones of long-dead warriors cached by the myalls in their sacred place.

He wondered whether they would accord him the same privilege after they had killed him—whether even this primitive decency would be denied him. Not that it mattered. Not that anything mattered now, except a comfortable exit from the ruins of his life.

He had never had any religious faith. Philosophy was a scholastic mystery to him. His whole life had been dominated by the pragmatic cycle of birth, increase, acquisition and death. A man's only survival was in his offspring, and he was lucky if he died before they disappointed him. Death was the ultimate fear, but once one passed beyond this fear, there was only the calm disappointment that life had meant so little.

Suddenly the arid stillness of the air was broken by a sound, a single clear note, as if someone had flipped a fingernail against a crystal goblet. The overtones hung a moment in the conical cave and then died. For a full minute Dillon lay listening, but the sound was not repeated. His thoughts drifted away from it.

. . . The drover's son who wanted to be a cattle king. . . . The snot-nosed boy, holding a stirrup leather for the great Kidman himself and gaping in wonder at the gold half-sovereign tossed for him to catch. . . . The stripling stockrider, plugging his first thousand head of beef over five hundred miles of drought-stricken country to the railhead. . . . The leather-faced gunner in the Japanese war, trading his cigarette and beer ration for a few extra pounds in his paybook. . . . Keeping away from the girls on leave, because a night on the town was half the price of a yearling heifer. . . . The day his number came up in the repatriation ballot for a lease of Crown Land in the Territory. . . . The tent in the middle of nowhere, while his stock grazed on the river flats. . . . All the years of sweating and penny-pinching and denial, of meager checks and lean credit, until he could build his first house and pay off his first mortgage and make his first trip to the east to buy decent stock. So long as he was small and struggling, dealing in scrub bullocks and stringy beef, the big combines were prepared to leave him alone. . . . But from the day he made his first leap into the breeding business, they began to put pressure on him—always on the same tender spot: credit. When he married and began to build a household and a staff, the pressure increased, but the greater the pressure the tougher he became, the more determined and single-minded, so that in the end his whole hope of life, security and happiness became centered in the genitals of a bull.

Looking at it now, in the thin twilight of his burial place, he saw it as a monstrous folly, next door to madness. Yet it was the truth. Other men had laughed and kissed and got drunk and bred sons they couldn't afford and laid their last shillings on a filly hammering down the straight; while he had lived, disciplined as a monk, in the service of a sacred animal. Who now was in profit—he or they? Who would be mourned longer, with more of love and pity?

As if to punctuate the unanswerable question, the tiny musical note sounded again. He strained at the tenuous echoes, but the next moment they were gone, while his mind still groped for the tag of association. . . . Sunday dinner at the homestead. . . . The meal all but over. . . . Two people with nothing fresh to say to each other, idling over the coffee and the last of the wine. Mary tapping absently at the rim of her wineglass with a coffee spoon, so that the heavy air was filled with the thin, repetitive note. His own voice, sharp and surprisingly loud:

"For God's sake, Mary! Must you do that?"

And then Mary's wintry, sidelong smile. "Wears you down, doesn't it?"

"Why do it then?"

"Cattle for breakfast, cattle for lunch, cattle for dinner, cattle in bed."

With each repetition, the spoon tinkled on the glass.

"That wears me down, Lance. I'm a woman, not a breeding cow. Don't you see what's happening to us? I want a husband, not a studmaster."

"For God's sake, Mary! Be a little patient! I've told you a dozen times, we're battling now; but it won't be for long. A couple more years and . . ."

"And we're building bigger herds and better ones—while love gets smaller and smaller; while our marriage goes from bad to worse."

"I've always thought it was a pretty good marriage."

"You've hardly thought about it at all. And I'm beginning to lose interest!"

"You don't damn well know what you want. . . ."

And so on and on, through the dreary dialogue of disillusion, with its meaningless accusation and its hidden rancours that each was too proud to put into words. . . .

Now, when there was no pride left, it was already too late. When he was ready to speak the truth, his swollen lips could not frame the words—and there was no one to hear them if he did.

Again the solitary crystalline sound rang through the vault. This time he understood what it was: the fall of a single drop of water into a pool. Behind his matted eyelids a picture formed: the slow seepage of minuscule droplets through the earth; their agglomeration at the root of a rusted stalactite; their slow, trickling course down the spear of limestone; the moment of suspension at the point; the final plunge into a basin where a million other drops had gathered safe from the sun and the thirst of man and beast.

89

Water . . . ! The last demand of the dying on a world of such varied richness. He waited until the sound came again and fixed its direction in his mind. Then he rolled himself over on his belly and began to drag himself towards it, hoping desperately that he would not find it beyond his reach.

Finally his hands touched the base of the wall and felt it swell into a kind of pillar above him. The next sound of water seemed to come from directly above his head. The problem was to raise himself to reach it. He drew his trunk and feet as close as possible to the pillar of limestone, and then, grasping the nearest projection, he began to haul himself upward, dragging with his hands, thrusting with his feet, holding himself by friction to the rough surface when each installment of strength gave out.

Then the pillar broke off and his fingers clung to a ledge. With a last convulsive effort he reached it and threw the upper part of his body across it so that he hung by his torso, with his face dipping into a shallow basin of icy water. The touch of it was like knife blades on his torn skin, but he lapped at it greedily and felt it burning his gullet as he swallowed. Even when he had drunk his fill he still hung there, waiting for the little infusion of strength to seep outwards to his members.

His fingers explored the ledge around the basin and found it wider than their compass—wide enough perhaps for a man to lie within reach of the water. They found other things too: knobs and shards of limestone fallen from the roof, stalactites, long as daggers and almost as sharp. His fingers brushed some of them into the water, but closed on one, long as a man's forearm, thin and smooth and pointed like an awl.

Again the cool reminder that he was not to be allowed to die in peace; that the last moment would be one of violence and terror. He had not cared before. But now, in this quiet place, a coal of anger began to glow inside him. He had suffered enough. He had run to the edge of the last dark leap. Why should be wait tamely till they thrust him over it? His fingers crisped round the smooth butt of the stalactite, then slowly relaxed.

First he must haul himself onto the ledge near the water. Here he could lie, husbanding his residue of strength, cooling himself when the fever rose again. From here he could make the final despairing leap at the first of his attackers, the stone dagger in his hand, all the anger, disillusion and regret arming him for the hopeless fight.

It was the last hour of the dark when Neil Adams got up, settled the blanket around Mary and walked down to the riverbank to take over the watch from Billy-Jo.

The blacktracker had nothing to report. The kadaitja men had been silent a long time. They would probably remain so until the first light of day. He shambled up the beach, threw himself down on his blanket and curled into sleep like a bush creature.

Neil Adams sat down on a rock ledge, lit a cigarette and let his mind drift with the smoke spirals, while his body relaxed into the sad, sweet contentment that follows after the act of love.

He had known many women, but this was the first with whom possession had seemed more like a surrender than a conquest. The ramparts of egotism had been tumbled down, the barricades of the Book of Rules had been taken without a fight. The legend of impregnability was destroyed for ever. He was a man who had taken another's wife, a policeman who had betrayed his trust and was open to attainder by any man who cared to dig deep enough into his secrets.

It was a bitter dreg to poison the aftertaste of love, but it was there, and gag as he might he had to swallow it. Get it down then at one wry gulp. Adultery and professional dereliction. It is done. There is no way to mend it—and perhaps, after all, there is no need. The odds are all on Dillon's death, and what's the harm in a tumble with a new and willing widow? If he's alive, he doesn't know; and who's to tell or care—unless my lady has an unlikely attack of remorse? . . .

Even as he thought it, he knew it for a cynic's defense, harder to sustain than the simple truth. For the first time in his life he had come close to love— the pain and the power and the mystery of it. Mary Dillon had come to it too; and even without the consummation, the love would still be there—the pain too, and the haunting questions: Will it look the same when the sun comes up? And if it does, what's to do about it?

He stared across the water at the driftwood pile behind which Lance Dillon had hidden only twenty-four hours ago. Again he was touched with reluctant admiration for the endurance and resource of the man, naked, wounded and alone, pitting himself against the primitive to whom the bush was an open thoroughfare. How long had he lasted? How had he died? Had he known beforehand that his wife was lost to him? Did he end hating her or regretting his own failure to hold her? What would he have done in Neil Adams's shoes? Fruitless questions all of them—except one: Where was Dillon now? If anyone knew the answer, it was Mundaru, the buffalo man, and he was coming nearer to death with every minute that ticked away towards the dawn.

Neil Adams listened to the night, waiting for the calls of the kadaitja men. None came. If Billy-Jo was right, none would come until the death chant began and the banshee howling of the bull-roarer. He tossed his cigarette into the river and watched the current whirl it away into darkness. All his other loves had been like that—a swift enjoyment, a swift extinction. But who could tell how long this one might last and what fires might blaze up from its still-warm embers?

At the sound of a footfall in the sand he turned sharply to find Mary standing over him, her face pale but smiling in the moonlight. He stood up, took her in his arms and they held to each other for a long, quiet moment of renewal. Then they sat down together on the flat rock, hands locked but faces averted from each other, lapped in the tenuous content of new lovers.

"Neil?" Her voice was soft and solicitous.

"Yes, Mary?"

"There's something I want to tell you."

"Go ahead."

"Remember the old gag: 'The hardest thing about lovemaking is knowing what to say afterwards'?"

He turned at the hint of mockery in her voice, but there was no mockery in her eyes, only a smiling tenderness. He grinned and nodded.

"I remember it. Is that your problem?"

"No." The denial was emphatic. "And if it's yours, Neil, forget it. There's nothing to say and nothing to pay. I'm glad it happened and I'll always remember. But if you don't want to remember, I'll never remind you. That's all, darling."

"Is it?"

"From me, yes."

"Is that a dismissal?"

Her face clouded. She shook her head slowly.

"It's an act of love, Neil. It's the only way I can tell you that you're as free now as—as you were with any of the others."

"I may not want to be, Mary."

"Then you're free until you find out."

"And then?"

"Then perhaps I'll be sure too."

He gripped her arms brutally and slewed her round to face him. His eyes and mouth were hard.

"Understand something, Mary! This isn't a bush meeting where you can back 'em both ways and hedge your bets on the outsider!"

"You think that's what I'm trying to do?"

"Yes."

Her head went up proudly and she challenged him.

"All right, Neil! Here it is. What happened tonight was real for me. I wouldn't take back any of it, even if I could. If Lance is dead, I'm free. If he's alive and well, I was going to leave him, anyway. . . . And I love you, Neil. Now, what do *you* want to do about it?"

His grip on her arms relaxed. His eyes dropped away from hers. His voice lost its harsh commanding note.

"I—I think we should both wait and see."

"That's all I was trying to say, Neil," she told him coolly. "I love you enough to leave you free. But don't ever tell me I'm hedging my bets. I did once, but never again."

"I'm sorry, Mary."

"I don't blame you. But I can't let you blame me, either. If I blame myself it's a private business, and I'll never ask you to carry the load of it. Now kiss me, darling—and let's not talk anymore."

But even in the kiss there was still the sour taste of regret, the comfortless revelation that guilt is a lonely burden—and that a man needs a special kind of courage to carry it in silence. Mary Dillon had it, but he wished he were half as sure of himself.

When the grey of the false dawn crept into the eastern sky, Mundaru, the buffalo man, halted, just inside the fringe of the grasslands. He was cold, weary, hungry, and above all confused. All night long he had been creeping in the tracks of the white man. At every moment he had expected to come up with him, living or dead, but still he had not found him.

Ten paces ahead the grassland faded out into tussocks and stunted mulga trees, a wide waterless area limited by the limestone ridge where painted poles were grouped around the sacred bottle tree. The whole space was empty of life or movement. The white man had disappeared and Mundaru lapsed into the final despairing conviction that he had died long since and that what he had followed was a spirit shape, luring him to destruction.

With the conviction came a kind of calm. Death was already lodged in his carcass. He could hope no more, run no farther. When the kadaitja men came, as soon they must, they would find him waiting for them, a passive participant in the ritual of propitiation.

Stiffly he got to his feet and pushed through the grasses into the open space beyond. The light was spreading now, the stars receding to pinpoints in the grey firmament. A little breeze was beginning to stir in the leaves of the mulga trees. The bullfrog chorus died slowly into silence and the first bird of the morning rose, a black sinister shape in the sky ahead of him. It was a kite, and soon there would be more of them, many more, wheeling above him, waiting for him to die.

Halfway to the ridge he halted, laid down his spears, unwrapped his fire sticks and squatted down on the ground to coax a little flame into a handful of dry, spiny grass. It was a meaningless action. He had no food to cook. The fire would have no warmth in it. But the motion of twirling the stick between his palms, spinning its point against the hardwood of its mate, blowing the first spark into a tiny flame, required a concentration that took his mind from the men who were stalking him.

When he himself had worn the kadaitja boots, he had found his victim crouched like a frightened animal, vomiting on the ground. He did not care to die like that. He could not fight. There was no challenge to the sacred spears, but at least he could go through the last motions of manhood, with the first gift of the dream people flowering into flame under his hands.

Eastward the sky brightened, blood red, as the sun pushed upward towards the rim of the world. The point of the spinning stick ran hot against the hollow of hardwood, and a thin whiff of smoke rose from the tuft of grass. Mundaru grunted with satisfaction and blew steadily to coax out the first spark. A long shadow fell across the ground in front of him, and he looked up to see six men, painted and motionless as rocks, standing in front of him. In their upraised arms they carried throwing-spears, and the long, barbed heads were pointed at his breast.

The fire sticks fell from his hands. The smoke was extinguished. Mundaru's arms hung slack to the ground and his eyes searched the painted faces above him. Between the bars of yellow ochre, their eyes looked down at him, cold as granite.

Then from behind him the bull-roarer began, a thin howling, growing in volume and tone to a deep, drumming roar. The air was full of it. The ground vibrated to it. It hammered at his skull and crept into the hollows of his bones and filled his entrails like wind. It stuffed his ears and seared his eyeballs and choked his nose so that he could not breathe.

The kadaitja men watched and listened immobile, their spear points ready. The roaring went on and on for nearly twenty minutes, then stopped abruptly. Blind, deaf and shivering in the silence, Mundaru waited. There was a sound like a rush of bird wings at his back, and he pitched forward with the sacred spear in his kidneys.

Long before the bull-roarer began, Billy-Jo had the horses saddled and the pack pony loaded. Mary Dillon and Neil Adams were standing by the fire drinking pannikins of scalding coffee. The tension between them had eased and they talked gravely and companionably of the day ahead.

"I'd like you to understand my reasoning, Mary. It could be wrong, but it's the only logic I can see."

"You can't ask more of yourself than that, Neil. Go ahead."

"Strictly speaking, I should forget about the myalls and concentrate on a search for your husband. The tribal blood feud is secondary, I can deal with that anytime. But the fact is, we could cast about all day and still find no trace of your husband. Billy-Jo's the best tracker in the Territory, but even he can't work miracles. You understand that?"

"Of course."

"So I'm working on the assumption that your husband is dead. All the signs point that way. This is the third day, and we know he was quite badly wounded. The only man who can give us any information is the man who's been tracking him—Mundaru. The kadaitja men are after him, and they'll get him—sure as God."

"How can he help you then?"

"In a kadaitja killing, the victim lives for some hours. That's the point of it. He dies by a magical power, not by a man's hand. If I can come up with him before he dies, I may be able to get something out of him. But I can't promise. . . . If we fail there, then Billy-Jo and I will beat the swamp for the rest of the day."

"Neil?" There was tenderness in her voice and a curious touch of pity. "You're a good policeman. Believe it always."

"I'm glad someone thinks so." He bent and kissed her lightly, tossed the

94

dregs of his coffee into the fire and turned away towards the horses, just as the first booming sound of the bull-roarers sounded across the swamp. The three of them froze: Billy-Jo in the act of tightening a girth, Adams in midstride, Mary with the tin mug halfway to her mouth. Even in the cold light of morning, the primitive terror held them strongly.

Billy-Jo cocked his head like a hound listening. He flung out his hand in an emphatic gesture.

"Over there, boss. Long way. Outside swamp."

Adams nodded.

"We'll try to skirt the billabong. No point trying to hack our way through." He turned to Mary. "Before we go, Mary . . . you ride between Billy-Jo and me. No matter what happens, no matter what you see, keep your head. And do exactly as I tell you. Understand?"

"I understand."

"Let's get moving."

He hoisted her into the saddle and they moved off, Neil Adams in front, Mary behind him, with Billy-Jo last and leading the pack pony. They splashed across the ford, struggled up the steep bank and began to work their way upstream along the narrow strip of clear ground between the bushes and the grass fringe.

They had gone perhaps a mile when the bull-roarer stopped. Neil Adams reined in and they waited while he stood in his stirrups and scanned the swamplands, stirring lightly under the morning breeze. After a couple of minutes he lowered himself into the saddle, dug his heels into the pony's flanks and set off at a canter with the others trailing behind him.

For the next mile Mary Dillon found herself moving in a kind of waking dream, conscious of all her surroundings yet absorbed in an inner contemplation. She felt everything, saw everything: the thrusting muscle of the pony, the twigs and branches that whipped at her, the wind rushing in her face, the new light spilling over the land and the sky, Neil Adams a galloping centaur ahead of her. Yet her thoughts were all bent backward—to the riverbank, to the homestead, to the swift passion that had driven her into the arms of Neil Adams, to the slow death of her love for Lance, to the one vaulting moment in which the world and her relationship to it had changed completely.

She had seen the change before, in other women, but she had never understood it until now. There was an alchemy in the act of union. The transmutation for better or for worse was terribly final. One emerged from it curiously free, yet free in a new country, the contours of which hid mysteries unguessed at in the time of wholeness or fidelity. It was the old drama of Eve and the Tree of Knowledge, when the world changed overnight at the first bite of a strange fruit.

She was a wife, but not the same wife. From a creditor in marriage she had become a debtor. Her rights in law had been forfeited. The wholeness of herself had been broken and parcelled out, valueless to one man, to the other worth only what he cared to pay for it.

95

How much would he pay? How much was his hesitation dictated by fear for himself, how little by concern for her? How much did she care whether he paid or not, provided she could still read love in his eyes and a respect, however reluctant? And Lance? Was it only because he was dead that she could still think of him with tenderness? If he was alive, could she still face him with dignity? Even the most merciless self-scrutiny told her that she could. Few marital contracts were breached without fault on both sides, and the moralist's finger often pointed in the wrong direction.

Ahead of her Neil Adams reined in suddenly and her own horse reared up on its haunches, and it took all her strength to hold and steady him. Adams turned in his saddle and pointed out across the grassland to where a thin column of brown smoke was rising into the sky.

"What do you make of it, Billy-Jo?"

The blacktracker called back, "Kadaitja men, boss. Takim man. Burnim spirit snake in back."

Adams nodded and turned to Mary.

"This is it. Close in."

She edged her mount close to him so that their stirrups were almost brushing.

"How far, Neil?"

"About half a mile. We'll take 'em through the grass."

"I'm scared, Neil."

His hand reached across and closed over her own. His voice was very gentle.

"Don't worry. We'll be together from here on."

As they urged their horses through the high, rank grasses, she wondered what meaning she should read into those eight simple words.

Mundaru, the buffalo man, was lying spread-eagled in the dust. The kadaitja men were squatting round him, holding his twitching body, while their leader extracted the spearhead from his back. Beside them, a small fire was burning, and in the center of the fire lay a stone, elliptical in shape and flattened on both sides. As the coals built up around it, they brushed them carefully to one side so that the sacred object was always visible, like a heart absorbing heat from the fiery body that encased it.

When the spearhead was extracted, there was a small rush of blood, and the kadaitja man held the lips of the wound together while he rummaged in the small bark bag which Willinja had given into his hands. He brought out a small sliver of white quartz, about the length of a finger, and this he inserted deep in the wound, covering it with a plug of brown gum resin. Mundaru twisted and heaved convulsively at this magical invasion of his body, but the kadaitja men held him down and forced his mouth into the dust so that he could not cry out.

The leader stood up and walked to the fire. Without a moment's hesitation, he plunged his hand into the coals and picked up the sacred stone. It was

96

nearly white-hot, but he grasped it firmly. He felt no pain, and when he laid it over the wound in Mundaru's back, the flesh and the resin were instantly cauterized, while his own hand was unharmed. When the operation was over, he laid the stone on the ground, filled his mouth with water and squirted it with his lips on the stone to wash off any evil which might have clung to it from Mundaru's body. When it was cool he put it back in the bark bag and stood up. The others stood with him and looked down at Mundaru, jerking and groaning at their feet.

It was all but done. There remained only the death walk. They hauled Mundaru to his feet and held him until they felt him steady, then they pushed him forward. At the first step he collapsed, but they dragged him up again, set his face to the sacred place and prodded him forward with their spears. Miraculously he stayed on his feet and, one hand clamped to the torn muscles of his back, he began to shamble ahead. The kadaitja men followed, with pointing spears, measuring their pace to his.

A foot outside the circle of painted poles they laid hands on him again and held him, turning his head this way and that so that his glazed eyes might see the symbol of all the power he had outraged. Now for the first time he began to struggle. This was the final vision of death. No matter how long more he survived, this was the ultimate agony. But they had no pity for him. With one concerted heave, they tossed him forward into the leaves and watched the ground swallow him up.

The echoes of his last despairing scream were still in the air when the shot rang out, and they wheeled to face the riders pounding towards them over the plain.

The scream woke Lance Dillon out of a doze, filled with the phantasms of fever. He was lying on the edge near the pool, one arm dangling numb and helpless in the water, the other still grasping the pointed stalactite. When he opened his eyes, he saw at first only a formless blur of light; but as his vision cleared, he understood that it was the sunlight slanting down from the entrance to the cave.

It was morning then. He had lasted the night. He wondered whether he would see the noon. He eased himself carefully on the rock ledge, trying to work a semblance of life into his numbed arm. The effort brought him perilously close to the edge of the platform, and as his angle of sight shifted he was able to focus on the spot where the sunbeam struck the sandy floor of the cave.

Terror flooded through him like a purge. Crouched on all fours in the sunlight was the figure of a myall black. As he looked, the myall raised his head, and Dillon could see the bulging eyeballs and the mouth drawn back in a grin from the white teeth. Recognition was complete. This was the man who had wounded him in the valley, who had led the trackers through two nights and a day, and who had found him at last, cornered and ready for the kill.

The myall moved forward out of the sunbeam, and Dillon lost him for a moment, when his head drooped and his body melted into the darkness. He could still hear him breathing in short savage gasps as he moved closer to the low pillar of limestone. Any moment now he must stand up, and as soon as he did he must come leaping to haul him off his pedestal.

He must not die like this, trapped like a rat in a dark hole. Every nerve in his body was alive with the instinct of survival. His fingers tightened round the stone dagger and he could feel the remnants of his will gathering themselves like a spring inside him.

With a huge effort he forced himself up to his knees, slewed his body so that his legs dangled over the edge of the platform and he was sitting more or less upright. The effort made him groan aloud; pieces of limestone, dislodged by his movement, splashed into the pool. When his dizziness had passed, he wondered why the myall had not come for him. His heavy animal breathing was closer than ever.

Dillon blinked away the sweat that bleared his eyes and peered about the dark hollows of the cave, searching for his adversary. Then he saw him, a pace away from the foot of the platform, still on his knees and snuffling at the sand. A faint highlight outlined the shape of his shoulder muscles and the line of his dorsal bones.

It was now or never. If the myall lifted up his head, it was the end. Dillon's fingers crisped round the thick butt of the stalactite and, holding it forward in both hands, he plunged downward onto the body of the myall.

He felt the point of it dig deep into flesh, heard the sound as the limestone snapped under his weight, then darkness swept over him like a wave, tainted with the smell of death.

Chapter Nine

JUST OUTSIDE THE RANGE OF A THROWN SPEAR, Neil Adams halted his little troop and sat, erect in the saddle, watching the painted men, drawn up in line across the entrance to the sacred place. They were tense and watchful. Their spears were notched to their throwing-sticks, and a single untimely gesture would bring them running to outflank the riders and cut them down. He might hold them off with gunfire; but this would mean killing, and in the code of the Territory policeman this was barbarism, a confession of failure, a destruction of twenty years' work in the management of the nomads.

He turned to Mary and said quietly, "I'm going to talk to them with Billy-Jo. If there's trouble, don't hang around. Ride like hell for the river and get the stock boys. Understand?"

"Yes, Neil."

"For the present, stay here. Don't move until the first spear is thrown."

"Do you think . . . ?"

"Just do as you're told."

"Yes, Neil."

"Billy-Jo!"

"Yes, boss?"

"We'll go on foot."

The tracker shrugged and dismounted. Neil Adams made an ostentatious gesture of shoving his rifle back into the saddle bucket, then he too dismounted, and the two of them walked slowly towards the painted men, holding their hands wide from their bodies, palms upturned, to show that they came in peace and without weapons.

Mary Dillon watched, white-faced and fearful. The kadaitja men watched too, measuring their paces, the fingers tightening round the throwing-sticks, their muscles contracting for the throw. Twenty yards from the enclosure of poles, Adams and the tracker halted, straddle-legged, arms outstretched. The hostility in front of them was like a wall.

Adams moistened his dry lips and said to the tracker, "Tell them we come in peace. Tell them we know what has been done to Mundaru and that we know what they do not—that he raped and killed the wife of Willinja. Tell them where the body is and that they should take it back to their camp."

The tracker grunted assent, paused a moment collecting himself, then raised his husky voice in the manner of the tribal orator. It rang in the emptiness, now high and dramatic, now rolling in long, resonant periods. His gestures were ample and expressive, and as he spoke Adams saw the kadaitja men look at one another in doubt, felt their hostility relax a fraction.

When Billy-Jo had finished speaking, they muttered a while together, then one of them laid his spears on the ground and stepped forward into the open space and began to speak. Billy-Jo translated for Adams:

"Mundaru dead. Eaten by spirit snake. Leaveim in spirit place. Blackfella business. White man no touch."

"Tell them we understand blackfella business. Tell them Boss Dillon is lost and we think Mundaru killed him. This makes it white man's business. I want to go down into the spirit place and talk with the spirit of Mundaru. If they try to stop me there will be trouble for them and the tribe. Say that we have done service to Willinja and that we tried to help his wife. He has a debt to us. They will earn his anger if they prevent him paying it."

Billy-Jo took up the theme again, embellishing it with the symbols of the people, translating the pragmatic logic of the white man into the involved spiritistic reasoning of the primitive. Adams knew enough of the language to understand that the tracker was drawing heavily on the personal credit of the policeman with the tribes. He was emphasizing time and again that Adams had always paid his debts, that he had never infringed legal custom, that he had never spoken with the forked tongue of the liar, that he had defended the black against the predatory drifters, that his friendship was strong and his vengeance terrible.

The answer of the kadaitja man was clear and emphatic. He accepted all the claims of the policeman—but the life of Mundaru was forfeited to the spirits, and the white man must not enter the spirit place.

When the answer was translated to him in clattering pidgin, Adams found himself in a neat dilemma. The myalls knew that the white man tried to save the victims of tribal vengeance and bring them to trial in their own fashion. They knew, too, the unwritten law that their own secret places must be respected. Defiance of this law would destroy his credit and earn him nothing but a spear thrust in the ribs. He decided to play for time.

"Ask them, Billy-Jo: do they know Mundaru killed the great bull? And do they know that he was hunting Boss Dillon to kill him also?"

The answer came back: yes, they knew.

"Do they know what happened to the white man?"

No. They did not know. But if he were dead this debt was paid by the death of Mundaru.

Adams took a deep breath. He was gambling now—with his own life, with Billy-Jo's, and possibly with Mary's.

"Then tell them this: I believe that Mundaru tracked the white man to this place and either drove him into the spirit cave or killed him and hid his body there. If this is true, his spirit will not rest, but will haunt the place forever and destroy the magic of the tribe. . . ." And he added in sardonic parenthesis: "For God's sake, make it sound good!"

The tracker shot him a swift, dubious glance and spoke again. This time the myall's answer was less hostile, more bargaining.

"He say you not sure, boss. You go down, maybe come up with Boss Dillon, maybe not. But you no take Mundaru. Mundaru belong spirit snake."

For all the danger of the situation, Neil Adams felt a flicker of sardonic amusement at the neat way they had trapped him. They wanted Mundaru at all costs. He understood why. They were the official executioners. They must report a successful killing—otherwise they themselves would fall under sanction. To get what he wanted, he had to wrench the law in their favour, but their spears were at his breast; he had no choice. He turned to Billy-Jo.

"Tell them I agree. Tell them to go and pick up the girl. I will leave Mundaru in the spirit cave. Give them a message from me to Willinja. I will see him at sunset."

The message was relayed. The answer came back.

"They want to stay, boss. Watchim go down. Watchim come up."

Adams's face clouded with dramatic anger.

"I have never spoken a lie. If they do not believe me, let them kill me now!"

Even as Billy-Jo was speaking, he advanced, ripping open his shirt and baring his breast to them. It was the kind of theatrical gesture the primitives understood: man asserting his maleness by boasting and provocation. Three feet from the kadaitja spokesman he halted, and they faced each other, the painted man, the policeman, their eyes locked, their faces stony with mutual defiance. Then the kadaitja man grunted assent and turned away; Adams did the same. He had won his point. There was no profit in making his adversary lose face.

The kadaitja men moved off, heading back to the grasslands and the river. Adams and Billy-Jo walked back to the horses. Adams's hands were twitching as he climbed into the saddle and picked up the reins.

Mary questioned him shakily: "You looked so small and lonely out there. What was it all about?"

He shrugged and grinned at her.

"A piece of haggling. They didn't want me to go into the sacred place. I talked them into it—or rather Billy-Jo did."

The blacktracker chuckled huskily.

101

"Boss Adams big fool gambler, missus. Maybe win, maybe all get bellyful of spears."

"Maybe."

He dismissed the subject casually, but Mary's concern and admiration warmed him like whisky and restored a little of the confidence he had lost on the riverbank.

As they cantered across the open ground towards the big bottle tree, she asked him gravely, "You have nothing more to tell me, Neil?"

"About your husband? Nothing. All we know is that Mundaru is down in the cave. We saw them push him into it. The chances are he's still alive. We take it from there."

"I was afraid for you, Neil. When I saw you walking out towards the spears, I—I thought, if anything happened to you, I couldn't bear it."

He mocked her lightly.

"Wonderful what you can take when you have to."

"Don't laugh about it, Neil."

"I'm not laughing, Mary. Just reminding you that what happens from here on may not be pleasant."

"I know. I've been thinking about it."

A few yards from the painted poles they stopped. Adams dismounted and handed the reins of his pony to Billy-Jo. The blackfellow stared at him, puzzled. Adams answered his unspoken thought.

"First I'm going in alone, Billy-Jo. The myalls will be watching to see what happens. I've got to keep the promise. If Mundaru's alive, I'll send you down to talk to him. Wait here with Mrs. Dillon."

He rummaged in the saddlebag and brought out a flashlight encased in rubber. He tested it and stepped towards the gaping hole in the leaves. Mary's voice stayed him.

"Please be careful, Neil."

He grinned and waved a reassuring hand.

"It's just a cave, full of bones and bats. I'll be back in a few minutes." He stood a moment, shining the light down into the vault, then stepped down the ramp of sand and was lost to view. For one wild second, it seemed to Mary Dillon that he had gone down into a deep, private hell from which he would never come back.

Halfway down the ramp Adams halted, listening and probing the darkness with his flashlight. There was no sound but the rasp of a tiny runnel of sand cascading down from his boots. The air smelt dry and musty, but tinged with the acrid odour of blood and human exhalation. The moving fingers of light picked out the bats hanging from the vault, the cavities stuffed with sacred objects, the glittering fall of the stalactites.

Adams focussed the light on the floor and moved it in wide sweeping arcs as he stepped down the last slope. From the shadows there came the single

102

musical note of dropping water, and when he swung the light towards the sound he saw the two bodies, one flattened on the sand, the other flung over it like a sack.

He gasped with the sudden shock and drew back, then edged his way carefully towards the prone figures. They were motionless, silent. When he knelt to examine them, he saw that the upper one was that of a white man. He reached out a tentative hand and rolled it onto its back. At the sight of it he gagged and turned away, retching violently.

The face was a swollen mass, the eyes and nostrils puffed, the mouth frothy and distorted. One shoulder was a suppurating wound and the skin about it was streaked and swollen with infection. The whole trunk was scored with scratches, blistered raw from the sun and caked with dust and dried blood. The hands were joined under the diaphragm and held a stump of limestone between their clenched fingers. One rib had caved in under the impact.

Adams switched the beam to the body of the myall and saw the stalactite projecting from the small of his back, and near it the cauterized spear wound. He reached out his hand and withdrew it sharply from the cold and rigid contact. He slanted the beam upward and saw the rock platform where Dillon had lain. The picture was brutally clear to him. Dillon cornered in his last refuge. The dying aborigine blundering about the cave. The last panic leap of the white man onto the body of his hunter. Now they were both dead, with all their problems solved—and a lot more than either of them had ever guessed.

A wave of relief washed over him, and when it passed he felt strangely elated. The slate was clean, the report could be written with truth and discretion. The obsequies could be arranged to spare Mary any of this grisly spectacle, and after a decent time they could begin to think about their own future.

Then the policeman's habit asserted itself once again and he bent to make a final examination of the bodies. He raised the myall's arm and felt for the pulse. There was none. The cold of death was already creeping into the members. He jerked out the stalactite and tossed it far into a corner of the cave. No point in complicating the report. Cause of death—spear wounds. A kadaitja killing. Period.

He turned away and bent to make a similar examination of Dillon. He prized open the puffed lids and saw the eyes rolled upward into the head. He put his ear to the broken rib cage and listened. There was no sound of a heartbeat. But when he felt the pulse, his heart sank like a stone in a pool. It was still there, weak, thready and uncertain. But it was there. Lance Dillon was alive.

For the first time in his life he understood the meaning of murder. The motive, simple but monstrous. The compulsion, overwhelming in its urgency, to sweep away at one stroke an obstacle to happiness. The opportunity, complete and flawless. Leave Dillon alone for another few hours and he would most certainly die. He had only to go aboveground, tell Mary and Billy-Jo that he found both men dead and then, to spare the widow the grisly sight of the body, head back to join the stock boys, who would later return to pick up the body and carry it back to the station for a postmortem, whose finding would be inevitable: death from a spear wound, infection and exposure.

For one horrible, timeless moment the thought possessed him like a madness. He could do it. He wanted to do it. Immunity was guaranteed. Here in the naked country, Neil Adams was the law. His word was beyond question. He needed only the courage to turn his face away and walk into the sunlight.

The horror receded slowly and he stood there, sweating and trembling, with Lance Dillon lying at his feet like a rag doll, muddied from a playtime of children. Then, before the madness could take him again, he stooped, hoisted Dillon onto his shoulders like a sack of carrots and staggered up the steep incline into the day.

They covered Lance Dillon with blankets and laid him under the shade of the bottle tree. They bathed his face, forced water and whisky between his teeth, felt the thin trickle of life in him surge a moment, then ebb again. They did all these things with a fierce, wordless concentration as though the simplest exchange might shout their secrets to the sky.

Mary Dillon bent, tearless, over her husband, sponging his lips, wiping the suppuration from his eyes, holding his head up to take the liquid from Adams's pannikin. After the first cry of shock at the sight of him, she had relapsed into silence, but her face was ravaged by an inner struggle. Her cheeks were bleached of colour, the skin was drawn tightly over the cheekbones, her lips were drained of blood. Her eyes were a staring confusion of pity, of revulsion, of pain, puzzlement and sheer physical horror. Yet she worked gently as a lover, competent as a nurse, over the wreckage of Lance Dillon.

Neil Adams stood a little apart, smoking a nervous cigarette and conferring in low tones with Billy-Jo. After a while he came back to her and said carefully:

"It's time we moved. Gilligan's coming back this morning. I want to make sure the strip's ready for him to land."

Mary Dillon nodded and asked in a dead voice, "How are we going to get Lance there?"

"We'll straddle him on the pack pony and then let him lie forward. We'll pad him with blankets and tie him on. He'll be as comfortable that way as any other."

"Will he last the distance?"

Adams made a small, helpless gesture.

"God knows, Mary. Down in the cave, I thought he was dead. I wouldn't say he was any better now. We'll have Gilligan radio to Ochre Bluffs and get the doctor to stand by. The hospital will have a bed ready for him. It's the best we can do."

"I'd never have believed he had so much endurance."

Her voice had the same flat, toneless quality and her face was a white mask.

"We shouldn't waste too much time. Give him another sip of whisky and then we'll get moving."

Her next words shocked him like a blow.

"If he dies, Neil, you mustn't blame yourself. You could have left him there in the cave and no one would have known—though I might have guessed. If I have to, I'll tell him that."

It was another lesson in the complex logic of women. He was still trying to digest it when they crossed the river and came to the landing strip to lay out the message for Gilligan.

The aircraft made two low circuits before it hit the strip, bounced along the rough surface and taxied to a stop abreast of the little group clustered in the shade of the paperbarks. Gilligan cut the engine, climbed out and came towards them at a run. When he saw Lance Dillon lying under the blankets, his eyes hardened and he gave a low whistle of surprise.

"The poor devil! Where did you find him?"

Adams jerked a thumb over his shoulder and answered crisply, "Over the river. He's in bad shape. You'll have to fly him straight to Ochre Bluffs. Radio the doctor and the hospital. Spear wounds, sunburn, massive infection and exposure. Mrs. Dillon will go with you. Have them make a bed available for her as well. Call for me at Minardoo homestead first thing in the morning."

Mary shot him a quick, troubled glance.

"Aren't you coming with us, Neil?"

He shook his head.

"No room, for one thing. Second, I've got to get over to the myalls' camp and investigate this kadaitja business. Then I've got to return your horses to the homestead. Besides, you need a doctor now, not a policeman. I'll see you at the Bluffs tomorrow."

"Of course. I—I'm not thinking very clearly."

Adams turned away to talk to Gilligan.

"Can you make him comfortable in that crate of yours?"

The pilot nodded.

"We can slide back one of the seats and lay him on the floor. It's only an hour's run if we push it. He won't be too uncomfortable."

"Let's get moving then."

The stock boys lifted Lance Dillon and carried him across to the aircraft. Gilligan climbed in to prepare a space for his passengers. Mary Dillon and Adams stood a little apart, watching. Adams said awkwardly, "I'm not running away, Mary. I've still got to clean up this job. There'll be time for us to talk later."

She did not look at him but said quietly, "I understand, Neil. It's better this way. And—and I need to be alone for a while."

Gilligan stuck his head out of the cockpit and yelled, "All ready? Lift him in!"

105

They hoisted the slack body, wrapped in the grey soiled blankets, and settled it carefully inside the fuselage. The pilot stretched out his hand, helped Mary into the cockpit and closed the door. He gunned the engine, turned the plane and headed it back into the wind for the takeoff.

When she looked out through the Perspex window, she could see Neil Adams talking to Billy-Jo and the stock boys. She waved to him, but he did not see her, and before the wheels were off the red ground it seemed as if he had already forgotten her.

The Auster climbed steeply, banked and headed towards Ochre Bluffs. When it levelled off, Mary bent down to look at her husband, wedged against the wall of the fuselage, padded with packs and blankets against the bumping of the aircraft. His eyes were still closed, his puffed, distorted face lolled slackly on his shoulder, and when she felt his pulse, it was still a faint, hesitant beat. She knelt down awkwardly and prized open his mouth to give him a few more drops of water and whisky. Some of the liquid spilt and ran down from his mouth. She wiped it away with the corner of her handkerchief, then eased herself back in the bucket seat behind the pilot.

Gilligan turned and shouted above the noise of the engine, "How's he doing?"

She shrugged and spread her hands helplessly. Gilligan nodded in understanding and tried to encourage her.

"Sit tight and keep your fingers crossed. I'll make the best time I can."

She was glad when he turned back to the controls and she could look out the window away from the accusing face at her feet. They had left the river and the grasslands, and the naked country spread itself beneath them, an emptiness of red plains, sparse, gnarled timber, sandstone ridges and dotted anthills like lilliputian mountains. Heat struck down from a bleached blue sky and rose from the hot earth in waves and whirlpools through which the little aircraft bucketed like a live thing.

A clammy sweat broke out on her forehead and she fought against air sickness, bending her head down to her knees until the nausea passed. Now, of all times, she could not afford another failure, another humiliation. Now, more than ever before, she needed a dignity to face the final act of the drama. After a few minutes the plane steadied itself, the faintness passed, and she wiped her face and hands with a soiled handkerchief.

She had spoken the truth when she told Neil Adams that she needed to be alone. From the moment he had come, carrying Lance out of the cave, every gesture had seemed like an actor's mime, every word a shameful lie. The rush of tenderness and pity she had felt for Lance had been dammed back by the presence of the man with whom she had betrayed him. Everything had happened so quickly that it still wore an air of unreality, like a game played in front of an audience. A game of truth and consequences, in which the truth was only part-spoken and the consequences still beyond assessment.

Hung out in the bright emptiness between earth and sky, her senses dulled by the drone of the aircraft, she felt the numbness of shock slipping away and reason beginning to take hold again. Her husband was alive. She could still feel for him and with him. The feeling was changed from what it once had been, diminished, confused with other feelings for another man; but it was still alive—a residue of love for what was left of a husband.

How long either would last was another matter. The first love had slow weathering and swift assault. The man had succumbed too, and even if he survived how much of him would be left—how much of the tough sinewy body, of the thrusting, disciplined but myopic spirit?

And Neil Adams? He too had gone through the scene tongue-tied, jerky as a puppet. What was he thinking now? What did he hope or fear from the brief, passionate encounter under the stars? What private devils had he talked with down in the spirit cave? How would he greet her twenty-four hours from now?

There were so many questions—and the answer to all of them hung on the same slim filament by which Lance Dillon clung to life. She closed her eyes and let her head rest against the resonant hull of the aircraft, while the wide empty carpet of the land unrolled itself beneath her.

The land . . . ! This was one thing she knew with certainty. She would never be afraid of it again. She might loathe it or love it, live in it or leave it, but she would never be afraid. She had seen the worst of it—the pain, the blind cruelty, the blood drying into its dust. Yet she had heard its music, had slept under its stars, surrendered to its harsh enchantment in the act of love. It was her country now and she belonged to it; just as she belonged to each of two men, unknowing still whether to stay or go with either.

Willinja, the sorcerer, sat in the shadow of the pointed rock and watched the two horsemen take shape out of a mirage and head towards him across the flat plain. He was not afraid of them, but he would be glad when they had come and gone. There were days, and this was one of them, when the years were a weariness in his bones, and care of his people was like a stone on his shoulders. He wished he could shed them, as a snake sheds his skin, and sit in the sun like other old men and let his young wives feed him and keep him warm at night.

He could not do it yet, because so far there was no young man fit and ready to undergo the ritual death and assume the burden of his power and his knowledge. Perhaps there never would be. More and more of the young bucks were drifting away to the white man's towns, to the homesteads and to the prospectors' camps. Those who were left were too preoccupied with the daily problems of living to devote themselves to the long preparation. It had happened in other tribes, whose names were now lost to the land. First they had neglected the knowledge which was the key to their survival, then their skills had begun to fail, their women become less fruitful, the totem spirits more hostile. Then one day there were only old ones left, shrivelled women squatting in the sand, toothless ancients mumbling at lily roots because they could no longer eat the strong meat of the hunters.

In the two men ambling towards him Willinja saw both the symbol and the cause of the change. The black man become the servant of the white, aping his manners, his dress and customs, rejecting the old knowledge in favour of the new. The white man taking possession of the land, thinning out the game, setting up barriers, bringing new laws, new diseases, breeding slowly into the tribes, yet destroying them as he did so. Even now, today, the white police-man could impose a penalty that would bring the day of extinction two steps closer.

The kadaitja men had come back to report the death of Mundaru, the murder of Menyan, the encounter with Adamidji outside the spirit cave. They had told of their bargaining, tried to justify it; but Willinja had shrugged them away. The bargain meant nothing if the white man was not disposed to keep it. His eyes narrowed, peering out across the hot dancing air. If they were bringing back the body of Mundaru, it was a bad sign. If not, there was some hope of a favourable outcome. But the riders were still too far away to distin-guish the bulky shapes on the back of the pack pony.

The body of his wife, Menyan, was buried on the riverbank. They would leave her there, marking it perhaps with a strip of bark or a heap of stones. The casual burial was good enough for a woman, provided that she were sung to rest in the proper fashion. Even now, back in the camp, they were making the preparations: gathering every article she had worn or touched, piling them in a hole in the ground to be burned when the sun went down. If they were not burned, the "wingmalungs" would cling to them and bring sickness to the tribe. Even the name of the dead woman could call them up, so no one spoke it anymore—not even her husband, who was a man of power.

Willinja would not grieve for her. He was too old for anything but regret and he could soon buy himself another girl-wife. But he could still be angry and his anger was directed against the dead Mundaru, whose wanton folly had destroyed a breeding woman and brought the whole tribe in jeopardy. Justice had been done; the blood price had been paid; but only Willinja understood that the consequence of crime was a continuing curse that no penance could ever totally remove.

The riders were closer now, and Willinja relaxed a little when he saw that the pack pony was loaded normally and that no body hung across its cruppers.

When they dismounted and came up to him, he gave no sign that he had seen them but still sat, cross-legged, tracing patterns in the sand with the tip of his finger.

Neil Adams sat down in front of him and waited. Billy-Jo remained standing a pace to the left of Adams. It was perhaps three minutes before the sorcerer raised his head and looked at the policeman. It was longer still before they began to talk, but even though Billy-Jo acted as interpreter it was as if he were not there and they were talking in a common tongue of matters mutu-ally understood.

"There has been a killing," said Neil Adams calmly. "Mundaru, the Ana-buru man."

"And Menyan, my wife," said Willinja. "And the white man?"

"The white man is still alive. Though he may yet die."

"I tried to prevent it." The sorcerer traced a complicated pattern and then rubbed it out with the palm of his hand.

"You sent out the men in feather boots," Adams told him bluntly. "This is forbidden. You know that."

"Would the white man be still alive if the spirit snake had not killed Mundaru?"

A thin smile twitched at the corners of Neil Adams's mouth.

"Would not all be alive if your bucks had not killed the bull?"

Willinja stared at him with brooding eyes.

"You say we are under white man's law. Is the white man here to hold my bucks in check? Is he here to protect my wife? He comes and goes, and when he is not here, who is afraid of him? But they are always afraid of the kadaitja boots."

The logic was as plain to Adams as to the man who uttered it. Black or white, no one would heed a law without sanctions. If you are not here to apply them, then we must apply our own! Adams nodded gravely, considering the proposition.

After a while he said, "You are the man who talks with spirits, Willinja. You will answer me this question. Who killed Mundaru? The kadaitja men, or the spirit snake?"

"The spirit snake."

"If it had been the kadaitja men, you would understand that I must take them to Ochre Bluffs for punishment?"

"I would understand that."

"But a spirit snake is different and I cannot touch such a one. So I believe what you tell me. . . ."

A faint gleam of approval brightened the old eyes of the sorcerer. This was a man who understood the subtleties of rule. This was one who gave ground when he must but whose spear was still sharp and well-barbed. He said gravely:

"Today, Mundaru is eaten by the spirit snake. Tonight, we sing the 'wing-malung' out of . . . that girl. Tomorrow, the white man's cattle will be safe."

"I am happy," said Neil Adams.

But Willinja had already dismissed him and was tracing a new set of patterns in the warm sand.

As they remounted and rode towards the homestead, Adams felt a small, familiar glow of satisfaction creeping over him. He had done well with Willinja. He had conceded a point but kept a principle. He had maintained respect but allowed another man to keep face. He had lubricated a little the rasping contact between twentieth-century man and his Stone Age brother. And though no one would ever thank him for it, it helped him to feel a whit more at ease with himself. So long as a man stuck to the job he knew, to situations that he could control, he would sleep soundly at night. One step outside them and he was in bother. A policeman's follies were public property. He lived in a glass house and the taxpayers liked to keep him there, because they paid his salary and because they wanted value for money, security for their families and no shady bargains under the office desk.

So far, in the argot of the cattle country, Sergeant Neil Adams had been a cleanskin with no brands on his hide. But tomorrow, back at Ochre Bluffs, would he brand himself—lover to Lance Dillon's widow, or co-respondent in his divorce? By moonlight and starshine it was easy to talk of love; but by daylight there were a dozen dirtier names, and the raw realists of the Territory knew them all.

As they rode he found himself turning to look at Billy-Jo and wondering how much the blacktracker had seen on the riverbank, and how he had judged this unaccustomed commerce of Boss Adams.

All of a sudden he was sick of his own cynicism. He loved this woman. He had been tempted to murder to hold her. If love meant anything, it meant honesty, courage, a high head and a clear eye and a challenge to the world to wreck it if it dared.

Why then was he skulking away—from Mary, away from himself, away from the catcalls of a backcountry bar?

Then at one stride he came up with the truth. It was not the love that was in question, hers or his. It was the cost—his own willingness to surrender the whole or a part of himself to any woman. To be a lover was one thing—all care taken and no responsibility. To be a husband was quite another—all care, all responsibility, and the wedding ring worn like a hobble chain on a brumby stallion. It was pleasant to finger the price tag, but to put the money on the counter, wrap up the goods and carry them away for better or for worse—eh! this was much, much different.

The ponies ambled homeward through the dust and the heat haze, while Neil Adams lolled in his saddle and thought of Mary Dillon flying back to face, alone, the crisis he had precipitated for her.

Chapter Ten

LANCE DILLON WAS CLIMBING out of a spiral pit of darkness. The climb was slow and painful, full of checks and reverses. Sometimes he fell dizzily into emptiness. Sometimes he groped against a solid handhold and felt on his eyeballs the weight of a light he could not see. Sometimes he was cold as death, sometimes burning in a black furnace.

The darkness in which he moved was alive. Bat wings brushed his face, black hands reached out to hold him, spear points pricked at him, water dripped in maddening monotony, the palpitant air lay over him like a blanket. There were voices too, talking without words, uttering words without sense. Some of the voices were strange, some vaguely familiar, like faces seen in a fog.

Even in this blind world there was a perspective, a sense of extension and relation. But the perspective was always changing—now rocketing away into infinity, now contracting on him like a concertina. The sounds swelled in wild climaxes, then died into haunting cadences, elusive as whispers in a twilit street.

In the galactic darkness he seemed to have undergone a strange metamorphosis. The small core of himself was the same, but the rest of him, the conformation of trunk and limb and feature, seemed to have slipped out of mould and into fluidity. He might have been a snake in a hollow log, a wombat in a tunnel, a chrysalis in a cocoon, for all the certainty that was left.

For a long while the darkness was absolute, but then a light began to show, blurred and transient, always a long way beyond the reach of his groping fingers. Later it solidified, stayed a little longer, haunted him with its suggestion of an outline. By now he was higher in the pit, sensible of some faint progress—though towards what he could not tell. Then, at one moment in the timeless continuum, the light took form and he found himself looking into Mary's face. He tried to reach for her, but made no contact. He tried to call to her, but no sound came. Then her face melted into light and the light was snuffed back into blackness.

For a long time afterwards it seemed that he hung suspended near the peak of the spiral, a breath away from some kind of revelation. What it was he could not guess, nor even care greatly, being weary from the long climb out of nowhere. Finally, without knowing how, he drifted out of limbo and into sleep; and when he opened his eyes, he saw a man bending over him, a black-haired fellow with stubbled cheeks and a wide grin and a stethoscope dangling from his ears. Dillon was still fumbling drowsily for his name, when a raw, cheerful voice said:

"So you're awake, eh? They breed 'em tough on Minardoo."

It was the voice that jogged the wheels of memory into motion. Dillon tried to grin back, but his lips were numb and his own voice issued in a husky squawk.

"Black Bellamy! The mad doctor! How am I doing, Doc?"

Dr. Robert Bellamy took the stethoscope out of his ears and hung it round his neck. He sat down on the edge of the bed, chuckling.

"By rights you should be dead. I've never seen such a bloody mess."

Dillon struggled to sit up, but pain broke out over his body and he lay back, sweating, on the pillows. Bellamy cocked a cynical eye at him and grinned again.

"Let that be a lesson to you; take it slow and easy. You're burnt raw, back and front. You're full of formic acid, and there's still enough sepsis in that shoulder to kill a bullock. You're going to be with us a long time yet."

Dillon blinked away the pain and asked thickly, "How long have I been here?"

"This is the third day."

"How did I get here?"

"Neil Adams found you. Your wife brought you in."

"Mary. . . ." Just as he had come to the end of his groping, the darkness was clouding in on him again. "Mary . . . where is she?"

"Resting. She's been with you night and day since you came. You're going to rest yourself now. Then you can talk to her."

He felt the prick of a hypodermic in his arm, saw the dark, stubbled face ballooning into a fog above him, then the blackness swallowed him up once again.

Dr. Robert Bellamy frowned and wiped the sweat from his forehead with a khaki handkerchief. He had had a rough week—two hard deliveries, an outbreak of measles in the aborigine settlement, one punctured lung after a brawl in the bar and a smash on the Darwin road that added up to a crushed arm, a ruptured spleen and some quick, if unbeautiful, plastic surgery. And for the last three days, Dillon had been fighting a drawn battle with death while they pumped penicillin into him and had Gilligan screaming up to Darwin for fresh supplies.

Now it seemed Dillon had won his battle. But it was a partial victory at best. Every auscultation confirmed it. The human heart is the toughest organ in the body, but Lance Dillon's had taken one round of punishment too many. He would recover. He could lead a normal, temperate life. But his hard-driving days were over. He had ridden to his last muster, thrown his last steer. And Black Bellamy wondered how he would take the news.

He folded his stethoscope, shoved it into the pocket of his bush shirt and walked across the dusty little compound of the hospital to the grey iron-roofed bungalow that was the nurses' quarters. He pushed open the screen door and walked into the cool dim lounge with its rattan furniture, its piles of old fashion magazines and its pots of struggling cactus and trailing creeper. Mary Dillon swung her legs off the settee and stood up to greet him.

"Sit down, Doctor. I'll pour you a drink."

She walked to the kerosine refrigerator in the corner and brought out a bottle of beer and two glasses. As she stood pouring for him and for herself, Bellamy watched her with hooded, speculative eyes. In the last three days she had grown visibly older—no, older wasn't the word; maturer, that was it. The skin was still young and unlined, the figure firm, the walk springy and confident. But the lines had hardened somehow. The skin had tightened over the bones of her face, the mouth had thinned a little; the eyes looked into farther distances; there was an air of deliberation and control about her, as if she were walking a little strangely in a new estate.

She handed him his glass, carried her own to the settee and sat down. They toasted each other ritually and drank. She questioned him calmly.

"How is Lance?"

Bellamy took another long draught of beer and refilled his glass before he answered.

"Pretty well, considering what he's been through. The infection's under control. The broken rib will mend in time. The burns are clearing up, slowly. We'll have him up and about in a few weeks."

"Is that all?" She was watching him over the rim of her glass, her eyes, shadowed with weariness and want of sleep, probing him.

He hesitated a moment, then shrugged and gave it to her bluntly.

"Not quite all. There's a certain amount of damage to the heart."

"How much damage?"

"Well . . . we'd need more tests than I can make to establish it fully. But in general terms, he'll have to slow down. No heavy work, no violent exercise. A regular routine, as little anxiety as possible. On a careful regimen, he could outlast both of us."

"Can he still run Minardoo?"

Bellamy shook his head.

"Not the way he's been doing it. With a good manager and a good foreman, maybe, yes. But I understand you've been having a rough time lately?"

"We've been short of money, yes."

"And now you've lost the bull."

"Yes."

"That makes it very rough. I wouldn't like to see Lance going back to that." Her eyes were cool as ice.

"Any other suggestions, Doctor?"

He cocked his head on one side and spread his hands in a comical gesture of deprecation.

"Cut your losses. Get out. Get Lance a desk job with the pastoral company, handling other people's mortgages."

"That would kill him quicker than anything."

"It probably would at that."

"Have you told Lance?"

"Not yet. I'd like to wait till he's stronger. It'll give you some time to think things out too."

"I've already done that. We're going to carry on Minardoo. I'll run it myself until Lance is well. Then we'll share it."

His bushy eyebrows went up in surprise, and she gave him a little ironic smile.

"You don't think I can do it?"

"I didn't say that. I've confined too many women not to know how tough they are." He chuckled and buried his nose in his drink; then he quizzed her shrewdly. "One small point—what will you use for money?"

"I called the pastoral company and asked for a new loan."

"What did they say?"

"They refused—at first. Then I told them they could foreclose any day they wanted, provided they could get someone to work the place. And I'd plaster the story all over the country about how they put a returned serviceman off his land because the blacks had killed his bull and damn near killed him."

"And they took it?"

"They took it and liked it, Doctor. They'll give us another three years and enough capital to see us through."

For a moment he stared at her in amazement, then threw back his dark, tousled head and laughed.

"For God's sake! That's the best damn story I've heard in years. But you . . . you of all people! The city chick chirping up to the crows and the bush hawks. Lord love you, girl, I didn't think you had it in you! I remember the first night Lance brought you to a dance at Ochre Bluffs. I thought it and I said it: 'Give her eighteen months and she'll be scuttling home to mother!'"

"A lot's happened since that night, Doctor."

The tone of her voice, the chill, appraising look in her eyes, choked off his laughter and reduced him to blushing embarrassment. He mumbled an apology, finished his beer with indecent haste and went out, wondering.

Strange things happened to the folk who lived in the naked country. What had happened to Mary Dillon in the three years of her marriage, in the five

114

days of her search and vigil for her husband? And what would happen to the husband when the soft hands of the city girl took over the reins of the power?

Alone in the dim room, Mary Dillon poured the last of the beer into her glass and drank it slowly. She had behaved like a shrew and she knew it—regretted it too, because she had always felt a softness for Robert Bellamy, bush doctor, old Territory hand and kindest of souls this side of the sunset. Yet she could not help herself. It was as if she had called up every last reserve—of pity, gentleness, courage—to bolster her decision to stay with Lance. Now there was nothing left, just the hard stone of resolve set where her heart had once been and no love or laughter or tenderness left to spend on anyone.

The feeling terrified her. It was as if she had signed her own death warrant—or vowed herself to a closed convent while the sap of youth still ran sweet. The future stretched before her, bleak as the Stone Country under a dry moon. Why had she done it? Not for the moralists with their pointing fingers. Not for guilt and penance. You can live with the guilt and there are twenty rougher substitutes for a hair shirt. Why then? She could answer it now, in the wintry calm of decision. . . . Because it takes a tougher woman than Mary Dillon to sit with a man—any man—for three days and two nights and watch him battling for breath, battling for life, to hear him call your name while the microbes are eating at his blood and the poison is clotting in his heart muscles, to hold his hand and feel it grip yours as if it were the life strand, to watch death take hold of him and see him fight his way free—and then take your own table knife and cut his throat. There's a whore in every woman, but there are things even a whore won't do for love or money. So you sit here, sipping your beer, a brave little woman taking on a man's job, bargaining with the bankers, bullying the stockmen, bolstering a husband old before his time and wondering what it will feel like when your womb dries up and the callouses grow on your hands and there's leather in your voice and the sour taste of disillusion on your tongue. . . .

She could answer it now and know that, right or wrong, it was the only answer for her. Lance might have a different one; Neil Adams too. But this was another lesson she had learned—you live with a man for breakfast and dinner and the Sunday roast. For eight hours of bedtime you love him or loathe him. But the only one you live with twenty-four hours of a day is yourself. And for so much of living you need so much of self-respect if you're not going to hit the bottle or run crazy with a meat cleaver.

The glass was empty now. She put it down on the table, lay back on the settee, closed her eyes and thought about Neil Adams.

She had seen him once and briefly on his return from Minardoo. He had come to the hospital and found her sitting at Lance's bedside, screened from the rest of the ward. He had made solicitous inquiries, he had held her hand for a few furtive moments. They had kissed, quickly, without passion. Then he had gone, too quickly, with too little regret. She did not blame him. It was too much to ask of the most devoted lover to enjoy an embrace at the husband's deathbed. But he had not come to her since, whether from decency or discretion—and there had been moments when heart and body cried out for the comfort of his arms. Had he urged differently she might have decided differently about her future with Lance; but he had not spoken, and when the choice was made there was a kind of stale satisfaction in the thought that she wanted him still, but needed him not half so much.

Soon it would be her turn to go to him. But not yet. Not for a little while. Until the words were spoken, he belonged somewhat to her and she to him. She had earned the right to dream a space, hold a mite longer to the last illusion. The weariness of the long vigil crept in on her and she slept, dreaming of Neil Adams with the moon on his face and his arms reaching up to draw her lips to his.

In the fall of the afternoon, while the shadows of the bluffs lengthened across the dusty town, Sergeant Neil Adams sat in his office writing the last pages of his report on Lance Dillon and the kadaitja killing. It was a neat piece of work and he was proud of it. The facts were laid out in order—all facts that Headquarters needed to know—dates, times, places, the simple sequences of physical events. It leaned—but not too emphatically—on the action taken by the officer in charge. It lingered—but not too long—on the reasons for the action, the fortunate outcome, the preventive diplomacy which was a guarantee against further trouble with the tribes.

It would read well in Darwin. It would read better still in extract on the Minister's file in Canberra. And the memorandum scribbled on the margins would read best of all: "Action approved. An efficient and far-sighted officer, with profound knowledge of the area and its indigenous peoples." These things were important to an ambitious policeman. They would be read and noted and recalled when the names went into the hat for appointments and promotions.

It was equally important to know what to leave out. Many a good servant of the State had died in obscurity because he had a garrulous pen. Many a promising man had written his own epitaph when he lapsed from fact into speculation. Neil Adams had much to ponder in the case of Lance Dillon and his wife, but he was too canny to commit it to paper.

So he wrote on, slowly and thoughtfully, until a shadow fell across his desk and he looked up to see Mary Dillon standing over him, pale but composed, a little smile breaking on her lips. He cast a quick sidelong glance at the window, but there was no one to be seen, except Billy-Jo sitting by the veranda post whittling a stick. He stood up and took Mary in his arms. Their lips brushed, and then, gently but firmly, she disengaged herself.

"Sit down, Neil." Her voice was calm, but remote. "I'd like to talk to you."

He hesitated a moment, but she put her hands on his shoulders and pushed him back in his chair. Then she sat down opposite him, hands folded in her lap, her eyes fixed on his face.

He said gently, "It's nice to see you, Mary. I'm sorry we couldn't get together before, but it didn't seem wise. This is a small town. People talk."

"I understand that." There was no rancour in the level tone. "But we had to talk sooner or later, didn't we?"

"Of course. How is your husband?"

"Dr. Bellamy says he's out of danger now."

"I'm glad to hear it."

"Are you, Neil?"

He had not expected to be cornered so quickly. He flushed and stammered. "Well—you know what I mean. It's . . . it's the thing you say. . . ."

"What did you really mean, darling?"

"I'm glad for him—and sorry for us."

"Why sorry, Neil? If we love each other, we can still arrange things—one way or another."

"It's not as easy as that. Don't you see . . . ?"

His face was troubled. His eyes fell away from hers. Her heart went out to him in his humiliation and perplexity, but she still pressed him brutally.

"Neil, answer me one question. Do you love me?"

"You know I love you, Mary. But . . ."

He could not complete the sentence. The single word hung between them like a suspended chord of music—minor music lost and plaintive. She knew it was no use hurting him or hurting herself anymore. Everything had been said. The rest was postscript and dispensable.

She stood up, took his face between her hands and kissed him full on the lips. There were tears in her eyes, but her voice was steady.

"I love you, Neil. Not as much as I did. Not as much as I could. But wherever I am, whatever happens, there'll still be a corner of my heart that belongs to you. Good-bye, darling."

She turned away and he sat like a stone man, watching her go. With her hand on the door knob, she turned back.

"I almost forgot to tell you—I decided before I came—I'm staying with Lance. I'll be running Minardoo from now on."

Before he had time to think, he was halfway out of his chair, and the words were on his lips: "Are you going to—tell him about us?"

For a long moment she stared at him, shocked, silent and contemptuous, then she opened the door and walked out into the sunlight. Neil Adams sat down heavily at his desk, buried his face in his hands, and for the first time in his life found grace to be ashamed of himself.

Three days later, Lance Dillon lay behind white screens and wrestled with the black imps of despair. Bellamy had given him the verdict, calmly, precisely. Then, wise fellow that he was, he had left him to digest it in privacy. His first reaction was to reject it utterly. He was getting stronger every day, healing as a healthy man should. A fellow was halfway into the grave when he

117

could not sit a horse and plug round the herds and hold a yearling under the iron for a mere five seconds.

Then cold reason told him that Bellamy had no cause to lie. He knew better than any the loads a man had to carry, with the bankers yapping at his heels every step of the way. If Bellamy said it, it was true. If it were true, he was a cripple for life, and this was a cruel country for the halt and the maimed.

Then the whole hideous irony of it broke on him. He had survived so much—hunger, thirst, the spears of the black hunters, the terror of death in a dark place. Now he was reduced to this—a young-old man, nursing his heart in the shade, while herds wheeled under the whips and came thundering home through the paperbarks. It was too much for one man to take. Soft curses came bubbling out of his lips. Tears forced themselves out from his shut lids and trickled down the raw new skin of his cheeks.

Then Mary came in, an unfamiliar figure in jodhpurs and a starched shirt, her hair windblown, her face tinged brown from the afternoon sun. She kissed him lightly on the forehead, wiped the tears from his cheeks and sat down beside the bed.

She said gently, "So Bellamy told you?"

"Yes. . . ." He caught at her hands and his voice broke in desperate appeal. "I can't take it, Mary. It's too much. I can't . . . I can't . . . !"

"Listen to me, Lance!" The command in her voice checked him abruptly. He stared at her, puzzled, vaguely afraid. "You're going to take it, because it isn't half as bad as it looks. When you're out of here, we're going back to Minardoo. We're going to run it together."

"Together?" The word seemed unfamiliar to him. "You—you don't know anything about the cattle business, and besides, we're broke . . . flat broke."

For the first time she smiled at him, an odd, secret smile.

"No, Lance. We're in business. I've got us a three-year extension and some extra working capital to get us going again. You know where I've been this afternoon? Down at the stockyards watching an auction."

"My God, Mary!" Panic made him seem for a moment like his old self. "You didn't buy anything?"

"No." She patted his hand in maternal assurance. "But I learned a lot. I'll learn more and quicker as time goes on. . . . If you want me to, that is."

He stared at her, unbelieving.

"You . . . you've changed, Mary. I don't know how, but you've changed."

Her face clouded. The sparkle went out of her voice. She nodded slowly.

"Yes, Lance. I've changed. I'm going to tell you how and why. I want you to listen. Afterwards, you will tell me what you want to do."

"I don't understand." He frowned, searching her face with troubled eyes.

"I'm going to try to make you understand. Before all this happened, I was going to leave you."

"Leave me?" It was a high note of panic. "You mean for good?"

"Yes."

He closed his eyes and grappled with the thought. When he opened them again, she saw that he understood.

He said gravely, "I don't blame you. I know I didn't give you much of a life."

"It wasn't the life, Lance. It was you I wanted."

"I know that too. It—it was in the cave . . . I was waiting to die. Everything seemed suddenly futile. Except you. Did I make you very unhappy?"

"Yes." She was sparing him nothing. "You made me want someone else."

"Did you find him?"

"Yes."

"Did you . . . ?"

"Yes."

"Oh!" The word came out on a long whisper of weariness. He closed his eyes again and lay back on the pillow, his head turned away from her. He asked dully, "Do I know him?"

"It was Neil Adams."

"I should have guessed that."

"He saved your life when he could have let you die."

"I suppose I should be grateful." There was no anger in his voice, only a dull recognition of fact. "Why are you telling me now?"

His eyes were still closed so that she could read nothing of his feelings, but she went on, calm and unhurried, piecing out the theme she had lived and dreamed for days and sleepless nights.

"Because I've learnt something, Lance—and I think it's important to both of us. You can't live in this country with a lie. Even if you live alone, you've got to face the truth or go mad, because the lie festers up and eats at you like a tropical ulcer. When you've heard me through, you may not want me anymore. I can take that. I'll go away and start a new life of my own. If you do want me, just as I am, I'll stay and try to make you a good wife, and build you a good property. But not with a lie, Lance. Not with a hate buried somewhere in either of us. We've got to look at each other and see everything, the good, the bad, the failures, the virtues, and say: 'I'll take it, just as it stands!' No recriminations, no afterthoughts! If we come together again, I want to try to have a child. If we can't make one of our own, I want to adopt one and rebuild our love around it."

"Do you think you can, after all this?" His eyes were still closed. There was no more animation in his voice.

"I don't know. I've got to be honest about that too. I think it's possible. I think we need to try, both of us. Everybody makes mistakes. The lucky ones make them before they're married and start fresh from there. Others spend their lives regretting the mistakes they didn't make—and that's a kind of lying too. People like us—what do we do? Throw it all down the drain and start again? Or take a good long look at the truth and admit that every man's got a streak of the beast in him and every woman a touch of the tart?" For the first time her voice wavered and the tears began prickling at her eyelids. "I can't say it any other way, Lance. I've used up all the words. I'm sorry, deeply sorry. But I'm not going on being sorry all my life, with every act and every word a repetition of guilt. I want to live again and laugh, and sing sometimes and go to bed happy. There's a bit of the whore in me. And more than anything else, I want to be able to say one day: 'I love you' . . . and to hear you say it to me. That's all, Lance. . . . If you'd like some time to think, I'll go away and . . ."

"No, Mary!" His hands reached out across the coverlet and caught at her wrist. She looked up and saw that his eyes were open. They were grave and hurt, but not bitter. He said soberly:

"I don't know if it will work any more than you do. But a man who's come back from the dead like I have, ought to know the value of what he's got. I'm hurt, shamed too. I'll admit it. If I weren't tied to this bed, I'd take you out and thrash you . . . and Mister bloody Adams too. But even while I was doing it, I'd know you were a better man than both of us, Mary Dillon! I need you, girl, more than I ever did. I'm no damn good to any other woman. Maybe it's a rough justice that you should be saddled with me. I'd—I'd like to give it a try."

"On those terms?"

A ghost of a grin brightened his sunken eyes.

"I'm too tired to think of any others." His eyelids drooped and he lay back on the pillows, all the strength drained out of him. They did not kiss. There was no gesture of reunion but the slight tightening of his grasp on her wrist before he released her. Already he was on the borders of sleep and she was glad for him. Tomorrow would be time enough to care.

She walked out onto the veranda and watched the sun go down, a glory of gold and purple and crimson behind the ramparts of the naked country.

GALLOWS
ON THE SAND

Chapter One

THE LETTER WAS DELIVERED to my room at a quarter past twelve on Wednesday, the thirtieth of June. It was addressed to Mr. Renn Lundigan, Department of History, University of Sydney, Sydney, Australia.

There was a baroque seal on the flap of the envelope and an address in Spanish in the lower left-hand corner. The postmark was slightly askew and the typescript was fine and clear.

I remember all these things so clearly because I looked at the envelope for a long, long time before I dared to open it.

Finally I picked up a paper knife, slit the envelope carefully, took out the folded sheet and sat down, lit a cigarette and began to read.

The man who had written the letter was the Chief Archivist of the City of Acapulco, Mexico.

He told me with Latin flourish of the interest my inquiry had awakened in his department. He told me of his eagerness to establish so definite a link between the Spanish navigators of the eighteenth century and the new continent, Terra Australis Incognita. He told me how gratified he was to cooperate with so scholarly a gentleman on so important a piece of historical research.

He told me that in October 1732 the *Doña Lucia* had left Acapulco with twenty chests of minted gold for the colonies of His Most Catholic Majesty in the Philippine Islands.

That the *Doña Lucia* had never arrived at Manila and was presumed either to have foundered in a storm or fallen victim to pirates in the China seas.

That the gold coin of which I had sent such an excellent rubbing was of a minting contemporary with the *Doña Lucia* and could in fact have been part of her cargo.

He told me . . .

But the rest was courtesy and I was no longer interested.

I was thinking of a tiny island off the coast of Queensland, one of the hundred islands and atolls strung like chips of jade and emerald along the coral thread of the Great Barrier Reef.

A two-horned island, sheer to the sea on one side, with a narrow crescent of white beach on the other. An island where the winter tourists never came, because the surveys of the Queensland Government said there was no water there, and no channel through the reefs and no shelter for fishing boats or cabin cruisers.

But I knew there was a channel. Jeannette and I had run a thirty-footer clean through the reef and beached her without a scratch on her copper sheathing. We had camped for days under the pandanus and found a spring at the foot of the western horn. We had walked the reef and gone spearfishing at high tide, and one day Jeannette had brought up a gold chain, defaced, encrusted with coral.

Then, before our honeymoon was past a month, Jeannette had died of meningitis and I was left—with a junior lectureship, a battered coin and the dream of a golden girl on a white beach in the sun. And the dream of a Spanish treasure ship under rioting coral branches.

The memory of Jeannette faded slowly, faded to a dull ache in my heart that flared occasionally into savage pain and drove me to wild nights of drinking and chasing my luck with the baccarat boys and the hardheads round the poker table, and the strappers who stood round the tracks in the misty mornings trying to pick Saturday's winners.

The memory of Jeannette faded, but whenever I opened the drawer of my desk the old coin, burnished from daily handling, seemed to glow like fire. My girl was gone, lost to me for life, but my treasure ship was there. It must be there—timbers rotted, decks canted under the coral and the sea grasses, while the rainbow fish swam round and round the treasure chests in the hold.

It must be there. I was a historian. I could prove it must be there. At least I must prove it *could* be there.

It was old Anson who gave me the clue—George Baron Anson, not yet an Admiral of the Fleet, not yet First Lord of the Admiralty, cruising months on end between the Ladrones and the Carolines, waiting for the galleons that came every year from Acapulco to Manila. George Anson, who literally lashed his leaky hulk together so that he could wait another month and another while the barnacles grew on his hulk and his water casks split and his men died of scurvy under the tropic sun.

The old Spaniard would come nosing out of Acapulco, sniffing for the northeast trades that would drive him westward along the equatorial belt until it was time to tack north again past the Ladrones to Manila . . . but October would be late for him. Summer would be drifting down towards Capricorn, and if he drove too far south the hurricanes might catch him. And if the hurricanes caught him—they would whirl him down, past the Bismarcks and the Solomons, and westward on to the Great Barrier. He would be under jury rig by now, listing perhaps and leaking, in no condition to thread his way through the islands and the reefs. And if the weather did not blow itself out, one day, one night, perhaps, the coral claws would rake him open and he would founder—on the outer reef of an island with twin horns.

It could have happened like that, it must have happened like that. Else where did my doubloon come from, that dull golden eye that mocked me from the bottom of my drawer?

There was a knock at my door and the little blonde from the registrar's office came in with a wire tray stacked with pay envelopes.

She smiled and fluttered her eyelashes and shifted the tray so that I could see what her sweater did for her figure, and made her little joke when she handed me the envelope.

"Don't spend it all at once, Mr. Lundigan."

I smiled and said thank you and then made my little joke.

"Let me take you out one night and I'll spend some of it on you."

She giggled as she always did, lifted her chest a little higher, picked up her tray and walked out, swinging her hips.

I tore the top from the envelope and tipped its contents on my blotter. Two fivers, eight singles and some assorted silver, the weekly stipend—less tax—of a junior lecturer in history.

Take a week's board out of that and cigarette money and tram fares and the pound I'd borrowed from Jenkins on Tuesday, that left enough for a stake at Manny's. But not enough, not nearly enough to buy an island and a boat and diving gear and stores and help and all the other things a man needs when he starts looking for sunken treasure, and then trying to raise it when he has found it.

Still, it was a stake. And last week I had seen a fellow turn a fiver into five hundred and then into a thousand and then into two thousand. After which Manny sent him home in a hired car, with one of his own bruisers for safe conduct. I had seen it done. Perhaps I could do it myself.

I wouldn't even need two thousand. One would be enough. Five hundred for the island. The Queensland Government sells cheap when there is no water and no channel and no harbourage. Two hundred for a boat—no cabin cruiser at that. A hundred for new diving gear. That would leave two hundred for incidentals and there'd be more than enough of those, but it could be done . . . if I won a thousand pounds at Manny's.

I folded the letter from the Chief Archivist of Acapulco and put it in my pocket. I took the gold piece from the drawer and slipped it into my fob, for luck. I counted out eight pounds, ten shillings, and sealed them in an envelope. At least I would eat and sleep with a roof over my head and take a tram to work and smoke twenty cigarettes a day . . . if I didn't win a thousand pounds at Manny's.

The junior lectureship in history does not carry a private telephone, so I had to walk down the hall and fumble in my pocket for pennies before I could make my call.

A laconic voice said, "This is Charlie."

"This is the Commander. Where is it?"

"Same as last week. It's a clear night."

"Thanks."

I hung up. It was a clear night. The police had been paid and Manny would not be raided tonight. I would have my chance to win a thousand pounds.

You should meet Manny Mannix.

He's quite a boy. Brooklyn Irish on his father's side, Brooklyn Italian on his mother's. Manny was a supply sergeant with the United States Army who fought a gallant war from King's Cross and, when the war was over, decided to stay in Sydney.

Sydney, according to Manny, was New York cut down to workable size, and Manny was ready and willing to work it. He worked the disposals racket and the sly-grog racket and the used-car racket and the immigration racket, and when the profits started to slide, Manny slid out, too, with a bank balance that bought him a block of flats, a slice of a nightclub and a string of assorted fillies whom he paraded for the decorative effect. Manny was never a man to let love interfere with business. Manny also bought himself a small piece of the gaming squad—enough to guarantee him a phone call before the cars turned into his street.

For Manny that was more than enough . . . life was too sweet to spoil it with a conviction. Manny dressed well and ate well and drove a Cadillac as long as a housefront, but no matter what he wore or where he dined, he carried always the stink of the city, the smell of stale women and the reek of racket money.

You should meet Manny Mannix.

He calls me Commander because in an unguarded moment I told him I ran a lugger round the Trobriands in the last years of the war. He pumps my hand and slaps my shoulder and offers me a drink which I never refuse. While we drink, Manny talks. About Manny, about money and Manny, about girls and Manny and Manny's plans for Manny's future. And while he talks he smiles, but never with his eyes, which dart from the bouncers at the door to the tense little groups round the tables and the stewards moving about with trays of drinks held shoulder-high.

You should meet Manny.

You would hate him as much as I do; but you might not hate yourself as much as I do, because I drink his liquor and listen to his patter and smile at his jokes, because I want to preserve the privilege of losing my money at his game and having Manny pat me tolerantly on the shoulder and tell me better luck next time.

If I won tonight, there would be no next time. I would cash my chips and go, and turn my face to a green island and a white beach and a golden hoard where the reef dropped down into deep water.

So, at nine o'clock on Wednesday night, the thirtieth of June, I hailed a taxi and drove out past the flying-boat base at Rose Bay to a discreet crescent near Vaucluse. On the loop of the crescent there was a high stone wall, broken by gates of wrought iron.

The gates were locked, but there was a bell push on the pillar, and when I pressed it a man came out from the lodgekeeper's cottage. I told him it was a clear night. He made no argument about it but opened the small side gate and let me in.

I walked up the gravelled drive to the house. The curtains were drawn and the shutters were closed, but the front door was open and I saw men and women who might have been guests at a cocktail party and a waiter in a white coat crossing the carpeted hall.

I nodded to the sad-eyed Pole who kept the door, handed him my overcoat and went upstairs to the big room with the black-glass bar and the great windows that would show you the lights of the harbour, if they were opened—but they never were.

To run a business like Manny's, you need to shut out the moon and the stars and the wind that comes in from wide waters. You must draw the drapes and close out the cheep of crickets and the silken wash of the ebb tide. You must have music and laughter and the click of the wheel and the clack of the counters stacked and unstacked on the baize. You must have strong liquor and stale smoke and the shabby illusion of friendship and community.

To run a business like Manny's, you wear shining pumps and knife-creased black trousers and a silver-grey tuxedo with a burgundy tie and a red carnation in your buttonhole. You take your elbow off the bar when your guest comes in, you toss a wink to the model draped on the corner stool, and you say:

"Hiya, Commander! Long time no see."

"Hiya, Manny! Long time no money."

I delivered my line with a little smile and Manny laughed and choked on his cigar smoke. He took me by the elbow and steered me to the stool next to the model. He tapped the bar and called to the steward.

"Set one up for the Commander, Frank. Pink gin. Commander, I'd like you to meet a friend of mine, Miss June Dolan. June, this is Commander Lundigan. Watch out for him, sweetheart. You know what these navy boys are."

Manny choked again and grinned, and the model gave me a small professional smile and a long professional look that set my six-foot figure against Manny's six-figure prospects and found me wanting. Which was exactly what Manny knew she would do. Otherwise he would never have introduced me.

Manny said, "You feeling lucky tonight, Commander?"

I shrugged and spread my hands and made a rueful mouth. It's a little act. I do it very well. Jeannette used to tell me it was part of my boyish charm. Now I felt rather ashamed of it. It was so like the smile of Manny's drooping model.

"Not more than usual, Manny. But I could use it, if it runs."

"I guess we all could at that," said Manny. "Say, Commander, what do you think of this?"

He closed his hand round the model's limp fingers and lifted her forearm to display a heavy gold bracelet hung with coins.

"I bought it for her today. It's the little sweetheart's birthday and I thought,

127

that's for my baby. So I waltzed right in and bought it. Cost a packet, too. But I reckon she's worth it. What do you think of it, Commander?"

"I think it fits the lady's personality."

"See, there's room for more coins on it. So I say to her, if she's a good girl and brings me luck, I'll fill it up for her, link by link."

"I'm dry, Manny," said the model. Her voice was flat and bored.

Manny frowned and tapped the counter and the steward sidled up to refill the lady's glass. The coins jingled dully as she took her hand away from Manny and began to fumble in her handbag. It was then I had my foolish idea.

I took the gold piece out of my pocket, spun it in the air and laid it on the bar.

"Talking of coins, Manny—have you ever seen one of those before?"

A flicker of interest showed in Manny's guarded eyes. He took the coin, examined it and made a tiny nick in the edge with his diamond ring.

"It's gold?"

"Pure gold. I keep it for a good-luck piece."

I popped the coin back in my pocket and watched with some satisfaction the gleam in Manny's eyes.

"What sort of coin is it, Commander?"

"Spanish. Eighteenth century. There's a story about it."

"I'd like to hear it sometime."

This was the lead I had hoped for. Manny smelt gold. Manny might be prepared to lay out paper to catch gold. I said, as casually as I could, "As a matter of fact, Manny, there's a proposition behind that gold piece. One that might interest you."

Manny's eyes were instantly hooded. His voice took on the flat, incurious tone of the huckster.

"Well, you know me, Commander. Always interested in any proposition, provided it's profitable—and safe. Like to talk about it now?"

I shook my head.

"Later, Manny."

Later I might have a thousand pounds and then I wouldn't have to discuss any proposition with Manny. I wouldn't have to say a single word to Manny— ever again.

"Later it is, Commander," Manny said, and turned back to the bar and the drooping model with the round bosom, the flat voice and the shrewd professional eyes.

One hour and seven minutes later I was back at the bar—flat broke and busted.

Chapter Two

"DRINK, COMMANDER?" said Manny.

I refused, wearily.

"Sorry, Manny, can't afford it. I'm cleaned out."

Manny clicked his tongue and made little soothing gestures.

"Too bad, Commander—too bad. It comes and it goes. I figure the house owes the loser a drink. Sit down."

"No thanks, Manny. It's a nice thought, but I'll be running along."

I moved towards the door, but Manny followed me. I had never known him so reluctant to speed the losing guest.

"Commander?"

"Yes, Manny?"

"You said something about a proposition. Like to talk about it in my office?"

So I had hooked him after all. My heart was thumping and my mouth was dry. I had to clench my fists to stop the trembling of my fingers, but I tried to make my answer sound indifferent.

"Just as you like. There's no hurry."

"This way, Commander," Manny said, and steered me through a leather-studded door onto an acre of mushroom carpet under a chandelier of Murano glass.

There were mushroom draperies with gold cords. There was a buhl desk with a high-backed chair in Italian walnut. There was a fabulous settee in gold brocade in front of an Adam fireplace, and the drinks were served from a cabinet concealed in the pastel panelling. The fairies from the Cross had done Manny proud. Everything was genuine, everything was expensive, and the final effect was as true to character as the foyer in the House of All Nations . . . and as depressing.

Manny gave me a sidelong look as he bent over the drinks.

"You like it, Commander?"

I clicked my tongue and said, "It must have cost you plenty, Manny."

Which Manny took for a compliment and grinned and said, "It even frightens *me*, how much. Still, I work here, so I figure I might as well be comfortable. Besides, it impresses the clients."

"I didn't think the clients ever got in here, Manny."

I winked and smiled at him over the glass, the brothers-in-lechery smile, which makes a man like Manny push out his chest and forget that he has to buy what other men have for love.

Manny winked back and raised his glass.

"To the fillies . . . God bless 'em."

We drank. Then Manny waved me to the settee, while he himself stood back against the Adam fireplace, his elbows resting on the marble mantel. I recognized the gambit. It's hard to sit down and sell anything to a man who is standing up. You should try it sometime. I decided to make myself as comfortable as possible. I leant back against the gold brocade, crossed my knees and tried to feel relaxed, while I waited for Manny to open the discussion.

Manny's eyes were hooded again, filmed over like a bird's, so that there was no light or luster in them. When he spoke his voice was soft, almost caressing.

"What line of business are you in, Commander?"

"Does it matter?"

Manny pinched the end from an expensive cigar and took his time over lighting it. When it was drawing well, he blew a cloud of smoke and waved the cigar in the direction of the door.

"Out there at the tables—no, it doesn't matter. A man pays for his drinks. If he loses he pays for his chips. If he wins he doesn't make a fuss. That's all I want to know. You're a man like that, Commander. I like to have you here. But this is different. This is business. In business you've got to work together. So I've got to know."

He put the cigar back in his mouth, drew on it and waited.

I grinned at him—a nice friendly grin, no malice in it at all. I said, "Just for curiosity, Manny, what do you think is my business?"

Manny blew out more smoke and pursed his lips and said, "I've often tried to figure that, Commander. You're not Service, although you've got the Service look. Guess a navy guy never really loses that. You could be wool money, but you don't spend big enough. You play cautious, and when you're out of chips you quit. You could be an agent, though you don't have the salesman look. Doctor, dentist, maybe. Like I told you, I've never been able to figure for sure."

"I'm a historian."

His cigar almost fell out of his mouth.

"A what?"

"A historian. I lecture in history at the University of Sydney."

Manny was puzzled. It showed behind the film that covered his eyes. I had made ground. If I could hold it I might have a chance. Manny gave himself time to recover before he shot his next question at me.

"How much does that pay?"

"Eleven hundred a year . . . twelve with extension lectures."

"Peanuts," said Manny concisely. "For a guy with brains—peanuts."

"That's why I'm interested in business."

Manny shook his head. "For business, you need capital. What have you got?"

I stood up and spun the coin under his nose again.

"I've got this."

"How much is it worth?"

"For the gold—about six pounds, Australian. As an antique, about thirty. I've had it valued."

"With that, maybe, you could start in the popcorn business, Commander, but that's not for Manny Mannix."

This was the critical moment. If I said the wrong thing now I was lost and my treasure ship was lost, too. I said nothing. I smiled. I took my glass over to the cabinet and made myself another drink. This made Manny puzzled again, puzzled and interested. I brought my drink back to the fire and toasted him. Then I said, "The trouble with fellows like you, Manny, you think you know all the answers. Nobody can tell you."

Manny flushed but he kept his temper.

"So you should tell me anything, Commander. I got all I want . . . and it's all paid for with dough to spare in the bank. What should you tell me that I don't know?"

"Where this coin came from, for instance."

"Well, spill it. Where did it come from?"

"From a Spanish galleon that left Acapulco for Manila in October 1732 and was lost with all hands."

Manny relaxed and grinned skeptically.

"Treasure stories, huh? Oldest sucker bait known. You got a map, too? Old pirate map maybe? Pick 'em up for five dollars apiece anywhere round the Caribbean. Like shrunken heads, the locals make 'em for the tourist trade."

I shook my head.

"No map."

"Well, go on, what have you got?"

I took the letter out of my pocket and showed it to him. He read it painfully, fumbling for the facts behind the courtly phrases and the stilted English. Then he looked at me and tapped the letter with his thumb.

"This genuine?"

"It is. Nobody forges a document like that. Only costs a cable to prove it true or false."

Manny nodded. So much he could understand.

131

"Yeah . . . yeah. Guess that's right. But it doesn't say enough. There was a treasure ship. This coin could have come from it. Doesn't say it did come from it."

"That's where I come in. I'm a historian, as I told you. It's my job to collect, weigh and determine the value of historical evidence. I've collected enough evidence to show that the lost galleon could have been wrecked near the spot where I found that coin."

"Where was that?"

I was sure of him now. He wasn't waving his cigar anymore. The film had slipped from his eyes and I read greed and interest and the calculations of the trader weighing cost against revenue to determine the percentage profit. I could play him more firmly now, like a tiring fish at the end of his run. I told him bluntly.

"The place is my secret. I know where it is. I found this coin there myself. I'm not prepared to reveal it until we've made and signed a legal agreement."

"How much do you want?"

"For a half share—a thousand pounds, and all expenses paid."

So it was done. The chips were down. There was no more to do or say. The next play was up to Manny Mannix.

But Manny wasn't ready to bid yet. He had more questions to ask.

"Suppose we did find this ship—where you say it should be—how much of this stuff could we expect to get?"

"The letter says twenty chests of gold. I couldn't guess what it might be worth . . . twenty thousand, thirty . . . something like that. Could be a lot more, of course."

"Could be. Could also be that this place was salted and then we'd get nothing."

"Could be," I agreed. "But it wasn't. I know that. My wife and I brought up the coin."

Manny shot me a quick inquiring glance. "You didn't tell me you were married."

"My wife died a month after the wedding day."

Manny clucked and said, "Too bad," then handed me the next inquiry. "You said you wanted a thousand for yourself and all expenses paid. What sort of expenses did you have in mind, Commander?"

"Two thousand pounds—more or less. You might do it on less, but you'd be working the hard way."

"What sort of items would that include?"

Manny was so obviously interested, we had so obviously progressed from speculative bargaining to practical thinking, that I forgot to be cautious.

I gave him the answer, clear and simple.

"Five hundred to buy the island. That would give you land and water rights and a way round the law of treasure trove. Then there's a cabin cruiser and diving gear equipment and stores and perhaps a professional diver for the later stages. I could give you an itemized list when we get round to it."

132

I had dug my own pit and walked myself happily into it, but I didn't know it then. I didn't know it till much later. At that moment I didn't even know why Manny was smiling. When he turned away to mix our third drink, I thought he was preparing to seal our bargain. Which proved I didn't know Manny. Which proved I was what Manny thought I was: a simpleminded historian, who couldn't read the elementary lessons of history, which are the vanity of human wishes and the fickleness of women and the fact that no sucker ever gets an even break—because he doesn't deserve it.

Manny came back with the drinks. We raised our glasses and smiled at each other across the rims. Then Manny said, quite gently, "Sorry, Commander . . . no dice."

It was as final as a smack in the mouth.

And Manny smiled and smiled and smiled.

I wasn't smiling. I felt sick and tired and humiliated, and I wanted to go home. Then Manny moved in for his final punch.

"Tell you what, Commander. Just to show there's no ill feeling, I'll buy the coin for the market price—thirty quid. Look nice on the little girl's bracelet."

I laughed myself then. God knows why, but I laughed. I spun the coin and caught it and said to Manny, "Give me a free night at the bar as well and it's a deal."

Manny looked at me with cold contempt, then went over to the buhl desk and counted out thirty pounds in crisp new notes. He snapped a rubber band round them and laid them flat in my outstretched hand. He said, "If you're wise, Commander, you'll leave the tables alone and stick to the bar. The drinks are on the house like you wanted."

"Thanks, Manny," I said. "Thanks and good night."

"Good night," said Manny. "Good night, sucker."

I remember walking to the bar and ordering a double Scotch.

After that, nothing.

At nine o'clock the next morning the dean found me snoring in the shrubbery outside his front window.

At four o'clock the same afternoon the faculty accepted my resignation and gave me a month's pay in lieu of notice. Which left me with a screaming hangover, no job, no prospects and a little better than a hundred pounds in cash. For Manny had been kind to me. When he had bundled me out into the street, he had pinned his thirty pounds into my inside pocket with a note:

"Too bad, Commander. It was a nice play."

Manny is like that. A friendly fellow, with a sense of humour.

Chapter Three

On Friday morning I went out to collect a debt.

I took the early train to Camden, which is a small, smug little town built on the wealth of the oldest landed gentry of the youngest country in the world. The green pastures sweep up to its doorsteps and the black bitumen highway winds through acres on rolling acres of fat grazing land, dappled with shade from the great white gums and the willows that fringe the homestead creeks. The mellow grey houses are set far back in the folds of the land and the families who own them go back to the First Fleet and the raw, roistering days of a convict colony.

This is stud country, all of it; dairy country, merino country, sleek, horse-breeders' country where a drought never comes and the creeks are never dry and the roots go deep and where I, a rootless man from the city, had no place.

In Camden I hired a taxi and drove out five miles along the highway to a chain-wire gate, over which was raised, pergola fashion, the legend— McAndrew Stud. It's a longish walk from the gate to the homestead, and the taxi man stared at me when I paid him off and told him to call back for me in an hour's time.

He couldn't know that I was ashamed of my errand and of myself and that I needed the walk between the flowering gums to prepare for my meeting with Alistair McAndrew.

The drive rose gently for a while and then dipped down to the house, a low spreading sandstone building nestling in shrubbery and ringed by white out-buildings and the fences of the home paddocks.

To the left was a broad pasture with some of the McAndrew stock at grass.

To the right was a small enclosure of tanbark, where a group of men were watching a young colt being broken to the saddle.

McAndrew was with them—a stocky black Celt in khaki shirt and riding breeches. He leant on the rail fence in the relaxed attitude of the country man, but his puckered eyes missed no detail of the exercise and from time to time he called a quiet direction to the strapper in the saddle.

He turned at my footfall, hesitated a moment, then came towards me with a wide smile and hand outstretched.

"Lundigan! Well, I'll be damned! Man, it's good to see you!"

I grinned foolishly and pumped his hand and said, banally enough, "Hullo, Mac."

"What brings you out Camden way?"

"Well, I . . . I wanted to see you, Mac. If you've got time, that is."

My voice, or my eyes, betrayed me then, because he looked at me with odd concern and said, "Of course, man. All the time in the world. Excuse me a minute while I have a word with the boys."

I watched him as he turned away to give directions to the men around the training enclosure. He walked with assurance, talked with authority, a man at home and at ease with his men and his horses and his dappled acres. I remembered the day when I had dragged him across a beach in the Trobriands, a yellow, shrunken skeleton, last survivor of a raiding party whom the Japanese had cut to pieces two days after they landed. Shaking with malaria, knotted by dysentery, he had made his way to the rendezvous, and we had brought him off under fire from the patrol in the palm groves . . . and now I had come to claim payment.

McAndrew came back and we walked together towards the house.

"It's been a long time, Renn."

"Eleven years . . . twelve. Yes . . . a long time, Mac."

"My wife's in town for the day. She'd like to meet you. You'll stay, of course. I've a lot to show you."

I shook my head. "I'm sorry, Mac. I have to leave in an hour."

He was puzzled and a little hurt. He pressed the point.

"But you can't blow in and blow out like this. Of course you must stay."

"Perhaps you'd better hear why I've come, first."

It was a graceless, mumbling sort of answer to give to a man you haven't seen in twelve years; and yet, what else was there to say? I felt awkward, loutish. I was sorry I had come.

He took my elbow and steered me gently across the veranda and into the living room, a wide expanse of polished floor with bright rugs and good pictures and leather chairs grouped about a great stone fireplace.

"Make yourself easy, Renn. I'll fix a drink. Scotch?"

"Thanks."

The armchair was deep and comfortable, but I could not relax. The muscles of my face were tight, my mouth was dry. My hands were unsteady and I pressed them hard against the arms of the chair to stop their trembling. McAndrew brought the drinks, handed me mine and then sat down, facing me across the fireplace.

"Good health, Renn—and happy meetings!"

"Good health, Mac."

The whisky went down, smoothly, as a good whisky should, and then lay like a warm coal at the pit of my stomach. McAndrew watched me with sober concern.

"Renn, are you ill?"

"Ill?" I tried to laugh, but it was a dry, coughing sound in my throat. "No, not ill. At least not the way a doctor would read it."

"A friend might read it differently."

His gentleness, his puzzlement, his genuine kindness, made me suddenly angry with myself. I heaved myself out of my chair and stood by the fireplace looking down at him. The words seemed to force themselves out, rasping my throat as they came.

"Look, I'm a bad risk for friendship. I didn't come here today for the pleasure of seeing you. I—I came because I need a thousand pounds and you're the only man I could think of who could help me get it."

McAndrew showed no surprise. He stared into his glass and said, "Then I'm glad you did come to me, Renn. A thousand pounds is little enough to ask of a man whose life you saved. I'll write you a check for it before you go. Now, will you relax and enjoy your drink."

It was so simple, so bland and casual, that it took my breath away. And yet I had not, even then, the grace to accept and be done with it. I talked on, brashly, foolishly.

"But I don't want it that way."

"How do you want it then?"

"I want to tell you first why I need it."

"That's not necessary."

"Just the same I want to tell you."

And I told him. I told him of Jeannette and myself and our island in the sun. I told him of the old coin and the old ship from which I believed it had come. I told him of Manny Mannix and my final folly at Manny's tables and my ignominious exit from the university. I poured it out in an orgy of self-flagellation, and when I had finished I felt suddenly empty and tired.

McAndrew didn't say a word. He got up and refilled my glass and handed it to me.

"Drink it up, man. It'll make you feel better."

I grinned sourly. "That's an old wives' tale. I've tried. It doesn't work."

McAndrew smiled and clapped a friendly hand on my shoulder.

"You've been drinking in the wrong company, that's all. If you'd had sense enough to come to me in the first place . . ."

We drank. I put down the glass carefully and, just as carefully, I explained to him.

136

"Mac, I want money, yes. I want it more than I can say, for more reasons than I can explain, but I don't want your money."

"Call it a loan then, to be paid when you raise your treasure ship."

"No, Mac. Not a loan either. I want it to be my money. If I find what I'm looking for, I want it to be mine, too . . . I don't know if I can make you understand this. But I want something like you have here . . . your land, your horses, your own life. That's what I want from my treasure ship. A place of my own, a life of my own."

"Would you be happy in it? Without her?"

"I don't know. But if I can't have Jeannette, I want the other things. The things I hoped she would share with me. Can you understand that?"

"Yes, I can. But I don't see what you mean about the money."

"Then I'll tell you. Call me crazy, if you like. But this is how I want it. You race horses. You race winners. When you have a good one coming up, at a good price, tens or better, I want you to tell me. I want you to give me the same chance as the stable, to lay my money on it. It's only a hundred. It won't kill the market . . . and if it comes home, I'll have my stake and a small revenge on the bookies. That's all I want."

McAndrew stared at me in amazement.

"Renn, you're crazy. Every race is a gamble. Every horse is a gamble. The best horse in the world can lose. What then?"

"Then I'll go to Queensland and cut cane or get myself a job as shearer's cook. All I ask is the chance, Mac, the same chance that the stable has. A good horse trying to win."

"But if it loses, you lose everything."

"I lose a hundred pounds. That isn't everything."

"It's everything you have. My way, you could have the money without risk, without obligation."

"That way I lose the one thing I still have—independence."

There was a long, long minute while McAndrew considered the proposition. It was plain that it was distasteful to him. By all rules I was making a damn fool of myself. I was also cheating a gentle, good man of the chance to repay a debt with generosity. Had I known then what I know now I should have taken his check and kissed the hand that offered it to me. But I was a cross-grained historian who refused to learn the lessons of history, so I let McAndrew piece out the answer himself. He gave it to me quietly, without restraint.

"All right, Renn. If you would let me give you the money, or even lend it to you, you'd make me very happy. You won't. I think I understand why. Black Bowman is running in the third at Randwick tomorrow. He'll open at twelves and start somewhere about threes. So get your money on early. We think he'll win. If he doesn't, it won't be our fault or his. I wish you luck."

I held out my hand. He took it. And before he released it, he said to me, "You've had a stormy passage, Renn. It isn't over yet. But there's a safe landfall at McAndrew's. Remember that."

137

"I'll remember it. I'm more grateful than I can say. But I'm sailing my own course, and if I don't make harbour it'll be no one's fault but my own."

I left him then and walked down the long drive to the highway. Across the far side of a paddock a black stallion picked up his heels and set off at a gallop round the perimeter. For a fleeting moment I thought it was Black Bowman. But then I remembered Black Bowman would be in his stall by now, resting his strength for the third race at Randwick.

I arrived at the course in the middle of the second race. The crowds were roaring as the favourite was being beaten in a canter by a rank outsider from the country. The bookies' ring was deserted, as I knew it would be, and I took up my position near the rails of the enclosure, where the big men laid the odds to big money and a hundred-pound bet wouldn't send the market tumbling.

It's a touchy business when the stable is set for a strike. There are thousands of pounds to invest before the odds tumble to threes or worse, and every bookmaker in the ring is warned to close the betting before the betting closes on him. There are a dozen commission men in the ring, each with the stable's money in his pocket, and the pencillers are busy totting up the risks and the runners watch beady-eyed for the familiar faces of these men who make a business out of beating the books for owners and trainers and the big gambling syndicates. I had to beat the bookies and the commissioners both. I had to place my bet as soon as the odds were called. So I took up my position near the stand of Bennie Armstrong, the biggest bookie on the course, and waited.

A groan went up as the outsider came home, lengths ahead of the field. Two minutes later the betting opened on the third race.

On Australian courses the odds are displayed on every bookmaker's board and changes are made on numbered rollers rather like markers in a billiard saloon. Bennie Armstrong showed twelve to one against Black Bowman. Five yards away a colleague was offering fourteen. I calculated the time it would take me to push through the crowd and take the longer odds. It wasn't worth the risk. The commissioners would be spreading their money and the odds might tumble in thirty seconds. I turned to Bennie, held up a bundle of five-pound notes and called my bet.

"Twelve hundred to a hundred, Black Bowman. . . ."

Bennie shot me a quick glance. His clerk grabbed my money, counted swiftly and stuffed it in his bag; he nodded to Bennie, who pencilled a ticket and thrust it at me.

"You're on. Twelve hundred to a hundred."

Then he twisted the roller on his board and the odds were down to ten. I glanced across at the other board. Eights! I had been lucky. The stable money was going on now . . . and before the barrier went up Black Bowman would be offering at evens.

I put the ticket in my wallet and walked across to the grandstand to find myself a seat. My mouth was dry and my stomach was knotted with excitement. I needed a drink badly, but the thought of the bar with its clamour of voices and its smell of spilt liquor turned me sick. I swallowed and licked my lips to moisten them and wiped the clamminess from my hands, then mounted the steps near the broadcasting booth on the main stand.

It was a clear day, but there was no heat in the sun. The women on the lawns seemed touched with the drabness of autumn. The flower beds lacked colour and the crowd was thinner than usual. But the track was firm and the air was still and that was enough for me. I saw the strappers lead the horses into the enclosure. I watched the small men in bright silks carrying their saddles to the scales. I saw the purple and gold of the McAndrew stable and my heart beat a little faster. McAndrew had Minsky riding for him, and if God had made a horse to win the mile and a half he would have picked Minsky to ride him.

They were saddling up now. Minsky and McAndrew and McAndrew's trainer were talking together. They stood in the relaxed attitudes of men who know their business, who know that they have done all that can be done and that from this point everything depends on the horse and jockey and God Almighty.

The trainer hefted Minsky into the saddle. He tried the girth and tightened the leathers. Then Minsky reached down and McAndrew reached up and they clasped hands along the sleek, rippling shoulder of Black Bowman. It was an odd, intimate little ritual in which I had no part. Black Bowman was carrying my money and my future, but I had no part in him, or he in me. If he won, it would be because McAndrew had bred him and McAndrew's men had trained him and a gnome in the McAndrew silks crouched over his neck. I was a punter, and a punter is a parasite on the pelt of a noble horse.

Now the clerk of the course was leading them out onto the track. His thick-barrelled hunter made a laughable contrast with the fine, nervous lines of the thoroughbreds. Minsky was taking the Bowman at a gentle walk and the black stallion was stepping as daintily as a ballerina. He started and sidestepped as a big bay passed him in a warming canter, but Minsky quietened him and tightened the reins a fraction. A good man, Minsky, a wise old Jehu. I was glad my money was riding with him.

Black Bowman was drawn number ten at the barrier. It was a good position in the middle of the field. They couldn't pin him against the rails or jostle him on the turns, and if Minsky could get him away to a clean start, he could run freely with the field until they came to the last five furlongs that make proof of a horse's muscle and heart and of his jockey's cunning and skill.

The air was full of a metallic buzzing as the commentator called the positions and tried to convey to his unseen audience the small confusion at the barrier. I couldn't distinguish the words, but I raised the glasses and saw Black Bowman standing steady at the tapes while the starter moved the last three mounts into line. One was in and the other two were turning away. The jockeys pulled them round and faced them in again. They moved forward. The tapes went up. The crowd roared. They were racing. . . .

I saw the flash of purple and gold as Minsky moved out to a clean start.

Then I lost him in the press of horses that settled down behind the pace-makers for the first half mile.

A roan gelding and a big grey were out in front. There was a straggle of bad starters coasting along for the exercise. But the winner was somewhere in the tight bunch in the middle of the field, and nobody could begin to guess at him till they thinned out at the three-quarter mile and the boys who were riding to win nosed up into position.

The roan dropped out at the mile, and at the seven the grey was in the lead, but dropping back into the field. By the time they hit the five the bunch was split in two, and I saw Minsky and Black Bowman striding comfortably at the tail of the first eight horses. At the half mile there were still eight, but two were falling back and Black Bowman was still tailing the first half dozen. Minsky was riding a copybook race until they turned into the straight. Then my heart sank. The favourite moved across to the rails. Three more riders moved abreast and Black Bowman was a length behind the fourth. I tried to focus on him, but the horse ahead of him blocked my view. I saw the favourite's rider take to his whip. I saw the first three horses lengthen strides as the riders crouched forward in their irons. If the Bowman didn't move now, he was finished and so was I.

Then I saw. And the crowd saw. And we leapt to our feet and roared. Minsky had moved Black Bowman to the outside. He was four lengths behind the leader. But he was out of the saddle, cramped by his skinny knees right up on the shoulders of Black Bowman. His head was down behind the rear of his mount, he was giving him rein, as much as he wanted, and the big stallion was stretching out. Three lengths—two—then he was level with the leader. Then Minsky laid the whip across his flank so lightly that you wondered that he felt it, and the Bowman leapt forward to win by a length and a half.

I waited to see the numbers go up. I waited till correct weight had been signalled. I patted my pocket to assure myself that the bookie's ticket was safe. Then I walked from the course and caught a taxi to my lodgings. I was richer by twelve hundred pounds. I wondered that I felt so little excited by it.

On Monday morning I went to the settling at Tattersalls Club. Bennie Armstrong paid, as he always did, with a smile and an invitation to do more business with him.

I was counting the crisp new notes and stuffing them into a briefcase when Manny Mannix slapped me on the shoulder.

"Looks like you had a good day, Commander."

I nodded briefly and said, "Yes, quite good."

"More than a grand in that little lot," said Manny.

I stowed the last of the notes in the briefcase and snapped the catch.

"That's right, Manny. More than a grand."

Manny grinned shrewdly.

"So now you've got your stake, eh, Commander?"

"As you say, Manny, I've got my stake."

He smiled then—the old, hearty, no-hard-feelings smile—and held out his hand.

"I guess you had it coming, Commander. I wish you luck."

I ignored his hand and looked him full in the eyes.

"You're a bastard, Manny," I said softly.

Then I tucked the briefcase under my arm and walked out of the club.

That was the second mistake I made. Call another man a bastard and he'll punch you on the nose. But a man like Manny wants to show you how much of a bastard he really can be.

Chapter Four

My money was stowed in the bank. My seat was booked on the aircraft. There was a letter in the post to the Lands Department of the Queensland Government telling them of my arrival to negotiate the purchase or lease of an inner-reef island noted thus and thus in the surveys. My gear was packed and my rent was paid. I took a ferry ride up the Lane Cove to talk to Nino Ferrari.

Nino is a Genoese, a spare, stringy brown man with crow's feet at the corners of his eyes. Nino had been a frogman with Mussolini's navy and Nino had sent more than a few thousand tons of Allied shipping to the bottom of the Mediterranean.

A migrant now, he ran a small waterfront factory fabricating diving gear for the navy and the spearfishermen and the boys who have fallen under the spell of the blue deeps. His work is precise, reliable. His knowledge of deep-water skindiving is encyclopedic.

I told him what I wanted—diving gear and cylinders.

He questioned me gravely.

"This is for pleasure, Signor Lundigan—or business?"

"Does it make any difference, Nino?"

"Sì, sì . . . it makes a great deal of difference."

"Why?"

Nino shrugged and spread his hands in deprecation.

"Why? I will tell you why. You buy this thing for pleasure, you will find yourself a nice interesting rock hole twenty feet deep maybe and you will play for hours without much danger. You will take a holiday in the sun and go down and look at the coral—spear fish maybe . . . and that is that. You are

142

careful of the sharks, you observe a few simple rules and no harm can come to you. But for business . . ."

He broke off. I waited a moment, then prompted him gently.

"For business, Nino?"

"For business, my friend, you need training."

"I haven't time."

"Then you will probably kill yourself, very soon."

That stopped me in my tracks. Nino wasn't fooling. Nino was a professional. Nino had nothing to lose by telling me the truth. I asked myself whether I had anything to lose by telling Nino the truth. His cool, level eyes answered that I had not. So I told him.

"I'm looking for a ship, Nino."

To Nino this was a commonplace. He nodded soberly.

"Salvage?"

"Treasure."

Nino's weathered face relaxed into a smile. "You know where this ship is?"

"I know where it should be. I have to find it first."

"Where do you expect to find it?"

I told him. I told him what I believed had happened to the *Doña Lucia*. I plotted her course. I showed him how I pictured her end . . . foundering on the outer reef of the Island of the Twin Horns.

Nino listened carefully, nodding approval of my historian's logic. When I had finished he reached for a pencil and a draftsman's pad and began to question me.

"First you will tell me what sort of island this is. Is it an atoll?"

"No. It's a mainland island. A hump of ironstone and earth with cliffs on one side and a strip of beach on the other. The coral reef has grown round it."

"All around it?"

"That's what the surveys show. But there is a channel. I found it years ago."

Nino sketched rapidly on the pad. He showed the elevation of an island . . . a small mountain heaving up above water level. He showed a long shelf of sand fringed with ragged coral. And beyond the coral a shorter shelf, then a steep drop into deep water. Then he shoved the sketch in front of me.

"It is something like that, perhaps?"

"Very like that."

"Good."

He took up the pencil again and began to make a picture that grew as he talked.

"There are two things that could have happened to your ship. The first: she drives onto the reef in moderate weather. She is holed. She founders. She settles here . . . sliding down the shelf into the deep water. . . . How deep water . . . How deep would you say it is here?"

"I don't know. That is the first thing I have to find out."

Nino nodded. "It is also the most dangerous thing. But we shall return to that. If it is not too deep and if the ship is not already eaten by the coral, then you may have a chance. But . . . if the second thing happened . . . if she foundered in a storm . . . she would have been battered to pieces by the surf. Then, I tell you now, you have not one chance in a million. Her timber would have been shattered, her treasure chests, too, perhaps . . . but even if they were not, they would have sunk to the bottom and two hundred years of coral growth would have devoured them . . . and you will never find them—not till judgment day."

Nino raised his head from the drawing. His frank eyes searched my face.

I put the question to him bluntly.

"If you were in my place, Nino, what would you do?"

He smiled and shook his head.

"If I were in your place, with the experience I have now, I would forget all about the treasure ship and save my money. But . . . if I were you, as you are now, with a dream in your heart and a few pounds in your pocket . . . I would go and look for it."

I grinned at that. The tension between us relaxed. We settled down to talk of practical matters.

"First," said Nino briefly, "you will buy yourself a marine survey map. You will note the depth of the water off this shelf. If it is no more than twenty fathoms . . . then you have a chance. A man can train himself to be comfortable and to work at that depth, provided he observes the decompression tables. Below it . . . no. After that there is the zone of rapture, where men get drunk on the nitrogen in their bodies . . . where every movement is a danger, even to the experienced. You understand enough of this business to know what I mean."

I nodded agreement. I knew the terrors of the bends, when free nitrogen explodes like champagne in the joints and vertebrae and the careless or luckless diver is twisted into fantastic contortions. I had read of the strange, deathly rapture that comes to men in the blue zone, that urges them to talk to the fishes, to rip off their masks, to dance strange sarabands while death waits grinning in the underwater twilight.

Nino returned to his interrogation.

"You realize that you cannot do this thing alone?"

"I shan't be alone. I'll have a . . . a friend with me."

"A lung diver?"

"No . . . a skindiver. An old hand from the trochus luggers. He's a Gilbert Islander. Worked with the Japanese. He's used to deep waters."

"So . . ." Nino pursed his lips. "He will dive with you. But he will not be able to work with you."

"That's the way I want it, Nino. I'll work alone."

He shrugged. "It is your life. I simply tell you the risks."

"I want to know them."

"Then I repeat that you will need training."

"Can I train myself?"

"Ye-es. I will give you a set of rules and exercises. You will practice them daily, rigidly, increasing the dives each day, observing the stages for de-compression. You will on no account deviate from the exercises or the direc-tions. Is that understood? Your life will depend on that. This is a new world that you are entering. You must make friends with it—or perish."

I knew that I was foolish not to accept Nino's offer of a training course before I left for my island. But the black devils were at my back, goading. It was up stakes and away, for me, before the dream faded and the sour taste of disillusion settled on my tongue. Nino understood, I think, but he could not approve my folly.

He showed me the equipment, taught me how to maintain its simple mech-anism. He put it on me and took me down in a series of short test dives in the rock pool below his workshop.

Then we dressed again and, while we sat over a glass of Chianti in his workshop, Nino listed the items with which he would have to supply me: the lung itself, goggles with safety glass, a weighted belt, flippers, cylinders of compressed air . . .

"Mother of God!" Nino swore quietly. "I am a fool. I had forgotten!"

"What, Nino?"

"This island of yours. Is it far from the mainland?"

"Fifteen miles, more or less. Why?"

"Is there a town nearby?"

"Yes, but once I've bought my stores and moved out, I don't want to go back. It's a small town. Visitors are a curiosity. Tourists make talk among the locals. That could be bad. But what's the fuss about?"

"This." Nino slapped his hand on the metal air bottle. "You wear two of these. You have enough air for an hour and a half under water. But they have to be refilled, and that needs a three-stage compressor, which is heavy equip-ment. Probably there is not such a machine even in your town."

It was my turn to swear. I swore . . . competently.

"What's the alternative?"

"There is none. I will sell you twenty bottles, which is nearly all my stock. You will have to freight them to your island. That will give you enough for fifteen hours under water. After that you will have to send them to Brisbane to be refilled."

Twenty air bottles at seven pounds each was a hundred and forty pounds—plus air freight. When I left Nino's I would be two hundred and eighty pounds poorer and all I would have would be fifteen hours to find my treasure ship. On the other hand, if I didn't find it in fifteen hours I would never find it.

Nothing to do but pay with good grace and hope that my money would turn to yellow gold, stamped with the head of His Most Catholic Majesty of Spain.

We closed the deal. We talked of technicalities. Then, when the wine was finished and I stood up to leave, Nino Ferrari laid his hand on my shoulder. There was more than a hint of irony in his smile, but whether the irony was directed at me or at himself I could not tell.

145

"Signor Lundigan," he said, "I will tell you something. When I was diving first round the Mediterranean, you could walk into any bar and meet a man— half a dozen men—who knew about a treasure ship waiting to be raised. In all my life I never met one who had brought up more than a few shards of pottery or a piece of marble or a bronze figurine. And yet you know, and I know, that the treasures of Greece and Rome and Byzantium lie still on the continental shelf. And if you ask me why I tell you this, it is to say to go, go, dive for your ship. Find her if you can. And even if you fail you will have done what the heart demands . . . and that is a more precious thing than all the gold of the King of Spain."

Nino Ferrari is a Genoese. Genoa is a fine, bright adventurous town with a statue of Christopher Columbus in the public square. The craggy old visionary would have been proud of Nino Ferrari. I know that Nino Ferrari made me, for a brief while, proud of myself.

The gentleman in the Lands Department was cheerful and courteous—and quite convinced that I was a lunatic. He pointed out that the Queensland Government was disinclined to alienate any more offshore islands but would be happy to lease my island for ten years or twenty or ninety-nine if I really wanted it so long. He made it clear that no man in his right mind would want a place like that for more than ten minutes. There was no water and no channel through the reef. When I told him there was both water and a chan- nel, he clucked dubiously and asked me to send information on both to the Chief Surveyor—that is if I still wanted to become a tenant of the Crown.

I did want to. I wanted it even more when I discovered that the leasehold would cost me only twenty pounds a year and that I could secure my base of operations without paying out a large slice of hard-won capital.

The lease was drawn, attested, stamped and lodged with the Registrar- General, and Renn Lundigan, Esq., became a tenant of Her Majesty's Govern- ment with rights to free and undisturbed possession of a green island with a white beach and a coral reef, fifteen miles off the coast of Queensland.

The whole transaction was so simple, so obviously trivial, that I quite forgot one important fact. To sign, seal, stamp and deliver a document is a legal act, irrefutable as the shorthand of the recording angel—and a damn sight more public. But of this I had no slightest thought as I tucked the copies in my pocket along with my letter of credit and the consignment notes from Nino Ferrari and walked in the raw sunlight towards the freight office of the airline.

My equipment was waiting for me, packed in three wooden crates. I was faced immediately with the problem of getting them out to my island. They could be taken by air up the coast, railed to the small town opposite the island and then taken out by launch. But this did not suit me at all. There was the risk of delay and damage. There was the even greater risk of gossip and unwelcome interest when such bulky stores were shipped out to an island where even the tourists could not be landed for their picnics and their paddles round the Barrier Reef.

Cautiously, I discussed the problem with the freight clerk.

He told me there was a biweekly flying boat which served the tourist islands in Whitsunday Passage. My packages could be landed on one of these. I could collect them in my launch. He presumed I had a launch. I told him I had—which wasn't strictly true. I hoped to have a launch. But I had to find one first and then buy it at my price. I paid the stiff freight bill, signed insurance papers and accepted his personal assurance that my crates would be available for collection any time after Thursday—provided the weather was right and the engine didn't fall out of the ancient Catalina.

Then I bought a ticket for a northbound flight the following afternoon and walked round to Lennon's Hotel to buy myself a drink.

July is the tourist season in Brisbane. The sun has moved north from Capricorn to Cancer. The rains are over and the sky is blue and the air has a crispness that is worth a fortune to the land sharks and the publicans and the keepers of guesthouses and the owners of furnished flats from Southport to Caloundra.

The wealthy move north from Melbourne and Sydney. The playboys flourish their bankrolls and the playgirls peddle their charms. The social weeklies send in their spies, and the cameramen have a field day with the mannequins from the rag houses. You can't get a room for love, though you may get one for money—big money. The tourist islands are packed and the rotogravures turn out colour pages and special supplements on the Riviera of the South Pacific and the Waikiki of the near north.

The shrewd, drawling businessmen in tropic suits smile over their drinks in Lennon's bar and add another thousand to the price of a hundred feet of sand hills in the sucker belt.

I was a stranger among them. They would be friendly to me as they always are to southerners, but I would still be an outlander.

I moved from the bar into the lounge and toyed with a mug of beer while I watched the tourists staging through to the reef islands north or the bikini parade south.

I envied them their freedom and their small or great opulence. True, they had no islands of their own. True, they had neither hope nor thought of bullion chests among the coral branches. But they had no devils on their shoulders either, no goading imps thrusting them out into lonely sea roads to desolate landfalls under the cold moon. They had no compulsion to dive into deep waters, to keep company with painted monstrosities in the forests under the sea. I envied them—but envy is a dangerous vice and self-pity is a more dangerous one still. I had risked too much and lost too much and won my stake too painfully to indulge myself again.

I had just made up my mind to finish my drink and take myself to a theater, when I saw her.

A waiter in a silk shirt and a red cummerbund was showing her to a table under the palms. He was giving her the treatment reserved for the known and the favoured guest. He added a little something of his own, because he was

147

young and she was beautiful—and too careful to show that the beauty was cracking at the seams.

He bent close to her as he drew out the chair. She smiled at him over her bare shoulder and gave her order with the practiced gesture of the mannequin. When she raised her hand, I heard the rattle of her bracelets and saw the dull-gold flash of my Spanish piece.

It was Manny Mannix's girl, the model with the shrewd eyes and the drooping mouth, the girl who had seen me busted at the tables and boosted into the street when I was too drunk to care.

I felt a small cold hand tighten round my heart. If his girl was here, Manny must be here; and Manny was a carrion bird forever circling round a kill.

Then I lit a cigarette and told myself I was a fool. The girl was here alone. She wasn't Manny's girl anymore. She had been paid off as the others had been paid off and she had come north to the gold coast to invest her winnings in a new man with a promising bank balance.

The waiter brought her drink. She paid for it. That was a good sign. Girls like this one never paid for their drinks if they had someone else to pay for them. I saw the coins flicker as she raised her glass to drink, delicately, self-consciously, like a trained animal. Then I had a sudden foolish idea. It restored my confidence and good humour like a drug.

I stubbed out my cigarette and walked across to the quiet corner under the palms. She saw me coming over the last ten paces, but her eyes were blank and her lips held no hint of welcome.

I bent over the table, smiled my little rueful smile and said, "Remember me?"

"I remember you."

Her voice had changed as little as her face. It was still flat, sulky, unlovable.

"Mind if I sit down?"

"No."

"Thanks."

I sat down. She finished her drink and pushed the glass towards me. The gesture was a patent insult.

"You can buy me another if you like."

"You mean if I can afford it."

"Oh, I know you can—Manny told me you were in the money."

Again the small, cold fingers crisped round my heart, but I managed a grin and the words came flatly enough.

"Trust Manny. He's a clever boy."

"He doesn't like you very much, Commander."

"It's a mutual feeling."

She blew a cloud of smoke full in my face and handed me the terse little tag, "That makes three of us, Commander."

"Meaning what?"

"I don't like Manny, either."

"I thought he was here with you."

148

"No. Manny has other interests. This one's a brunette."

I said I was sorry to hear it. I was about to say that men who treated girls the way Manny treated girls were no kind of men at all. She cut off my little philippic with a gamin gesture.

"Save it, Commander. You don't like me. I don't like you. Let's not make pretty speeches. You know Manny gave me your coin?"

She held out her wrist so that the old piece dangled provocatively under my nose.

"Yes. He told me he'd give it to you."

For the first time she smiled. She moistened her lips with a small darting tongue. Her eyes were alight with malicious amusement.

"Like to have it back?"

"Yes."

"How much will you pay?"

"Thirty pounds. That's what Manny gave me for it."

"Make it fifty, Commander, and you can have the rest of the junk as well."

I took out my wallet, counted out ten five-pound notes and laid them on the table without a word. She unclasped the bracelet and tossed it across to me, then picked up the notes and stuffed them into her handbag.

"Thanks," she said flatly. "I was down to my last fiver. Now you can buy me that drink."

I took out a ten-shilling note and put it carefully under the ashtray. Then I stood up.

"I'm sorry. I'm moving out of town. You'd do better with the tourist traffic. They're playing. I'm working."

It sounded cheap and it was cheap. Manny Mannix himself couldn't have made it any dirtier. I tried to find grace enough and words to make an apology.

"I—I'm sorry. I shouldn't have said that."

She shrugged and reached for her compact.

"I'm used to it. There's one thing, Commander . . ."

"Yes?"

"You overpaid me for the bracelet. To make up the difference, I'll tell you something."

"Well . . . ?"

"Manny told me you've got something he wants."

"That's the way Manny lives—wanting what someone else has."

"This time he swears he's going to get it."

"He'll have to find me first and he'll be a long time looking. And even if he does find me . . ."

I was moving away as I spoke, but she stopped me in my tracks.

"When he finds you, Commander . . . when he finds you, he's going to kill you."

149

Chapter Five

THE AIRCRAFT LEVELLED OUT AT EIGHT THOUSAND FEET and through the starboard port I could see its shadow darting like a bird across the green carpet of the hinterland.

Eastward was the sea and the reef and the jade islands. Westward, far beyond our view, were the parched brown plains of the cattle country. Below us was the lush coastal belt, where the monsoons watered the low hills and filled the swamps, where the ibis gathered and the brolgas made their mysterious bird ballet on the mud flats.

Here were the cane fields and the pineapple plantations and the groves of papaws and the spreading mango trees. Here were the lush pastures of the milking herds. Here were the lean, slow-spoken men of the north—the cane cutters, the mill hands, the drovers who walk with the lounging roll of saddle-bred men. Here are the sad, lost people bred from the old race and the new, whose blood is tinctured with the blood of China and Japan and the Gilberts and the Spice Islands.

Here the houses were built on stilts so that the wind could blow all about them and cool them after the steaming lazy days. Here was the riot of bougainvillaea over creaking veranda posts and galvanized roofs. Here men were rich because they had time to spend. Here men were poor indeed if they could not find a friend among the open-handed people of the Queen's own land. Here there was work for any man who cared to put his hand to it. And if he cared for nothing but to nibble a grass twig on the veranda steps, why, he might do that, too, and be damned to the rest of you.

To me, Renn Lundigan, riding high between a blue heaven and a green earth, there came a curious calm, a sense of release, as if a navel cord had

150

been cut and I were born into a new, free world, remote from danger, emptied of memory, beyond the ache of desire and the pain of loss.

I was headed for Bowen—a small harbour town where the tropic lushness covers the scars of the cyclones and the sudden storms. From Bowen I must travel south again, doubling back on my tracks for fifty miles. At first sight this might have seemed a folly, since the aircraft would have set me down at my destination without the fatigue of three hours on the antique railway service. But this did not suit my book at all.

My town was smaller even than Bowen. A stranger arriving by air is either a tourist or a commercial traveller. As such, he is an object of courteous but lively interest. His every movement is a subject of gossip among the fraternity in the bar or the lounges under the shopfront verandas.

Come in by train, dusty, crumpled, irritable, and they are prepared to take you at any value you care to set—stock inspector, commission agent, fisheries man, or a clerk from one of the sugar mills. If you pay your score and don't talk too loudly or spend too much and show some knowledge of the local scene, they'll leave you to your own devices and forget the questions they meant to ask you, because it's too hot to remember.

My knowledge of the local scene was pitifully inadequate, but I was counting on Johnny to fill in the gaps for me.

His full name was Johnny Akimoto. He was the son of a Japanese trochus diver and a Gilbertese woman. The mother's blood was stronger, and except for a curious greyness of complexion and an Oriental tightness about the eyes and cheekbones, Johnny would have passed for a full-blooded islander. Ever since the blackbirding days, when island men were shanghaied for work on the cane fields, these curious racial mixtures have been found all along the Queensland coast.

Johnny himself had worked the trochus luggers. He had sailed with the pearlers and dived on the deep beds. But when the war came and there was no more work for a skindiver, Johnny became an odd-job man. He had been houseboy to the Americans, roustabout on a tourist island, engine hand on a fishing boat, truck driver for a local contractor. Everybody knew Johnny. Everybody liked him, and when Jeannette and I had run ashore in cyclone weather, it was Johnny who mended our sails and repaired our sheathing and painted the hull and read us wise lectures on the offshore weather in the bad season.

It was Johnny who had helped me trace the course of the Acapulco galleons. When I had told him of our first wild hopes of the *Doña Lucia*, he had nodded approval and promised that one day he would dive with me round the reef of the Island of the Twin Horns. A wise, quiet man, Johnny Akimoto. A gentle, loyal man. A lonely, lost man among the friendly people of the coast.

I thought of Johnny as the plane thrust northward. I dozed and dreamt of Manny Mannix and the girl who had sold me back my coin for fifty pounds. I woke to find the hostess at my shoulder warning me to fasten my seat belt. The plane banked sharply over a stretch of blue water. I closed my eyes, and when I opened them again I saw a bellying wind sock and a huddle of iron-roofed sheds. We were coming in to land.

We sweltered in the dusty waiting room while they unloaded our baggage. It was midafternoon and the sea breeze would not come for another hour. I found myself in conversation with a tubby fellow in an alpaca suit. He told me he was a retired bank manager. He told me he was going to join his wife and daughter on a luxury island offshore from Bowen. He told me how much it was going to cost him. He told me how little he was going to enjoy it. He told me how the heat gave him rashes and the cold gave him bronchitis. He told me his golf handicap and his ambition to raise prize dahlias. He told me . . .

"Mr. Renn Lundigan?"

The airport clerk was at my elbow.

"That's right."

"Telegram for you, sir. Came in just before you landed."

He handed me a buff envelope with a red border. It was franked "Urgent." I slit the envelope and unfolded the message form. The office of origin was Brisbane. The filing time was half an hour after midday. The message was brief and hearty as a handshake:

GOOD FISHING COMMANDER STOP BE SEEING YOU STOP

And it was signed "Manny Mannix."

I crumpled the paper and thrust it into my pocket. The tubby bank manager looked at me curiously. He wanted to get on with his story. I turned away and left him gaping. I felt suddenly sick and lonelier than I had ever been since Jeannette was taken from me. I wanted very much to talk to Johnny Akimoto.

The train journey was a slow torment. I was hot, dusty, beset with flies and badgered to insanity by a pair of small boys who whined continuously for sweets and drinks while their mother nagged vainly for peace.

We stopped at every siding while the guard exchanged news with the station staff. We were shunted onto a loop and waited three-quarters of an hour for the northbound train to go through. The green country which had seemed so rich and desirable from the air was now in the grip of a drooping misery which matched my own depression. The friendly people of the north were a drab and garrulous race. Their children were monsters. Their transport service was a primitive horror. Their greetings were an intrusion on my privacy. Their gifts of newspapers and fruit and lemonade were a presumption not to be borne. By the time the journey was over they had written me down as a cross-grained boor. Looking back, I find I agree with them.

Manny's telegram had shocked me deeply. The first blind rage passed quickly and then fear took hold of me. I did not believe for a moment that Manny's threat to kill me was anything more than a boast to impress a woman. But the fear remained—fear of losing something I did not yet possess, but which I had struggled and schemed and gambled to attain.

More than this, I knew the power that lay in Manny's hands. Money power. Power to buy a man here and a piece of information there. Power to plan his moves like a chess game, to check me here and circumvent me there, to match any move of mine with another, shrewder, swifter and more effective. I thought of the three crates of equipment in the airways office at Brisbane and wondered if he could do anything to divert them.

I remembered that Manny could pay for a charter flight and might even now be waiting to greet me at the hotel. I wondered what I would do if he were.

But he wasn't. I was the only guest. I could have the best bedroom with the iron bedstead and the big mosquito net and the cracked ewer and basin. I could have free use of the single bathroom and walk fifty yards to the lavatory in the yard. I could drink alone in the commercial room. I could rise at seven-thirty and breakfast alone at eight. I could accept mine host's wheezy invitation and join the mill hands and the fishermen telling bawdy stories in the bar. They were good boys. They'd make me very welcome. But I wanted none of that. I wanted a shower and a drink and a meal—and then I wanted to see Johnny Akimoto.

I found him where I had found him the first time. In a small slab hut with the bush at its back and the sand dunes in front. The coral paths were raked clean every day. There was a trailing of bougainvillaea and a hibiscus tree and a border of sweet gardenia, and a tall frangipani whose naked branches thrust out like the symbols of some ancient phallic cult.

A kerosine lamp hung on a nail in the door jamb, and Johnny was sitting on a packing case splicing hooks on a trawl line. He wore a hibiscus flower in his frizzy hair and his only clothing was a pair of denim shorts.

He looked up sharply when he heard my footfall and his face broke into a gleaming smile of surprise and welcome.

He came to me, hand outstretched.

"Renboss!"

"That's right, Johnny. Renboss."

It was the old name, from the old happy time. It brought me very near to tears. Johnny pumped my hand and patted my back and made me sit down on another packing case which he dragged out of the shadows into the small circle of light.

"What brings you here, Renboss? You staying long? How are things with you? You are well? You look tired, but that's the travelling, eh?"

The questions came tumbling out in Johnny's precise Mission English, and all the time he was looking into my face, searching like an anxious mother for the truth about a child.

I told him the truth.

153

"I came to see you, Johnny."

"Me? That's nice, Renboss. I often thought about you . . . and the missy."

"The missy is dead, Johnny."

"Oh, no. When?" His mild eyes were full of sympathy.

"A long time ago, Johnny. A long, lonely time."

"You got no other woman?"

"No other woman."

"And you came back here to see Johnny Akimoto. That's good, Renboss. I've got a boat now. A good boat. We go out on the reef, eh? You come out and fish with me, eh? We take a trip together to Thursday Island . . . Moresby, maybe."

"We take a trip, Johnny . . . yes . . . but not to Thursday . . . to my island. . . ."

"Your island?" He looked at me in momentary puzzlement, then he grinned happily. "Oh, yes, I remember. The island of the treasure ship, eh? You say she's your island?"

"I've leased it, Johnny. It's mine. We're going diving for the *Doña Lucia*. I want you to come with me."

Johnny was silent. He turned his hands palm upwards and seemed to study the lines and creases in the flesh. Then after a moment he fished in his pocket for a cigarette and handed one to me. We lit up. We smoked for a few moments, listening to the wash of the water and the searching voice of the wind.

Then Johnny spoke, quietly, professionally.

"To do a thing like this, Renboss, you need a boat."

"I've got money to buy one, Johnny."

"You need a diver and equipment."

"We skindive, Johnny. We use diving gear."

"You have dived before, Renboss?"

"A little. A practice dive or two . . . no more."

"Then you have to learn much before you make a working diver."

"That I want you to teach me, Johnny. Also, I have a list of exercises from the man who made the diving gear. He says I can train myself to work in twenty fathoms."

"Twenty fathoms!" Johnny was shocked. "Too deep, Renboss . . . too deep for skindives. . . ."

"It can be done, Johnny. This is not naked diving. A man can breathe down there. . . ."

Johnny shook his head. "This is new to me. I don't like the sound of it."

"Will you come with me, Johnny? Will you help me buy a boat and get stores and—"

"No need to buy a boat," said Johnny quietly. "We use mine. She's lugger-built. Old when I bought her, but I patched her up and she will sail you anywhere. The engine is new. She will make eight, ten knots if you want."

"All right, then, I rent the boat. I pay you wages. You come to the island and work with me. Is that the way you want it?"

Johnny nodded soberly. "That's the way, Renboss. Easy, quick—no trouble. You try to buy a boat around here. They sell you a bad boat for a good price. Or a good boat you can't pay for. This is the Reef, Renboss. A man who does not look after a boat finds the teredo eating it. Then he tries to sell it to someone who doesn't know about teredo . . . you see?"

I saw. I knew the teredo, the small mollusk that bores into the timbers in the warm latitudes, eating a boat as the white ants eat a house. There is only one remedy—sheathe your boat with copper to the waterline or paint her over and over with bronze paint till she has a new skin impervious to the sea worm. The boatmen on the Queensland coast are like the horse copers of Kerry . . . and more than one is a lineal descendant of the same fabulous rascals.

Besides, another thought had occurred to me. Johnny's boat was a lugger, a lolloping, awkward craft if you try to sail her too close to the weather, but a deep-water boat nonetheless, safe as a bank and comfortable in the trades. If we raised the treasure chests from the *Doña Lucia*, the whole find would be treasure trove, the property of the Crown, and I was at the mercy of the Crown for whatever payment might be made by way of reward. But with Johnny's lugger, with Johnny's knowledge of the islands, we could up anchor and head north until we found a Chinese who would pay notes for minted gold, or an agent who needed gold to pay for smuggled guns. It's flourishing business in the Celebes and in the China Straits, and for gold you can name your own price and your own currency. I didn't speak the thought to Johnny. Johnny might not approve. Besides, there would be time enough later.

Johnny smoked quietly, weighing his next question. His face was in shadow, but his eyes were intent on my face.

"Renboss, you are afraid of something. What is it?"

"I'm coming to that, Johnny. It's a long story."

"If we are to work together, Renboss, I should know the story."

I told him. I told him about Manny Mannix and the girl in Lennon's Hotel. I told him about the telegram. I told him how I feared Manny Mannix and the power that money put into his hands.

Johnny blew smoke rings and watched them drift away on the eddies of the wind.

"We should get out quickly," he said.

"I'm ready to move whenever you are, Johnny."

"We need stores, first."

"When can you get those?"

"Tomorrow. Stores and a medicine chest. Accidents can happen on the Reef and in the water."

"I'll make a list of them tonight. There's a chemist in the town?"

Johnny nodded. "There is a chemist. Better, I think, you buy the medicines. I will see to the stores. If you start to buy yourself, people will ask questions."

155

"When can we leave, Johnny?"

"The day after tomorrow . . . first light."

"Not before?"

"No," said Johnny firmly. "What good does it do? We have to make the boat ready. We have to go down to the tourist island to collect your gear. Then we have to sail a lugger through a narrow reef passage. That is daytime work. Silly to risk a boat for no profit."

"But what if Manny comes before we're ready to move?"

"Why should he come?"

"Simple enough, Johnny. The one thing Manny doesn't know is where I'm going. He knows there's an island. He doesn't know its name or its location."

"Don't fool yourself, Renboss," said Johnny gravely. "Don't try to make yourself believe what is not true. You bought this island, didn't you? Like I bought this hut and this little piece of ground."

"I leased it."

"The same thing. You signed papers. The papers are registered with the Government office in Brisbane. Anyone can go in, pay two and sixpence and find out everything he wants about the transaction. You see?"

I couldn't fail to see. It was too simple, pat and final. I was a historian. I could trace the decline of empires and the fall of heroes, but I had forgotten one of the simplest legalities of modern living.

Manny Mannix didn't have to do anything. He just had to wait and then move in for the kill. And all it would cost him was two and sixpence.

I laughed. I couldn't help it. I laughed until hysterical tears ran down my face and the birds nesting in the bush behind the hut began chattering in sudden fright.

Johnny Akimoto stood and watched me with quiet concern. The laughter spent itself in a fit of coughing. I asked him, rather foolishly, for another cigarette. He handed it to me, lit it and then said, "You feel better now, Renboss?"

"I'm all right, Johnny."

"Good. Tomorrow I buy the stores, you see to the medicine chest. I meet you here at three o'clock in the afternoon. We get the stuff on board and make her shipshape before nightfall. We sleep on board and raise anchor at first light."

I took out my wallet and handed Johnny fifty pounds in notes.

"That see you through for the stores?"

"More than plenty, Renboss."

"The rest of the money is in the bank, Johnny. I'll settle with you tomorrow or later, whenever you like."

"You settle when we finish the job, Renboss."

Johnny smiled his rare flashing smile and clapped me on the shoulder.

"And if we don't finish it, Johnny?"

"Then we do like I said the first time. Go north to Thursday, to New Guinea, and maybe catch ourselves some trade, eh? Go home, Renboss, go home and get some sleep. Things always look better when the sun shines in the morning."

"Good night, Johnny."

"Good night, Renboss."

I walked back to the hotel under a sky that was full of stars. I drank with the mill hands in the bar. I don't remember finding my way to bed. I don't remember anything until the raw sun woke me at ten in the morning.

Chapter Six

I CRAWLED PAINFULLY OUT OF BED and made my way down to the bathroom to wash the sleep out of my eyes and the stink of liquor off my skin. I dressed slowly, resigned to the thought that it was now too late for breakfast. I packed my bag and paid my bill, declining the offer of a drink on the house in favour of a cup of tea in the kitchen. Then, leaving my bag behind the bar to be collected later, I walked down to the low timber building that was the town's only bank.

The manager was a tall, ruddy man in a fresh linen shirt and starched shorts. When I presented my letter of credit, he greeted me as if I were a millionaire and invited me into his office for yet another cup of tea. His manner cooled considerably and he gave me a sidelong look when I told him I wanted to lodge my letter of credit for safekeeping, and that if I did not return within three months the whole amount of the credit was to be paid to the personal account of Johnny Akimoto. He drew some papers from the drawer of his desk and laid them on the blotter in front of him.

Then he began to quiz me.

"Is there any reason why you should not return in three months, Mr. Lundigan?"

"None that I can think of at this moment, but it's as well to be prepared, don't you think?"

"Of course, but what for, Mr. Lundigan?"

"Accidents do happen, don't they?"

"True enough, but . . ." He realized that he was on the verge of an indiscretion. He stopped short and gave me his practiced, professional smile. "Of

158

course the bank will make any dispositions you wish. You have only to sign the papers and . . . Well, that's all there is to it. I was just curious."

This sort of question and answer could go on indefinitely. I decided there was no harm in telling him at least half of the story. I told him.

"I've leased an island off the coast. I'm a naturalist. I'm making a study of marine life at depths of fifteen and twenty fathoms. I use diving gear. That entails certain risks. I've rented Johnny Akimoto's boat and I'm paying him a weekly wage in addition. If anything happens to me, I want him to be able to claim payment and to have whatever is left over by way of a bonus."

The bank manager relaxed again. He might be dealing with an oddity, but at least I was not the lunatic he at first thought.

The tea came at that moment, and he began to make small talk again. I endured it for a while with reasonable courtesy, because I had a question to put to him.

"Tell me . . . do you know anything about water rights?"

"Water rights?"

His eyebrows went up again.

"Yes, water rights. What rights, if any, has the freeholder or leaseholder of an island over the surrounding waters?"

He thought for a moment and then said, "It is not a question that normally arises. In law as I know it, the holder's land rights extend to the low-water mark, in practice they are presumed to extend to the inner fringes of the reef surrounding the island. You might possibly have an action for trespass, but I think it would be a long and costly business to sustain. In any event, the question is hardly likely to arise, is it?"

"No, I suppose it isn't, but one likes to be sure of these matters."

"Impossible to be sure in this case, I'm afraid, Mr. Lundigan. But"—he spread his hands in a gesture of smiling disparagement—"there is a lot of water and a lot of islands on the reef. Your island is off the tourist tracks anyway. If you make it clear that you want to be private, I don't think you'll be bothered very much."

I couldn't tell him about Manny Mannix, so there wasn't any point in pressing the question. I nodded and smiled and made some fatuous remark about students being odd cattle anyway. Then he handed me the papers to sign.

We finished our tea, we shook hands and I walked out again across the street. Halfway down on the other side was a small single-fronted shop with gold lettering on the window and an old-fashioned glass jar full of coloured water behind the dusty pane.

I walked across and introduced myself to the proprietor. He was young, which was fortunate for me. He was talkative, which was an annoyance, but he accepted my story with more readiness than the bank manager had done and was quite ready to waive the formalities of prescriptions and doctors' signatures when I asked him for Atabrine tablets and penicillin and sulfanilamide. I bought iodine and bandages and aspirin and a small scalpel and had them packed in a small wooden box provided by the garrulous young druggist.

But I was not to escape so easily. Time is at discount in the north, and the most casual customer is expected to make his own contribution to the conversational gambits of the community.

I listened with mild interest to a curtain lecture on the stings of bluebottles and sea urchins and the danger of the dreaded stonefish. I heard, without too much concern, that another naturalist had passed through the town only a fortnight before—a girl, this time, quite young, very attractive according to the young chemist, who, fresh from the university, was no doubt finding the local fillies something less than interesting.

I escaped at last, clutching my little wooden box under my arm, only to find that I had hours yet to kill before I made rendezvous with Johnny Akimoto at his hut behind the sand dunes.

Sudden panic overtook me as I stood on the cracked pavement bubbling with hot tar and saw the rickety town peter out at either end of the single main street. The riot of green, the raw colours of bougainvillaea and poinsettia seemed to close in on me, weigh me down, with their rioting strength. Johnny Akimoto's warning came back to me, and this, added to Nino Ferrari's caution about the dangers of an inexperienced diver, made me afraid and set me cursing my own foolhardiness for embarking, with so little preparation, on a project that scared even the professionals.

The thought of Manny Mannix nagged at me, too. I wondered what he would do next, where I should meet him, what would happen when we came face to face. Then I saw that I was standing opposite the post office.

On an impulse I crossed the street, presented myself at the counter and placed a trunk call to Nino Ferrari. The wilting clerk looked at me as if I had ordered the Eiffel Tower, then he scribbled the number on a slip of paper and told me to wait by the phone booth outside.

I waited. I waited a full hour, and when Nino finally came on the line his voice sounded faint and far away, as if it had been filtered through wet linen. He said. "This is Ferrari. Who is calling?"

"This is Lundigan, Nino—Renn Lundigan."

"So soon? Didn't your stuff arrive?"

"The stuff's all right, Nino. It's being shipped from Brisbane today."

"Then why do you call me?"

"Because I'm scared, Nino."

I thought I heard him chuckle, but I couldn't be sure.

"What are you scared of, my friend?"

"I think I'm crazy, Nino."

He really laughed this time: a full-bellied laugh that came crackling in fantastic distortions over the thousand miles of cable.

"I know you're crazy. There was no need to spend good money to tell me that. Is there anything I can do for you?"

"Yes, Nino, there is. I'm expecting trouble."

"Trouble? What sort of trouble?"

I had to be cautious now. There is no privacy in a public telephone booth in a Queensland country town.

"I told you, Nino, there is someone who doesn't like me."

"You told me, yes. Has anything happened?"

"Not yet, but I want to ask you, if there is trouble, would you come up and help me out?"

There was a long pause. I thought for a moment we had been cut off. Then Nino's voice crackled again over the wire.

"What sort of help do you want? Diving?"

"And other things, too, perhaps. I don't know yet. I can't predict what may happen. I'm just taking out insurance, that's all."

There was another pause. I knew what Nino was thinking. He was a newcomer to this country. He had once been an enemy. If he got into any trouble, it could prejudice his chances of naturalization. I was asking more than I had a right to ask. I knew it, too, but I was too scared to care.

Then Nino spoke. "All right, friend, if you want me, you send for me. I will come on the first plane. You can pay the bills?"

"I'll pay the bills, Nino . . . and thanks."

Nino chuckled. "I'll thank you better if you stay out of trouble and let me run my business."

"I'll try, Nino, but I can't promise it. I'll send you the rest of the story in today's mail. Good-bye for the present and thanks again."

"Good-bye, my friend," said Nino, "and stay out of trouble as long as you can."

The line went dead. I hung up the receiver. I walked back into the post office, bought myself an air letter and scribbled a note to Nino Ferrari.

When I dropped it in the mailbox I felt less lonely and less afraid. There were three of us now. Three men and a good boat and a friendly island. Manny Mannix could do his damnedest. I picked up my little box of medicines and walked down the track to the sand hills to meet Johnny Akimoto.

Johnny's boat was lying a hundred yards offshore, rolling a little in the oily swell. She was ketch-rigged, freshly painted, and her brasswork shone under the loving care of Johnny's hands. Her sails were old but carefully patched. A workmanlike boat run by a good workman. She had a hold amidships and cabin space aft. Her decks were swabbed clean, and her movables were stowed with the sailor's careful precision.

It took us three trips in the dinghy to get the stores aboard, and when we had stowed them and closed the hatch down Johnny busied himself with the small fuel stove in the galley.

I sat on the bunk and talked to him while he worked.

"She's a good boat, Johnny. I like her."

He grinned at me over his shoulder.

"A good boat is like a good woman. Look after her, she looks after you. You

161

saw her name, *Wahine*. In island language that means 'woman.' This is all the woman I have."

I grinned back at him.

"That makes two of us, Johnny."

He nodded and turned back to his stove, talking as he worked.

"Sometimes it is like that—there is one woman who is all woman, and when she is gone it is as if there were no women at all."

"You're a very wise man, Johnny," I said quietly.

I saw his dark shoulders lift in a shrug.

"We are the lost people, Renboss. But we are not all children or fools."

"Have you ever had a woman of your own, Johnny?"

He shook his head. "Where in this country would I find a woman of my own kind? Where, if I left this country, could I find the life which I have here? It is better this way, I think."

There was a small silence after that, while I smoked my cigarette and Johnny heated a can of stew and cut thick slices of bread which he buttered and laid on a tin plate.

When the meal was ready, he laid it on the cabin table and we sat down together. I felt again the curious sensation of separation and release which had come to me on the flight north. This man was my friend, my brother in adventure. The small, confined world between decks was the only real world, the rest was all illusion and fantasy.

When we had finished eating, we washed the plates and went up on deck. Sitting on the hatch cover, we saw the sun go down in a crimson glory, and then it seemed, at one leap, the stars were out, low-hung, in a purple sky. The wind was blowing inshore, and we heard the slap of the water as the *Wahine* rose and fell to the rhythm of the small waves.

Johnny Akimoto turned to me.

"Something you should understand, Renboss."

"What's that, Johnny?"

"This boat. She is mine, as if she were my woman. I understand her, she understands me. So long as we are on board, I must be the master. On the island it is the other way. It is your island—you say what is to be done, I will do it. We understand that, both of us."

"I understand it, Johnny."

"Then there is nothing more to be said between us."

"There is one thing, Johnny."

"What is that?"

"Before I came on board today, I telephoned a friend of mine in Sydney. If there's trouble, he'll come up and join us."

"This friend of yours—what sort of man is he?"

"He is an Italian, Johnny—a skindiver. He was a frogman with the Italian navy during the war."

"Sounds like a good one. He has promised to come?"

"Yes."

"It is always good to have friends at a time like this. Come below. I want to show you something."

We tossed our cigarettes into the water and went back to the cabin. Johnny Akimoto opened a cupboard under the bunk and took out two rifles. They were .303s, army pattern, but they were freshly oiled and the bolts slid home smoothly and true.

Johnny looked at me and grinned.

"I have had these a long time. I have never used them, except for rabbits and wallabies. If there is trouble, we shall not meet it unarmed."

"What about ammunition?"

"Two hundred rounds. It goes on your bill."

He put the rifles back in the cupboard and closed the door.

"Now I think we should sleep. We start at first light."

I peeled off my clothes and threw myself on the bunk, drawing a single sheet over me for covering. I heard Johnny go on deck to set the riding lights. I saw him come down and turn out the hanging lamp in the cabin. Then I slept and I did not dream at all.

We woke to fresh sunlight and a flat calm. I dived overside for a freshener, while Johnny stood on the deck with the rifle in case of sharks. When I hauled myself aboard on the anchor cable, Johnny went over in his turn.

Then we started the diesel, hauled in the anchor and nosed the *Wahine* out, eastering first, then turning southward to the Whitsunday channel and the bright islands where the tourists come.

Johnny was at the wheel, standing straight and proud—proud of the boat which was his woman, proud of himself and his mastery of her. We ate in the sun, watching the coast slide green and gold past our starboard quarter and the small smudges ahead grow to green islands with the lacework of white water round them.

It was a three-hour run at cruising speed. Allowing another hour for loading, Johnny proposed that we should lunch before we left for our own Island of the Twin Horns. There was a matter of courtesy, he explained. The tourists were one thing. They came and paid their money and had their fun and went away, leaving little but a memory of laughter by day and whispers under the palms by night. But with the island people themselves it was a different thing. There was the drink to be taken together, the news to be exchanged, the small local news which they made themselves and in which the transient tourists had neither interest nor part. There were favours to be done: the repair of a generator, a fault in the refrigeration system, a note to be taken to a guesthouse on a neighbouring island. We must attend to our own business, to be sure, but we would not cut ourselves off from the concerns of the small family of which we were now a part.

I pleaded caution, remembering that one day, sooner or later, Manny Mannix would come flaring like a hunter for the traces of Renn Lundigan. To Johnny Akimoto my reason was unreason.

"These are good people," he said. "Make yourself one of them, they will be one with you when trouble comes. You never know how or when you may need them."

I had no choice but to agree with him. I asked myself what I should have done without this grave, strong islander, alien in blood but still no stranger, who stood at the wheel like some ancient god, his muscles rippling to the play of the wheel, his skin shining like silk in the sun.

We were halfway there when Johnny gave me the wheel while he went up to the forepeak and stood whistling like the old lugger captains for a wind.

We didn't need a wind. The diesel was throbbing smoothly and pushing us through the flat water at a steady eight knots. But Johnny wanted a wind. Johnny wanted to hoist sail and show me how his woman performed, when the sweet wind filled the canvas and laid her over on her side. But the calm persisted and I was glad of it. There was no work at the wheel, and I could surrender myself to the soft magic of sun and water and the silence of men who understand each other and have no need for words.

It was eleven in the morning when we made our landfall—a small island of coral with a long, low building in the center and small white huts dotted among the palms. The coral beach dropped sharply into six fathoms of water and we cut the motors and let the *Wahine* drift in to close anchorage.

The tourists came down in a body to meet us—brown girls in bright bathing suits, brown boys with their arms round the shoulders of the girls, the island staff in print frocks or khaki shorts, following behind like shepherds of the holiday flock.

Some of the bathers swam out to us and tried to clamber up the anchor cable, but Johnny Akimoto refused to allow them on deck. His ship was his own and none might come aboard except as his guest. We dropped into the dinghy and rode the few yards to the beach, where Johnny returned the familiar greetings with grave courtesy and introduced me as his friend, Mr. Lundigan, who had bought a place nearby and had come to pick up his stores. The island folk gave me a warm greeting but asked few questions, content to accept me at the value Johnny had given me.

They told me that my crates had arrived safely. I was able to relax again and enjoy the cold beer and the tropical salad and the easy hospitality of these dwellers on the inner reef.

When I told them the name of my island, they laughed. When I confounded them with news of a channel and a water supply, they nodded sagely and pointed the moral that the Government didn't know everything—even though it might pretend to. When I talked in cagey generalities about underwater exploration, they were frankly and embarrassingly interested. The island dwellers have a naïve and touching pride in the wonderland that surrounds them. Each has his tally of small discoveries or his small hoard of collector's pieces—cowries, quaint corals, bailer shells, flotsam and jetsam from forgotten wrecks.

Again they repeated the chemist's story of the girl student who had passed their way, making the short hops between the islands in an open skiff with a puttering outboard motor. I was sorry to tell them I had never met her. I was happy in the private thought that I never would.

Then, mercifully, the meal was over. We had no errands to run. We had only to hoist the crates on board the *Wahine*, up anchor and head north by east for the Island of the Twin Horns. I smiled my way through the small ceremonies of farewell, passed some banal backchat with the tourists who came down to cheer us off . . . and then we were free again, with a freshening breeze to gladden the heart of Johnny Akimoto and a bellying jib that gave us two knots better than the steady, chugging diesel.

Johnny nursed the *Wahine* onto the wind like a lover. He held her on the tack like a master. He stood at the wheel, strong legs straddled against the buck, head thrown back, eyes shining and white teeth grinning in triumph. He shouted to me, "She's a beauty, my *Wahine*, eh, Renboss?"

"She's a beauty, Johnny. What time do we raise the island?"

"Hour and a half. Two, maybe."

"Nice work, Johnny. That gives us daylight to unload and make camp."

He nodded, grinning still, and twitched the wheel a fraction, to follow the faint shift of the wind. Then he began to sing, a warm, crooning island song in the language of his mother's people. The words were a mystery to me, but the melody caught at my heart and I was glad for him and sad with him and very grateful that Johnny Akimoto had made me his friend.

It was three in the afternoon when we raised the island. I stood in the forepeak, braced against the stays, and watched it grow from a grey smudge to a green blur and then to a horned island with a crescent of beach. In a little while I could trace the contours of the rocks and distinguish the separate trunks of the great pisonia trees. There was the group of pandanus that marked the spring. There was the surfline on the outer reef and the shifting green of calm water inside the lagoon. I watched it grow and grow, filling our horizon, and I felt like a man coming home from the wars to his father's house.

I turned and shouted to Johnny, "You know the channel, Johnny?"

He raised a hand in acknowledgment and shouted back, "I know him, Renboss!"

"You going to take her in with the engine? It's fast and narrow."

He shook his head. His eyes were full of bright challenge.

"I sail her in, Renboss . . . I sail her."

And sail her he did. With every stitch of canvas she could carry. A hundred yards from the reef he brought her round on a short tack. He lined her up with the western horn and the single beach oak, and set at the reef like a horse to a hurdle. I felt her leap as she hit the first roller, then Johnny laid her hard over and drove her like a racer through the rip, while I watched open-mouthed and waited for the coral trees to rake the bottom out of her and strip her to the keelson.

A minute later we were through, sliding with way on through glassy water, with the white beach in front and fear and uncertainty and Manny Mannix a thousand miles behind.

I shouted and cheered and danced the deck for sheer happiness, while Johnny nosed the *Wahine* into anchorage.

We dropped the hook and stowed the canvas and were just preparing to take the dinghy ashore on the first run when I saw something that killed my happiness with one stroke and set me cursing obscenely in a cold fury. . . .

At the head of the beach, where the trees began, a small tent had been pitched—and below it, careened above the tidemark, was a small skiff with an outboard motor.

Chapter Seven

"EASY, RENBOSS . . . take it easy now."

Johnny Akimoto was at my elbow, his warm voice chiding gently, talking me from madness to anger, from anger to common sense.

"It's only the girl, Renboss. You know—the one they told us about at the guesthouse."

"I know! I know!" I shouted the words at him. "The bloody little naturalist with her put-put and her collection of bloody sea slugs. Why the hell did she have to come here? Doesn't she know this is my island?"

"No, Renboss, she doesn't know that," said Johnny quietly.

"Then she damned soon will. Come on, Johnny, get the dinghy. I'll have her off the beach in twenty minutes."

"You can't do that, Renboss."

There was that in Johnny's voice which gave me pause. He laid his hand on my arm in a gesture of restraint.

"Why can't I? She doesn't have to stay here, does she?"

He pointed back to the reef and the channel we had just passed.

"You see? The tide is running in now. In the channel it makes five, six knots. With a boat like that, and a toy motor like that, how would she get through? And if she did, she could not reach the nearest island for three hours. By that time it is dark and dangerous."

I had no answer to that. I stared moodily across the water to the beach and wondered vaguely why the girl didn't show up. She must have seen us coming.

Johnny spoke again. "Renboss?"

"Yes?"

"In a minute or two we go ashore. We meet this girl. We tell her who we

167

are. We tell her that she must leave us soon as possible. But we do it gently."

"Why?"

"Because she is young. Because she will be a little afraid. Because it is easier to be kind to someone than hard. Because it would be bad to have her spread the story that you are an unpleasant man who does not understand the manners of the Reef. . . . And because we are both gentlemen, Renboss."

I looked up at him. His mild, wise eyes pleaded with me not to disappoint him. I gulped down my anger and gave him a crooked smile of apology.

"All right, Johnny. Be damned to you. We'll be kind to little bluestocking. But I tell you now, I'll have her off this island tomorrow or my name's not Renn Lundigan."

His face broke into a wide smile of approval. He clapped me on the shoulder and walked aft to haul in the dinghy for the first load of stores.

We were halfway to the beach when I gave voice to the thought that had been plaguing me for the last ten minutes.

"Funny thing, Johnny, the tent's there . . . the boat's beached. . . . Where's the girl?"

"Round the other side, perhaps, in the rock pools."

"She's a damn fool if she is, with the tide running in. There's a sheer wall round there. If she's not careful she'll be spending the night on a ledge."

"Maybe she's sleeping."

"Maybe."

Johnny grinned at my ill humour and bent to the oars again. Nothing more was said until we had beached the dinghy and were striding up towards the tent. The flaps were open and the guys were slack. A careless job. She'd be lucky if it didn't tumble about her ears at the first puff of the night wind. I hailed her.

"Hello, there! Anybody home?"

My voice was flung back at me from the circling ridge, but there was no answer from the tent. I was two strides ahead of Johnny when we reached it, so I was the first to see her.

At first glance I thought she was dead. Her dark hair was lank and matted about her cheeks and temples. Her face was the colour of old ivory. Her cotton blouse was torn open, exposing her small round breasts. One hand trailed limply on the sandy floor, the other lay slackly across her belly. She wore a pair of faded denim shorts. One leg was outflung on the stretcher. The other dangled over the side. It was swollen and blue from knee to instep.

Then I saw that she was alive. Her breathing was shallow, laboured. I felt her pulse. It was thready and flickering. There were beads and runnels of perspiration on her face and neck and breast. She looked like a limp rag doll left by little girls at playtime.

I looked up at Johnny Akimoto. He said nothing, but bent and examined the swollen limb. He flexed the ankle joint so that the sole of the foot tilted upwards. The girl stirred in a sudden spasm of pain but did not awaken.

Johnny motioned to me to look. Then he traced with his finger the small lines of punctures stretching from the ball of the toes to the ridge of the heel. Seven of them. He shook his head gravely and said one word, "Stonefish."

The stonefish is the ugliest fish in the world. Its grey-brown body is a mass of wart-like growths. It is coated with thick foul slime. Its mouth is a gaping semicircle, opening upwards and livid green inside. Along the ridge of its spine are thirteen needle-sharp quills, each with its own poison sac. Its sting can kill a man or cripple him with racking agonies for weeks. There is no known antidote to its poison. The natives of the north dance the stonefish dance in their initiation ceremonies so that young bucks may know the danger that lies in wait in the crevices of the coral reefs.

I questioned Johnny Akimoto.

"Will she die, Johnny?"

"I don't think so, Renboss. She is very sick. She has fever, as you see. She sleeps because she is worn out with that and the pain. But she will not die, I think, unless the poison in the leg gets worse."

"We shall have to get her to a doctor, Johnny."

Johnny shrugged. "I have seen what the doctors do with this sort of thing. They know as little as we do about the poison of the stonefish."

"But, damn it all, Johnny, she can't stay here! We can't look after her."

"Why not? We have the medicine chest. We have sulfa and the other drugs. We know what to do. Besides, if we take her to the mainland, we lose two days. A day there . . . a day back."

A wise fellow, Johnny. A shrewd, secret man from the old islands. He knew better than I did, myself, what would bend me to his wishes. I resigned myself to the situation.

"All right, Johnny, have it your way. Get back to the *Wahine* and bring the medicine chest—and a couple of clean sheets while you're about it."

"Yes, Renboss," said Johnny.

He gave me a small ironic smile and walked swiftly out of the tent.

When he had gone, I settled the girl more comfortably on the stretcher and looked around. There was a small folding table loaded with stoppered jars of marine specimens. There were bottles of acetone and formaldehyde. There were scalpels and tweezers and scissors and a good microscope. There was a canvas chair and a bucket and a collapsible canvas basin. There was a rucksack with clothes and towels and a small cosmetic case. On the face of it, the girl was a genuine student who knew her job and worked at it.

Against this was the fact that she had walked the reef in bare feet . . . an intolerable folly that had nearly killed her and might well wreck my plans for the raising of the treasure ship.

I settled her more comfortably on the narrow stretcher, then took the bucket and walked up to the spring under the pandanus tree. Had I come to the island as I had hoped to come, I might have gone running and singing. Now I was full of the flat taste of disappointment. I filled the bucket with

169

fresh, cool water, and as I walked back I saw Johnny Akimoto casting off the loaded dinghy for the pull back to shore.

He waved to me and I waved back, but in spite of the comradely gesture I was irritated with Johnny Akimoto. All very well for him to be bland and logical about the situation. This was my island, as the *Wahine* was his boat. This was . . . Then I saw the humour of it, saw what a cross-grained creature disappointed greed can make of a frustrated don. I began to chuckle, and by the time I reached the tent I was in reasonable humour again.

I poured water into the canvas basin. I rummaged in the rucksack for clean clothing. I found a fresh towel and a washcloth. Then, turning back to the girl on the bed, I began to bathe her. I stripped off the dank clothing and sponged the fever sweat from her body.

She groaned and opened her eyes as the cold water flowed over her. But her expression was blank and she mumbled unintelligibly, then fell limply back against the sodden pillow.

Sickness is never beautiful. The service of a sick body provokes pity but not desire. The girl, cradled in my arms, was beautiful, there was no doubt of that; but fever and shock and the wrenching pains of the poison had marred her beauty and left her like a wax image, without pulse or passion, almost without life.

I had just finished dressing her in the fresh clothes when Johnny Akimoto came back. He nodded approval, then set the medicine chest on the table and took out the scalpel, which he sterilized carefully in the flame of a cigarette lighter. There was a delicacy and precision about his movements that made me wonder what education and opportunity might have done for this calm, deep man, whose alien blood had condemned him to isolation among his white brothers.

"Let her lie back," said Johnny. "I want you to help me."

We knelt at the foot of the stretcher and I took the girl's foot in my hands, tilting it and holding it firm, while Johnny made a deep incision along the line of the spine marks. The girl groaned and writhed, while a great gush of fetid matter spurted from the puffy flesh. Johnny drained the wound, washed it, dressed it generously with sulfa powder and bound it with clean gauze. I watched, gaping, while he took a syringe and injected a careful measure of penicillin into the girl's arm.

"Where did you learn this, Johnny?" I could not keep the surprise from my voice.

"In the army, Renboss," said Johnny calmly. "I was a medical orderly at Salamaua field hospital."

He took the ampule out of the syringe and laid it carefully back in its container.

"We sterilize these things later, when we have hot water."

I agreed meekly. "Yes, Johnny."

The girl was moaning now, fighting her slow way back to consciousness. I

170

lifted her and held her in my arms while Johnny stripped the stretcher and remade it with one of our palliasses and a pair of clean sheets. Then we laid her down again, drew the sheet over her and watched a little till the moaning subsided and she slept again, breathing more regularly and deeply. Then we left her. We had work of our own to do.

We pitched our tent in an angle of rocks a few paces from the spring. It was out of the wind and sheltered from the heat by the spreading green of an ancient pisonia. We dug a drain round it to carry off water if the rain should come. We built an oven of stones against a rock wall. We unrolled sleeping bags on the framed stretchers and disposed our few personal belongings out of the reach of ants and spiders.

We filled our big canvas water bag and hung it, dripping, on the tent pole to cool. We slung a tarpaulin between four tree trunks and stacked our crates of equipment underneath it, draining the ground round them as we had drained the tent. Only fools like to rough it. The secret of a working camp is to keep it tidy, clean and dry.

Now at last we were at home. Johnny Akimoto lit a fire while I brought a billy of water from the spring and set it on to boil. We lit cigarettes and sat down to smoke while the dry wood sputtered and crackled and the small flames rose round the blackened sides of the billy.

It was a placid moment, a good moment. Had it not been for the girl in the tent on the beachhead, it would have been a perfect moment. I turned to Johnny Akimoto.

"Now, Johnny, suppose you tell me."

"About what, Renboss?"

"About tomorrow, Johnny."

"Tomorrow?" said Johnny calmly. "Tomorrow we start work."

"But the girl, Johnny. What about the girl?"

"The girl is ill, Renboss. She will not be able to move for days yet."

"But she'll be able to talk, won't she, Johnny? She'll be curious, won't she, Johnny? All women are, Johnny. What do we tell her when she asks questions?"

"We tell her the truth, Renboss. We tell her that you are learning to be a skindiver and to use the apparatus for breathing under water. That is what you will be doing, isn't it?"

"Yes, I suppose it is. But I'll be doing more than just training."

Johnny flicked the butt of his cigarette into the flames.

"If you are wise, Renboss, you will do nothing more than that. You will find from the first moment that you put on the mask and make your dive into deep water that you are like a child learning his first steps. You will be uncertain. You will be afraid. You will be surrounded by monsters. You will have to live and move among them like one of themselves. You will have to learn which of them are enemies to be feared. You will have to learn to manage your own body in the simplest exercises of going down and coming up and moving

171

yourself from one place to another. I tell you now, so that none of the time you give to this will be wasted. You will need all your courage and all your skill when you come to dive for the treasure ship."

Try as I might I could not shake the logic of this calm-voiced islander. I might defy it; but that could mean my own destruction and the end of all my hopes. I shrugged in wry resignation.

"All right, Johnny. We practice, we practice for days—a week, maybe. By then the girl's moving around. She's bored. She wants company. She's curious about what is going on. She's a scientist, remember, Johnny. She won't buy the fairy tales we sold the others."

"Then," said Johnny simply, "I load her stores on the *Wahine*, take the boat in tow and deliver her to the mainland."

I was beaten and I knew it, but I was irritable and refused to let the matter drop so easily.

"She's ill, Johnny. We've still got to feed her and nurse her."

"We have to feed ourselves, too, so that is nothing. As for the nursing, it is a matter of changing the dressing, morning and night. Medicine she can take herself. We make her comfortable, then leave her till mealtime."

The water was bubbling in the billy. I heaved myself up to make the tea, but Johnny Akimoto laid a hand on my shoulder and drew me down again. His eyes were steady. His voice was firm.

"Renboss, there is something that must be said. I will say it and then perhaps you will tell me to take my boat and the girl and leave the island. If not, then I will stay and we will never mention it again between us. I know what you want to do. I know how much and why you want to do it. It is a good thing for a man to want something at the limit of his strength. It can also be a very bad thing. When I was diving for the pearling masters, there were those we hated and feared. They would go out to a new bed in the deep waters. They would find good pearls—enough to pay the divers and the crew and the expenses of the boat, and still leave a fine profit for the master, but they would not be satisfied. They would send the boys down again and again, deeper and deeper, until their eardrums burst and blood spurted out of their mouths and nostrils, and the bends knotted them up so that they could never work again. It is a bad thing, Renboss, when a man is so hungry for money that he can spare neither thought nor pity for anyone else in the world. . . . Now it is said. If you want, I will leave in the morning."

The billy boiled over. The steam rose in hissing clouds from the blackened coals at the edge of the fire, but neither of us moved. I tried to speak, but the words were slow in coming. Shame stifled them in my throat. Johnny Akimoto sat silent, a gentle man waiting without regret for me to accept or reject him.

Then mercifully the words came. I turned to him and held out my hand.

"I'm sorry, Johnny. I'd like you to stay."

He took my hand, his dark face split into a smile of sheer delight.

"I stay, Renboss. Better we make tea now. The girl will be awake soon and she will be hungry."

172

Together we prepared a simple meal, and when it was ready we carried it together down to the girl's tent.

She was feverish again. Her face was flushed. She was soaked with sweat and she tossed and moaned and plucked at the sheet as her temperature rose and the pains racked her. She shivered violently and drew the sheet up to her neck for warmth.

I sponged her again and held her up while Johnny forced water and a couple of tablets between her chattering teeth. Then we laid her back on the pillow and made our own meal, while the shadows lengthened outside and the first stirring of the night wind raised small eddies in the sand.

"She is worse than I thought," said Johnny. "If the fever does not break tonight . . ."

He left the rest of it unsaid.

"One of us should stay with her tonight, Johnny."

He nodded. He was pleased that I had said it.

"We should take her up to our tent, Renboss. She can use my stretcher. Then, maybe, you can get some sleep. If she needs you, you are there."

I looked at him, curiously. I could not read what was in his mind. I questioned him.

"But what about you, Johnny? There's no need to move out. We can both—"

"No, Renboss. I will sleep down here."

"I don't see what you're driving at."

Johnny smiled with gentle irony.

"She is young, Renboss," he said. "She is young and sick and lonely. If she woke tonight and saw a black man bending over her, then she would be afraid."

Johnny Akimoto's father was a Japanese exile. His mother was a dark woman from the Gilbert Islands. Johnny himself was one of the lost people who would live without love and die without a son to succeed him. But of all the men I have ever met, Johnny Akimoto was most a man.

We wrapped the girl in the sheets and carried her up to the big tent. Leaving Johnny to settle her, I walked back to pick up the medicine chest. As I bent to pick it up, I noticed a small leather wallet wedged between two bottles on the folding table. I opened it.

There were a few bank notes, some postage stamps and a letter of credit from the Commercial Banking Company. It was endorsed "Miss Patricia Mitchell." Now at least we knew her name and the fact that she was single. I folded the paper and put it back in the wallet. The rest she could tell us herself when she recovered—if she recovered.

Johnny seemed to have his doubts about that and I didn't care to dwell on what might happen if she died while she was in our hands: police inquiries, a coroner's inquest, stories in the newspapers, gossip along the coast. The secret of the *Doña Lucia* and the gold of the King of Spain would be a secret no longer.

The sun was going down when I left the tent: a golden ball rolling off the edge of the world into a sea of yellow and crimson, ochre and royal purple. I stood and watched it disappear behind the rim of creation. I saw the brief glory of the afterglow. I watched the colours fade from the surface of the ocean and the peach bloom brushed from the sky by the swift fingers of the night. Then I turned slowly and walked up to the tent.

The girl was still in the grip of fever and Johnny Akimoto was waiting to bid me good night.

Chapter Eight

I STRIPPED DOWN TO A PAIR OF SHORTS and stretched out on the camp bed. But I could not sleep. My nerves were tight as piano wires, and I could not shut my mind to the mumblings of the sick girl on the other side of the tent or to the steady beat of the sea and the small creaking of restless birds in the flame tree outside.

I got up, lit the kerosine lamp, fished in my bag for the notes Nino Ferrari had given me and began to study them. They were simple, dry, precise; an elementary exposition of the principles of free diving with a static air supply. They spoke of the relation of pressure to depth; of the accumulation of free nitrogen in the bloodstream; of the dynamics of motion in deep water; temperature variations and symptoms of narcosis; and positive control of the Eustachian tubes.

I read them, line by line, but they made no impression on me. I was a man beset with visions. Visions of coral gardens, and monstrous fish in rainbow colours, and a shadowy ship festooned with sea grasses in whose holds lay chests of gold guarded by antique horrors.

I heard the girl chattering and moaning as the fever shook her again. I got up and held the lamp high to look at her. I was shocked and frightened. Her lips were blue. There were great shadows round her sunken eyes, which stared blindly at the yellow light. I put the lamp down while I bathed her face and neck and hands. I forced two tablets between her lips and washed them down with water, which splashed on the covers as I held the glass to her chattering mouth. Then I settled her back against the pillow and, pulling a packing case to the foot of the stretcher, I sat down to wait.

It was three in the morning when the fever broke. Great spasms racked and twisted her and her moaning rose to a high bubbling sound. Then suddenly she seemed to collapse. A foul sweat broke out over her body and ran down her cheeks into the hollows of her neck and breast. She seemed to struggle for air and then lay very still. I felt her pulse; it was weak but steady. Her breathing became regular again; and, when I held a glass of water to her lips, she opened her eyes and said firmly, "I don't know you."

I grinned at her and said, "You soon will. I'm Renn Lundigan. You're Pat Mitchell. I saw the name in your wallet."

That puzzled her. She closed her eyes and turned her head slowly from side to side on the pillow. When she looked at me again, I could see she was afraid.

"I've been sick, haven't I?"

"Very sick. You stepped on a stonefish. You're lucky to be alive."

Memory was stirring slowly now. She struggled to sit up. I pressed her gently back onto the pillows.

"Just lie there. There's plenty of time. It'll come back if you take it easy."

She sighed fretfully like a child.

"I don't remember this place. Where am I?"

"You're on my island. This is my tent."

"Did you bring me here?"

"To the tent—yes. To the island—no. You were here when I came. You needed looking after, so we brought you up here for the night."

"Who's—we?"

"Johnny Akimoto and myself. Johnny's a friend of mine."

"Oh."

Suddenly she seemed to droop. The worn body was refusing its functions. She closed her eyes, so that I thought she had fallen asleep. Then she opened them again.

"Please . . . could I have a drink? I'm thirsty."

I held the glass to her lips, raising her head while she drank greedily, choking on the last mouthful. Then I lowered her to the pillow and she thanked me gravely, like a small schoolgirl.

"That was nice. Thank you very much."

I turned away to get rid of the glass of water and then, when I looked at her again, she was asleep.

I drew the covers over her and closed the flap of the tent to keep out the wind. I threw myself on the stretcher, bone-weary, but no longer depressed. It was as if we had fought a battle together and won it. In a few minutes I, too, was asleep.

Johnny Akimoto brought us our breakfast: coral trout, fresh caught and grilled on the coals, thick buttered bread, tea sweetened with condensed milk. He grinned broadly when he saw the girl awake and with an anxious, puzzled smile on her worn face. I made the introductions.

176

"Pat Mitchell, this is Johnny Akimoto, my good friend. Johnny, this is Pat."

"I should thank you both. I . . . I don't seem to remember very much."

"We were worried about you, Miss Pat," said Johnny. "This morning I thought you might be dead. I looked in and saw you both sleeping. I thought maybe you would like fresh fish for breakfast."

He laid the tin plate on the side of the bed and watched anxiously while she propped herself on one elbow and began to pick at it.

"You like it, Miss Pat? He was a big fellow. All of four pounds."

His eyes lit up when she smiled at him and said quietly, "It's very nice, thank you, Johnny."

We ate together—talking little. The fish was sweet eating, and the new sun warmed us through the grey canvas of the tent. I saw the colour flow slowly back into the girl's face as she nibbled at the food and drank mouthfuls of the steaming tea.

She raised her head and looked at me. The question seemed to worry her. She took time to phrase it.

"It was a stonefish, you said?"

"That's right. Don't you remember?"

"Not very well. I was walking on the reef . . ."

"Silly to walk on the reef barefoot."

She was instantly angry.

"I wasn't barefoot. I know better than that. I was wearing sandshoes. There was a pebble in one of them. I stopped to take it out. I overbalanced and slipped into a pool. My bare foot must have landed on the stonefish."

Johnny and I grinned at her small, weak anger. She flushed and went on.

"I don't remember how I got back. The pain was frightening. I seemed to be paralyzed. I fell several times. I remember wondering if I'd be caught by the tide. After that . . . nothing. How long have I been sick?"

"We don't know. We only arrived last night. You were unconscious when we found you."

A sudden thought came to her. Cautiously she drew back the sheet and looked at her bandaged leg.

"You dressed this for me?"

"Johnny did. He had to open it. You won't be able to walk for a while."

"No . . . I suppose not." Again the cautious framing of the question. "These . . . these aren't the clothes I was wearing on the reef."

I turned away and fumbled for a cigarette, but Johnny Akimoto answered her with never a smile.

"You were very sick, Miss Pat. Renboss had to change your clothes and wash you."

She blushed ripe red; then her chin went up bravely and she said, "You've been kind and gentle to me. I'm very grateful."

"More tea, Miss Pat?" said Johnny, the courtly gentleman.

"Thank you, Johnny. I seem to be dried out."

177

Johnny took the tin mug and went out to the fire to fill it again. She turned to me.

"You told me last night this was your island."

"That's right."

"I didn't know that. I didn't mean to trespass."

"You weren't trespassing." I stumbled over it, lamely. "When you're well again, Johnny can take you back to the mainland."

"There's no need for that. I've got my own boat. I don't want to give you any more trouble."

It was an awkward moment. Courtesy might betray me into the very situation I wanted to avoid. The girl had been ill. She was handling an embarrassing interlude with some charm and more dignity than I myself could muster. But the fact remained: I wanted her off the island as quickly as possible.

Then Johnny came back with the tea and a suggestion that gave me time to think.

"You have been sick, Miss Pat. You are still sick, although the fever is gone. You must rest as much as you can. If you like, we will carry you down to the beach. We can make a shade for you with the tent fly, and you can watch us while we work."

Her face brightened. "I'd like that. I could sleep. I could write up some notes. And as you say, I could watch you work. What sort of work is it?"

"Renboss, here, wants to learn skindiving. I have come out to teach him."

She laughed at that, strongly, happily.

"That's not work. That's play."

"The way Johnny teaches, it's hard work. You wait and see."

My bluff adventurer's manner didn't deceive her for a moment. She gave me a long, level look and said quickly, "This is your island, Mr. Lundigan. Whatever you choose to do here is your own affair. I promise you I'll mind my business and leave you as soon as I can travel."

Johnny Akimoto choked convulsively, spluttered something about a fishbone and rushed from the tent. Miss Patricia Mitchell gave me a sidelong smile and settled back on her pillow.

"Renn Lundigan, eh? You were quite a legend in your day. I never thought I'd meet you face to face."

"I don't know what the devil you're talking about—"

"That's natural enough. They sacked you, didn't they? Dead drunk under the dean's window at nine in the morning."

I gaped at her, speechless. The smile died on her lips, and she laid a small, clammy hand on my own.

"I'm teasing you and it's not kind—after all you've done for me. I'm from Sydney, too, you see. I'm a reader in natural history at the university. Small world, isn't it?"

A small world, indeed. Too damned small, when a man's past follows him out to the last island on the last reef before the wide ocean. Anger boiled in me swiftly and spilled out in a spate of bitter words.

"All right . . . so you know me. But I don't want to know you. I don't want you here, but you're ill and I can't do anything about it. Understand this: so long as you're here, we'll care for you. We'll feed you, nurse you and make you as comfortable as may be. But as soon as you can walk I want you gone. If you can't handle your own craft, Johnny will take you back. Until then, don't talk to me about the past. It's dead—done—finished. Don't talk to me about friends. I have none. And when you go, leave me in peace. Forget you've ever seen me."

I turned on my heel and walked out of the tent. I thought I heard her weeping, but I didn't turn back. She was the past and I wanted no part of her. The past was dead and best forgotten. It was an illusion, of course. A wild, crazy illusion. But I was still fool enough to cherish it.

Johnny Akimoto rowed me out to a rock pool on the inner fringe of the reef. He pulled easily across the oily water, and when I looked back I could see the small shelter on the sand where Pat Mitchell lay on her stretcher looking out to sea. It was Johnny who had set it up for her, Johnny who had carried her down and made her comfortable and set the water bag within reach, and dressed her wound and left the tablets at her hand.

Johnny. . . . Always Johnny. . . . Johnny's was the strength and mine the weakness. Johnny's the calm wisdom and mine the folly of frustration and flight. He was sober and subdued as we rowed out, and if there was pity in his eyes, I could not read it.

We moored the skiff to a niggerhead, one of those jutting stumps of dead coral which are found all over the reefs, and which have the look of a frizzled skull on top of a stumpy neck. I took off my sandshoes and put on the pair of flippers that Nino Ferrari had given me. They were not the orthodox model with half sole and a heel strap. They were made with a full sole and a heel grip so that the diver might walk on the coral floor without too much danger from stonefish and spiny urchins.

I buckled on the wide canvas belt, weighted with seven pounds of lead slugs, with the long knife of tempered steel in a sheath of plaited leather. Now I was ready for the lung pack.

The two cylinders of compressed air were fixed to a frame of light alloy, and they fitted on my back as a knapsack fits on the back of a climber, with an arrangement of canvas braces slung on the shoulders and buckled under the breast. Two tubes of corrugated rubber, coated with cotton webbing, led from the cylinders to the polished metal disc of the regulator, which is the main-spring of the mechanical lung. Another tube of the same material terminated in a small rubber mouthpiece with slotted rubber lugs to be gripped between the teeth of the diver.

I set the regulator and Johnny Akimoto lifted the pack onto my back, settling the spine pad comfortably, while the straps were buckled and tested.

Now I was ready for the mask. I dipped it in the sea to wet the rubber and wash the Perspex so that it would not mist over under water. Then I slipped it over my head, moulded the rubber into my cheekbones and tried a breath to test whether it was watertight. Then I adjusted the strap at the back of my skull and slipped the mask up on my forehead.

Johnny Akimoto watched me with careful interest.

"Ready now, Renboss?"

"Ready, Johnny."

"Take a look first before you go down."

I sat down in the thwarts and looked over into the clear water. Coral pools vary in depth from a few inches to fifteen or twenty feet. This one was perhaps a dozen yards long and fifteen feet wide. Its depth was no more than two fathoms. Yet, like all the others on the reef, it was a perfect microcosm of the colourful and abundant life of the coral sea.

Soft sea grasses, green and red and gold, moved gently as if to an underwater wind. Purple-lavender corals spread like flowers in a summer garden. Red and white anemones spread their tentacles like the petals of a Japanese chrysanthemum. Soft corals in rainbow colours lay like primitive frescoes on the rocky walls. Shoals of small fish, striped and dappled, darted about among the foliage. A blue starfish lay motionless on the sandy bottom, and a hermit crab made a tentative foray from the speckled cone shell which was his home. It was a world of riotous colour and teeming life, and I felt a sudden thrill at the thought that I was soon to be made free in it. I looked up at Johnny.

"Ready, Johnny."

He grinned and nodded. I slipped the mask over my eyes and nostrils, moulded it once more to my skin, clamped the mouthpiece between my teeth, tested the airflow and lowered myself over the stern into the pool. The weighted belt took me down instantly. I sank to a depth of four or five feet and hung suspended in a liquid world.

My first sensation was one of utter panic.

I was surrounded by monsters. Magnified by the mask and the water, the waving grasses were primeval forests. The anemones were gaping mouths. The corals were trees in an antediluvian forest. The shoals of fish were armies from another planet. The hermit crab was a huge and horrible deformity. I gasped and gagged and spat out the mask and kicked myself to the surface to find Johnny Akimoto leaning over the gunwale laughing at me.

He gave me his hand and pulled me up until I got a grip on the timber, and I hung there, gasping and spluttering.

"What happened, Renboss?" said Johnny Akimoto, his white teeth flashing in a broad grin.

"I got scared. That's what happened. Everything's different when you get down there."

Johnny nodded. "It is always like that, Renboss, the first time. Now look again."

I looked down into the pool. There were no monsters. It was the same narrow world of rare Lilliputian beauty that I had seen the first time.

"Go down again, Renboss," said Johnny. "Take it easy this time. Breathe slow and even. Swim a little. Dive to the bottom. Take a good look at the things that frightened you the first time."

I nodded agreement, slipped the mask back over my face, clamped on the mouthpiece and let myself slide back into the pool.

For a long minute I hung suspended below the surface, forcing myself to concentrate on the simple involuntary act of breathing. After a while the rhythm returned to me. The air flowed freely from the cylinders. The bubbles from the regulator rose to the surface in a steady steam, with a soft palpitating hiss that matched the rhythm of my breathing.

My courage returned to me. I kicked gently with the flippers and found myself floating easily towards the coral wall.

Then I stopped short. A new terror confronted me. Naked hands, big as the branches of a tree, reached out to grasp me. From a shadowy recess between waving sea grasses a great mouth gaped to devour me and a pair of eyes as big as oysters surveyed me with calm malevolence. For a moment I was petrified. I wanted to do as I had done before, spit out the gag and kick myself to the surface. Then reason returned and self-control with it. The hands were stag-horn corals. The eyes and mouth belonged to a small coral trout, which turned and flickered away with a flash of princely scarlet when I reached out my hand to touch it.

I kicked more strongly now. I found myself moving with a fabulous ease. The corals and the grasses slid past me with surprising speed. The labour of breathing at increased pressure was no longer apparent. I was seized with the illusion that I was a bird suspended between earth and heaven, that my arms were spreading wings and that the element surrounding me was air instead of water. I emptied my lungs and saw the air bubbles stream upwards as I dived downwards in a steep trajectory. There was a sudden pressure in my ears, a sharp pain in the sinus cavities. I swallowed as one does in a landing aircraft. The tubes cleared themselves and the pressure and the pain were gone. My hands clutched the sandy bottom.

With a series of movements that made me think, irrelevantly, of an acrobat on the high trapeze, I stood upright. There was no weight in my body, no hint of labour in the liquid motions of my limbs. When I walked it was as if I floated. When I floated it was as if I walked. Happiness took hold of me. A great goodwill pervaded me. I walked to the coral walls and swam along feeling the sea grass brush my face, reaching out to touch the branches, gin-gerly at first, then with more confidence, as if they were trees on my own land. I touched the anemones with my finger and saw the bright tentacles withdraw in fright. I hung motionless while the striped fish swam round my body and flashed away in terror at the slightest movement.

I don't know how long I stayed there, tasting the pleasures of my new citizenship in a new world. Then suddenly I was cold. I looked down at my body. It was covered with goose pimples. The skin of my fingers was white and crapy. It was time to go. With a flurry of hands and flippers I shot to the surface and hauled myself into the dinghy. Johnny told me I had been underwater for twenty-five minutes.

I shed my gear and sat quietly for a while, feeling the warmth flow out again from the core of my body to meet the warmth of the sun on my naked skin.

Johnny questioned me intently. "You did not find it hard this time, Renboss?"

"Not hard at all, Johnny. Once the first fear left me it was easy—child's play."

"The first part is always easy," said Johnny soberly. "The pool is shallow and enclosed. There is no work to do. There is no danger to think of, so you enjoy yourself. But this"—he reached forward and ran his finger along the seams of my shrunken hands—"this is the first danger—cold. You think you are not working, because you move easily. But your body is working all the time. It burns itself up to keep you warm. And when you go into deep water it is colder still . . . suddenly cold, as if you had crossed a fence from summer into winter. That is why a man cannot stay down too long in deep water. For a naked diver like me it is not so bad. I stay down only for a short while, so long as my lungs can hold the last mouthfuls of air, but you breathe down there and the cold creeps on you, makes you tired without your knowing it."

I nodded, remembering that Nino Ferrari had told me the same thing in other words, remembering his advice to wear a woolen jerkin for underwater work.

"We should go in now," said Johnny. "For the first time you have done enough. This afternoon we will try again. When you are not diving, you should eat well and exercise yourself. When we come to work, you will find that your strength spends itself quickly."

We unhitched the dinghy from the niggerhead and pushed off. The tide was running out fast now, and in an hour the lagoon would be a naked stretch of sand and the reefs would be exposed, dead and ugly in the sun, save where the pools remained guardians of the multitude of lives which spawn in its coral reaches.

As Johnny sculled steadily back to the shore, my eyes were fixed on the beach where Pat Mitchell lay under the canvas awning. I asked myself what I was going to say to her. I wondered what words would bridge the gap that I myself had cut between us. My decision was unchanged. I wanted her gone. But we would be together for days yet; and a tropic island may be a paradise, but it may also be a hell, if the people on it cannot live in harmony.

Johnny Akimoto sent the dinghy forward with one long powerful stroke; then he shipped his oars and spoke to me. "Miss Pat is sorry for what she said, Renboss. She wants to tell you, but she does not know how."

"Neither do I, Johnny, that's the trouble."

Johnny smiled gently. "She is a good one, that; what she promises she will do. When the time comes, she will go and she will leave you in peace. She has told you that, and she has told me, too."

I grinned at him then. I couldn't argue with Johnny.

"All right, Johnny. I'll talk to her. You get something to eat and leave me alone with her. I'll find something to say, though God knows what."

He dipped his oars again without saying another word. And when we came to the beach there was peace between us.

Chapter Nine

THE NOON SUN WAS BLAZING on the canvas canopy; so we carried Pat Mitchell up to the big tent in the shade of the trees. Leaving Johnny to settle her, I walked outside to change into dry clothes—and to prepare my opening gambit.

When I came back she was alone, propped up on the stretcher with a small vanity case in her hand. I looked at her and saw that she was beautiful. Her cheeks were no longer yellow with sickness but tinged with brown from the sun, and lit from within with the growing fire of health. Her hair was no longer lank and matted but brushed soft and shining, drawn away from the face so that you could see the fine bones of the cheek and the small proud lift of the firm chin. Her eyes were dark but veiled in shyness. Her hands were capable and controlled on the coverlet.

She was all woman, this one, small, rounded and perfect like those statuettes of golden girls out of antique times. The stretcher creaked as I sat down on the foot of it. I took out a cigarette and offered her one, but she refused with a gesture. I lit up, smoked for a few moments to steady myself, then started to speak.

"Miss Mitchell . . . Pat . . ."

"No, Mr. Lundigan, let me say it."

She bent forward and spoke earnestly, carefully, as if she were afraid to forget the lines she had rehearsed, as if the lines once spoken should fail to convey their meaning.

"What I said to you this morning was unpardonable. It was unnecessary and cruel, and I don't know why I said it. Or rather I do. It was because . . . because you had seen me with my clothes off, and you hadn't any right and

184

. . . well . . . that's it and I'm sorry and I'll go away whenever you want me to and nobody will ever know that I have been here . . . nobody."

Then she lay back on the pillows as if exhausted. She looked at me as if afraid of what I might say or do. I tried to smile, but it wasn't a very successful effort. The smile is a sign of confidence. I was far from confident. I said, "I'm sorry, too. This is the first time I have been back to this island since . . . since my wife and I were here together. I can't explain how I felt about it. It was like—like a homecoming. I couldn't bear the thought of anyone else . . ."

"Intruding?"

"Yes—I must say it—intruding. But it wasn't your fault—it was mine. You couldn't know, even, that the island was mine. You were ill. You . . . Oh, to hell with it! I was a bloody boor. I'm sorry. Now can we talk about something else?"

She was smiling now; the breach was healed. She asked me for a cigarette. I gave it to her, lit it, and our talk led us away from the old dangerous grounds.

I told her how I had heard about her on the mainland. I told her of the young chemist who had lost his heart to her. I told her how she had impressed the islanders—a solitary girl put-putting between the islands in a tiny work-boat. She laughed at that.

"Impressed? They thought I was crazy."

"I think you are, too. That's no sort of a boat for deep waters."

She shrugged. "It's all right if you're careful and wait for the weather. I've been lucky most of the time."

"Most of the time?"

She nodded. "I had my worst moment when I came here. The wind was high and the sea was freshening. I wasn't particularly worried. I was so close inshore. Then I couldn't find a channel."

"What did you do?"

"Rode up and down the reef until I found it."

"Dangerous."

"Yes, very. There was nothing else to do. Even when I got into the tide rip it was like trying to ride a bucking horse, but we got through all right."

I looked at the small firm hands on the sheet. Her mouth was firm, too—firm and smiling. A girl with heart and courage. I found myself beginning to warm to her. I thought that could be dangerous, too. I asked her some more questions.

"You're a naturalist. That's an odd job for a woman, isn't it?"

Her chin went up at that.

"I don't see why. I like it. I'm good at it. It pays fairly well and leaves me free to do the things I like."

"Such as—this?"

"That's right."

"What are you working at now?"

"A doctor's thesis. The ecology of *Haliotis asinina*—muttonfish to you, Renn Lundigan."

185

She had popped me back in my box and closed the lid with a bang. I couldn't help but be amused. Then it was my turn to be questioned.

"What about you, Renn? What are you doing now?"

"Johnny told you. Learning to dive."

"For pleasure?"

"For pleasure. Anything against it?"

"No. It makes a fascinating holiday, but what are you going to do afterwards, Renn? For a living, I mean. You can't beachcomb here all your life."

I needed notice for that question. This was no playtime girl to be put off with fatuous backchat. I shrugged and made my little rueful mouth and said, "Well, I can't teach anymore. No university would have me. But I'm not a bad historian, and there is enough material around this reef to make a book or two. You know"—I waved my hands in a vague all-embracing gesture—"you know, the early navigators, the blackbirders, the pearling days . . . none of it's ever been properly documented."

Her eyes brightened. She leant forward with eager professional interest.

"That's good, Renn. "That's very good indeed. This is the Barbary Coast of Australia, you know. There's all sorts of material here—piracy, violence, romance . . . everything. If I could write, that's what I'd like to do. Look, I'll show you something."

She snapped open her vanity case, tilted the lid back, lifted out a small tray and took out a small round object which she laid in the palm of my hand. For a long moment I stared at it, not daring to raise my eyes.

It was an exact replica of the old Spanish coin which Jeannette and I had found on the reef. I felt the blood drain from my face. My lips were dry. My tongue was too big for my mouth. I closed my eyes and saw my dreams blown down like a house of cards. I opened them again. The coin stared up at me from my palm, a golden eye, unblinking.

I looked at Pat Mitchell and asked her softly, "Where did you get this?"

Her explanation was eager and guileless. "Here, Renn. On the reef. It was the second day. I was poking round in a rock pool when I saw what looked like a piece of dead coral, flat and round. I don't know why I picked it up, except perhaps that its shape was a little unusual. When I did, I saw that there was metal underneath—tarnished, of course, and overgrown. I brought it back to the tent, cleaned it up and . . . that's the result."

"I see."

"But you don't seem to understand, Renn." She was puzzled by my sudden change of manner. "You don't seem to realize what that coin means. It confirms the theories that the old Spanish navigators came down this way and that some of them were wrecked on the reef islands. You're a historian, Renn. Surely you see the significance of it?"

I saw it all right. I couldn't fail to see it. I saw that this girl would go back to the mainland and tell her little story and flourish her antique coin until some bright press man saw it and made a filler paragraph out of it, and then the jig would be up. Every damned holidaymaker on the coast would descend on my island in search of buried treasure, unless . . .

I must have spoken the word aloud, because Pat Mitchell laid her hand on mine and quizzed me with anxious puzzlement.

"Unless what, Renn?"

I was caught between the devil and the deep. To fob her off with a story would bring the world to my doorstep. To tell her the truth would make her an unwanted partner in my enterprise—an arbiter of my fortunes and my destiny.

Involuntarily I closed my fingers on the coin. I felt the edges of it biting into my palm. Then I thought of Johnny Akimoto and what he had said to me. "She is a good one, that; what she promises she will do." If I trusted Johnny, I should trust Pat Mitchell also. My fingers relaxed. I looked at her again. Her eyes were full of grave concern.

She said quietly, "Have I said something wrong, Renn?"

I shook my head. "No, nothing wrong. I want to show you something."

I walked over to my bed, pulled my bag from underneath it and took out the bracelet I had bought from the girl in Lennon's Hotel. Then I laid it in Pat Mitchell's hand.

"There's the mate to your gold piece."

Her eyes widened. She held the two pieces together, examining them closely. When she spoke again, her voice was a small breath of wonder.

"Is this yours, Renn?"

"Yes."

"Where did you get it?"

"My wife and I found it on the reef, years ago. Probably in the same place that you found yours."

"What—what does it mean?"

The words came out slowly and deliberately, like coins dropping into a pool.

"It means, my dear, that the treasure ship *Doña Lucia,* bound from Acapulco to the Philippines, was wrecked on this island in 1732. And Johnny Akimoto and I have come here to find it."

There was a long, long silence. The two coins lay unnoticed on the white sheet between us. Neither of us looked at them. We were looking at each other. Then Pat Mitchell spoke, quite calmly.

"Thank you for telling me, Renn. You did me a great honour. You have nothing to fear from me. When I am better I shall go away as I promised. I'll leave my coin with you. Nobody else will ever know."

I said nothing. On the face of it, what was there to be said? I felt tired and spent. My eyes ached. I buried my face in my hands and pressed the palms hard against the lids . . . in the old familiar gesture of the harassed student working by night light. Pat Mitchell reached out, took my hands away and tilted my face up towards her.

"Does it mean so much to you, Renn?"

"Everything, I think."

"The ship went down two hundred years ago, Renn. You may never find her."

"I know that."

"What then?"

"I don't care to think about it."

"One day," she said softly, "one day you may have to think about it. I hope for your sake you will not be too unhappy."

She lay back on the pillows and closed her eyes. She looked very small and very tired and very, very desirable.

I brushed her cheek with my fingertips and left her.

Johnny Akimoto was bending over the fire, stoking it with driftwood. He straightened when he saw me. His calm eyes were full of questions.

I told him bluntly. "She knows, Johnny."

He looked at me, wondering. "Knows what, Renboss?"

"Why we are here—about the treasure ship—everything."

"You told her?"

"I had to, Johnny. She found this on the reef." I spun the coin in the air, caught it and slapped it into his palm. He looked at it for a long time without speaking.

"I had to tell her, don't you see, Johnny? If I hadn't . . ." He looked up at me. His dusky face was beaming.

"I understand, Renboss. I understand very well."

"Did I do right, Johnny?"

"I think you did right, Renboss," said Johnny Akimoto. "Now there are three of us."

It was easier now that there were no secrets between us. Every morning Johnny and I carried Pat down to the beach and made her comfortable under the awning. She was growing stronger now, and the area of infection was receding down the calf towards the ankle. Soon she would be able to hobble about, but for the present she had no choice but to lie on the stretcher under the canvas and read or doze or write up her notebooks or watch the small bobbing shape of the dinghy, where Johnny and I were diving.

We were working the outer fringe of the reef now—the small narrow shelf where the anchor hit sand at ten fathoms. We had not yet begun our search for the *Doña Lucia*. I was still training, adapting body and brain to new conditions of depth and pressure. I was learning the art of decompression—staging slowly to the surface ten or fifteen feet at a time, resting after each ascent to prevent the accumulation of nitrogen in the bloodstream. At first I clung to the anchor cable, measuring my ascent as if on a notched stick. In the fantastic underwater world it seemed at first like a link with reality, and in my first contacts with the strangeness and terror of deep waters I clung to it desperately, while I struggled to regain my self-control.

I made new acquaintances, too. Acquaintances who might become enemies but who seemed content for the present at least to regard me as a curious phenomenon in their undisputed territory: the long, slim Spanish mackerel with his predatory saw-toothed mouth; the big groper, huge and bloated; the scarlet emperor; the big snapper whose flanks are striped with broad arrows; and now and again a cruising shark.

At first I was terrified. Then I learnt to lie still, suspended in the blue water, while the fish stared at me coldly and then whisked off when I blew out a stream of bubbles or clapped my hands in the fashion of a child.

Johnny said little until he saw me gain confidence and then he talked to me calmly, logically, about danger.

"There is always danger, Renboss. Never forget that. We do not know how a fish thinks, so we cannot tell what he will do. A dog—yes, a horse—yes. They belong to our world. They have lived with us for thousands of years. But a fish—who knows? One day a shark may come at you. You will have little warning. He will swim towards you. He will stop. He will circle. Then go away, perhaps. And the next second he will be coming at you like a bullet."

I grinned sourly. "What then, Johnny?"

He shrugged. "You are in the world of fishes. You must fight like a fish—by swimming, by twisting and turning away, by trying to frighten him."

"And if he won't be frightened?"

"You have a knife. You must try to strike him in the belly. There is no other way."

Always it was the same lesson—conquer fear by understanding. Conquer danger by courage and common sense. Naked in the underwater world a man has no other weapons.

Sometimes Johnny himself would come down with me. I would see him swimming about fifty feet above clad in nothing but a mask and a breechclout and a belt with a long knife in a leather sheath. I would lie on my back and watch him. I would see his dark body double up like a jackknife, then stiffen into a long, shearing dive that brought him down eight, nine fathoms in a matter of seconds. Then I would see how the pressure of the water squeezed his belly and his lungs and his rib cage until I thought the bones must crack under the enormous strain, but he would still swim with me a little and grin behind his goggles and raise his hand in a comical gesture before he slanted upwards into the sunlight.

I was proud of my newfound skill, but Johnny's was an older one and a greater one. I could breathe. I had air in bottles on my back to keep me comfortable for an hour or more, but Johnny had nothing but two lungfuls and his own strength and skill and calm courage. Then, when the lessons were over, we would row back to the beach, totting the small sums of my new knowledge. And when the shadows lengthened we would sit beside the fire and eat the meal Johnny had cooked, while Pat Mitchell lay on the mattress and added her small, wise voice to the quiet flow of our talk.

One evening in the warm darkness she gave voice to a thought that had vexed me for a long time.

"About your treasure ship, Renn . . ."

"What about it, Pat?"

"I've thought about it a lot these last days. It was wrecked outside the reef, wasn't it?"

I nodded. "I think so. I think it must have been. When I was away from the island I used to believe there might be a possibility that she had been flung onto the reef itself and broken up. The finding of my coin seemed to confirm that. Now that I'm here, I'm not so sure."

Then Johnny Akimoto spoke. "I think it was outside, Renboss. I am sure it was outside."

"What makes you so sure, Johnny?" asked Pat.

"I will tell you, Miss Pat. This Spaniard—she is a bigger ship than my *Wahine*, yes?"

"Much bigger, Johnny," I said. "Two hundred tons—three hundred, maybe."

"So . . . Now look at the *Wahine*. She is a small boat, yet she draws five feet of water. It takes a big sea to lift a boat like that and throw it into the middle of the reef. More likely I think that your Spaniard drove straight onto the outer reef, stuck there, perhaps, until the water and the wind hauled him off and he sank on the ledge."

"It reads all right, Johnny," I said, "but how do you explain the coins in the rock pool?"

"That's the point I was making, Renn." Pat's voice was eager and full of conviction. "It wasn't the ship. It was the men."

"The men?"

"Yes. Think of what happens in a wreck. They are out of control in uncharted waters. They know there is land, but they have no idea whether it is inhabited or not. It's the natural instinct of men in danger to cling to whatever possessions they have. The ship strikes. They know she must founder. The boats are useless on the reef. They jump and try to swim to the island. What would a man take with him when he jumped?"

Johnny Akimoto's voice came out of the darkness.

"I can tell you that, Miss Pat. His knife and his money belt."

And there it was. A neat hypothesis, certainly. A piece of logic that gave me new respect for this small brown girl with the proud chin and the dark, flashing eyes. But there were other things I wanted to know.

"If that's the way it happened, some of them must have reached the shore. I've been all over the island and I've never seen any traces of them."

"No, Renboss," said Johnny. "If the ship broke up on the night of the storm, none of them would have survived. The surf would have rolled them over the reef and torn them to pieces. After that there would be the blood and the sharks. You see?"

"Yes, Johnny. I see. I see something else, too. If your theory and Pat's are right, then we've an even-money chance of finding the *Doña Lucia* on the outer shelf."

190

"That is if she did not break up, but foundered immediately."

"That's the even-money chance."

For the moment nothing more was said. It was a working theory. We should have to test it. And to test it, Johnny Akimoto and I would have to dive over hundreds of yards of shelf outside the reef, ten fathoms down. Deeper, perhaps, because the shelf was narrow in places and the *Doña Lucia* could have slid and rolled down the sloping edge into the blue depths of the ocean. And if she did, I would have to go down alone, because the limit of Johnny's dive was ten fathoms higher than mine.

Johnny Akimoto stood up and began to pile more brushwood on the fire. I went into the tent and brought back a blanket for Pat's shoulders. When we were seated again she made a small announcement.

"I walked today."

"What?"

"I walked. It was painful at first, but after I'd hobbled about for a while it wasn't too bad."

Johnny's deep voice chided her. "You shouldn't have done that, Miss Pat. You can't afford to take chances."

"It wasn't a chance really, Johnny. The swelling's gone down—most of it, anyway. If I do a little each day, it won't hurt me. . . ."

I caught the odd note in her voice and looked towards her, but her eyes were in shadow and I saw only the defiant lift of her chin.

"So now you can send me home any time you like."

Chapter Ten

A TWIG EXPLODED into a shower of sparks. New flames leapt up among the driftwood. The noddy terns in the giant pisonia tree chattered stridently and then fell silent. There was the distant boom of the surf, the steady whisper of the wind, the creak of branches and the small rustle of leaves and beach grasses.

Between the three people on the outer edge of the circle of firelight there was a long silence. Then Pat Mitchell spoke again. Her voice was steady and controlled.

"Will you take me back, Johnny?"

Johnny's voice answered her from the shadows.

"That's for Renboss to say, Miss Pat. I work for him. This is his island."

And there it was laid neatly in my lap. A decision that I had to make at a moment when I had neither wish nor need to make it. Abruptly and unreasonably I was angry. I said bluntly, "Do you want to go back?"

"No."

I stood up. I tossed my cigarette away irritably. I heard the words come tumbling out and did not recognize my own voice.

"Then, if you can walk, you can damn well work. You can cook the meals and keep the camp tidy. You can plot the reef where I want it plotted. You can stay in the boat while Johnny and I go down together. And for God Almighty's sake keep your mouth shut and don't get under our feet."

With which courtly little speech I left them and walked down to the beach with the uneasy conviction that I had made a fool of myself.

The moon was rising, a great cold disc in a purple sky. Its track lay across

192

the water in a broad blade of rippling silver. The *Wahine* lay in the middle of it, riding at anchor with bare spars, like a ghost ship.

Far out on the rim of the reef I could see the white froth of the surfline. I could see the uneasy water with the channel cut through the coral. I knew, almost to a yard, the position of the rock pools where Pat Mitchell had found her coin and where Jeannette and I found ours.

Jeannette . . . I realized with a shock that I had not thought of her for a long time. When I tried to recall her face I could not. There was a new face there, engraven on the tablets of memory, a small, brown, lovely gypsy face, crowned with dark hair. I knew that I had just committed a singular folly. I knew that I could not recall it. I looked out again towards the dark water beyond the reef. I told myself that the time of preparation was over. Tomorrow we would begin work.

Tomorrow Johnny and I would plot a line on the outer edge of the reef and we would search it, step by step, on the sea floor for a ship that had died more than two centuries ago. And if we did not find it, I would have to summon my small courage and move out from the safety of the shelf into the blue pelagic deeps beyond.

I would go down into a continent of giants—among the manta rays which fly like great bats through the blue twilight, among the killer sharks and the giant gropers. I would go down to the fringe of madness, where the detritus of life from the upper levels filtered down to feed the other lives, nameless, primitive, in the ooze of the ocean floor.

I was suddenly cold and afraid.

Johnny Akimoto's footfalls in the sand made me start like an animal.

"Miss Pat says to thank you, Renboss."

"I'm a fool, Johnny . . . a bloody fool."

"No, Renboss," said Johnny quietly. "No man is a fool when he does what his heart tells him to do."

"It's not a question of my heart, Johnny. It's a question of . . . of time—and convenience. We start work tomorrow."

"Yes, Renboss."

I raised my arm and pointed, drawing a wide arc across the sector of the reef where the coins had been found.

"That's where it will be, Johnny. Thirty, forty yards to the right of the channel and from there to the big niggerhead."

"That's a lot of water, Renboss."

"That's why we start work tomorrow."

"Miss Pat says to use her boat, Renboss. It is bigger than our dinghy and easier to work in the outside water."

"She is a shrewd one, isn't she, Johnny?" I said, with sour admiration.

"No, Renboss, she is not shrewd. She wants to show us that she is grateful for letting her stay."

I shrugged. "Perhaps, but she knows what she wants, doesn't she?"

"Yes, Renboss. She knows what she wants."

"And what does she want, Johnny?"

"Why not ask her yourself? Good night, Renboss."

He gave me a wide grin, turned on his heel and left me.

I walked slowly up the beach to the big tent. I brushed my teeth and sluiced my face from the water bucket. I doused the warm coals and watched the fire die in small clouds of smoky ash and hissing steam. I slacked off the guy ropes a little against the damp of the night. Then I took off my shirt and shoes and went into the tent. I lay down on my stretcher, pulled the sheet over me, lit a cigarette and lay back, watching the small hypnotic glow of the tobacco tip in the darkness.

From the other side of the tent came a small, uncertain voice. "Renn?"

"Yes?"

"Thank you."

"No need to thank me. I did what I wanted to do."

"Thank you for that, too."

I said in a flat voice, "Do you want a cigarette?"

"Yes, please, Renn."

I threw back the sheet, crossed the tent, handed her a cigarette, then lit it for her. In the brief flare of the match her face looked like an old cameo, timelessly beautiful. I stood looking down at her while the flame burnt down and scorched my fingers. Then I threw it on the floor and kicked sand over it. I said bluntly, "Tomorrow you'd better go back to your own tent."

"Yes, Renn."

"Good night."

"Good night, Renn."

I went back to bed. I drew a blanket over me because I was cold. I did not go to sleep for a long, long time.

In the morning over breakfast we made our plans. The tide was high, so our search of the rock pools for more relics of the ancient wreck would have to wait till later. There was a flat calm; we would be able to work the boat close to the reef and move gradually outwards to the extreme edge of the shelf. My training exercises had already used a third of our air bottles. We would have to conserve the rest, not only for the search, but for salvage operations if we did find the *Doña Lucia*. This worried me. Underwater work is slow. We had a big area to cover, and if I had to go down into deep water it would be slower still. Then Pat Mitchell came up with her suggestion.

We would weight the anchor cable of the workboat with pig lead from the *Wahine* ballast. We would trail it a fathom short of the shelf bottom. I would go down and cling to it and, with the motor at half speed, they would drag me along in continuous sweeps along the whole length of the search area. Given a few hours of calm, we could make our first survey of the shallow water. A fishing line attached to my belt would be held at the upper end by Johnny Akimoto, and if the lines fouled or I wanted to stop and examine a given area,

194

or if danger threatened, I could tug on the line and signal. It was simple, time-saving and economical. Pat Mitchell was childishly gratified when we agreed to it.

Leaving Pat to hobble about cleaning the dishes and tidying the camp, Johnny and I took the workboat out to the *Wahine*. Johnny fastened the pig lead into a bag of heavy fishnet and secured it at the top with stout cord. We took fresh air bottles from the crates—three sets—enough for four hours' work, with a little to spare for safety. Then Johnny took one of the rifles from the cabin locker and shoved three clips of ammunition into the pocket of his shorts.

"Just for safety, Renboss." He grinned.

Then he took out a long rod of polished wood, like the shaft of a golf club, with a barbed spearhead at the top.

"What's that for, Johnny?"

"Fish spear."

"For me?"

His teeth showed in a flashing grin.

"For me, Renboss. In case you get into trouble and I have to come down after you."

It was a grim reminder that we were engaged, not in holiday sport, but in a dangerous enterprise, with wealth or death at the end of it.

We loaded the gear into the workboat, and Johnny, meticulous as ever, oiled the outboard motor, cleaned it, primed it and filled the small tank with gasoline. Then we went back to the beach.

Pat Mitchell was waiting for us. She had made our lunch and packed it in a wooden box with a billy of cold tea. My harness and flippers were ready on the sand. She smiled happily when I acknowledged her forethought.

Desire stirred in me when I saw her standing there—small, brown and perfect, boyish in a checked shirt, open at the throat, and denim shorts, a canvas cap flopping comically over her forehead.

We loaded the boat, pushed off, started the engine and puttered across the glassy water to the channel entrance. Then I noticed two things which must have escaped me while Johnny and I were loading the gear. They were glass floats covered with fishnet, each with a small lead weight hanging on the underside.

"Marker buoys," said Johnny. "We used them for the lobster pots. Now we use them to mark where we start and where we finish. We cruise between them, working farther and farther out. When we have finished we bring them in again."

We rode easily through the channel and cruised along the reef, dropping the markers one at each end of the search area. Then we cut the engine and heaved over the anchor cable with its bag of ballast.

Now it was time to go. My stomach cramped with sudden fear. A little sweat broke out on my upper lip. I wiped it away with the back of my hand. Johnny Akimoto shot me a quick glance but said nothing. He and Pat helped me into the lung pack, and I was acutely aware of the touch of her hands, silken against my skin. I reached for the billycan and gulped big mouthfuls of cold tea. The cramps in my stomach relaxed.

"Two tugs on the line, Johnny, and I'm ready to go. Three, if I want you to stop. Four and you come overside, fast—I'm in trouble. Clear?"

"All clear, Renboss," Johnny said, and gave me the thumbs-up sign for luck.

"Good hunting, Renn," said Pat Mitchell, and she leant forward and kissed me full on the lips.

I slipped the mask down over my eyes and nostrils, tested it and set it comfortably. I clamped my teeth round the lugs of the mouthpiece and went overside.

The weight of the belt and equipment took me down a few feet, until I could see the flat bottom of the workboat and the fins of the small propeller and, below them, stretching down into the twilight, the furry thread of the anchor cable.

I jackknifed and went down in a steep dive, following the angle of the cable. I felt the familiar pain in my sinus cavities and the relief when I swallowed and the Eustachian tubes cleared themselves. A school of harlequin fish flirted away from my descent, their tube-like bodies flashing blue and gold, their ugly faces smiling like a circus clown's. The reef was on my left, thirty feet away. Its colours were muted by the watery distance, and the waving grasses and the branching corals and the shadowy caverns gave it the look of a forest on a hillside. A small ray slipped out under my breast. His long barbed tail was as stiff as an arrow, and he moved with little flickering motions of his wing pinions.

In the shadows of the reef I saw the constant coming and going of other fish, small and large, and in the blue distance on my right I saw a mackerel school coast lazily by, flecked by the shafts of sunlight refracting through the clear water. Then I hit bottom.

There was sand under my feet—sand and small nodules and broken pillars of coral—but I could not see them. I was walking through waving grasses, green and red, and yellow and dark brown. Some of them brushed me with the touch of wet silk. Others rasped my skin like rough and scaly hands.

The ballast net at the end of the anchor cable hung clear of the bottom by perhaps four feet. I looked up and saw the shape of the boat, a pointed shadow against the surface.

I had grasped the anchor cable and was just about to signal Johnny to start the engine, when I saw the shark.

He was no more than twenty feet away, a big blue fellow, twice as long as a man. I could see the suckerfish clamped on the underside of his belly and on the upper edges of his dorsal fins. In front of his nose three striped pilot fish hung as motionless as their master.

He was watching me. His big tail fin flickered, but he did not move. I blew out a stream of bubbles, but he refused to be frightened by such childish tricks. I clung to the cable and leapt and waved my arms, clowning for him.

Still he hung there. I leapt out towards him. He moved away, then came back towards me in a long, lazy sweep that brought him a pace or two nearer.

I took firmer hold on the anchor cable and tried to reason out my situation, all the time keeping a wary eye on the big fellow, who, if he attacked, would come with the speed of an express train. I had two alternatives.

I could tug my belt line and Johnny Akimoto would come shooting down with his knife and the long fish spear. Then the shark might attack him, too. If he wounded it, there would be blood in the water and other sharks might come, scavenging like cannibals on the flesh of the wounded brother. Then, even if we escaped, work would be over for the day. This obviously was a last resort. I tried the second alternative.

I gave two tugs on the line and seconds later I heard a sudden clatter, magnified by the water, as the outboard started and the propeller spun with the meshing of the gears.

That was the end of Johnny Shark. He flicked himself round with his big caudal fin and shot off into the shadows so quickly that even the pilot fish were surprised.

I felt the anchor cable jerk and the next minute I was trailing out behind it, lying flat on my belly, as comfortably as on a feather bed, while I scanned the twilight ahead and the coral cliffs to the left and the shafts of sunlight in the deep waters on the right.

The grassy floor below me rose and fell like a country landscape. There were rounded hills and small depressions. There were small escarpments made by ridges of growing coral, but there was nothing large enough to indicate the presence of a wreck. Many things can happen to a sunken ship in coral waters. If it founders on a submerged reef, the corals will devour it, growing over it as the jungle grows over the lost temples of the Incas. If it falls on a sandy bottom, the sand will cover it, perhaps, but it will still show like the tumuli of ancient tombs. It may be that the tricks of tide and current will leave it exposed in whole or part while its metalwork is pitted and eaten by galvanic action and the sea worms bore into its timbers and the sea growths cover it with branches and plumes and the fish swim through the gaping holes of its wounds. But always, to the end of time, there will be a sign, a mark, a scar on the bottom of the sea.

I was looking for such a sign now.

The cable went slack for a moment, then wrenched me round in a wide arc. The boat had reached the first marker buoy and was heading seaward for our second traverse of the search area. After about thirty yards we turned again and headed backwards in the direction from which we had come. I looked down at the sea meadow beneath me and saw with a curious thrill that it fell away steeply about three yards to the left.

The land shelf was narrower than we had thought, and if the *Doña Lucia* were here we must find her soon or not at all. Without warning, a dark shadow blotted out the sunlight streaming down from the surface. I looked up, startled. A huge manta ray was flapping his lazy way over my head. I

197

watched, fascinated, while the whole ton weight of him hung over me and then moved on with the same easy motion as a bird uses in flight. I watched him go, lying on my back against the course of the boat. For perhaps ten seconds I followed him, then I rolled over and scanned the blue twilight ahead.

Then, with the stunning shock of a monstrous revelation, I saw it—twenty yards ahead of me.

A great blunt mass heaved itself up from the sea floor into the underwater twilight. Waving sea growths covered it. Sand and coral outcrops surrounded it like altar steps. Shoals of fish, large and small, darted in and out of the dark hollows of the seaweed. One side of it was a rounded shoulder, the other a steep incline softened by the fluid contours of the moving weed. At the foot of the incline a short stumpy pillar was visible, festooned with grassy growth. As the towline drew me closer, I knew that I had made no mistake. The rounded shoulder was the high stern of a Spanish ship. The incline was her canting deck. The pillar was her shattered mast.

I had found the *Doña Lucia.*

Chapter Eleven

I caught at the line with my free hand and tugged it—once, twice and again. I heard the motor cut and, looking upwards, saw the last flurries of the propeller. The way of the workboat carried me onwards and over the sloping deck of the *Doña Lucia*. I loosed my hold and, blowing out air, let myself float down.

I landed, gently as a leaf, among the slimy sea grasses. But when I groped for a handhold the coralline growths and the seashells scored my palms. I took the knife from my belt and, working with a sort of frantic energy, scraped away a small area of weed and coral and clustered mollusks to reveal the spongy timber of the deck.

The riot of startled fish passed by me, unheeded, as I worked my way upwards along the edge of the slope and stopped to scrape away two centuries of sea growth from the broken timber of the handrail. Halfway up the incline was a gaping square hole fringed with brown weed. I looked in but withdrew in sudden fear from the blackness and tore the skin from my hands on the coral crust on the edge. I had not counted on finding our ship so quickly. I had forgotten to bring the flashlight. But now that we knew where she was there would be a time, and times, to see all that she had to show us.

At the top of the slope was a high canted platform and above that another, smaller and narrower. On the top of the shoulder was a small structure that would probably show itself as the finial ornament of the high Spanish poop deck.

It was a triumphant moment. But I needed someone to share the triumph with me. I jerked four times on the line and, before I had counted five seconds,

199

Johnny Akimoto came cleaving down like an avenging angel, with the spear in his hand.

I danced for him on the ancient deck. I pointed and waved my hands in clownish gestures, mumbling helplessly against the gag of the mouthpiece.

When he saw the reason for my madness Johnny clasped his hands above his head and drew back his lips in a grin. Then he swam close to me and clasped my shoulder and I saw his eyes wide with wonder behind the goggles. Then he kicked upwards, motioning me to follow him.

I staged upwards more slowly, remembering, just in time, the lessons I had learnt, knowing that even a treasure ship is poor payment for the crippling agonies of the bends.

Pat and Johnny hauled me into the boat, and the next minute we were shouting and slapping one another on the back and laughing like idiots and Pat was kissing me and I was kissing her, with the boat rocking dangerously beneath us.

It was Johnny Akimoto who recalled us to sanity.

"Before we drift, Renboss, we should take bearings, so we find this place easily again."

"Right you are, Johnny. There's too much work to do now, without trawling all over the ledge every time we want to go down."

We did a simple triangulation, lining one of the peaks with a tall pandanus and the other with a jutting rock that Pat named the Goat's Head. We tested our method by sailing round in a wide sweep and then trying to set ourselves in the diving spot. Then, more for a monument than for any sort of reliable marker, we hauled in one of the glass buoys and dropped it over the resting place of the *Doña Lucia*.

I wanted to go down again before lunch, but Johnny Akimoto shook his head.

"No, Renboss. No more today."

I protested vigorously.

"To hell with it, Johnny. We've got the whole afternoon yet."

"Johnny's right, you know, Renn," said Pat Mitchell calmly. "You've done in half a day what you were quite prepared to spend days and weeks doing. Besides, what more can you do down there today?"

"I want to have a look at that hold."

"You've got no light, Renboss," said Johnny mildly. "Besides, I can tell you what's in that hold now."

"Treasure chests, Johnny?" I grinned at him.

"No," said Johnny slowly, "not treasure chests."

"What then?"

"Water, Renboss. Water and fish and sand . . . tons and tons and tons of sand."

I was shocked into silence. My triumph was destroyed, like a pricked bubble.

"It's true, you know, Renn." Pat Mitchell laid a sympathetic hand on my knee. "That's what happens to all wrecks, isn't it? The sand piles up, round and inside them. You expected that, didn't you?"

I shook my head glumly. "I should have, but I didn't. I was so set on finding the damn ship that I didn't give half a thought to what would happen when we did find it. Well . . . what do we do now?"

"We have lunch," said Pat promptly.

From her wooden box she produced thick sandwiches of beef and damper, biscuits spread with tinned butter and cheese, and four bars of creamy chocolate. She poured tea from the billycan into our tin mugs and, as we ate and drank, rocking the ground swell, we talked.

"Renboss," said Johnny deliberately, "today we have found our ship. That is the first thing and the biggest thing. What we saw down there, you and I, shows us that her nose is well down in the bank. Something less than half of her is showing. I ask you this. You know about these things. She was carrying gold. Where would she carry it?"

"My guess, Johnny, is the stern, in the captain's quarters, under the poop deck. When we get back to shore I'll draw you a picture . . . show you what a ship of this kind looks like."

"So, then," said Johnny, "our first chance—our only chance—is that the treasure is still in the stern of the ship under the first layers of sand."

"That's right."

"If it is anywhere else, then we can never reach it, except, perhaps, with a salvage ship, which might pump away the sand. Even then"—he shrugged and spread his hand—"these things do not always succeed. You know that."

Pat Mitchell had been listening carefully. Her dark intelligent eyes were alert and questioning.

"You've got something in your mind, Johnny. What is it?"

"It is this, Miss Pat," said Johnny. "Renboss here, and myself, we know little about these things. I am useless, because I am only a diver. I learnt to work naked on the trochus beds, but I cannot stay down long enough to be of any use. Renboss, here, has learnt to dive and explore. He knows little more than that."

It was all too true. I had no answer to the relentless logic of the islander.

Pat Mitchell questioned him again.

"What do you suggest, Johnny?"

"Renboss, here, has a friend . . . the man who made these things for him."

Pat looked at me. I nodded.

"That's right . . . Nino Ferrari. He was a frogman with the Italian navy during the war."

"So you see," Johnny went on, eagerly, with his exposition, "this man is a professional. He understands salvage. He knows the tools we need and how to use them. Renboss tells me he has promised to come if we need him. I say we need him now."

201

Johnny again. Johnny the lost man, the alien man, with a first-class brain ticking over behind his shiny dark forehead.

I grinned at him and clapped him on the shoulder.

"All right, Johnny, that's it. Let's have ourselves a picnic. You sail us over to Bowen first thing tomorrow morning. I'll telephone Nino Ferrari in Sydney and tell him to get up here as quick as he can, with all the equipment he can lay his hands on. While we're there we'll freight the empty air bottles down to Brisbane to be refilled. What do you say, Captain?"

Johnny's dark face beamed.

"I say yes, Renboss. We take Miss Pat?"

"We take Miss Pat."

"Good. Then I show her my *Wahine* and how she sails, eh?"

From then on it was a light-hearted meal. And when it was finished we tossed our scraps overside to feed the fishes and washed our mugs in the water and stowed our gear and hauled up the ballast cable.

Then we saw the plane.

It was an old Dragon Rapide, like the barnstormers use on the country fields and the outback cattlemen charter when they can't get through in the rainy season. It came from the west—from the direction of Bowen. It was flying low and we could hear it chattering like an ancient chaffcutter. As he neared the island the pilot banked and made a wide circuit that took him round the cliffside and then back towards us round the edge of the reef. He was flying on the deck, and we saw his face and the face of his single passenger, blurred behind the cabin window. Then he was past us, banking again for another circuit of the island. This time he flew low over the beach, then made a figure eight round the back of the island and swung out again for another look at the reef and ourselves. After that he sheered off and headed back to the mainland.

The three of us looked at each other.

"That," said Pat with a smile, "would be a wealthy tourist."

"That," I said grimly, "could be Manny Mannix."

Johnny's mouth was shut in a tight line. He didn't say anything.

"Who's Manny Mannix, Renn?"

"Tell you later," I said briefly. "Come on, Johnny, let's go home."

Johnny spun the starter wheel and the engine stuttered into life. We turned and headed home, through the lazy water.

That night, for the first time in years, I held hands in the moonlight with a girl. We sat in a small grassy hollow sheltered from the breeze and leant our backs against a bank of springy turf. Around us the spidery roots of the pandanus made a trelliswork for privacy. High above us their broad-bladed leaves made a muted clatter when the wind moved them. Above us a white ginger blossom spread its heavy perfume and a bank of wild orchids drooped from a rocky ledge. The sea was a murmuring voice and a thin ribbon of silver beyond the rim of our retreat.

We were uneasy at first. We talked banally to conceal our thoughts and made small jokes and laughed like strangers who had met at a cocktail party. Then, as the languid night relaxed us and the sea voices sang, we drew close to each other and talked more quietly of things that lie near to the heart. I told her of my brief, beautiful love for Jeannette . . . of how I came to the island . . . of why I had left it . . . of all the restless, barren years between my leaving and my coming back.

I told her the things I feared and the things I hoped. I told her of the eerie, teeming world under the water. I told her of my small odyssey in search of the *Doña Lucia* and of the morning's adventure with the shark. Her hand tightened on mine and I felt her shiver a little, as if someone had walked over her grave.

Then, shifting her position, she squatted in front of me and looked at me squarely.

"Renn, I want you to tell me something."

"What?"

"Are you really interested in money?"

It looked like thin ice. I tried to skate away from it.

"Isn't everybody interested in money?"

"Everybody needs money, Renn. Most people would like to have more of it than they have. But not everybody makes a lifetime hobby of it."

I couldn't quarrel with that. I couldn't but admire the shrewd probing of my small dark lady.

"Would it matter to you whether I were interested in money or not?"

"Yes, Renn, it would." She was earnest now, almost pleading. "I know what you want to do. I know what you think: if you can raise the treasure it will buy you freedom from a life you hate. It may—I doubt it."

"What then?"

"I think it will put gyves on your hands and chains round your heart."

Her voice was so bitter, there was so much pain in her eyes, that I was shocked. I drew her down on the bank beside me. I tried to jolly her.

"Here now, sweetheart. What is this? A sermon on the seven deadly sins?"

She blazed at me, "Yes! If you look at it that way. Look at it my way, and it isn't a sermon at all. It's—it's something I hate and fear."

"What? Money? The thing we work fifty weeks of the year for?"

"No, Renn. Not money. But the greed for it. The horrible, twisted yearning. The fear and hate I saw in your eyes this morning when you looked up at that plane and thought of Mannix."

The blade was out of the velvet now. I felt it prick painfully against my heart. I didn't relish the feeling. I said, curtly, "Greed? Hate? Fear? What the hell do you know about these things?"

"A great deal, Renn," she said simply. "I lived with them for twenty years. My father's a very rich man, and he's never had a happy moment in his life."

There was nothing to say to that. My irritation died. I said gently, "Is that all?"

She faced me, eyes bright, chin tilted proudly.

"No, Renn, not all. For the first time in my life I've met a man I can respect and admire—even love, if he would let me. I want him to fight, to stretch out his strength for a prize. But if he loses it I'd like to see him smile, so that I could still be proud of him. It's out now, Renn. Shall we go?"

"Damned if we'll go!"

I caught her in my arms and crushed her to me. I kissed her and her lips were willing. She clung to me and her body leapt and her brown arms were strong.

The sea was suddenly dumb. The stars were blotted out. And if the moon tumbled over the rim of chaos, we did not see it.

Next morning Johnny took us across to Bowen in the *Wahine*. A light wind was blowing offshore, and Johnny nursed the *Wahine* into it with skill and a naïve pride in himself and his boat. It was a picnic sailing on an easy sea under a clear sky. But when we came to Bowen the town was sweltering in the midday heat and the dust rose in little puffs about our feet as we walked from the jetty into the main street.

Johnny strode over to the garage, swinging a pair of oil cans, to buy diesel fuel. Pat had purchases of her own to make and she left me to walk over to the post office and telephone Nino Ferrari in Sydney.

The trunk service was better this morning, and twenty minutes after I had lodged my call I was talking, cautiously, to Nino Ferrari.

"Nino, this is Renn Lundigan."

"Trouble, Renn? So early?"

Nino's voice sputtered over the cables, but I caught the tension in it.

"No, Nino. No trouble yet. That comes later, possibly. I don't want to say too much. You ask the questions, I'll answer them. We've found her, Nino."

"Found her? The ship?" Nino's voice was a high, distorted squeak.

"That's right."

"How deep?"

"Ten fathoms."

"How much of her?"

"About half. The stern half."

"Sand or coral?"

"Sand."

"Much?"

"Lots of it, Nino. Lots and lots of it."

I could almost hear the cogs whirring in Nino's methodical brain.

"I get it, my friend. I get it. You want me to come up?"

"Yes, as soon as you can. Bring whatever gear you want with you. I'll pay the air freight."

"There's a little gear—not much. If we cannot do it with that, then we cannot handle it without a big operation. Understand?"

"I understand. Could you get up here this evening?"

Nino hesitated a moment. Then he chuckled and said crisply, "Where is 'here'?"

"Bowen. There's an evening plane out of Sydney. Can you make it?"

Nino chuckled again.

"You work fast, my friend."

"I have to, Nino. We may have . . . er . . . interruptions."

"Then I had better come prepared, eh?"

"It might be a good idea at that. We'll pick you up with your gear at the airport. We'll go straight down to the ship. That's all, Nino. If you miss the plane send me a telegram at the airport."

"I'll do that," said Nino. *"Arrivederci."*

"Good-bye, Nino. Make it snappy."

I hung up. As I walked out of the booth I jostled a man in a white tropic suit who was leaning against the wall of the next one. When I turned to apologize, he took the cigar out of his mouth and grinned at me.

"Nice work, Commander," said Manny Mannix.

Chapter Twelve

MANNY STUCK THE CIGAR back in his mouth and blew a cloud of smoke full in my face. Then he took it out again. His lips were smiling, but his cold eyes measured me with the familiar veiled huckster's stare. He was still lounging back against the door of the empty phone booth. He was relaxed and watchful as a cat.

"So you found her, eh, Commander?" he said softly.

"I tell you, Manny . . ."

He waved his cigar. "Save it, Commander. Save it. This is business. You've found her. I saw you yesterday working outside the reef. You were just telephoning to a friend to bring some gear up from Sydney. Check?"

"Check, Manny," I said quietly. "Check something else, too. If you try to move in on this deal, I'll kill you."

"Nuts!" said Manny Mannix. "Why don't you get wise to yourself, Commander? We could make a split."

"No, Manny."

Manny shrugged indifferently and blew out another cloud of smoke.

"O.K.! I buy you out. Two thousand. Cash on the barrelhead. Plus your expenses to date. Take it or leave it. If you don't, I move in and move you out. Well, Commander?"

Out of the corner of my eye I saw Johnny Akimoto mount the steps in front of the post office. I heard him put down the oil cans with a clatter. I beckoned him and he came and stood beside me.

"Look at this man, Johnny," I said gently. "Look at him and remember his face. You may possibly meet him again. His name is Manny Mannix."

There was a deadly hate in Johnny's dark eyes as he towered over Manny Mannix and looked down at him as if he were some noxious animal. When he spoke his voice was like silk.

"Stay out of this, Mr. Mannix. Stay out of this."

Manny shifted his feet a little and tossed his cigar onto the sidewalk.

"Back to the kitchen, black boy," he said easily, and put one hand on Johnny's chest to thrust him away.

Johnny caught his wrist with one hand in a grip that made Manny's eyes pop and his mouth drop open and great beads of sweat start out on his sallow cheeks. "I have never yet killed a man," said Johnny precisely, "but I think it very possible that I shall have to kill you, Mr. Mannix."

His hold relaxed and Manny's hand dropped at his side, nerveless. Then we left him. Johnny picked up his oil cans and we walked down the street to meet Pat Mitchell. Our thoughts were written on our faces, and she questioned us with instant concern.

"Renn! Johnny! What's happened?"

We told her.

"But what can he do?"

"He can do a lot of things, sweetheart. We have no water rights. We have no salvage rights, either, because we haven't registered a claim. He can do just what he threatens—move in and move us out."

"By force?"

"Yes."

"But you're not doing anything wrong. Can't you claim police protection?"

"From what? Manny hasn't done anything wrong either—yet. We'd only make fools of ourselves. More than that, we could find ourselves in a legal tangle that might take years to unravel. . . . The laws of salvage and treasure trove have kept the lawyers in pin money for centuries. You see?"

"Yes, Renn, I see."

There was a sadness in her voice that made me remember our talk of the evening before. I turned to Johnny.

"Any thoughts, Johnny?"

"No thoughts, Renboss. Only this. Your friend arrives tonight with his equipment. We meet him. We take him back to the island and start work."

"And after that?"

"We wait and see, Renboss . . . we wait and see."

Fear and depression lay over us as the heat lay over the sleepy tropic town. We walked slowly back to the jetty, unmoored the dinghy and rowed out to the *Wahine*, riding sleepily at anchor.

Johnny spread an awning over the forward hatch cover and we lay under it, sipping iced beer, eating sandwiches, talking, smoking, dozing, as the afternoon wore itself out into the slackness of evening. Always the subject of our thoughts was the same—Manny Mannix.

"I don't understand how he found us so easily," said Pat.

"Very simple, Miss Pat," said Johnny. "He knows in Sydney that Renboss has won enough money to begin his search. He knows there is an island. So far he does not know where it is. But the airlines tell him when a passenger named Lundigan leaves for Brisbane. The Lands Department in Brisbane collects a fee of two shillings and sixpence and tells him Renn Lundigan, Esquire, has bought the lease of an island latitude this and longitude that. The rest is a matter of common sense. He knows Renboss must have a boat. He knows the boat can put in at one of the ports convenient to the island. He comes to Bowen because there is an airfield and he can charter a plane and begin his inquiries. It is just unfortunate that he should have come to the post office at the same time as Renboss was making his telephone call."

"Put it that way, it's easy, isn't it?"

"Too easy," I growled. "Too damned easy for a smart operator like Manny."

"I am trying to think, Renboss, what he will do next."

"So am I, Johnny. There are a dozen things he could do. But what he will do is something else again. Manny knows too many people—can buy too many people. He doesn't have to bid till he's stacked the deck just the way he wants it."

"So we just wait," sighed Pat.

"We wait," said Johnny.

"Damned if we wait!" I snapped. "Johnny, can you make the channel at night?"

Johnny gave me a sharp look, thought a moment and then nodded.

"Yes, Renboss, I can make it. The moon is later tonight."

"Good. Then we pick up Nino Ferrari at the airport, come back on board and raise anchor straightaway. We start work first thing in the morning. Even Manny Mannix can't work that fast."

The plane landed at twenty past ten. Nino Ferrari stepped off it—a small, compact eager man in a light suit and an open-necked shirt. We collected his luggage—a small suitcase and three wooden crates. We lashed the crates on the carrier of an ancient taxi which rushed us down to the jetty at breakneck speed over the broken and rutted roads.

By midnight we were in open water, with Johnny at the helm and the rest of us dangling our legs in the cockpit beside him, while we discussed the situation.

Pat's dark eyes flashed approval of Nino's crisp, professional exposition.

"First, you must understand, there will be no miracles. You have a whole ship full of sand. Even a salvage vessel with heavy pumping equipment could not shift so much."

"We understand that, Nino."

"Good. Our best hope is that the treasure chests are in the exposed stern of the ship, near enough to the surface of the sand for us to dig them out with our hands."

This was disappointing. I said as much.

Nino answered trenchantly. "You thought I would come up here with a little box of tricks that would blow away a hundred tons of sand when I pressed a button. No. That is a schoolboy dream. This is what I have brought. Extra air bottles, because we must work long hours, two at a time, below water. Flashlights with battery replacements. And limpet mines and fuses."

"Limpet mines?" Pat was wide-eyed.

"Those I will explain in a moment. First, you will tell me, Renn, is there a current down there by the ship?"

"Yes, there is. It sets along the direction of the reef and crosswise to the way the ship is lying."

"Strong?"

"Moderate."

"*Ebbene*. . . . Now I will tell you. Your friend, Johnny here, will understand better than you what I try to explain."

Johnny turned his head and acknowledged the compliment with a wide smile. They would work well together, these two. Nino Ferrari went on . . .

"You will remember that when you first saw this ship you saw that the sand was piled about its sides. You did not go into the hold because the water was too dark. But when you do go into it, with the flashlights, you will see that the sand is piled up there also—but it is continually in motion. You understand that?"

I nodded.

"Now, this is how we work. We explore first the area that is out of the sand. If we find nothing, we go down into the hold. We dig there—all over it. . . ."

"With our hands?"

"With our hands. We are under water, you see. We raise too much sand, it floats about us and obscures our view. Best then to work quietly."

"And if we don't find anything in the hold, Nino, what then?"

"Then," said Nino, "we use the mines. They are small, because we are dealing with an old wooden ship and we don't want to blow her to pieces. We fix the mines, one on either side of the hull, and detonate them with a time fuse. They will blow holes in the side of the hull and the current will remove at least part of the sand inside. You see?"

It was not hard to see. Nino's trenchant phrases spoke of confidence and experience. Our courage, sadly shrunken after our meeting with Manny Mannix, grew again to man size, but Nino wasn't finished yet.

"This I want you to understand clearly. This is the last stage of the operation. If, after the mines, we go down and find nothing, we ourselves can do no more. If you want to go farther, you must think of a salvage expedition with heavy equipment. I tell you this because you must not have false hopes. They are costly and dangerous."

I told him that we understood. I told him that so far as diving operations were concerned we would work to his orders. Then I told him about Manny Mannix.

Nino's dark eyes snapped fire and he snorted contemptuously. "This I have seen often before. There is a smell of gold and all the vultures come flapping as if to a dead body. Sometimes there are dead bodies. So I brought this."

He fished in his pocket and brought out a small blue Beretta that gleamed dully in the starlight. He sighed.

"I hope I never have to use it. I came to this country to find peace. But where gold is, there is never peace."

I knew Pat was looking at me from the other side of the cockpit, but I dared not meet her level eyes.

It was after midnight and we had a three-hour run ahead of us. If we wanted to make an early start in the morning we would have to snatch what sleep we could. I took the wheel from Johnny and sent the three of them below to rest. When I raised the island I would wake Johnny and he would make the tricky passage through the reef.

Before she went, Pat put her arms round my neck and kissed me.

"Good night, sailorman."

"Good night, sweetheart."

Then I was alone. I heard the brief murmur of their voices as my friends and my lover settled themselves to sleep. I saw the cabin light extinguished and caught, through the open door, the small red glow of Nino's cigarette. Then that, too, went out, and the night was mine and all the wonder of wind and stars and bellying white sail.

In the morning Nino Ferrari took command of our small company. He squatted on the sand in front of the big tent, the sun gleaming on his small muscular body. He gave his orders simply and bluntly.

"First we must dive from the *Wahine*. The workboat is too small."

I looked across at Johnny. He nodded agreement.

"All right with me, Renboss. I run her wherever you want."

Nino went on, "We keep all our stores on board—lungs, bottles, lamps—all of it. We keep a day's food and water on board and the medicine chest, in case there are accidents."

"I'll look after that part of it," said Pat.

Nino nodded briefly and continued, "We are working in ten fathoms. That is not too bad. We will work for half an hour at a time, then come up and rest for two hours before going down again."

This sounded like an expensive waste of time. I queried the point. Nino answered me without rancour. "If we were working in deeper water I should say only fifteen minutes' work and three hours of rest."

"But why?"

"Because to this point you have been diving only. You have not been working. When you work under water the exertion causes a greater and a quicker

210

discharge of nitrogen into the bloodstream. The danger of the bends is therefore greater. This way we diminish risk and fatigue."

"We'll do as you say, of course. I just wanted to know. But couldn't we save time if we went down singly and worked that way? One man resting—the other working?"

Nino's bright eyes twinkled ironically.

"If you were an experienced diver, I would say yes, by all means. But you are not. It is better that we work together—better and safer."

I grinned submission. Then I asked another question, "How do we tell the time?"

"I have a watch," said Nino, "a watch that the makers say will work under water. But when one is busy it is easy—and dangerous—to forget time. So Johnny here will fire a bullet into the water for a signal. The noise when it strikes the water will be very clear down below. When we hear it we come up."

"What happens if you find anything down there?" asked Pat.

"For small things there is a weighted fish basket, which Johnny lets down on a line each time we descend. For big things like"—Nino grinned broadly—"like a treasure chest, we put a sling under it and haul it on board. . . . Now, if there are no more questions, we should take the gear aboard and get to work."

"I've got a simple question," said Pat. "It's got nothing to do with diving. Where does Nino sleep?"

It was Johnny Akimoto who answered that one—a little too quickly, I thought, though I could not imagine why.

"Nino sleeps in the big tent with Renboss. I will sleep aboard the *Wahine*."

And that was that. A simple question, a simple answer, with no dark thoughts behind them. I could not even tell myself why they worried me.

Forty minutes later the *Wahine* was anchored outside the reef, with the *Doña Lucia* sixty feet under her keel.

Nino Ferrari and I sat on the hatch cover drinking strong sugared tea, while Johnny spliced a cord handle on a fish basket and Pat squatted native-fashion beside me, listening to Nino's final instructions.

"When we go into the hatch you will have to be careful. Outside the light you will not be able to see very much. But remember there will be beams, covered with coral and shellfish, and small projections of all kinds. Brush against them and you may cut your breathing tubes."

The same thought had occurred to me. It wasn't a happy prospect. Pat shivered with excitement at the thought of the nameless terrors of the world she had never seen. She turned to Nino.

"What about the other things, Nino? The sharks and . . . and . . ."

Nino laughed. "And the monsters that they show you on the films? There are monsters in the deeps, yes, but they do not normally live in the holds of ships. There are fish that are dangerous to the diver, just as there are animals that are dangerous to him on land. But for the most part the fish is as wary of

211

the diver as he is of them. For the rest"—he crossed himself simply—"the hand of God reaches down even into the great waters."

" 'They that do business in great waters, these see the works of the Lord and His wonders in the deep.' "

The quotation came simply and surprisingly from the girl at my side.

" 'They cry to the Lord in their trouble and He brings them out of their distress.' " Nino added the tag in liquid Italian, then smiled and stood up. "Time to go down, my friend. Harness up."

We buckled on our gear and went overside, steadying ourselves on a cleated rope. This time I had a large flat rubber-sealed flashlight with a big reflector clipped on my belt. We swam round to the anchor cable and followed it down into the blue twilight. Nino was behind me as we went down, and I looked back to see him give me a small signal of approval. Then we were on the bottom, two men-fish standing in a waving meadow whose grasses were stirred by a soundless wind. The wreck of the *Doña Lucia* was thirty feet away, straight ahead of us.

I swam over to Nino and floated beside him. I touched his shoulder and pointed eagerly. He grinned behind his mask and gave me a thumbs-up. Then we saw Johnny's weighted basket sliding down to us through the twilight, and we moved off.

I led Nino up the sloping weed-covered deck and showed him the dark gaping hole with its fringe of weeds. He shone the flashlight into the blackness, and in the pool of light I saw a waving of red sea grasses, the naked arms of small branch coral and a cavalcade of small bright fish, which swam leisurely out of the light into the surrounding darkness.

Nino snapped off the flashlight and motioned me upwards. At the top of the incline, under the first canted platform, there was a bulkhead, broken by a door which was now no more than a narrow dark hole fringed with weeds. Nino flashed the light again, snapped it off after a brief scrutiny and went on again. Whether the opening led to cabin or companionway we could not tell—yet.

The bulkhead on the first platform was similarly broken. But the opening led this time obviously to a cabin. Possibly the captain's. This would be our first area of search after we had completed the survey of the poop. The next deck area was narrow and surrounded by carved bulwarks and surmounted by some sort of finial carving. I should have liked to scrape away the weeds and barnacles and coral to examine it more closely, but our time and our air supply and our strength were all limited. We could not spend them on antiquarian trifles.

Then Nino took control. Motioning me to follow him, he turned and swam downwards to the cabin deck and waited for me outside the narrow black entrance.

It was an eerie moment. I had subdued, by practice, my first fears of the twilight world under the water . . . subdued but not destroyed them. Now they came trooping back full-size with new fears added—fear of the darkness, fear of the unknown monsters that might lurk where the light did not shine. My flesh broke out in goose pimples again. Then Nino smiled behind his mask and laid his hand on my shoulder in a gesture of reassurance. He snapped on the flashlight.

There were no monsters. There were only fish. Fish and weeds and water and beyond them a new darkness which my own flashlight would help to dissipate. I switched it on and followed Nino through the festooned weeds into the cabin.

Out of the corner of my eye I saw a pair of big round eyes staring at me and a round, thick-lipped mouth that slobbered continually. I whirled and flashed the light.

It was a big blue groper. He flicked his tail and swung off into the shadows. Nino turned and signalled me to come beside him. We stood together on the sandy uneven floor and played our lights on the wall of sea growth ahead of us.

To me, the novice, it was a disappointing sight. There were projections that might have been beams. There was a recess that might have been a bunk alcove. There was a shapeless mass, waist-high, that might have been a cabin table. Beyond that—nothing . . . nothing but the shifting outlines of weeds and sea grasses and the flutter of small fish in and out of their roots.

We turned the light upwards. Hanging weeds brushed our faces. I put up my hand and felt the faint outline of a beam under the slimy growth. I shone the light ahead of it and saw a large incrustation that looked vaguely like a hanging lamp. I struck at it with my knife. It snapped off and dropped slowly and weightlessly to the sandy floor.

Nino made an impatient gesture that said, "Leave it," and knelt down on the weed-covered sand.

I did the same. I saw him scraping with his knife among the weeds and sand and coral stumps. He was testing the depths of incrustation over the planks. Eighteen inches down we struck wood, pulpy and waterlogged.

Nino stood up and made a gesture of negation. No treasure chests can be hidden under eighteen inches of sand. Nino then moved over to the far corner of the cabin where the slope of the floor had caused the sand to pile up into larger and deeper drifts.

A canny professional, Nino. He knew his business. He went down on his knees again and began scraping the sand away with knife and hands, probing carefully ahead with his fingers. I chose a spot three feet away from him and began to work in the same fashion.

I had not been digging for more than three minutes when my hand struck something that was unmistakably wood. I shifted the flashlight, but I could see nothing.

Sudden fever took possession of me and I started digging frantically, like a dog for a buried bone. In an instant Nino was beside me, wagging his finger in a reproving gesture, showing me in dumb show that this was a dangerous way to work. Then he knelt down and began digging with me. The sand rose in

213

swirls and eddies above us, blinding us. No sooner had we clawed out a handful than two more flowed in to fill the space we had left. But, after an interminable labour, we managed to clear enough to identify my find.

It was the brassbound corner of an old sea chest.

At that precise moment we heard a crack that sounded like the snapping of a tree branch. It was the warning shot. Time to return to the surface.

I looked at Nino. I pointed to the box. I made gestures, pleading with him to stay down a little longer. He shook his head. His eyes were grim behind the mask.

"Topside!" he signalled.

Slowly, terribly slowly, we staged upward to the *Wahine,* while the sand settled once more round the sea chest in the *Doña Lucia.*

Chapter Thirteen

NINO AND I STRETCHED ON MATTRESSES under the canvas awning amidships. Pat served us cool beer and cigarettes, while Johnny, singing in the galley, prepared the pashas' meal—fillets of red emperor, caught while we were at the bottom of the sea, fritters of sliced bully beef and potato chips, canned peaches and preserved cream, fresh from the icebox. We must eat well, rest well. So Nino had ordered, so it was done.

And, as we lay there in the warm shade, rocked by the gentle swing of the sea, Nino read me lesson number two.

"You are a damn fool, Renn. After all I tell you about the way to work under water, you scrabble and scratch like a child looking for a lost toy. You work slowly, man . . . slowly. You save your air and your strength and you keep the nitrogen poison down as low as possible. Think you are making love to your girl here." He cocked a wicked eye at Pat, who blushed and retreated to the galley. ". . . Gently, gently. You reach the same end in the same time. And the going is much more pleasant."

"All right, Nino. Round one to you. But why the blazes couldn't we have stayed down a little longer? We'd have had that box clear in ten minutes."

Nino heaved himself up on his elbow and jabbed an accusing finger at me. His eyes flashed. His anger was theatrical.

"So! The young cock wants to crow his own song, eh? Let me tell you something, smart one. You know how long it will take us to uncover that box? Fifteen—twenty minutes. You know what would have happened if we had stayed down? We would have needed another twenty minutes to stage up, another hour to rest. And still no box. Why? Because there was no sling ready

215

to lift it up. When we go down this time, the sling follows us; and if we are lucky—if we are lucky, I repeat—we may get the box up in time."

"And if we don't?"

"Then we leave it," retorted Nino. "Do you think the fish will eat it? Do you think a mermaid will tuck it under her flipper and walk off with it?"

He clapped his free hand to his forehead with a gesture of contempt and despair and rolled back onto his pillow. There was a roar of laughter from Pat and Johnny who had watched Nino's triumphant little drama from the safety of the cockpit.

Then dinner was served and, while we were eating, Pat put the question direct to Nino Ferrari.

"This box you've found. Is there any chance of its being a treasure box?"

Nino shrugged eloquently.

"Who knows, *signorina*? Maybe yes—maybe no. In my experience of these things, it is generally no. It is as well not to build up too many hopes. From the look of that cabin down there I should say we will not find too much. If we went scavenging through the rubbish, we might find small things—a drinking cup, a knife, a pewter plate. But they would be hard to distinguish under the growth and not worth the trouble." He grinned engagingly. "I'm sorry to disappoint you, *signorina*, but this business of treasure hunting is one long disillusion. I knew a man who made a fortune when he salvaged a load of plastic sheets. I knew another who found a treasure ship—a real one, too—and lost his whole fortune because he couldn't pump the mud away as fast as the sea could spread it."

Johnny Akimoto nodded his approval. This small, dark fellow from Genoa was a man after his own heart. The sea had spawned them both and they were both wise in her ancient ways. Then Johnny's face clouded with sudden recollection. He hesitated a moment, then he spoke.

"Renboss, Miss Pat thought I should not tell you this while you are working. I think now that I should tell you."

"Let's have it, Johnny."

"While you were working down there, the airplane came again."

"The same plane?"

"The same plane. The same movement. Round the island twice, three times. Then home again."

"Hell and damnation!"

I leapt up from my mattress. Nino Ferrari pulled me down again.

"If you want to go down this afternoon, you stay where you are. What has happened that is new? You know this Manny fellow will spy on your work. No sense to spoil the work because you are angry with the spy."

Reluctantly I lay down again. I was boiling with anger. Johnny's next words echoed my own thought.

"I think this time it is more serious than the last."

"Why, Johnny?"

It was Pat's voice this time, questioning, earnestly.

"Because, Miss Pat, this time he sees the *Wahine* instead of the workboat. He knows that we have begun to work the wreck. He knows that whatever he plans to do must be done quickly."

I turned to Nino. "Johnny's right, you know. Manny can't delay too much longer. We've got to move faster."

Nino waved an eloquent hand. "Can we work any faster than we are working now? Can we do any more than we have planned to do? No. So why spoil your own digestion and mine? Today we work the cabin. Tomorrow we work the hold. We keep on working until this Manny fellow turns up—"

"Sure, sure! And what do we do when he does turn up?"

"I think maybe if we use our brains instead of our bottoms we give him the surprise of his life."

Nino chuckled and closed his eyes, and not another word could I get out of him until it was time to go down again.

We checked the pressure in our air bottles and tested the regulators, and while Pat helped us to harness up, Johnny tied the ballast net on the end of the long sling cable. This would go down with us. We would carry the cable end over to the wreck and dump the ballast bag inside the door of the cabin. Then, when we had uncovered the box, Johnny would haul it to the surface while we were staging up.

Before I put on my mask, Pat kissed me on the lips and said, "Good luck, Renn. And try not to be too disappointed."

"I won't. There's a treasure topside, even if there's none below."

Then I followed Nino Ferrari over the side and felt the shock of the water on my skin, warm after its two-hour broiling on the deck. The ballast bag followed us down and we carried it between us as we swam over the now familiar deck and up to the door of the cabin.

The dark held no terrors for me now. The staring fish eyes, the secret scurrying movements in the shadows, were all forgotten as I knelt with Nino on the rough floor and began steadily, rhythmically, to scrape away the sand from the sea chest. Nino watched me shrewdly and nodded his satisfaction when he saw that I had learnt my lesson.

Try to bury a kerosine can in your kitchen garden. You'll be surprised at the size of the hole you have to dig. Try to get rid of the same can six months later and you'll find you have double the work on your hands. Tackle it on a wet weekend and you'll be up to your knees in slush within ten minutes. Imagine two men attempting the same task in sixty feet of water, shifting with their bare hands two hundred years' accumulation of fluid sand and trailing seaweed and coral growths. You will understand that Nino had not exaggerated the size of the job.

I was working on the underside of the box, Nino on the upper. No sooner had I scraped away one handful of sand than more flowed down into the hole to take its place. The water around us was full of drifting particles which blurred our masks and vexed our patience. We had been working for perhaps fifteen minutes when Nino tapped my shoulder and beckoned me to look at his side of the box.

I saw it—and my heart sank. The top of the box had been stove in, probably on the night of the wreck, and the inside of it was full of sand.

The brass strips which had bound it were corroded and broken; the metal studs still left in the spongy wood were coated with coral cells and tiny mollusks. They scraped our hands as we plunged them into the box, screening the liquid sand for any trace of gold or jewels or ornaments.

My hand closed round something hard, but when I brought it up it proved to be a corroded buckle—brass, probably, or pinchbeck. Nino brought up a broken, rusted knife. This too was of common metal. When he found another buckle, larger than the first, he made a rueful mouth behind his mask and signalled me to stop. His miming told me only what I knew already.

The box was a very ordinary sea chest. It had held nothing more valuable than its owner's shore suit and his buckled shoes and his sea knife. The voracious sea organisms had eaten everything but the knife and the buckles of his hat and shoes.

For a moment we stood looking down at our pitiful find. Then Nino motioned me to help him, and we lugged and heaved the rest of the box clear of the sand and tipped its contents out among the seaweeds on the floor. We found nothing more than a pitted metal handle with a piece of porcelain still fixed to one end.

Then we heard the smack of the bullet on the water. We tossed the box on the pile of sand in the corner and watched it settle weightlessly among the weeds.

Clutching our few childish relics in our hands, we made our hesitant way to the surface.

"Tired, Renn?"

Pat and I were sitting on the forward hatch cover while Johnny steered us home through the channel and into the lagoon, and Nino, calm as a cat, was asleep on one of the bunks. Pat's hand was in mine. Her dark head was resting against my shoulder.

"Yes, sweetheart, I'm tired. Nino was right. It's wearing work."

"Are you disappointed, Renn?"

"Yes. It's crazy and childish and I don't want any sympathy. I'm new to the business. I'll have to learn to be patient. That's all."

"Nino says you'll start working the hold tomorrow."

"That's right."

"Will it be difficult?"

"No more difficult than the cabin. Except that there's a lot more of it and the sand is ten times deeper."

"It doesn't sound very promising, does it?"

"No. It's a matter of luck, that's all."

She hesitated a moment, then went on, "Renn, I've been thinking."

"About what?"

"About the coins on the reef. Do you think it's possible that any of the crew reached the island?"

"And took the treasure boxes with them?"

"Yes."

"Sweetheart," I said patiently, "we've been over all this before. You heard what Johnny said about it. I tell you, I've been over the whole island. There's not a trace of any such happening."

"Aren't there any caves?"

"Nary a one. There are a few rock holes and overhangs on the cliffside. But they're either too shallow or too high up in the wall. There's a sort of narrow cleft up on the eastern horn. Jeannette and I looked at it once, but it was so dank and musty and full of goat smell that we didn't go inside. Apart from that, nothing . . . nothing at all."

She sighed and made a little rueful mouth.

"Well, so much for my fine theory. Looks as though it's up to you and Nino, doesn't it?"

"Yes, it's up to us."

Johnny was slacking off now and we were sliding in to anchorage. I stood up and walked forward to be ready with the hook. Pat followed me up.

"Renn?"

"Yes."

"Johnny's worried about something."

"Did he say what it was?"

"No, but he wants to talk to you tonight, Renn . . . after dinner. Alone."

I tossed the anchor overboard and the cable went whipping down after it. Then the cable tightened. The *Wahine* stopped drifting and her stern swung round into the current. The first day's work was over. We were home again.

Dinner was over. The stars hung low in a soft sky. Nino squatted beside the fire, carefully taping the hose joint of his diving gear and crooning happily to himself. Pat had gone down to her tent to write up the thesis that would make my brown girl, incongruously, a Doctor of Science. I saw her shadow cast by the lamp against the glowing canvas of the tent. Johnny was going back to the *Wahine* to sleep. I walked down with him to the beach.

When we were out of earshot of the others, Johnny told me, "Renboss, I am scared."

"Of what, Johnny?"

"Something is going to happen with this Manny Mannix."

"We know that, Johnny. We've always known it."

"Yes, Renboss, but . . ." He stumbled and groped for the words that would frame the thought and make its urgency clear to me. "How can I explain it, Renboss? It is like the old days on the trochus beds. Word would go round that this one or that one had found a new place and was working it quietly. When

219

he walked into the bar the others would watch him silently, with greedy eyes. They would measure his strength and his courage and the loyalty of his crew. If he were strong and his men loved him, they would fawn and smile and offer him drinks and try to wheedle his secret out of him. But if he were weak or cowardly or unloved, then they would growl and mutter. Someone would start a fight. A bottle would be thrown and the shell knives would come out, and they would fight like animals. . . . This Manny is animal, Renboss. That is the way he will fight."

I nodded gravely. Johnny was right. Manny Mannix was an animal with an animal's courage. But Manny was a businessman, and where money was concerned, Manny would take no chances. If he moved at all, he would move in strength. And if you stroll round the waterfronts of the north with money in your pocket you will find plenty of tough characters who are not too particular how they earn it. Johnny watched me with troubled eyes.

"You agree with me, Renboss?"

"I agree with you, Johnny."

"What are you going to do, Renboss?"

"What do you want me to do, Johnny?"

He considered the question a long time before answering.

"For myself and for you and for this diver fellow, Nino, I would say we stay and fight. But there is the girl."

I saw the point. There was the girl. If there were violence, she would be caught in the midst of it. She would be there when the animals began to rend and tear each other. And afterwards . . . ? It was not a thing that should happen to any girl, and this was the girl I had come to love. There was only one answer.

"All right, Johnny. We send her back in the morning. If it's flat weather she can take the workboat. She needn't go to the mainland. There are two or three islands where she can put up and wait till it's over."

Johnny Akimoto straightened up. It was as if a great load had slipped from his shoulders. He smiled and shook my hand.

"Believe me, Renboss, it is best. You will not want her to go, I know that. But when she is gone you will be able to fight with free hands. . . . Good night, Renboss!"

"Good night, Johnny!"

I watched him push off the dinghy, step lightly over the stern and scull out to the *Wahine* with long, easy strokes. I turned away and walked up the beach to Pat's tent.

She got up when I entered. We kissed and clung together for a moment, then I sat her down in the chair again and perched myself on a packing case beside her. I said flatly, "Sweetheart, I'm sending you away tomorrow. There's going to be trouble. You'll take the workboat and go over to South Esk or Ladybird Island and stay there until we come for you."

She looked at me a long time without speaking; there were tears in her eyes and her lip trembled. Then she took hold of herself and asked me, calmly enough, "Do you want me to go, Renn?"

"No. I don't want you to go. I think you should go."

"And Johnny?"

"Johnny thinks the same."

She turned her face away and dabbed at her eyes with a small handkerchief. When she faced me again her mouth was firm and there was a proud lift to her chin. There was a note in her voice that I had not heard before.

"You are going to fight, aren't you, Renn?"

"Yes."

"For the treasure ship?"

"Partly . . . yes. But not only for that." Slowly, painfully, I tried to piece out for her the thought that had been growing in my mind for the past days. "I know now that we may never find the cargo of the *Doña Lucia*. There is still a chance, of course. There is an even greater chance that it may be buried so deep under the sand that we could never come to it in a million years. In that case the fight would be a monstrous and costly folly. But don't you see? It's not only that. It's all the other things. It's this—this life, my friends, this island. For the first time in my life I've stood a free man with my own land under my feet. I'll fight for that, sweetheart. I think, possibly, I will kill for it."

"And your own woman, Renn?" The words came out in a whisper. "I am your woman, aren't I?"

"You're my woman, Pat. From now to crack o' judgment."

I stood up. I reached out to draw her to me, but she pushed me gently away.

"Then I'm staying with you. You're my man, and you can't send me away."

I tried to argue with her and she closed my mouth with kisses. I tried to threaten her and she laughed in my face. I tried to charm her to submission and she dismissed me, reluctantly.

"Go to bed, Renn. Tomorrow's a working day. When this is over we'll have all the time in the world—till crack o' judgment, as you say."

I was shorn like Samson. I kissed her again and went back to my tent.

Nino Ferrari was still squatting by the fire, tinkering with the delicate mechanism of the regulators. He looked up when he heard me and gave me a crooked smile.

"A fine girl you got yourself there. She'll make a good wife for a diver. A deep-water man needs plenty of sleep."

I grunted irritably and squatted down beside him. He flipped me a cigarette.

"Something on your mind, my friend?"

"Yes. We're going to have a fight on our hands. Johnny thinks so. I think so."

Nino cocked his dark head and whistled soundlessly.

"So! It is going to be like that, eh? I have seen these things before, with the

221

sponge fishers in the Aegean. They can be ugly. When the wine flows and the long knives come out." He jerked his thumb over his shoulder in a significant gesture. "What about the girl?"

I shrugged. "I wanted her to go, she refused. Short of running her off the island by force, there's nothing I can do about it."

Nino tightened the last screw in the regulator and folded it carefully in clean cloth to keep the sand away from it, then he put the whole apparatus back in its case and snapped the lid.

"First rule for a lung diver," he said irrelevantly. "Clean the regulator after every dive. If it fails in deep water you are a dead man."

There was a silence between us. I heard the cheep and clack of insects in the bush behind us. I watched the dipping flight of a bat. Then I turned to Nino again.

"Out there, this morning, you said you had something we might use against Manny Mannix when he comes. What is it?"

His dark eyes gave me a long, sidelong stare. Then he bent his head and seemed to be studying the backs of his hands. When he spoke his voice was level, without emphasis.

"My friend, one does not put a knife into the hands of a child, nor a loaded pistol into the fist of a man who is angry. The knowledge that I have came to me in a sad time, a time of violence and bloody destruction. If it is necessary to use it again, I will do so. Even though you are my friend, I will say what is to be done and how, and for the consequences, I will take the responsibility. I am sorry, but this is a thing that I feel deeply—here in my heart."

And with that I had to be content. I grinned, got up, clapped him on the shoulder and took myself off to bed. I dreamt of a wartime beachhead with dead bodies rolling in the backwash and a man pinned down in a foxhole by machine-gun fire from the palms.

The man in the foxhole was myself. The man behind the gun was Manny Mannix.

Chapter Fourteen

At SEVEN O'CLOCK THE NEXT MORNING we dropped anchor in the diving area. We planned to make three dives a day and, allowing for rest periods and staging time, each dive would cost us three hours of daylight. I wanted to make four descents, but Nino was adamant. The gain would be an illusion, he said. After two days or three the strain would tell and we would begin to feel the effects of long immersion and nitrogen narcosis.

Today we were to make our first survey of the hold. We harnessed up quickly, and I felt the tenseness of expectation as I climbed overside and followed Nino down, watching his air bubbles stream upwards past my face.

Once more we swam over the waving growths on the deck until we came to the gaping hole with its fringe of slime and sharp corals. Nino motioned me to wait. I saw him dive, slanting downwards along the beam of his own flashlight. I noted the care he took to avoid fouling his airlines against the jagged edges. Then he shone his light backward, and I dived in to him along the beam.

The space in which we found ourselves was, perhaps, three times as large as the cabin we had visited the day before. The sand sloped upwards and the timbers with their coating of sea grass canted downwards wedge-fashion towards the rear of the chamber. The beam of my flashlight picked out a colony of lobsters clinging to the roof timbers in one corner. I told myself I would take one up to the *Wahine* for lunch. I felt something brush my shoulder blades. I turned sharply and flashed my light on a large squid. I saw his black parrot beak and his saucer eyes, then his tentacles stiffened beneath him and he shot upwards, leaving a puff of ink, like a ghost image, behind him.

Nino beckoned me to his side; together we made the circuit of the hold, standing where the roof was high, swimming on our backs or our bellies where the space narrowed between the sand and the timbers.

Our groping hands traced the outlines of ancient deck beams under the sleek waving growths. We marked them carefully. They would serve as guides when we came to divide the area into sections for our daily searches. When we had made the circuit, we swam back and forth across the bottom, groping with our hands among the weeds and sand and coral for anything that might resemble a box. It was superficial, unsatisfying work, but we had to do it. Later we would begin the heartbreaking task of turning over hundreds of square feet with our hands and our knives.

When we had traversed the whole area, Nino motioned me to stop. For a few minutes we hung suspended in the new element, grimacing at each other and making crazy dumb show with our hands. Then Nino signalled to me to shine my flashlight along one wall of the hold. I did so. He swam over to the corner, measured with his outstretched arms a width from the corner, then swam from that point parallel with the wall to the other end of the hold. The beam of my light followed him. I understood what he meant. He was marking out a narrow strip of sand for our first search.

He swam back to me and side by side we began to work. We scraped and scrabbled and probed, pushing ourselves backwards with our hands while our bodies hung suspended behind us like the bodies of fish.

We had not been working more than a few minutes when we heard the familiar impact of a bullet on the surface of the water. We stopped. I looked at Nino. Nino looked at me. We had not been down more than fifteen minutes. Then we heard a second impact and, immediately after it, a third.

Something was wrong on the *Wahine*. Nino gestured to me. We swam out of the hold and made our way as quickly as we dared to the surface.

Johnny and Pat hauled us aboard and, as we stood dripping on the deck, Johnny pointed across the water, westward.

"They're coming, Renboss," he said quietly.

She was a lugger, like the *Wahine* but bigger, broader in the beam. Her hull was black. Her spars were bare. She was coming under engines, fast, at about twelve knots. She would be with us in twenty minutes.

Johnny Akimoto handed me the glasses. I focussed and saw that her deck space was cluttered with machinery under canvas. I saw more bulky shapes forward of the main hatch. I saw men stripped to the waist moving round her decks. I saw a figure in a white duck suit braced against the forward stays— Manny Mannix.

I handed Nino the glasses. He scanned the lugger for a few moments, then lowered them.

"Diving gear," he said curtly. "Pumps and a winch. A lot of other stuff for'ard. Could be anything."

I turned to Johnny Akimoto. "Do you know her, Johnny?"

"Yes. She is a trochus boat, Renboss. Twin diesels. The number says she is registered on Thursday Island."

224

Clever Manny. Clever, clever, Manny. Never forget a face, never neglect a contact. Manny had chartered a boat like this before, when he went north, with a legitimate buyer's license to buy war surplus in the islands. Manny had brought it back with a false manifest, loaded with gear he had plundered from forgotten dumps in a hundred lonely bays. A simple telegram would bring the same boat and the same tough skipper and the same crew of plug-uglies racing down the reef to pick him up at Bowen. And if the business turned out to be dirty business, a cut for the skipper and a bonus for the boys would guarantee Manny silence and security.

"What do you want to do, Renboss?" said Johnny.

"Wait for her, Johnny. Just sit here and wait. Stow the gear, Nino. Pat, get below and make us something to eat. If we're going to have trouble, I'd like to be fed first."

She gave me a wan smile and padded aft. Nino picked up the lung packs and began drying them carefully. Johnny Akimoto stood watching the black shape of the lugger as she raced towards us across the flat water.

As she drew closer I could see the white numerals on her bows. I could see the bearded faces and tanned bodies of her crew. I could see Manny Mannix waving his cigar as he talked. I was still puzzled by the curious shapes under the canvas in the forepeak. I pointed them out to Johnny. They meant nothing to him, either. He bent down, picked up the rifle from the hatch cover, ejected the spent shell, slid another shell into the breech and rammed the bolt home. Then he slipped on the safety catch and laid the rifle carefully in the scuppers, out of sight.

Then Pat and Nino came on deck with mugs of tea and a plate of beef sandwiches. We sat on the hatch and ate together, watching the black lugger move closer and closer. The warm sun streamed down on us through the canvas awning. The *Wahine* rocked gently in the quiet water. We might have been a fishing party, out on a picnic cruise, had it not been for the tension between us and the menacing black hull with its motley crew.

We had hardly finished our meal when they came up with us. Thirty yards to starboard they cut the motors. The way brought her across our bows. The helmsman swung her beam to and we saw the anchor go down with a rattle and a splash. Then we were lying broadside to with no more than ten yards of water between us.

The crew lined the rail, laughing and shouting. They whistled and called ribaldries when they saw there was a woman among us. There were perhaps a dozen of them—black, white and in-between. Some were young and some were not so old. Some were bearded—others wore careless stubbly growth. But all were brown and tough and dangerous—veterans of the shabby towns on the fringe of the law.

In the midst of them stood Manny Mannix, incongruous in his white suit and his gaudy tie. His panama hat was tilted on the back of his head. The inevitable cigar was stuck in the corner of his mouth. He took it out to hail me.

"Hiya, Commander! Nice weather we're having!"

I said nothing. I felt Pat stiffen beside me.

"I'd like to come aboard, Commander. Business talk. Private."

"Stay on your own deck, Manny."

Manny waved a tolerant hand. He shouted back, "Just trying to be friendly. The market's still open if you're interested."

"I'm not interested, Manny."

"I'll split with you, Commander—fifty-fifty. Look, I've got the gear and the men to work it." He made a sweeping gesture that embraced the whole boat and her ragged crew. "If you don't like that, I'll still buy you out on the same terms."

"The answer's no, Manny. If you want it, you've got to take it."

"It's open water, Commander. Show me a salvage claim and I'll leave you to it."

"No claim, Manny. We were here first, that's all."

The men lining the deck sent up a great bellow of laughter. I saw Johnny's hand go down to the rifle lying in the scuppers. I stopped him before he touched it.

Manny Mannix hailed me again. "I've got witnesses, Commander. Witnesses to say that I made you a fair offer for something you don't own anyway. Now I'm moving in."

I bent and picked up the rifle and showed it to him.

"I told you you'd have to fight for it, Manny."

There was another bellow of laughter. Manny swung round and called an order to a seaman standing apart in the eyes of the boat.

In an instant the canvas was thrown back. My puzzle was solved. The humped shapes were depth charges, looted from some island dump. Behind them was a small machine gun mounted on a tripod. There was a full belt in the magazine and our man had his finger on the button.

"Still want a fight, Commander?" yelled Manny.

The gallery roared at his wit. Then his face darkened and his voice took on a new, venomous note.

"I'm moving in, Commander . . . as of now. You take your boat and sail her back inside the reef and stay there. If you so much as stick your ears out before we're finished, you'll be cut down. And just in case you and your little Wop think of any frogmen's tricks—like working the bottom when my boys are resting—remember those." He pointed to the sinister metal cans lying on the forward deck. "We'll take a little run and drop 'em on you as we go."

And there it was—the royal flush. And Manny was sitting on it. The last hand and we could do nothing but watch him scoop the chips into his pocket and go home. For the second time I was broke and busted in a game with Manny Mannix.

But I wouldn't give Manny the satisfaction of hearing me say it. Out of the corner of my mouth I spoke to Nino and Johnny.

"Nino, get the anchor up. Johnny, get the engines started, and we'll take her home. Don't hurry. Take it slow and easy. Pat and I will stay here."

They didn't ask questions. They moved quietly, almost languidly, to their posts, while Manny and his minions watched the gambit with silent puzzlement and the man behind the gun stood tense and ready.

Nino got the anchor up. I heard the cough of the *Wahine*'s engines and the stern flurry as the gears meshed and the screw bit into the water. Then, mercifully, we were moving. Pat and I still leant against the rail and I still held the rifle tucked under my arm with the safety catch off. Manny didn't want a shooting war—yet—but if he started it, I wanted him as the first casualty.

The watchers on the rail were silent as we nosed out, still broadside to, and Johnny swung the wheel and headed eastward along the reef to the channel entrance. The man behind the gun slewed it round to follow us. Then suddenly a great roar of laughter went up. It rang like a monstrous obscenity across the clean sunlit water.

Nino, Pat and I walked aft to join Johnny Akimoto in the cockpit.

"That's the most horrible, brutal thing I've ever seen." Pat's voice was low and controlled, but her dark eyes were black with anger. "It was so cold-blooded and—and stark."

I grunted unhappily. "It was no more than I expected. The gun and the depth charges were the only surprise. But, knowing Manny, I should have been prepared for those, too."

"I think," said Nino Ferrari with judicial calm, "I think I do not like this Manny fellow very much. I think he is the son of a whore. He called me a Wop, but my people were civilized gentlemen when he was a dirty thought in his great-grandfather's mind. I shall think about him, very seriously."

Johnny Akimoto said nothing. He stood aloof at the wheel—a dark, lonely figure, nursing the *Wahine* homewards with a kind of pathetic carefulness. Something had happened to this gentle man. It was as if he and the boat he loved had suffered a defilement from the mere presence of the black lugger and her tatterdemalion crew. His wise eyes were full of cold anger. The skin was drawn tight along his cheekbones and the line of his jaw.

Not another word was spoken until we cleared the channel and dropped anchor in the placid water of the lagoon.

Then we held a council of war. We would transfer the stores and the diving equipment to the beach camp. We would move Pat's tent up the beach close to our own. We would keep a twenty-four-hour watch on the black lugger and her activities. We would beach the workboat and the dinghy in sight of the camp and we would all sleep ashore. At this point Johnny Akimoto disagreed.

"No, Renboss. You and your friends will stay ashore. I stay with the *Wahine*."

"I don't know if that's wise, Johnny. I think we're safer together. No harm can come to the *Wahine*. They'll see us unloading the stores. If they decide to move in on the island—which I doubt—they will leave her alone and come to the camp."

Johnny shook his head. He said in a level voice, "No. This island is your island, Renboss. The *Wahine* is my boat. Each of us will guard what is his own. I will keep one rifle and half the ammunition. You will take the other gun to the camp. Nino has his pistol, so the division is fair. Believe me, Renboss, it is better this way."

Nino Ferrari nodded agreement when I looked at him.

"Johnny is right, my friend. Let him do as he wants. One of us can come out each day to keep him company and bring him fresh water. Besides, the *Wahine* is our lifeline. She must be kept safe and in running order, in case we need her."

So it was agreed. It took us four trips in the dinghy to get all the gear ashore, and from the black lugger outside the reef Manny Mannix watched us through the long afternoon. When evening came, Nino, Pat and I sat round the campfire and saw the riding lights of the *Wahine* rise and fall on the lonely water and, farther out, the yellow glow that streamed from the cabin hatches of the big lugger.

In his detached professional voice Nino Ferrari discussed the situation.

"What happened this morning was a shameful thing, but it does not profit us to curse and sweat and be angry about it. In the end it may turn out to our advantage."

"The hell it may!" I burst out angrily. "Manny's in possession. Manny's got the equipment. Manny's got the time and the money. If we make a single move he can shoot our heads off. We've just got to sit here, and—"

A small firm hand was laid on my arm, and Pat's calm voice brought me up short.

"Let Nino finish, Renn."

Nino chuckled and winked at me.

"I told you, you got yourself a good woman, my friend. I did not tell you before, but when I saw that hold this morning, my heart was down in my flippers. I have seen these things before, you understand, and I can tell you now that more than three-quarters of that hold is buried in the sand. You saw the angle of the deck. If you will think about it you will realize that when her nose went down everything movable would slide down also. So if the chests are there they are most probably far down under the sand. There are freaks, of course, and accidents, but that is the way I read the story."

"Read it any way you like, Nino, the fact remains that Manny's got suit divers and pumps. He can work longer than we can. He can hose away the sand. He can stay out there till he does it."

Nino chuckled and shook his head.

"You amateurs! He has a pump, sure. But what sort of a pump can you work from a small crate like that? How long will it take him to shift a thousand tons of sand? You talk of time. Sure he has time, but time is money. He has the wages of the crew and the skipper and the divers. He has the charter of the boat. He will work so long, and if he does not find the treasure chests he will pack up and go home. Why? Because he is a businessman. Because there is always a limit to the amount of money he can spend. Then, when he goes, we move in. He has made our job easier for us, you see?"

Nino's logic was unshakable. I had no answer to his argument. I was an angry man. He was cool as a judge. Pat nodded her approval of his calm reasoning. I felt ashamed of my helpless anger.

Then we saw a spotlight switched on aboard the lugger. Its naked beam made a great pool of light on the water outside the reef. We heard the rattle of a winch and the steady, distant beat of a pump. We saw a monstrous shape lowered over the side of the lugger into the lighted pool.

Manny was a businessman. He knew that time was money. He was going to work round the clock.

Chapter Fifteen

WE WOKE EACH MORNING to the steady thudding of the pumps. We saw the
black lugger riding still at anchor over the wreck of the *Doña Lucia*. We saw
the sleepy movement of men about her cluttered decks. We saw Johnny
Akimoto perched on the bows of the *Wahine* dangling a line overside to fish
for his breakfast.

We would race down to the beach to wash the sleep out of our bodies; and
then, while Pat made breakfast, Nino and I would tidy the camp and scavenge
in the undergrowth for our day's supply of wood. Then one of us would take
the workboat and putter out to spend the morning with Johnny aboard the
Wahine. His anger had gone now; he was able to smile again, and he moved
comfortably about the decks of the *Wahine* like a householder in his garden
plot. But there was about him a quality of wariness and caution, the attitude
of a man waiting for the inevitable in the midst of a brief, illusory peace.

Then, because there was nothing else to do, I would take Pat on small tours
of inspection of my embattled island kingdom. I taught her the names of the
trees—casuarina, tournefortia, umbrella tree, native plum. I showed her the
great hoop pines, whose seeds had been carried by birds from the mainland. I
showed her where the noddy terns rested under the soft leaves of the pisonias.

We picked wild orchids on the rock ledges. We sat for coolness under the
drooping fronds of tree ferns. We watched the green tree-ants sewing leaves
together, using their babies as a living shuttle from which came the long silky
thread that bound and cemented them together. We watched them spin their
stables, pens and galleries of fine silky mesh where the mealybugs lay im-
prisoned like domestic cattle until their time came to be killed and eaten.

We sat entranced at the angling spider who hangs from his web and fishes
for fluttering moths with a drop of moist glue hung beneath his body.

230

We tried, and failed, to make friends with the lean and shaggy goats, protected by an old law against the needs of shipwrecked mariners. Their tracks were everywhere in the bush, and we followed them up to the saddle between the twin horns and looked down on the brown cliffs, with the white water beating at their flanks. Perched solitary, like dawn people, between the sea and the sun, Pat and I watched the glory of green islands strung on the broken strands of the reef. We saw the blue turn to green and yellow where the deeps ended and the shallows began. We saw the light slant off the heaving bodies of porpoises, and the skimming arrowheads of flying fish, and the small dark shape of an ancient turtle that had seen, perhaps, the coming of the *Doña Lucia.*

We climbed the twin peaks and I pointed out the narrow cleft in the rocks which was the only semblance of a cave on the island. But we withdrew hurriedly from the heavy animal smell that greeted us. A bearded goat thrust his head out of the shadows and grinned at us.

Then we would go back to the camp to find Nino, stretched on the sand, sunning his dark body and grinning at us like the god of the goats himself.

Nino was a constant wonder to me. Time meant nothing to him. His spare, muscular body was endowed with a feline grace. He moved like a cat and he had the cat's capacity for instant relaxation and repose. He refused to spend his energies on profitless speculation or activity; yet his mind was clear and sharp as a knife edge.

"I am counting the days, my friend," he would say, "but I am also enjoying them. I am telling myself that, in a week—ten days—two weeks at most, they will lose heart and go away. Until then, I am enjoying myself. I have not had a holiday like this in years."

I felt an odd sense of guilt when I realized that I was thinking the same thing. Locked in the small circle of the reef, denied all opportunity for action, I had resigned myself to the calm of the lotus days and to the pastoral peace of my love for Pat Mitchell. We told ourselves that this way of life we could enjoy forever. We would build a house on the island. We would buy ourselves a boat like the *Wahine.* We would see our children grow brown and sturdy in the sun. We wove a tapestry of lovers' dreams, shot with the colours of the sunset and the sea.

Then, one day, something happened aboard the black lugger. I was watching her through the glasses when I saw a sudden flurry of movement on her decks. I heard a distant shout above the beat of the pumps. I saw the group playing cards on the forward hatch break up and scurry aft. I saw the dark body of one of the island boys scramble up from the cockpit and make as if to dive overboard. I saw him caught and held and dragged forward and flung, face down, on the hatch cover.

I saw him beaten, mightily, while the crew stood round grinning and Manny Mannix took the cigar out of his mouth and laughed and laughed.

I handed the glasses to Nino Ferrari. He stared at the scene for a moment, then passed them to Pat. She handed them back to me without a word, then walked away and retched on the sand.

The beating continued, steadily, methodically, monstrously, until the black boy had ceased to struggle and lay bloody and broken on the hatch cover.

Then I saw a horrible thing.

Manny Mannix made a curt gesture with his cigar. There was a moment's hesitation, and then four men stepped forward, took the limp form by the arms and legs and heaved it overboard. For perhaps a minute it floated, a dark mass on the smooth water, drifting slowly away with the current from the side of the lugger.

Suddenly I saw the black dorsal fin of a shark. Then another and another. There was a flurry and a threshing of water as the scavengers fought over their meal, then . . . nothing. But I thought I saw a dark stain spreading out with the ripples. I put down the glasses.

Nino Ferrari spat in the sand.

"Now," he said quietly, "now I think it is time we did something."

That evening I rowed out to the *Wahine* and brought Johnny Akimoto ashore for a discussion. He, too, had seen the terrible little drama and his eyes were smouldering with anger.

The four of us sat in the circle of firelight and watched Nino Ferrari bend forward, smooth the sand with his palm and begin to draw a map. . . .

"Here," he said, "is the island, with the beach in front and the cliffs behind. Here is the lagoon. Here is the line of the reef. Here it swings wide out in front of us. There it comes in close and becomes one with the rock shelf at the back of the island. Here is the camp. Here is the *Wahine*. And there"—he made a cross in the sand with his finger—"there is the lugger and the wreck."

He straightened up, lit his cigarette, inhaled deeply and blew out smoke from his mouth and nostrils. Then he spoke. His voice was low and even, but full of deep feeling.

"Before I tell you any more, I want to say this. A man's life is a precious thing. It is worth more than all the gold of the *Doña Lucia*, more than all the wealth in the world. I have seen many men die, some of them because of things I have done. I have seen a few men beaten and killed, as that one was killed today. In that I had no part. But the older I get, the more I know that each man's death is the death of a part of myself, because my life is sharing in theirs. I tell you this so that you will understand that what I propose is not a light thing, not a thing done for gain, but for justice."

He broke off. He smoked for a moment, silently. His eyes were veiled. The rest of us watched him, tense, expectant. Then he went on.

"I am going to blow up the lugger."

The words dropped into the silence like pebbles into a pool. Johnny Akimoto breathed out with a small sound like the hissing of a gas jet. I felt Pat stiffen. Her hands caught at my arm. She was shuddering violently. Nino Ferrari talked on calmly.

"The limpet mine is a very simple weapon. Very safe for the man who uses it. It is fixed by suction to the underside of a hull. It has a time fuse which is set to give the attacker a margin of safety in which to escape. I brought four of them with me to use on the *Doña Lucia*—now I shall use them against the lugger."

He bent forward and began again to draw in the sand, while the rest of us watched in speechless fascination.

"Here"—he pointed to a spot where the reef came close to the island under the shadow of the western horn—"here is where the current begins. It sets along the reef and runs out along the edge of it towards the spot where our friends are working. When the tide is full it makes three, perhaps four, knots. A man could enter the water here and swim down with the current. It would take him no more than half an hour to reach the ship. He would come up to it on the opposite side from that on which the divers are working. He would fix the mines and swim, still with the current, in the direction of the channel. He would shoot the channel and swim back to the *Wahine*. The whole operation would take an hour and a half—no more."

He straightened up and looked at us. His dark eyes searched our faces. It was Johnny Akimoto who spoke first.

"I think it is a good idea, Renboss. If Nino will have me, I will go with him."

Nino shook his head. "No, Johnny. This swim must be made under the water. I go alone."

Now it was my turn.

"If you go at all, Nino, I'm coming with you."

Nino looked at me. He darted a swift, warning glance towards Pat, who still clung to my arm, white and shaken. Then he said slowly, "You should understand, my friend, that in a thing like this there is always a certain risk . . . and time fuses, you understand, and the depth charges which are still lashed to the deck."

"It's my party, Nino," I said. "If you go, I go with you."

Then, sharp and high, Pat Mitchell's voice cut into our discussion.

"None of you will go. This morning we saw murder done. That's a matter for the police. We'll take the *Wahine*, or I'll take the workboat, and we'll go straight to Bowen and report what's happened here."

It was Johnny Akimoto who answered her, gravely, somberly, like a father telling a painful truth to a child.

"No, Miss Pat. The moment we try to move out of the channel, they would turn the machine gun on us. Besides"—he hesitated and then went on—"what was done this morning was done in daylight in full view. They know that we saw, and they are not frightened. Because I think—I know—that when they are ready, they have it in mind to kill us also."

To Nino and to me the logic was plain, but Pat protested it, violently.

"They couldn't, Johnny. They wouldn't dare. They couldn't hope to get away with it."

"Why not, Miss Pat? You know where we are. We are three hours' sailing from the mainland. Out there is the big ocean. I will tell you how they would do it. They would kill us first and feed our bodies to the sharks. Then they would destroy all trace of the camp. They would load the stores on the *Wahine* and tow her out into the big waters and let her drift. Then one day, perhaps, she would be washed inshore and the newspapers would call it another mystery of the sea. It would be very simple."

In the face of this stark revelation Pat was horror-stricken. She buried her face in her hands and sobbed. I put my arm round her shoulders and drew her to me to comfort her. I said gently, "I'm sorry, sweetheart, but Johnny's right. Nino's way is the only way. It's their lives or ours."

"I think," said Nino quietly, "I think, maybe, the lady should go to bed. These are not pleasant matters."

"No!" The word snapped like a lash. She lifted her ravaged face, still wet with tears, and challenged us. "I will not be turned out like—like a waitress. My life is involved as yours are. I will stay and listen to what you have to say."

If I had ever loved my small tanned woman, I loved her at that moment. I was proud of her and grateful for her and humbled by the bright courage of her. I bent and kissed her while Nino grinned and Johnny Akimoto smiled his wise, slow smile of approval. Then we settled to our planning.

"It is important," said Nino Ferrari, "that there should be no moon. We have seen that each night they keep a watch on deck. The men on the pumps are busy, but this fellow walks the deck with a gun. We shall be under the water, but there are still the bubbles. If the sea is flat they are unmistakable."

Johnny Akimoto made a quick calculation.

"Tomorrow night the moon does not rise until eleven o'clock. The tide is full by eight. That will give you three hours to work."

Nino nodded and went on briskly, "Good! But it is still important that we make full use of the time." He turned to me. "Is there a place where we can get into the water without having to float ourselves across the reefs? We shall be carrying explosives, remember."

I thought for a moment, and then I remembered. Just behind the first shoulder of the western horn there was a place where the rocks dropped down into deep water, and where the sea ran in like a long tongue, into a deep cleft in the side of the island. The reef was broken at this point and, if we had strength enough to fight out twenty yards against the wash, we should strike the current that would carry us down towards the lugger. I pointed it out to Nino on the map. He questioned me meticulously. Then he was satisfied.

"So! The next thing is to plan our movements so that tomorrow will look like any other day. They watch us from the lugger, remember. They know, therefore, that Johnny stays aboard the *Wahine* and I sunbathe on the beach and you and the young lady trot about the island. Tomorrow we must do exactly the same thing. Johnny stays on the boat, one of us visits him. This time it had better be me. I can fix the mines down in the cabin. You two will take your little walk, but tomorrow it will be to the point where we are to enter the water. Then you can lead us there, quickly, when we are ready to go."

234

I was filled with admiration for the little Genoese. He was planning his small campaign like a great general. The stone man on the pedestal in his native town would have smiled his approval. There was one point that worried me. I put it to Nino.

"If Johnny stays on the *Wahine,* that means Pat is left here alone. I don't like that."

"Neither do I," said Nino, "but I think it is necessary. We cannot afford to make any change in our routine. She will light the fire and make the meal at the same time. She can finish her meal and go to bed, if she wants. She will have the rifle and my pistol, but I do not think she will have any need of them. On the lugger they work right through the night; besides, they will not risk her in the channel in the darkness."

Pat nodded and gave me a brave smile.

"It's all right, Renn. Really it is. I'm used to it, remember? I was alone on the island before I met you."

I submitted, of course. I had to. But I told myself that if I survived the following night I would never leave her alone again. Nino went on, patiently detailing the final stages of the operation.

"As soon as it is dark we will leave the camp. The *signorina* will have sandwiches and hot tea ready for us. We will carry them to the place where we enter the water and eat there. Better, you see, that they do not see too much movement in the camp after dark. When we enter the water, remember that we have a long swim ahead of us and we must save our strength for the swim home. Do not hurry, do not thrash about. Content yourself with keeping on course and let the current do the rest. Then, when we come to the ship, stay well under her counter, so that the bubbles will dissipate themselves out of sight of the watch. We will fix four mines . . . two amidships, the others fore and aft. I will do that myself. You will float beside me and hand me the two which you will carry. And after that . . ."

He shrugged and spread his hands in a gesture of comic resignation. For myself, I was less good-humoured about it. After that would come the half-mile race to the channel, before the mines went off and the depth charges exploded and the killing shock waves battered our tired bodies. After that, the millrace of the turbulent channel and the final swim to the *Wahine.* For most of it we would not dare surface because of the machine gun in the bows of the black lugger.

"Now," said Nino abruptly, "we go to bed. And you, young lady"—he thrust a bony finger at Pat and grinned like the father of all the goats—"you go to bed first. Kiss your man and tell him you love him. Then go to bed. Love is a tiring business, and tomorrow he will be swimming for his life."

She laughed and kissed me and clung to me a brief moment. Then she walked to her tent, a brave small figure, shoulders squared, head high.

When she was out of earshot Nino turned to me. He wasn't grinning now. He was dead serious. He said bluntly, "I made it sound as simple as I could for the lady. But it is not simple. We are swimming in bad waters to the limit of our air supply. By midnight tomorrow night we may both be dead. Understand that."

"I understand, Nino."

He turned to Johnny Akimoto. He spoke tersely, crisply, a general giving the last battle orders to his staff.

"Johnny, this is an operation that runs to time. If it does not, it fails, and we are dead men. We should be back by ten o'clock. That is the extreme limit of the air supply. Give us till eleven. If we are not aboard then, you will know that we are dead."

Johnny nodded gravely. Nino continued.

"What you will not know is whether we have managed to fix the mines or not. So this is what you will do. You will take the dinghy and row inshore as quietly as you can and pick up the girl and bring her out to the *Wahine*. Then you will start the engines and head out through the channel at full speed. You will have a little start, because they will have to get the men up from the bottom of the sea and that takes time. After that they will come for you, shooting. You understand?"

"I understand very well," said Johnny.

I understood, too. In his dry, crackling, professional voice Nino had been discussing our funeral arrangements.

236

Chapter Sixteen

JOHNNY WAS GOING BACK to the *Wahine*. I walked with him down to the beach and stood with him on the damp sand under the bright, cold stars. Each of us knew that this might be our last meeting.

"Look after my girl, Johnny," I said.

"With my life, Renboss," said Johnny Akimoto.

I told him about the money in the bank on the mainland. I told him how, if anything happened to me, the money would be paid to him. He shook his head.

"No, Renboss. Not to me. You have your own wahine to look after."

"She doesn't need it, Johnny. She wouldn't take it anyway. I want you to have it."

"Thank you, Renboss," said Johnny.

It takes a great gentleman to accept a gift gracefully. Johnny Akimoto was a very great gentleman. I thanked him—banally enough, God knows—for all he had done for me. I tried, with halting, awkward phrases, to convey all that I had come to feel for him: respect, admiration, the kind of love that grows between men who have drunk the wine of triumph together and tasted the stale, sour lees of defeat.

He heard me out with embarrassment. Then, quite simply, he said a strange and beautiful thing which I shall remember till the day I die.

"Wherever you are, Renboss, my heart will be with you. Wherever I am, your heart will be with me. Good night . . . my brother."

Then he took my hand and pressed it to his naked breast, released it and was gone. I heard the rattle of the oarlocks and the ripple and dip of the oars as he sculled back to the *Wahine*. God has made few men like Johnny Akimoto. I have often wondered if he made all of them black.

The next day began like all the other days.

We swam before breakfast. We pottered about the camp. And when the chores were done, Nino took the workboat and went out to the *Wahine*. He carried with him a small wooden box in which were the limpet mines and the detonators, packed in cotton wool. Pat and I strolled out, hand in hand, to explore the tracks that led to our launching place. The whole island was crossed and recrossed with goat pads, but we needed a path that we could follow without difficulty in the darkness and which would be screened from the beach and the watchman on the black lugger.

We found it without difficulty. We calculated that Nino and I could walk it comfortably in fifteen minutes. We climbed down to the launching place and studied it carefully, noting the juts and hollows in the rocks and the snags that would be hidden by the high water. Then we retraced our steps, checking the landmarks that would guide us in the darkness—a twisted tree trunk, a jutting rock, a clump of tree ferns, the perfumed blossoms of a solitary ginger flower.

Then, our survey completed, we made our way through the bush to the small valley with the grassy bank and the drooping of rock lilies. The shade was grateful to us, and the cool was kind. The words we spoke were simple, private, pitiful. We were a man and woman who loved each other and who knew that the next twelve hours might see the end of all love and the death of all desire. Yet we were like the old, old lovers turned to marble in the market square whose hands are clasped, whose eyes look always into each other's but whose lips are parted a hair's breadth from a kiss and whose bodies ache eternally for ecstasies that will never come.

Nino Ferrari was right—love is an expensive luxury when a man must swim for his life.

We turned our backs on our disappointed paradise and walked out of the bush into the sun.

Nino was in his usual place on the beach. This time he was not sunbathing. He was sitting propped against a small mound of sand, scanning the black lugger through the field glasses. When we came to him, he grunted a greeting, told us with a curt gesture to sit beside him and continued his scrutiny of the boat. Then he handed the glasses to me. He was frowning.

"Tell me what you make of that, my friend."

It was a curious and puzzling little scene. One of the divers was sitting in the midst of a small ring of spectators with a square, dark object at his feet. His helmet had been unscrewed and was lying on the deck beside him, but the rubberized fabric of his suit was shining and dripping with water. He had evidently just come up. He was pointing to the dark object and gesticulating awkwardly as if explaining where and how he had found it.

The crew were grouped round him in a broken circle. Manny Mannix stood facing the diver. I could not see his face, but I caught the familiar flourish of the cigar. I knew that he was questioning the diver closely.

"Well, my friend, what is it all about, do you think?"

I lowered the glasses and turned to Nino.

"I don't know exactly. On the face of it, the diver's brought up something from the wreck and they're just standing round discussing it."

"You know what it is they have brought up?"

"No. It's dark and squarish—that's all I know. Every time I tried to get a better look, some fool shifted his feet and I couldn't focus on it."

"I saw it," said Nino soberly. "It is our box. The one we found in the cabin."

I burst out laughing. The thought of Manny Mannix, frustrated and fuming over that empty sea-rotten box, was too much for me. I threw back my head and roared.

"I'm glad you think it's funny, my friend."

Nino's icy voice was like water thrown in my face. I stopped laughing and looked at him. Then I looked at Pat. Her face was as troubled as Nino's.

"I don't get it," I said. "I'm sorry to be so dull, but I don't get it. Maybe I have a peculiar sense of humour, but I think that's very funny . . . very funny, indeed."

"No," said Nino tersely, trenchantly. "Not funny. Not funny at all. Very unfortunate for all of us. They have found our box. They have been working for many days now, with divers and pumping equipment. They have found nothing but that single broken box. Now they are telling themselves that perhaps we have found the treasure and carried it ashore. They are telling themselves that is why we did not put up a fight, but let ourselves be pushed off the diving area without so much as a dirty word. Soon, I think, very soon, they will come in to take us."

I was horror-struck. The stark simplicity of the situation, the sudden wreck of all our careful plans, left me for a moment without power of thought or speech. I looked out towards the *Wahine* and saw that Johnny Akimoto was standing in the bows, shading his eyes with his hand, watching the men on the deck of the lugger. I wondered if his thoughts were the same as ours.

I raised the glasses again. I saw the circle of men break up. I saw them moving about the decks with the disciplined hurry of those turning to an urgent but familiar task. I saw the pump hands stripping the diver of his heavy suit. I saw the winch man winding in his cable, making it fast on the drum and throwing the canvas cover over it. I handed the glasses to Nino.

"You're right, Nino. They're making ready to move."

"Then," said Nino curtly, "it is time for us to move also."

I pointed to the *Wahine*.

"What about Johnny?"

"Johnny knows what is going on as well as we do. We cannot help him, he cannot help us. If he wants to join us he has time to do so, but I do not think he will leave the *Wahine*.

239

"Nino's right, Renn," said Pat quietly.

"But they'll kill him!"

"I think," said Nino dryly, "they will try to kill all of us. Johnny has the rifle and ammunition. He has the same chance as we have—a slightly better one, I think, unless they try to board him, which I doubt they will do."

There was a moment's silence. We watched them get the anchor up. We heard them start the engines. We saw the flurry of water under the stern of the lugger. Then they were moving.

"Come," said Nino briskly. "Back to the camp. There is work to do."

We turned and went up to the camp at a run. We arrived panting and breathless, but Nino would brook no delay. His voice crackled in a running fire of orders.

"We have twenty minutes, perhaps half an hour. No more. They have not run the channel before. They will take it carefully. They will go to the *Wahine*. After that they will come for us. Sooner or later you will have to stand and fight. Is there a place where you can do that?"

I tried to marshal my thoughts. They were like sheep, scattered by fright on a country road. It was Pat who answered for me. Her voice was cool and controlled.

"The western horn. The cleft in the rock. It goes in a long way. It is in the angle between the main saddle and the shoulder that falls down to the sea. There's only one way to reach it. They must come up the goat track. With a rifle we can hold them off a long time."

Nino grinned sourly.

"Didn't I say you'd got yourself a good woman? Now, listen, and listen carefully. You will take a water bag and food. You will take the rifle and the ammunition. You will take the knife from your diving belt in case . . . in case the ammunition runs out, or you have to fight quietly in the bush, then the two of you will make your way up to the cleft in the rock. Is that clear?"

"Quite clear, but what about you? Aren't you coming with us?"

"No, but what I will do concerns you as well, so you must understand clearly what I am telling you. They cannot run the lugger inshore. So they will send a party to the beach in a boat. They will be armed. They will search the camp first. Then they will beat the island, looking for you."

I nodded agreement.

Nino talked on crisply. "When you are gone, with the *signorina*, I will take the lung pack and the pistol and two of the limpet mines, which is all I can carry. I will go through the bush and find a place where I can hide myself in the rocks and enter the water without being seen. Then, when I can, I will enter the water and swim out to the lugger and fix the mines. I will set them on a three-hour fuse, then I will swim to the *Wahine* and float myself under her blind side until I have a chance to get myself aboard. That is my party. This is yours."

He paused and wiped the sweat from his face with the back of his hand. Pat and I watched him silently, full of admiration for this small dark fellow with the icy courage and the brain like an adding machine.

He continued. "You will go up to the cleft in the rock under the western horn. Soon—in an hour, ninety minutes—they will come up for you. You will have to pin them down with rifle fire so that they do not move out of the bushes. Then—I cannot think how, but you will know—you will have to work your way out of the rock hole into the bush and down again to the beach. Then you will swim to the *Wahine*. If God wills, I shall be waiting for you. We shall run her out through the channel before the big blowup. Is it clear now?"

It was as clear as water. Our small force would be broken up—Johnny on the *Wahine*, Nino keeping his solitary vigil behind the rocks, Pat and I penned in our hole in the hill waiting for the chance to slip through the bush like hunted beasts and make our way down to the water. There was nothing to add, nothing to subtract, the tally was made. It was time to go. I stretched out my hand, Nino took it.

"Good luck, Nino!"

"Good luck, my friend—and to the little lady!"

Pat took his small lean face in her hands and kissed him.

"Thanks, Nino. God keep you."

I slung the field glasses round my neck and hooked a small flashlight to my belt. We picked up the rifle and the ammunition and the water bag and a small package of food and walked off into the bush. Nino stood a moment looking out across the water, then he turned away and went into the tent.

Halfway up the hill we stopped and looked back. A break in the trees gave us a clear view of the lagoon and the outer reef.

The black lugger was coming through the channel now. We saw her buck a little in the troubled water, then slide forward into the calm. They cut the engines and she moved slowly forward towards the anchorage of the *Wahine*. She was about three cable lengths away when they dropped the hook. I swore softly. The boys knew their business. They were moored slap across the channel. The *Wahine* could not get out without a wide detour through which the machine gun could rake every inch of her decks. We saw a boat lowered and half a dozen men climb into her. There were four at the oars and one in the stern with a rifle on his knees. There was another in the bows.

We looked at the *Wahine*. Johnny Akimoto was standing amidships, a little back from the rail, the rifle trailing easily below his hip. The rowers rowed the boat with long, easy strokes across the intervening water, until they were almost under the counter of the *Wahine*. Then they backed water and held her, rocking a little against the wash. Johnny Akimoto did not move.

I glanced back at the black lugger. Manny Mannix and the rest of the crew lined the deck. There was a man behind the machine gun in the bows. He was squatting and sighting it across the decks of the *Wahine*.

When I shifted the glasses back to her I saw that Johnny was still standing in the same position, while the fellow in the bows of the rowboat was talking and waving his hands. He wanted to come aboard. Johnny shook his head. The fellow talked again; his gestures were jerky, like those of an angry puppet. I saw Johnny raise the rifle slowly, ever so slowly. I caught the movement of his hand as he shoved the bolt home and threw off the safety catch.

Then a burst from the machine gun cut him down.

Chapter Seventeen

THE SEA BIRDS ROSE in screaming horror from the rocks and from the reefs. The echoes of the shots rang shatteringly along the ridge between the peaks. In one suspended moment of shock and terror we saw the body of Johnny Akimoto flung backwards into the air, fall, twitching and jerking against the cabin hatch, and then lie still.

Pat buried her face in her hands. Her body was shaken by deep, shuddering sobs. The echoes died. The sea birds settled again, and the silence of death hung in the bright air between the island and the sea.

Then my belly knotted and I vomited on the dead leaves. When I looked up again I saw that the men from the dinghy were scurrying over the ship like rats—diving down the companionway, ripping off the hatch covers, defiling every corner of the boat which had been Johnny Akimoto's woman. Then anger rose in me, deep, soul-wrenching agony, that set me gibbering obscenities and leaping and shouting like a madman at the men who had killed my brother. Then the anger died to blank wretchedness and we turned away, climbing slowly up the hill and along the saddle to the dark cleft in the rocks.

A stale animal smell hung heavily about the entrance. When I shone the flashlight inside, an aged goat bleated and shot out between our feet. His hair was long and matted and he stank foully. The floor inside was deep in his droppings. I shone the light on the rear wall and saw that it was broken by another narrower cleft beyond which was blackness. When I flashed the beam on the roof, a small colony of bats stirred and squeaked and made a small panic, then settled again as I shone the light round the walls.

Pat shivered and drew close to me. The flashlight pried out a small angle in the rock walls. I scraped the filth away with the sole of my shoe and set down

243

the food and the water bag and the clips of ammunition. I turned to Pat and pointed.

"When the shooting starts, sweetheart, that's where you'll be—head down and tucked well behind the angle of the rock. It's not much help, when they start shooting into the cave and the slugs start whipping off the walls, but at least you'll be able to pass the spare clips to me."

She nodded, as if she could not trust herself to speak. I took her hand and drew her out into the sunlight. In the bushes near the cave we found two large rocks, covered with moss. These we carried and set across the entrance so that they made a small crenellation that would give me some small protection when the shooting started and leave me a reasonable traverse of the path below.

We scouted the bush on either side of the cleft, noting with desperate precision every bush and rock and fallen log that might shield us when we made our desperate dash down to the beach. I clutched at the small consolation when I saw how steeply the goat track fell away in front of the cleft and how a man approaching it from below must walk straight into my sights.

Then, our survey made, our small fortress prepared as much as it could ever be against the coming siege, we stood together in front of the dark hole in the rock and looked down to the camp and the beach and the sea.

The rats had left the *Wahine* now. They had nosed and scampered and pried and then gone overside, their appetites unsatisfied. The dark, crumpled figure still lay against the cabin hatch, and the *Wahine* rocked in the water, like a woman nursing her lonely grief.

Now they were coming ashore—two boatloads of them this time—four men to a boat, with Manny Mannix sitting in the stern of the leading craft. The sunlight glistened on their sweating backs as they bent to the oars, and I saw their lips move in talk and laughter, though I could not hear a sound. They were armed—two with automatic rifles, the rest with pistols and standard .303s. They drove hard inshore and beached the boats high up on the sand. Then they spread out and advanced up the slope towards the camp, with Manny Mannix bringing up the rear, like the cautious fellow he was.

The noise of their shouting drifted up faintly, as we watched them scrambling about the camp, upending crates and boxes, ripping the tops off them, kicking them aside with angry disappointment. Then, when they found nothing, they stopped. They gathered round Manny and stood dejectedly while he harangued them. We could guess what he was telling them. The treasure must be on the island somewhere. If they found us they would find it, too. We saw him point upwards to the ridge, making a long sweep with his arm in the direction of the upper slopes. We saw him bend down and trace lines in the sand while the others bowed their heads to look at him. Then he straightened up. The men strung themselves out in a long line on the tussocky fringe of the sand. Manny took his place in the center of the line. I saw him put his hand into the breast of his white coat and withdraw it, holding a long-barrelled black pistol. Then he waved and shouted something which I could not hear, and the whole line moved slowly forward into the bush.

They were coming after us. It was time to retire to our fortress in the rock.

When we were inside, I made Pat lie down on her stomach on the floor, so that her head was protected by the skirt of the rock. I was worried about what might happen when Manny and his boys began shooting into the cave mouth. The bullets would go buzzing like angry bees, ricocheting between the walls. A sudden thought occurred to me.

I handed her the flashlight, warning her to shield the light with her hand, and sent her back to explore the narrow opening in the rear wall. She started to protest. I silenced her with a gesture. I heard her move gingerly into the darkness. I saw the small reddish glow of the light shining through her fingers. Then she called softly.

"It's quite large, Renn. I can't see all of it. But there's quite a big wall to the left of the entrance. The floor's clean, too."

"Good! Lie down behind it. Switch off the light. And don't come out, whatever happens. If anything happens to me, stay there. There's just a chance that they'll think I'm alone and leave you there."

I heard her give a small cry and I half turned to comfort her. Then, quite near, I heard voices and the crashing of clumsy men through the bush.

I called softly, warning her. She did not answer.

I took a long swig from the water bag, drew the clips of ammunition close to my hand and sprawled in the firing position between the two stones.

I worked the bolt of the rifle and then shot it home, shoving a shell into the breech. Then I thrust the barrel out between the rocks, enough to give me a traverse of the approach, laid the butt of it hard against my shoulder and sighted down the sloping path.

That was the way they would come. There was no other approach. They might strike down from the ridge, they might move upwards along the flank of the hill, but at the end they must come out on the goat track and I would see them.

I tried to think what I would do if I were planning Manny's tactics for him. I told myself that I would set two men with automatic rifles in the bushes on either side of the track. These two would begin pouring crossfire into the cave, enfilading me, pinning me down, while the others crept up along the bush fringe to jump me at point-blank range. One man, with a single-action rifle, could not long survive a maneuver like that. I took small courage from the thought that Manny had fought his war from King's Cross and might well have forgotten what they had taught him as a rookie.

My body was cramped; my arms ached. My elbows were frayed by the rough floor. The sweat was pouring down my face; the small nodule of the foresight wavered and trembled. I shifted and eased myself a little as the noise came closer.

They had lost formation now. Their voices were scattered. They stumbled and cursed and shouted to one another when they lost contact among the tree trunks and the thick bushes and the trailing vines. I pictured them, sweating and angry, their flesh torn by brambles and twigs, tormented by flies and buzzing gnats, and I smiled sourly to myself.

Then they seemed to come together. The footsteps converged on a spot near the bottom of the track. The shouting ceased. There was a babble of voices, then a murmur, over which I heard a single harsh voice crackling in a spate of unintelligible words. Then the murmuring began again—sullen, protesting.

Three seconds later Manny Mannix stepped out on the track. His white duck suit was crumpled and stained. He had lost his hat. His face was streaked with sweat and grime. He looked angry and unhappy. His mouth was working; I heard the nasal, snarling sound of his voice, but I could not distinguish the words. He waved his pistol dangerously and pointed first at the ground, then, with a wide sweep, at the surrounding bush. Then he raised his head and stared straight into the mouth of the cave.

I shot him between the eyes.

The impact carried him backwards down the path, spinning. He crumpled and lay still.

I heard the shot echo along the ridge. I heard the sudden riot of the sea birds. I ejected the spent shell and shoved another up the spout. Now, I thought, they would come.

But they didn't come. They broke and ran.

I heard a voice scream: "Manny's had it!"

Then the whole sorry crew ran, stumbling and plunging and yelling down the slope. Then I was standing in the mouth of the cave firing wildly into the bush. I heard a yelp of pain and the crash of a falling body and I shouted and fired again and again, laughing crazily as I heard the high whine of the bullets through the trees . . .

I wondered, irrelevantly, what had happened to Nino Ferrari.

Then Pat was beside me and we stood together watching the wild stampede break through the fringe of the bush and stumble drunkenly down to the waiting boats. I flung the hot rifle on the ground and propped myself against the rock face, sobbing and retching and trembling like a man with fever.

When the spasm had passed, Pat handed me the water bag and I drank, gagging at first, then gulping down the cool, flat liquid as if there were a fire in my belly. Then I upended it and poured the water over my face and neck and breast as if to wash away the slime of a nightmare that had clung to me even after waking. Her control broke, too, and she sobbed and clung to me, her face against my breast, kissed me, clinging to me, weeping and laughing at once, pressing my body to hers as if to assure herself that it was still living and whole . . . not lying as Manny's lay, a bloodied wreck on the goat path, with the flies buzzing round its ravaged face.

She took me by the hand and led me back into the cave.

246

I was too weary to question her, too spent to puzzle on small mysteries. Meekly I let myself be led across the filthy floor of the first chamber to the dark opening in the wall. Pat switched on the flashlight.

I saw a large vaulted chamber, three times as large as the first, with a sandy floor and walls of ironstone down which the water seeped slowly over a coating of green fungoid growths.

She swung the beam of the flashlight until it came to rest in the far corner. She said softly, "Look, Renn!"

I started back in momentary terror. Stretched on the sandy floor were the bleached bones of a skeleton. Two paces away was another, face downwards . . . its fleshless fingers clutched the sand. Its knees were drawn up under its ribs in a fetal attitude.

Pat's hand was trembling. The flashlight wavered on the weird latticework of naked bones. I took the flashlight from her and gripped it firmly. We moved closer.

The first skeleton was lying on its back. The bones were slightly displaced by the nuzzling of the goats which had stripped it of every shred of clothing that had not rotted and crumbled with the passing of the centuries. Just beyond the reach of its fingers was an ancient pistol. Its wooden stock was mouldy and wormeaten, and the metal was rusted beyond repair.

Round the little finger of the skeleton was a loose gold band in which a large cabochon ruby glowed dully under the dust of centuries. But this was not all.

Through the naked trellis of the ribs a long, thin knife had been driven, so that its rusted blade still stuck deep in the sand. The steel was pitted and corroded, but the hilt was crusted with jewels that winked and glowed under the beam of the torch.

"He was murdered," said Pat quietly.

I nodded and turned the beam on the other skeleton. The fingers were buried deep in the sand into which they had clawed in their last struggle for life. The face of the skull was buried, too, but the back of it was exposed—a smooth yellow spheroid of bone, pierced by a large round hole.

"He stabbed the other fellow," I said. "Then he was shot as he turned away."

"Yes. But there's something else, Renn. Look!"

I focussed the light and bent closer to the sand.

Clearly visible through the bleached ribs of the skeleton, clutched against his breastbone, as he must have clutched them in the last brief agony, was a pile of gold coins.

We had found the treasure of the *Doña Lucia*.

Pat caught at my arm. She was trembling violently, but she forced herself to speak.

"They escaped, Renn. Don't you see? They escaped the wreck in which all their shipmates died. They struggled ashore with these small remnants of a fortune—the jewelled dagger and the bag of gold coins." Her voice rose higher with the first onset of hysteria. "They were fortunate. They had been granted mercy. But they didn't value it. All they valued was this. . . ."

"Steady, sweetheart! Steady!" I put my arm about her shoulders to comfort her. "It was all a long, long time ago. It was done and finished two hundred years ago."

She pushed herself free and hammered at my chest with small fists. Her voice was an anguished cry.

"It didn't finish! It never finishes! It happens all the time. Men fighting and killing each other for this—this yellow refuse that even the goats reject. It happened today, Renn. It happened to you and me and Nino, and Johnny Akimoto."

Then it was as if she had been struck in the face. The wild light was quenched in her eyes. Her mouth dropped slackly. She stared at me in blank misery.

"Johnny's dead, Renn . . . Johnny Akimoto's dead. . . ."

She crumpled and I caught her in my arms and carried her like a sick child into the sun.

Chapter Eighteen

I LAID HER DOWN on a bed of leaves in the shade of a big pisonia tree. I ripped off my shirt and folded it under her head. I bathed her face and forced a little of the water between her lips. After a few moments she opened her eyes and stared at me blankly; then her head lolled slackly to one side and she lapsed into the deep sleep of utter exhaustion.

I stood for a moment looking down at her, touched with weary desire for this small perfect body and with pity and love and gratitude for the bright, brave spirit which it covered. Then I left her sleeping and walked the few paces back to the mouth of the cave.

Soon we would have a long walk and a long swim ahead of us, and my tired dark girl was in no condition to face them yet. I looked down at the lagoon and saw that the boats had come alongside the black lugger and their crew were being hauled aboard by the deckwatch. The *Wahine* was still riding at anchor. The body of Johnny Akimoto still lay untended on the sweltering deck. There was no sign of Nino Ferrari.

I sat down on a slab of brown rock, lit a cigarette and considered the situation.

Manny's small army of scalawags had broken and run at the first shot; but there was no guarantee that they might not regret their cowardice and come again, better led, to make another search for us and for the treasure. Even so, we could not leave the island until they came ashore again. We would have to make a surface swim to the *Wahine*, right under the muzzle of the machine gun.

On the other hand, if they delayed too long the limpet bombs would go off and the depth charges would explode when the lugger sank. The *Wahine* was moored so close to her that she could not possibly escape damage, even total wreck. Unmanned, she might easily be wrenched from her moorings and flung onto the reef by the first waves from the explosion.

If that happened we might be in a worse situation than before—killers and victims alike marooned on a barrier island. I shivered in the warm sun. The prospect was grotesque but very possible. Three hours, Nino had said. Three hours from the time he fixed the mines to the hull of the black lugger. I thought that not more than an hour and a half had passed since Pat and I had left the beach for the hill. Allowing time for Nino's swim, I thought there were not more than two hours to the blowup.

I scanned the green water of the lagoon for any sign of Nino's shadow in the refracted sunlight. There was no shadow. There was no flicker or ripple that could show where he was.

I looked over at the lugger. The crew were huddled in a shouting, gesticulating group amidships. They were arguing, accusing each other. They were discussing the merit of another foray for the treasure, or a quick run up the reef and into safe waters before news of the killing reached the mainland. There are a hundred islands between Macasar and Bandung where a man with a boat and a willing crew can name his own price for a little honest gun-running.

I noticed that the boats were still tied alongside, their oars inboard, their bows bobbing and thumping against the planks. I thought that if they did not get the boats inboard in twenty minutes they would mean to stay and search for us in their own time. If they hauled them inboard and lashed them, they would be leaving very soon. If they were not gone within two hours, the lugger would blow up inside the reef and there would be bloody murder done on the white sand of my island.

I decided that I would let Pat sleep a little longer; then we would go down to the beach and wait. If the lugger left, well and good. If she stayed, we would wait till after the explosion, then take the workboat and head for the mainland.

I realized with a start that I had no means of warning Nino Ferrari. I had no way of letting him know that we were even alive. Even if, half submerged under the counter of the *Wahine,* he had seen the wild rush to the shore, it could have meant any one of half a dozen things to him.

Then an idea occurred to me. Allow twenty minutes more for Pat to be rested enough for the walk back to the beach. Allow half an hour for the walk. There would still be an hour before the mines went off. Time enough for me to don my own diving gear and swim out across the lagoon to the *Wahine.* There was the problem of entering the water without being seen from the lugger. But Nino had done it; so could I.

Now that the decision was made, I felt suddenly weary and vaguely resentful of the new demand for effort and strength. I looked at Pat. She was still sleeping. Her breathing was deep and regular and the colour was flowing slowly back under the ivory skin. A small insect lighted on her face; she stirred uneasily and brushed it off with an instinctive gesture, but did not waken.

As I sat there, slack and tired, and saw my girl sleeping and all the green wonder of the island spread below me, and all the blue stretch of ocean running out to the rim of the world, I was conscious of a feeling new and strange to me. A sense of truncation and of loss, because my friend was dead and because the last shreds of innocence had been ripped away when I had seen the naked evil of the world and when I had killed the man who most of all embodied it. I felt no guilt, only distaste and disillusion. But I felt something else, too—a sense of possession and of permanence, as if I, the landless man, were now free of his own possession, as if I, the blind historian, had opened my eyes at last to see the wild wonder of the world and to know that I, too, was part of its turbulent history.

A man is fully grown when he has learnt this truth: There is no mercy in the world, except the mercy of the Almighty. There is neither peace nor permanence nor secure possession until a man straddles his small standing place and dares all comers to thrust him out of it.

I stood up, trod out my cigarette and walked back to the cave. I picked up the empty water bag, ripped open the top seam of the canvas and carried it into the big vaulted chamber. I turned over the huddled skeleton, surprised to find there was so little weight in it, and scooped the tarnished coins into the water bag. They filled it almost to the top. Then I put my hand on the jewelled hilt of the dagger and drew it out of the sand and put it on top of the coins.

The coins did not burn me. The dagger did not cut my hand.

Men had died because of them. I had fought and survived to enjoy them. They were mine to use or misuse as I pleased.

I straightened and stood a moment looking down at the pitiful bleached relics on the sand. They had nothing to say to me, nor I to them. The gulf of two centuries lay between us and their voices were blown away long since by the desert winds of time.

I snapped off the flashlight, picked up the water bag and walked out of the cave.

I wakened Pat and lifted her to her feet. She gave me a wan little smile and said, "I'm sorry, Renn. It wasn't very thoughtful of me, was it?"

I kissed her and held her to me for a moment. Then I told her what we were going to do. I handed her the glasses and showed her the deck of the lugger, where the shouting men were quiet now, squatting in a small circle round the skipper, discussing the next move. The boats were still in the water, bobbing. She handed the glasses back to me.

"Renn?"

"Yes, sweetheart?"

"Do you think Nino's still alive?"

"Of course. We can't see him because he's probably still in the water. He'd

251

be floating under the counter of the *Wahine*, saving the last of his air for the swim home. Nino's done this sort of thing before, remember."

She nodded and said softly, "Renn, I wish it were all over."

"It will be, sweetheart," I told her gravely. "It'll all be over before sunset."

I stuffed the remaining clips of ammunition into my pocket, gave her the small parcel of food, then picked up the rifle and bent down for the water bag that held the last of the *Doña Lucia*'s treasure. When Pat saw it, she looked at me oddly but said nothing. I answered her unspoken question.

"Yes, sweetheart, I'm taking it. I'm taking it because we fought for it and we've won it. I'm taking it because there are debts to pay and a house and a life to build for both of us."

She shivered a little and said, "There's blood on it, Renn."

"Yes, there is blood on it, sweetheart. There's blood on the island, too. There's blood on the decks of the *Wahine*. There's blood on every acre and every doorstep where men have come, first in peace, and then have fought against those who have come, in violence, to destroy their peace. Do you understand?"

"Give me time, Renn," she pleaded quietly. "Give me time and a little love. Then I will understand."

We walked down the goat path where the body of Manny Mannix lay festering in the sun. We stepped over it and, without a backward glance, turned downwards through the trees.

When we came to the last fringe of bush before the camp we dropped to the ground and pushed aside the leaves, looking out across the water towards the black lugger. One of the boats was already inboard. Two men were lashing it to its place on the deck. The other was just being hauled up.

They were going away.

For long minutes we lay there, hardly daring to hope.

Then we saw the anchor pulled up and we heard the engines start. Slowly the black lugger nosed out towards the channel. We stood up and walked into the camp.

Nino Ferrari was lying on the warm sand, smoking a cigarette.

"I thought you would come," he said blandly.

The sublime effrontery of the man took my breath away.

"What the devil . . ."

He waved a slim brown hand.

"I made better time than I hoped. I fixed the charges, then I swam over to the *Wahine* for a breather. I heard one shot, then when I saw them running like cattle onto the beach, I guessed what had happened."

"I killed Manny Mannix."

"I know. I waited until they rowed out to the lugger. Then, while they were busy explaining what heroes they had been, I swam back to shore. I was tired. I needed a rest."

Then I showed him the water bag with the gold coins and the dagger.

He whistled softly.

"Where?"

"In the cave, behind the cleft. Pat found them . . . with two skeletons. They had killed each other."

"They always do in the end," said Nino flatly.

Then I saw that there was no laughter in his eyes. His face was grey. He looked tired and rather old. In the same flat voice he answered the question I dared not put to him.

"Very soon now."

He heaved himself up from the sand and the three of us walked down to the water's edge.

The tide was running in strongly, and the black lugger was butting her way out through the channel. The men on her decks were looking back towards the island and pointing. The thought came to me that perhaps they intended to work the wreck again, or that, having seen us, they would put about when they had cleared the channel and return to the attack.

But they did not. The lugger thrust out of the rip and into the wide water. The man at the wheel held her firmly on a southward course until she was out of the reef current, then he turned her eastward and the westering sun threw long shadows from her spars across the water.

Then it happened.

We heard the dull boom of an explosion, then another. Great spouts of water were flung into the air. The lugger seemed to heave itself up until we saw the line of her keelson. Then she settled again with a great gushing splash, heeling over as she hit the water. We saw the bodies of men flung, like dolls, high into the air to fall back into the boiling sea. Then she rolled clean over. Her spars dipped and her hatches were covered and we saw the gaping holes that had been blown in her timbers. Then the waters closed over her, heaving and bubbling and churning, while the bodies of the crew were tossed about like corks and scraps of wreckage were flung like chips in the maelstrom.

We saw the waters subside slowly and great waves spread out and come racing towards the reef. Some of the men were clinging to pieces of wreckage; others lay in the rocking water as if dead. Two or three were striking out with pitiful slowness towards the island.

"It is not finished yet," said Nino Ferrari.

Seconds passed—long, inexorable seconds—while the three of us stood in silent horror at the water's edge. Then, one after another, the depth charges went off . . . four of them.

Again there was the leaping and spouting of water and the spilling of bodies, like drops from a fountain, back into the sea. Sand and fish and weed were vomited upwards from the ocean bed. The water spewed and bubbled like pools of volcanic mud.

There were no swimmers now, only bobbing, helpless shapes in a waste of wild water. For hours it seemed—though it could not have been more than ten minutes—we stood like stone figures, looking out on the last, horrifying act of an ancient, bloody tragedy.

Then the bubbling and the heaving subsided and the long waves spread out. The westering sun splashed gold and crimson on the open water. We saw the black fins of the sharks converging on the kill.

Pat Mitchell and I turned away and walked slowly up the beach towards the tent.

When I looked back I saw that Nino Ferrari was still standing, a lean, pitiless figure, at the water's edge. His back was straight. His head was unbowed. He shaded his eyes with his hand and stared out across the blood-red water.

His long, distorted shadow lay beside him . . . like a gallows on the sand.

Epilogue

BETWEEN THE CIRCLING ARMS of the island a house has been built. From its deep, shadowy veranda you look out across the lagoon to where the *Wahine* rides at anchor. There is a trailing of white trumpet flowers and a crimson burst of bougainvillaea.

There is a small browned smiling woman and a toddling boy who come down the coral path to the beach and wave me in from the channel, and wait for me while I drop the hook and loose the dinghy and scull home at the end of an island run.

We walk up the path, hand in hand, until we come to the small plot with its border of branched coral and its square white headstone. We stop. I pluck a scarlet hibiscus bloom and drop it in front of the stone, while the boy watches, fascinated, the familiar ritual.

The flower will wilt soon in the sun, but there will always be another and another, so long as we live on our Island of the Twin Horns. When my son is older, I will teach him the meaning of the plot and the cemetery, and the words which are cut into the headstone, . . .

In Memory
Of a Great and Courageous Gentleman
JOHNNY AKIMOTO
This Is His Island.
We, His Friends, Hold It in Trust for Him.
REQUIESCAT.

THE
CONCUBINE

Chapter One

When he woke, it was midafternoon.

The first thing he saw was the old-fashioned fan turning slowly and uselessly in the heavy air. It made no draft, only a sleepy drone as if the spindle were worn and needed oiling. Then he saw the sunlight seeping through the slats of the rattan blinds.

It was enough for a beginning.

He was in bed, in a room with a fan. It was daytime. The rest could wait until he was strong enough to cope with it. He closed his eyes again. His mouth was dry and there was a bitter, metallic taste on his tongue. His skin was clammy and strong-smelling. When he tried to move, his muscles were slack and reluctant.

He remembered that he had had the fever.

He wondered, idly, how long the attack had lasted and whether anybody had come to look after him. There must have been someone. His clothes had been stripped off and he was naked under the cotton sheets. There had been vague voices and hands mopping his forehead, holding him up while other hands held a glass to his chattering lips. Hands and voices, but never a name or a face.

Carefully, he opened his eyes and turned his head. He saw a bedside table of red carved wood, a glass jug, half full of water, and a tumbler. He eased himself into a sitting position and poured himself a drink. His hand trembled and the jug rattled against the tumbler and some of the water splashed onto the tabletop.

The drink disappointed him. It was warm and flat and the bitter taste was still in his mouth when he had finished. He put down the glass and began to take stock of the room: a long casement window shaded with bamboo blinds; white walls; a hanging cupboard, a dressing table, a writing desk, all of the same red wood; a sea-grass chair, with a cushion covered in batik; two doors, one of them carrying a framed notice.

Now he remembered the rest of it.

He was in a hotel—the Tanjil Hotel in Djakarta. He had flown in from Pakanbaru in Sumatra. The fever had hit him an hour after his arrival— a wrenching, shivering agony ending in darkness. His name was Mike McCreary. He was an oil man out of a job.

He drank another glass of water, then threw back the sheets and slid off the bed, steadying himself against the table until the first giddiness had passed. Then he walked slowly across the polished floor to the bathroom. From the shaving mirror a gaunt yellow face stared back at him: an Irish face, with bright, shrewd eyes sunk deep in their dark sockets, an inquisitive nose and a wide, thin mouth that grinned engagingly when he was happy and closed like a trap when the black mood was on him, as it was now.

For McCreary was on the beach, flat broke and busted, a long, long way from Kerry of the Kings.

He shaved unsteadily but carefully and rubbed his face with astringent. Then he turned on the shower and stood a long time under the jets, lathering and sluicing, until the fever reek was gone from his skin and he felt fresh again. Then he walked back into the bedroom and stood towelling himself, naked under the reluctant, droning fan. No sooner was he dry than the dank heat made him sweat again, and after a while he gave it up and began to dress, whistling an off-key version of "The Raftery Little Red Fox," which is a song made in Kerry by the great Raftery, himself a footloose, wandering man

There was a knock at the door. McCreary stopped whistling and called, "Come in." The door opened and Captain Nasa stepped into the room.

He was a small, compact Javanese with an oblique smile and a soft voice. He was dressed in a grey tropical suit of military cut and he wore a black fez cocked at a slight angle. He closed the door behind him and bowed stiffly.

"Good afternoon, Mr. McCreary."

McCreary said, "Good afternoon," and went on knotting his tie. Captain Nasa took out a cigarette, tapped it on his thumbnail and lit it. He grinned at McCreary through the smoke.

"You have been quite ill, my friend. How do you feel now?"

McCreary shrugged.

"I wouldn't be knowing yet. I'm just out of bed."

"You are feeling weak?"

"How else?"

Captain Nasa smiled and clicked his tongue and took another puff at his cigarette.

"You will feel better tomorrow."

"I hope so," said McCreary without conviction.

"Then I shall call for you at midday and escort you to the airport."

McCreary slewed round and faced him squarely.

"You're in a hurry to get rid of me, aren't you?"

"The extradition order has been in force for some days," said Nasa smoothly. "I am charged to execute it as soon as possible. Meantime"—he looked down at the backs of his small brown hands—"meantime, I should prefer you did not leave the hotel. It is unwise for a European to move about the city when his papers are not in order."

"I'm sure it is," said McCreary.

"Midday tomorrow then?"

"I'll be waiting for you."

"Good day, Mr. McCreary."

"The back of me hand to you, Captain!" said McCreary softly.

Nasa bowed again and went out, walking lightly, like a dancer, on the balls of his feet. McCreary waited until the door closed on him, then he cursed, fluently and foully. Nasa was a policeman, the representative of law and order—but the law worked strangely and deviously in this sprawling, gimcrack republic of three thousand islands and seventy-nine million souls. It worked better if you oiled the wheels a little. But McCreary's sole possessions were a plane ticket to Singapore, a month's salary in Indonesian rupiahs—and the luck of the Irish.

The plane ticket would lift him off one beach onto another. The rupiahs would drop 20 percent once the exchange sharks took their cut. And the luck of the Irish seemed to have run out.

McCreary put on his coat, walked down to the lounge and ordered a gin sling and a copy of the *Strait Times.* He thought it was time he started to look for a job in Singapore.

Even before he opened the paper he knew he was wasting his time. Singapore, Saigon, Bangkok, Hong Kong—entrepôt ports, hucksters' towns. There was nothing for him there.

There was nothing for him anywhere, except where the big steel skeletons reared themselves up into the sky and the rasping bits drove down through subsoil and rock into the black sands at the guts of the earth. He was an oil man, not a clerk or a merchant. He was a driller and his place was here, in the Islands, or in the Americas, or in New Guinea, or out on the fringe of the Australian desert.

But oil was a tricky business—political business. The big companies depended for their concessions on the favour of foreign governments and the expensive cooperation of local officials. They were apt to fight shy of a man who couldn't keep his fists in his pockets and his tongue between his teeth. After the business at Pakanbaru, his name would be on the blacklist, and he would have to turn to one of the smaller companies wildcatting in the marginal territories—provided he could get there.

He gave up reading the advertisements and turned to a half-page feature on the new fan dancer who had just opened a season at the Golden Dragon. But even a Eurasian fan dancer was no match for the drinks and the soggy air and the droning of the ventilators. The print danced in front of his eyes and the lush prose of the Singapore columnist made no sense at all.

Then a voice spoke to him, an English voice, but high and thin like the squeak of a bat.

"Are you McCreary?"

He looked up, startled, and saw a squat, stocky man in a tussah suit. His hair was black, his eyes were grey-green, his nose was a predatory beak and his mouth was small and red as a woman's above the square chin. His face was dead white, except where the razor stubble showed on his jawline. His hands were short and stubby and covered with thick black hair. It was hard to match him with the thin, reedy voice. McCreary looked at him a moment before he answered.

"I'm McCreary. Who are you?"

"Rubensohn. Mind if I sit down?"

"Go ahead."

He sat down and mopped his face and hands with a silk handkerchief. He took out a case of fat cigars and offered one to McCreary.

"No, thanks. I use cigarettes."

Rubensohn put the case back in his pocket. He laid his thick hands, palms down, on the table, pushed himself back in his chair and smiled at McCreary.

"I hear you're in trouble, my friend."

"You do now?" asked McCreary mildly. "What did you hear—and where?"

"You were drilling with Palmex in Pakanbaru. You beat up a Sundanese boy, who then reported you to the police. The company disclaimed all responsibility and the police took out a warrant for your extradition. You have been sick for three days. You are to leave Djakarta on the two o'clock Garuda flight tomorrow. Is that right?"

"That's part of the story."

"What's the rest of it?"

"If it's any business of yours," said McCreary in his soft Kerry brogue, "he wrecked a new bit and thirty feet of casing, through sheer bloody carelessness. He set our operations back more than a month. I'd warned him a dozen times before. This time I hit him."

"An expensive indulgence."

"So, it's my expense. Why should you worry?"

"I don't worry, Mr. McCreary. I'm interested."

"Why?"

"I'd like to offer you a job."

McCreary stared at him blankly. "I don't understand."

"Are you interested?"

"Sure I'm interested. But what sort of a job? Where?"

"Let's have a drink, shall we?" said Rubensohn in his high, piping voice.

He clapped his hands and a Malay boy in a cockscomb headdress and a batik sarong hurried over to take the order. While they waited for the drinks, McCreary smoked a cigarette and Rubensohn watched him with ironic amusement.

Abruptly he asked: "How old are you, McCreary?"

"Thirty-eight."

"Married?"

"No."

"Any vices?"

"The usual ones."

"And an uncertain temper?"

"I don't get on with fools. I don't like careless work."

Rubensohn nodded agreement.

"Put that on the credit side. Now tell me, what's your ambition?"

McCreary grinned at him through the drift of cigarette smoke.

"Now, that's the damnedest question I've ever had put to me."

"Haven't you any ambition?"

"Sure I have, but I doubt you'd understand it if I told you."

"Try me."

McCreary's eyes clouded. With a sudden gesture he stubbed out his cigarette and leaned forward across the table.

"I don't know who you are, Rubensohn, or what you want. I don't know, and I don't much care whether you'll like the answer I give. But here it is. I'm a damn-fool Irishman with itchy feet and his home on his back. My only real talent is plugging holes in the ground to get oil. My only real ambition is to make enough money to buy me a nice little stud farm twenty miles from Dublin and see if I can breed the winner of the Grand National. Now, if you want to laugh, go ahead!"

"I'm not laughing," said Rubensohn. "So you're interested in money?"

McCreary shrugged and said, "Who isn't?"

Then the boy came back with the drinks. Rubensohn paid him and waited till he was out of earshot. He raised his glass.

"Good luck, McCreary!"

"*Slainte!*"

Rubensohn sipped his drink and wiped his red lips. He said, deliberately, "Money is the least important thing in the world."

"When you have it," said McCreary flatly.

"Exactly. When you have it, you know what it really is: a bundle of soiled paper, a handful of base metal, a grubby token of something far more important—credit. Myself, for instance"—he tapped his barrel chest—"I never carry more money than is necessary for the expenses of the moment. Yet I have credit everywhere . . . Hong Kong, Djakarta, New York, Paris, London."

"Lucky fellow!" said McCreary dryly.

Rubensohn ignored the interruption and went on: "With that credit, I can do business all over the world—as, in fact, I do. I can make fifty thousand pounds by lifting a telephone. I can speculate on rubber in Singapore and pepper in the Celebes. I can send Palmex shares down three points in an afternoon. And I can send your shares rocketing in the same way."

"I don't own any shares," said McCreary.

"You can," said Rubensohn in his reedy, incongruous voice, "if you accept the job."

"What is it?"

Rubensohn smiled and shook his head.

"Not here, McCreary. People talk. Other people listen. The best business is private. Look, you are, on your own showing, a man with itchy feet, who carries his home on his back. I offer you three thousand American dollars to make a trip with me to look at the job. If you don't like it, you pull out with a profit. If you want it, you keep your money and make more—lots more. What do you say?"

"Where do we go?"

"A long way from here. Out to the Celebes."

"That's still part of the Indonesian Republic. I'm under an extradition order. The police have impounded my passport. I can't get it back till I'm on the plane tomorrow."

Rubensohn smiled gently and fished in his breast pocket. He took out a small book with the symbol of the Republic of Eire on the cover and laid it on the table between them. McCreary goggled at it.

"That's my passport! How the hell did you . . . ?"

Rubensohn waved a deprecating hand.

"Credit, my dear fellow! It is useful at all levels. Captain Nasa understands that. He is much less interested in you than in a sudden increase in his bank account. He is prepared to agree to another form of transport for you, and not ask too many questions about your destination."

"And so?"

"If you agree, you will sail with me on the midnight tide."

McCreary stared at him with puzzled, brooding eyes. He shook his head.

"I don't get it, Rubensohn. I don't understand a single damn word of it. You're a businessman. You want profit. You don't give charity. Why me? I'm a driller, out of a job. How can you hope to make a profit on me?"

"At this moment," said Rubensohn slowly, "I need a man to handle certain business for me in the eastern part of the Republic. I need him urgently. I had a man lined up in Singapore. Now he can't come. You are available and I am prepared to gamble on you. The only question is: Are you prepared to gamble on me?"

"For three thousand American dollars?"

"And the prospect of much more."

McCreary looked at him a moment, then his lean face broke into a lopsided grin.

"One of us is a damn fool, Rubensohn. I've got the feeling it's me."

"Why not call it the luck of the Irish?"

McCreary shrugged and held out his hand.

"Why not indeed? All right, Rubensohn, you've got yourself a man."

Rubensohn's handclasp was slack and flabby, but his grey-green eyes were sharp with interest. He said curtly, "Good. We'll call it settled. Now, let's go to my room and talk business."

They stood up.

McCreary, moved by an odd Celtic quirk, looked at his watch. It was four-

264

thirty. The date was the tenth of July. If there were omens in that, he had no wit to read them. And there were no prophets on hand to cry *"Cave"* to the voyager. He walked out of the room side by side with Rubensohn.

Rubensohn's room was a large, cool chamber furnished with carved teak. French windows opened onto a latticed balcony and the walls were hung with canvases by Javanese artists—misty mountain peaks, paddy fields bright with the passage of people, long beaches, gold between the hills and the iridescent sea.

But the pictures were pale and lifeless beside the girl.

She was small, high-breasted, perfect as a wax doll. Her hair was jet black. Her skin had the warm honey colour of the *métis*—the exotic bloom that flowers out of the grafting of East and West. Her body was sheathed in a dress of jade-green brocade, high to the neck. There were jewels on her fingers— diamonds and a blood-red ruby. Her feet were bare in high-heeled, open-work sandals made by a Chinese craftsman.

When they came in, she was preening herself at the mirror. She turned and looked at them curiously but said nothing. McCreary grinned at her, but there was no flicker of interest in her dark eyes. Rubensohn made a perfunctory introduction.

"This is Lisette. Lisette—a new colleague, McCreary. He will be travelling with us."

"A pleasure, ma'am," said McCreary with a flourish.

The girl said nothing. Rubensohn smiled thinly. McCreary felt faintly ridiculous.

Rubensohn jerked his thumb towards the French windows.

"Outside, Lisette. Wait for us."

The girl shrugged and turned away from the mirror. She walked to the French windows and opened them. McCreary saw a chaise longue set under the trailing greenery of the lattice. The girl went out, closing the door behind her.

"She's beautiful," said McCreary.

"She's mine," said Rubensohn, without emphasis. "I like decorative women."

"You're lucky to be able to afford 'em."

Rubensohn shrugged indifferently and walked across to a cabinet, unlocked the drawer and took out a small pigskin briefcase. He opened it and took out a long tube of transparent paper, which he spread carefully on the top of the table.

"Take a look at this, McCreary."

McCreary bent over the drawing. He whistled soundlessly. It was a survey chart made by a famous American company of geological surveyors. The signature was that of their best man. Both were familiar to McCreary. Rubensohn watched him shrewdly.

"Can you read it?"

"Sure, I can read it."

"What is it?"

"An oil survey."

"What does it tell you?"

"If it's genuine . . ."

"It's genuine. It cost me twenty thousand dollars."

"Cheap at the price," said McCreary. "I smell oil. Lots of it."

Rubensohn's stubby finger thrust at a point on the map.

"How long would it take you to bring in a well there?"

"Hold it a minute, Rubensohn!" McCreary straightened up and faced him. "Let's get a few things clear. A survey's one thing. To bring in a well is something else entirely."

"How so?"

"A surveyor," said McCreary easily, "is a man, not a mole. He lives on top of the ground. He can't see underneath it. Given science and skill, he can tell you a lot about earth and rock formations. He can plot you, as this fellow's done, a promising anticline, where by rights there should be oil. But he can't tell you whether the oil's there or not. There's a gamble—a financier's gamble, a driller's gamble."

Rubensohn nodded. The answer seemed to please him. He put another question.

"I'm prepared to take the gamble. But I'd still like an answer to my question. Suppose there is oil on the anticline. At the depth shown on this survey, how long would you take to bring it in?"

McCreary considered the question.

"Is the ground cleared?"

"Yes."

"What's your equipment like?"

"The best."

"Then I'd say anything from a week to a fortnight to get the rigs up and spud in. Then another month. If this fellow's right, we strike the sand anywhere between a thousand and fifteen hundred feet. Give us six weeks in all and we should have the answer for you—good or bad."

"Good!" The word came out in a long exhalation of relief.

McCreary looked at him sharply.

"Understand it, Rubensohn! I can't make promises. I can't provide against human error and acts of God."

"I don't expect you to do that. What sort of labour force do you need?"

"An engineer first—a man who can keep my plant in order and do tool dressing and machine-shop repairs. The rest I can handle with local labour, provided I have a free hand."

"I've got an engineer. Where we are going you'll have the labour—and the free hand."

"Where are we going?"

Rubensohn smiled and shook his head.

"Sealed orders, McCreary, until we're three days clear of Djakarta."

McCreary made a small gesture of indifference.

"It's all one to me, Rubensohn. You pay the piper. You name the song. But there's one thing."

"Yes?"

"Once we start work, I'm in command. I know my job and I don't like interference. Is that clear?"

"Perfectly."

Rubensohn rolled up the chart, put it back in the briefcase and locked them once more in the cabinet. He turned back to McCreary. His eyes were bright with satisfaction and his red mouth was smiling blandly.

"I like you, McCreary. I think we should go a long way together."

McCreary thrust his hands into his pockets and leaned back against the table. He said softly, "Before we go anywhere, Rubensohn . . ."

"Yes?"

"I'd like to know how much I'm getting paid, apart from the retainer."

Without a moment's hesitation Rubensohn laid down the terms.

"Three thousand dollars retainer, three hundred a week during the drilling period, a bonus of ten thousand if you bring me in a well, or the equivalent in shares in any company we form. All expenses paid during your employment and a free passage to any port in the world at the end of it. Unless, of course, you decide you'd like to continue working for me. How does that sound?"

"Fine," said McCreary coolly.

"Do you want it in writing?"

McCreary shook his head. "I'll take your word for it."

Rubensohn looked at him oddly and frowned.

"Never take any man's word about money, McCreary."

McCreary stuck a cigarette in the corner of his mouth. He grinned at Rubensohn through the first spirals of smoke.

"If a man's word is no good, his signature's no good either. But, if you want to write me a contract, do it by all means. The girl can witness it."

"I'd prefer it that way," said Rubensohn evenly. "Call her in, McCreary, and have her fix us a drink. And, McCreary . . . ?" Halfway to the French windows McCreary turned back. Rubensohn was smiling at him, but his eyes were as hard as pebbles. "Lisette is mine. Remember that, won't you?"

"With all that money," said McCreary gently, "why should you worry?"

He threw open the casement and stood looking down at the girl. She was like a bird, he thought, a bright gold-green bird under the trailing vines.

Chapter Two

AT EIGHT O'CLOCK THE SAME EVENING, McCreary packed his canvas bag, paid his bill at the desk and walked out into the warm darkness.

The stars hung low in a velvet sky and the lights of the city were spread below him—ten miles of them, bright round the new city, intermittent in the bungalow district, where the homes of rich Chinese retreated behind the lush greenery, yellow and flaring in the kampongs, sparse and winking in the fish traps beyond the harbour of Tanjung Periuk.

He could smell the city, too, even here, on the high ground far from the fever flats and the canals of the old town where the brown people swarmed and chaffered and poured their refuse into the sluggish canals. It was a strange, exotic smell compounded of spices and rotting vegetation and drying fish and swamp water and the exhalation of two million bodies sweating in the languid air. It crept into the nostrils and cloyed the palate and clung to the clothes. You could never shake it off. And, when you went away, it remained a disturbing memory, calling you back.

McCreary put down his bag and stood a moment against the bole of a big banyan tree to light a cigarette. Before he had doused the flame of his lighter, three betjaks pedalled up to him ringing their bells furiously. The drivers leapt out and began tugging at his sleeves, crying in parrot-like Malay about the speed and cleanliness of their vehicles. McCreary grinned and shoved them away and hefted his bag onto the seat of the first arrival. The driver laughed and mocked his rivals with a dirty word and a dirtier gesture, and the next minute they were racing down the road with plumes tossing and bells ringing and the air humming in the rubber bands stretched under the seat.

In the new town the traffic was light and McCreary leaned back in his seat and let the wind blow in his face. The driver's skinny legs threshed up and down on the pedals, and he sang and shouted and chuckled and rang his bell at every intersection and every passing car.

They were an odd people, thought McCreary, odd like the Irish. They were simple, courteous, lovers of colour and music. They walked like ballet dancers and talked like poets. But there was always the little yeast of madness fermenting under their brown skulls, and they were as apt as the Irish to run crazy with liquor or love or the simplest frustrations of living. "Amok, ' they called it—and when a man went amok with a hatchet or a swinging kris, he was killed quickly in a dark corner or in a police cell, because there was no hope for him anymore.

When they came to the old town, their progress was checked.

The houses of the old Dutch colonists were set back among the trees, but now four Javanese families slept in every room and their gardens were cluttered with atap huts from which the life spilled out onto the narrow streets—scuffling children, the spread baskets of the vendors, pecking chickens and peddlers with their baskets of bean curd and cooked rice and dried fish and pungent spices.

Rolls of batik were spread under matting shelters. A wood-carver squatted among his carved birds and his tiny, high-breasted girls. From an open doorway came the tinkle of gamelan music, and inside McCreary could see the grotesque puppets of a shadow show above the heads of the squatting audience.

The driver swerved and pounded his bell and kicked out at the skittering children, and ten minutes later they broke into the clear space round the harbour of Tanjung Periuk. McCreary paid off the betjak and walked down to the quayside to stand looking out across the oily water of the basin.

Here were the ships of all the world: tankers from Balikpapan, rusty coasters from the China Sea, a big white Italian with her ports ablaze, homing from Sydney with the summer tourists, high-tailed junks with winking eyes on their forepeaks, a rakish merchantman from Yokohama, and the small, trim packets of the new Republican fleet, with the Garuda bird spread-eagled over their nameplates.

There was the splay of lights and the rattle of hawsers and the cough of the big dredge chewing up silt from the channel. There was the flurry of a police launch and the slow homing of a fisherman's prau and the bump of lighters against the plates of a new arrival.

Then he saw what he was looking for.

She was moored at one of the oiling berths, two hundred yards away on the eastern curve of the harbour—a long white hull with the lines of a corvette, which she probably was. She was lit from stem to stern, and he could see the hurrying figures of the Malays tending the black hoses that ran into her fuel bunkers.

He read the name on her bows—*Corsair*, Panama. He picked up his bag and walked swiftly along the quay.

A Malay serang waved him up the gangway and, when he reached the top, a young deck officer saluted him smartly and inquired his business in passable English.

"I'm McCreary."

"You are expected, sir. I understand you sail with us. Arturo Caracciolo, Second Officer."

"Happy to know you, Arturo. Where's Mr. Rubensohn?"

"In the saloon, sir. He is waiting dinner for you."

"Kind of him. Where do I go?"

"This way, sir."

He picked up McCreary's bag and led him down the companionway. McCreary noticed that the bulkheads were freshly painted and that the passage was floored with new rubber. Arturo threw open the door of a cabin and stood aside to let him enter. McCreary whistled with surprise. The cabin was as large as a stateroom. There was a bed and a writing desk and an easy chair clamped to the floor. There were bright Italian watercolours on the wall and a modern spread on the bed and drapes at the portholes. There was a small shower recess and a spacious hanging cupboard.

"Well now!" said McCreary softly. "It promises to be a pleasant trip."

Arturo smiled with boyish satisfaction.

"She was built in England, sir, and converted in Genoa. We are very proud of her."

McCreary looked at him. A nice lad. Fresh out of officers' school by the look of him. He asked, innocently, "Who is 'we'?"

"The personnel, sir. Dutch captain. Italian officers."

"And the crew?"

"Malay deckhands. Lascars in the engine room. Chinese in the galley."

McCreary nodded. He thought Rubensohn was a shrewd fellow with an eye to detail. Divide and rule. There was small room for trouble with a crew like that. He tossed his bag on the bed and went into the recess to straighten himself for dinner. Then Arturo led him to the saloon and announced him with a flourish.

"Captain Janzoon, Mr. Rubensohn. . . . Mr. McCreary."

They stood to welcome him—a blond giant of a man with a cropped skull and a spade beard, Rubensohn himself and the girl.

Rubensohn greeted him with studied warmth. The girl gave him a distant nod. Captain Janzoon crushed his hand in a fist as big as a ham, slapped his shoulder and chuckled in his thick, asthmatic English.

"McCreary, eh? The wild Irish. That makes us a League of Nations. Dutch, Italian, English and a beautiful woman who is . . ."

Rubensohn's thin voice cut across the monologue. "A drink for McCreary, Captain."

Janzoon flushed but said nothing. He poured two fingers of whisky into a glass and handed it to McCreary, who tempered it carefully with water and toasted them. Janzoon and Rubensohn drank with him. The girl smoked a brown cigarette in a long holder with a gold mouthpiece and a jade tip.

Then Rubensohn put down his glass and said brusquely, "Something to remember, McCreary."

"Yes?"

"The four of us here are the only persons concerned in this . . . this enterprise. The rest are employed to run the ship and mind their own business. Is that clear?"

"Clear as me own conscience," said McCreary. "Anything else?"

"For the present, no. Do you like my ship?"

"I like it fine, the little I've seen of it. I think I'm going to enjoy myself."

"Twenty knots," said Janzoon in his thick voice. "Three thousand sea miles in her tanks. You should see my bridge. The latest! The best!"

"I always buy the best," said Rubensohn.

"We're fortunate in our boss"—McCreary grinned—"all of us."

For the first time a flicker of interest showed in Lisette's dark eyes, but McCreary did not see it. At that moment a Chinese steward came in. Janzoon spoke to him in Cantonese. When he went out, they heard him beating his little brass gong up and down the companionways and along the open deck.

Rubensohn looked at his watch and said briskly, "Dinner in fifteen minutes, gentlemen. Excuse us. Come, Lisette!"

He turned away and walked out of the saloon. The girl followed him without a word, without a glance at McCreary or Janzoon. They watched her go with speculative eyes. If there was coquetry in her walk, they did not see it. She was beautiful and cold as a wax doll.

McCreary and Janzoon looked at each other. McCreary grinned and Janzoon gave his throaty chuckle.

"What do you think of her, eh, McCreary?"

"I mustn't," said McCreary. "The stewards have warned me off the course."

Janzoon gave him a quick, shrewd glance from under his bushy brows.

"Wise fellow. We should get to know each other, you and I. I think we could be good friends."

"I'm sure we could."

Janzoon splashed more whisky into their glasses. He handed the drink to McCreary and asked casually, "Have you known Rubensohn long?"

"Four—five hours. Why?"

"He speaks highly of you."

"Nice of him."

"What do you know about him?"

"Not a thing that he hasn't told me himself."

Janzoon tossed off his drink at a gulp and wiped his lips with the back of his hand. He said bluntly, "You've got a lot to learn, my friend."

McCreary smiled comfortably and said in his gentle brogue, "I learn easily. Especially when I'm paid for it."

"He's a big man," said Janzoon deliberately. "He knows what he wants and goes after it. He has great wealth. His name opens doors in Rome and Paris and Geneva and New York. This ship—he bought her from the wreckers for thirty thousand pounds and spent another fifty thousand to make her what she is today. He thinks big. He does not stint money on a project. He pays well for good service."

"What's his real business?" asked McCreary cautiously.

Janzoon shrugged.

"A man like that is interested in anything that makes profit, anywhere in the world. Today it is oil. Tomorrow it may be guns or gold or cotton. He plays the market. He floats a new company here, buys an old one there. He has the golden touch."

"Have you been with him long?"

"Ever since the *Corsair* was commissioned, three years ago. Before that I ran tankers for Bataafsche Petroleum. This is the best berth I've ever had. Good pay and better pickings."

McCreary eyed him quizzically.

"Some of the gold rubs off, eh?"

"Sometimes."

"It's a promising thought."

"For the right man," said Janzoon softly, "more than promising: a certainty."

McCreary grinned and buried his nose in his drink. Janzoon was fishing for something, but he was damned if he'd rise to the lure. A man can feel the hooks in his mouth once too often. He'd do his job, collect his money and head for home, and to hell with this blond buccaneer with the big bell laugh and the cold, calculating eyes.

Then it occurred to him that he hadn't a home, only the vague dream of a grey stone house and a spread of green pastures where the stallions kicked up their heels, while himself in hacking jacket and wide breeches walked like a proper horse-breeding man and talked softly with the trainer and the strappers.

The humour of it took him by surprise and he laughed suddenly and gagged on his whisky, while Janzoon looked at him with puzzled hostility.

"I have said something amusing, yes?"

"Nothing! Nothing at all," said McCreary, as he mopped his mouth and his shirtfront. "A small private joke, with no malice in it."

Janzoon shook his head and clucked his disapproval.

"A thing to remember, my friend. Mr. Rubensohn doesn't appreciate jokes, especially jokes he doesn't understand."

"Then I'm sorry for the fellow," said McCreary. "It's a sad life that has no laughter in it."

"A better life than yours or mine," said Janzoon sourly, "with money and a woman like that, and the power to break a dozen men in as many minutes."

"If he doesn't enjoy it, what's the point?" McCreary shrugged and stuck a cigarette in the corner of his mouth.

Janzoon leaned forward with a lighter. He was still puzzled, but there was admiration in his eyes, a reluctant respect for this lean fellow with the lopsided grin. He said soberly:

"I like a man who can laugh at someone bigger than himself. But take a word of advice. Never laugh at Rubensohn. Never cross him in front of his woman. He's a big man, sure, but he has to feel big all the time. You watch him at dinner. Watch him any time where there is company. He must have the spotlight, the center of the stage."

McCreary shrugged and drew on his cigarette.

"So far as I'm concerned, he's welcome to it. But thanks for the advice."

Janzoon made an expansive gesture of deprecation.

"Don't thank me, McCreary. I only try to help. Like I told you, I think we should be friends—good friends. Now let's go to dinner. That's another thing to remember. Rubensohn likes punctuality."

McCreary looked round in puzzlement. The table was laid in the saloon and a Chinese steward was standing in the doorway that led to the galley.

"I thought we were dining here."

"Oh, no, my friend!" Janzoon chuckled again and steered him out the opposite door. "That is for the officers. We—we are the guests of the great man. We dine in his suite, with the beautiful Lisette for company."

"Who is she?"

The question was out before he knew it, and Janzoon gave him a swift, sidelong glance that belied his indifferent answer.

"Lisette? A *métis* from Saigon, by her skin and her accent. But whether she comes from the palace or the gutter, who knows? What she is now, Rubensohn has made her. She is his product and his property."

"So he told me," said McCreary softly. "I wonder if the girl thinks the same way."

Janzoon stopped dead in his tracks. He caught McCreary's arm and swung him round, hard against the steel bulkhead. His spade beard thrust forward into McCreary's face. His voice was an angry whisper.

"Listen to me, Irishman! There are ten million beautiful women from Djakarta to Dili. All of them you can have with my blessing. But this one you don't touch. She belongs to the big man. She keeps him happy. So long as he's happy, we all stay comfortable and get rich. Make so much as a smile at her and you have two knives at your throat—his and mine! Understand?"

McCreary's smile was as bland as a babe's, his brogue as soft as butter.

"Sure, I understand. But why should I give a tinker's damn for a cold one like that? I'm a warm-hearted fellow myself and I like a smile and maybe a gentle word or two at bedtime."

"So long as you understand," Janzoon grunted sourly, and slackened his grip on McCreary's arm.

McCreary faced him squarely. His mouth was still puckered in that lopsided grin, but his eyes were bright with anger. He said bleakly, "A word in your own ear, Captain."

"Yes?"

273

"Keep your hands in your pockets in future. The next time you touch me like that I'll break your bloody neck!"

Janzoon's mouth dropped open with the shock of it, then without a word, he turned on his heel and led the way to Rubensohn's stateroom.

When they entered, they saw Lisette sitting languidly on a settee under a flaring nude by d'Arezzo. Her small, perfect body was sheathed in cloth of silver and her ornaments were of jade and emerald. She was smoking a cigarette and flipping idly through the pages of a French fashion magazine. She looked up when they entered, murmured a greeting and then turned back to her magazine.

We might be the milkmen, thought McCreary sourly, or the garbage collectors or the men to mend the drains. But give me half an hour under the stars and I'll teach you different, dark one.

Then he remembered the warnings he had had and he turned his attention to Rubensohn.

He was dressed meticulously as if it were the Captain's Dinner on the Pacific run, yet the first impression was of a squat frog compressed into the trappings of a gentleman. His face was whiter still, now that it had been shaved and pomaded, and the small mouth was cherry red under the jutting nose. He greeted them briskly.

"Sit down, gentlemen. We have a few minutes before our next guest arrives. I have things to say to you before he comes."

Janzoon looked up in surprise. It was clear that he, at least, was expecting no more visitors before sailing time.

He said sharply, "No more trouble, I hope."

Rubensohn looked at him with cool contempt.

"Trouble, Captain? Why should there be trouble? We sail at midnight. Our papers are cleared, our pilot is booked. Unless, of course, there is something you have forgotten?"

"No, no! Nothing! An unfortunate remark. Please forget it."

Janzoon blushed and mopped his face with his handkerchief.

Rubensohn smiled grimly at his discomfort. Then he said, "Our next guest is a friend of Mr. McCreary."

"The devil he is! What's his name?"

"Captain Nasa."

McCreary almost leapt from his chair.

"Nasa! Now look, Rubensohn, if this is some sort of a joke . . ."

"No joke at all, I assure you, Mr. McCreary." Rubensohn waved a deprecating hand. "A simple business transaction. Captain Nasa comes to be paid for services rendered."

"It's your ship, of course," said McCreary, without enthusiasm. "If it was mine, I'd not have that little bastard within a mile of it. I'd pay him his money in a dark corner and give him a kick in the teeth for good measure."

"And then have your own teeth kicked out in a Djakarta jail?" Rubensohn smiled contemptuously. "Believe me, McCreary, my methods pay better."

McCreary grinned easily and spread his hands in defeat.

"Oh, I believe you. You've got the money to prove it."

"Good!" said Rubensohn briskly. "Now we get down to business. Captain Nasa comes to be paid. Unfortunately . . . ." He looked down at the backs of his short, hairy hands. ". . . Unfortunately, he now demands more money than we agreed. More money than I am prepared to pay. So I must talk to him privately. We will make a leisurely meal. Then, after the coffee, you, Captain, will have your business on the bridge. You, McCreary, will take Lisette and entertain her a little, in the saloon on the deck. When I have finished my business with Captain Nasa, I shall send for you. Is that clear?"

"It sounds like a pleasant evening," said McCreary.

"Let's hope so, for your sake," said Rubensohn dryly.

McCreary looked up sharply.

"And what does that mean?"

Rubensohn shrugged and smiled humourlessly.

"Unless I can come to terms with Captain Nasa, you, McCreary, are on the beach again."

"Would you like me to throw him in the harbour for you?" asked Mc-Creary, with grim irony.

"Later, perhaps. For the present, you will look after Lisette and leave Captain Nasa to me."

"Like I said, it'll be a pleasure!"

He turned and made an ironic, sweeping bow to Lisette. But she did not lift her head to look at him. She was still flipping over the big shiny pages where all the women had faces like her own, cold and beautiful and dead.

Five minutes later Captain Nasa came in and they all sat down to dinner.

It was an uneasy meal. The little Javanese was cagey and suspicious, parrying the simplest questions with a sidelong smile and click of his tongue. Janzoon was clearly unhappy. He was a Dutch captain in a country where his people had once been masters but where, now, they were treated with contemptuous sufferance and sometimes with open violence. He had a hundred thousand pounds of ship under his command and he would not be happy until he had cleared the channel lights and was well away outside the territorial limit.

Lisette made no contribution at all to the conversation, and McCreary was plagued with the Celtic temptation to bait the little policeman, who sat there grinning and clucking his contempt of the Westerners who had to pay him for the simplest service.

Only Rubensohn was completely master of himself and of the situation. He led them like a chamber group through the courtesies of the meal. His thin, reedy voice flattered and cajoled and admonished and tossed topic after topic round the table, so that, out of the hostility and conflict, there came a kind of harmony, illusory and temporary, but enough to last them to the coffee and the first brandy.

Then, without emphasis, Rubensohn dismissed them.

"If you will excuse us a while, Lisette, gentlemen, Captain Nasa and I have business to discuss."

They filed out of the stateroom and closed the door behind them. Janzoon left them without a word, and McCreary and the girl walked up the companionway to the afterdeck.

The air was warm and heavy with the smell of the city and the jungle, but Lisette shivered when McCreary linked his arm in hers. As he led her over to the railing, her sandals made a small dry clatter on the steel plates of the deck. They stood together, leaning over the rail and watching the play of lights on the slack, oily water. McCreary felt the skin of her arm, silken under his touch, but there was no pulse to it, no answer to the tentative pressure of his fingers.

He said gently, "Are you cold, dark one?"

"No. I'm quite warm, thank you."

Her voice had the upward, questioning lilt of the *métis*, but there was no life there either. It was like the tinkle of the little glass bells that fluttered outside the shrines of the old gods. McCreary wondered how it would sound when she laughed and how long it was since she had been touched to passion or to tears.

He asked her again, in the soft honeyed brogue of the Kerryman, "We're to be together for a long time, it seems. Could you not give me a smile sometimes and a word to pass the hour of the day?"

"Why should it matter to you whether I smile or frown?"

"It'd make me feel better," said McCreary lightly. "More of a man, maybe, and less of footloose gypsy with no hearth to warm his toes at and no wife to warm his bed."

"I'm paid to do that for one man now. Two would be too much."

She said it simply, inconsequently, staring out across the water to the banked lights of a passing tanker.

"There's no question of payment," said McCreary with a grin. "I'm as poor as a village fiddler. So what I get I must get for love, and what I give is out of a full heart and an empty pocket. So I'm out of the market. Is that any reason why you shouldn't give me the pleasure of a smile or two? Is the world such a sad place that you can't find a damn thing to laugh about? Look now . . ."

He pointed out across the bay to where the tugs were hauling the big white Italian ship, snout first, into the channel. "There's a sight for you. You know where she's going? Singapore first and then Colombo and afterwards Naples. . . ."

"I've been to Naples." Her voice was empty of interest.

"You have now? And you stayed no doubt in a fine hotel down on the waterfront in the best suite that Rubensohn's money could buy."

"I did."

"And you had every damn waiter in the place tripping over himself to give you service, and every damn huckster trying to sell you something."

"I did."

"Where else have you been now?"

She shrugged lightly and counted off the names: "Oh, many places—New York, London, Paris, Cannes, Madrid, Vienna."

"And every one of them was like the other, wasn't it?"

"Yes."

"Then, don't you see, dark one, you haven't lived an hour or a moment of it? You don't know what the world's about or what the taste of happiness feels like."

"Happiness?" She lingered on the word almost with scorn. "Happiness, no . . . that I do not know. But the world? I know it better than you, McCreary, much, much better."

"And how would you make that out, dark one? When I've wandered the world since I was sixteen years of age?"

"I didn't have to wander. The world came to me."

"Why shouldn't it? And you with all that dark and secret beauty."

She did not bridle at the compliment as another woman might have done. Her hand lay slack and unresponsive in his own. She said baldly, "In the Peacock Pavilion there were no secrets. All the doors opened to a man who had money."

"Where was this?" McCreary's voice came dry and harsh.

"Saigon."

"How did you get there? Is that where Rubensohn found you?"

"Yes. I had the talent to please him, it seemed, and he is a difficult man to please. More than that, it gives him satisfaction to present me to respectable people, to have men bow over my hand and women admire my clothes and jewels, and to know all the time that I am a woman he has picked out of the gutter in Saigon."

"And you?"

"Me?" Again he heard in her voice the brittle music of the old and ugly gods. "I am content. Why should I be otherwise? There are two hundred women in the Peacock Pavilion. Here I am only one. And better paid than any of the others."

"Until Rubensohn gets tired of you."

"Could you do better for me, McCreary?" There was no anger in her voice, only a thin, cool irony.

"I might," said McCreary soberly, "if the passion took me and took you at the same time and we could go far away to make a new beginning."

Then, for the first time, he heard her laugh. But there was no joy in it for him or her.

"You're a fool, McCreary."

"That's something I've known a long time, dark one. But I like my folly better than Rubensohn's wisdom."

"Why did you join him then?"

"Because he offered me good money to do the only job I'm trained for—drill for oil."

"Is that all?"

"What else should there be?"

"You were afraid of Captain Nasa."

Now it was McCreary's turn to laugh—a gusty bellow that rang out across

277

the harbour and startled the homing fishermen and the sea birds roosted on the anchored beacons. Lisette drew away from him, startled.

"Afraid of him? Why should I be afraid of a teak-faced jack-in-office like that? The most he could do was to put me on the plane to Singapore. I was prepared for that. There was nothing to be afraid of. Then Rubensohn came along and made me an offer and told me he'd squared Nasa to allow me to be extradited on the *Corsair*. It wasn't even illegal, though I don't doubt Nasa made it sound a big concession and charged him plenty for it."

"Then why has Nasa come here tonight, if not for you?"

"Whatever the reason, dark one, and whatever Rubensohn says, he didn't come here for me."

"Why then?"

There was an odd note in her voice that puzzled him, but her eyes were blank as a doll's and her face as beautiful. He leaned back against the rail and laughed at her.

"Should you care why? Should I? It's Rubensohn's business and Rubensohn's money. So long as we get paid, who cares? One thing you can be sure of, Nasa's doing better than either of us—except me!"

Then he took her in his arms and kissed her and she beat at his breast with small, helpless hands, but he held her until the coldness melted out of her and her lips were warm to his own.

Chapter Three

A LONG TIME LATER, it seemed, they sat together on the canvas hatch cover, McCreary smoking peacefully and Lisette repairing the damage to her lips and hair.

McCreary said softly, "So, now we know."

Her face was in shadow, so that he could not see whether she smiled or frowned, but when she answered her voice was no longer brittle, but low and strained.

"So we know—what? That you are a man who warms quickly to a woman?"

"And you a woman who can warm to me?"

"That, too. But where does it lead us?"

"Wherever you want," said McCreary. "Over the side and down the gang-plank and back to the city. We can start from there."

She shook her head.

"And you with a police order against you and no money in your pocket?"

His hand reached out to her in the darkness, but she drew back from it. He challenged her brutally.

"So we stay here, me wanting you, you wanting me, me trying to keep my hands and my eyes off you, night and day, and you in another man's bed, because he's got more money than I have. Is that what you want?"

"It's not what I want, McCreary. It's what I have. I intend to keep it until someone offers me better."

"Isn't love better? Even with the risks of it?"

"Love?" The word was a tinkling mockery. "You call this love? You think you are the only man for whom I have had this feeling? You think I believe I am the only woman who has moved you? Be honest, McCreary, as I am with you."

279

"So, Rubensohn does own you after all."

"He owns what he has paid for, nothing more. Look, McCreary . . ." Her voice warmed suddenly and she laid her small hand on his. "In another time, in another place, there might have been hope for us. But not here, not with him. Don't you see? If he knew what has passed between us just now, he would do everything in his power to hurt and humiliate us—destroy us even."

"It'd take a bigger man than Rubensohn to do that," said McCreary.

"You think so? You don't know him as I do. He stops at nothing to get what he wants."

"I'm a determined man myself," said McCreary lightly.

"You're a bigger fool than you know, McCreary," she said.

And before he had time to deny it, a Chinese steward came padding round the deck to tell them that Rubensohn was ready for them.

The first thing they saw when they entered Rubensohn's suite was Captain Nasa slumped across the table, snoring noisily. There was a champagne bucket at his elbow and an overturned glass in front of him. A runnel of spilt liquor dripped from the table edge onto his lap. Rubensohn himself was standing over by the porthole, smoking one of his fat cigars.

Lisette stared at Nasa in amazement.

McCreary swore softly: "Mother of God! He's out to it! Drunk as a fiddler!"

Rubensohn smiled and waved his cigar expansively.

"A good Moslem never touches hard liquor. Nasa forgot his faith—and this is the result."

"Did you finish your business with him?" asked McCreary.

"Oh yes. Satisfaction on both sides. I brought out the champagne to seal the bargain. I might as well have saved it."

"It didn't take him long to get like this. We've only been gone half an hour."

Rubensohn looked at him sharply, but McCreary's eyes were innocent of malice.

"These fellows can never hold their liquor," said Rubensohn flatly. "Now he presents us with another problem: how to get him home."

"Simple enough," said McCreary airily. "Call a betjak, bundle him into it and tell the boy to take him to police headquarters."

"Not so simple as it looks, McCreary."

"Oh, why not?"

Rubensohn gestured impatiently.

"Because he was here, unknown to his superiors, for the purpose of negotiating a bribe. If we call a betjak to the ship, the driver will know where he came from. He will be questioned and so will we—and we are due to sail in an hour from now."

"He's in no condition to walk home." McCreary grinned.

"No, but he can be walked away from the ship, down to the market area. Then he can be bundled into a cab and sent on his way."

"True enough."

"Then," said Rubensohn fastidiously, "I suggest you hoist him up and get him out of here as quickly as possible. He has fouled the place enough already."

"Now, wait a minute!" McCreary was instantly hostile. "Why me? Why not one of your deckhands, one of the lascars?"

Rubensohn smiled at him blandly.

"Because, at this moment, they are all busy preparing to put us to sea. Because they are ignorant fellows who could not possibly explain themselves as nurses to a drunken policeman. Because you, McCreary, are in my debt and I ask this as a small favour. . . ." He chuckled and went on in his high bird's voice. "And because now, at last, you have your chance to throw him in the harbour if you want to."

McCreary looked at him a moment, debating the question. Then he said coolly, "That's four reasons you've given me, Rubensohn, and the only one that holds water is that I owe you something. For that I'll do it."

He bent over the snoring Captain Nasa and slung one arm over his shoulder, then heaved him out of the chair by main force. Nasa's full weight hung on him like a coal sack.

"Put his fez on, Rubensohn, and steady him while I get my grip. I'll need a lift up the companionway."

Rubensohn clapped the black fez on Nasa's lolling head and McCreary half walked, half dragged him to the door like an old friend roistering home from a party.

Lisette stood aside to let him pass and watched him stagger down the passageway and up the companion ladder, while Rubensohn heaved and grunted to get the pair of them safely on deck.

"Get him well away from the waterfront," said Rubensohn tersely. "If he's too much trouble, toss him in the canal."

"I've been drunk myself," said Mike McCreary. "I couldn't do that to my worst enemy. Come on, Nasa me boyo, see if you can't walk a little and take the weight off my shoulders."

And, whistling a tuneless little jig, he staggered down the gangplank, while Captain Nasa breathed thickly and noisily down his collar.

The bunkering crew were too busy uncoupling the hoses to give them more than a passing glance, and once they were clear of the *Corsair*'s berth, the dock was almost deserted. But there was always the chance of a prowling waterside patrol, so McCreary decided to dive straight into the huddle of warehouses and work his way round by a longer detour to the fringe of the market area, where the betjaks had their stands.

At first he tried to make Nasa walk with him, but the little man's legs dangled slack as a puppet's and his polished shoes scuffed in the dust as McCreary dragged him into the shadows of the loading ramps between the warehouses. More than once he had to stop and lean against a wooden wall or a concrete pylon to take a breath and ease the weight on his shoulder. All the time his eyes and ears were alert for the coming of the dock police, and he wondered what answer he would give if they questioned him.

Finally he cleared the warehouses and found himself on a narrow path fringed with jungle growth, at the end of which he could see the shape of a bamboo bridge and the gleam of canal water and a huddle of yellow lights. To judge from the smell and the distant clatter of voices and the yapping of dogs, the night market was in full swing.

He decided it would be safe to give up all pretense of walking the captain and hoist him over his shoulder—easier, too, than dragging a dead weight as he had done for the last fifteen minutes.

In the shelter of a big banyan tree he halted and let the little captain slide to the ground. He stood a moment, to take a breath and flex his muscles and loosen his tie. He realized that his clothes were sodden with sweat and clung to his body. Then he realized something else.

Nasa wasn't snoring anymore. He wasn't breathing either.

He knelt swiftly and laid his ear to the little man's chest. He could hear no heartbeat. He felt for his pulse. There was none. The hands were cold, though the air was hot and reeking. McCreary fumbled for his lighter, snapped on the flame and held it close to Nasa's face. The eyes were open and staring. The mouth was slack and a small runnel of spittle had dried against the jaw.

By all elementary tests, Captain Nasa was dead.

Swiftly McCreary went through his pockets. In the breast pocket there was a wallet. In the fob of his trousers a handful of small notes. There was a handkerchief and a packet of American cigarettes and a cheap Japanese lighter. McCreary opened the wallet and went through it quickly. Letters, a police card, a photograph of a woman and a child, five hundred rupiahs in notes—nothing more. He wiped the wallet with his handkerchief and put it carefully back in the breast pocket. Acting on a sudden impulse, he shoved the lighter and the cigarettes into his own pocket.

Then he lifted Nasa's body by the armpits and dragged it behind the bole of the banyan tree. The fez rolled off in the process. He picked it up, dusted it carefully and cocked it over the staring eyes. Then he wiped his hands on his own handkerchief, stepped out onto the path and walked swiftly back the way he had come.

When he reached the shelter of the warehouses, he stopped, propped himself in a sheltered angle and lit a cigarette: a dead man's cigarette with a dead man's lighter. His hands were trembling and the small yellow flame wavered in front of his nose. A shiver went through him. The sweat on his body felt suddenly cold, as if the fever were coming on again. He leaned back against the slats of the wall and inhaled deeply, and battled to set his thoughts in order.

"Think about it, McCreary. Think! Think! Don't stand here like a bog-trotting idiot. A man's dead. He died in your arms. You're in a mess. Up to the neck. Nasa's dead, but a man doesn't die of half a bottle of champagne. Most men don't even get drunk on it, not snoring drunk. That's one lie chalked up to Mister goddamn Rubensohn. And here's another. Nasa came to be paid off. According to Rubensohn, he was paid off. But all he had in his pockets was spending money—not enough to pay for fixing an extradition order, not half enough to pay for whatever other services Rubensohn has had from him. Other services? But what? Big enough to make Nasa think of raising the ante. Rubensohn is in oil. Oil is a tricky business. You need friends in government quarters . . .

"A policeman doesn't have friends. But he does have power—lots of power in a gimcrack republic like this one, where squeeze and graft are the order of the day. So he raised the ante. And Rubensohn killed him. Poisoned his drink, or simply crammed the stuff down his neck at gunpoint, because it's easier for a man to die unconscious than to feel a bullet tearing into his guts. The rest is crude stage management: slop champagne over his chin and down his shirt-front and keep talking till a thick-headed Irishman like McCreary takes him off your hands. If there's any trouble, McCreary's the man. McCreary's the pea under the thimble. He killed him to get his passport back. He's got a charge of violence against him from Pakanbaru. If there's no trouble, you've got McCreary, too—to bring your well in and hand you a million on a silver plate. Clever fellow, Rubensohn . . . clever, clever fellow. And like the lady said, McCreary, you're a bigger fool than you look."

The cigarette was smoked to a stub and the stub was scorching his fingers. He dropped it in the dust and ground it out with his heel. Then he lit another. His hands were steadier now and his mind was clearer. He saw plainly the choice he must make.

He could cut loose from Rubensohn, here and now. Go back to town and take the two o'clock plane to Singapore the following day, and hope the police didn't catch up with him in the meantime. But they probably would catch up with him, and when they did they'd shove him in jail and work on him, in their aimless, pitiless Asiatic fashion, with rattan canes, until they'd killed him or beaten a confession out of him. After which they'd kill him anyway.

There was no profit in that. But there might be profit in Rubensohn. If he could command himself enough to put a grin on his face and a spring to his step, and walk back to the ship to tell Rubensohn that Nasa was still snoring his way home, Rubensohn would believe him, because he would want to believe him. And then . . . ? He would do the job he was paid for. He would watch and maneuver until one day he had Rubensohn where he wanted him, looking down the gun barrel and squealing for mercy. He would take Lisette and he would take his money, and then he would remind him of Nasa and hand him the cheap little lighter for a souvenir.

He knew it was a wild hope. He had even enough humour to laugh at it. But it would give him something to plan for and work for and—what a cross-grained Celt needed most of all—somebody to fight.

Slowly and with relish he smoked the last of his cigarette. Then he straight-ened his tie and smoothed his crumpled jacket and walked briskly back to the

Corsair, whistling the march of Brian-na-Kopple, who was the greatest fighter of them all in Kerry of the Kings.

When he reached the ship, he found Rubensohn pacing the deck, with a cigar stuck in his red woman's mouth and his hands clasped behind his back in the attitude of a pensive Napoleon. McCreary fell into step beside him, and Rubensohn questioned him sharply.

"You're back quicker than I expected. Did you have any trouble with Nasa?"

"None at all." McCreary's tone was as casual as be damned. "I pushed him into a betjak and paid the driver to cart him round till he sobered up. I told him he'd get a beating if he delivered him before he was respectable."

Rubensohn spluttered over his cigar and broke into his high laughter.

"Magnificent, McCreary! Magnificent! By the time he wakes, we'll be heading out of the channel and turning our noses eastward."

"I hope we'll be a long way farther than that," said McCreary. The irony was lost on Rubensohn, who strode out faster now, head thrust forward as if butting his way towards a new conquest. He took the cigar out of his mouth and stabbed it towards the open sea.

"There are big things ahead of us, McCreary, bigger than you dream. Do you know why I am here, in this stinking backwater at the wrong end of the world? For money? I am stifled with money. From now till the day I die, I can have the best and not raise a finger to work for it. But it is not enough. A man needs more than that. He needs the challenge to himself, the urge to exercise the power that is in him. And here"—he flung out his arms in a theatrical gesture—"here in this sea of three thousand islands, is one of the few places in the world where he can still do it. The wealth of Europe was built here, by the Portuguese and the Dutch and the British. But Europe is dying now, stifled by legalism and diplomacy and the controls that men impose on themselves for an illusion of security. You know what I am, McCreary?"

"I've been trying to find a name for it," said McCreary quietly.

"Then I'll give you the name. I'm a filibuster, a privateer—the nearest thing to the old merchant princes who hired their mercenaries and primed their own guns and plied the ports of the world under their own flag. The islands here, South America perhaps, are the only places in the world where a man like me can be free to breathe and build his own empire with his own brains and guts and money. Can you understand that?"

"I think so. It's a big thought. It needs time to brood on."

Rubensohn threw back his head and laughed his high, whinnying laugh.

"You'll have time, McCreary. I will show you things that beggar the thousand and one nights of Haroun al Raschid. I will show you a prince whose rivers run with jewels, who eats from gold plate and keeps five hundred women for his own pleasure. I will show you the slave routes, where the beauty of the world is brought for sale. I will show you how to multiply money like a gambler's dream . . ."

He broke off and stood a moment as if drunk with his own eloquence. The light from the bridge above fell full on his face, and when McCreary looked at it, he saw the bright, mad eyes of a visionary and the curling, cruel mouth of a caliph. The man believed every word of what he was saying, and McCreary had more than half a conviction that he should believe it too.

Then, abruptly, the mood of exaltation passed and Rubensohn was himself again, hard-eyed, canny, the man of affairs instructing his hireling.

"Bring me in a well, McCreary. Bring it in fast and you'll never regret it. There's a full rig and a full range of spares crated down in the hold. You can start work the day after we land."

"And where will that be?"

Rubensohn chuckled contemptuously and shook his head.

"Three days out, McCreary, and I'll show you on the map."

"You don't trust your staff very far, do you?" said McCreary tartly.

Rubensohn looked at him with cold irony.

"With money or a woman, trust nobody."

"Do you expect your staff to trust you?" McCreary was nettled. He was damned if he'd be put down by this putty-faced Napoleon.

Rubensohn's answer was as chill as a knife blade.

"I don't give a damn whether they trust me or not, McCreary. I expect them to give value for value received. If they don't, I take it out on their hides—now, or ten years hence. I've got a long memory. Do I make myself clear?"

"Sure," said McCreary easily, "it's clear enough. It's just that I'm new here. I like to know the rules. I don't carry a chip on my shoulder, but I don't like to feel that other people are trying to knock one off it."

Rubensohn shrugged and turned away. The discussion was closed. The subject was trivial. He had no further interest in it. McCreary bit back his anger and stood leaning against the rail, watching the last small traffic on the dock.

He saw the bunkering crew reel in their hoses and move away. He saw the small brown figures standing by the bollards, waiting to cast off. He saw the pilot come aboard, a bustling dapper little Javanese who bore an uncanny resemblance to Captain Nasa. He saw the gangway hauled inboard and the deckhands waiting with the officer of the watch.

He felt the slow shudder as the engines started, heard the shrill note of the bos'n's whistle and the thresh of water as the screw began to turn.

Then they were nosing out, slowly, tentatively, into the channel, past the dark skeletons of the fish traps, past the bobbing lights of the praus, eastward into the moonrise, towards a nameless island in a nameless sea.

The air was heavy as incense clouds, but McCreary felt suddenly cold and naked. He thought of Captain Nasa huddled in death among the spreading roots of the banyan tree. And, when a barefoot seaman padded past him on the deck, it was as if someone were walking over his own grave.

Chapter Four

THE SKY WAS A DAZZLE OF BLUE, the sea a flat mirror, broken only by the wash of their passing. Java was far south by now, slanting downward towards the ninth parallel. To port lay a huddle of islands, blurred in the heat haze. Their names were an exotic mystery: Pulau Pulau, Kemudjan, and the high peak that heaved itself sheer from the water was called Karimunjawa. Through the glasses they could see the feathery green of the hinterland, the sliver of gold that was the beach and the tiny, bird-like shapes that were the boats of the island people.

They were thrusting eastward, dead on the sixth parallel, towards the Makassar Straits and the southern tip of the Celebes. The steady beat of the engines never faltered and their day was a bright but languid monotony. A canopy had been stretched on the afterdeck and a canvas swimming pool slung beyond it.

McCreary and Lisette spent most of the first day stretched on towels under the canopy, stripped down to swimming costumes; but Rubensohn sat in a deck chair, immaculate in silk shirt and linen slacks, as if afraid or ashamed to expose his white, slug-like skin to the sun. A Chinese steward wandered by at intervals to serve iced beer, and when young Arturo came off watch, he, too, stripped down to swimming trunks and came to join the little group under the awning.

He looked with frank admiration on the lithe, perfect body of Lisette and tried at first to woo her with Latin compliments. But, when he felt Rubensohn's cold eyes on him, he flushed and lapsed into embarrassed small talk. Lisette, herself, was cool and composed, and McCreary was conscious of her secret contempt for her boyish suitor and for Rubensohn himself.

286

Since their brief interlude of the night before, they had had no moment of privacy or contact. Even when they swam together in the pool, Rubensohn's cold eyes followed them, and when they lay under the awning, Rubensohn dominated the talk, chopping off each theme that he could not share, capping each incident with a tale of his own. The man's boorishness irritated Mc-Creary, but he learned quickly to control himself. He needed Rubensohn happy and unsuspicious. He needed Lisette, too, but he knew he would have to wait for time and secrecy.

Meantime, he set himself to open diplomatic relations with the Italian officers—young Arturo, with his bright, guileless eyes and his pride in his first post; Agnello, the horse-faced Florentine who ran the engines, a sad fellow, who wandered up on deck, with a piece of cotton waste in his hands and his overalls sodden with oil and sweat, to take the air; Guido, the stocky little Neapolitan with the flashing eyes and the dark Arab face.

Guido was the wireless officer, and McCreary took special pains with him, chuckling over his first dirty stories, capping them with one or two of his own. Guido had all the Neapolitan's love of salacious intrigue, and McCreary had an eye to the time when he might want a quiet look at the *Corsair's* wireless log.

With the first officer, Alfieri, he was less successful. Alfieri was a tall, saturnine Venetian who ran the ship with cool efficiency and kept his party manners for Rubensohn and Lisette. McCreary judged him an ambitious fellow who would make his way in the world without too much care for the faces he kicked on the climb up.

Janzoon, himself, was at pains to heal the breach between them. On the afternoon of the first day, he made a fumbling apology, then took McCreary up onto the bridge for a tourist's lecture on the equipment. Then he took him into his own cabin and poured him a double whisky and soda and talked shrewdly and probingly about an alliance.

"Now, I think, you begin to see how it goes here, eh?"

McCreary shrugged and smiled at him over his glass.

"I'm learning. A little here, a little there. You know?"

"Sure, I know," said Janzoon. "You learn that the big man goes his own way and doesn't give a curse for anyone else. You learn that he is jealous of his pride and of his girl. After that, what does he care?"

"Nothing, I'd say."

"Right!" said Janzoon in his thick, emphatic voice. "So you do what he pays for, and for the rest you make a little trade on the side, eh?"

McCreary made a rueful mouth.

"I've never been a very good trader, Janzoon. Otherwise I'd be richer than I am now. My great-grandfather was a Kerry horse coper, but the talent seems to have died before it reached me."

"Pfui!" Janzoon's ham fist waved aside the argument. "It takes no talent, only know-how. Look, I'll show you!"

He got up and opened the clothes locker behind McCreary's chair. From the top shelf he took half a dozen bundles of notes, which he flapped under McCreary's nose.

"You know what that is?"

"Money," said McCreary. "I can smell it."

"Paper!" said Janzoon, with rambunctious contempt. "Unless you know where to spend it. Indonesian rupiahs! They wouldn't buy you a glass of beer in Singapore. In London you might as well use 'em to wipe your backside. But there, in the Islands, you can buy gold with 'em and jade, if you know where to look for it, and diamonds washed down from the inland rivers. And these things you can sell for good hard dollars or Swiss francs. You see how it goes?"

"Sure," said McCreary. "But I don't see why you need a partner. And besides, I've got a short-term assignment from Rubensohn. After that I'm out."

Janzoon bent forward, dropped his voice to a confidential whisper and tapped McCreary's knee with a stubby finger.

"Why else do I tell you about the market and the opportunities here, except to show you why you should stay?"

"It depends on Rubensohn, doesn't it?"

"It depends on you," said Janzoon, with throaty emphasis. "Rubensohn needs men. He wouldn't say so himself, but he does. If he sees that you play the game his way, keep your tongue still and your hands off his girl, there is nothing you cannot come to. Believe me, McCreary!"

He heaved himself up again, and this time brought out from the cupboard a chamois bag bigger than his own fist and tipped the contents out on the table. McCreary saw a medley of stones, cut and uncut, winking in the shaft of sunlight from the porthole. Janzoon lifted them in his hand and let them sift slowly back onto the table.

"Two more bags like that, McCreary, all on the one trip. A hundred percent profit made by bazaar haggling and scalping the percentage on the money market."

"Then why share it?"

Janzoon took the question in his stride, almost, thought McCreary, as if he had been briefed for it. He said earnestly:

"Because two men can make three, four times as much as one. It's a question of time, you see. I'm a ship's captain. The time I have in port for private business is half that of an ordinary officer or seaman. With someone like you, free to move, to make the contacts, we could do big business, really big."

McCreary grinned happily and poured himself another shot of the captain's whisky.

"I like the idea, Janzoon, but I don't see how I'm going to get time for trade when I'm supposed to be drilling for oil."

"The oil is for six weeks, two months, three. Afterwards is what you must think about."

"I'll do that," said McCreary genially. "I'll think about it very carefully. And thanks for the tip."

"Nothing," said Janzoon. "I help you to help myself. Down the hatch!"

"Up the Irish!"

They drank together like a pair of conspirators and McCreary walked out into the blazing sunshine of the deck, with two new thoughts buzzing in his brain. The first was that Rubensohn was trying, through Janzoon, to buy him, lock, stock and barrel, to make him a permanent member of the club. All the flash and flurry of easy money was unnatural, out of character for both men.

The second thing, and the more important, was that the oil venture was a short-term project—six weeks, two months, three. That in itself was a matter for suspicion. Oil wasn't handled like that. Oil was big business, developing business. You brought in one well, you tried to bring in others. You set about extending your holdings and opening up new areas. You thought in terms of pipelines and storage installations, of tanker contracts and harbourage and political protection and capital issues. Oil was a lifetime business, even for the wildcatters. Yet here, the talk was of bringing in a well in a couple of months, then peddling currency and stones in the bazaar ports. None of it made sense. Or did it?

He leaned on the rail and stood a long time looking down at the hypnotic wash of foam and water against the flanks of the *Corsair*. He thought he was being paid small compliment. He was a bull-headed Irishman with the wanderlust in him and a taste for the lighter side of living and loving. But he wasn't to be bought with a few dirty notes, and he thought he could see a hole in the wall as clearly as the next man.

He thought, too, that he understood why Captain Nasa had been killed.

He tossed the stub of his cigarette over the rail and watched it whirl away in the thresh of green water and white foam.

Then he walked slowly aft to join Rubensohn and Lisette under the awning.

To his surprise he found Lisette alone. She was sitting in a striped deck chair, leafing through a magazine. Her eyes were hidden from him by modish sunglasses.

He eased himself into the chair beside her and asked quietly, "Where's Rubensohn?"

Without lifting her head from the magazine, she said flatly, "Gone to his cabin. The heat was too much for him. He said he would rest till dinnertime."

"Good. Then we can talk awhile."

"Not for long. I'm going below, too."

"Listen, dark one!" His voice was urgent and angry. "We've rehearsed this part, remember? I know the lines by heart. This is the next act . . . new scene, new time, new complications. You're in it, too, like it or not."

"I've told you before, McCreary. I'm not interested. I refuse to be involved. I've told you why."

"It's murder, sweetheart," said McCreary softly.

He might have told her the time of the day for all the reaction he got. Calmly she turned another page of the magazine and went on scanning the photographs and the captions. Her small hands were steady on the glossy paper.

She said simply, "Whatever it is, it is not my business."

"Listen, Lisette! Last night . . ."

"Last night was a wild moment best forgotten."

"You told me I was a fool and . . ."

"And now you've found out?" Her voice was tinkling with mockery. "Then please don't make me part of your folly. Now, McCreary, will you go or must I?"

"I'll go." He hoisted himself out of the chair and stood a moment looking down at her. His tone was harsh with disappointment and frustration. "You've had it rough, Lisette, and you're scared to lose the little you've salvaged. But you'll have it rougher yet, and you'll find that Rubensohn won't help at all, at all. He'll throw you to the sharks and watch them eat you. When that time comes, you'll remember what I'm telling you now. I want to help you. But I can't unless you help me too."

Then, for the first time, she took off her sunglasses and he saw that her eyes were somber and rebellious. She looked at him a long moment and shook her head slowly.

"Nobody can help you, McCreary. Nobody can help me either. We're both lost. The only difference between us is that I know it and you don't. Now for God's sake leave me in peace!"

He turned on his heel and left, cursing softly and fluently to himself. She watched him striding swiftly down the deck and scrambling up the companionway that led to the wireless cabin. Then the magazine slipped from her hands and she sat a long time, numb and staring, while the warmth drained out of her golden body and the chill crept in around her frightened heart.

Guido, the wireless operator, was lounging in his chair, waiting for the English bulletin from Singapore radio. When McCreary stuck his head into the cabin, he looked up, and his swarthy face broke into a grin of welcome.

"Come in, *amico!* Come in! *S'accomodi!* Make yourself at home. You like a drink?"

"I could use one, Guido." McCreary sat himself on the bunk, while Guido lifted the cap from a bottle of Pilsener and poured it foaming into a tooth glass. "You sure you're not busy?"

"Busy?" Guido made grand opera gestures and reached for another bottle of Pilsener. "Nothing important—the English news from Singapore. Then nothing till the weather reports at seven and the confirmation at eleven. Unless anybody wants to send a radio or make a telephone call to his girl."

"Not me," said McCreary, with conviction. "I've given up women. *Salute,* Guido!"

"You what?" Guido was so startled by the news that he forgot to answer the toast. His beer remained suspended halfway to his mouth. "Give up women? Impossible. Unnatural. I've tried. It can't be done. The only way I can save my strength is to come to sea. Even then I have to remind myself that I am still a man. Look!"

McCreary slewed round to admire the double row of bosomy film stars gummed to the bulkhead at the foot of the bunk.

"You like them?"

"At least they're less trouble that way," said McCreary ruefully.

"Less trouble, sure, but less pleasure, too. *Non è vero?*"

McCreary chuckled. After his passage at arms with Lisette, the comic lechery of the little Neapolitan was a refreshing change.

Guido cocked his head on one side and looked at him like a speculative parrot. He jerked a knowing thumb in the direction of the afterdeck.

"Talking about women, *amico*, this one we got here . . . What do you think, eh?"

"Cold," said McCreary, with flat conviction. "Cold as a fish. No profit to any man."

Guido nodded vigorously and rubbed his thumb and index finger together in the familiar Neapolitan gesture that says "money."

"That's the only thing that warms them, *amico*. That's why they're no good to fellows like you and me who like a little honest loving without having to pay for every kiss and every caress. There was a girl once in Reggio . . ."

"Maybe . . ." said McCreary hastily, "maybe we should catch the news from Singapore, eh?"

"Sure, sure! You like to listen too? We can take it on the speaker."

"I'd like that."

Guido flicked the switch, and after a few moments the voice of the news announcer faded in:

". . . and no further student demonstrations were reported. A late message from our correspondent in Djakarta states that Indonesian police authorities are seeking to interview a former oil company employee, Michael Aloysius McCreary, in connection with the murder of a senior official of the Djakarta police department. McCreary, who was due to be extradited for an act of violence in the Pakanbaru area, has disappeared. A continual watch is being maintained on airport and dock areas in case McCreary tries to leave the country. . . ."

McCreary reached over and flicked the switch and the announcer was cut off.

Guido looked at McCreary with bright, shrewd eyes. He said, "That's you they talk about, eh?"

"That's me, Guido."

"Killed a policeman, eh? Big stuff!" Half of Naples is bandit at heart, and Guido's eyes widened with admiration. "What happened, *amico*? Did he steal your girl? Did he . . . ?"

"I didn't kill him, Guido."

Guido patted him paternally on the shoulder.

"Whatever you say, *compar'*. Your business, not mine. You can trust Guido."

McCreary slewed round sharply to face him.

291

"I can? Good! Can I trust you to say nothing of this to anybody for two days?"

"Trust me? *Senz'altro!* I would swear it on the bones of my mother, if I knew who she was."

"I'll take your word for it, Guido," said McCreary, with a wry grin. "But I still didn't kill him."

He stood up and slammed one bunched fist into the palm of his other hand. He was in it now, for good and all. He'd been named to every police department in the East as the man behind the gun. Like it or not, he was a member of the Outsiders' Club. It was time he learned the rules and started playing them—hard.

Chapter Five

On the morning of the third day, Rubensohn called McCreary to his stateroom. Captain Janzoon was there with Lisette, and Rubensohn's squat figure was bending over a chart spread on the table.

They looked up when he entered, a lean, gangling figure with his crooked grin and his bright, shrewd eyes. Rubensohn greeted him warmly enough and pointed to the chart.

"The big day, McCreary. The day of revelations. Come here and look."

The three of them bent over the chart, and Rubensohn's thick finger traced the last leg of their voyage. His voice was touched with a faint triumph.

"Here is where we are now. Sulawesi to the north. Sumbawa far to the south. Ahead of us—this long island here—is Selajar, which is the gateway to the Banda Sea. Captain Janzoon tells me we shall clear the southern tip about midday today. From there . . ." His finger veered slightly northward and traced a line that bypassed the clutter of islands at the southern tip of Sulawesi and came to rest almost at the center of the Banda Sea. He ringed the area with a pencil and McCreary saw that it was a small archipelago at the center of which lay a largish island. He strained to read the tiny script of the cartographers, but Rubensohn had already given him the name: ". . . We come to our destination—the island of Karang Sharo."

"It's a long way from anywhere," said McCreary.

"An advantage I have not overlooked," said Rubensohn with cool satisfaction. "Technically, the island is Indonesian territory. For all practical purposes, it is controlled by a hereditary sultan, whose power is absolute in Karang Sharo and the surrounding islands."

"And this is where you had your survey made?"

293

"That's right."

"How did you come to know there was oil there?"

Rubensohn answered without hesitation: "For that I am indebted to Captain Janzoon here. Back in the mid-thirties, the island was listed as a promising survey area by Bataafsche Petroleum Maatshappij. But, with the war, and the later restriction of their franchise by the Indonesian Republic, nothing more was done about it. The record was filed away and forgotten. When Janzoon brought it to my attention, I made overtures to the Sultan, secured his permission for a survey, and later secured a concession, on very favourable terms, from the Government in Djakarta."

"That's the part that interests me," said McCreary mildly. "How did you swing it? I'm an oil man myself, remember, and I know how hard it is even for the big outfits to extend their concessions."

Rubensohn's red mouth twitched into an oblique smile and his eyes sharpened with interest.

"A matter of influence, McCreary. Friends at court, you know."

"Sure," said McCreary softly. "It was a damn-fool question, anyway. By the way, what's the harbour like in this place?"

Rubensohn was watching him now, guarded and suspicious.

"What makes you ask that?"

McCreary shrugged.

"I was thinking of the future: shore installations, storage tanks, harbourage for tankers. It's one thing to pump the stuff out of the ground. You've still got to get it to market. In a place like that—at the rear end of the world—it's a major development project."

Rubensohn frowned and said tersely, "That's not your worry or mine. Our job is to bring in a well."

"Then you sell out as a going concern, eh?"

"Clever fellow," said Rubensohn softly. "Very clever indeed. Looks though we picked the right man, eh, Janzoon?"

Janzoon chuckled asthmatically and slapped a big fist on McCreary's shoulder.

"First time I met him, I told you so, didn't I, Rubensohn? A good fellow, intelligent, far-sighted."

"I like to see where I'm going," said McCreary easily. "Who's the buyer, Rubensohn? Obviously you've got one, otherwise you wouldn't have gone to all this trouble."

Rubensohn wasn't smiling anymore. His mouth was a thin line. His eyes were blank and filmed over like a bird's. His thin bat's voice was edged with anger.

"That's my business, McCreary."

"No!" The word came out, sharp as a whipcrack. "It's mine, too, Rubensohn. I want to know."

Janzoon's mouth dropped open. Lisette's eyes widened with astonishment. Rubensohn and McCreary faced each other, tense and unsmiling, across the table. Finally Rubensohn spoke. He measured out the words carefully, deliberately, like chips on a gambling table.

"You're a driller, McCreary. You are paid to make holes in the ground. The control of any enterprise belongs to the shareholders and directors. If you've any other ideas, I'd like to hear them now."

"Fair enough, Rubensohn." McCreary's brogue was as creamy as Irish butter. "I'll give 'em to you. You hired me as a driller. I do the job, you lay cash on the barrelhead, no questions asked. That was fine! But you set me up for something else that you didn't tell me about. The way I read it, I need a new contract."

"I don't understand what you mean."

"Do you want it here," asked McCreary gently, "or would you rather have it in private?"

"I want it here and now."

"Good! The man who negotiated your concession in Djakarta was Captain Nasa. I don't know what documents he got you. I don't know how good they are, but I imagine they'll hold water till you get your deal signed up with the buyers and pull out. Nasa tried to hoist the price, so you poisoned him. I walked him off the ship for you and he died in my arms. I left him under a banyan tree about a mile from the dock. Last of all, my name was broadcast over Singapore radio as a probable suspect for his murder. I don't like that. I don't like looking down the barrel like a sitting duck. I think you should tear up my present contract and write me a new one."

Rubensohn's eyes never left McCreary's face. He said in a high whisper, "Get out, Lisette! Get out and stay on deck till I call for you."

She went out swiftly. McCreary held the door for her and closed it again behind her. When he turned back, he saw that Rubensohn held a gun. The barrel was a black, unwinking eye, staring at his heart. Rubensohn was smiling bleakly.

"You're looking down the barrel now, McCreary. Death is very close to you. Have you anything else to say?"

McCreary grinned crookedly. He took out a cigarette, tapped it on his thumbnail and lit it with Nasa's lighter. He blew a cloud of smoke in Rubensohn's face and murmured:

"Put it away, man, and let's get down to business. You made a mistake. Why not admit it and let's make a new start?"

"And if I don't?"

"Then you'll probably blow the back of my head off. But"—he pointed down at the chart—"you'll have a long, long way to go to find a new driller."

Janzoon mopped his face with his handkerchief and said thickly, "He's right, Rubensohn. Unless we want to upset the whole schedule, we need him. What do we lose if we talk?"

Slowly, ever so slowly, the tension relaxed. Rubensohn laid the gun down on the table and eased himself into a chair. Then Janzoon sat down and, last of all, McCreary. They leaned back, hands on the table edge, eyes downcast, each waiting for the other to make the opening gambit. It was Janzoon who spoke first. His thick voice was unsteady and embarrassed, but he got the words out in the end:

"Maybe McCreary will tell us what he wants. Then we can go from there."

"McCreary?" Rubensohn looked at him with blank, filmy eyes.

McCreary drew placidly on his cigarette for a few moments, then he told them, "The first thing I want is full information on the project, a sighting of all concession documents, a look at all correspondence and cable messages. From here on, you can take it as read that I won't work in the dark. Next, I want a share in whatever company or partnership exists at this moment to control the concession and its working."

"How much?" asked Rubensohn flatly.

"How much is Janzoon getting?"

"Twenty percent."

"I'll take thirty," said McCreary genially. "That still leaves you in control, Rubensohn."

"Anything else?"

"Yes. I'll sit in on all sales negotiations and I'll take my cut from the sale by direct payment from the purchasers."

"And how do you expect to enforce your claims?"

McCreary shrugged and spread his hands in an eloquent gesture.

"Simple enough. If you don't agree, you don't get your oil. If you welsh on me later, I'll tell the buyers a little story about a policeman who was bribed and afterwards murdered. They may not believe it at first, but they'll probably take the precaution of checking with the Ministry in Djakarta. Then they'd find you had nothing to sell." He smiled at them amiably through the smoke. "I gather you'd rather not have that happen?"

Rubensohn's red mouth curled in a grudging smile.

"It's a nice play, McCreary. But you forget one thing. You're outside the law. You're wanted for murder."

"So are you," said McCreary calmly, "though it might take a little longer to prove it."

"It's too much!" Janzoon exploded into guttural anger. "He comes in at the last with nothing more than a threat and he wants more than me—the man who . . ."

"Be quiet, Janzoon!" Rubensohn's peremptory voice cut him short. "Mc-Creary is a good negotiator. He understands that one should always ask something more than one is prepared to accept. Say twenty percent, McCreary, and you're in business."

"Say twenty-five and I'll forget the cruel damage to my reputation."

"No!" Janzoon's cropped head thrust angrily across the table.

"It's a deal," said Rubensohn. "They're my shares, Janzoon, not yours."

Janzoon relapsed into hostile silence.

"Do I get the information and the documents?"

Rubensohn nodded.

"I'll give you a briefcase full of them. You can go through them at your leisure."

"And we'll put all this in writing the way it should be?"

"Before we land on Karang Sharo, yes. Anything else?"

"No, I think that's all."

"Good," said Rubensohn briskly. "Now we can discuss what brought us here in the first place. What happens when we reach the island."

And while Rubensohn went on to discuss the coming operation, McCreary listened with only half his attention. The rest was absorbed by a curious and disturbing question: why had Rubensohn handed a fortune on a silver plate to the man who had it in his power to destroy him?

Even Janzoon didn't seem to know the answer to that one, since for the rest of the meeting he scowled into his beard and said not a single word to McCreary.

Rubensohn, on the other hand, had much to say. His exposition was crisp, concise and businesslike, and McCreary was moved to reluctant admiration for his cool appraisal and his imaginative strategy.

"First, we have our concession from the Indonesian Government. As McCreary astutely points out, this is a dubious document, prized out of a senior official on whom Captain Nasa had an embarrassing dossier. It is, however, quite genuine, although I suspect that the Ministry knows nothing of its existence and the man who issued it will be happy to forget it for a while and repudiate it when it is called in question, by which time we shall have our profit in hand and can leave the legal problems to our successors. Our immediate problem is with the Sultan of Karang Sharo. As I told you, his authority is absolute in his own territory. The folk in Djakarta couldn't control him, even if they wanted to. As it is, they have enough trouble with the rebels in Sulawesi to keep them busy for the next ten years.

"When I first visited the island, the Sultan was well-disposed. He was prepared, for a price, to give us a concession and make labour available for us to work it. Considering the value of the concession, the price is negligible and childish—jewelry, radio sets, assorted European novelties, even a small automobile, though there's hardly a road on the island where he can use it.

"The important thing is that he is a primitive despot. He must be approached with ceremony. We must come as strangers bringing tribute to the man whose title is 'Navel of the Universe.' We'll do that. We'll do it as well as we can. We'll receive him on board and we will be received by him in his palace. Then, after the palaver, we hope to get from him a document under the palace seal, granting us a concession in his own name. Then, if we're lucky, we can start work."

"How long do you expect the junketings to last?"

Rubensohn shrugged dubiously.

"A day, two days, no more. Then you can start unloading the stores and get a permanent camp working. By the way, among the documents I'll give you is a full list of equipment and supplies. You can check it when you have time. I went over it carefully with experts. I think you'll find there's all you want."

"I'm sure I will," said McCreary, and he meant it as a compliment. "So we start work and we hope to bring in a well. When does the buyer come in, and from where?"

"The buyer is Scott Morrison. Do you know him?"

McCreary whistled. Scott Morrison was a big name in the independent oil business. He was a speculator, pure and simple, tabbing the operations of the small concessionaires, ready at the right moment to move in on an outfit that was short on capital but long on promise. He'd buy in on the ground floor, stack up a flotation, hoist the market and move out again, with a three-way profit and no risk except the original gamble. And the odds on that were heavily in his favour. He had the best advice that money could buy and the best nose in the business for a good field.

McCreary chuckled and Rubensohn frowned with irritation.

"Something funny, McCreary?"

"Yes. I've just thought of it. Morrison's a filibuster, too, isn't he? He's pulled a few fast ones of his own. I'll be interested to see how you make out."

"How *we* make out," Rubensohn corrected him sharply. "We're partners now, McCreary, remember?"

"I'm not forgetting. I'm just enjoying the joke while there's still a laugh in it. Later it gets serious."

"I'm glad you realize it."

"Where's Morrison now? When does he show up?"

"Cruising," said Rubensohn, with a hint of amusement. "Tahiti, Bougainville, Nouméa, Sydney. Then he's pulling in to New Guinea to take a look at some new operations up the Fly River. We can expect him at Karang Sharo about six weeks from now. If we need him sooner, we can send a radio. He insists on a personal inspection. That's why we must have something to show him."

McCreary grinned.

"He's a wise man. If I were in his shoes, I'd do the same. Do you think he'll take your Djakarta papers at their face value?"

"Give him a smell of oil and he'd take them written on toilet paper. Besides, the mere fact that we're working openly will be proof enough of good faith. All the same"—Rubensohn's full mouth smiled with sardonic satisfaction—"I'd give a lot to see his face when the Indonesian Government orders him off the island."

"You sound as though you don't like him."

"I've done business with him before," said Rubensohn grimly. "Ten years ago, when I was battling for a stake, he turned me out of his office. I've waited a long time to settle the score, but now, I think, we may do it. It depends on you, McCreary."

"I'm glad you said that," murmured McCreary. "It makes me feel better."

Rubensohn looked at him with cool and speculative eyes. He picked up the gun from the table and held it a moment slackly in his hands, then put it back in his pocket. His tone was elaborately casual.

"You play a nice hand, McCreary. I don't grudge you the jackpot. But don't bid too high. It can be dangerous."

McCreary shrugged casually.

"I'm a modest man, Rubensohn. I'm content with a cozy game. So long as it stays that way."

But all the time the black Irish devils were chuckling inside him and he thought, If only you knew, Rubensohn, just how high I am bidding!

Chapter Six

THE NEXT TWO HOURS McCreary spent in his cabin, wading through a brief-case full of documents and correspondence which Rubensohn had dumped contemptuously in his lap. The correspondence told him little that he did not know already. Scott Morrison was interested in buying an oil project on Karang Sharo as a going concern after the first proving well had been sunk. Assurances were given that full documentation would be available, and a tentative time had been fixed for a meeting on the well site itself.

What interested McCreary first of all was the fact that none of the correspondence had been signed by Rubensohn. All of it was franked by a certain Joao da Silva, Managing Director of Southern Asia Mineral Research Limited, whose registered address was in Singapore. Rubensohn had been thoughtful enough to include a copy of the memorandum and articles of this company, which showed that it had been incorporated in Singapore twelve months previously and that its directors were John Mortimer Stavey, Wilhelm Kornelis Janzoon and Joao da Silva, each of whom held one share each of an authorized capital of £50,000 sterling.

Still no sign of Rubensohn, but that would still mean nothing. The names were token names, used by the solicitors for the formalities of incorporation. The real information would be contained in the directors' list and the register of shareholders, but of these there was no sign.

The next document was rather more rewarding—as a measure of Rubensohn's confidence, and as evidence of his need for a quick settlement. It was a bill of sale with Southeast Asia Mineral Research as the vendor and Scott Morrison Enterprises Incorporated as the purchaser. It provided for the outright sale of the Karang Sharo oil concession, together with all plant scheduled at the time of signature. Space had been left on all copies for the insertion of monetary figures, and both the document and the space for additions had been signed for the company by Joao da Silva and witnessed by Elisabeth Mary Gonzalez.

There was also a blank space for a second director's signature on the day of completion, and this, he saw with interest, would be Janzoon and not Rubensohn.

The most significant clause in the agreement was the final one: that the sale should become effective on the cabled notification that the purchaser's check had been deposited and cleared to the account of the vendor with the Chase Manhattan Bank in New York.

Once the figures had been agreed, the whole deal could be concluded on the spot and radio messages could be sent off to New York for confirmation and payment.

When that was done, Rubensohn could up anchor and head to sea, richer by several million dollars, leaving Morrison and his lawyers a ten-year battle with the intricacies of international law and the liabilities of corporate bodies registered in foreign territories. Even then, it would be the signatories who would take the rap, not Rubensohn himself. Presumably they considered themselves well paid for the risk. It was fraud on a grand scale, but the odds looked better than even that Rubensohn would get away with it.

The odds were determined, of course, by the final document—the concession granted by the Republic of Indonesia to the Singapore company. This was a fifteen-page opus in Malay, with a certified translation in English, bound in manila and stamped with the massive seal of the Republic—the symbolic Garuda bird, with seventeen feathers in its spreading wings and eight in its splay tail.

There was no doubt of the authenticity of the document itself. The real problem lay in its origins and in the signatures at the foot of it.

Any official with access to files could draw a credible contract, scrawl in the necessary signatures and append the government seal. But if he lacked the authority, the signatures and the seals were of no value to anyone but himself. The man to whom he sold it was risking his whole enterprise on a scrap of worthless paper.

Rubensohn's gamble, however, was based on two very simple pieces of psychology. The first was that he would be working openly and with the personal approval of the local ruler. Even the canniest lawyer would hardly question the legality of his position. The second was that all businessmen mistrust all governments. They resent the restrictions imposed on them by the administrators and they walk in constant fear of the tax collector and the politician. Give them a document signed, sealed and delivered, they are only too happy to lock it in their files and be rid of it.

McCreary smiled with sour admiration at Rubensohn's audacity and astute-

301

ness. The man was a filibuster all right—quite amoral, quite fearless. And like so many of his fellows, he stood even chances of ending up with a bullet in his back or with an art collection and a reputation for philanthropy.

Thinking of bullets, McCreary thought of himself and of his all-too-easy victory in Rubensohn's stateroom. He bundled the papers back into the brief-case, lit a cigarette and stretched out on the bunk to consider his own position.

He had cut himself a quarter of the birthday cake, but he had made himself a partner in a criminal enterprise. That was the first bad taste in his mouth. He was a man who had lived rough and loved, at times, unwisely, but so far at least he'd managed to keep his hands clean. Now he was in a dilemma. He wanted to take Rubensohn—take him for his shirt and his girl. But it seemed he couldn't do it without climbing down to the man's own level. There was no immediate answer to this problem, so he pushed it to the back of his mind and hoped that the future might show him some answer to it.

The next problem was less easily shelved. He had to find a way of staying alive.

Until the well was brought in, he was safe, because he was necessary. After-wards . . . ? He would be not only unnecessary but an active danger to Rubensohn and a pointless charge against the profits. He would be alone, on an island. His only link with the outside world would be Rubensohn's own ship. His only friends . . . then he remembered that he had no friends. He was as rootless as a Galway tinker with no one to care a damn whether he lived or died.

He was still chewing on that sour truth when the door of his cabin opened and Lisette came in.

She closed the door carefully and locked it. Then she came to him swiftly and stood over the bunk. Her face was ashen, her hands were trembling and her voice shook with fear and anger as she blazed at him:

"Why did you do it, McCreary? No matter what happened, no matter what you knew, why couldn't you keep it to yourself? Don't you know he'll never forgive you for what you've just done?"

McCreary took the cigarette out of his mouth and smiled.

"Matter of fact, dark one, I thought he was being rather pleasant about it. He's given me a quarter share of the business and full director status."

"Dear God in heaven!" Her eyes filled up with tears of impotent anger. "Is there no end to your follies? Don't you know yet what sort of man he is? He may fill your lap with bank notes, your pockets with diamonds, but he'll never forgive you. He'll wait and wait, and one day he'll put a knife in your ribs and twist it till you scream for mercy. But there won't be any mercy. Why didn't you listen to me? Why? Why?"

"Holy Patrick!" McCreary swore softly. "Then you do care! God help me for a bog-trotting clown! You care!"

He heaved himself up on the bed and caught her in his arms and she clung to him desperately, and he felt her body against him shaken with deep, racking sobs.

He held her close to him, his lips brushing her hair, patting and coaxing her like a child in his soft, blarneying voice.

"Come now, sweetheart! Have your cry if it helps, but let's not make an elephant out of a fat toad like Rubensohn. He's not God Almighty, with the power of life and death. There's nothing he can do to either of us, if we've got guts enough to face him."

The words were hardly out of his mouth before she thrust him away again in tearful fury.

"Don't talk like that! I tell you, you don't know him like I do. Look!" She unbuttoned the high-necked Chinese frock and slipped it back from her shoulders.

With a shock of disgust, McCreary saw that her back and her breasts were crisscrossed with thin, angry weals.

"He did that to me last night. He laughed while he did it. He told me it was to teach me that my body was for his pleasure, not for other men to gape at on the deck. Now can you see what sort of man he is? Can you?"

For a long moment McCreary looked at her with pity and tenderness. Then his belly knotted and anger rose in his throat like bile. His eyes hardened and his crooked mouth was as tight as a trap. Very gently he bent and kissed her shoulders, then he drew the frock over them and buttoned it, while all the time she watched him with puzzled, questioning eyes. Then he made her sit down on the bunk while he talked to her, softly, deliberately, in a voice she had never heard before.

"I'm going to take him, Lisette. Not now, not yet, because here, on this ship, I'm as helpless as you are. So I'll smile with him and eat with him and drink with him and let him dream of all the things he's going to do to me after I've served my uses. Then, one day, I'll take him. I'll strip him down, stitch by stitch, till there's nothing left but his yellow soul and his white slug's body. Then I'll kill him for you."

She looked at him with a kind of forlorn tenderness and shook her head.

"You can't, McCreary. Others have tried and they've all ended the same way. He wears his money and his power like an armour. He's too big to touch. He'll kill you before you can get within reach of him."

McCreary gave her a somber, lopsided smile.

"You don't understand the Irish, sweetheart. They're an old dark people, with amazing powers of survival. They saw Herod the Great die with worms in his guts and Nero sobbing for a slave to kill him and the Lord Protector of England pelted to his grave with cabbage stalks and rotten fruit. A man like Rubensohn they can eat for breakfast and still be hungry for bacon and eggs."

He lifted her to her feet and kissed her again, long and passionately, and then sent her to the bathroom to wash the tears off her face so she could greet Rubensohn when he sent for her.

When she came out, her face was the same dead mask that she had shown him the first day they met, but her eyes were warm to him and grateful.

He opened the door to see that the passage was clear, then he beckoned her out swiftly and watched her go, a small, defiant figure with stripes on her shoulders and the wounds of the world on her heart.

Her perfume still lingered in the cabin and on his clothes, but he paid no heed to it. He lay on the bed with Captain Nasa's lighter in his hands and thought about killing Rubensohn.

Soon after lunch, when all but the duty watch had retired to sleep away the worst of the heat, he climbed to the wireless cabin to talk with Guido. He found the little Neapolitan stripped to his underpants, propped on his bunk, with a glass of beer at his elbow, cigarette in his mouth and a gaudy magazine propped on his knees.

He greeted McCreary with a flashing smile and a theatrical gesture of welcome.

"Come in, *amico*. Get yourself a beer! Sit down and share my women. They're all I have now, but you're welcome to them."

McCreary grinned and swept the magazine out of his hands.

"Save it till you get ashore, Guido! I've known men go crazy with too much reading like that!"

"I don't read!" protested Guido. "I just look and dream and bite my fingers."

McCreary chuckled and eased himself into Guido's chair. He propped his feet on the bunk, lit a cigarette and looked at Guido with quizzical interest.

"Any more news from Singapore, Guido?"

"Nothing." Guido shook his head emphatically. "I take all the transmissions, but nothing more comes in. You think maybe they found the killer by now?"

"I doubt it."

McCreary blew a couple of smoke rings while he considered his next gambit. He needed desperately to trust someone, and the cocky little wireless operator seemed the most likely and the most useful bet. But, if he made a mistake, he was finished. His chances of survival were cut to nothing.

Guido watched him with bright, intelligent eyes. He said shrewdly, "You got something on your mind, *compar'*. You want to talk about it, but you're not sure you can trust Guido. That's the truth, eh?"

"That's the truth, Guido," said McCreary soberly. "If I put myself in the wrong hands, I'm a dead man."

Guido's lips pursed in a soundless whistle.

"That bad, eh?"

"That bad, Guido."

Guido swung his feet off the bunk and sat on the edge of it. He talked swiftly and quietly with eloquent Latin gestures.

"Listen to me, *amico*. I try to explain something. You know what I am—

Napoletano! You know what people say of us—that we are liars, cheats, that we would sell our own mothers for a packet of cigarettes. It isn't true. If we don't like you—*sicuro!*—we squeeze you for what profit we can make. But if you are *simpatico,* we make you a *compar'*—a pal. We share our bed with you and our pasta and our wine. We hide you from the police or from an angry husband. If there are knives against you, our knives are out, too. You understand that. To me you are *simpatico.* You don't come in here looking down your nose at a cut-off fellow who looks like an Arab. You come with a smile. You drink my beer, I smoke your cigarettes. You call me Guido. So you can trust me, eh?"

"Thanks, Guido," said McCreary warmly.

Then he told him everything from the beginning in Pakanbaru to the last hour in his cabin with Lisette. He told him what he wanted to do and how the odds were stacked against his doing it. When he had finished, Guido's face was clouded with anger and his dark eyes were somber.

"Mamma mia! Che covo di ladri! What a bunch of crooks! You are in worse trouble than I thought. Anything you want, I do, you know that."

"There's nothing you can do yet, Guido. Just keep an eye on the radio traffic and let me know what goes through. When we get to Karang Sharo, I'll be working. But I want you to keep in touch with me—and keep an eye on Lisette. I'll tell her about you when I get a chance. I only wish I had a gun."

Guido brightened immediately.

"I got a gun, *amico.* I have not used it since the war, but I always carry it, in case I meet the wrong girl in the wrong house, eh?"

He slid off the bunk and fished in a battered suitcase to come up with a stubby automatic and two clips of ammunition. The gun was carefully oiled. McCreary tested the action, shoved a shell into the breech and slipped on the safety catch. Then he put the gun into his trouser pocket. His eyes were bright with gratitude as he held out his hand to Guido.

"Thanks, Guido. I won't forget this. And when we've taken our profit from Rubensohn's hide, you get your cut, too."

Guido shrugged.

"Forget the profit. Look after yourself and the girl." His face brightened into a grin of happy lechery and he thumped McCreary on the chest. "It shows, *amico!* You can never guess. A cold one like that and suddenly she is on fire like brandy on a *bombe!"*

"You've got a dirty mind, Guido," chuckled McCreary. Then he shoved the little fellow back onto the bunk and walked out into the raw tropic sunshine. He stood awhile at the rail, watching the green hump of Selajar receding westward.

He felt better now. The odds against him had shortened a little. He had allies now—Guido and Lisette—and when he shoved his hand into his pocket, the gun lay hard and comforting against his palm.

Chapter Seven

The night before they raised the island of Karang Sharo, Rubensohn called a conference of his staff.

McCreary was there, and Lisette, with Captain Janzoon and the ship's officers—all except young Arturo who had the bridge watch. They sat in a circle on the afterdeck under a sky hung with low, soft stars. Rubensohn was in an expansive mood. He brought out champagne and cigarettes and talked with more charm and consideration than McCreary would have believed possible from so gross a man.

Then, when they were at ease with him and with one another, he plunged briskly into business.

"Tomorrow, gentlemen, we make our landfall—Karang Sharo. We expect to spend some time there, six weeks, eight possibly. In the work we shall be doing there, all of you must take a share. All of you will have certain responsibilities in maintaining good relations with the island people, and through them with their ruler. Now . . ." Rubensohn gestured emphatically with his cigar and they bent towards him attentively. "We anchor offshore, because there is no adequate wharf. We have fifty tons of supplies to unload—some of these will be transported in our own lifeboats, the rest will be taken ashore on pontoon rafts which will be ready for us on our arrival."

McCreary looked up sharply. It was the first he had heard of a Rubensohn representative on the island itself. Rubensohn caught his quick, inquiring glance and smiled obliquely.

"A question, Mr. McCreary?"

"No, no! I'm just interested." McCreary waved aside the irony. "I've been asking myself how you were going to get a couple of generators, pumping gear and two thousand feet of casing onto the beach."

"We have someone organizing that for us," said Rubensohn. "His name is Pedro Miranha. He's a half-caste Portuguese from Timor, married to a local girl. He runs a trading post of sorts on Karang Sharo. He speaks the local dialect and some English and stands well with the palace authorities. I've arranged for him to act as interpreter, negotiator and recruiter of local labour. If you, McCreary, or any of you have problems, take them up with him. Is that clear?"

There was a murmur of agreement from the little group.

Rubensohn went on, his high voice tinged with sardonic humour.

"Some of you have visited the island before. You know that the people are mixed migrant stock, from Bali and Lombok, from Sulawesi and from Ceram. The women are beautiful and the men temperamental. You know also that any—er—arrangements for your comfort are best made through Miranha, and that offenses against the family code are liable to have frightening results. For this reason all non-European personnel will be required to report back to the ship before midnight, except those who are detached for duty in McCreary's camp. No women will be allowed on board at any time. We are running a ship, not a brothel. The responsibility for the execution of this order will rest on the officer of the watch. Any breaches of it will be reported immediately to the captain."

"Does the order apply to officers as well?" It was Alfieri who asked the question in his cool, fastidious voice.

"To all officers," said Rubensohn with terse humour. "They can make whatever arrangements they like, so long as they make them ashore and see that they remain fit for duty. Talking of fitness, we have no doctor on board. There is none on the island. Malaria is endemic here, so before we land you will all be issued suppressant tablets, and both the shore party and those living aboard will use mosquito nets at night."

Watching him in the starlight, listening to his crisp, well-reasoned commands, McCreary was touched again with admiration for his genius as an administrator and a strategist. If this was the way he handled all his business, he couldn't fail to make money. If his revenge were planned with equal care, it boded ill for the man he was gunning for. . . . Rubensohn's high voice took up the thread again.

"Our first job is to get the stores ashore and a work camp set up on McCreary's drilling site. Our next is to get the derrick erected and the motor and generators installed and storehouses built. There's enough unskilled labour on the island, but for installation and maintenance, McCreary, you'll be able to call on Agnello and the engine-room staff for whatever help you want."

"The installation's the biggest part," said McCreary. "Once the stuff is running, it's only normal maintenance, barring accidents, of course."

"I hope we won't have any accidents," said Rubensohn coldly.

"So do I," said McCreary blandly. "But they do happen and it's wise to be prepared. We'll be running the motors day and night. I'll want Agnello to have a look at 'em every third day."

The horse-faced Florentine nodded.

"For the beginning, I stay ashore with you. After that I come visiting. How far is this camp from the beach?"

"Three miles," said Rubensohn.

"A damn nuisance without transport," said McCreary. "Every time I want something from the ship, I've got to send a runner."

"Maybe I can help," said Guido.

McCreary looked across at him and caught his flashing smile and the faint suggestion of a wink.

"How?" asked Rubensohn.

"I got two emergency transceiver packs. One of those we can set up on board for me or for the officer of the watch. If McCreary wants anything, he calls up the ship and we organize it. Presto!"

"Suits fine!" said McCreary with enthusiasm.

It suited better than they knew. It gave him a link with Guido, a link with Lisette, who, once he was working, would be too far away from him for comfort. It wasn't so important now, but later his life might depend on it.

Rubensohn nodded agreement and passed briskly to the next part of the agenda.

"Formalities, gentlemen. Our estimated time of arrival is ten-oh-oh hours tomorrow morning. We expect to receive the Sultan and his retinue on board at midday. All officers and crew will be mustered to receive him. Full dress for officers, clean clothing for crew. Captain Janzoon will meet the Sultan and bring him down to the saloon. Then lunch will be served on deck. That's for you, Alfieri—ten, fifteen people in addition to our personnel. Champagne for the visitors, fruit drinks for the rest." He grinned at them sardonically. "This is only the beginning. There is the night to be got through as well. I want no incidents until I've completed certain business with the Navel of the Universe. In the evening, I understand, we'll be received in the palace—officers only, but each man will choose one of the crew to attend him as personal servant. I'd like to make an impressive showing. The ship will be manned by a dock watch of one officer and skeleton crew in engine room and galley and on deck. And that's all, except for a final word from Captain Janzoon."

Janzoon coughed over his cigar and began to talk in his thick voice: "For the lady this is no concern. For the men, all of you, it is very important. I do not make jokes with you, I will tell you the truth. Until the war I lived in these parts most of my life. I know something about these people—and about their women."

He chuckled throatily and went on: "Like Mr. Rubensohn says, we don't mind what sort of entertainment you make for yourselves, so long as you don't make trouble for us. But I give you all a friendly warning. Have yourself a playmate, if you want. But do not take yourself a mistress or a lover. If you do, you find maybe when you come to go home, you can't go. You are lying on the mats in an atap hut retching your guts out because your girl has poisoned your drink or chopped up her hair and put it in your curry. There's no cure for that. You get the biggest bellyache of your life and you bleed inside and you swell up with peritonitis. And don't touch a married woman or you get another sort of bellyache when her husband cuts you up with his kris."

Guido's voice piped up forlornly, "A man should stay with his picture books."

Janzoon smiled grimly.

"He should, my friend, but he won't. So I give you a friendly warning, eh? Sometime, later, I've got to sail this ship. I don't want to sail her short-handed."

There was a ripple of laughter round the deck and Rubensohn signalled to the steward to bring out more champagne. They toasted the enterprise and toasted one another. Then, after a while, Rubensohn and Lisette went below and the rest of them dispersed.

McCreary walked over to the starboard rail and lit a cigarette. The moon had not yet risen and the ship was a small moving island of light in a dark sea, pricked only by unfamiliar stars and touched, here and there, by faint phosphorescence. There was no land now, no winking signals from passing merchantmen. They were heading northeasterly off the trade routes into the old pirate waters of the Chinese and the Buginese and the Portuguese filibusters. Now they were the filibusters, sailing under the flag of a tatterdemalion republic, on errands far outside the law.

There was a footfall behind him, and a moment later Captain Janzoon's burly figure was propped on the rail at his side.

"A nice night, my friend."

"Sure," said McCreary amiably. "A nice night."

"You should feel very pleased with yourself, McCreary."

"Why so?"

Janzoon spread his big hands in a grasping gesture.

"Why not? The big play—the big profit. You cut yourself in for a lot of money."

"If I don't bring in a well," said McCreary coolly, "there's no money in it for anybody."

Janzoon gave him a quick, sidelong glance.

"Perhaps you'd like to lay off some of the—the risks."

McCreary shrugged with apparent indifference.

"What's the risk for me? Only time and effort. They cost me nothing."

"There's your life," said Janzoon softly. "And the girl's."

McCreary held tightly onto the rail and stared out to sea. The knives were out again, pricking round his ribs. At the first flicker of doubt or fear they would slide in, up to the hilt.

After a long pause he said lightly, "We all take risks, Janzoon—me, Ruben-sohn, you. It's not so bad if you carry insurance."

Janzoon licked his lips. The conversation was taking an unexpected turn. This lean-faced Celt had more reserves than he had counted on. He tried another maneuver.

"Listen, McCreary! I'm trying to tell you something. There are three of us in this deal: Rubensohn, me and you. Rubensohn's the big one, but you and me together, we are pretty big, too. You see? We should be allies, not enemies."

McCreary slewed round sharply to face him. His voice was low but tight and cold.

"You've given me this before, Janzoon. The big spiel. Friends and neigh-bours. Brothers in arms! Now let's get some facts on it. I don't like mysteries. I don't like threats. I don't like card games with five aces in the pack. If you've got a proposition, let's hear it—all of it. And let's be blunt! It'd better be good because at this moment you need me much more than I need you!"

Janzoon grinned at him behind the thick spade beard. His eyes twinkled maliciously.

"So! Plain talk you want? The open game? Good! I show you what I hold—three aces!"

"Let's see 'em."

"First, you have a yen for Rubensohn's girl."

McCreary shrugged.

"That's not an ace, Janzoon, that's a deuce. I've had a yen for lots of girls. Not one of 'em was worth a quarter of a million."

Janzoon spread his hands in a wide gesture of disbelief.

"No one asks you to pay so much. You have the want for her. If Rubensohn hears it, he will kill her first and then you. So it comes out an ace anyway, McCreary—the ace of hearts."

"Go on!" McCreary's voice was bleak.

"The next one is the ace of diamonds." Janzoon was enjoying the metaphor. "You asked for thirty percent. You got twenty-five, more than me—and I'm the man who put the thought in Rubensohn's mind. You make what you think is a clever condition. Your share of the money must be paid to you direct. Rubensohn agrees to that, too. You think you have touched the horn of plenty. You bloody fool!" Janzoon's grin changed to a crooked sneer. "You think you know everything. But you know nothing. You don't touch that money till Scott Morrison comes. And Scott Morrison doesn't come till Rubensohn sends for him. He doesn't send for him till the well blows in. Before he comes, you are dead! No pockets in a winding sheet, McCreary. But I can keep you alive—at a price."

"We'll come to the price in a minute," said McCreary easily. "I'm inter-ested in the last ace of yours."

"The ace of spades," said Janzoon. "The gravedigger. You read the docu-ments Rubensohn gave you?"

"I read 'em, yes."

"You read the bill of sale?"

"Yes."

"And the articles of association of the company? You see that Rubensohn's name does not appear in either?"

"I thought that was very clever of him," said McCreary tartly. "He takes the money, but he doesn't take the risk. You're liable for any action that's brought in this part of the world because your name's on the Singapore registration."

Janzoon looked at him in swift surprise.

"So you saw that, too? Good! But did you reason to the next step? Rubensohn's signature is not necessary to the sale. If there are any alterations necessary to the drawn document, I can countersign them under the articles. So maybe it's better if we both stay alive and Rubensohn dies, eh?"

"Holy Patrick!" McCreary swore softly. "That's one I hadn't thought of!"

Janzoon chuckled.

"It makes a nice hand, eh, McCreary? You got any cards to beat it?"

"Depends on which way you want to play it," said McCreary.

"What do you mean?"

"There's three ways, Janzoon. Take your pick. First, I can sit back and bid against you on the strength I hold—and you're still not quite sure what that is. Otherwise you wouldn't be here now. Next, you can buy me out of the game altogether, cash on the nail—here and now. I become a paid employee again, no questions asked; except that I want a very good offer and a guarantee of safety when the job's done, and Lisette would have to be part of the purchase price. Last of all, we play together and against Rubensohn and split the stake fifty-fifty. But understand something . . ." McCreary faced him squarely. His lean jaw was set, his eyes bright with challenge. "I won't be threatened, I can't be scared. I've not got a soul to care whether I live or die, so I can gamble my life with a free conscience. I don't care, you see? I'd like to come out of it with a whole skin and a nice profit, but if I can't, then by the living Harry I'll give you both a hot run for your money! Does that make it plain?"

Janzoon looked at him with sober, speculative eyes.

"Very plain. I think I can make you an offer that will attract you. But I like to think about it first, eh?"

"Does that mean *you'll* think about it or Rubensohn?"

"God in heaven, no!" For the first time, there was real fear in Janzoon's voice. He laid a big hand on McCreary's arm and his fingers bit desperately into the flesh. "At the beginning, sure! I sound you out for Rubensohn. But this, no! This is a private thing. I know how close we sail to the wind. I am not happy about it. I want the profit, but I want the risks better than they are for me. If Rubensohn knew . . ."

"He won't," said McCreary curtly, "so long as you play straight with me. And another thing . . ."

311

"Yes?"

"Rubensohn lied about Scott Morrison's cruise, didn't he?"

Janzoon looked at him in surprise.

"How did you know that?"

"Easy enough. Rubensohn said he was up the Fly River in New Guinea. That's combine territory, all of it. No interest there for a freelance speculator like Morrison."

Janzoon nodded slowly.

"Rubensohn does that always. He makes a maze of little lies for no good reason. Unless you ferret it out for yourself, he will never give you the real truth. That's one of the things that makes me uneasy now. We are trying to sell a big lie to Scott Morrison and yet Rubensohn still tries to sell little lies to me—his partner."

"Where is Scott Morrison now?"

Janzoon cast a quick, scared glance around the deserted deck.

"He's in Darwin Harbour. He's looking at oil claims in the north of Australia and waiting for word from us."

"How many days' sail from here?"

"Three, four at most. This is the good time in these waters."

"Thanks," said McCreary, in his most genial brogue. "That makes it easier for all of us."

Janzoon seemed suddenly remote and abstracted. He nodded vaguely and stood irresolutely, as if trying to put an uncomfortable thought into words. McCreary lit a cigarette and waited.

After a while Janzoon said uneasily, "I think we can do business, McCreary. I know we should. But—but—there are promises I can't make."

"Such as?"

"The girl. How important is she to you?"

"Why?"

"Because . . ." Janzoon fumbled awkwardly for the phrase. "Because I don't want to spoil our business . . . because of what Rubensohn may . . . may have in mind for her."

"Do you know what he has in mind?"

"No, but—"

"For God's sake, Janzoon!" McCreary's voice was edgy and impatient. "Out with it, man! What are you trying to tell me?"

Janzoon gestured wearily.

"I try to tell you that if you want her, you fight Rubensohn, not me. If you lose, you blame him, not Janzoon. Do you understand?"

McCreary smiled crookedly.

"Sure! I understand! Women are private business. I'll handle it when the time comes."

"Good!" Janzoon was obviously relieved. "For the rest of it, I think over a figure and terms and I make an offer. Yes?"

"Take your time," said McCreary with a grin. "I'm in no hurry."

But when he was alone again, looking out at the flat sea and the march of the pendant stars, his face grew somber.

Janzoon he could handle, playing on his greed and his fear of Rubensohn. But Lisette was a different matter. He knew now that he was in love with her, and a threat to her was a knife held to his own throat.

Chapter Eight

"THERE IT IS, McCreary! Karang Sharo." Rubensohn's voice was higher than usual with the excitement of the landfall. "Here, take the glasses!"

They were standing on the bridge with Captain Janzoon, watching the island grow from a blur on the horizon to a sharp contour, while Alfieri called to the helmsman the new bearings that would bring them round to the south-eastern entrance to the harbour.

McCreary took the glasses and focussed carefully. He saw a long serrated spine of mountains rising slowly to a high truncated cone over which a small mushroom of smoke hung lazily in the still air. He whistled and turned to Rubensohn.

"Volcanic, eh? You didn't tell me that!"

"Is it important?"

"Could be. You might find natural gas instead of oil."

Rubensohn smiled his low, oblique smile and nodded, approvingly.

"You know your job, McCreary. You continue to impress me. It's a question I had already taken up with the surveyors. They tell me the odds are on oil."

"They'd know, of course," said McCreary, with mild irony. "Just thought I'd mention it."

He turned back to scan the approaching coastline. Black cliffs rose sheer from the water, and after the cliffs came mountains coated with smoky greenery, clear to the peaks, except for a small barren area below the mouth of the volcano.

"Nothing on this side," said McCreary. "What's it like on the other?"

"A paradise!" said Rubensohn with enthusiasm. "The mountains break down into foothills and the foothills spread out into a wide, flat plain cut into

314

plantations and paddy fields. There is a gold beach and a circle of harbour fringed with palms and the huts of the fishermen. We have to tack round to come into it through the archipelago."

McCreary raised the glasses again and saw a scattering of smaller islands, jade and emerald, strung out from the southern tip of Karang Sharo. He saw the changing colours where the sunlight lay on shallow reef water and the small shapes of the sails clustered like sea birds over the fishing grounds.

"You see those mountains?" Rubensohn put his hand on McCreary's shoulder and turned him back to Karang Sharo itself.

"I see 'em, yes."

"They are full of swift waters, McCreary—streams that rush down to feed the canals and irrigate the paddy fields. And the streams are full of diamonds. You can pan them like gold. The people will sell them to you for tobacco or betel nut or trade goods. Miranha himself buys a few to sell in Timor, but he is too far away from the market to do very well. You should think about it while you're here."

"I'll do that," said McCreary. "Thanks!"

He handed the glasses back to Rubensohn and stood watching the helmsman bring the nose of the *Corsair* onto the new tack.

Janzoon said tentatively, "Maybe Lisette would like to see this. Something new for her, eh?"

"Women have no taste for scenery," said Rubensohn indifferently, "except as a background for their own beauty."

"I'm going below to have a shave." McCreary's voice was as casual as he could make it. "I'll be back to see us enter the harbour. Like me to knock on the door and tell Lisette where you are?"

"As you wish," said Rubensohn over his shoulder. "And ask her to bring up my sunglasses. I'll need them shortly."

"I'll do that."

He waited a moment longer lest even a suspicion of haste betray him, but Rubensohn was still peering through the glasses at the dragon-like mountains of Karang Sharo. Then he turned away and walked swiftly down the companion ladder.

His heart was pounding when he reached the door of the stateroom. This would be the first private moment he had had with her since she had come to his cabin. They had met, to be sure, at meals and on the deck; but they had been like people shut off from one another by soundproof glass, their conversation soundless, their gestures a meaningless mime. He knocked on the door.

Lisette's voice, glassy and impersonal, answered: "Who's there?"

"It's me—McCreary. Open up, quickly."

There was a moment's pause, then the door opened.

"McCreary, what . . . ?"

He moved swiftly inside, closed the door and took her in his arms, stifling her questions with a kiss. Then he released her and talked swiftly and urgently.

315

"Rubensohn's on the bridge. He wants you up there. Take his sunglasses. I told him I'd look in as I was passing. So I daren't stay more than a moment."

"God, I've missed you!" She came to him again, fiercely and passionately, drawing his face down to her own, pressing her body against him, then thrusting him away with the same abruptness. "I'm frightened, McCreary. Today is the beginning of it and I'm frightened."

"So am I, dark one," said McCreary. "Frightened for you more than for myself. I've got to talk to you. And this isn't the time or place for it. How can we get together?"

"I've been thinking that, too. Perhaps when we anchor first Miranha will come aboard. They may want to talk privately. If I can get away then . . . ?"

"I'll be in my cabin. I'll wait for you."

"I'll try to come."

"Good. Now get up on the bridge as quickly as you can, and don't forget the sunglasses."

"Kiss me, please."

When the kiss was done, she reached up with her small ivory hands and touched his cheeks and said softly, "It is a small thing, I know, to be loved by a woman from the Peacock Pavilion; but I love you, McCreary. Whatever happens, I love you."

"I love you, dark one," said McCreary gravely. "And nothing is going to happen but good for both of us."

Abruptly as he had come, he left her, and she stood looking at the blank door, wondering how she would bring herself to tell him of the bargain that Rubensohn had proposed to her.

Two steps from the door of Rubensohn's stateroom, McCreary cannoned into Guido, on his way down to the saloon for a late cup of coffee. The dark fellow whistled and wagged a warning finger.

"*Mamma mia!* How crazy can a man be? In full daylight, with the whole ship astir! What happens if it is not Guido but Rubensohn or Janzoon?"

"Shut up, Guido. Come with me. I want to talk to you."

Before he had time to protest, McCreary caught him by the arm and hustled him inside his own cabin.

"I'm thirsty," mourned Guido plaintively. "I got up late. I have a taste in my mouth like old boot leather. I need my coffee."

"You'll get it in a minute," said McCreary unfeelingly. "I want to talk to you."

Guido sighed mightily and sat on the bed while McCreary began laying out his shaving gear and talking to him from the washroom alcove.

"When was the last time you had any radio traffic from Rubensohn?"

"Not since before Djakarta."

"How does he send? In code or clear?"

"In code—it comes cheaper that way."

"What's the code—a private one?"

"No. He uses Bentley's."

"Who does the encoding?"

"Me." Guido reached for one of McCreary's cigarettes and lit it, all unknowing, with a dead man's lighter. "Listen, *compar'!* Maybe we come at this quicker if you tell me what you're driving at, eh?"

"I'm trying to establish two things, Guido. First, if a code message comes in for Rubensohn, can we read it?"

"Sure," said Guido confidently.

"Second, if I want to send a message in Rubensohn's name, can I do it and get away with it?"

"*Senz' altro!* You can get away with it, provided you remember two little things."

"What are they, Guido?" McCreary stuck his head out from the alcove. His face was smothered in lather, but his eyes were bright with interest.

Guido blew a succession of careless smoke rings and gave McCreary a wide, urchin grin.

"All this information and I don't even get a cup of coffee!"

"I'll buy you a bottle of cognac instead. Give, Guido! Give!"

Guido dropped his voice to a stage whisper and told him.

"I pick this up because I am an observant fellow. Nobody tells me. I just see it as the traffic goes through. When he cables Singapore, he begins 'For Silva' and signs himself 'Rex.' When he cables New York, he begins 'For Mortimer' and signs himself 'Imperator.'"

"Rex—Imperator. King—Emperor." McCreary gagged on a mouthful of lather. "That's a little much, isn't it? What does he think he is—Napoleon Bonaparte or God Almighty?"

"From the way he handles his girl," said Guido, "he might be Nerone or Caligula."

"I didn't think you'd know about them," said McCreary, with a wry grin.

Guido made an airy gesture of condescension.

"I got a cabinet of books about them, full of dirty pictures!"

"I wouldn't doubt it for a moment. Now tell me something else, Guido. Have you seen any traffic from Rubensohn to Scott Morrison?"

"Only two messages."

"How were they addressed?"

"Morrison—M. V. *Melanie.*"

"And the signature?"

"Asmin."

"Come again, Guido?"

"Asmin—it is a cable address for Southeast Asia Mineral Research, Rubensohn's company."

"No other signature?"

"Oh, yes. Always Janzoon."

"Janzoon?"

Guido nodded emphatically. "I thought it was funny, too, seeing that Rubensohn wrote the messages and delivered them to me. But I am not paid to ask questions. I send them as they come."

"Damn!" McCreary was so absorbed in his questioning that he nicked a neat triangle out of his jaw.

Guido chuckled and said, "Keep your mind on your job, *amico*. I'm still here, and dry as a . . ."

"Get it straight, Guido!" McCreary dabbed his face with styptic and talked rapidly and tersely. "Once we drop the hooks, we're not going to have much time together. From now on, I want a copy of all incoming messages. And hold any outgoing traffic until I've given you a clearance to send it."

"Body of Bacchus!" Guido's eyes popped and the cigarette fell out of his mouth. "You know what you're asking? The incoming stuff—sure! That's easy. But the other? You know what Rubensohn does? He brings it to the radio cabin and stands over me while I code it and send it. I try to help you, McCreary, but this is suicide you want!"

Wiping the last fluffs of lather from his face, McCreary stepped back into the cabin. His lean face split into a lopsided grin and his voice was full of the blarney.

"We can still do it, Guido, and spit in Rubensohn's eye at the same time. Look! You're giving me a transceiver pack for the camp. You're giving me a Morse key, too. We arrange morning and evening schedules to keep in touch. If Rubensohn wants to stand over you while the message goes out—fine! If it looks like normal business, you send the damn thing like a good operator and let me know the contents on the next schedule. But—and this, me bright bandit, is where you must use your judgment—if it looks odd or urgent, or dangerous to me, then you're professional enough to fake a breakdown until you've checked with me. Now, does that make sense or not?"

Guido brightened immediately. His dark eyes sparkled.

"If you talk to the girls like you talk to me, McCreary, you'll never want for a bed. That way we can do it—*sicuro!*"

"Fine!" McCreary reached for the cigarettes and shoved one in Guido's mouth and one in his own. "Now, there's something else. Janzoon has approached me with a proposition."

"What sort of proposition?"

McCreary snapped the lighter and lit their cigarettes before he answered.

"I don't think he's quite clear on it himself yet. But it boils down to two alternatives: buy me out at his own price in return for protection from Rubensohn, or team up with me against Rubensohn and split the profit fifty-fifty."

Guido cocked his head on one side and looked quizzical.

"You know why he makes this proposition, McCreary?"

"I'm not sure, but I think he's scared that Rubensohn is going to sell him down the river."

"I know he is," said Guido simply.

"And how the devil would you be knowing a thing like that?"

318

"I think it out for myself. You know Alfieri—how he walks about with his nose in the air and his chest stuck out as if he were the Doge of Venice?"

McCreary nodded.

"Last night he was so full of news, he had to share it with someone. He comes to my cabin with half a bottle of grappa and tells me that Rubensohn has sounded him out for the captain's job. Told him Janzoon might be retiring at the end of the trip, going into business. He mustn't say anything, of course. But he has to say it, or burst his breeches."

"Hell and damnation!" McCreary cursed softly. "What's Rubensohn driving at?"

Guido grinned and stabbed a bony finger at his chest.

"Ask me, McCreary! This is the way it goes in Naples. We call it 'schiffo.' You tell a small truth here and a big lie there. You buy this one a dinner and seduce that one's wife and write a letter to the bishop about the morals of the mayor—and at the end of it everyone is at his neighbour's throat and you walk off with the money and the girl. That's what Rubensohn will do, watch!"

"The hell he will!" said McCreary. "If it's rogues you want and shysters and monumental liars, they come biggest of all inside the ring of Kerry!"

"I'll take your word for it," said Guido dolefully. "Now, please, *amico,* can I have my coffee?"

Chapter Nine

Now THEY WERE THREADING THEIR WAY through the outer ring of islands, the slow water curling away from their bows and rocking the small craft that put out from the beaches and the praus that rode with slack sails on the fringe of the reefs.

The beaches were lined with people, bare-breasted women in gaudy sarongs, scrabbling children and small brown men with bright turbans and carved combs in their hair. Behind the people were the roofs of the kampongs peering between the palm boles and the lush green of the undergrowth.

Karang Sharo lay ahead and to port, but the harbour was hidden behind a long flank of hillside that tapered down from the peak of the volcano.

The sky was clear and cloudless and the sun struck back cruelly from the smooth water and made vivid patterns of light and shadow in the folds of the land.

McCreary stood with Rubensohn and Lisette and let the warmth and the colour seep into him. Lisette was cool and remote—her eyes an enigma behind the dark glasses. Rubensohn was elated and voluble. He gestured widely and talked in his high, emphatic voice with an enthusiasm odd and disturbing in so devious a man.

"You see now what I mean, McCreary? The new land of promise! No tax collectors, no policemen, no jacks-in-office sitting behind their papers like shabby kings! There is the sun, the sky, the sea, the land—and all that a man cares to wrench out of it with his own two hands. Where have they all gone, the old adventurers? There are a hundred places like this, waiting like women to be taken, but the adventurers never come. Where are they?"

"It's an interesting question." McCreary's eyes brightened with mischief.

"The way I've heard it, some of 'em died of strange diseases, some of 'em died of drink, some of 'em were eaten by cannibals, some of 'em lopped by the public executioner, the best of 'em were killed in the war, and the rest are sitting in Lombard Street with hardened livers and fat cigars."

Rubensohn gave a little high cackle of laughter.

"You're an amusing fellow, McCreary. I should keep you near me always."

"You'd get tired of me," said McCreary blandly. "The Irish make good playmates but uncomfortable bedfellows."

"Do they make good lovers?"

"I'm not a woman," said McCreary softly. "I wouldn't know that."

"What do you think, Lisette?" Rubensohn's voice was barbed with malice.

Lisette shrugged indifferently.

"I know nothing about love."

"A neat point, McCreary!" Rubensohn's red lips smiled, but his eyes were bleak. "Lisette is a woman of some experience. When I met her first, she was . . ."

Janzoon's voice called to them from the helmsman's side.

"We're rounding the cape now. You should see the harbour in a moment. You'll get a better view from the port side."

As they moved through the wheelhouse to take up their new positions, Lisette brushed against McCreary and he felt the light pressure of her hand against his own. It told him plainer than words:

"He guesses, McCreary. Be careful of him. Don't let him goad you."

She walked ahead of him to join Rubensohn on the port wing of the bridge, but McCreary stayed inside with Janzoon.

Janzoon gave him a swift, warning glance, then began scanning the tip of the cape as it slid toward them.

"Port ten!"

"Port ten!" came the parrot voice of the helmsman.

Slowly they rounded the green finger of land and then, like the dawning of a revelation, the harbour of Karang Sharo came into view.

It was a great semicircle of still water fringed with golden sand. Behind it the land rose slowly, terrace on broad terrace, to the flanks of the hills. The paddy fields were broken by patches of plantation and swaths of jungle and the shining dams and canals of the irrigation systems. The kampongs were spread along the shore fringe and dotted intermittently on the higher ground. The roofs of the huts showed brown and yellow against the flaring green of the vegetation, and the flowers of the flame trees were red flecks on the carpet of leaves.

But most startling of all was the palace. It was built on a broad plateau at the foot of the volcano, and the land before it fell away in a series of hanging gardens bounded by elaborately carved palisades. At the back the volcano cone reared up majestically and the buildings themselves were splayed against it, like the spread tail of a peacock, fretted gold and turquoise and dark amber.

Its windows and terraces stared straight into the morning sun, but at noon the shadow of the mountain would begin to fall across it, a grateful easement from the equatorial heat.

"Well, McCreary!" Janzoon looked at him and chuckled huskily. "What do you say to that?"

McCreary shook his head.

"What do you say? It's beautiful—and the man who designed it was a genius."

"Join us, McCreary!" Rubensohn's high voice summoned him into the sunlight. "I told you I would show you wonders. Now do you believe me?"

"I never doubted you," said McCreary dryly. "It's a great and marvellous thing, to be sure. Like a goldsmith's work."

"And there are as many wonders inside," said Rubensohn with relish. "There are rooms for a hundred concubines and their children. There are state chambers and a hall for the dancers and a theater for wayang puppets. There are painters and musicians and masters, for the girl dancers and the royal treasures are housed in tunnels driven right into the mountain itself."

Rubensohn's eyes glittered behind the dark sunglasses. It was as if he were describing the fulfillment of his own dreams, the proper climax to the career of every filibuster.

More from resentment than from immediate interest, McCreary changed the subject. He said, "Where will I be drilling?"

"Over there!" Rubensohn pointed northward, away from the palace to where a secondary range of hills broke into the terraces and formed a small re-entrant with the main range. "There's a road that runs along the bay to the mouth of the valley. That's the way your stores and equipment will go in. It's away from the main villages, as you see. You'll have a certain amount of privacy."

"Looks as though we'll need it." McCreary pointed to the beach, which was crawling like an anthill with a colourful press of people. Canoes were being pushed off the beach and brown bodies were clambering into them, while small boys and girls plunged into the water and began swimming out to the ship. A figure in white ducks was standing on the spindly jetty and waving frantically. Rubensohn waved back.

"That's Miranha. He'll be out as soon as we're anchored."

As he spoke, they heard Janzoon ring down to cut the engines, and then they were sliding, with way on, through the flat water, while the men in the bows waited for the signal to let go the anchor.

Janzoon bellowed an order and the hooks went down, and the engines started again to make head and take up the slack of the chains. The bell rang again—"Finished with engines"—and they were riding at anchor in the slack water with that curious feeling, half surprise, half disappointment, that comes with the last landfall.

McCreary and Lisette looked at one another. Rubensohn stood a long moment, staring up towards the palace and the smoking mountain. When he

322

turned back to them, he was smiling and rubbing his thick hands together. He chuckled shrilly.

"The overture is finished. Now the opera begins. I hope you both enjoy it very much."

"I'm sure we will," said McCreary. "I know the producer. He's very competent. And besides, he's got a very good leading lady."

Rubensohn flushed with sudden irritation and snapped at him.

"You're impertinent, McCreary!"

"I am, I know that," said McCreary cheerfully. "But I'm also a damn good driller, and a man who's good at his job can afford to speak his mind."

Rubensohn opened his mouth to speak, then closed it again. A wintry anger seemed to take posession of him. His eyes filmed over and the big beaked nose clamped down over his small feminine mouth. Deliberately, he turned his back on McCreary, linked his arm in Lisette's and stood watching the small white figure of Miranha stepping off the jetty into a shabby motor launch manned by a pair of Sharo boys in batik sarongs.

McCreary propped himself against the bulkhead and lit a cigarette. Then he, too, turned away and strolled into the chart room, where Janzoon was talking to Alfieri. They were stripping the chart from the navigator's table and locking the instruments away. Their work was done, it seemed. His own was just beginning.

The launch ground awkwardly against the plates of the *Corsair,* and a moment later Pedro Miranha came scrambling up the monkey ladder. Rubensohn and Janzoon received him on the bridge, while Alfieri stood at Lisette's elbow and McCreary waited in the background and studied the newcomer.

He was a skinny, narrow-faced fellow with a turned eye and a malarious complexion. His teeth were stained with betel and his thinning hair was plastered across his scalp with palm oil. His hands were knotted and stained and the threadbare ducks hung on him like sacking. His English was surprisingly good, but his voice was a rasping whine and, as he talked, he shifted nervously from one foot to the other.

"Good morning, gentlemen! Welcome to Karang Sharo. A big day for the island. Everybody is out, as you see. Even from the palace they will be watching. Everything's ready for you. . . ."

"Did you get the pontoons built?" Rubensohn asked curtly.

"All built, ready to haul out. Four of them—solid logs underneath and a bamboo decking. Fifteen feet square, take anything!"

"Good! You've got labour lined up for us?"

"Labour!" Miranha giggled foolishly and flung out his skinny arm. "Look at it! Men, women and children. You've only got to whistle and they'll come like ants."

"When can we start unloading?"

"Oh, for that"—Miranha wagged a cautionary finger—"best wait till you've paid respects at the palace."

"Is anything wrong?"

"No! No! No! Nothing wrong, only . . ." He dropped his voice to a confidential whisper. "But you know the way it is up there. We're the Navel of the Universe. We like to be tickled to make us feel better. You've brought the . . ."

Rubensohn cut him short with a gesture.

"Yes, I've brought everything. We can talk about it below. Janzoon?"

"Yes?"

"You and Miranha come down to my cabin. There's a lot to talk about."

Without a word to Lisette or McCreary, he turned on his heel and walked down the companion ladder. Miranha and Janzoon followed him, leaving McCreary and Lisette with Alfieri.

McCreary said quietly, "Now, there's a dock rat, if ever I saw one!"

Alfieri stiffened and said coldly, "Miranha is an important person on the island. Mr. Rubensohn has great confidence in him. He has connections at the palace and . . ."

"They always have," said McCreary contemptuously, "at the tradesmen's entrance and the back door to the women's quarters. He's got a pimp's face and a huckster's eyes. I don't like him."

"You, of course, have much more experience of such people than I."

It was a patent insult, but McCreary took it with a grin. He said in his gentlest brogue:

"You should relax more, Alfieri. I've known men grow ulcers worrying the way you do. You're not captain yet, and if you're not nice to your friends you never will be!"

Alfieri flushed angrily and stammered.

"I—I don't understand what you mean."

"I think you do," said McCreary softly. "Mr. Rubensohn has been dangling promotion in front of your nose, like a carrot to a donkey. But Lisette here will tell you, there's a long way to walk before you reach it. That's right, isn't it, Lisette?"

Lisette laid a restraining hand on his arm.

"Please, McCreary, let us have no unpleasantness."

"I'm not being unpleasant, dark one. But Alfieri is young and innocent. I've seen fellows like him taken for their shirts because they gambled in the wrong company. Take a tip from me, Mister Mate. Don't believe everything the owners tell you. And don't count on promotion till you've got the braid on your arm and your backside in the captain's armchair."

Then, while Alfieri was still goggling at him, he linked his arm in Lisette's and led her down the companion ladder and towards his own cabin.

With the door closed and bolted behind them, they clung together for a long moment, and McCreary was amazed at the pent passion in her small doll-like body. Slowly they relaxed and McCreary made her sit down on the bed beside him.

324

He took her hands in his own and said gravely, "There's a lot to talk about, dark one. Let's get that over first."

"I know that, Mike." It was the first time she had used his Christian name. "But first I want you to listen to me."

"Sure, I'll listen. I like your voice better than my own. What do you want to tell me?"

"Give me a cigarette, please."

He opened a new pack, handed her a cigarette and lit it. She smoked greedily for a few moments, then she began.

"He guesses about us, Mike."

McCreary nodded.

"I gathered that, on the bridge. Has he said anything to you?"

"Not in so many words. But you know how he is—secretive, probing, waiting for the moment when he can hurt most."

"I know, yes."

"He wants to destroy you, Mike."

"I know that, too," said McCreary simply. "But he can't do anything until I've brought in a well for him. And before that I hope to make a few arrangements of my own. That's what I want to talk to you about. I'm going to . . ."

"Please, Mike! Let me talk first."

There was so much urgency in her voice, so much pain in her eyes, that he had no choice but to let her go on.

"I want to tell you about myself, Mike. I want so much that you should understand. If you don't understand, you will do something foolish, something that will be no profit to either of us."

"Before you go on, Lisette . . ." McCreary's voice was grim. "I'll tell you bluntly. What touches you touches me. If I have to blast our way out of this rat hole, I'm going to do it and take you with me."

"I know, Mike, I know. But please . . . please listen!"

"Go ahead, sweetheart."

"I told you where Rubensohn found me—in the Peacock Pavilion in Saigon. I never told you how I came there."

"I've never asked to know."

"But I want to tell you. I did not belong to Saigon. I was from the north—Haiphong. My husband was an official of the French administration."

"Your husband?" The word shocked him like water splashed in his face.

Lisette nodded simply.

"His name was Raoul Morand. He was a *métis* like myself, half-French, half-Tonkinese, so that when the war started and Ho Chi Minh's army moved down from the north, we were not evacuated. We joined the refugees moving south. We made it, too. We came to Binh Dinh and even found a modest lodging outside the town. Raoul went out each day to try to make contact with a French official with power to give him back his old job. Then, one evening, the soldiers came—three of them, from the Binh Xuyen. They were looking for spies, they said. And they stood Raoul against the wall and made him watch while they stripped me. They mocked him all the while and told him what they were going to do to me and, when he tried to break away and help me, they shot him. Then, when they had finished, they took me with them to Saigon and sold me to the Peacock Pavilion, because the Binh Xuyen collected the revenues from such houses for Bao Dai, and his troops stocked them and controlled them for him. I was alive, though I did not wish to be. But after a while I began to be grateful even for that small mercy. Then, one night, Rubensohn came and was pleased with me and offered to take me away. He bought me from the Pavilion for a big price and made me his mistress, and I have travelled with him ever since."

"Is that all, dark one?" McCreary's voice was somber.

"No, it is not all!" Her eyes were bright with challenge. "There is a moral to my story, Mike, I want to read it to you. First I will tell you, truthfully, that even in the Peacock Pavilion one can be grateful for the gift of life. And then I will say that when Raoul died for me, he did a useless thing. Had he not tried to help me, had he been able to bear what they were doing to me, we might have been together now. I might never have come to the Peacock Pavilion, and there would have been nothing but the memory of that one night, and, in time, we might have forgotten even that." Her voice rose sharply and she reached out and grasped his hands again, desperately. "Death is so pointless, Mike! It is the end of hope, the end of love for the one who is left. So that's what I want you to promise me . . . whatever happens, whatever Rubensohn tries to do to hurt me, you will stay alive. Will you promise, Mike?"

"I promise, sweetheart," said McCreary softly.

His arms went round her and drew her to him so that her head was pillowed on his breast, her small, perfect body pressed against his own. But for all the love he poured out on her, she could not bring herself to tell him the truth.

Chapter Ten

Just before noon Miranha went ashore again, and shortly afterwards the Navel of the Universe came to pay his state visit to the *Corsair*.

They saw him first a long way off, carried in a golden palanquin on the shoulders of ten men along the terraces of the palace, then down the winding path to the flatlands. There were guards in front of him and behind, each with a kris strapped between his shoulder blades and a long musket of ancient design over his shoulder.

The procession lost itself in the green overhang and they did not see it again until the crowds on the beach parted suddenly, fell to their knees and uttered a long, wailing cry that drifted faintly across the water. From the mouth of a canal a long canoe with a carved prow shot out, propelled by ten oarsmen. When they came to the opening in the crowd, they beached it swiftly and the Navel of the Universe was carried down to it on the shoulders of his servants. When he was seated, the courtiers joined him, one of them holding a large yellow umbrella over his head.

Then the canoe shoved off and the oarsmen drove it swiftly with long sweeps of the big, carved paddles.

The gangway was down and a Malay seaman stood with a boathook to bring the visitors neatly alongside. Arturo waited on the lowest step to hand the visitors aboard. The rest of the ship's company lined the deck, the officers in freshly starched uniforms, the seamen and the lascars and the galley staff all dressed in their shore clothes and standing stiffly at attention. Janzoon and Alfieri were posted at the top of the gangway, but neither Rubensohn nor Lisette were to be seen.

McCreary thought it was another piece of shrewd stage management. The

Navel of the Universe must be brought to the great man, alone, in the privacy of the saloon. Lisette would be displayed as a prize possession. It gave him grim satisfaction to think that soon this fiction, too, would be destroyed and Rubensohn would lose Lisette with all the rest.

When the small procession reached the top of the gangway, McCreary saw, with a shock of surprise, that the Sultan was a young man—thirty at most— with finely chiselled Balinese features, set now into a rigid ceremonial mask. He was as colourful as a jungle bird in his ceremonial silks, embroidered with threads of silver and gold. There were jewels at his throat and on his fingers. A dagger with a golden haft was thrust into his sash, and in the center of his round skullcap a great ruby glowed with dull fire.

Behind him came a fat figure, who looked more like a Chinese than a Malay and whom McCreary took to be the vizier. His silks floated about him like a widow's drapes, but his slant eyes were shrewd and appraising. The rest of the courtiers were small brown men, like their master, and their costumes and their jewelry were in descending order of magnificence.

When they reached the deck, Alfieri called the officers to attention and the crew bowed deeply. Captain Janzoon saluted formally, then held out his hand and made a short speech in Malay.

The Sultan made a curt acknowledgment and Janzoon led the party down to the saloon. Alfieri hustled the crew about their business of setting the afterdeck for the meal, and McCreary and Guido strolled forward to smoke a private cigarette.

Guido quizzed him shrewdly.

"You're a shareholder now, McCreary. Shouldn't you be down there when the business is being done?"

McCreary shrugged off the question.

"The business was done a long time ago, Guido. This is ceremony. Each telling the other what a big shot he is and waiting to see the size of the glory box."

"But the girl is there—your girl."

"She's not all mine—yet. We both know we've got to wait and plan for that, Guido."

Guido gave him an odd, sidelong look.

"You said that like a man in love."

McCreary turned on him sharply.

"What the hell do you think I am?"

"I don't know." Guido made a wry mouth and looked at McCreary with puzzled eyes. "I know you have a want for her; sure, I know you get some satisfaction when you take her from a *maledetto* like Rubensohn. But love! That's a serious thing, *amico*. Love reaches higher than the belly and stabs like a sharp knife. I'm sorry for you."

"Why sorry?"

Guido shook his head.

"The world is full of women—and you fall in love with a packet of trouble.

328

Tell me"—he changed the subject abruptly—"has Janzoon made his proposition yet?"

"No. Not yet. He's waiting to watch the cat jump. So far there hasn't been a real trial of strength between me and Rubensohn. Janzoon will wait for that."

"I don't think he will have to wait long."

There was a note in Guido's voice that brought McCreary up short. The little Neapolitan wasn't joking anymore. His face was puckered with doubt and indecision. McCreary questioned him bluntly.

"There's something on your mind, Guido. Let's have it!"

"No!" Guido was quite definite in his refusal. "I have a thought, but it is mine and private. If I am right, you can do nothing about it. If I am wrong, then you fret for nothing when you should be attending to other things. But this I tell you. If I am right, the first trial of strength with Rubensohn will come tonight."

And with that McCreary had to be content. Before he had time to ask another question, there was a babble of voices on the deck and Captain Janzoon appeared with the vizier and the courtiers of Karang Sharo. The Sultan was still below with Rubensohn and Lisette.

For the next two hours they stood, sat or lounged under the awning, entertaining the visitors, while the galley staff bustled round with dishes and trays of drinks. The officers spoke only shipboard Malay and the brunt of the conversation fell on Janzoon and McCreary, but their patience soon frayed under the grinning politeness of the envoys, who gave oblique answers to their simplest questions and made not a single contribution of their own.

When, halfway through the affair, Rubensohn and the Sultan appeared, the situation was even worse. The attendants stood in attitudes of submission while the Navel of the Universe ate and drank and talked only to Janzoon and Rubensohn.

McCreary stood it as long as he could, then tried to slip away to see what had happened to Lisette. But Rubensohn caught sight of him and called him back to present him to the Sultan, and from then till the end of the ceremony he was anchored, sweating and uncomfortable, trying to answer a hundred questions on the mechanics of oil search, with a vocabulary limited to bed, board and the simpler transactions of living.

Then, finally, it was over. They were mustered again for leave-taking and the royal party was shepherded down into the big canoe. But before they were halfway to the shore, hatch covers were off and Alfieri was standing by the winches to superintend the unloading of the gifts that were to be presented at the evening's reception in the palace.

They heard the put-put of Miranha's launch and saw him towing a string of rough pontoons, each loaded with a bunch of boys to unhook the slings and settle the freight for its journey back to the shore.

Rubensohn kept Janzoon and McCreary with him until he was satisfied with the way the work was being handled. Then he said briskly:

"We have business to talk, gentlemen. Let's go to your cabin, Janzoon.

Lisette is resting, I don't want to disturb her. She will want to look her best for the evening."

McCreary looked at him quickly, but there was no malice in his eyes. Rubensohn was at his best when there was work to be done. The mischief and the malice were playtime indulgences. They could not be allowed to interfere with the project in hand.

Janzoon settled them in the cabin and poured three tots of whisky from his private store. He and Rubensohn lit cigars and McCreary smoked a cigarette. Rubensohn came quickly to the point.

"We're a going concern, gentlemen. The Sultan is happy with the gifts we've offered him and with our promise of a royalty on the oil produced, to be paid in kind and in American bank deposits."

"Which he'll never get, of course," said McCreary dryly.

"Precisely!" Rubensohn waved his cigar. "But by the time he finds that out, we'll be away with a profit in hand. Then Scott Morrison can start worrying."

Janzoon chuckled asthmatically.

"I like that touch. The final nail in the coffin, eh?"

Rubensohn hurried on.

"The document of concession will be presented to us tonight at the palace. It has no value in law, but in fact it will be one more piece of evidence to present to our friend Morrison. And he can raise no question of its authenticity."

"When can I start unloading my stores?" asked McCreary.

"First thing in the morning. Miranha will be out at sunrise with his barges. He'll take the crated stuff first. The rest he will leave until you're on deck to superintend, which I imagine will be much, much later."

"What makes you say that?"

Rubensohn sipped his whisky and smiled at him over the rim of his glass.

"Because tonight, McCreary, you will see yet another of the wonders I promised you. We are to be entertained in the palace. We shall be carried up the hill in litters, feasted, entertained and presented each with a royal gift, and carried back again, I suspect, somewhat the worse for wear."

Janzoon spluttered happily over his cigar.

"Watch out for the palm toddy, McCreary. However they spice it, whatever they serve it in, it carries a hundred headaches."

"I'll remember," said McCreary with a grin. "It sounds like the biggest come-all-ye of the season."

"Bigger than you dream, McCreary."

Rubensohn turned to Janzoon

"A change in orders, Captain. At least until other arrangements can be made onshore, officers will be permitted to bring women aboard ship."

"Is that wise?" Janzoon frowned and looked puzzled. "I like my fun as much as any man, but I like a clean ship better."

"Unless you've any other suggestions? I am informed by the Sultan that each officer will be presented with a concubine for his use during our stay in

Karang Sharo." He smiled and licked his red lips. "An ancient custom, I believe, which has, unfortunately, fallen into disuse in other parts of the world. I thought it unwise to refuse, but I must depend on you, Janzoon, to see that discipline is maintained and that suitable arrangements for shore residence are made as soon as possible. We're doing well, McCreary, don't you think?"

"Too damn well," said McCreary without enthusiasm. "Why take so much trouble with a bunch of interlopers who are getting a damn good bargain anyway?"

Rubensohn brushed the objection aside with an airy gesture.

"Perhaps I'm a good negotiator. Perhaps the Navel of the Universe has made a better bargain than he expected. In any case, who are we to complain?"

"Who indeed?" said McCreary dubiously. But, remembering Guido's warning and Lisette's desperate plea, he was troubled and afraid. The prospect of the evening's celebration gave him no pleasure and he wanted desperately to talk to Lisette. But Rubensohn and Janzoon kept him talking through the afternoon. When the time came to dress, Lisette was still in her cabin and Rubensohn was with her, so they had no chance at all to see each other.

The sun went down swiftly behind the spine of the mountains, and at a single stride darkness came down on the islands and on the sea. The stars pricked out, and the yellow lanterns in the kampongs, and the glow of the volcano was spread softly against the night sky.

Then, as if at a signal, the torches were lit—on the beach first, then all the way up the winding path and along the climbing terraces of the palace. Their flames tossed and waved in the hands of the torchbearers, so that it seemed as if a long, fiery serpent were writhing down the mountainside.

When McCreary came on deck, dressed for the evening, he found the other officers on the deck watching the display, stiff as pouter pigeons in mess jackets and starched whites and scarlet cummerbunds.

The gangway was down and the boat was bobbing below it, with the oars shipped and the bo's'n standing below, waiting to hand them aboard. Each officer had a crew member allotted to him, and these stood apart, self-conscious in their clean clothes, their eyes rolling with excitement, their voices a sibilant whisper in the shadows.

Alfieri stepped up to him and said curtly, "Captain's compliments, Mr. McCreary. You will go ashore in the first boat with the other officers. Litters will be waiting for you and you will proceed immediately to the palace. Your servant will walk beside the litter and will stand behind you during the ceremony."

He called a name, and a moonfaced Chinese cook boy stepped forward to attend McCreary.

Guido sidled up to him and said softly, "I'm in the first boat, too, McCreary. I'd like to stay near you."

"Suits me fine, Guido. I'm in need of company."

"I thought you might be."

Then Alfieri summoned them crisply and they filed down the gangway, with their attendants following, into the waiting boat.

When they came to the beach, they found the litters drawn up between the lines of torchbearers, and behind the lights they could see the gifts piled for the pack carriers and covered with cloths. Under one of the covers McCreary made out the shape of a small car lashed to long, stout poles for its passage up the mountain. Farther away stood a line of palace guards holding back a press of people whose murmur was like the buzzing of a hive of bees. The torchlight flickered on their shining brown faces and made queer highlights on their goggling eyes.

A litter bearer touched McCreary lightly on the arm and pointed to his place. McCreary climbed awkwardly onto the platform and seated himself on a low chair covered with patterned silk that smelt of spices and sandalwood. Ahead of him he saw Guido being hoisted awkwardly into his place.

Then, at a word of command, the bearers bent and lifted the long poles onto their shoulders, and McCreary found himself riding high above the torches like a captain in some barbaric triumph.

All the way up the mountain there were the lights and the people. The lights were scented with incense and the incense mingled with the smell of the people and the dust and the warm exhalation of the kampongs and the jungle.

Above him the trees hung slack in the heavy air, and over the leaves were the sky and the soft, low stars. Sometimes he heard the clatter of night birds, but it was a small sound against the cries of the villagers, who laughed and shouted and beat their hands as the guests of the Sultan passed by.

Once the torchlight fell on a broad stretch of water banked on the hillside, where great lily pads gleamed and the giant flowers were folded for sleep, and, because the people were rarer now, he heard the deep drone of insects coming to the lights and the croak of frogs in the green water fringe.

Ahead of him, Guido turned and clasped his hands above his head and shouted back, *"Che passeggiata, amico!* You enjoying yourself?"

McCreary waved and called a warning.

"Watch yourself, Guido! You'll fall off and break your damned neck."

Then, abruptly, they were at the gates.

Two great pillars of teak reared themselves up, sculptured with flowers and writhing monsters and capped with the spread wings of birds. There were guards at each pillar and they waved the procession forward, and as they passed, McCreary saw the big wooden gates, carved as intricately as a pair of screens, and beyond them the climbing gardens, tier on tier, through which they must pass to the palace itself.

There were lights at every window and in every arch and colonnade so that the fretwork of stone seemed featherlight, apt to blow away in the first wind.

But there was no wind. The air was heavy with flowers and burnt incense and a faint, tinkling music of gamelan bells.

Lulled by the swaying of the litter, McCreary felt that he was floating disembodied in an opium dream, incapable of decision or action.

Then, at last, the dream ended.

The procession stopped. The litters were lowered to the ground and, as they stepped out stiffly, they found themselves in a wide, open courtyard, at the end of which a flight of steps led up to the glowing fretwork of the palace. At the top of the steps stood the fat vizier, waiting with a retinue to greet them.

Slowly they mounted the steps, their servants walking a step below them. The vizier greeted them in soft Malay and led them through the portico, along an elaborate colonnade carved in Hindu fashion and into a huge chamber lined with pillars, at the end of which was a raised throne backed by a fretted stonework screen.

They looked at each other, dumb with amazement.

The hall was large enough to deploy an army. The walls and the pillars and the throne itself must have been carved by the craftsmen who came in the ninth century with the Hindu rulers of the spice islands.

The center square was brightly lit and set round the edge with piled cushions and low tables of carved wood and pearl inlay. In the shadows behind the pillars, servants in embroidered blouses and colourful sarongs waited silently and, to the left of the throne, a gamelan orchestra played its tinkling monotonous rhythms. From behind the stonework screen came a murmur of women's voices and an occasional smothered giggle, as if the women of the household were watching the arrival of the strangers.

The floor in front of the throne and between the tables was clear to allow the passage of the servants and the entertainers, and the throne itself shone with changing lights as the jewels reflected the wavering flames of the lamps that hung from the ceiling and from the pendants on the pillars.

On the right of the main throne a smaller one had been raised, less richly jewelled, obviously movable. McCreary wondered whether it had been set for Rubensohn or for the senior member of the household. There was no firm protocol in these petty sultanates. Their customs were a baroque compound of migrant manners and strangely mixed faiths.

The vizier led them to the row of cushions immediately facing the throne and seated them a little to one side of the center trio. Guido squatted next to McCreary and watched wide-eyed as the vizier clapped his hands to bring a small troupe of servants, each carrying a tray of beaten silver on which was palm liquor in a silver goblet and a box of strange sticky sweetmeats.

They bowed, presented their offerings and withdrew. As they sipped the sweet, flat liquor, Guido chuckled impishly.

"Poor Arturo! Left with the dogwatch on a night like this. I weep for the boy."

"He's better out of it," said McCreary with a grin. "I'm told it can turn into a willing evening. Where's Rubensohn, I wonder?"

Guido shrugged theatrically.

"He'll be here! The big entrance, with Janzoon in all his gold braid and your girl on his arm. I wouldn't be surprised if he marched straight to the throne and took over from the Sultan."

"I wouldn't either," said McCreary. "But not tonight."

Guido grinned and turned away, chattering in Italian to the other officers. McCreary sipped his liquor and surrendered himself to contemplation of the barbaric splendour around him.

Now, he thought, he could understand the dreams of the filibusters. This was the thing that had beckoned them out, century after century, under alien flags, in leaky ships, with tatterdemalion crews—this vision of peacock thrones and gods with jewels for eyes, and treasure stores under the foundations of fairy palaces.

For them, power was a tangible thing, measured by weight of bullion, by number of slaves, by the size and splendour of palace or mausoleum.

They were the primitives, stifled by civilization. There was no rest for them in the cities, no hope for them in the old world. And if they died too soon, they died with incense in their nostrils and the music of strange tongues in their ears.

Rubensohn had that streak in him and it was the best part of his complex character. It showed in his moments of exaltation and in the cool daring of his roguery. He was a big man; he might even have been a great one but for the taint of cruelty and perverted cunning.

The music stopped suddenly, then began again on a new and stronger beat. There was a rustle of draperies and a murmur of voices and the courtiers filed in, gaudy as parrots in silk blouses and embroidered vests and sarongs stencilled in bold jungle designs. They bowed formally and showed their betel-stained teeth in a grin of welcome, then took their places on the cushions at either side of the hollow square. The servants came forward again with the drinks and the sweetmeats, then withdrew into the dim arches.

A moment later the vizier entered again. Rubensohn, Janzoon and Lisette followed him.

The beauty of her was breathtaking. Her small body was clothed in a sari of gold, draped ceremonial fashion over her hair and falling in soft folds to the golden sandals. There were emeralds at her throat and on her wrists, and her skin glowed like alabaster with the light behind it.

Her face was a sculptor's mask, immobile, perfect, in which her dark eyes were the only sign of life.

Rubensohn and Janzoon led her to the center cushion and settled her comfortably. Then she drew her sari round her face like a veil and sat, silent and absorbed, waiting for the ceremony to begin.

The fat vizier moved to the foot of the throne and stood waiting. Then a gong sounded, brazen and terrible, echoing through the colonnades and up among the sculptured figures on the ceiling. The whole assembly stood up and waited with bowed heads and closed eyes, while the vizier chanted the ten ceremonial names of the Sultan of Karang Sharo, ending with the greatest name of all—Navel of the Universe.

When they looked up, he was standing on the dais, a small boyish figure against the spread of the peacock throne, with his guards ranged about him and the chair at his side still vacant. He sat down. The company waited till he had raised his hand, and they, too, settled themselves on the cushions.

McCreary thought it was a pretty piece of stage management. He wondered whether Rubensohn had had a hand in it. He also wondered when they were going to bring more drinks. His mouth was dry and the cloying taste of the sweetmeats was still on his tongue.

Then the fat fellow took the floor again.

He spoke, he said, unworthily in the name of the great, whose voice was a thunder that might wake the sleeping mountain. His voice—which he prayed might be like flowers in his mouth—was raised to welcome the strangers whose coming would bring prosperity to the land and wealth to the people. They came as friends, bearing gifts, which were the promise of greater gifts. But the great one, he of the ten names and the greatest name of all, was not to be outdone in generosity. So now to each of the strangers he would give his own gift, a jewel to wear on his heart, a flower to perfume his pillow. . . .

He raised a pudgy hand and the gongs sounded again, and from the shadowy colonnade came seven girls, small and perfect, bright as blossoms, bearing each a small cushion on which lay a jewel set in the soft filigree of the local craftsmen. They came and knelt in front of Rubensohn and McCreary and each of the officers and tendered the gifts. Then they knelt beside the cushions in attitudes of submission to their new masters.

The gongs sounded again and Rubensohn stood up. McCreary watched him, fascinated. Hate him as you might, there was no denying the power that went out from him. His clothes were drab beside the bright finery of the Asiatics, yet he dominated the assembly and seemed even to dwarf the figure on the peacock throne. He paused a moment and then began to speak in perfect Malay, full of allusion and hieratic hyperbole.

He was grateful, he said, for the princely honours done to him and to his friends. The gifts he had brought were small and unworthy beside those of the Sultan, but they were a promise of greater ones. Moreover, they came from a new world, where wonders sprang up like mango trees from the hands of a magician . . .

As he spoke, the servants began carrying the gifts from the rear of the hall and ranging them a little to the side of the throne.

There was a box which would bring the voices of the world into the palace of Karang Sharo. There was a machine which would light the whole palace at the touch of a finger. There was a palanquin on wheels which would carry the Navel of the Universe wherever he wished, as soon as roads were built to accommodate it. There were guns for the royal armoury and glassware such as the princes of Europe used. There were silks for the royal household and jewelry for the fingers of the royal wives. There were gifts for every officer of the palace. . . .

He paused, while the last boxes were stacked around the shining runabout, incongruous and laughable amid the ancient magnificence.

And finally, the greatest gift in his power to bestow, a pearl of incomparable quality, a personal gift for the Navel of the Universe, which he begged humbly to present in person. . . .

Slowly he raised Lisette to her feet and walked her step by step down the empty space to the foot of the throne.

"Dear God no!" McCreary's voice was a whisper of horror and he started to his feet, but Janzoon and Guido clamped their hands on him and held him down, and Guido's voice spoke desperately in his ear.

"Not now, for pity's sake! They will cut you down and you cannot help her! Control yourself—for her sake!"

He sank back on the cushions, feeling their fingers bite into his arms, and he watched Lisette prostrate herself like a slave at the feet of the Sultan. Then he saw the brown hands lift her to her feet, unveil her and lead her to the throne beside his own, while the courtiers sighed in soft wonderment at her beauty.

He saw Rubensohn bow and walk slowly back to his place, a thin smile on his lips, his eyes bright with triumphant malice. He longed desperately to leap at him and tear him down and trample him on the pavement, but Guido and Janzoon still held him and he could not find even voice to curse his tormentor.

Then the document of concession was presented and the music began again, and with it the long procession of waiters, bearing food and drink. The jugglers came and the acrobats, and the dancers, moving like jointed dolls in the rhythms of the old mimes.

But McCreary saw none of it. He sat silent and stone-faced, filling himself with liquor and watching Lisette perched beside the peacock throne, being fed like a bird from the brown fingers of the Sultan.

When the evening was over, they hoisted him, dead drunk, onto the litter; and when they came to the ship, Guido and the little brown slave undressed him and put him to bed.

Chapter Eleven

He woke, deathly sick. His head was hammering and his tongue was too big for his mouth. His skin was clammy and smelt of stale liquor, and the sheets were wrapped round him like a shroud. He saw that the cabin was full of sunlight and that a brown girl was sitting in his chair, watching him with wide, solemn eyes.

Then he remembered—and the memory was like a blow in the belly. He heaved himself off the bed and staggered to the bathroom, and after a while the brown girl came in and helped him to clean himself up and get shaved and bathed. Her service was simple and unquestioning. Her hands were soft, her movements were deft, and McCreary found her a small comfort in his manifold miseries.

He had hit rock bottom, and he knew it. He knew, too, that his own blind faith in the luck of the Irish had landed him there. He had tried to fight out of his own class and had ended on the mat with Rubensohn kicking his teeth and Lisette handed over, helpless, as part of the price of an oil deal. He asked himself why she had never told him what Rubensohn had in mind for her. The answer was very simple. She had known he could do nothing about it and that he was liable to act like a bull-headed Irishman and get shot for his pains. Which left him where he was now, sitting on the edge of the bed in his underpants, holding his aching head and wondering what he should do next. The others would be wondering too—Rubensohn and Janzoon. They would be waiting for his reaction, judging him by it, preparing to counter it.

What would they expect? A red-eyed rebel, sour with hangover, charging in with his head down, easily subdued by another smack in the teeth. No profit in

337

that for Lisette or for himself. He needed time to get a grip on himself and plan the gambits before he saw Rubensohn.

The brown girl helped him to dress and then he sent her to the galley for coffee and a sick man's breakfast. She answered quickly enough to his own Malay, but he was too fuddled to piece out much of her exotic island dialect.

The stewards were apparently dispensing for others than himself. They sent him a large jug of coffee, a slice of papaya and a small grilled fish with buttered toast. The sight of the food revolted him, but he forced himself to eat it, and by the time the last of the coffee was gone he began to feel better. His skin was yellow and blotchy, his eyes were like two holes burnt in a blanket. And when he tried to light a cigarette, his hands trembled as if with malaria.

He sent the girl back to the galley for more coffee and breakfast for herself. Then he sat down and tried to gather his strength. Outside he heard the clatter of the winches and the high voices of the loading crews. Miranha was at work and the first of the drilling equipment was on its way to the shore. Soon he would have to go on deck to superintend the loading of the motors and generators, and then, he thought, his real test would come.

For all the sickness in his belly and the ache in his heart, he would have to face them with a grin, make them uncertain of their victory, uneasy about his future actions. He had one trump left—without him they couldn't get oil. Everything depended on how and when he played it.

The girl came back with his coffee and a plate of rice for herself. She squatted, native fashion, at his feet, and while she ate McCreary questioned her gently.

"What's your name, little one?"

"I am called Flame Flower, tuan."

"It's a pretty name."

"I am glad it pleases the tuan."

"You understand that you belong to me now?"

"I understand, tuan."

"Shortly I must go to work. While I am gone, you will wash my clothes, and when they are dry you will pack them with the others as I will show you. We are going away from here."

"Where are we going, tuan?"

"Back to Karang Sharo. We shall live there awhile."

She looked up at him with shining, guileless eyes.

"And I shall be the tuan's woman and care for him and . . ."

"You'll care for me, little one," said McCreary hastily, and added for himself, "and we'd better leave the rest for a later time. I've got problems enough as it is."

He drank the last of his coffee, got up, tossed his laundry into a heap and showed her his bag and how to pack it. Then he put on a pair of dark glasses to hide the worst ravages of the night and went up on deck.

Alfieri was standing by the winches, snapping orders at the deck hands. He greeted McCreary with curt distaste and turned away quickly. McCreary hoped he felt as green as he looked.

Captain Janzoon was pacing the for'ard deck. McCreary waved and shouted a greeting. Janzoon looked up with faint surprise and waved back, hesitantly. There were no other officers in sight, but a couple of the girls were squatting against the bulkhead, dipping into the same rice bowl and talking in high voices like the piping of birds.

McCreary walked over to the rail and watched the island boys standing on the bobbing pontoons and juggling the heavy slings while Miranha sat in his boat and shouted orders at them.

He looked across the dazzling water to the palace below the mountain and thought of Lisette. A moment later Rubensohn's high voice spoke at his elbow:

"You're stirring early, McCreary."

"Habit of years," said McCreary coolly. "The morning's the best part of the day."

"You enjoyed your evening?"

"Sure. It was a good night."

"The best come-all-ye of the season?" Rubensohn was baiting him cruelly, but McCreary forced a grin, thankful that his eyes were hidden behind the dark glasses.

"The best. What I saw of it, that is."

"Lisette looked beautiful, I thought."

"So did I."

"You don't disapprove of my bargain?"

"I think you're a bastard," said McCreary, without rancour. "But then I've known that all along. Besides, it's no skin off my nose. I'd had my share of her before she left."

It was a calculated crudity, but he saw no shame in it. He felt a grim satisfaction when he saw Rubensohn's recoil and watched him battle to control himself.

"You're tougher than I thought, McCreary." It was a high whisper, soft as silk.

"I have to be," said McCreary. "I'm playing in a tough school. And while we're talking business, there's the small matter of an agreement to be signed and delivered before I start work."

"I'll have it ready for you in an hour," said Rubensohn flatly.

"And before we sign it . . ."

"Yes?"

"I'd like to see your passport."

It took Rubensohn completely off guard. His head flicked back, his eyes narrowed and his reedy voice was unsteady.

"What are you driving at, McCreary?"

McCreary leaned back against the rail and smiled at him.

"I want a legal document, with a verifiable signature. So I'd like to see your passport."

For a long moment Rubensohn looked at him, then, surprisingly, he smiled "I'll let you see it before we sign. Anything else?"

"Yes. Janzoon has approached me with a proposition."

"What sort of a proposition?"

This, too, was news to Rubensohn, and in spite of his control he could not conceal the first shock of surprise.

"It's a double," said McCreary sardonically. "At the moment he can't make up his mind which leg he wants. Either to buy me out for cash and guarantee protection from you, or team up with me to oust you. We could probably do it, too."

Rubensohn gave him a long, speculative look.

"Then why do you tell me?"

"You're a big man, Rubensohn. I think you can do a lot for us," said Mc-Creary deliberately. "But even big men can make mistakes that, in the end, destroy them. Your biggest mistake was to pick the wrong fellow to kick in the face. Janzoon will take it—and has—because he's scared. I'm not scared. I've got nothing to lose and a lot to gain. I've told you that before. It's time you understood it."

"You've changed a lot since that first night in Djakarta."

"I learn fast," said McCreary, with genial good humour. "The Irish are good horse copers."

Rubensohn nodded slowly and leaned against the rail, absorbed in a new, private thought. After a moment he turned to McCreary.

"I'd feel happier if we could trust each other more."

"So would I," said McCreary. "But I don't doubt we'll come to it in time." He changed the subject abruptly. "The loading'll be finished in a couple of hours. As soon as we've got the agreement fixed, I'd like to be off. You'll be down often, of course, to watch progress?"

"Every day," said Rubensohn, "until the well blows in."

"Then you're thinking of killing me?"

"I had thought of it," said Rubensohn, with surprising frankness. "Now I've changed my mind. I'll get you to kill Janzoon instead."

"You're lying again," said McCreary amiably.

Rubensohn flushed angrily.

"Now look, McCreary . . ."

"Look yourself, me bright boyo! Why not admit it? You'd like us both out of the way so you can take the whole profit for yourself. Else why did you offer Alfieri the captain's job?"

"Did Alfieri tell you that?"

"A little bird told me."

"Have you told Janzoon?"

"I've thought about it," said McCreary carefully. "Just as I've thought about dropping a word about the island that the Sultan's new wife came from

340

the Peacock Pavilion in Saigon, and about leaving a message for Scott Morrison that the deal is phony and that there's a dead man in Djakarta to prove it; just as I've worked out every damn trick in the book to stop you getting a drop of oil, if there's half a chance I'm going to be killed when it comes in. Now, Rubensohn, don't you think it's time you played at least one honest hand?"

And with that he turned away and walked over to the winches to watch the first generator being hoisted overside. He didn't count too much on all his brave talk. It was a nice Irish gesture, and he hoped it might give Rubensohn a headache or two, but it was rather like old Paddy Moynighan, drunk as a lord, prancing at the crossroads and waving his shillelagh at the cows. Come close to him and he'd fetch you a crack or two, but he always ended the same way, with a broken head and a bloody nose, lying in the ditch in the morning.

Two hours later, accompanied by Guido and Agnello, the engineer officer, and Flame Flower and Agnello's girl, McCreary left the ship for the drilling site. He had the survey charts in his pocket and with them Rubensohn's contract giving him, in return for services rendered, a quarter share of the proceeds of the sale and the right to claim payment direct from the purchaser.

He had no illusions about the validity of the document. There is no law in the world that can enforce a payment to a criminal accessory. He was more interested in the fact that Rubensohn's name really was Rubensohn and that he had a specimen of his legal signature verified from the passport. The passport had given him other information, too. Rubensohn was a British subject, Polish by birth, who had been naturalized ten years before. His age was forty-eight, and his names were Joseph Ladislas. The passport itself was a double-sized book to cope with Rubensohn's peripatetic existence.

The day might come when he could make use of these facts. For the present there were other matters to occupy him.

When they came to the beach, they found Miranha waiting for them with a couple of boys to carry the bags and the radio pack. The rest of the equipment was already on its way, carried on poles and bamboo hurdles by a small brown army.

They set off along the winding track that led through the villages of the littoral towards the low spur beyond which lay the drilling area.

Agnello walked ahead with Miranha, and Guido and McCreary strode along together, with the girls trotting like excited children behind them.

The dust rose in small clouds from their feet, parching their lips and settling in the nostrils. The broad green leaves hung listless, and the air was crackling with insects and the chatter of the villages.

Slowly the drink sweated out of him and McCreary began to be absorbed in the strident, colourful life of the huts that lined the road. Women, naked to the waist, suckled children at the doors or stood knee-deep in the roadside pools washing themselves and the family clothes. A smith beat out the wavering blade of a kris over a small charcoal fire. A vendor padded by with long

341

bamboo poles over his shoulders, from which hung bunches of bananas and baskets of bean curd and brown rice. Laughing girls sat weaving the big palm mats which would make the walls of the houses and the beds on which they would sleep. A water buffalo wandered by, goaded by a toddler with a sharp bamboo stick, and a flight of swallows dipped down from the blue sky into the shade of the pathway. High up in the bare branches of a flame tree a boy was picking the scarlet blooms and putting them into a basket hung round his neck. A silversmith, old and blear-eyed, was tapping a bowl with a tiny hammer, and beside him a boy with honey-coloured skin and tiny hands like a woman's was whittling a comb from soft white wood.

For a while Guido, too, was absorbed in the spectacle; then he broached the subject that was troubling him.

"It was bad last night, *amico.*"

"Very bad, Guido."

"You—you understand I had to do what I did. Otherwise they would have killed you."

"I know that, Guido. I'm grateful."

"What are you going to do now?"

"Work," said McCreary tersely. "Work and plan to get Lisette out and bring Rubensohn down."

Guido whistled.

"Get her out? You think you can?"

"I'm going to try."

"But how? You saw what the palace is like. The women are kept in their own quarters. There are guards . . ."

"I know." McCreary nodded gravely. "But we can make a beginning. These girls . . ." He pointed to the two small figures giggling behind them. "They come from the palace, remember. They know the layout. They can help."

"If they will, yes."

McCreary looked at him sharply.

"What do you mean . . . 'if'?"

Guido grinned at him like a wise goat.

"These are women, too, McCreary. They look like children, but they could be any age from fifteen to twenty-five. They have been given to the tuans— they regard themselves as our women and us as their men. It would be wise to remember that. If you want help, you will have to pay for it, one way or another. If you want your Lisette back, you must have an ally, not a rival."

"Hell!" said McCreary succinctly.

"That's what I mean," chuckled Guido. "Another thing . . ."

"Yes?"

"You get your Lisette out. It is still not enough. You have to get her away from the island, otherwise you both end in the hands of the torturers. You think Rubensohn will give you a free passage on the *Corsair?*"

"I doubt it."

"So you think of that, too. You remember that we are three people—you, me, the girl—anchored on an island, and the man who owns the transport is a man who wants to kill you."

"I've thought of it," said McCreary. "I've thought it over and over, and it all adds up to the one answer. Someday, soon, I'm going to kill Rubensohn. But before I do, I'm going to strip him of everything he's got. Don't ask me how, but I'm going to do it."

"I wish you luck," said Guido, without conviction.

"Tell me." McCreary dropped his voice and jerked his head at the pair ahead of him. "This Agnello. What sort of man is he? He's going to work with me most of the time. I'd like to think I could trust him."

Guido shrugged and kicked out at a pecking chicken.

"You know engineers. They eat cotton waste and bathe in machine oil. Sometimes I think they want nothing better than to marry an engine and breed little ones. Agnello is like that. He has a sad face like a horse, and he never says more than two words. What he thinks or feels you will have to find out for yourself. If you can make him a friend, we are much stronger. Without him, they cannot run the ship."

"I'll spend some time on him," said McCreary thoughtfully.

Now they had left the last of the villages and were rounding the low spur that divided the drilling area from the rest of the island. The track led upwards through thick jungle, and beside it a small stream tumbled downwards over green rocks overhung with ferns and the skeleton roots of breadfruit trees.

After about half an hour's tramping they came to the area itself, a wide clearing that looked eastward over the sea and the scattered islands. Behind it was the serrated spine of the mountains rising slowly to the palace itself and the humped cone behind it.

The clearing swarmed with brown, chattering men, and the equipment was piled along one side of it in neat stacks.

McCreary looked about him with a practiced eye. It was a good spot, easy to work in. There was clean mountain water, free from the pollution of the kampongs. There was good timber close, handy, and bamboo and palm boles in abundance for the lighter construction of the huts. When the day was ended, they could sit and look out over the sea, away from the plague of mosquitoes, and, if they climbed the spine of the mountains, they could look down on the approaches to the palace. Perhaps, even, he might catch a glimpse of Lisette as she walked in the walled gardens among the women. He reminded himself to ask Guido to get a pair of field glasses from the ship.

Miranha came up to him, waving his arms and hopping from foot to foot, and talking in his huckster's whine.

"Here we are, senhor. You are the number one here, they tell me. There is your gear, there are my workmen. You tell Miranha what you want and we get busy, eh?"

343

"Right!" said McCreary crisply, and calling to Agnello and Guido, he began pacing out the locations.

"The derrick goes here, slap in the center. Motor housings here. Machine shop and maintenance over there. You'll find all the stuff numbered on the schedule, Agnello, together with a working diagram. The crates are stencilled to correspond with the number on the list. Get yourself a team and start work. Over against the hill, facing out to sea, we'll have the living huts—two of them; next to them a storehouse for machine parts, a long, roofed shelter for the piping and the big stuff. A cook house here. The radio goes in my hut, Guido. Below the derrick, shelters for the labour crew. Over here, the fuel dumps—a thatch cover will be enough for them . . ."

For a while it was a babbling chaos, but by midafternoon they had sorted themselves out and McCreary was able to stand with Guido on the upper edge of the clearing and watch the job take shape. Agnello and his boys were working on the foundations for the big splay legs of the derrick; the logs for the engine beds were being cut and hauled in from the jungle; the frames for the living huts and the shelters were already in position, and the brown figures were swarming over the roofs, laying the thatch of alang grass.

McCreary found a deep satisfaction in this ant-like activity. He had seen it before many times, in many places, but each time it was new, because each well is a new challenge, and the day the bits bite in for the first time is like a new race for an unknown yearling, with the crowds waiting and the sleek bodies shining at the starter's gate and the silks fluttering in the small wind and no one knowing what number will go up at the finish.

It was sacrilege to think of it as a criminal enterprise, with death and disaster at the end of it.

Guido squatted on his haunches and chewed reflectively on a grass stalk. He said hesitantly, "I've been thinking, McCreary."

"What?"

Guido pointed down the hillside to where the flapping scarecrow figure of Miranha was hustling a line of boys cutting alang grass.

"There's the man who can help you. He knows this place. He knows the back doors to the palace. He's got a boat, too—that ketch moored in the main harbour. He's a trader, isn't he? He knows these waters. At least he could get you to Timor . . ."

"I don't trust him," said McCreary. "He's a dock rat. He'd sell his own mother for a fistful of coppers."

"You don't have to trust him," Guido persisted. "You only have to frighten him."

"And how would I do that?"

"Simple enough. When this thing blows up, as it must do one day, like a bomb, who is here? Not us, not Rubensohn—Miranha! If the Sultan wants to roast somebody's toes, who's the nearest? Who's the interpreter and the agent? Miranha! I think if you talk to him someday and tell him the facts and

344

offer him a nice fat reward, you will have yourself an ally—and a boat as well."

McCreary looked down at the little Neapolitan and laughed.

"We'd better change jobs, Guido. Seems you're the only one with brains around here."

"Not me!" said Guido firmly. "Not for a million pounds would I sleep in your bed! Every night I would have nightmares, thinking my throat was cut."

"I've got 'em now," said McCreary somberly. "But somehow I've got to learn to live with 'em."

Chapter Twelve

By sunset, the living huts and the main storehouses had been built. The base frame for the derrick was in place; the teak logs had been stripped and laid out near the engine positions. Miranha had marshalled his workers and checked their tools back into storage and herded them homewards. Guido had gone with him, after setting up the radio pack and giving McCreary detailed instructions for its operation. They had arranged a morning schedule, when Guido would call McCreary and give him half an hour's practice on the key, passing on at the same time any news from the ship.

Guido had wanted to stay the night, but McCreary had refused. It would be unwise, so soon, to let Rubensohn see too close an association between himself and the little radioman. Their communication system was sketchy enough, and at all costs it had to be kept open.

The huts were modest but habitable. Each had two bunks framed with bamboo and covered with palm matting. There was a rough table and a couple of bamboo chairs, knocked together at astonishing speed by Miranha's workmen. For the rest, they were furnished from the ship with clean bed-covers and eating utensils and mosquito netting and a basic stock of first-aid gear, suppressant tablets and liquor—half a dozen cases of beer and two bottles of whisky per man. Their food would be tinned stores supplemented by local produce supplied under contract by Miranha.

McCreary and Agnello were sitting together outside McCreary's hut, drinking beer and looking down over the jungle fringe to the luminous water of the small bay between the two spurs of cliff. Twenty yards away the two girls were giggling over the cook fires, from which rose the pungent, exotic flavour

346

of native cooking. This would be the first meal they would serve to their new masters, and the girls were making it an elaborate production.

They sipped their beer and smoked contentedly, saying little.

The horse-faced engineer had a quality of relaxation that contrasted sharply with the bubbling temperament of Guido. He talked sparsely, a man content with his own company, and his simple, pragmatic phrases carried their own quiet conviction. McCreary found him a satisfying companion for the long evening hours when he, too, was busy with his own thoughts.

They were halfway through their second bottle of beer when Agnello said calmly, "I like this. It satisfies me."

"What—the beer?" McCreary was miles away—up the mountain with Lisette.

"No. This work. To see something building under your hands. To make a hole in the ground and see good oil come out of it. I am an engineer. I have great respect for oil."

"So have lots of other people," said McCreary, with offhand irony.

"No. They see it as a commodity, a source of profit. An engineer sees it as a source of life to the things he loves most in the world—good engines turning sweetly on their bearings."

"It's a good thought," said McCreary. "Better than many I've heard lately. Tell me, Agnello, how did you come to join this outfit? Why do you stay with it?"

Agnello puffed placidly at his pipe and considered the question.

"Simple enough. Here I am number one. On a big ship I would be number two. Nobody bothers me and I get good pay. That's important. In Florence I have a wife and two daughters who must soon be provided with dowries. So it suits me."

"Lucky fellow."

Agnello smoked his pipe and sipped his beer and looked out into the moonrise. For all his horse face and his melancholy eyes, McCreary thought he must be a singularly happy man. His next question brought a smile to McCreary's lips. Agnello coughed and fidgeted and jerked his thumb in the direction of the girls at the cook fires.

He said awkwardly, "What—what am I expected to do with that?"

McCreary chuckled.

"It depends on you, Agnello."

Agnello frowned and mumbled unhappily.

"I know, but—but I am not interested. When I was younger, I was happy to make a fool of myself. Now, when I see my friends going down to the houses near the docks, when I see things happen like last night in the palace, I think of my daughters, and I have no taste left for it. I just ask. I don't want to criticize what you do, but for me . . ."

McCreary dropped his cigarette on the ground and trod it out with his heel. He grinned wryly in the darkness and said, "It's fine with me, Agnello. So long

347

as you're here, we'll share my hut. You'll keep me out of mischief, too. The girls can bunk in together."

For the first time a slow smile dawned on the engineer's long face. He said gratefully, "A thousand thanks, my friend. Now I can enjoy my supper."

Then they both laughed, and McCreary thought that he, too, might eat better and sleep sounder, and build a little hope on a new ally.

The girls brought out one of the tables from the huts and laid on it dishes of steaming rice and curried fish surrounded by smaller masses of spices and side meats, cradled in green leaves. Then they squatted on the grass and watched the men pick gingerly through the unfamiliar dishes and finally settle down to enjoy them.

They giggled self-consciously when McCreary praised the meal and dismissed them to their own supper.

Flame Flower hesitated a moment and asked, "When do I come to the tuan?"

"Not tonight," said McCreary gently. "When I send for you. Tonight I have things to talk about with my friend."

"All night?" The childish eyes widened with disbelief.

McCreary grinned and patted her sleek, perfumed hair.

"No. Not all night. But we are tired. Tomorrow we work early. We need sleep."

The girl nodded and her small brown face split into a flashing smile. This she could understand. So long as she pleased the tuan, there would always be tomorrow and the nights after. The real shame was when a woman lacked the power to attract a man, and she was very anxious to attract this lean fellow with the soft voice and the laughing eyes.

She turned away to join her companion and, a long time later, while Agnello snored contentedly, McCreary could hear their twittering voices from the farther hut. They reminded him of Lisette penned with all the other alien women in the fretwork palace on the hill. The thought of her was an ache in his heart and a sharp torment in his flesh.

Early next morning, when Agnello was out with Miranha and the labour gangs, Guido sent him word on the buzzer.

"Rubensohn's on his way up to see you. He's given me a radio message for Morrison."

"What is it?" signalled McCreary awkwardly. It was a long time since he had worked a key and his fingers were slow and his groups uncertain.

"Test begins . . . Operations begun stop. Expect early result stop. Stand by further reports stop . . . Message ends. I sent it."

"O.K.! Any more news?"

"Argument Janzoon-Alfieri still in progress. Subject *Corsair* command. More when I see you. Palace courier arrived first light with message for Rubensohn. End news."

"Thanks. Remember field glasses."

"Will bring this afternoon. Practice sending. Hard to read."

McCreary spelt out: "Go to hell!" then switched off the power, laid aside the headphones and lit a cigarette. He was smiling to himself. His talk with Rubensohn was beginning to have effect. To cover his own maneuvers, Rubensohn must have talked with Janzoon and given him a doctored version of Alfieri's ambitions. It was part of his technique, to muddy up the water and make profit from the confusion of his subordinates.

Well, McCreary had stirred some mud of his own, and like a cranky Celt, he found a deal of pleasure in it. He stepped out into the raw sunshine, called Flame Flower to tidy his hut, then walked down the slope to the work gangs, whistling jauntily to himself.

It was an old tune this morning, called in Kerry "The Hounds of Glenloe." It told of the hunt slavering up hill and down dale while the canny old fox sat in his earth and thumbed his nose at the lot of them. For a long time now McCreary had had great sympathy with Brother Fox.

Miranha was directing a bunch of boys stacking the big fuel drums under a thatched shelter. When McCreary came up to him, he showed his teeth in a betel-stained smile and immediately launched into a rasping monologue.

"We're doing well, senhor, aren't we? See! It begins to look like something. But you've got to understand these fellows. Smile at 'em, but keep driving all the time. You're satisfied, I hope. If there's anything you want, tell Miranha. I get it fixed, pronto. I promised Mr. Rubensohn cooperation, fullest service. When I say that, I mean it. Value for money, eh? That makes good business for both of us."

"Sure," said McCreary coolly. "You're doing fine. Just keep the work rolling. I'll let you know if there's anything I want."

Miranha licked his lips. His bloodshot eyes looked both ways at once. He said in a confidential whisper:

"You—er . . . you couldn't sell me a bottle of whisky, senhor? This native toddy ruins a man. I'm prepared to pay . . ."

"I'll give you a bottle," said McCreary curtly.

Miranha began to pour out a profuse speech of gratitude, but McCreary cut him short.

"Tell me, what are you getting paid for this?"

"Three pounds sterling a day, in Indonesian rupiahs. It's only a pittance, of course, but . . ."

"But it's more than you'd earn otherwise, and you get a cut from the boys' wages and a profit on any materials you supply and on the food rations. . . ."

Miranha shrugged and spread his hands in deprecation.

"Oh, a little here and there. But that's normal trade, eh? That's what I am after all—a trader. This job keeps me from my normal trips. I'm entitled to a small profit. Isn't that right?"

McCreary grinned at him ironically.

"Don't ask me, Miranha. Your contract's with Rubensohn. I just work here." He brought out a packet of cigarettes and handed one to Miranha. "Tell me, where do you trade normally?"

Miranha puffed out a cloud of smoke and talked as offhandedly as a merchant prince.

"Oh, Ambon, Buru, east to Kai Ketjil and south to Timor Laut and Timor."

"What sort of trade?"

"Foodstuffs, spices, trade cloth, normal things—it's mostly barter here. A few stones sometimes, gold and silverware. There's a small market in Dili for European export. Sometimes a girl or two, to keep the Sultan happy. You know how it goes."

"Sure," said McCreary.

"Maybe . . ." Miranha hesitated. "Maybe you do a little trade yourself sometimes?"

"A little." McCreary cocked a quizzical eyebrow. "You know how it goes?"

"I could put some business in your way, perhaps?"

"What did you have in mind?"

"This stuff." Miranha jerked his thumb at the stacks of fuel drums. "It costs like gold in Dili, which is the only place I can buy it. Then I can't build up a store because it cuts down my cargo space. So half my trip I run the ketch on sail. That doubles my time and halves my profit. You got more than you need there. I can make you a nice offer. Stone, some jade, nice pieces, and other things. If you're interested, I'll show you."

"Bring 'em up to the hut one evening. We'll talk about it."

Miranha showed his stained teeth in a wide and understanding grin.

"Good, good! I think you'll like what I show you. And we keep it private, eh? Another thing. If you want a girl any time."

"I've got a girl," said McCreary bluntly, "and she's more than I can handle. Now, jump to it! I want this stuff stacked in the next twenty minutes. Then you can start on the steel sections."

"Yes, senhor." Miranha flapped away, cursing the Malays in fluent and obscene dialect, and McCreary looked after him with sardonic satisfaction.

Then he saw Rubensohn coming into the clearing, riding like a rajah on a litter carried by six men. He was dressed in a tussah suit and a white panama and was smoking one of his long cigars.

They lowered the litter and he stepped out awkwardly, then stood a moment looking round the clearing, measuring the progress with a critical eye. McCreary tossed away his cigarette and walked over to him. Rubensohn greeted him cheerfully.

"This is what I like to see, McCreary! Good organization, fast work. You've got everything you want?"

"For the present, yes."

"When do you think you can spud in?"

"Early to say. But we'll be ready in a week at the outside. Six days maybe."

"Good. You're satisfied with Miranha?"

"So far, yes."

"You've got all the labour you want?"

"Yes."

"One thing, McCreary. I'm sorry about it, but I'll have to take Agnello away from you for a couple of days."

"Why?"

Rubensohn shrugged and waved his cigar.

"A message from the palace. We made the Sultan a present of some mechanical equipment: a lighting plant for one thing, an automobile . . . He wants them put into running order. The lighting's the biggest job—lots of wiring to be run and . . ."

"You can't have Agnello!" said McCreary.

Rubensohn frowned.

"You don't understand, McCreary. This is . . ."

"I understand damn well!" McCreary was curt and determined. "You gave me a free hand here. You see the stage we're at. If I don't have Agnello, I can't get this gear running on time. It's as simple as that."

Rubensohn was apologetic.

"I'm sorry, McCreary, but you know the way things are run here. The Sultan is the Navel of the Universe—first cousin to God Almighty. I can't refuse him. He could shut us down with a twitch of his finger."

McCreary thought about it for a moment. The point was clear enough, but if anyone were going to the palace, it should be someone who could make a profit out of it for Lisette and for himself.

He said, irritably, "Why waste a good engineer on a simple job like that? Any electrician's apprentice could do it. Why not leave me Agnello and send Guido instead? He's a radioman—he could run the wiring and connect it to the generator. He can drive a car, surely. Damn it all, Rubensohn, let's be sensible about this thing! I don't give a curse whether the Sultan goes to bed by candlelight for the rest of his life, but we both care if this rig isn't working on schedule. I want Agnello here!"

Rubensohn was obviously glad of the suggestion. He said heartily, "Of course! Wonder I didn't think of it myself. Guido's the obvious man. I'll send him up there this afternoon."

"Leave it till the morning," said McCreary. "I've got him coming over here this afternoon. My radio isn't satisfactory. I want him to have a look at it."

Rubensohn chuckled shrilly and patted him on the shoulder.

"You're a prickly fellow, McCreary. But I like the way you work. It gives me great confidence for the future."

"I'm sure it does," said McCreary sourly. "Now, if you want to look around, I can give you ten minutes. Agnello doesn't know enough Malay and I've got to teach a dozen of these boys how to handle and bolt the derrick sections."

But Rubensohn was not to be shaken off so easily. Even after McCreary had left him to begin work on the steel frame of the derrick, he strolled about the

351

clearing watching the work with shrewd, appraising eyes. McCreary began to be afraid that he would not leave before Guido arrived and that he would lose this first, slender chance of communicating with Lisette.

Just before noon, however, Rubensohn began to show signs of tiring. His tussah suit was staining under the armpits and his pale face was streaming with sweat. He sat down on a log and mopped his cheeks and tried to smoke another cigar. Then, abruptly, he surrendered. He signalled to the litter bearers, shouted farewell to McCreary and left, a crumpled white figure swaying down the hillside and into the jungle overhang.

McCreary climbed down from the framework and called to Agnello to join him.

"Let's have a beer, Agnello."

"As you like. But it's not noon yet."

"The boys are doing all right. We can leave them to it. I want to talk to you."

Together they climbed the small slope to the living huts and went, gratefully, into the shade, which smelt of leaves and fresh grass and the lingering musky perfume of Flame Flower.

McCreary brought out the beer. They toasted each other, then sank the first glasses in a long, thirsty gulp.

"Another one, Agnello?"

"Thanks. It goes down easily."

This time they sipped it slowly, tasting it with relish.

McCreary said blandly, "I've got things to tell you, Agnello—a long story." Agnello nodded.

"You woke me last night, shouting in your sleep."

"Did I say much?"

"Enough."

"Right! I'll tell you the rest of it. When I've finished, I'm going to put it up to you to help me. I'll understand if you refuse, but I must count on your secrecy."

"You can count on it," said Agnello, in his grave, practical voice.

McCreary told him.

When he had finished, Agnello's face was longer than ever and his limpid eyes were angry. He said simply, "A dirty business. And to sell a woman like that is the dirtiest of all. I have daughters—good girls. I feel that part most."

"Will you help me then?"

"I'll help, if I can. What do you want?"

McCreary told him about the Sultan's summons and how he had persuaded Rubensohn to send Guido. Then he went on:

"I have the idea that Guido may be able to make contact with Lisette. At least he'll be able to get some idea of the layout of the palace and of the women's quarters in particular. When he comes this afternoon, I'm going to take him up the mountain there and see what sort of a view we get from this side. I may want to spend more and more time up there over the next few days. Can you run the camp and keep the work going? And answer any questions of Rubensohn if he comes when I'm not here?"

"No trouble at all," said Agnello. "But you must think further than that."

"I know," said McCreary. "But I can't think too far yet. I've got to play the cards as they fall. The big problem is to lift ourselves off the island once I get Lisette out."

Agnello put down his beer and began filling his pipe with maddening deliberation. Then he said calmly, "Miranha's got a boat."

"I can't trust all this to Miranha."

"You don't have to do that. You tell me he wants you to sell him fuel. Good. You point out to him that you can't do it openly or all at once. You suggest he move his ketch out of the main harbour and down to the bay there, so you can let him have a drum now and others later. He can take the stuff down at night. He will stay there so long as there's a chance of getting more out of you. So you have your boat, fuelled and ready to move, whenever you want."

McCreary whistled softly.

"Holy Patrick! It might work at that! And if I were to get myself one of these native dugouts and interest myself in some night fishing, so they'd be used to seeing me around . . . Let's have another drink to celebrate a noble thought."

"Not for me," said Agnello, with his slow smile. "I'll walk down and see how the work goes. These boys are intelligent—but they are like the southerners in my country. They would rather sing and sun themselves than do an honest day's work."

McCreary watched him walk slowly down to the derrick site, puffing his pipe, a picture of guileless contentment, the man who ran the engines while the passengers drank and seduced each other's wives and the captain took coffee with the owner's representative.

He turned back into the hut, took out a pencil and paper and began to sketch a plan of campaign.

The little brown girl came in and squatted down at his feet, watching him with expectant eyes. McCreary stroked her head absently and she leaned against him, purring like a contented kitten.

It took him twenty minutes to realize that here was yet another ally, perhaps the strongest of all.

He leaned down and lifted her, feather-light, and sat her on the table in front of him. She sat there, smiling like a small brown doll, perfect as a doll, with her small, pointed breasts and the honey skin and her tiny expressive hands.

He asked her gently, "What did you do in the palace, small one?"

"I served the Sultan's women. Sometimes, when one of the others was sick, I danced in the *djoged* dances."

"Were you shut in, like the Sultan's women?"

She laughed, amused at his ignorance.

"No! Only the wives and the concubines were kept like that. We others were free to come and go. We were neither married nor betrothed nor concubines."

"What would have happened to you if you had not come to me?"

She pouted and shrugged indifferently.

"One of the servants might have asked to marry me. The Sultan might have given me as a gift to one of the court. We were his property, to keep or give away."

"Were you born in the palace?"

"No. I was born in the town. But my parents gave me to the palace, because they were too poor to pay the Sultan's tax."

"What do the women do—the Sultan's women?"

"They sit and talk. They listen to the musicians beyond the screens. They eat sweetmeats and sew and have babies. Sometimes they walk in their own garden, in the cool."

"And no man comes near them—only the Sultan?"

"No man. There are guards on the doors and it is death to any man to enter."

"Do they never have lovers then?"

Her eyes widened with surprise and a hint of fear.

"Oh, no! Who would risk the torturers and the fiery death?"

"What do you mean?"

She told him, making a pantomime with her small, fluent hands.

"If a woman were unfaithful to the Sultan, she and her lover would be tortured first, under each other's eyes. Then they would be bound and thrown together into Gurung Merapi, the mountain of fire."

A grim prospect, thought McCreary. Enough to cool the ardour of lovers. He thought of Lisette penned among the twittering, idle concubines, eating her heart out in the walled garden, and he was filled with anger against Rubensohn for what he had done to her. Flame Flower watched him with puzzled, questioning eyes. He took out a cigarette and stuck it between his lips. When he made to light it, the girl took the lighter from his hands and laughed with delight when finally she snapped it into flame. He smoked a few moments in silence, wondering how to frame the next question. He reminded himself of Guido's warning that this, too, was a woman—apt to jealousy and subtle revenge. Then he hit on an idea.

He said carefully, "The woman who was given to the Sultan was my sister."

To his surprise, Flame Flower laughed happily and clapped her hands.

"Then you are both fortunate. To be the Sultan's woman is a great honour."

"No!" said McCreary gravely. "I am lonely for her. We were like flowers on the same stem, beans in the same pod. She did not want to go. She wanted to marry one of her own kind. I wanted her to be near me when I, too, married my woman. Can you understand that?"

"Yes. Sometimes there were women who did not wish to come into the palace. They were sad and wept often—but only when the Sultan was not there."

"I want to get a message to my sister," said McCreary carefully, "and have her send a message to me. If I knew she was happy, I could be happy, too. Do you know how I could send it?"

"I could take it for you."

"You could?"

"Of course. That is how news comes and goes in the palace. We belong there. We can go back at any time. The guards know us and let us pass freely."

"Well, I'll be damned!" said McCreary, in English. "As simple as that."

"And when you know she is happy," said Flame Flower, guilelessly, "you will begin to be happy with me?"

Then he knew it wasn't simple at all. It was damnably complicated. If he didn't watch his step with this girl, he'd be getting poison in his rice bowl and Lisette might well fall into the hands of the Sultan's executioner.

Chapter Thirteen

"WHAT DO YOU MAKE OF IT, GUIDO?"

"Narrow," said Guido cryptically. "Narrow like the beam of a ship. When you look at it from the front it spreads lengthwise all along the flank of the hill. But from here, end on, it has no depth. The hill is like a cliff behind it and the plateau is narrow. It is the gardens that make the illusion."

They were lying on their bellies, high up in the neck of the re-entrant above the drilling side and looking southward along the flank of the hill to the Sultan's palace. Below them lay the jungle fringe and above them the sparser vegetation of the heights. Two big boulders hid them from view and the binoculars brought the building almost to finger-touch.

"What else, Guido?"

"There is a colonnade at this end and the garden has a fountain in it, half hidden by trees. No . . . wait! This garden is completely enclosed. It does not join the hanging gardens in front!"

"Can you see anybody?"

"No. It's full of shadows."

McCreary looked at his watch.

"It's three o'clock! Flame Flower said they came out to walk in the cool."

"But this may not be their garden."

"It's got to be!" said McCreary desperately. "It's on the same side of the palace as the screen we saw. It's closed off from the other gardens. It must be!"

"Here, look for yourself!"

Guido handed him the glasses, then hoisted himself up against the rock and lit a cigarette. McCreary focussed again and scanned the dappled garden behind the high wall and the elaborate colonnade at the end of it. The fountain was playing gently, but, unless they were hidden by the trees, there were no women in the garden. They would show up quickly enough in their bright clothes. Perhaps if he waited awhile, they would come. The afternoon was still young.

He shifted his position and began to scan the green sloping hillside that lay between their observation post and the boundaries of the palace.

When the time came to bring Lisette out, this would be the way they would have to come—along the hillside and over the secondary hills and down the re-entrant to the drilling site. The normal approach would be closed to them by the guards and the milling villagers.

Carefully, he swept the hillside, up and down, along the jungle fringe, higher up in the sparse savannah towards the saddle. There was no path. The green carpet was unbroken. It was as if by custom or interdict this approach to the palace was barred to the population of Karang Sharo.

McCreary put down the glasses and rubbed his eyes.

"Nothing yet. We'll wait awhile longer."

"Relax a moment, *amico,* and tell me what you want me to do tomorrow."

McCreary propped his back against a shaded rock and began to give his instructions. They were crisp and detailed. He had thought them out carefully.

"First, you're going up to the palace in the morning to install a lighting plant. It isn't very big, so it won't light the whole palace. My guess—which could be wrong—is that you'll be instructed to light the Sultan's apartments. My hope is that you may be asked to extend it to the women's quarters. Even if you're not, you'll be moving about the palace. You'll have to find an outside location for the motor first, then you'll have to work out a wiring plan. That gives you an excuse to use a pencil and paper and draw me some plans—exits, entrances, positions of guards, and, most important of all, the various approaches to the women's quarters. If you can work in a master switch somewhere accessible, that might help, too. Are you clear so far?"

"Like crystals," said Guido cheerfully.

"How much Malay do you know?"

"Oh . . . sailorman's needs. You know—money, food, liquor . . ."

"And women!"

"Clever fellow," said Guido genially. "How did you guess?"

"My grandmother had second sight," said McCreary. "It's a pity you're so damned ignorant, otherwise you'd be able to find out a lot from chatting to the servants or the vizier or whoever's showing you around."

"Leave it to me, *compar'.* I might surprise you."

"I hope so. Now listen, Guido, this is the most important part of all. I don't know what hope you've got of making contact with Lisette—precious little, probably. You can't risk passing a note. You can't risk a direct approach even if you do catch sight of her. But, somehow, you've got to try to tell her that we're planning to get her out, that this side of the palace is where she must

357

watch and that when she gets a message from me—no matter how—she's to act on it without question."

"I'll sing it to her," said Guido, with heavy irony.

"That's just what you will do," said McCreary sharply. "And for God's sake sing it in English, not Neapolitan. Even the Pope of Rome can't understand that!"

"You offend me, *amico!* Neapolitan is the language of lovers. Even my girl is beginning to learn it. And talking of lovers, you didn't give me time to tell you of our lovers on the *Corsair.*"

"Who's that?"

"Janzoon and Alfieri!" Guido leaned back against the rock face and laughed happily. "*Mamma mia,* what a spectacle! It started the moment Rubensohn left the ship. My cabin is near the bridge. I hear Janzoon call for Alfieri over the speakers. When he comes, Janzoon tells him he had word from the owner that Alfieri had asked for the captain's post when Janzoon retires. Alfieri splutters and denies it. He would like to call the owner a liar, but he doesn't dare. Janzoon strips him down like a banana, gives him extra duties and cancels his shore leave and tells him he will write him in the log. All the time Alfieri looks down his Venetian nose and snuffles, because he doesn't know whose bed he's in and who pays at the end of it. Oh, and another thing . . ."

"Yes?"

"Janzoon gave me a message for you. He's coming ashore in the morning. He'll be paying you a little visit."

"Now, I wonder . . ." chuckled McCreary, ". . . I wonder why he'd want to do that."

He slewed himself round again and focussed the glasses on the palace garden. At its lowest point the wall looked anything from ten to twelve feet high; at its highest there was a drop of fifty feet to the jungle trees. A man would need rope and a grappling hook to scale it. It would be simpler to get out than to get in. There was a big tree near the lower corner and its branches were thick and hung low to the level of the garden. Suddenly his eye was caught by a flash of colour in the shadows of the colonnade. He lost it for a moment, then it appeared again and two figures in bright sarongs and blouses appeared and walked hand in hand towards the fountain.

McCreary handed the glasses to Guido and said sharply, "Look at 'em, Guido, and tell me—men or women? They all look the same at this distance."

"Not to me, *amico!*" said Guido, with a connoisseur's conviction. "Let me see . . . No, they're women. There are two more coming out, but neither of them is Lisette."

"We're right!" said McCreary excitedly. "That's the women's quarters and the women's garden. Now we know where to look for her!"

But though they waited and waited, taking turns with the glasses, they could not find Lisette among the bright, bird-like women walking in the dappled shade. After a long time they gave it up and walked slowly down through the jungle to the drilling site.

358

The Sharo boys were still scurrying, ant-like, through the clearing, and the steel skeleton of the derrick was rising like a giant spider web against the peach-coloured sky.

That night, after they had eaten, Miranha came to see him.

Agnello winked solemnly at McCreary and walked out to smoke his pipe. The two girls crept into the hut and sat on the bed, curious as children, while Miranha spread his offerings on the table under the kerosine lamp.

The first was a wash-leather bag of river diamonds, rough and lifeless, which Miranha spilled out on the table. McCreary looked at them with concealed interest. A lapidary could have guessed at their value, but to McCreary they might have been a handful of pebbles. There were other stones, emeralds and rubies, cut cabochon fashion and set in the flimsy filigree of the native craftsmen. There were two small jade figures, exquisitely carved, a set of Indian ivories representing the manifestations of Siva, a clutter of carved ornaments of fine workmanship and a pair of jewelled daggers.

McCreary turned them over in his hands, stirred by their odd, exotic beauty, yet careful to conceal his interest from the huckster's eyes of Miranha.

He said indifferently, "What are they worth?"

Miranha waved a dirty hand and gave him a gap-toothed smile.

"More to you than to me. You see I'm honest with you. My best market is in Dili. There they offer me perhaps a tenth of their value and I have to take it. But you, when you go away you have a chance for a big profit. It's good stuff. You can see that."

"What's it worth to you, now?"

"Say, three hundred gallons? Thirty drums?"

"Three hundred!" McCreary laughed in his face and pushed the stuff back across the table. "What do you take me for, Miranha?"

"Say twenty drums?"

"Say fifteen and we might do business. I say 'might' "—McCreary held up a warning finger—"because there's a risk in this. If Rubensohn found out, I'm in the fire and so are you. I lose my job, you lose your profit and your fuel. Those are ten-gallon drums. How do you expect to get 'em away without being seen? You can't just roll 'em down to the beach under Rubensohn's nose."

"I could come at night and siphon it out."

"To hell with that! Once we start drilling, God knows who's likely to be here at night. No, if you want the stuff, we'll do it this way. Run your ketch out of the main harbour and anchor her in the cove down there. Then you can come up at night and take a couple of drums at a time. Not all in one week either. Any fool with half an eye could see if they all went off at once. Spread 'em over a month or six weeks, and nobody will be any the wiser. We're going to be running our motors day and night during the drilling time, and I want this to look like normal usage."

Miranha looked unhappy and tried to haggle.

"Fifteen drums—a hundred and fifty gallons . . . it's too little for what I pay."

McCreary waved him away.

"It's no worry to me, Miranha. You opened the deal. Take it or leave it."

"Maybe . . . maybe for another bottle of whisky . . . ?"

"I'll throw in the whisky because I'm Irish and generous. Is that settled?"

"I'm being robbed," said Miranha unhappily. "But all the same . . ."

"You're doing damn well and you know it," said McCreary with a grin. "Half the stuff is junk and the other half will cost me boot leather and commission trying to . . ."

There was a noise like an express train and the ground rocked crazily under their feet. The girls screamed and the lamp swung high against the ceiling thatch and back again. Then the noise passed and the ground steadied again and they looked at each other with wide, startled eyes.

"Earth tremor," said Miranha uneasily. "We get them sometimes. We are in the belt. But that was a big fellow. Sometimes . . ." He licked his lips and gestured towards the rear wall of the hut. "Sometimes I wonder if Gurung Merapi isn't going to wake up and blow the lot of us to hell. He's been sleeping a long time now."

"Happy thought!" said McCreary laconically. He walked to the doorway and called out into the darkness: "Hey, Agnello! Are you all right?"

Agnello's voice floated up from the derrick site.

"I'm all right! The framework looks all right, too. I'll check it in the morning. No other damage."

A good engineer, thought McCreary wryly. He thinks of his engines like he thinks of his children.

He turned back to the hut to gather up Miranha's trinkets and hand over the bottle of whisky.

"Tomorrow," said Miranha anxiously. "Tomorrow night I run the boat round the point, then I can start to collect, eh?"

"That's right. But spread it out, remember. The longer you take, the better I'll like it."

"And if you strike oil, maybe you make me a better deal, eh?"

"If I strike oil," said McCreary genially, "I'll give you the lot. Every damned drum of it!"

He thrust the whisky into Miranha's arms and hustled him out of the hut. Then he sat down at the table and began turning over the stones and the trinkets and fingering the soft, cool surface of the jade. The two girls came peering over his shoulder and whispering excitedly.

He handed them each a small golden brooch, then patted them on their small round rumps and packed them off to bed. It was one way of keeping them happy, but he'd need to be richer than he was now to go on doing it.

He wrapped the rest of the stuff in a soiled shirt and shoved it in his bag; then he walked out into the soft moonlight to smoke a last cigarette with Agnello.

They paced slowly round the clearing, checking for signs of damage by the

360

tremor, but they found none. As they walked, McCreary gave Agnello a terse commentary of the day's doings.

When he had finished, the engineer summed up soberly.

"So far, it is all profit. You have two possibilities of communication within the palace—Guido and your girl. You have a boat, fuelled and ready, to take you off the island. You have two allies—me and Guido; three if you count Flame Flower. You have a small stake in saleable stones to start yourself somewhere. You know what I should do now in your shoes?"

"What?"

"Get out!" said Agnello stolidly. "Plan swiftly and surely, take your girl and leave the island. Forget the oil. Forget Rubensohn. Think only of your safety and a new start." He pointed with the stem of his pipe towards the cone of Gurung Merapi, whose smoky glow seemed angrier now, after the tremor. "Look, if you want a warning, you have it there. You are sitting on top of a volcano. Get off, before it blows up!"

"No!" said McCreary grimly. "I want Rubensohn. I want him pulled down and stripped to what he really is, and I want to take everything he's got."

"Why?" The long, comical face was somber and puzzled.

"Now that," said McCreary with a smile, "that would be the jackpot question, wouldn't it? I'm not sure that I know the answer, but I think it goes something like this. There are a million women in the world that you could bed with, breed children by and live with in moderate contentment. But there's only one who's so right and perfect for you that all the others are stale and tasteless. There are twenty million bastards in the world, too, any one of whom you'd be happy to kick in the teeth. But there's always the number one, the biggest of 'em all. Whatever he does, it's twice as bad to you, you hate him twice as much, you want him twice as dead and hurt a dozen times over. Probably," McCreary conceded ruefully, "because he's so very like your own secret image that you can't bear the sight of him. I wouldn't be knowing that either. But that's the way I am with Rubensohn. If I pull out now—even with Lisette—Rubensohn goes on in his own sweet way, untouched, untouchable; while we wander the world like a pair of fugitives. There's a murder charge against me in Djakarta—and that means in three thousand islands between New Guinea and Singapore. My girl's been sold for a scrap of paper, so that Rubensohn can clean up a few million. I'm not going to let him get away with it. I can't. And that, Agnello, me boy, is the longest damn speech I've ever made, and I'm still not sure there's sense in it at all."

Agnello sucked his pipe and pondered silently. But if he found an answer, he had no time to deliver it. The roaring came again and the ground shook under their feet, and the frightened girls rushed screaming from the hut and down the slope towards them.

When the silence came and the earth was still again, Agnello looked up at the angry mountain and said softly, "Someday it will all blow up. I pray that I am not here to see it."

361

Chapter Fourteen

THE NEXT DAY was unbearably long.

The Sharo boys came at daybreak and they marshalled them swiftly to work on the derrick itself, strengthening the foundations against further tremors, building up the steel sections into a tall, tapering cone. McCreary and Agnello worked on the engine beds, trenching the big logs solidly in the earth and bolting the blocks hard into the flat ax grooves.

Rubensohn came in midmorning, sweating and anxious over the effects of the tremor. They gave him scant courtesy and had him on his way in half an hour.

Miranha, red-eyed and dishevelled, with a bottle of whisky under his belt, shambled among the gangs, cursing them to greater activity, while the boys sang softly and grinned at him behind their hands.

McCreary worked with merciless intensity, trying to keep his mind off Lisette and wondering at every moment what Guido was doing in the palace. At midday he drank a bottle of beer and ate a slice of papaya and was back again in twenty minutes, scrambling up the ribs of the derrick to check the work of the Sharo boys.

At three in the afternoon Captain Janzoon came to see him.

McCreary led him over to the fringe of a clearing, sat down on a log and offered cigarettes. Janzoon was red in the face and dripping with perspiration. His spade beard jerked nervously and his thick voice stumbled over the preamble.

"The proposition, McCreary—I thought about it, as I promised. I think . . . I know . . . we can do business."

"You do now," said McCreary dryly. "And what's your offer?"

"We join forces," said Janzoon eagerly. "We work together, get rid of Rubensohn and split fifty-fifty. That was your own idea, remember?"

McCreary threw back his head and laughed. Janzoon looked at him, angry and puzzled, while the startled birds squawked in the branches of the big casuarina tree behind them.

"If there is a joke, why not tell me?"

"The joke's on you, Janzoon."

"Why?"

"Rubensohn's asked me to team up with him and get rid of you."

Janzoon's jaw dropped slackly and his eyes were frightened. For a big man, with a captain's braid on his arm, there was very little fight in him.

He said unsteadily, "You—you mean that?"

"I mean it," said McCreary coolly. "He asked me to kill you. He thought Alfieri could run the ship for him and he and I could take over your share."

"But . . . but you don't believe that? You know what he's trying to do, don't you? Play us both off. Make us destroy each other!"

"I knew that, too." McCreary's voice was bitter. "So, I'm better able to look after myself. I'm going my own way, and be damned to the pair of you."

"But listen, McCreary!" Janzoon's ham fist caught at his sleeve.

McCreary brushed it aside and faced him. His eyes were hard and his crooked mouth was tight.

"You listen to me, Janzoon. Two days ago you could have had yourself a deal. Now, no. You knew what was going to happen to Lisette, but you never told me. You didn't lift hand or voice to stop it. You walked her into that palace with Rubensohn and watched her handed over as blood money. And you're still trying to squeeze a profit out of it! Well, go ahead! I wish you luck! But you'll be working on your own. And the joke is that you'll never know who's going to pull the trigger—me or Rubensohn. Now get to hell out of my camp. We're busy."

McCreary stood and watched him stumbling across the clearing, a big bull of a man with itchy fingers and a coward's heart. He felt no pity for him. He could not even bring himself to make use of him. He was sick of the backstairs whispers and the huckster's chaffering. He was spoiling for a fight—knockdown, drag-out and come again; and the sooner he could start drilling, the sooner he was likely to get it. He tossed away his cigarette and walked down to the right, where Agnello was wrestling a compressor unit over the bolt holes.

By sunset, the main frame of the derrick was completed and the machines were bedded down. It was fast going and they were pleased with themselves. McCreary yelled to the girls to bring clean clothes, and they walked down to the stream to bathe themselves and freshen up for dinner. They stood under the overhang of a small waterfall and let the cool water sluice over their bodies while the girls sat on the bank and watched them and made comments in the local dialect.

Then, dried and dressed, they tossed their soiled clothes to the girls and left

363

them washing and scrubbing them against the smooth stones. As they emerged from the screen of bushes, they saw Guido toiling up the path.

McCreary went to meet him at a run.

"What's news, Guido? Good or bad? Did you see her? Were you able to get a message . . . ?"

Guido waved him away with weary humour.

"The news is good, *compar'*—most of it. I didn't see her, but I got a message to her. And if I don't have a wash and a beer right now, you'll never hear the rest of it! *Che brutta giornata!* What a hell of a day!"

They hustled him down to the creek and waited while he sluiced the dust off himself. Then they walked him swiftly back to the hut, poured a brace of drinks into him and sat, bent over the cane table under the hanging lamp, while he laid out in order the day's discoveries.

Guido's narrative style was vivid and theatrical, but his eye for detail was sharp and accurate.

". . . First we go in, the same as on the night of the big *festa*, only this time it is daylight and I see what goes. The gates are teak, twelve feet high and topped with spikes. All the front wall is wide, like a rampart, and the guards walk along the top. They have long guns, like you saw. God knows if they ever fire, but it is the kris that I should fear. Now the gardens—just terrace and steps between. They take me up through the same entrance—carved doors, open but guarded, one man either side. Now I am inside. It is an entrance so . . ." He sketched it swiftly in plan. "To the left, screen doors guarded. I find later these lead to the Sultan's apartments and, above him, to the rooms of the courtiers. Now, we get this first. It took me time to work out, but it is important. The ground floor and everything in it is for the Sultan—his personal apartments, the reception rooms, the women's rooms and the kitchens. All the others are upstairs—two, three floors, because the Navel of the Universe mustn't do anything so strenuous as walk up steps. Now, we come to it. I am to fix the lights in the big hall where the throne is—it makes a show when the Sultan is there with all his court. Also I think it frightens him to have such novelties in his private rooms. A disappointment, but I remember that there is the screen and behind it the women's quarters. Then I try to explain that I must find a place for the motor and generator. They smile and chatter, but make no sense to me. Then, at last, they take me out into the garden, not the women's garden, but the terrace below it, so I can see the wall and the big tree. I set the machines, then I run the lead along the top of the wall to give myself a look inside. I also measure the drop, and it is much like it looks through the glasses. Anyone can get out by climbing the big tree and going over the wall, but to get in is hard without a rope and a hook."

"You mean, Lisette could get out herself?"

"*Sicuro!*" Guido nodded vigorously. "And if there is someone on the outside to meet her, it is easier still."

"Go on!"

"Then I go inside to wire the hall. I make a messy job of it—hang the flex from pillar to pillar, with naked bulbs between—but nobody cares. It's beautiful, they think. And while I work, I sing, loud and clear, so that at first they think I'm mad, and afterwards they start to laugh. I make up a song to go with the music of 'Marechiare,' and I tell of a girl who goes every night after dark into a garden to watch the mountain where her lover will come and signal with a lamp, once, short and sharp, no more. Then I say that one day she has a message, and the same night the signal is three flashes, which means that her lover will come inside an hour and she must be ready to climb the tree and go over the wall to meet him. I sing it over and over, loud and clear, so that even on the ship they must have heard it."

"Let's hope they didn't," said McCreary. "What then? Did you get a reply?"

"I don't know what you'd call it," said Guido, with a slow grin. "But after I finish, I hear giggling and talking behind the screen, and after a while a child comes out with a red flower in her hands and she says, loud and clear, but not knowing what it means: 'For the man.' Then I hear them laugh again, so I pat the head of the *bambina* and I give her my black flashlight for a return gift, an afterthought, but this way she can signal back to you. Then the men laugh, too, and everybody thinks I'm a *pazzo*, but nice. So they give me a drink and a plate of sweets which make me sick. I start up the engines, switch on the lights, show them how they work and know they don't understand. Then they give me a litter to take me back to the ship, and before I get here, I send the litter away and walk. And that's the news! Do you like it?"

"I like it fine!" said McCreary softly. "I like it more than anything I've heard for a long time. Pour the man another drink, Agnello. Pour him all the drink he wants. And when he's had dinner, I'm going to give him . . ."

"Oh, and another thing . . ." Guido's eyes were bright with malice. "Just to prove it really happened . . ."

He fished in the pocket of his shirt and brought out a small scarlet hibiscus, crushed and dying already, but still bright, and laid it in McCreary's palm.

"I think she would mean it for you. My voice isn't all that good, especially not in English."

"Thanks, *compar'*," said McCreary shakily. *"Mille, mille grazie!"*

Then Agnello took his pipe out of his mouth and said calmly, "Now, perhaps you can tell me something."

"What?" asked McCreary absently.

"Just this. You begin now to see a way to get yourself and your girl off the island. What happens then?"

"Murder!" said Guido, with relish. "Murder and riot. The Sultan's bride is stolen. *Mamma mia!* Then they call out the *guardia*—the boys with the wavy knives."

"That's right!" Agnello's long face grew longer still. "And there is the *Corsair* in the harbour with a mixed crew of whites and Chinese and lascars and Malays. What happens to them? They are here—all except Rubensohn and Janzoon—as simple seamen. They have no part in this filthy business.

365

What happens to them when the long knives come out and the villagers run amok in search of the Sultan's bride? Have you thought of that?"

"I've thought of it," said McCreary.

They looked at him, startled at the unfamiliar note in his voice.

The light from the lamp fell full on his face and they saw the lean, jutting jaw and the tight trap mouth and the shrewd Irish eyes that were not laughing anymore.

"You've thought of it," said Agnello flatly. "So . . . ?"

"So now I'll tell you. And every day and every night for the next weeks you'll ponder it waking and dream it sleeping, so that when the time comes, you won't make a single mistake."

Then they bent, tense and attentive, across the bamboo table, and he told them exactly what would happen the day the well came in.

Chapter Fifteen

THREE DAYS LATER they began to drill.

Rubensohn wanted to make a ceremony of the spudding in: muster the officers and crew, bring down the Sultan and his court, bring out champagne, and then start the motors and watch the bits gouge in for the first time. There was a streak of the dramatist in him and a perverted humour.

McCreary rejected the idea out of hand. He was less than polite about it.

"Look, Rubensohn, if this were a normal project, sure! It makes a nice job for the publicity boys, keeps the shareholders happy, the stock market lively. But this isn't normal. It's a very dirty piece of grand larceny that started with a murder. You want your oil, I'm trying to get it for you. Why waste a day with this sort of humbug? If you want to get rid of your champagne, send it up to me. I'll have a lot of time on my hands to drink it."

Rubensohn looked at him sharply and then shrugged.

"Just as you please, of course. You're the boss. But why so prickly about it? Are you worried about something?"

"You're damn right I'm worried." McCreary was determined not to spare him a moment of anxiety. "Any one of these tremors could topple the rig, and we'd have to start again from scratch. If they get any worse, they could cave in the well and we'd lose our bits and our casing."

"Do you think they will get worse?"

"How should I know? I warned you, I can provide against technical hitches, but not against acts of God. If you watch that mountain up there, you'll see it's hotter and brighter than it was when we first came. That's normal, too—it's a kind of safety valve. But it's what goes on under the ground that starts the trouble."

Rubensohn frowned and turned away. McCreary grinned sourly at his retreating back. The man was sweating under the fans. There was no insurance on a job like this, and he had a lot of money on the table. That was the trouble with a crooked game. The jackpot was big, but a man could grow ulcers waiting for the draw. McCreary knew. He was in the game himself.

So, when they started the motors and the big bit began chewing the soft topsoil, there were only McCreary and Agnello and Rubensohn and Janzoon, with the girls and a gaggle of workmen. After they had watched for a while, McCreary led them back to the huts, poured them drinks and said crisply:

"From here on, it's a waiting game. You'll be anxious, so will I, but I don't want to be bothered with anything but tending the rig. Agnello can come every third day to check the motors and dress the tools. Send me up a typewriter from the ship and some graph paper. I'll write up a daily log and plot the drilling progress on a chart that corresponds with the surveyors' elevation. I'll send it down each morning by runner, so you'll know what's going on. Guido will call me morning and evening on the buzzer for any other messages. If I want anything from the ship, it's up to you to see that I get it smartly. For the rest, I want to be left alone. Is that clear?"

"Quite clear," said Rubensohn. "But you'll be up here a long time. Won't you need some company?"

McCreary grinned.

"I'll have Flame Flower—and Miranha, if I develop a taste for dirty stories. When Agnello comes up, he can stay the night. For the rest, I might do some fishing, I might take a few walks, and, if I'm still lonely, I'll invite myself to dinner on board."

"Do that," said Rubensohn genially. "We'll be happy to see you."

"I'm sure you will," said McCreary.

"Will you be working all night, too?" asked Janzoon.

"I won't," said McCreary, "but the plant will be. You'll be able to look up at night and see the lights on the derrick and think of the millions you'll have when it blows in."

"You'll have them, too, McCreary," said Rubensohn tartly. "Don't forget that."

"I won't forget," said McCreary. "I'll be thinking of them all the time."

When they had gone, he stood in the middle of the clearing and listened to the steady thud of the motors and saw the long steel spindle like a shining needle plunging down from the peak of the derrick. There was satisfaction in it, the deep, simple satisfaction of the professional. But it was marred by the thought that this was one project that would never grow beyond its infancy. There would be no pipelines running down to the water, no clutter of storage tanks and pumping stations, no town springing up on the harbour fringe, no ships in the bay. The derrick would rust in the monsoon rains and the jungle would surge back and devour the small impermanent relics of his stay.

When night came, he climbed once again to the neck of the valley from which Guido and he had first looked down on the palace. He carried the field glasses slung round his neck and a flashlight in his pocket. He set a brisk pace and timed the journey meticulously: twenty-three minutes.

When he reached the shelter of the two boulders, he lay down on his belly and scanned the garden and the colonnades behind it. There were lights in the palace, but the garden and the colonnades were all in darkness. If Lisette were there, he could not hope to see her.

He took the light out of his pocket, thrust it out, clear of the rocks and the undergrowth, and flicked it on. A second, no more—then he flicked it off again. He waited, his heart pounding, then from the shadows of the garden came a faint pinprick of light, like a lonely star. It was gone so quickly he might have dreamed it, but it told him what he wanted. Lisette was there. She had had the message. She had Guido's flashlight. She would wait and wait till he was ready to take her.

He raised the glasses again and swept the shadowy area that lay between his aerie and the wall of the garden. A mile and a half perhaps—no more. But there were no paths and the jungle grew thickly with undergrowth and trailing vines. It would close over his head like a canopy and he would have to navigate by the gradient of the land. It would need practice—one trip and another and another, till he had made a track for himself and had reduced the time to the lowest possible. When the final night came, time would be the deciding factor. Once Lisette's flight had been discovered, the alarm would be raised and the island would swarm like an anthill with searchers.

Well, this was the beginning of it. He stood up, scanned the hills again and tried to lay himself a course up the slope and down again, to end under the wall of the enclosed garden. Then he moved off. A minute later the jungle had swallowed him up.

It took him eighty minutes of sweating misery to make the trip. Trailing vines caught at his ankles, moss-grown logs crumpled under his feet, thorns tore at his clothes and whipping branches scratched at his cheeks. Roosting birds clattered in alarm and monstrous insects flicked angrily in front of his face. His body was streaming with perspiration and his nostrils were filled with the stench of rotting vegetation.

When, finally, he saw the dripping stones of the wall, he realized with a shock of terror that he was a hundred feet below his objective and that a guard with a long musket was standing on the parapet high above him. He crept back into the undergrowth like a frightened animal, and it took him another fifteen minutes to scramble up to the place where the big magnolia hung from the parapet.

He listened. There was no sound from the garden, only a faint tinkle of gamelan music from far inside the palace. He looked up at the dank, mossy stones of the wall. It was better than it looked from a distance—ten feet, no more. The branches were almost low enough for a man to leap and hold and hoist himself to the top of the wall. He fought against a wild impulse to try it then and there. Lisette was so near, yet he could not come to her, dared not even raise his voice to call her.

He looked at his watch, then turned back into the sweating shadows of the jungle.

When he reached the camp, he found Flame Flower squatting outside his hut, her eyes wide and terror-stricken. He had been away nearly four hours. With luck and practice, he thought he could get it down to two and a half. If he couldn't, their chances of survival were cut to a minimum.

He walked down to the creek to bathe and change into clean clothes, and when he came back Flame Flower had his meal ready. She squatted at his feet while he ate, and when he had finished, she brought him a cigarette and lit it for him. The little trick with the lighter never failed to amuse her, but tonight her small child's face was troubled.

She looked at him a moment and then said hesitantly, "Tuan?"

"Yes, little one. What is it?"

"Now that the other tuan is gone, do I sleep here with you?"

McCreary looked at her with grave, gentle eyes. She was young and ripe and perfect as a tropic flower, and he was alone and susceptible to comfort. He had lived and loved lightly enough in his time. Why hesitate now? He could take her, without question. She was a prince's gift, at his own disposal. He could use her and leave her with child and forget her, like all the other filibusters whose offspring people the islands and the Asian coasts. Lisette would not blame him. There was no one else to care. Only himself, and he did care, strangely and strongly. He had a momentary vision of her, on the night of the knives, haled before the Sultan's torturers, with McCreary's child in her belly.

But how to explain it to her in his halting Malay? How to make her understand without shame to her and danger to himself and Lisette? He said carefully:

"Do you know where I went tonight, little one?"

"Where, tuan?"

"I walked a long way through the jungle."

"No, tuan!" Her hand went to her mouth. "The spirits of the dead are abroad in the jungle and the Goddess of Death rides on a striped beast."

It was an odd echo of the old Hindu beliefs distorted, but persistent still in the scattered islands.

McCreary nodded.

"I walked through the jungle and I came to the wall of the Sultan's garden, and I heard my sister weeping on the other side. I dared not call to her. I could only sit and listen. After a while she went away."

"What then, tuan?" Her eyes were bright with sympathy.

"I swore a vow to my gods that I would not touch a woman until my sister was taken away from the palace and given back to me again."

"But that will never happen, tuan. No woman leaves the palace, ever."

"This one will. One night she will leave and I shall take her away from

370

Karang Sharo, and I shall take you with me, where the Sultan will never find us."

"Do you swear that, tuan?"

"I swear it."

"Then—then—if I may not come to you, may I sleep here in your hut? When I am alone and the ground shakes, I am frightened."

McCreary grinned at her and patted her sleek, perfumed hair. He said in English, "Whatever I do, you're a thorn in my flesh, little one. I suppose you might as well move in."

"What did you say, tuan?"

"I said, I would take you away, little one. Does that make you happy?"

"So long as I am near the tuan, I am happy."

He thought that if every woman in the world were like that, things would be a lot easier for the men in it. He undressed and lay down on the bed, and Flame Flower crawled into Agnello's bunk.

For a long time McCreary lay wakeful, listening to her soft, regular breathing and to the steady, thudding beat of the motors driving the drill. Then he fell asleep, exhausted. There were two more slight tremors during the night, but neither he nor Flame Flower wakened, and in the morning he found the rig still intact and the bit still clawing its way down through the first rock layer.

In the weeks that followed, McCreary's days patterned themselves into a comforting professional routine. He rose early and bathed in the stream, then walked back to the hut where Flame Flower would serve him his breakfast. Guido would call him on the radio, and they would chat back and forth on the keys, cautiously, for fear of eavesdroppers on the ship.

No messages were being received by Rubensohn, except a cable to the company in Singapore asking them to replenish bunker credits for the *Corsair* in Luzon and Hong Kong. McCreary let it pass without comment. The credits might come in handy later.

After the morning transmission he would go down the rig, fuel and tune the motors and direct the small team of Sharo recruits whom he had kept on the rig. They learnt quickly, he found. Their hands were apt at mechanical skills and, with a smile and a little flattery, they could be handled very easily.

As the bits went deeper and deeper and the casing followed them, McCreary began to take core samples, checking them against the geologist's survey for variations in the strata.

At night he would mark up the log and the chart, then he would tramp up the slope to the observation post and signal to Lisette—only once. Then, when he had seen the small answering light, he would plunge into the jungle again and time his walk back and forth from the garden wall. After half a dozen trips he found he could strike a bearing accurately and make the return journey in two and a half hours. He began to think of getting it down to two.

On the evenings when Miranha came to pick up his cans of fuel, McCreary would walk down to the beach with him and spend an hour fishing in the placid water between the shore and Miranha's mooring.

Miranha had prized two more bottles of whisky out of him, and now there was a dugout canoe beached under the bushes and ready for his use at all times. It was big and awkward for one man to handle, but, when the time came, it would have to carry a full load.

Every third day Agnello came up and spent the daylight dressing the used bits and tuning the motors and checking the electrical circuits. After the evening meal he would walk up to the observation post with McCreary and wait for him to come back from the palace wall. Then they would sit in the hut and drink beer and smoke placidly, turning over their plans for the final day.

Agnello had made a new ally—the young deck officer, Arturo. They would need him on the final night. For the rest, the news from the ship was negligible. Rubensohn spent much time in his cabin, writing and studying McCreary's reports. Janzoon and Alfieri were at daggers drawn, and the girls were proving more of a nuisance than a recreation.

McCreary chuckled happily at Agnello's dry reportage. He knew how Rubensohn's temper must fray under the waiting. He regretted only that he couldn't string it out to breaking point.

One thing was worrying them all, it seemed—the volcano.

It was more active now than at any time since their arrival. Sometimes they would hear it grumbling, a low, thunderous sound, like a giant snoring in his sleep. At night a bright red glow lit the cone, and sometimes they would see a fiery shower blown high into the air and spreading out like sparks from a Roman candle. The tremors were slighter now, but more frequent, and there had been radio reports of severe shock waves in other areas.

"It may not mean much." Agnello sucked his pipe and talked in his calm, flat voice. "Etna plays up like this sometimes. Stromboli is always growling. But if it does . . . Mother of God!"

"Let's forget it!" said McCreary, uncomfortably, "and hope we're miles away when it does blow."

But he couldn't forget it, and more than once he woke from a shouting nightmare in which he saw the mountain spill over with fire and engulf the palace and the gardens, while Lisette's voice screamed for help, and he was held back from her by invisible hands.

Finally, one afternoon, a new core sample was brought up. It was black and porous and it looked like a crust of old cement. As he fumbled it, it left a brown, tarry stain on his hands. McCreary looked at it a long time, his lips moving soundlessly, his heart pounding. He knew what it was. He'd seen it before, many times.

The bits had driven down into an old porous layer which sometimes covers the main oil bed and sometimes is the oil bed. To bring in the well, it would be necessary to lower a long section of casing loaded with steel-jacketed

372

bullets. When these were fired by electrical contact, the crust would break up, releasing the oil and sending it gushing to the surface. The surveyors had been right. Rubensohn's gamble had been right. There was oil on Karang Sharo, and tomorrow Mike McCreary would bring in his well. Tomorrow!

For the rest of the afternoon and long after sunset, McCreary drove his crew with a madman's energy. The drill was stopped and winched to the surface. The long steel bullets were loaded into the firing casing and the contents fused. The casing was lowered slowly down the shaft, and, when this was done, McCreary ran a long pair of cable leads to his own hut and carried the contact box there, too, and stowed it under his bed.

Then he dismissed the boys and stood a long time staring at the big derrick with its naked struts crisscrossed against the stars. Tomorrow!

But even tonight there was much to be done. He switched on the radio, put on the headphones, and after a few moments he heard Guido's impatient signal. He was late for his schedule.

"Tomorrow . . ." He tapped out the letters with trembling fingers. "Warn Agnello. Come yourself in the afternoon, early. No word to anyone. That's all. No more tonight."

"Understood," Guido's message came back. "Understood." And McCreary knew he could rely on them. They had been pondering it for a long time.

He sat down at his table, drew the typewriter towards him and, slowly and painstakingly, began to tap out the letters. There were two long documents and one very short one. When he had finished, he folded them carefully and put them in his wallet, which he placed under his pillow. Tomorrow!

Flame Flower brought him his meal and he ate it, sweating and filthy as he was, and drank two bottles of beer and smoked three cigarettes.

He took out his gun and oiled it and tested the action carefully, loaded it, put on the safety catch and placed it under the pillow with his wallet. Tomorrow!

Now he was deathly tired. His head was buzzing and his hands were trembling, and his whole body reeked with fatigue. He walked down to the creek to bathe himself and Flame Flower followed him, and, when he stepped under the racing cool water, she came with him and soaped and sluiced his body with her soft hands, dried him and led him back to the hut walking like a man in a dream.

When they reached the hut, she urged him to lie down and sleep, but he refused. He lifted her onto the table and perched her in front of him and told her, very carefully, what she herself must do when tomorrow came. How she must go to the palace and to the apartments of the women and entertain them with her stories of life with the tuan, and how she must say to Lisette, foolishly, as if it were a child's mimicry: "Tonight . . . three lights . . . wait!"

He made her say it over and over again, like a parrot, so that there could be no mistake. Then he told her how she must leave the palace early in the afternoon and come back to him to confirm that Lisette had his message. She nodded wisely, and he made her repeat the directions slowly and carefully; when he asked for the words again, she gave them to him clearly and without hesitation:

"Tonight . . . three lights . . . wait!"

Now there was nothing more for him to do, until tomorrow. He lay down on the bed, fully clothed, and fell instantly asleep. But Flame Flower heard him muttering and wrestling with his nightmares, and she came to him and soothed him with crooning voice and soft hands, and, after a while, she lay down on the sheets beside him and cradled his head on her breasts, so that even when the tremors came, he did not hear them, and when he woke again it was already—tomorrow!

Chapter Sixteen

THE SHARO BOYS CAME STRAGGLING UP THE HILL, laughing and chattering as they always did. McCreary set them restacking the stores, polishing the engines, cutting new timber—everything he could find to keep them busy and create an illusion of normal activity.

When Miranha came up, blear-eyed and inquisitive as a weasel, McCreary took him up to the hut and told him what he wanted of him. The fellow's eyes started from his head and his mouth gaped with the shock of it.

"Mother of pity! I can't do it. You know what this means? Ruin for me! I lose everything."

"You've got a hut and a clutter of trade junk!" said McCreary brutally. "I'll replace it for you two over. You've got a wife and children I can't replace and your own worthless throat that I wouldn't replace, if I could. If you stay, you'll be murdered. If you try to double-cross me, I'll kill you myself. Make up your mind!"

"No . . . no . . . no!" Miranha was gibbering with terror. "Anything you say. But you'll pay me for the boat, give me a new start?"

"Yes! Now, listen carefully. Get your wife and kids onto the ketch—not yet, late in the afternoon! Then come up here. If you're not here by sunset, I'll send Guido gunning for you. Is that clear?"

"Clear, yes . . . but how can you be sure?"

"I am sure," said McCreary. "I've got to be sure. Now get to hell out of here and be back by sunset. I want you to take a message down to the ship."

McCreary watched him shambling down the path, then he turned back to Flame Flower. Swiftly he led her once more through the catechism. She answered him without hesitation, and the four words she must speak to

Lisette came back to him clear as a bell. Then she, too, left him and his heart followed her small colourful figure flashing like a parrot's plumage under the first green overhang of the jungle.

Shortly after noon Guido arrived, sweating and excited.

"Big things, *amico! Festa* day! And on the ship they doze and drink and snarl at each other as if it were any other day of the month. The mountain worries them. They don't like the way it rumbles and spits. I laugh at them and tell them how old Vesuvio blew his top. They like that—like poison. Their eyes pop and they give themselves indigestion worrying about it."

"They won't have to worry about it much longer, Guido. Tonight will see the end of it."

"I hope so," said Guido, with fervour. "Even for me it gets too much."

"Everything set on the ship?"

"Everything. Agnello and young Arturo are primed. They know the movements, the timetable."

"The timetable—everything depends on that."

"Everything," said Guido.

They sat down to go over it again.

Just after four, Flame Flower came back. She had been to the women's quarters. They had welcomed her and petted her and listened avidly to her stories of the tuans and their strange ways. She had recited her little words to Lisette and the other women had laughed at the mimicry, not understanding a sound of it.

When she had left, they had given her presents, fruits and sweetmeats and a comb for her hair and a bracelet for her wrist. Lisette had given her a cambric handkerchief, scented with her perfume. Her message was written on the handkerchief in bright red lacquer.

"Mike, come early. Two hours after sunset latest."

McCreary smiled thinly. Two hours after sunset and she should be back here, in the hut, waiting for Rubensohn and Janzoon. There were no margins in the schedule. He hoped and prayed that Rubensohn and Janzoon would arrive on time.

At five o'clock they dismissed the Sharo boys, and within ten minutes the clearing was deserted.

At five-thirty Miranha arrived, red-eyed and unhappy. His family was aboard the ketch. He, himself, would like to join them. He was worried . . . he had no talent for this sort of thing . . . they were sure of their promise to make good his losses and give him a new start . . . ?

They were sure. They were even surer that they would kill him if he lost his nerve. McCreary sat down and wrote a brief note to Rubensohn.

"Drilling site tonight. Urgent conference, self, Janzoon. Expect good news. McCreary."

He folded it and handed it to Miranha.

"You'll leave here at six by Guido's watch. At normal going, you'll be aboard before seven. Don't dawdle, don't hurry, and above all don't be diverted by anything. If you make a mistake in timing, we're all dead men. Understand that."

Miranha understood, but he needed liquor and cigarettes and a mixture of threats and encouragement to bolster his small courage.

It was twenty minutes to six when McCreary himself set off up the mountain path to his observation post. In his pockets he carried the flashlight and the gun. The field glasses were slung round his neck, and, looped over his shoulders, mountaineer fashion, was a length of rope, with a large grappling hook at the end of it. Agnello had made it for him, covering the hook with rubber tubing so that it would not clatter against the stonework.

He walked swiftly up the slope, thinking of Lisette, thinking of all that must be done in the next hours, and how a few minutes could make the difference between success and disaster.

By the time he reached the rocks, the swift-striding dark had come down on the island and the cone of Gurung Merapi glowed angrily against the night sky. There was a deep rumbling and the hills shuddered under his feet, then settled again, slowly. From the cone of the volcano a fountain of fire erupted, then fell back again through the smoke.

He stood upright against the rocks, holding the glasses in one hand and the light in the other. Carefully, as if aiming a gun, he thrust it out beyond the rocks and flashed it—once, twice and again. The answer came back swiftly this ·time. Three short flashes, magnified a little by the glasses, but still small and uncertain, like his own hope.

He put the flashlight in his pocket and set off down the slope and into the jungle. The way was more familiar to him now, its hazards fewer. Long practice had given him the feel of the ground, and his quickened senses led him now to this fallen trunk, round that tangle of lianas, down the dip and over the hump and past the sound of water on the left. . . .

Panting and staggering, he came to the base of the wall and leaned against it, fighting for breath. He looked at his watch. He had covered the full distance in forty minutes. The margin was a mite better, but he could not afford to waste it.

He eased his way up the slope to where the big magnolia tree hung over the wall. The ground was slippery with the drainage from the hill and he had to go carefully or risk a crashing tumble down the slope.

He unslung the rope and paid out a length of it from the coil, holding the covered hook in his hands. He tried one throw, but he was too cautious and the hook fell back at his feet with a soft thud. He tried another; the hook hung on the wall, but when he put weight on it, the lip of the wall crumbled in a shower of loose rubble. McCreary splayed himself against the stones, trembling. No sound came from the garden, only the distant muted noise of the falling fountain.

Carefully, he tried again. This time the hook held. He tested it with a strong pull, and another, and another. It was still firm. He eased his weight onto it and began to hoist himself carefully up the wall under the shadow of the branches.

When he reached the top, he hung there, peering into the garden through the small gaps in the leaves.

A moment later his heart stood still.

The Sultan, himself, was in the garden, and Lisette was with him, walking slowly by the fountain under the blossom trees.

He dared not hoist himself up any farther. He could not go back for fear that Lisette might leave the garden without his knowing it. He hung there, bracing himself on the rope, till his muscles screamed and the sweat broke out all over him and he had to bite his lips to keep from crying out. The ticking of his watch was loud as a death knell, and he knew that both time and strength were slipping away from him.

Then they stopped walking. The small brown figure of the Sultan turned away, then came back, as if on an afterthought. He talked a few moments in a low voice and Lisette bent her head in acknowledgment. Then, abruptly, he turned on his heel and walked swiftly through the colonnade, leaving Lisette alone.

McCreary eased himself a little higher on the rope and struggled to find breath enough for a whistle. It issued from his lips with startling shrillness. He saw Lisette's head turn sharply. She cast a quick, scared look towards the lighted colonnade, then moved unhurriedly towards the big magnolia tree.

"Is that you, Mike?" Her voice was a whisper, but he heard it louder than drums.

"It's me, dark one." His own voice was strained and harsh. "Up into the tree now—hurry!"

He stayed long enough to see her safely into the first branches, holding his breath lest the dry snapping of twigs should bring them running and screaming after her. Then he slid down the rope and waited, tense as a spring, until he saw her, like a white moth, coming over the wall and out of the dark leaves.

"Jump, sweetheart! I'll catch you!"

He saw her hesitate a moment, then she jumped. The impact rolled him over on the slippery incline, but he was on his feet in an instant and, without a kiss or come-hither, he was dragging her into the shadows and stumbling with her over the rotting floor of the jungle.

Before they had gone half a mile, she was gasping and retching with fatigue. McCreary brought up short and held her to him, taking her weight on his breast and shoulders, feeling her small body wrenched with sobbing weariness. He looked at his watch. Three minutes after seven. No time to spare, if they were to be back before Rubensohn arrived.

He lifted her face to him and kissed her gently. Then he spoke swiftly and sharply.

378

"Listen, Lisette. Time's against us. We've an hour to be back in the camp and then maybe half an hour of comedy that you must see out, because I've prepared it for you and no other. Then we'll kiss the backs of our hands to this place and be on our way. I'll carry you pickaback part of the way, then I want you to walk, and walk with all the strength you've got. Don't fail me now, dark one! You won't, will you? Tell me you won't!"

"I—I won't, Mike."

"That's my fine dark woman."

He hoisted her onto his shoulders and carried her a little way until her strength came back, then she walked, plugging and persistent, behind him, until they came to the camp, with ten minutes to spare before Rubensohn and Janzoon arrived.

Guido laughed and stammered and swore and patted them both on the shoulders, while Flame Flower stood goggling at the tattered apparitions. McCreary rounded on them impatiently.

"That's enough! Both of you! Time, remember! Time! Get Lisette into the other hut, Flame Flower. Help her to clean up, lend her clean clothes. I'm sorry, sweetheart, but I want you looking like a queen when Rubensohn comes, for all you're dead on your small, brave feet!"

"I'll be ready, Mike!" Her head went up proudly and the weariness seemed to fall away from her.

"Stay in the hut till I come for you. Don't move outside. Hurry now! Guido!"

"Yes, *amico?*"

"Connect the plunger box."

"I've done it, Mike—it's just outside the door. I thought you'd want it there."

"Good! There's a bundle of assorted stones and jade in my bag. Take it and give it to Flame Flower. Tell her to bring it with her when we go down to the boat."

"Yes, Mike. Anything else?"

"Yes, Guido." His voice was soft now and very deliberate. "There'll be a small ceremony when they come. I want no risks at all. If Rubensohn makes half a move, kill him! No questions, no hesitations. Kill him!"

"A pleasure, *compar',*" said Guido, feelingly. "A very great pleasure indeed."

McCreary grinned crookedly and went into the hut. It took him three minutes flat to change and clean himself, and when Rubensohn and Janzoon came tramping up the hill, he was waiting for them, cool as bog water, with a cigarette stuck in his mouth and the light of triumph in his eyes.

"Well, McCreary?" Rubensohn's voice was shrill and edgy. His eyes were bright with anticipation and his red lips were startlingly vivid against his pale, perspiring face. "Your message said good news. We hope you'll make up for our spoiled dinner."

"I think you'll find it worth the trip," said McCreary, with a grin. "You'll forgive me for being a little elated myself. It's the Irish in me. Come in, gentlemen, and sit down."

He led them into the hut and sat them down at the bamboo table with their faces to the door of the hut. He made a little ceremony of it, so that they looked at him curiously, wondering if he'd been drinking. McCreary smiled and smiled and leaned against the bamboo upright of the door.

Then he said in his gentlest brogue, "Gentlemen, I have good news for you! I'm going to bring you in a well!"

"My God!" Rubensohn's voice was a high bat's squeak.

"You mean it!" Janzoon's voice was a hoarse whisper. "When?"

McCreary looked at his watch. Fifteen minutes after eight. Time was running out fast.

He said briskly, "Very soon now! Tonight! You'll see me leaning on a plunger and you'll count three—or maybe five—and you'll see one of the most wonderful sights in the world: a gusher spouting black, filthy oil towards the stars. Does it please you, gentlemen?"

"So much!" Rubensohn chuckled shrilly. "You don't know how much, McCreary."

"But before I do that," said McCreary, "there's something else I want to show you, more wonderful to me than all the oil in the world." He raised his voice and shouted, "Guido!"

A moment later Guido stepped into the hut with Lisette.

Janzoon goggled at her open-mouthed. Rubensohn leapt up from his chair.

"Sit down, Rubensohn," said McCreary's soft voice. "Sit down or I'll kill you!"

Rubensohn saw the gun in his hand and death in his Irish eyes. He sat down. Lisette stood watching him, a small, queenly figure with a strange smile playing about her lips.

"You're mad!" cried Rubensohn shrilly. "You're raving mad! Any minute from now there'll be gongs beating from the palace and the whole island will come swarming over us, like soldier ants."

"I know," said McCreary. "I've thought about it—often. Take their guns, Guido!"

Guido moved swiftly round the table and came back with two guns. McCreary smiled his lopsided smile.

"So you were going to kill me? That makes it easier all round."

"Listen, McCreary . . ."

"Shut up, Rubensohn!" The smile was gone now and his mouth was tight with anger. "Cover them, Guido! If they move, kill 'em!"

"I know," said Guido, with a flashing smile. "I've thought about it too."

McCreary put his hand into his breast pocket and brought out a fountain pen and the folded typescripts over which he had laboured the night before. He opened them out and laid them on the table before Rubensohn.

"Sign the first two, please."

Rubensohn looked up at him with cold, hating eyes.

"What am I supposed to sign?"

"The first is a will, which is to be witnessed by Guido and Agnello, leaving all your property, real and personal, to Lisette Morand, late of Saigon, except the *Corsair*, which comes to me because you owe me money and a lot else that you can't repay. The second is a confession, similarly witnessed, to your murder of Captain Nasa in Djakarta on the tenth of July."

"You're mad, McCreary! I'm not going to sign those."

McCreary looked at his watch.

"If you don't," said McCreary calmly, "Guido will shoot you both in five seconds from now. And I'll guarantee to have a signature out of you before you die."

"And if I do sign?"

"I'll bring your well in for you and you can both go back to the *Corsair*."

"Now I know you're mad!" said Rubensohn. "A will has no value until a man's dead."

"You're dead already," said McCreary very softly, "but you don't know it yet. I'm counting now. One . . . two . . ."

"Sign it, Rubensohn . . . for God's sake, sign!" Janzoon was sweating in his chair.

"Three . . . four . . ."

"Give me the pen!"

"I know your signature now, Rubensohn," said McCreary, easily, "so make sure it's the right one."

Rubensohn scrawled his signature on the first two documents. McCreary took them from him, folded them and put them back in his pocket.

"What's this?" Rubensohn was staring down at the last sheet of paper.

McCreary said coolly, "That's the message Guido's going to send to Scott Morrison in Darwin telling him there's no oil on Karang Sharo and that the deal is off. And, as you see, it will be signed, like all the others, by Janzoon."

Rubensohn's face was ashen; for the first time since McCreary had known him, there was fear in his eyes and in his twitching lips.

"But . . . but there is oil here! You said . . ."

"I know," said McCreary. "I promised you oil and I'm going to give it to you—enough to choke you. Then I'm going to . . . Listen!"

They all heard it, a great throbbing brazen gong, echoing out across the lowlands from the palace on the hill. It went on and on, rising into the hills and falling into the valleys of sound, and from the villages there rose a shrill crying like the wailing of lost souls.

"That's it!" said McCreary. "The alarm. The Sultan's wife has disappeared. Twenty minutes from now they'll be scouring the island. It should be interesting. You'll both be here to watch it. Then, of course, you'll be taken and killed. At this moment the *Corsair* is steaming out of the harbour with young

381

Arturo at the wheel and Agnello down in the engine room and Alfieri beating his head against his door. If I can talk sense into him in the next day or two, maybe I'll give him the command after all, Janzoon!"

Then the full horror of their situation seemed to dawn on Rubensohn and Janzoon. They gaped, slack-mouthed, and Janzoon tried to lurch forward, but Guido thrust him back. Rubensohn burst into a gibbering plea:

"For God's sake, McCreary! Listen! I'll give you . . ."

"You've got nothing to give me," said McCreary. "Stripjack naked! The game's over, Rubensohn! You're busted! And here's a small souvenir of the moment—Nasa's lighter! I took it from his body."

He tossed the lighter on the table. Then, while Rubensohn still stared at it, he turned and led Lisette out of the hut. Guido brought the others out with a beckoning jerk of the pistol.

The island was still full of the clangour of the great gong, but McCreary stood steady as a rock with his hand on the plunger, and Lisette was beside him, head high and proud.

"Watch it!" said McCreary exultantly. "Watch it! Count three or maybe five and you'll see it come—the thing you killed a man for and sold a girl for, the thing you're going to die for, Rubensohn—oil!"

His hand went down on the plunger and they waited, one . . . two . . . but before the count was done, the ground rocked under their feet and they heard a noise louder than a hundred gongs and, as they staggered on their feet, they saw that the top of the mountain had blown off and the air was full of flying particles, as if from a blasted sun tumbling out of the sky.

Then they were running, helter-skelter down the path, McCreary dragging Lisette, Guido with Flame Flower at his heels and Janzoon and Rubensohn stumbling after them, shouting, as explosion after explosion rocked the ground and the fiery missiles rained down like thunderbolts.

The path gave them a small shelter from the red-hot lapilli, but they could hear them clattering and hissing among the arching trees, and if one brushed them as it fell, it scorched them so that they cried out with the pain of it.

When they reached the path that led back to the village, they saw for a brief moment the growing terror of the situation. All along the coastline the kampongs were ablaze as the fallout from the explosions touched off the grass roofs like torches.

They saw the flames and heard the wild, panic screaming, then McCreary dragged them off the path and through the last green tangle before the sea.

The four of them reached the beach fifty yards ahead of Rubensohn and Janzoon. The sea was in a turmoil, tossing wildly and roaring like storm water. They could see the ketch heaving and straining at its anchor, but Miranha was cowering under the bushes, staring with terror. They kicked him out of his stupor and between them they manhandled the canoe down the sand and into the water.

As they climbed into it and pushed off, Rubensohn and Janzoon broke out of the bushes and onto the beach.

382

"McCreary!" It was Rubensohn's voice, high and despairing.

McCreary did not turn his head. He and Guido bent to the paddles and sent the canoe bouncing out across the waves to where the ketch was straining at its anchor in the lurching water.

"McCreary! McCreary!"

They were both shouting now, their voices shrill with terror, and, when at last he turned his head, he could see them wading out, waist-high, into the water.

It was desperate, back-breaking labour to hold the plunging craft head on to the waves and save it from being swamped. But after an eternity of clawing their way through the surf, they brought up under the lee of the ketch. When they scrambled aboard, they found Miranha's wife and children screaming in panic, but McCreary drove Miranha like a maniac.

"Get those damned engines started! Guido, get the anchor up! The rest of you get down below, if you don't want to be burnt! Hurry! Hurry! Hurry!"

Red-hot pellets were raining down on the deck, and already it was beginning to smoulder. The ketch was bucking like a wild horse as great shudders shook the sea floor and tossed the waves higher and higher. Guido was straining and cursing to get the anchor up. It seemed an age till McCreary heard the splutter of the engines and Guido's shout and felt the boat yaw drunkenly at the first drive of the screws.

The sea was chopping all ways at once, but when the big waves broke over the decks, they were grateful for it, as for a small mercy, because the smouldering pellets doused themselves and the new falls spluttered out in the wash.

Miranha was driving the engines full throttle now and the little boat was thrusting out, bucking and yawing, towards the lights of the *Corsair*, miles to seaward.

McCreary stood in the stern looking back at the shoreline where Rubensohn and Janzoon stood neck-deep now, still shouting their desperate plea.

"McCreary! McCreary!"

Then a new shower of blazing particles rained down, and their voices trailed off in a long-drawn scream of agony, quickly quenched as the wild waters swallowed them.

I've stripped him down, he thought. I've stripped him down to this—a face I can't see and a voice drowned in a few seconds. I've taken his girl. I've taken his money. I've taken his life. And though I don't feel very proud of myself, I'm damned if I can feel any pity for him.

Then they rounded the small cape and saw for the first time the blazing horror of the spectacle. The volcano was still spouting fire and roaring like a mad giant, the air was full of a stinking sulfurous smoke and the whole of the shoreline was blazing as if it had been sprayed with gasoline.

The brown people were scurrying like ants, in a panic stampede to the water. Even above the roaring of the mountain, their cry was a high shriek across the leaping waves.

383

"Dear God Almighty!" McCreary's voice was a hoarse whisper.

"Mike! Mike! Can't we do something for them?" Lisette was at his shoulder, steadying herself against the yaw. "Can't we go back a way? Pick some of them up?"

McCreary shook his head and shouted to make her hear.

"We'd be burned and swamped in two minutes. Best we can do is stand in as close as we dare with the *Corsair* and try to pick up survivors. Look . . . !"

She followed his pointing finger and saw the first canoe loads pushing off from the beach and the small stubby praus lurching out into the water with people fighting to cling to their thwarts.

Before they were twenty yards from the beach, the water spun them up and around, spilling the bodies out like matches and dumping the heavy hulls down on their bobbing heads.

"It's horrible, Mike! Horrible!" She buried her face in his breast and he held her close to him, swaying with the boat as Miranha pushed and cursed her out towards the *Corsair*.

"Close your eyes to it, dark one," McCreary urged her desperately. "Close your eyes and shut your ears and your heart. You've had pain enough and this you can do nothing to mend. Hold to me, sweetheart, and you'll feel the soft, cool wind stirring over the grass, and you'll catch the pipe of the blackbird and hear the drumming of the hooves as the sweet fillies turn over the rise and come pounding homeward over the hills of Armagh. Listen to 'em, dark one! Listen. . . ."

But even as he spoke, they heard a sound like an enveloping thunderclap, and, as they watched, dumb with shock, they saw the whole hillside open up and a great river of fire slide slowly over the palace and down towards the villages and the sea.

KUNDU

Chapter One

IT WAS FOUR IN THE AFTERNOON. The sun was westering along the green valley. The first streamers of cloud were creeping along the northern barrier, whose peaks heaved themselves up, cobalt against the peach tints of the sky.

It was still summer in Capricorn. Down on the coast, in Lae and Madang and Wewak, they sweltered and swore and whistled for the cool night winds. Up here, in the Highland valleys, five thousand feet above the sea, the warmth was waning, and, when darkness came, it would be cold.

On the broad stoop of his bungalow, thatched with Nipa palm and framed with bamboo, Kurt Sonderfeld stood looking out across the valley where the young coffee was growing under the rows of shade trees, towards the huts of the Chimbu village and the formal avenue of the dancing park.

He was restless, though few would have guessed it. The quality of containment, which was so much of his nature, the capacity for control, so long and painfully developed, were armour enough against betrayal.

But even had they guessed, they would have been hard put to name a cause. He had a wife whose brooding Slavic beauty was a legend from Madang to Mount Hagen. His coffee was healthy. His past was safely buried. The Administration approved him. He was master in his own valley, fifty miles from the scrutiny of the District Commissioner at Goroka.

Yet he was restless. His fine cigar tasted sour. He found no pleasure in the prospect that began with the green lawns of his bungalow and swept away to the foot of the purple mountains, whose brown people served him as they served few other white men, with awe and with alacrity.

Tonight, of all nights, he needed privacy. Tonight, of all nights, it would be denied him. Within an hour his guests would arrive. They would sit on his veranda and drink his whisky and eat his food and talk, volubly, emphatically, as lonely men do, far into the darkness, while the kundus throbbed and the chants of the villagers drifted up on the breeze.

Zum Teufel! Let them come!

He tossed his cigar away and watched it smoulder on the black earth of the garden.

He was a tall man, broad-barrelled, square-shouldered, straight as a pine tree. His deep forehead rose, dome-like, to the line of his red, cropped hair, and a brown scar ran clean along the line of his jaw from the earlobe to the cleft of his blunt chin. His mouth was tight as a trap.

For a long moment he stood there, moving his hand along the shining bamboo rail as if smoothing out his own ruffled temper. Then his mouth relaxed and he stepped off the veranda and strode down the gravelled path towards a small bamboo hut on the fringe of the plantation.

This was his laboratory, compact and efficient as he was himself. Here he was no longer Kurt Sonderfeld, migrant by necessity, medico by grace and favour, lessee planter under the Trustee Administration. Here he was Kurt Sonderfeld, Doctor of Medicine—Freiburg and Bonn, Honorary Adviser on Malarial Control in the Eastern Highlands, contributor to learned journals, correspondent of learned societies in Europe and the United States. He grinned sourly as the ripples stirred in the pools of memory. So many of his colleagues had found their past a handicap in a new country. Kurt Sonderfeld had turned his own dubious history to handsome profit.

He pushed open the door of the hut and walked in.

There was a girl sitting at the long bench under the window. She had a microscope in front of her and a pad of notes at her elbow. As Sonderfeld entered, she looked up and her mouth parted in a wide grin.

She had a broad nose and the full, thrusting lips of the mountain people. Her skin was brown as bush honey and her hair was crisped in tight ringlets close to her skull. Yet she was beautiful—beautiful with youth and health. Her skin glowed warmly and her round breasts were firm and challenging under the gaudy, pink print dress.

Sonderfeld towered over her, smiling in cynical approval.

"Well? What do you find, N'Daria?"

His voice was deep, and one had to listen carefully to catch the telltale intonation of the Continental.

She answered him in mission English, husky and precise.

"These are the eggs we took from the lower pond."

"Yes?"

"Anopheles."

Sonderfeld nodded.

"I expected it."

"So now we have the fever in the valley?"

"Not yet. But when the boys come back from the coast they will bring the fever with them. These fellows—"

He tapped the barrel of the microscope. "These fellows will carry it to the rest of the tribe."

The girl said nothing. She was watching him, lips parted, eyes wide, head tilted back, so that he could see the hollow of her throat and the slow downward curving of her breasts.

Sonderfeld watched her with satisfaction and amusement. This was his own creation. This he had wrought meticulously, patiently, as a man might make a delicate instrument, calculating each movement and function, balancing it against the next until he could say with mathematical certainty: "This is mine. Use it so . . . and it will work thus and thus."

She had come from Père Louis' Mission School as house help to Gerda. But with N'Daria the veneer of the Mission was thin and cracked before it was fully dry. Underneath was the primitive, full of the old fears, the old superstitions, the old violent passions. But he had tamed her—tamed her with subtlety and severity and rare gentleness. And as he tamed, he taught, so that she could work with him accurately, scrupulously, as he worked himself.

Now she was ready. But the work he had in mind for her was ten thousand years away from the bright instruments of the laboratory.

Still smiling, he laid the tip of his finger on her neck, pressing it gently into the hollow behind the ear. She shivered at his touch but did not draw away. Slowly, deliberately, he drew his finger down and across her throat so that his nail raised a thin weal under the honey-coloured skin. She trembled. Moisture formed at the corners of her mouth and split on her dark lips. Her eyes were flecked and lit with sudden desire.

"Do you care?" said Sonderfeld softly. "Do you care if the whole village dies of the fever?"

Her answer was a throaty whisper. "No."

"Do you care if Kumo dies?"

"No."

"Good."

He withdrew his hand and she bent forward as if to renew the touch. Her whole body was alive with passion.

Sonderfeld grinned and shook his head.

"Not now, N'Daria."

"Tomorrow?"

"Perhaps . . . if you do well tonight. Get dressed now. Then come and show yourself to me."

Submissive, but heavy with dissatisfaction, she got up and walked to the screen door at the end of the hut. Sonderfeld watched her go, and when the door closed behind her, he chuckled and bent over the microscope.

The small nodules of the mosquito larvae were monstrous under the powerful lens. N'Daria was right. They were anopheles, carrier of malaria. Now that the valley was open to traffic from Goroka and from the coast, it would be immune no longer. The pack boys coming over the mountains would bring the disease; the patrol officers and the police boys, the research men from the

Department of Agriculture. Then it would break out in the villages and the children would sicken and die, and those who survived would have swollen spleens as big as pineapples, like the pitiful scarecrows on the Sepik Delta—unless Kurt Sonderfeld did something about it.

He would do it, of course, because order was necessary to his nature and to his plans. And because disease was a disorder, repugnant to him, he would stamp it out—tomorrow.

Tonight there were other matters. Tonight, if N'Daria did her part, the kundus would thunder the march of the conqueror and the chant would ring like a paean of victory. For a long time he sat, absorbed in his own thoughts, then the door creaked and he turned sharply.

N'Daria was standing before him.

Bark cloth was wound about her loins and her pubic apron was of dyed and plaited grass. From navel to diaphragm, her belly was bound with a belt of plaited cane. Her upthrust breasts were bare, and ropes of red and blue beads hung down in the hollow between them. Her septum was pierced with a curved sliver of pearl shell, and her fuzzy head was crowned with a casque of iridescent beetles, surmounted by the scarlet feathers of the bird of paradise. Her naked skin was shiny with tree oil. . . .

Sonderfeld stared at her with admiration. He felt the slow, dangerous itch creep into his loins. He fought against it, angrily. The girl was his to take at any time—but not tonight. He saw her grin at his discomfort and cursed himself for a fool.

"Come here, N'Daria!"

She came to him, slowly, rolling her hips. She stood before him, head tilted back, and he smelt the oil and the heat of her body.

Perhaps, in spite of himself, the big man would take her now. Again she was disappointed.

Her eyes pleaded with him. He laughed at her frustration.

"Tomorrow, N'Daria—tomorrow. Now, show me!"

She plunged her fingers between the broad cane belt and her skin and brought out a small tampon of cotton wool.

"Good. Put it back!"

She replaced the cotton wool and waited, slack and submissive.

"Now tell me."

"Tonight I am to bring you—"

"No. Tell me from the beginning."

She took a deep breath and began again, her husky voice piecing out the directions slowly in the alien tongue.

"Tonight, in the village, the unmarried ones make kunande. We sit and sing and roll our faces together. Kumo will be there and we will make kunande together. Then we will go to my sister's house. We will eat and drink and Kumo and I will carry-leg. He will play with me and I will play with him. Then, when he is full of desire, we will go into the bushes and he will take me."

"Can you be sure of that?"

Her plumed head went up proudly.

"I am sure. Kumo desires me. I always please him."

"See that you please him tonight. What then?"

"When he takes me . . ." said N'Daria with slow relish, ". . . when he takes me, he make spittle on my mouth. I will draw blood from his breast and from his shoulders. . . . Then he will leave me."

"And when he leaves you?"

"I will come back to you and I will bring with me the blood and the spittle and the seed of Kumo—and you will hold his life in your hands."

"So!" The word came out, a long, sighing breath of relief. The tension in him relaxed. His irritation drained away and power flowed back to him in long, smooth waves. He laid his hand on the brown shoulder and stroked it gently, caressingly.

"What you do for me tonight, N'Daria, you do for yourself. Remember that."

"I remember. And tomorrow . . . ?"

He smiled and brushed her breast with his fingertips.

"Tomorrow, N'Daria, as you say. Go, now."

She was halfway to the door when he called her back.

"Tonight, when you return, I shall be at the house with the visitors. Light the lamp and hang it near the window. I will see it and will come when I can."

He took her to the door and stood watching her as she walked down the track to the village. She was like a bird, he thought, a small bright bird, with scarlet feathers, fluttering under the tangket trees.

He closed the door of the laboratory and walked swiftly, purposefully, back to the house.

The canvas chairs were set on the stoop. There were glasses and a bucket of ice and jugs of frosted rainwater on the cane table, and Wee Georgie, with tender care, was cutting the seal of a new bottle of Scotch.

He looked up as Sonderfeld mounted the steps, and his bloated face was distorted into a smile that displayed his gapped and rotten teeth. His voice was a piping cockney, incongruous in so large a man.

" 'Arf a minute, boss, and we're all set for the party. Care for a pipe-opener?"

"In a moment."

Sonderfeld surveyed him with weary distaste. Wee Georgie was one of his less successful enterprises. He was a head shorter than Sonderfeld, but his stumpy body was monstrous. His tousled head was set on two rolls of blubber, his breasts were pendulous as a woman's and his belly was an obscene barrel scarcely covered by his shirt. His trouser belt slipped under it like string round a rubber ball. His bowlegs were knotted with blue veins and discoloured by ulcer scars. His misshapen feet were thrust into canvas shoes slit at both sides for comfort. When he laughed, which was often, he quaked like a jelly and his eyes were lost in the folds of his purple face. When he moved—which was as little as possible—he wheezed like a broken-winded nag.

"For God's sake, man, why don't you tidy your hair?" snapped Sonderfeld.

"I try, boss. Strike me dead, if I don't. Me girl tries, too, but it won't lie down. Not unless I douse it with oil. And you wouldn't want me stinking of pig fat while I serve the drinks. Now would you? Besides, me shirt's clean, isn't it—and me pants?"

"We should be thankful for so little, I suppose. Pour me a drink. A strong one."

He sat down in the nearest chair and watched Wee Georgie with sardonic amusement. The fellow's hands were trembling. He moistened his lips continually as he sniffed the liquor. It was one of Sonderfeld's small pleasures to calculate how long it would be before Wee Georgie would ask for a drink.

Wee Georgie was a survival from the prehistory of the Territory. His origins were misted with legend. He had been deckhand on the copra-luggers, prospector, recruiter, waterfront pimp, and a dozen other things, mercifully buried when the Japanese destroyed the records. Sonderfeld had picked him off the beach in Lae, cured him of clap, stones in the kidney and a score of minor ailments, and brought him up to the valley as foreman to the boy labour and contact man with the tribes. He had settled down in squalid comfort with a pair of village girls, and Sonderfeld thought he would die in twelve months of cirrhosis of the liver.

But by some miracle he managed to survive, and Sonderfeld had made much profit from his alcoholic Caliban. Wee Georgie was a slovenly old reprobate, but he "thought kanaka" and he had no scruples. With care and caution and a judicious ration of liquor, he, too, had served the master-plan.

"There's your drink, boss."

"Thanks."

"Er— Ah— What about a small one for the help—eh, boss?"

Sonderfeld grinned and looked at his watch.

"Thirty seconds! You're doing well, my friend. You may have a drink."

"Thanks, boss—thanks."

He wheezed and chuckled and shuffled to the table to pour a stiff noggin.

"Mud in yer eye and pretty girls in yer bed!"

"*Prosit!*" said Kurt Sonderfeld absently.

Wee Georgie tossed his drink off with a practiced gulp. His master drank slowly, savouring the spirit, feeling the slow warmth gather like warm coals in his belly. Drinking, for Sonderfeld, was a princely pleasure and he took it like a prince, with leisure and deliberation.

"Lansing's arrived, boss."

"Mr. Lansing to you, Georgie."

"Mr. Lansing, then. He came about half an hour ago."

"Where is he now?"

Sonderfeld put the question with studious indifference; but Wee Georgie's little eyes were lit with malicious humour.

"Out back. Looking at the flowers with Mrs. Sonderfeld."

"The poor fellow has few pleasures," said Sonderfeld smoothly. "Who are we to deny him this one?"

Wee Georgie spat contemptuously over the railing.

"Few pleasures is right! What does he *do* down there in the village? Lives like a kanaka, he does. Eats their food. Sits round the cook fires. Never even touches the girls. What's the point in that, for Gawd's sake?"

"He's an anthropologist."

"Yup, I know. But what does he *do?*"

Sonderfeld stared into the golden liquor. His tone was velvet.

"He studies, Georgie. He studies the language, the beliefs, the manners, the customs and the mating habits of the indigenous population. He is paid, I understand, by grant from an American foundation which finances such worthy enterprises."

"Paid? For what? Gawdstrewth! I could tell 'em twice as much as Lansing'll ever know—and for half the price."

"I know. I know," said Sonderfeld gently. "But Lansing leaves out the dirty words."

"You're not very fond of Lansing, are you, boss?"

The whisky caught him full in the face. As he gasped and whimpered and rubbed his eyes, Sonderfeld jerked him upright by the hair and smacked him, full on the mouth. Then he chided him gently, without anger, as one admonishes a child.

"You will remember, Georgie, that you are a servant in this house. You will attend to my guests and mind your own business. You will remember that you are filth—alive by my skill and favour. You will have no more to drink this evening. Now clean yourself up and pour me a drink. Père Louis will be here any minute."

Wee Georgie backed away, a cowed, repulsive animal. Sonderfeld wiped his hands on a silk handkerchief and waited calmly for the arrival of his second guest.

The little priest came hurrying up the path, arms flailing, square beard bobbing on his chest. A small canvas bag hung over his shoulder and slapped up and down on his rump. His wizened, walnut face streamed with perspiration. He was like a goat, thought Sonderfeld, a wise and ancient goat with his grey beard and his bright, canny eyes. And yet of all the men who came to share his table, this was the one for whom he had most respect. He must have been more than sixty, yet he had the gnarled and stringy strength of an old tree. More than thirty years of his life had been spent in the mountains of Papua and New Guinea. When the first prospectors came through the southern valley, Père Louis was there waiting for them. When the recruiters came in to the Highlands to find new labour pools, Père Louis was there to see that they kept their hands off his girls.

The years had not robbed him of his spry, peasant humour and, for all the isolation of his life, he was as modern a European as Sonderfeld had ever known. When they met, they spoke French first and then German. They talked books and medicine and politics and morals and philosophy; and when they parted, Sonderfeld had the uneasy feeling that the little man had been sounding him, tapping the hollow places of his soul as a cooper taps a barrel.

If he feared any man—and this he was not prepared to admit, even to himself—he feared the little priest. Therefore he was careful with him, careful and courteous and humorously attentive as to a fellow exile on the outposts.

"Sit down, Father. Sit down. Get your breath back. Georgie will fix you a drink. My wife will be here presently. She has taken our friend Lansing to see the flowers."

"Madame is well?"

"Very well, thank you. The climate here is kinder to women than on the coast."

"She is still happy in the valley?"

Sonderfeld shot him a quick glance, but finding no malice in the bright eyes, he smiled and shrugged.

"If she is unhappy, she has not told me."

"Good, good. I have brought her an orchid. One of the big gold fellows. My boys found it in the gorge this afternoon."

He reached down into the canvas bag, took out the plant and laid it on the table. Its long, fleshy stalk carried one full bloom and a row of bursting buds. Its roots were clotted in rich, black earth and bound in bark cloth. Sonderfeld smiled, approving the gentle gesture.

"Thank you. Gerda will be pleased. She has wanted one of those for a long time."

" 'Ere's your drink, Padre." Wee Georgie shuffled over and laid the glass on the table. His hand trembled and a few drops splashed on the tabletop. Sonderfeld frowned but said nothing. Père Louis looked up, grinning.

"You have the shakes again, Georgie."

Wee Georgie sniffed petulantly.

"Always 'appens when I'm on the wagon, Padre. Stands to reason, don't it? A man's only flesh and blood."

"Try this, Georgie. It's easier on the liver than the native toddy."

The fat man's eyes lit up as the little priest produced a small bottle of altar wine. He reached out and, with a look of sidelong triumph at Sonderfeld, rammed it into the torn pocket of his trousers.

"That's charity, Padre. Real Christian charity. If there was anyone could get me singin' 'ymns at my age—which there ain't—but if there was, it'd be you."

Père Louis chuckled and waved him away. He raised his glass.

"Santé, mon ami."

"À la vôtre, mon père."

They drank comfortably, a pair of exiles twelve thousand miles from home. Sonderfeld offered a cigar. The little priest refused it, grinning as he produced a foul briar and a wad of trade tobacco.

"You would waste your cigar. I have smoked this stuff for so long, I cannot taste a good tobacco."

He lit up, puffing frantically to light the treacly plug. Then, when it was drawing comfortably, he said, "The tribes are still moving into the Lahgi Valley."

"I know." Sonderfeld's tone was indifferent, but he was prickling with interest. "It's the usual thing, isn't it? They always come for the pig festival."

The Lahgi Valley was a great green crater over the lip of the northern barrier. Here was the principal village from which all the scattered colonies had spread over the surrounding mountains in search of new garden plots. Here they returned for the pig festival once every three years. Their coming was a mass migration spread over many weeks. When the festival was over, they would return to their own villages and their separate tribal lives. Sonderfeld's people had not yet begun to move; before they did, his preparations must be completed if his whole project were not to fall in ruins about his ears. Père Louis chewed irritably at his pipe and went on.

"As you say, it is the usual thing. But this time it is different. Something is stirring."

Now, thought Sonderfeld, now we come to the bones of it. He probed gently, cautiously, masking his anxiety with the tolerant smile of the philosopher.

"There is always something stirring in these people. They are restless as children. In the old times they could work it off with a war or a raid on their neighbour's taro patch. Now they are controlled. The Administration disapproves of cathartic killings." He shrugged ironically. "Don't worry about it, Father. They will get rid of their fleas at the festival. They will sing and dance and get drunk, and come home quietly to cure their headaches."

"No." The little priest shook his head. "No, my friend, it is not so simple as that. You do not know these people as I do. They are not children. They are old—older than Greece and Rome, older than Babylon, old as the men who left their pictures in the sunken caves of the Pyrenees. Evil is rooted deep among them. Ancient evil, dark and frightening. It is stirring now. I know it, though I cannot put a name to it."

"But there must be signs, rumours—"

"There are signs—yes." He frowned. His weathered face seemed suddenly shrunken and tired. "My Christians tell me the elders are saying that the Red Spirit himself will appear at the festival. He will come in human shape and will lead his people to prosperity and power beyond their dreams."

Sonderfeld chuckled tolerantly.

"The old, old wish fulfillment. It appears in a thousand forms among the primitives and always at times of celebration or tribal crisis. It disappears as quickly—when the hangover starts. Look a little further, you will find the rumour begins with some witch doctor who wants to make a name for himself—and a profit, too, when all the people come together."

"I know the man already," said Père Louis flatly. "His name is Kumo. He lives in your village."

"Kumo, eh?" He must be interested now, but not too interested. "I have

395

heard of him of course, as one hears of tribal identities. I have never paid any attention to him. A local charlatan, a little more intelligent than his fellows. How can such a man be important?"

"Kumo," said the priest, carefully. "Kumo was one of my mission boys. He was intelligent beyond the average. I hoped that he would become a catechist and even, one day, a priest—the first, possibly, from the Highlands here. Then there arose"—he hesitated, groping for words—"a problem of conscience. I cannot tell you what it was since it came to me under the seal of the confessional. I pointed out to Kumo what he must do. He refused. I denied him the Sacraments. He left me—left the Mission, too. He went up to the mountains to the teachers of the old, dark mysteries. He became a sorcerer." Again Père Louis paused, as if reluctant to put the thought into words. "I—I have reason to believe that he sold his soul to the Devil."

Sonderfeld exploded into laughter.

"No, no, no, Father! Not from you! You are too intelligent for that! Werewolves in Carinthia, with the village priest as ignorant as his flock? A scrubby curate in Sicily with his weeping Madonna! But not from you. You are too wise, too old for this—this *Kinderspiel*. Look—we can be frank with each other. After all—"

"Mother of God!" Père Louis crackled into fiery anger. "How great a fool can a man be! You sit there rocking on your chair laughing—at what? The monstrous evil of ten thousand years."

Sonderfeld was swift in apology. He had made a mistake. The luxury of laughter would come later. He could not afford it yet.

"Forgive me, my friend. I was tactless. I did not mean—"

Père Louis shook his head. His anger died as suddenly as it had quickened. His voice was somber and sad.

"I know very well what you mean. Evil is an accident of the cosmos. The cosmos itself is an imperfect evolution of primal chaos. God is a name without substance. Satan is a medieval myth— Bah!" He took the pipe out of his mouth and laid it on the table. Hands and voice and eyes pieced out the low, passionate exposition. "Look, Kurt, try to understand. For your own sake, not for mine. I am too old to be troubled by laughter. But I am afraid for you. You cannot dismiss the mystery of creation with a shrug and a phrase. No man is big enough for that."

"You will forgive me if I doubt your explanation of it."

"Doubt it if you must, but do not dismiss it. Look!" There was a note almost of pleading in the old voice. "You know how I live here. You know how long I have lived here. I have no plantation as you have. I have no wife as you have. Yet I could have enjoyed them both, as you do now. Why did I choose to give them up? Because I believe in God and I believe in the Devil. I know that they exist, really, personally, actively. That is the whole meaning of a priest's life. To serve God and to fight the Devil—and to strengthen his flock to the same service and the same struggle."

"It is a notable belief, Father. It is also a harsh one. It is my loss, perhaps, that I cannot accept it. I have never seen God. I have never seen the Devil. Until I do . . ." He shrugged eloquently.

"The footprints of God are on every acre of your valley. His handiwork is there on your table." He lifted the golden orchid bloom and held it up for Sonderfeld to examine.

Sonderfeld waved it aside.

"And the Devil, Father? Where do you see the Devil?"

Something akin to pity showed in the bright, wise eyes.

"If I were to tell you, my friend, that I have seen women dash the brains from their firstborn and turn calmly to suckle a pig, if I were to tell you that there are magicians in the mountains—and this Kumo is one of them—who change themselves into cassowary birds and travel between the villages faster than man can run, if I were to tell that I have seen a girl suspended in the air, so that six men could not drag her down, that I have heard her screaming curses in the Latin of Saint Jerome while I, myself, pronounced the exorcism— and she a mountain girl who could not even speak pidgin—what would you say then?"

"Then," said Sonderfeld blandly, "then, Father, I should say that you have lived longer than I—and a good deal less comfortably. Now, if you'll excuse me, I will fetch my wife."

He heaved himself out of his chair. The little priest stayed him with a gesture.

"A moment, please."

"Yes?"

"You are concerned in this."

"I? How am I concerned?" His voice was harsh but steady.

"As I came up the path I met N'Daria. She was dressed for the sing-sing tonight."

"And how does that concern me? The girl belongs here. It is natural that she should want to join in the amusements of her own people. Even if I wished, I have no authority to prevent her."

"There is no question of prevention," said the old priest wearily. "It is simply that N'Daria is the chosen lover of Kumo. I thought you should know that."

"Thank you, Father." Sonderfeld's voice was cold. "Now that I know, I find it interests me not at all. Georgie! A drink for Père Louis. Forgive me, I shall not be a moment."

He turned on his heel and walked into the cool half-light of the house. Wee Georgie poured himself a double slug of whisky and tossed it off in one furtive gulp.

Père Louis sat slumped in his chair, staring out across the valley and the lengthening shadows of the mountains.

397

Chapter Two

GERDA SONDERFELD's GARDEN was a riotous miracle of colour and bursting life.

Two garden boys, the summer rains, the tropic warmth, the mountain cool, and Gerda's own careful hands, had turned a quarter acre of black volcanic soil into a private Eden.

Here in the high valleys there is no quartering of the seasons, no cyclic symbol of childhood and youth and maturity and age. Here there are only the big rains and the small, the sun in Cancer, the sun in Capricorn. Here you may plant what you will and when it pleases you. It will burst into life, bud, flower, as if in a forcing house.

In Gerda Sonderfeld's garden there were salvias, red as live coals, gladioli with long spears and monstrous velvet blooms, beyond the avarice of temperate gardeners. There were dahlias and delphiniums, tall poppies and asters and white trumpet vines, giant coleus with mottled leaves, crotons and pied lilies, rock orchids and drooping ferns, and a passion vine trailing over a bamboo summerhouse. There were casuarina trees and clumps of bamboo, and shrubs with berries, red, purple and shining orange. There were plants that might have graced an English garden, and wild grotesques that belonged only to the jungles and the rain forests. The air was still and heady with perfume.

It was a masterwork, as full of contradictions as the woman who planted it.

She was in the summerhouse now, with Max Lansing.

She smoothed down the bright cotton frock, moulding it back over her full breasts and downwards to where it flared away from the roundness of her hips. Then she repaired her smudged lips and rearranged her dark hair in the small formal bun on the nape of her neck. Lansing watched her, impatient and puzzled.

A moment ago she had been in his arms, clinging to him, pressing his mouth down upon her own, exciting him almost to frenzy with the urgent straining of her tight strong body. Then, suddenly, she had thrust him away without regret or apology and begun this maddening little ritual of the toilet.

The passion had died in her, abruptly as a light dies when the current is switched off. The flush was gone from her skin, leaving it smooth as old, fine ivory. Her small hands were steady and patient in the intimacies of restoration. Her dark eyes were enigma. He could not tell whether they mocked or caressed him. Her parted lips were cool and dry.

Yet she was neither capricious nor a coquette. There was a bluntness in her desire, a blandness in her acceptance that had shocked him at first, then pricked him to greater need. It was the suddenness of the transformation that angered him and affronted his vanity. His own nerves were ragged and screaming with want. She was as calm and comfortable as a kitten on a hearth rug. He made as if to take her in his arms again. She moved a step beyond his reach, still pinning up her hair.

"No, Max. Not now. Kurt will be here any minute. It would be embarrassing for all of us."

"Embarrassing!" It was as if the word gagged him. His flat midwestern voice was full of disgust and petulant anger. "Goddammit, Gerda! What do you think I am? I love you, don't you know that?"

"Keep your voice down, Max," she said calmly. "I can hear you. There is no need to shout at me."

"I'm not shouting. I'm trying to make you see—"

"But, darling, I see everything very plainly."

She patted the last hairs into place, then reached up and laid a cool hand on his cheek. The maternal gesture irritated him and he drew back from it abruptly.

"O.K.! You see everything. You understand everything. Do you understand how much I love you? Do you understand what it's like to lie in my hut and listen to those goddamn drums night after night, while you're up here with him? If I could just pack up and take you out of here. . . ."

She smiled at him then—the tolerant, pitying smile of the adult for the stamping child.

"But you can't, can you, Max? You must stay here until your term is out— otherwise you lose the grant from the University. And even if you could, where would you take me?"

"Home—to the States."

She shook her head.

"To what? To a little apartment in a big city? To a little cottage near the campus? I would stifle there. Besides, for me, it would be hard to enter the United States. Be sensible, my dear. Let us enjoy the little we have. Look, tonight, if Kurt goes down to the village, you can come to me—"

"For God's sake, Gerda!"

His anger went out like a snuffed candle. He stood before her, shoulders stooped, arms dangling, in an attitude of weary despair. Looking at him, she thought how sick and tired he was. His face was lined and yellow with suppressed malaria. His long, bony fingers were discoloured with tobacco. His clothes hung loosely over his big bones. His eyes were hollow and burning. Soon, she thought, he would be old and all his dreams would have cheated him. One day he would go home with his notes in a little canvas bag and his heart still hungry in his gangling body, and he would write his thesis and give his modest lectures and they would raise no ripple on the wide waters. For Max Lansing would always be the wrong man in the wrong place—too late, too early. His plans a little out of scale, his work out of rhythm, his life lonely and out of kilter.

Sudden pity took hold of her and she caught his hands and raised them gently to her lips. He bent over her and smelt the perfume of her hair.

"Listen to me, Max!" Her voice was gentle. He caught the faint gutturals that marked her for an alien. "I have said this to you before, I say it again. You are not meant for this sort of life. You are not one of those who can live alone. Give it up. Go home. Find yourself a nice American girl who will keep your house and give you children—"

"I can't go home." It was almost a cry. "This is my big chance. Don't you see that? This is one of the few places in the world where a research man can break new ground. If I can stick it out, I can make a name for myself, get myself a Chair at one of the big colleges—"

"All right, Max, all right." She had no heart to rob him of this last illusion. "But if you must stay, then at least accept what is here. Make yourself comfortable. Get yourself a village girl to look after you." She smiled up at him. "You would learn more from her in a week than you would in a year alone."

He thrust her away roughly.

"And come to you afterwards? Hold you in my arms? Make love to you?"

She shrugged and spread her hands in a small disarming gesture.

"Why not? It would not worry me. If you were content, I should be glad for you."

"And you say you love me!"

He turned away and began to fumble, defensively, for a cigarette.

"I have never said I loved you, Max," said Gerda quietly.

He whirled to face her.

"What then? In God's name, Gerda, what sort of a woman are you?"

She was still smiling. She would neither break nor bend nor give any hint of need to match his own.

"My husband," she said quietly, "calls me a whore. And yet I do not think I am. I have need of tenderness, as I have need of food, of the flowers in my garden. Kurt does not give it to me. I take it where I find it."

"From me or from the next man!"

400

"That's right, Max. From you or from the next man. Admit at least that I am honest about it."

"Sure, sure, you're honest about it!"

He let out a long, shuddering breath and ran his fingers through his cropped hair.

"Well . . . thanks for telling me. I know where I stand now. I guess I'd better push off."

"My dear fellow," said Kurt Sonderfeld from the doorway, "you can't leave now. You are our guest. Your room is prepared. The others are expecting you. Shall we go in, Gerda?"

There were two new arrivals sitting in the canvas chairs drinking Wee Georgie's iced whisky—a blond youth in stained khaki, and a round, ruddy-faced fellow, immaculate in starched shirt and tropic shorts. They had come up from the Kiap house, a large thatched hut on the edge of the village, built and maintained by the tribe as a staging camp for the officers of the Administration.

The blond youth was Lee Curtis, cadet patrol officer under the command of the District Commissioner at Goroka. His appointment constituted him policeman, judge, census taker, and semi-military controller of three thousand square miles of territory and fifty thousand human beings. He had blue eyes and a baby mouth, and he sweated uneasily in the polyglot company of his elders. His frank adoration of Gerda was a constant amusement to Sonderfeld.

His companion was a Britisher, representative of an international coffee combine, investigating the resources of the Highlands under the auspices of the Agriculture Department of the Trustee Territory. He had the bland and easy manner of the seasoned traveller. He smiled continually, but his eyes were wary and shrewd behind his horn-rimmed spectacles. His unlikely name was Theodore Nelson. He was an expert in crop estimates and the diseases of the coffee plant, but his principal value to his employers was as a canny judge of the men who would one day come to them for finance, when the thrips destroyed a crop or the cost of clearing caught up with their bank balance.

They stood up, smiling, when Gerda came in, and shuffled for positions as Sonderfeld ushered her into the company with practiced charm. Each of them wanted the chair beside her, and Sonderfeld was bleakly amused when she ignored their invitations and settled herself beside Père Louis and eagerly began to admire the golden orchid. Still they could not take their eyes off her. The panic unease was stirring them as wind stirs a wheat field, as the kundu drums stir the heavy silence of the uplands.

Strange, thought Sonderfeld sourly, that a woman could set fires in other men and yet be colder than stone to the man who married her.

The reflection irritated him. He put it away and turned to the entertainment of his guests.

"You have seen my coffee, Mr. Nelson. What do you think of it?"

The Englishman was enthusiastic.

"Excellent! Excellent! I can safely say it is one of the best plantations I have seen on the Highlands. The soil is good and well manured. You have chosen the best shade trees. I watched your boys spraying. You have trained them well."

Sonderfeld nodded, acknowledging the professional compliment.

"I made a close study of the problems before I opened the land here. The soil is rich. The climate is perfect. Given normal care, there is no reason why this country cannot produce the best coffee in the world."

"There is one thing that worries me," said Nelson carefully. "At least, it may worry the company, should we ever come to do business together."

"What is that?"

"You have no road. You are fifty miles from Goroka. How are you going to get your crop out to the market?"

Lee Curtis cut in, stammering a little in his eagerness to join the discussion.

"Tha—that's what everybody in the Highlands would like to know. It—it's been a sort of a standing joke ever since Sonderfeld came up here. All the rest of the settlers took up land along the road. There's three hundred miles of it from Lae to Mount Hagen. Even the old hands in the Territory wouldn't come out as far as this."

Sonderfeld smiled tolerantly. This was an old question. It had long since ceased to be dangerous to him.

"There, in part at least, is the answer to your question, Mr. Nelson. This is the newest country in the world—the least exploited. Germany held it first, but before she could capitalize her holding, it was taken from her with the rest of her colonial empire. The League of Nations handed it over as a mandate to the Commonwealth of Australia. Then the Japanese came and occupied the northern coast and some of the hinterland for the best part of the Pacific War. When Japan was defeated, Australia resumed the Administration under a new mandate from the United Nations."

Nelson looked puzzled.

"I don't see what that's got to do with the economics of coffee."

Sonderfeld smiled tolerantly.

"You would be surprised how much it has to do with coffee, my dear fellow. The Administration is a trustee, not an owner in perpetuity. As a trustee her prime duty is the welfare of the indigenous people. Under the terms of the United Nations Mandate, land must not be alienated permanently from the native population in favour of private individuals. Land which is not essential to the tribes may be acquired by the Government and leased by them for terms up to ninety-nine years. I was a latecomer. By the time I was ready to acquire a lease, the best land—that which borders the Highland road—was already preempted. So I had to move farther out. As you have seen yourself, I have not done badly."

"No," said Nelson dubiously. "But you still have the problem of getting your crop out. Load the freights too high and you price yourself out of the market."

402

Sonderfeld shook his head.

"I am not so short-sighted as that, believe me. By the time my crop is ready to flush, I shall have a road—my own road."

"You'll build it yourself?"

"My people will build it for me," said Sonderfeld calmly.

Père Louis looked up sharply. Max Lansing started, as if at a monstrous revelation. Only Nelson and the young patrol officer seemed to find nothing strange in the simple assurance of their host.

Nelson looked inquiringly at Curtis. The youth nodded agreement.

"It could be done—provided the tribes cooperate, of course. At the moment they're very cooperative." He laughed loudly, like a self-conscious schoolboy. "Hope they stay that way. Makes my job easy."

Sonderfeld bowed in ironic acknowledgment.

"A compliment from the Administration! Thank you, my friend. Unfortunately, it would seem Père Louis does not agree with you."

"Oh? Why not?" Curtis rose truculently to the bait. The Missions were an old burr in the pelt of the Administration. The doctrine of the immortal soul raises more than one problem for colonial officials.

Père Louis chewed on his pipe. His eyes were veiled. His mouth was an enigma behind the square, Trotsky beard.

Theodore Nelson studied him with mild disapproval. He had the Englishman's distaste for clerics who ventured beyond the cathedral close. There was a time and place for everything, and the Gospel of Saint John needed organ voluntaries and gothic gloom to make it half palatable. Among the Stone Age men it was Gallic indiscretion.

Père Louis looked up. His answer was mild and without emphasis.

"I happened to mention to our friend that the tribes are restless. The pig festival is approaching, as you know. The sorcerers are spreading rumours that the Red Spirit will appear in person at the time of the big sacrifice."

"So that's it!" Lansing almost leapt from his chair. His voice cracked like a dry stick. The others looked at him in amazement. Only Sonderfeld seemed unmoved. He questioned Lansing with quizzical irony.

"Come, come, my friend. Don't tell me it surprises you. You live with these people, don't you? It is your profession to study the social patterns of primitive peoples. You must have heard these rumours, as Père Louis has?"

"Sure, sure, I've heard 'em."

"Père Louis tells me they begin with a man named Kumo, a sorcerer in my own village."

"I disagree with Père Louis!"

Lansing was tight as a fiddle string. His chin was thrust out in nervous challenge. He was like a fighter moving in to his first opening. Sonderfeld was still smiling, but his eyes were wary.

"I am sure Père Louis would be glad to hear your views."

Lansing grinned.

"They might interest the Administration as well."

403

The patrol officer looked up. His boyish face took on an expression of comic gravity.

"We're always interested in the views of local residents. They help us considerably in making our own appreciation of the situation."

Lansing spread his long, bony hands and laid them fingertip to fingertip in a careful academic gesture. He was silent a moment, choosing his words. The others watched him silently. Gerda's eyes were troubled. Then he spoke, slowly, flatly, precisely.

"It is my considered opinion that the coming pig festival will be the occasion for an outbreak of the cargo cult in this area."

His words dropped into the silence like pebbles counted into still water. A ripple of interest stirred the small company. It was Theodore Nelson who spoke first.

"Cargo cult? That's new to me."

Lee Curtis was eager to explain.

"The cargo cult is—"

Lansing brushed aside the interruption and plunged into his own exposition.

"The cargo cult has many forms, but in essence it is very simple. It is the direct result of the impact of modern civilization on primitive man. The coming of the white man has revealed to the tribes a new heaven and a new earth, a way of life beyond their attainment. Time was when a man's wealth was measured by the number of his pigs or by his store of gold-lip shell. His manhood was rated by his skill in battle and the tally of his slain enemies. Now, tribal killings are a crime. The boys who come back from the coast after serving their indentures are discontented. They have seen bicycles and automobiles and refrigerators and moving pictures. They are no longer satisfied with pigs and trochus shell. The glory of the plumed headdress and the sing-sing costume is a matter of secret contempt. Knowledge has come into Eden, and Adam is ashamed of his nakedness."

He paused, gauging their interest, savouring the secret discomfort of Sonderfeld. Then he went on:

"That is the beginning of the cult—the new need, the new heaven beyond the stretch of dark fingers. Next comes the new prophet of the new promise. He uses the old symbols—the Pig God, the Red Spirit. He practices the old magic, the old rituals of sacrifice and propitiation. But the promise is new—'Follow me and I will give you the riches of the white man, a share in the powers of the white man. The great droning birds will fly at my command. The cargoes they carry will be cargoes of wealth for you.' Ask any of the old hands. They will tell you of Black Christs and Black Kings. They will tell you how American Negro troops were hailed as liberating legions. Ask Patrol Officer Curtis, here, and he will tell you of wireless houses with vines for aerials and little armies carving wooden guns like those of the native police boys."

He broke off, a little breathless from the fervent monologue. Then he made his final sober summation.

"That is how I read these rumours of the Red Spirit and his promised revelation at the pig festival. To this point, I believe, Père Louis will agree with me."

The little priest nodded, still chewing on his pipe.

"But," said Lansing, "this is where I disagree with him. The prophet is not Kumo. Kumo is the mouthpiece. The voice is the voice of another."

"What other?" Père Louis' question was deceptively mild.

Lansing turned to him and jabbed an emphatic finger at his shirtfront.

"You have lived in the Territory longer than any of us, Father. You know how often trouble among the tribes has been fomented by white men for their own ends—by gold seekers and labour exploiters and crazy kingmakers, who think that a mountain barrier can stop the march of civilization and enlightenment."

"I know it—yes," said Père Louis placidly. "I know also that their power has been brief and their end violent. Are you suggesting that the man behind Kumo is a white?"

"I'm stating it as a fact," said Lansing bluntly.

Darkness had come upon them unawares. The first stars were pricking out, low and bright, in the purple sky. As if to set a dramatic period to Lansing's speech, the black drums thudded into rhythm across the valley. Caught in the sudden mystery of the moment, no one spoke. Then, clear, boyish, pragmatic, the voice of Lee Curtis shattered the illusion.

"From here to the Lahgi Valley and fifty miles north there are only five whites—Père Louis, Mr. Lansing, myself, Mrs. Sonderfeld—"

"And me!" said Kurt Sonderfeld. Then he laughed, a great deep bellow that rang out over the throbbing counterpoint of the kundus.

He was still laughing when he made up his mind to kill Max Lansing.

They dined by candlelight in the long room that looked out beyond the valley to mountains and the rich sky. The table was dressed with fine linen and silverware and flowers from Gerda's garden. At each place was laid a single bloom of scarlet hibiscus. The wine glowed in long goblets of Bohemian crystal.

The servants were tall mountain boys in starched lap-laps that made a small rustling as they padded about on silent, naked feet. The candles glowed on their brown breasts and the rippling muscles of their shoulders.

The tension that had built up between Sonderfeld and his guests relaxed under the suavity of good food and wine and conversation that ranged beyond the mountain barriers to the old countries over the sea. The drums were still throbbing in the village; but they were muted now, and distant, subdued to monotone like the beat of surf on a sheltered beach.

Here, in the shadowy room under the grass thatch, was Europe—Europe of the old, decaying beauties, of the checkerboard frontiers, of the buried empires, Europe of the subtle centuries. Here woman was enthroned, soft under the candlelight, warm over the wine, smiling on her small court of churchman, trader, scholar and functionary, served by her dark, dumb slaves from the outer march.

Sonderfeld watched them as they bent to her, laughed at her small jokes, preened themselves to her coquetries. Theodore Nelson forgot his caution and told her stories of his travels in Brazil and Africa and Ceylon. Père Louis poured out his drolleries of mission life, while Lee Curtis rummaged in his shallow grab bag for trifles to divert her. Only Lansing refused his tribute. He sat, silent and resentful in the buzz of talk, while Sonderfeld watched him and sipped his wine and measured the harm that this unhappy man might do to him.

Gerda herself was a woman transformed. The brooding calm that normally enveloped her was shed like a cloak, revealing a nature of warmth and vitality. Her eyes sparkled, her gestures were vivid and expressive. As she became excited, she lapsed into little gaucheries of accent and idiom that added sauce and charm to her talk. The candlelight gave life to her ivory skin and made deep shadows in the curve of her throat and the hollow between her breasts. Small wonder, thought Sonderfeld, that other men desired her, when he himself could still be moved to fruitless want.

When the meal was over, they tuned the radio to music from Moresby, and Gerda danced with Curtis and Nelson and Lansing, while Père Louis and Sonderfeld sat by the big window with coffee and brandies. They heard the tinkle of the music and the shuffle of the dancers and the occasional burst of laughter from Gerda; but under it all was the kundu beat, louder now and faster, as the drummers sweated over the black snakeskin.

Sonderfeld selected a cigar, slipped off the band and pierced the butt with more than usual care. The drums were making him restless again. His nerves were frayed by the vapid chatter behind him. The memory of the scene on the stoop nagged him with its insistent warning of danger. He needed time and solitude to compose himself and complete his plans. Yet he was forced to play out this little comedy of leisure and good manners.

Cradled in a chair three sizes too big for him, Père Louis puffed contentedly at his pipe and studied his host through the smoke haze. For a long time now he had been worried over the big man. Outside he was hard and polished as teakwood, but the worms were chewing at the core of him, and Père Louis had a care even for those who were not of his faith. That Sonderfeld was distant from his wife was plain enough, though he gave no sign of being jealous of her. But an unsatisfactory marriage was not enough to explain the cold pride, the urgent, disciplined ambition of the man. Carefully as a chess player, Père Louis made his opening gambit of inquiry.

"You know, Kurt, I am very grateful for these evenings in your house."

"I am glad to hear it, Father," said Sonderfeld placidly.

406

"After all these years, you would think the need should grow less. It does not."

"The need for what, Father?" He was glad of this desultory, calm exchange. It soothed him to patience, gave him time to set his thoughts in order.

Père Louis shrugged.

"Comfort. The comfort of civilized food and good wine and music. Companionship. The talk of one's own people. Even the sight of a beautiful woman, the sound of her voice and of her laughter."

Sonderfeld grinned.

"I thought, Father, you renounced these things when you took your vows."

The priest made a wry gesture.

"To renounce is one thing. To stifle the need is quite another. I think perhaps it never dies until the body itself is destroyed. You should be very grateful for what you have here—a beautiful wife, a comfortable house, a serene living."

"Grateful?" He rejected the word with angry contempt. "Grateful? To whom? To myself, for what I have attained with brains and patience and courage? To my wife, who makes herself a harlot in my own house? To these who eat my food and drink my liquor and lust after my woman? To the tribes, who would steal the last shovel from my store if they were not afraid of me? To the country, which would devour my coffee in a month if I were not here to keep it in check?"

If Père Louis was shocked by the outburst, he gave no sign. He shot a quick glance over his shoulder to see if the others had heard. They were still laughing and chattering and tapping their feet to the music. Gerda was pouring another round of drinks. He turned back to Sonderfeld. His canny eyes were hard. His mouth was grim.

"My friend," he said softly, "you are a very unhappy man."

"You are mistaken, Father. I am not unhappy. On the contrary, I am a very contented man. Why? Because I regard the follies of others as I regard the looseness of my wife—with contempt. They do not touch me. I have my own road to walk. I walk it alone and in peace."

"Alone, yes. But not in peace. And where does it lead, this road of yours?"

Sonderfeld grinned crookedly and shook his head.

"Oh, no! I am too wise a fox for that. You will not bring me to your confessional, Father. Try my wife. She was a Catholic once. You may be able to lead her back to the fold. When she is too old for lust, she may develop a taste for piety. Who knows?"

"You are a fool, Kurt Sonderfeld," said the little priest softly. "I know this road of yours, because I have seen many men walk it. I have heard them cry out in despair when it was too late to turn back. I know where it leads."

"Where?"

"To death," said Père Louis simply. "To death—and damnation."

He stood up, brushed the ash from his shirt and stuffed his pipe in his pocket.

"I must leave you now. It is a long walk to the Mission. I have an early Mass."

Sonderfeld bowed ironically.

"I am sorry you have to leave. Remember that you are welcome here at any time."

Père Louis shook his head. His lined face was tired and sad.

"No, Kurt. I shall not come again unless you need me and call for me. But I will give you a warning."

"A warning?" Sonderfeld's eyes were hard as pebbles. His mouth was a thin, stringent line.

"Look, Kurt," the old man made a last, weary plea, "you tell me you are an unbeliever. The tribes on the other hand are believers. They believe intensely, passionately, in the old faiths. No matter that they are false, debased, cruel, they are part of the fabric of life for these people. For that reason, if for no other, their belief is stronger than your disbelief. If you tamper with it, if, in pride and ignorance, you try to turn it to your own advantage, it will destroy you. Believe me, it will destroy you utterly."

"Nonsense, Father!" Sonderfeld said, and smiled as he said it. He stood up. Père Louis heaved himself out of the chair and stood looking up into the stony, mocking face of the big German. Anger blazed in his old eyes and his voice was charged with the biblical menace of the prophets.

"Stay away from the tribes, Kurt. Stay away from Kumo and the sorcerers. You are dealing with matters you do not understand. To call up devils is a simple thing. To exorcise them, one needs faith, hope, charity and the abundant mercy of God. Good night, my friend!"

Brusquely, Sonderfeld led him through the brief rituals of farewell and shepherded him out of the house. He stood a long time on the veranda listening to the drums and watching the small bat-like shadow flapping homeward under the casuarina trees. He felt no regret. He had rid himself of one possible obstacle to his plans. The next was Max Lansing. But his death was already written on the palm of his hand. Sonderfeld was prepared to wait a little longer.

He looked down at the laboratory hut. There was no light yet. N'Daria was still in the village. He shrugged indifferently. The nights were long for mountain lovers and the throbbing drums had not yet reached their climax.

Chapter Three

Down in the village they were making kunande.

There were perhaps a hundred of them, bucks and girls, squatting two by two round the little fires in the long, low hut. Behind them, in the smoky shadows, sat the drummers, crouching over the kundus, filling fetid air with the deep, insistent beat that changed from song to song, from verse to refrain, with never a pause and never a falter.

The couples around the fires leant face to face and breast to breast, and sang low, murmurous, haunting songs that lapsed from time to time into a wordless, passionate melody. And, as they sang, they rolled their faces and their breasts together, lip to lip, nipple to nipple, cheek to brown and painted cheek.

The small flames shone on their oiled bodies and glistened on the green armour of the beetles in their headdress. Their plumes bobbed in the drifting smoke, and their necklets of shell and beads made a small clattering like castanets as they turned and rolled to the rolling of the drums.

The air was full of the smell of sweat and oil and smoke and the exhalation of bodies rising slowly to the pitch of passion. This was kunande, the public love-play of the unmarried, the courting time, the knowing time, when a man might tell from the responses of his singing partner whether she desired or disdained him. For this was the time of the woman. The girl chose her partner for the kunande, left him when she chose, solicited him if she wished, or held herself cool and aloof in the formal cadence of the songs.

N'Daria was among them, but the man with her was not Kumo. Kumo would come in his own time, and when he came she would leave her partner and go to him. For the present, she was content to sing and sway and warm herself with the contact of other flesh and let the drumbeats take slow possession of her blood.

A woman moved slowly down the line of singers. She was not adorned like the others. Her breasts were heavy with milk, her waist swollen with childbearing. Now she would throw fresh twigs on the fire, now she would part one couple and rearrange the partners. Now she would pour water in the open mouth of a drummer, as he bent back his head without slackening his beat on the black kundu. This was the mistress of ceremonies, the duenna, ordering the courtship to the desires of her younger sisters, dreaming of her own days of kunande when she, too, wore the cane belt of the unmarried.

The drumbeats rose to a wild climax, then dropped suddenly to a low humming. The singing stopped. The singers opened their eyes and sat rigid, expectant. Distant at first, then closer and closer, they heard the running of the cassowary bird. They heard the great clawed feet pounding the earth—chuff-chuff-chuff—down the mountain path, through the darkness of the rain forest, on to the flat places of the taro gardens and into the village itself. Tomorrow they would go out and see the footprints in the black earth. But now they waited, tense and silent, as the beat came closer and closer, louder than the drums, then stopped abruptly outside the hut.

A moment later Kumo the Sorcerer stood in the doorway.

He did not enter, stooping as the others had done under the low lintel. He was there, erect and challenging as if he had walked through the wall. He wore a gold wig, fringed with green beetle shards. His forehead was painted green and the upper part of his face was red with ochre. His nose ornament was enormous, his feathered casque was scarlet and blue and orange. His pubic skirt was of woven bark, and his belt was covered with cowrie shells. His whole body shone with pig fat.

The boy who had been singing with N'Daria rose and moved back into the shadows. N'Daria sat waiting. Then Kumo gave a curt signal to the drummers, and they swung into a wild, loud beat as he moved down the hut and sat facing N'Daria. No word was spoken between them. They sang and moved their faces together as the others did, but N'Daria's body was on fire and the drums beat in her blood, pounding against her belly and her breasts and her closed eyelids.

Then, after a long time, slowly the drumbeats died and the fires died with them. Quietly the couples dispersed, some to sleep, some to carry on the loveplay in a girl's house, others to seek swift consummation in the shadows of the tangket trees.

Kumo and N'Daria left the hut with them and walked through the darkness to the house of N'Daria's sister. Here there was food and drink and a small fire, and when they had eaten, two of the drummers came in with two more girls and they sat in pairs, backed against the bamboo walls, to make the greater love-play, called in pidgin "carry-leg."

Kumo sat with his legs stretched out towards the center of the hut. N'Daria sat beside him, her body half turned to him, her thighs thrown over his left leg, his right leg locked over hers. Then began a long, slow ritual of excitement, tentative at first, then more and more intimate and urgent. At first, they sang a little, snatches of the kunande songs; then they laughed, telling stories of other lovers and scandalous doings in the village and on the jungle paths. They made laughing flatteries of one another's bodies and their skill in the arts of love. Then, gradually, their voices dropped and their whispers became fiercer and more desirous.

"Does the white man touch you like this?"

"No—no—" She lied and half believed the lie in the warmth of the moment.

"Is the white man as great a man as I am?" His fingers pressed painfully into her flesh.

"He is not a man. Beside you he is a lizard."

"If he touches you, I will kill him."

"I would want you to kill him."

"I will make his blood boil and his bones turn to water. I will put ants in his brain and a snake in his belly."

"And I will watch and laugh, Kumo."

He caught her to him suddenly. His nails scored into her body, so that she gasped with the sudden pain.

"What does he teach you there in the little hut?"

She buried her face in his shoulder to hide the small smile of triumph. Kumo was a great sorcerer, the greatest in the valleys. Kumo could change himself into a cassowary bird and travel fast as the wind. But even Kumo did not know the secrets she learnt in Sonderfeld's laboratory.

"Tell me. What does he teach you?"

She giggled and clung to him.

"What will you give me if I tell you?"

"I will give you the charm that makes children and the charm that destroys them. I will make you desired of all men. I will give you the power to strike any woman barren and make any man a giant to embrace you."

"I want none of these things."

His mouth pressed to her ear, he whispered urgently so that the others could not hear.

"What do you want? Tell me and I will give it to you. Am I not the greatest sorcerer in the valleys? Does not the Red Spirit speak to me in the thunder and in the wind? Ask me and I will give. What do you want for the secrets of the white man's room?"

"Only that you should take me—now!"

His body shuddered with the flattery and the triumph of it.

"And you will tell me, when?"

"Tomorrow or the day after, when I can come without being seen. But not now—not now!"

Kumo laughed. His plumes tossed. His teeth shone. He swept the girl to her feet and half ran, half carried her out of the hut.

The consummation was a wild, brief frenzy that left her, bruised and crumpled, alone in the tall and trodden kunai grass.

The drums were silent, and the last fires were dying as N'Daria stumbled up the path to light the lamp in Sonderfeld's laboratory. Her body was aching and her head was swimming with fatigue and drunkenness, but between her belly and her belt was a piece of cotton wool which carried the life of Kumo the Sorcerer.

Wee Georgie was waiting for his wives to come home. In the small squalid hut on the edge of the track, he sat shivering under a ragged greatcoat, lamenting his misfortunes like Job on his dunghill.

First was the irregularity of his marriage, unblessed by the Church, the Administration or the tribes. The plump brown sisters were happy enough to share his rations and warm his rumpled blankets, but they counted themselves still among the unmarried and went to the kunande and solaced themselves regularly with the village bachelors. Wee Georgie was a tolerant fellow, frankly admitting his own impotence, but the mountain nights were cold and his blood was so thinned with alcohol that he could not sleep without the companionable warmth of an oily body, fore and aft.

More than this, his kidneys were suffering from half a century of systematic abuse and he was forced to make repeated trips to the base of the big casuarina tree while the cold seeped into the fatty marrow of him.

But worse than all, theme of the longest lamentation, was the liquor shortage. Père Louis' altar wine was thin comfort and soon gone—and Sonderfeld's ill humour had robbed him of his weekend ration of hard spirit. There was only a quarter of a bottle of whisky between himself and the terrors of the night, and this he was saving until the girls came home, so that he could sit and listen to their spicy gossip of village love and piece out the scraps of scandal that might one day earn him an extra bottle from Sonderfeld. It was the only pleasure left to him in the days of his decline, and he clung to it jealously, cursing the shameless lusts that kept his women late from his pillow.

A sharp pain in the region of his bladder brought him unsteadily to his feet, and he lurched out into the moonlight to relieve himself. He saw N'Daria stumbling wearily up the track, and when he looked up towards the big bungalow, he saw the big figure of Sonderfeld leaning on the veranda rail and, behind him, silhouetted against the window, the gesticulating shadows of three men in the lighted living room. The girl must have gone to bed, leaving the men to drink late. He grinned lecherously and wondered how long she'd stay there. Lansing would sleep at the house as he always did, and when the others had gone, Sonderfeld would come down to the laboratory and the lamp would burn long after midnight. Did he work there—or play? Wee Georgie had his own ideas, but he was wise enough to keep them to himself. This was the softest berth he'd had in many years—he wanted to keep it. Another mistake like tonight's could mean disaster.

He shivered and swore and reeled back into the hut. Then, far down the track, he heard the pad of feet and the high giggling of the girls. He wondered whether he should beat them, but decided against it. He uncorked the bottle and took a long, gurgling pull that ended in a belch of relief. Then he stretched himself out on the dirty blanket roll and waited for them to come in. With whisky in his belly and girls in his bed, Wee Georgie was the Caliph of the high valleys. He speculated amiably on the scandalous tales that Scheherazade and her sister would bring—he had a shrewd suspicion that N'Daria and Kumo would have their parts in it.

Sonderfeld saw the light go on in the laboratory and smiled to himself in the darkness. He was desperately eager to know the result of N'Daria's seduction of the sorcerer, but he was too careful a man to betray himself by even the smallest indiscretion. Gerda was safely in bed, but his guests were still drinking. He would go in to them, join the last hazy rounds, and tell them a dirty story or two to send them on their way to bed.

Lansing he would conduct with ironic courtesy to the guest room. With Curtis and Theodore Nelson he would walk a little way down the path that led to the Kiap house; he would tell them one last story; he would stand and watch them weaving homewards under the dark, drooping trees. Then he would go to N'Daria.

He straightened up, tossed the butt of his cigar over the railing and walked into the bright light of the living room.

Theodore Nelson, flushed and voluble, had reached the tag of his story:

"She said to me, 'What sort of woman do you think I am?' I said, 'My dear lady, I thought we'd already established that.' After which, of course, it was plain sailing from Aden to Bombay."

Lee Curtis gave his braying, boyish laugh. Max Lansing, grey-faced and weary, stared into his glass. They looked up as Sonderfeld came in, smiling and hearty.

"Forgive me, my friends. I was having myself a little fresh air between drinks. Now the clergy are gone and the lady is retired, let's have ourselves a private nightcap, eh?"

"If you don't mind," said Lansing flatly, "I'll take myself to bed. I'm very tired. I'm not good company."

"My dear fellow!" Sonderfeld was instantly solicitous. "Of course we don't mind. Are you sure you are not unwell? You're not getting the fever, are you? Have you been taking the tablets?"

"No, no . . . it's not the fever. I'm just tired, that's all. If you'll excuse me— good night, Sonderfeld. Good night, gentlemen!"

413

Before they had time to speak their own farewells, he had left the room, a tall, stooping figure bowed under the burden of his own ineptitude.

"That's an odd fellow," said Theodore Nelson, as Sonderfeld poured him a generous slug.

"They're all odd, these anthropology boys," Lee Curtis chimed in, with his shining new knowledge. "Lots of 'em scattered round the Highlands. Queer as coots. They—"

"You mustn't be too hard on the poor fellow." Sonderfeld's tone was a careful blend of tolerance, amusement and genuine affection. "He's a clever and devoted scholar. A little prickly in company, of course, but that comes of living alone. Add to which he is a very sick man. He has had one bout of scrub typhus. If I had not been here, I think it would have killed him. Gerda and I are very fond of him. That is why we like to have him here as often as we can."

Theodore Nelson clucked sympathetically and plunged his snub nose into his drink. His own reading of the Lansing story made a very different text. But when a man made his living drinking other men's whisky and eating at other men's tables, it paid him to keep his thoughts to himself.

Lee Curtis was a less practiced diplomat. Lansing's views on the cargo cult had been nagging at him all the evening. If they were correct, they spelt trouble for himself. The District Commissioner was a hard man and a subtle one. He had neither patience nor mercy for weak administrators and slipshod investigations. Curtis stifled a hiccup and put the question to Kurt Sonderfeld.

"He's a clever scholar, you say. But you laughed at his ideas on the cargo cult. Why?"

"My dear fellow," said Sonderfeld smoothly, "there is no contradiction, believe me. Lansing is a scholar, a man of books and theories. He lacks the practical experience of, say, a man like yourself."

Nelson grinned into his drink. You clever bastard, he thought. You clever, clever bastard. There's weather blowing up and you know it. Lansing knows it, too. But you're not making any forecasts. You're leaving it all to this boy, who hasn't finished cutting his milk teeth. If there's storm damage, you'll be high and dry with a handsome profit.

Lee Curtis hiccupped again. The compliment was sweeter to him than the whisky and just as heady. He jabbed an unsteady finger at Sonderfeld's shirt-front. His voice was thick and furry.

"That's what I always say. It's the men that do the job that really know. You do it—in a small way—on your plantation. I do it—in a big way—in my territory. The rest of 'em—the missionaries and the anthrop—anthrop—" He giggled happily. "Christ, I'm drunk! Better take me home, Nelson, before I fall flat on my face."

Deftly, Sonderfeld maneuvered him through the last drink, smiling like a genial conspirator at the moonfaced Britisher who had survived a thousand evenings like this one. Nelson was no danger to him. Nelson was a bird of passage, hovering high above the storm waters. Nonetheless, it would pay to

414

keep him friendly. With Curtis swaying between them, they walked out of the house.

When the cold air hit him, the boy gagged suddenly and vomited on the path. In the darkness, Sonderfeld grimaced with disgust, but he handled the situation with the ease and competence of long experience. He locked one arm round the boy's waist, supported his head with his free hand and held him until the spasm had passed. Then he cleaned him with his own handkerchief and handed him over to Nelson with a good-humoured grin.

Nelson watched the performance with bibulous approval. The fellow was a gentleman at least. In his peripatetic career he had met a few originals and many imperfect copies, but Sonderfeld had earned the seal of the connoisseur. If it came to a showdown between the big man and the Administration, Nelson would back private enterprise every time.

Which was exactly what Sonderfeld expected him to do.

He stood a long time, watching, as their shadows swayed down the narrow path. Then he turned and walked swiftly back to the laboratory.

N'Daria was waiting for him.

She had stripped off the ceremonial costume and wrapped herself in an old housecoat that had belonged to Gerda. She was drooping with sleep and her body gave off the smell of fatigue and stale oil. There was no desire in her smile, only a furtive triumph. She held out to Sonderfeld the evening's prize, carefully laid in a small tube of bamboo.

He took it from her without a word, slid off the top of the tube and gingerly extracted the wad with a pair of tweezers.

Strange, he thought, strange. Between those two steel fingers he held the key to power and dominion. That small foul relic of an animal act was a talisman whose touch would call up armies, rear a throne in the mountains, set on the forehead of its possessor the crown of a new empire. It was a giddy thought.

Yet it was true. The tribes were ruled in secret by the sorcerers. Chief of the sorcerers was Kumo. The man who held the blood and seed and spittle of Kumo was greater than he because at any moment, by a simple willful act, he could compass the death of Kumo. Such was the power of ancient superstition that once Kumo knew his vital juices were held by another man, he would be in perpetual bondage. Burn the tube in the fire and Kumo's body would burn to agonizing death. Crush the tube with an ax, Kumo would feel the stone grind into his own skull and would die of the impact. Warm it a little, beat on it with a stick, Kumo's body would burn with fever or his ears would ring with maddening noises.

It was the old, dark, fearful magic of primitive man turned against him by a twentieth-century despot.

For a long time Sonderfeld stood there, lost in the secret joy of his own triumph. The girl watched him, smiling uneasily. Then, abruptly, he replaced the tampon, closed the tube with a snap and thrust it into his pocket. He turned to her and grinned.

"You have done well, N'Daria."

Her eyes lit up. She moved forward to touch him. He drew back in disgust. It was as if he had struck her.

"But . . . But . . . you said . . ."

"You stink!" said Sonderfeld softly. "You stink like a village pig. Before you begin work in the morning, wash yourself clean."

With that he left her. She heard the door slam and the key turn in the lock. She flung herself on the low cane bed and sobbed.

Chapter Four

Gerda was asleep when he came in.

She lay on her side, her face pillowed on one hand, the other lying slack across the curve of her hip. Her hair was a dark cascade against the white sheets. Her skin was like warm marble. Her lips were smiling softly, like the lips of an innocent child. He turned up the lamp and stood looking down at her. She stirred faintly, then settled again, still smiling. It was as if she mocked him, even from the frontiers of sleep.

She had been with Lansing. He knew that. She had been as warm to him as she was cold to her legal partner. She had been tender and passionate and wanton—to a straw man, limp with his own self-pity. She had put horns on her husband in his own house and there was nothing he could do about it—yet. He could strike her and she would laugh in his face. He could kill her—as soon he would kill Lansing—but her death would bring him loss instead of profit. So he must wear the horns and endure the dreaming mockery night after night, until his triumph was perfected and she was delivered once more into his hands, as she had been that winter's day, twelve years ago . . . when Sturmbannführer Gottfried Reinach stood in the compound at Rehmsdorf and slapped his cane against his polished jackboots and looked over the new batch of women from Poland.

There were more than fifty of them, old and young and in-between. They were dirty and in rags. Their faces were pinched with hunger, their eyes glazed with fear. Their feet were bound with rags and old newspapers, and their skin was blotched with cold. They stood ankle-deep in the slushy snow, humble under the professional scrutiny of Gottfried Reinach.

He was an important fellow, the Sturmbannführer, ambitious, too, and careful of his career. He held medical degrees from two universities. His brief civilian practice had given him the name of a brilliant pathologist. His repugnance to Army service and his desire for rapid advancement had turned his thoughts to politics. He had joined the Party. He had made good connections—right to the door of Himmler himself—and now he was established comfortably, almost spectacularly, as Chief Research Officer, with the rank of Sturmbannführer in Rehmsdorf concentration camp. Here he directed the researches of a group of junior men on typhus vaccines, using as his subjects the decaying wrecks who were the camp inmates. He had other duties, too: the choice of subjects for the gas chambers and for the Sonderbau, the sterilization of young women of inferior race, lest childbearing interfere with their duties or increase the percentage of helots among the master men.

He had little taste for the work or for his associates, but he was a calculating fellow and, having chosen his road, he walked it resolutely—and circumspectly. His files were carefully kept. His success was minuted to the highest authorities. His failures were stifled as soon as they were born.

So, on this winter's morning, he walked down the line of women like a buyer in a cattle yard, pointing with his little stick, sorting them into categories—this for the work commandos, that for the brothel, this other for the Officers' Mess, these for the scrap heap. . . .

Until he came to the end of the line and saw Gerda Rudenko.

She was tattered and travel-stained like the others and the same fear was in her eyes, but her beauty was like a banner and her youth was still unravaged. She was a student, according to his lists. Her crime was consorting with suspected persons. She was nineteen years old.

To Sonderfeld she was a percentage profit. He had her sterilized like the others. He had her examined with more than usual care for venereal and other diseases. Then he took her into his service—clerk by day, bed and body servant by night. She was diligent because she was afraid of him and of his power to consign her to the crematorium. Because he was kind to her sometimes and not too often cruel, she was grateful, tender when he permitted it, passionate when, more and more rarely, he touched the deep spring of desire in her young body. There were even moments when fear and need brought her almost to belief in him; but as the years of her servitude spun out and she came to know him more intimately, belief became impossible. She served him still, but only with fear and with a deep and hidden hate.

Then came the last wild madness of defeat, the frenzy of murder, when the bodies piled up in the compounds and the gas chambers were choked, and the furnaces could not keep pace with the fuel that was fed to them. For the first time in his life, Gottfried Reinach was afraid—afraid of the haggard beasts in their wire pen, afraid of the vengeance that rolled in with the tanks and the gun limbers and the troop carriers.

So he struck his bargain with Gerda Rudenko.

He would take her out of the camp, save her from the final holocaust. He

418

would marry her—not as Gottfried Reinach, but as Kurt Sonderfeld, Doctor of Medicine, bachelor, dead long since and burnt in the fire; but Sonderfeld's records lay, complete and carefully preserved, in the steel filing cabinet.

When the final collapse came, they would merge themselves in the tide of stateless wanderers and claim protection from the liberating armies. And, lest she be tempted to accept now and betray him later, he pointed out that she, too, was compromised by her long association with Gottfried Reinach. She had enjoyed the protection of the defeated; she might well share their punishment.

She was trapped, and she knew it. She made the bargain. Three days before Rehmsdorf was taken, they left the camp. Reinach was now Sonderfeld. The dead man's number was tattooed on his forearm; the list of his works and days was etched in his memory. He wore the filthy rags of a camp inmate, starved himself for a week and had Gerda shave his skull to complete the change of identity.

The plan worked. Slowly they sifted through the inadequate machinery of relief organizations and reestablishment camps. They answered questions and filled in papers and lived in daily fear of recognition, until one day their names were posted on the camp notice board as migrants acceptable to the Commonwealth of Australia.

A new life was opening to Kurt Sonderfeld and his wife, Gerda. A new horizon challenged his cold ambition. This time he would follow no banners; he would walk alone.

They were a week out from Genoa when Gerda had her first affair with a fellow migrant. When he taxed her with it, she smiled. When he threatened her, she laughed in his face. When he struck her, she told him, gently and without anger:

"If you ever do that to me again, Kurt, I will tell everything I know. No matter what happens to me, I will tell. Remember that. We are bound together. We cannot escape each other. But from this moment I do not wish to sleep with you, to kiss you, even to touch you ever again."

At first he thought of divorcing her as soon as he could. Then he realized he would never sleep in peace so long as she was free and able to tell his secret. He toyed with the idea of killing her, but before he could frame a plan, she had forestalled him. They had not been two months in Australia when she told him that she had lodged papers with a bank—papers that would incriminate him if she should die before him.

No, it was he who was trapped, bound to a body he had maimed, denied its pleasures, shamed by its defiant wantonness.

As for Gerda herself, she was a woman without illusions. Cheated of love, cheated of children, she had made a bargain that guaranteed her security and comfort—and the bitter sweets of a protracted revenge. On this rickety foundation she and Kurt had built for themselves a kind of permanence, even a kind of peace. They were polite to each other. They cooperated on projects of mutual benefit. If they made love in other beds, they did so with reasonable discretion. In the new land bustling and bursting with vitality they were accepted even if they were not loved.

One of the conditions of their entry into Australia was that they should serve, each of them, for two years in any employment to which they were directed. Sonderfeld worked as a tally clerk on a dam construction project, Gerda as a waitress in the men's canteen. Strangely, the big man was not irked by the humble work. He was learning the language, adapting himself to a new, rugged environment. Every scrap of information was scanned and filed away for future reference. He had made one mistake in his life; he was not going to risk another. Sometime, somewhere, in this young, thrusting country, a door would be opened to him and he must be ready to enter into his new estate.

Then one day he read a notice in a Government Gazette. Migrant doctors who could produce evidence of medical qualifications in Europe would be permitted to practice in the Mandated Territory of New Guinea without renewing their courses.

This was his chance. He grasped it with both hands. Within a month he and Gerda were in Lae. Within three years he had built a practice, a bank balance and a reputation. He was offered a permanent appointment under the Administration. He refused, smiling. Kurt Sonderfeld had served long enough. Now he was ready to rule.

The rich Highland valleys were being opened up. Land was being leased to settlers of energy and good character. His application was approved—the more quickly because he was ready to push out over the mountains, where even the old hands were not prepared to risk their money.

So he had come to the valley, trekking over the mountains with Gerda and the cargo boys. He had made friends with the tribes. He had earned the goodwill of the District Commissioner by his gratuitous care of their health. Within a year his ground was cleared, his house was built, his coffee was planted under the shade trees—and his dream of wealth and empire was near to fulfillment.

The first step was the domination of the tribes through Kumo and the lesser sorcerers. The next was the exaction of tribute: labour, pigs, gold washed from the Highland streams, lumber from the rich stands in the tribal territories, a tithe of every man's garden patch, basket- and cane-ware, cinchona bark and galip nuts, to sell as the Missions did on the coast. Territory law compelled him to feed and clothe and pay his boy labour, but these payments would be returned to him less a nominal deduction by the sorcerers for their sumptuary service. It was a grandiose project, but simple and feasible in practice. So long as he could keep peace among the tribes. Before the Administration caught up with him—if they ever did—he would be ready to quit. And this would be the final stage, the return of the freebooter, rich and acceptable, to the luxury of life in Europe.

Yet wealth alone was too low a peak for his leaping pride. He must stretch out farther to the pinnacles of power. Power was an obsession with him—a brooding, secret lust that blinded him to the lessons of his personal and national history and showed him only the sweet illusions of attainment.

In the isolation of the high valleys where authority was represented by puling boys like Lee Curtis, the prospect of imperial rule seemed dangerously possible.

There was no garrison strength in the Territory, only the small, scattered force of native police. Airfields were few and fit only for small aircraft. Communications were sketchy and unreliable.

There were thousands of square miles of unexplored country peopled by tribes who had never seen a white skin. For a bold man, a shrewd man, leagued with the sorcerers, there seemed no limit to the extension and exercise of god-like authority.

All this, and more, would flow, like wealth from Fortunatus' purse, out of the small bamboo tube whose glossy surface shone dully in the lamplight.

Gerda stirred and murmured uneasily. He thrust the tube back into his pocket and began preparing himself for bed. Tonight he would rest well. Tomorrow was the beginning of a new chapter in the saga of Kurt Sonderfeld.

Five minutes later he, too, was asleep, smiling, like Gerda, in his golden dream.

It was two in the morning before Père Louis reached his mission station, a small, poor village sprawling along a narrow defile between Sonderfeld's property and the Lahgi Valley. To reach it, he had walked six miles along the flanks and the ridges of the mountains, through stretches of rain forest and occasional patches of kunai grass taller than himself. As he walked, he prayed, fingering the worn beads of his rosary, and as he prayed, he pondered . . . on what he had heard in Sonderfeld's house, on what he knew of the trouble simmering among the tribes.

Much of it was secret to himself. It came to him in whispers when his converts shuffled into the tiny chapel to make their confessions. This one had been threatened by the sorcerers and needed reassurance. Another had bought herbs to procure an abortion and begged absolution.

A boy had taken his girl into the bushes after the kunande and the carry-leg. His catechist demanded to know whether to take part in the pig festival was an act of idolatry or a harmless enjoyment of a village feast. But all the whispers were fragments of one story, the story of a wavering minority, clinging desperately to a new faith, afraid of the mockery of the old believers, more afraid of the dark powers of which they had daily, terrifying experience.

Père Louis himself was afraid. Not of the legends, not of the childish superstitions and the primitive spells, but of the ancient evil working in them and through them. He believed in the human soul. He believed in sin. He believed in God. He believed in the Devil who walked the valleys, not roaring like a lion of Saint Paul, but muttering and chanting, threatening and bribing, through the sorcerers.

Some of them were charlatans, as Sonderfeld had said. These he could ignore or discredit. But there were others, the powerful few like Kumo, intelligent, proud, dedicated to evil and the Prince of Evil. If, as he now believed, Sonderfeld had joined forces with them, the stirring in the valleys might grow to a whirlwind.

The big man puzzled him. He was not, like others, a wencher, chasing the village girls, a tippler, a ragged adventurer chasing gold or oil like folly-fires through the valleys. Sonderfeld was intelligent, cultivated, controlled. If he were to take a risk, it would be a calculated risk, and the reward would be calculated with greater care. The man was devoured by a cold pride and a ruthless ambition—but for what? Money, perhaps. But money was too low a goal for such a man. Power?

Père Louis shivered, though he was hot and sweating from the walk. Power was the greed of Lucifer. The lust for power was the sin against nature and the Holy Ghost, the sin beyond mercy.

In the tiny, rustling chapel, lit by a guttering taper that floated in a bowl of oil, the priest lay prostrate in supplication before his God. The god of the tribes was a Great Pig and beyond the Great Pig was the Red Spirit. The God of Père Louis was the Crucified, who lay on the crude altar in the form of a white wafer of bread. The old man's lips framed the familiar cadence of the Office of Compline. . . .

"*Scuto circumdabit te veritas eius.* . . . His truth shall compass thee with a shield. Thou shalt not be afraid of the terror of the night."

"A *sagitta volante in die, a negotio perambulante in tenebris.* . . . From the arrow that flieth in the day, from the plague that walketh in darkness, and from the noonday devil. . . ."

In the high secret valleys the sorcerers cast their spells; Kurt Sonderfeld slept in his white bed and dreamed of dominion and power; but Père Louis prayed in his bamboo church until the stars waned and the sun crept up on the ridges and his catechist found him lying face down, exhausted, on the altar step.

Chapter Five

WEE GEORGIE WAS MUSTERING the plantation boys. It was seven-thirty in the morning and they came loitering up from the village, torpid, red-eyed, scowling, to squat in little groups outside Wee Georgie's hut.

Stripped of their finery, their skins dull and dusty, their teeth stained and their mouths drooling with betel juice, they were an unpromising crew.

Wee Georgie surveyed them with regal contempt and spat in the dust before them. He was leaning against the big casuarina tree, an obscene and rumpled figure, with bleary eyes and the sour taste of hangover on his tongue. His shirt flapped raggedly outside his breeches, his belt hung precariously below his navel. His hair was a towy mess and his bare feet scuffed irritably in the dirt of the path. One trembling hand held a cigarette, the other scratched constantly under a sweaty armpit.

His two girls peered out of the doorway behind him and giggled softly. Their lord was in a fouler mood than usual. The performance would be worth watching.

The last stragglers arrived and stood shuffling uneasily under Georgie's baleful eye. He took a last long drag at his cigarette, coughed till he was purple in the face and spat again.

Then he started.

"On your feet, you black bastards! Get into line. Jump to it!"

Slowly they heaved themselves up from their haunches and moved into file in front of him. His ugly face twisted into a grin; he took a deep breath and began to curse them, softly and fluently. He cursed them in pidgin and place-talk and bawdy Billingsgate. He cursed them for the colour of their skins and the lechery of their women; he cursed them by the names of birds and beasts and crawling things; he cursed them as eaters of the dead and crammers of offal. They were a stink in his nostrils, an offense to his sight, an obscene pollution of the mountain air. They coupled with pigs and brought forth monsters. Their fingers were a black blight on the coffee and when they died, even the ants would reject their foul carcasses.

By the time he had finished, they were grinning all over their dark faces. Their ill temper was dissipated and they nodded to one another, approving this intoxicating eloquence. But this was only the beginning, the overture to the comedy.

Wee Georgie hawked again. A great gob of spittle landed at the feet of a tall buck and threw up a puff of dust as high as his ankles. The boys guffawed happily. The girls squealed with shrill delight. Georgie eased himself away from the tree bole and lurched over to his target. Slowly he surveyed him, from his frizzy crown to his scrabbling toes, and began his gallery speech.

"This is Yaria. This is Yaria, who talks like a taro root and performs like a bud of bamboo."

The boys hooted with laughter. Yaria was a well-known boaster, whose girls were never satisfied. The white man was a clever fellow who knew all the gossip of the village. Wee Georgie grinned happily. His play was running well.

"This Yaria was at the kunande last night. He changed partners three times—and still couldn't find a girl to sleep with him."

There was laughter and jeering while Yaria hung his head and scuffed his feet in embarrassment.

"Yaria wants to get married and have a son. But he can't find the bride-price—and even if he did, he'd need another man to help him—"

And so on, through the cheerful ritual of obscenity and insult until the sullen workers were bubbling with good humour and filled with gossip enough to last them through the working day. When he had finished with Yaria, Georgie moved to the next man in the line, and the next, spitting at their feet, parading them like hacks in the knacker's yard, spreading his ridicule so that no man escaped and none could feel resentment or loss of face.

It was a canny performance that guaranteed him the goodwill of his labour force and gave him leisure to sit in the shade with his straw hat tipped over his eyes, while the boys moved up and down the lines of trees, cultivating, spraying, clearing the irrigation ditches and chewing the spicy cud of the morning's entertainment.

He was nearly at the end of the line when he saw Kumo. The big fellow was standing a little apart from the others, arms folded on his chest, his face a blank mask, his eyes full of cold hatred.

Wee Georgie shivered and his tirade limped to a close.

Hurriedly, he set them their tasks—these to the sprays, these others to the new clearing, half a dozen to the drainage ditches from the upper pond, two to rake the paths and clip the lawns, the rest to weed and mulch the coffee rows.

Grinning and chattering, they dispersed to pick up their tools and start work. Kumo stood aloof and impassive as if challenging the fat man to assert his authority. Wee Georgie was too shrewd to engage the sorcerer.

"You wait there, big boy. The boss wants to see you," he snarled.

Then he spat contemptuously and lurched back to the hut where the girls were making his breakfast.

Kumo squatted at the foot of the casuarina tree and waited for Sonderfeld to come to him.

The big man walked slowly down the path, flicking at his calves with a thin switch of cane. It was a gesture that, in another time and another country, might have betrayed him. It recalled the shining jackboots and the trim black uniform of a discredited elite. Here in the bright mountain morning it was as meaningless as brushing away flies.

As always, his arrival was carefully timed to coincide with the end of Georgie's oration and the dispersal of the boys. They would see him coming the full length of the path, and they would stumble over one another in their eagerness to get to work and avoid the disapproval of his cold stare. Their fear flattered him and fed the fires that consumed him.

This morning his entrance was staged with even greater care. When he saw Kumo on his hunkers in the dust, he stopped and spent long minutes examining the big coleus plants that bordered the path. He took a cigar from his pocket and lit it with care and deliberation before he resumed his walk.

As he walked, he rehearsed the scene he was about to play. He would not use pidgin, which was the language of subjection, or English, which was the language of equality. He would speak to Kumo in his own tribal tongue, and this would say more clearly than words: "I know you. You cannot deceive me with a double tongue or with the blankness of ignorance. I share your secrets and yet I am greater than you."

He would speak privately, in the shelter of the tangket trees, so that the sorcerer would not be humbled and lose face with his fellows. His influence must be preserved, while his will was bent and his spirit humbled to the service of Sonderfeld. He would rebel, of course. He would rear against the yoke, because he was a proud man. Because he was an intelligent one, he would try to bargain, shrewdly, deviously, with the threat of betrayal to the patrol officer and the Administration. But Sonderfeld would reject the bargain and break the rebellion.

He grinned crookedly and fingered the bamboo tube in his pocket. He wondered what Kumo would do when he saw it for the first time.

The sorcerer did not stir when Sonderfeld came up to him. He remained squatting against the tree, eyes downcast, his jaws champing on the cud of betel nut. Sonderfeld stood a moment, watching him, then he flicked the cane switch sharply across his cheek. Kumo's head came up with a jerk. His eyes blazed.

"Get up," said Sonderfeld softly. "Come with me. I want to talk to you."

Then he turned away and walked into the shelter of the trees out of sight of the hut and of the house. Slowly Kumo got to his feet and followed him.

425

In the dappled shadow under the purple leaves they faced each other, black man, white man, each master in his own domain.

Sonderfeld smiled comfortably.

"Kumo, we have talked before. We talk again. I offered you friendship. Are you ready to accept it?"

Kumo's eyes were full of sullen anger.

"No. You take everything, you give nothing. That is not friendship."

"I told you I would make you chief of all the valleys."

Kumo's head came up, defiantly.

"Already I am chief of the valleys."

Sonderfeld laughed in his face.

"There is a luluai in every village appointed by the Kiap in Goroka. These are the chiefs. You are still a work boy, eating the offal of the lowly."

Kumo grinned with cunning and contempt.

"The luluais do as I tell them. But you are still the servant of the Kiap. How can you do for me what you cannot do for yourself?"

Sonderfeld shook his head.

"You do not believe that, otherwise you would not have told the tribes of the coming of the Red Spirit. I am no man's servant. I am the Red Spirit, who is the ruler of all—of the Kiaps and of the Pig God himself."

Kumo squirted a stream of betel juice at a passing lizard.

"You say so. But you do not speak in the councils of the Kiaps. Among the tribes you do no magic."

"Because I am not yet ready?"

Now it was Kumo's turn to laugh, a deep throaty chuckle that welled and gurgled behind his scarlet teeth. Sonderfeld flicked up the cane and struck him viciously on the cheek, raising a long, thin weal from mouth to ear. Kumo yelped and clapped his hands to his face.

"Now," said Sonderfeld calmly, "you will listen to me."

The sorcerer glared at him in helpless fury.

"You are a fool, Kumo. But I am prepared to forget your folly and make you my friend."

"No! You are not my friend. Does a brother strike his brother? The Kiap's law says the white man shall not strike the black man. I shall tell the Kiap and you will be punished."

Sonderfeld shrugged and spread his hands in a gesture of indifference.

"Tell the Kiap. But first listen to me."

"No."

He turned and made as if to go. Sonderfeld's next words stopped him dead in his tracks.

"Last night, after the carry-leg, you lay with a woman in the grass."

Slowly, fearfully, Kumo turned to face him. Sonderfeld grinned in mockery.

"When the elders made you a man, Kumo, did they not tell you that he who puts his seed to a strange woman puts his life in great danger?"

"This was no stranger. She was a woman of my village."

The words were defiant, but there was uncertainty in his voice.

"The woman was my woman," said Sonderfeld calmly. "Her name is N'Daria. She serves the Red Spirit."

A gleam of confidence showed in the red, sullen eyes of Kumo. He remembered the protestations of the girl, her passion and her desire for him.

"Does the Red Spirit share his women then?"

"No. He does not share them. He uses them to do his work. Look!"

The bamboo tube was in his hand. He thrust it under the nose of the sorcerer. Kumo drew back, startled and puzzled.

"What is that?"

Sonderfeld's voice rose to hieratic thunder.

"You lay with a woman, Kumo. Your spittle was on her lips and your blood was under the nails of her fingers . . . and you lay with her. I hold your life in my hands before you."

Kumo's reaction was sudden and horrible.

His spine arched backwards, his head fell back. His eyes rolled upwards. A bubbling imbecile sound broke from his lips. Then, as if he had been kicked in the belly, he doubled forward, retched and crumpled, trembling and gibbering, at Sonderfeld's feet.

Sonderfeld was startled, but only for a moment. Then he smiled, looked down at the twitching body and knew with absolute certainty that he had only to walk away and the sorcerer would crawl to the nearest bush and lie there, without food or water or speech, until he died. Kumo had killed others in the same way. Now the sword of the spirit, the terrible two-edged weapon of fear and belief, had been turned against his own unarmoured flesh.

For Sonderfeld it was a moment of pure triumph. Alone he had joined battle with the dark and secret rulers of the valleys. The evidence of his victory lay dusty and abject at his feet. He stooped and hauled Kumo upright by his thick, greasy hair. Then he propped him against a tree and stood, arms akimbo, mocking him.

"Now do you believe me, Kumo?"

"Yes." It was a drunken nod.

"You know that I am the Red Spirit with life or death in my hands?"

"Yes."

"You know that I can burn you with fire, or crush you with stones, or have the ants devour you even as you walk?"

The sorcerer's face twisted in hypnotic agonies.

"Yes . . . yes . . . yes."

"You know also that I can preserve your life if I wish it?"

Kumo opened his eyes. There was no hope in them, only an animal pleading.

"I know."

"If you serve me, I will preserve it."

"I will serve."

"If you serve me well, then one day, perhaps, I will give it back to you."

Kumo tried to speak, but no words came from his slack and babbling mouth. The impact of even this small hope robbed him of human speech. Satisfied with his little comedy of cruelty, Sonderfeld walked up to him and slapped him hard on both cheeks.

"Stand up!"

Kumo stood up.

"Your life is safe, so long as you do as you are told."

Kumo nodded vigorously, still without the power of speech.

"Now," said Sonderfeld quietly, "you will listen to me. You are a great sorcerer. You understand how a man may be killed so that none can tell who struck him?"

Kumo found tongue at last.

"I understand."

"Good. There is a man in my house whom you know. He is the one who lives in the village and sits with you by the cook fires and asks questions of the women."

"I know him."

"Today he goes back to his own house in the village. Tonight you will kill him—but so that the Kiap Curtis will think he died in his bed. Can you do that?"

The man's eagerness was horrible.

"I can do it. There is a powerful magic that—"

Sonderfeld cut him off with a gesture.

"I do not want to hear. Do it and tell no one. Come to me when I send for you but not before—and, Kumo—" His voice was a silken thread. "When the Red Spirit appears at the pig festival, will you proclaim him to the tribes?"

"I will proclaim him."

"Good," said Kurt Sonderfeld in his own tongue. "Good and good and— *wunderschön!*"

He threw back his head and laughed and laughed while the birds rose fluttering and squawking from the thicket, and Kumo the Sorcerer watched him with the fear of death in his heart.

Down in the Kiap house, Patrol Officer Curtis was groaning in the grip of a hangover. His head throbbed, his eyes were full of gravel, and his mouth was parched and foul. His stomach heaved at the first taste of the bitter tea brought to him by the police boy.

Theodore Nelson scooped the sugary pulp from a paw-paw and grinned at him across the yellow rind.

"Try some of this, my dear chap. Cleans the palate, settles the digestion. Wonderful stuff."

"Go to hell!"

"Drink your tea then. You're as dry as a chip. You won't feel better till you get some liquid inside you."

Curtis groaned and gagged over another mouthful.

"Dunno why I drink whisky. It always hits me like this."

428

"It was a very good whisky." Nelson chewed happily on the soft fruit. "I'll say this for Sonderfeld, he's a perfect host."

"I think he's an arrogant swine."

Curtis buried his nose in the tin pannikin while Nelson studied him with shrewd and twinkling eyes. There was truth in whisky, and it was one of his subtler pleasures to pry out the truth in other people's lives and savour its folly or its tragedy without involving his own transient person.

"Arrogant, yes. But a swine? You know him better than I do, of course."

Curtis rose like a trout to a well-cast fly.

"Any man who treats a woman the way Sonderfeld treats his wife is a swine for my money."

Nelson hid his smile with another spoonful of fruit. He nodded gravely. His eyes were full of sympathy for the bruised and knightly spirit of youth. Curtis took another mouthful of tea and wiped his lips with a stained handkerchief.

"Sonderfeld's as cold as a fish. Gerda's a warm person, full of life, hungry for affection."

"I gathered she was getting at least half a meal," said Nelson dryly.

Curtis's chin came up defiantly.

"What do you mean?"

"Lansing's the man of the moment, isn't he?"

For a moment Nelson thought the boy was going to strike him, then quite suddenly the anger went out of him, his face crumpled childishly, his eyes filled with tears of self-pity.

"I suppose he is. But I don't blame Gerda. She's alone up here. Lansing's close and—well, I don't begrudge her what she gets from him."

"Why should it matter to you one way or the other?"

There was a queer pathetic dignity about him as he raised his head and looked Nelson full in the eyes.

"Because I'm in love with her myself."

Theodore Nelson sat transfixed, the spoon halfway to his mouth, the great yellow fruit held precariously on his open palm. The blunt admission shocked him. A mild flirtation, a casual accommodation, would have amused him, but the grand passion was a different matter altogether.

"God Almighty!" he swore softly. "You are in a mess, aren't you?"

Curtis nodded miserably.

"That's why I got drunk last night. Never touch the stuff usually. Can't afford to when I'm on the round. Never know when you're liable to wake up with an arrow in your guts or a hatchet in your skull. But . . . to sit there at the table with her. To hear her laugh. To know that when we were gone she'd . . ."

He buried his face in his hands as if to shut out a tormenting vision.

Nelson scooped out the last mouthfuls of fruit, laid the empty skin on the floor of the hut, wiped his hands and lit a cigarette. Then he stood up.

"It's none of my business, of course, but if you'd take a word of advice from an old stager—"

"Yes?" Curtis raised his head slowly.

"Get out of the valley today. Finish the patrol, go back to Goroka and ask for a transfer to another area. If you don't, you're going to be in trouble—up to the neck."

"You think I don't know that?"

Nelson looked down at the boy's face, yellow with hangover, ravaged by the grief and torment of young passion. Pity touched him rarely, but he felt it now—pity and scorn and distaste for the folly from which his own cautious nature had preserved him.

"If you know it, why stay?"

"Because there's trouble brewing and it's my job to find out what it is and put a stop to it."

My God, thought Nelson, there's the makings of a man in him. He's flabby with puppy fat still, but there's a sound, stiff core underneath.

"Trouble? You said last night there was no trouble. You laughed at Lansing and that little parson fellow."

"I was drunk last night," said Curtis slowly. "I made a fool of myself in more ways than one. But I sobered up after I was sick. I lay awake for hours thinking about it, trying to fit things together."

"What did you make of it?"

"Nothing definite—except that Sonderfeld's involved. That means Gerda's involved, too. I'm going to stay around for a few days, visit a few of the other villages and see what information I can pick up."

"From whom?"

"From the luluais, from the tribal gossip and"—he hesitated a moment—"from Lansing and Père Louis."

Nelson grinned, savouring the irony of the situation.

"I thought you didn't like either of 'em."

Curtis frowned.

"I don't. But this is Administration business. My love life doesn't come into it, nor my religion. Lansing's got information that I want. The missioners live closer to the tribes than any other people in the Territory—especially the R.C.s, because they don't marry and they have to share the tribal life or live like hermits."

"Why don't you like the missionaries?"

Curtis shrugged.

"We're not ready for 'em. Make a man a Christian and you tell him that all men are brothers in Christ. His next question is, why can't I sit at a table with my brothers and marry the white women and say my piece in the Kiap councils and earn the same money as a white worker? It's too early for that— half a century too early."

Nelson was puzzled. This was no longer the braying youth of last night's dinner party. This was a sober young official who knew his job and was prepared to do it at some cost to himself and some damage to his heartstrings. Give him confidence and polish, teach him the art of silence among his elders, the boy would make a good administrator—provided Delilah didn't shear him of his strength and bed him down to messy marital scandal.

The boy's face broke into a rueful smile.

"Don't worry, Nelson. I'll get you back to Goroka in one piece. Take it easy and enjoy yourself. You'll probably find it very interesting."

"I wasn't thinking of myself," said Nelson soberly. "I was thinking of you."

Curtis's eyes darkened.

"You mind your business. I'll mind mine."

"And Mrs. Sonderfeld's?"

"Go to hell!"

He stalked out of the hut and Nelson heard him shouting angrily to the police boys. When he looked out of the doorway, he saw Curtis standing naked in the bright sun while a pair of grinning fuzzy-wuzzies doused him with water from canvas buckets. His skin was shining. His muscles rippled as he gasped and danced and swung his arms. His belly was flat and hard as a board.

Nelson was filled with sour admiration for his youth and his vitality and his resilient, glowing strength. He wondered what would happen if Gerda Sonderfeld should fall in love with them.

Chapter Six

In the warmth of the rich mountain morning, Max Lansing walked home to his village. It lay in a deep saucer-shaped depression between Père Louis' community and the Lahgi Valley. To reach it, he had to make a wide traverse westward of Sonderfeld's property and cross two steep saddles before he struck the path that led over the lip of the crater and downwards into the taro plots and the banana groves and the dancing park. He would not reach it till the middle of the afternoon.

He had a water bottle hooked to his belt and a canvas knapsack filled with food from Gerda's kitchen and a bottle of Sonderfeld's best whisky. By midday he would have crossed the first saddle and he would rest and eat by the swift water that came singing down over the rocks from the high peaks. Then he would push on, with neither joy nor impatience, to the small bamboo hut on the outer edge of the village—his home for the years of his subsidized exile.

As he topped the rise that overlooked the plantation, he halted a moment and looked back. He saw the blaze of Gerda's garden, the nestling of the bungalow under its thatched roof, the long, serried lines of the plantation trees. He saw the work boys moving about like leisurely ants and the tall white figure of Sonderfeld standing at the head of the first grove. He saw them all as a symbol of permanence and possession, a mockery of his own rootless, pointless existence.

Long, long ago he had been fired with zeal for knowledge—knowledge for its own sake, knowledge without thought of gain, profitless except in human dignity and spiritual enlargement. But the fire had burnt out years since, and he saw himself, not great among the solitary great ones, but a poor and tattered pedant, piling his dry facts like children's blocks, while the laughing,

432

weeping, lusting, suffering world rolled heedless past his doorstep. Without faith in himself and in his work, he found himself without strength for dedication. He could no longer walk happy among the scholars, and he had forgotten the speech of the marketplace. Even his love was a pedantry, dusty and dry beside the welling passion of Gerda.

When Sonderfeld had left the house, he had sat with her at breakfast on the veranda and had tried to recapture the brief warmth of their night's embrace. But Gerda refused to match his mood. She had talked, cheerfully enough, about the dinner party, the guests, the plantation, the news from Goroka. But when he had urged her to discussion of their own relationship, she had refused, gently but with finality.

"No, Max. All that can be put into words has been said between us. I am here, whenever you care to come. I will be with you as I have always been. But I will not talk—talk—talk! Better to kiss or make love, or simply walk among the flowers together. But why rake our hearts with words that mean nothing?"

To which, of course, there was no answer. Take it or leave it. He had not courage to leave it and he lacked the wisdom to take without question. He must itch and scratch and itch and scratch again, until the warm and willing heart was scarred into a running sore.

He had risen abruptly from the table and gathered his things to leave. She had come to him then and kissed him with that maddening maternal gentleness.

"Don't be angry with me, Max. I am as I am. I cannot change. But before you go, let me tell you one thing."

"Yes?"

Let her tell him she loved him and he would be happy again. Let her give him one small hope and ambition would soar again, mountains high.

"Be careful, Max, I beg of you. Be careful!"

"Careful of what?"

Her hands made a helpless, fluttering gesture.

"I don't know. I wish I did. But after what you said last night, my husband—"

"To hell with your husband!"

He caught her to him, crushing his mouth brutally on hers. Then he released her, picked up his knapsack and without a backward glance strode off, a lost and angry man, storming up the hillside.

When he came to the river, he was sweating and exhausted. It was a long walk at the best of times, but for a lonely and unhappy fellow, it was twice as tedious. He plunged down to the water and felt the humid air close round him like a curtain. A cloud of insects enveloped him. He beat at them irritably with his handkerchief and by the time he reached the sandy hollow near the ford he was free of them.

He slipped off his knapsack, took a long pull at the water bottle and flung himself down at the edge of the clear singing water. He was too tired to eat, so

433

he lay sprawled on his back, head pillowed on the knapsack, looking up into the dappled green of the jungle overhang through a cloud of bright blue butterflies. He saw the flash of brilliant scarlet as a bird of paradise made his mating dance on the branch of an albizzia tree. A tiny tree kangaroo peered cautiously between two broad purple leaves. A lizard sunned himself on the rock beside him, and in the undergrowth he heard the scurrying of small animals, rooting for food.

The thought struck him that in his four-hour walk he had seen not a single human being. This was unusual, for the mountain paths were the highways of the tribes. Since the white man's law had abolished war and killing raids, there was a modest traffic between the villages in canes and birds of paradise feathers and gum and galip nuts and pigs and the produce of the gardens.

This traffic had been increased of late by the movement of the tribes for the approaching pig festival. Yet today he had seen no one. Because he was tired, the thought nagged at him uneasily. He fumbled for a cigarette, lit it and watched the blue smoke spiral up towards the green canopy.

Then he heard it, distant but distinct—chuff-chuff-chuff—the unmistakable beat of a running cassowary. The sound was unusual enough to interest him. The cassowary bird was native to the high valleys, but the breed was being thinned out by killing and the survivors were retreating into the less populated mountains.

The footsteps came closer, thudding like the muffled beat of a train on steel rails. Lansing sat up. The bird was coming down the same path that he had followed. He wondered if it would break out onto the beach. He was not afraid, only interested. The big, ungainly bird was easily frightened and would not attack a human being unless it was angered or cornered. The footsteps came closer and closer. Then they stopped.

He judged the bird was probably a dozen yards away, hidden by the dense screen of undergrowth. He could hear its rustling among the leaves and low branches. Then the rustling stopped, and after a moment Lansing lay back drowsily against the knapsack. He thought he would sleep a little, then eat before he continued his walk. He worked a hollow for his hip in the warm sand and turned comfortably on his side.

Then he saw it.

A yard from his face was a small white snake, dappled with black spots. In the suspended moment of shock he saw the trail of its body in the white sand. It had come from the bush at his back, the deadliest reptile in the whole island. If it struck him, he would die, paralyzed and beyond help within two hours. Cautiously he moved his hand to get purchase on the sand, then, with a single movement, he thrust himself to his feet. In that same moment the snake moved, fast as a flicker of light, to the spot where his head had lain. Its jaws opened and it struck at the stiff canvas of the knapsack. Before Lansing had time to snatch up a stick or stone, it was gone again, a dappled death, slithering into the fallen leaves at the fringe of the bush.

Sick with terror, he stood looking down at the knapsack and the tiny dark stain of the ejected poison. Then he shivered, snatched up the bag and plunged across the ford, heedless of the water that swirled about his knees and hidden stones that sent him half sprawling into the icy current.

Gerda's parting words beat in his brain.

"Be careful, Max, I beg of you. Be careful!"

Breathless, he scrambled up the steep bank and looked back at the small white beach. It was bare and empty of life. The jungle was like a painted backdrop, motionless in the heavy air.

Then he heard it again—chuff-chuff-chuff—the running feet of the cassowary, retreating into the stillness.

Suddenly he remembered. The cassowary men! They were an old story in the valleys, an old fear among the tribes. They were sorcerers who, by common repute, had power to change themselves into cassowary birds and run faster than the wind. They were the Territory counterpart of the Carpathian werewolves and the jackal men of Africa. The tribes believed in them implicitly and for proof pointed to the claw marks on the soft ground after a nocturnal visit from one of the sorcerers. Newcomers to the mountains scoffed at such rank superstition, but the old hands—traders, missionaries, senior men in the district services—were less skeptical. Each had his own stories to tell of phenomena apparently beyond physical explanation. But all had one thing in common, a healthy respect and a prickling fear of the dim borderlands of primitive mysticism.

Lansing himself had at first rejected the manifestations as pure charlatanry. But the more he studied, the less certain he became; and now, in the eerie solitude of the upland paths, he, too, was gripped by the cold, uncanny fear of the bird-man.

It was late in the afternoon when he came to the village. The mountain shadows were lengthening and the first faint chill was creeping down the valley. He was hungry and tired and trembling as if with the onset of fever. He paid no heed to the curious stares of the villagers but went straight to his hut, crammed a couple of suppressant tablets in his mouth, stripped himself naked and sponged himself with water from the canvas bucket.

When he was clean and dressed in fresh clothes, he poured himself a noggin of Sonderfeld's whisky and tossed it off at a gulp. He poured another, tempered it with water and stood in his doorway with the glass in his hand, looking out on the village.

The women were coming up from the taro gardens, naked except for the pubic belt, their thick bodies bowed under the weight of string baskets full of sweet potatoes which they carried suspended from their broad foreheads and supported on the small of their backs. In the far corner of the compound a young girl was feeding the pigs. They were blinded so that they could not run away and tethered to stakes of casuarina wood. They grunted and snuffled and squealed as she passed among them with fruit rinds and bananas and taro pulp.

The pigs and the gardens and the children, these were the charges of the women—and in that order. A woman would suckle a child at one breast and a piglet at the other. The men would make the gardens, laying them out, breaking the first soil, marking each patch with the small blunt mound of the phallic symbol crossed with the cut that represented the female principle. But it was the women who tilled them and dug the big ripe tubers that were the staple diet of the tribe.

As for the men, they sat as they sat now, one making a ceremonial wig of fiber and gum and flaring feathers and green beetle shards, another plaiting a cane socket for his obsidian ax, this one chipping a round stone for the head of his club, that one stringing the short cane bow which would bring down birds and possums and the furry cuscus, whose tail made armlets for the bucks and the unmarried girls.

Looking at them there, bent over their small tasks, Lansing thought how like children they were, intent, mistrustful, jealous of their trivial possessions. The second thought came hard on the heels of the first. They were not children. They were adults, intelligent within the limits of their knowledge, bound by sanctions older than the Pentateuch, preoccupied with the problems of birth, death—and survival for the years between.

To the outsider their tasks were trivial, but in the small stringent world of the tribal unit they were of major importance. Let a blight come on the taro patch, the whole village must move to new territory. If the pigs should be stricken with swine fever, they would have no protein in their diet—the ancient island of New Guinea is poor in all but the smallest animal life.

They went naked because there were no furs to give them warmth. They practiced abortion and birth control because there was a limit to the crops that could be raised in the narrow gardens, and because the pigs were decimated at festival after festival by a meat-hungry people, bound, moreover, by the primal need to propitiate a hostile Pig God in whom lay the principle of fertility. They had no written language. They had never made a wheel. Their traditions were buried in ancient words and phrases that even the elders could not translate.

In their narrow, uncertain world, love, as the white man knew it, did not exist. The girl who made the love-play in the kunande would be raped on her wedding night, and her husband would scowl if she wore any but the simplest ornament. In certain villages a man chose his bride by firing an arrow in her thigh—an act of hostility and enslavement.

In this climate of fear, behind the closed frontiers of the razorbacks, superstition flourished like a rank growth and the old magical practices of the dawn people were the straws to which the simple clung for security and the clubs which the ambitious used to bludgeon them into submission.

As he sipped his whisky and watched the small but complex pattern unfold itself, Lansing was conscious of his own inadequacy. Two years now he had lived among these people. His notebooks were full of careful observations on every aspect of their life pattern, yet he was as far from understanding them as he had been on the day of his arrival. It was as if there were a curtain

436

drawn between him and the arcana of their secret life, and unless he could penetrate the curtain, his work would be without significance.

The missionaries did better. The old ones, like Père Louis, did best of all. They came unabashed to make commerce in souls and spirits. They had secrets of their own to trade. They offered protection against the sorcerers, an answer to the ambient mystery of creation.

But when you didn't believe in the soul, when you were committed by birth and training to the pragmatic materialism of the twentieth century, what then? You were shut out from the sanctuary, condemned to walk in the Courts of the Strangers, denied access to the mysteries and the sacrifice.

He tossed off the dregs of his whisky, rinsed the glass carefully and set it on the table. Then he walked out into the compound.

There was a girl in the village whom he had trained to look after him, to wash his clothes and tidy his hut and prepare his food with moderate cleanliness. He had not seen her since his arrival; he was going to look for her.

First he went to her father's hut. The girl was not there. The old man was sitting outside the door sharpening a set of cane arrows. When Lansing questioned him, he gave him a sidelong look, shrugged indifferently and bent over his work. Accustomed to the moodiness of the mountain folk, Lansing made no comment but walked over to a group of women bending over a fire pit.

They giggled and simpered and exchanged smiles of secret amusement, but they would tell him nothing. He was irritated, but he dared not show it for fear of losing face. He hailed the women coming up from the taro gardens. They shook their heads. They had not set eyes on the girl. He tried the children, but they drew away from him and ran to hide their faces behind the buttocks of their mothers.

Then, suddenly, he became aware that the whole village was watching him. They had not paused for a moment in their work, but they were following his every movement, eyes slanting and secret, their smiles a silent mockery. They were not hostile, they were simply amused. They were watching a dancing doll, jerked this way and that by forces beyond his control.

Anger rose in him, sour and acid from the pit of his belly. He wanted to shout at them, curse them, strike them at least into recognition of his presence. He knew he could not do it. The loss of face would be final and irrecoverable.

He turned on his heel and with elaborate slowness walked back to his hut. He closed the door and lit the lamp. His hands were trembling and his palms were clammy with sweat. This concerted mockery was new in his experience. Sullenness he had met and had learnt to ignore. Suspicion had been rasped and honed away by the daily, familiar intercourse. This was something different. It was like—he fumbled for a tag to identify the strangeness—like being sent to Coventry. But for what?

He knew enough of ritual and custom to make him careful of their observance. He had crossed no one of the elders. He was aloof from village scandal. There was no reason why they should turn against him. Then he thought of

437

Sonderfeld and of Kumo and of Gerda's cryptic warning, and he was suddenly afraid.

He thought of Père Louis and the dappled snake and the sound of the unseen cassowary bird, and his fear was a wild, screaming terror. He was alone and naked and defenseless among the secret people in the darkening valley.

Desperately he struggled for control. At all costs he must show a brave face to the village mockery, must maintain the simple order of his studious existence.

He broke out Gerda's package of food and tried to eat. The cold food gagged him, and he thrust it away. He lit the spirit lamp and tried to work over his notes, but the letters danced confusedly before his eyes and his trembling fingers could not control the pencil.

Then, with the abrupt coming of darkness, the kundus began their maddening climactic rhythm. He felt as though they were throbbing inside his skull case, thudding and pounding till his brain must burst into wild, incurable madness.

Then he knew what he must do if he were to get through the night. He set the whisky bottle and the water canteen on the table in front of him, broke out a fresh packet of cigarettes, pushed the lamp to a safe distance from his elbow and began carefully and methodically to get himself drunk.

He drank slowly at first lest his empty stomach revolt and cheat him of relief. Then, as the liquor warmed and relaxed him, he poured larger tots and used less water, until finally he was drinking neat spirit and the level of the bottle was below the halfway mark.

Long before the drums were silent, long before the singers were dumb, Max Lansing was slumped across his table, with his head pillowed on his unfinished manuscript, one nerveless hand lying on an overturned bottle, the other dangling over a broken glass and a pool of liquor that soaked slowly into the earthen floor.

Then Kumo came in.

All through the solitary orgy he had been squatting outside the hut watching Lansing's slow collapse into insensibility. He was dressed in the ceremonial costume with the tossing plumes and the clattering ornaments of pearl shell. His long, crescent nose ornament gave him the air of a tusked animal. Tucked in his fur armband he carried a small closed tube of bamboo.

For a long moment he stood over the unconscious man, then with a sudden gesture he lifted his head by the hair and let it fall with a thump on the table. Lansing made no sound. His head lolled into equilibrium on one cheek and one ear. Kumo grunted with satisfaction and took the bamboo tube in his hands.

First he rolled it rapidly between his fingers, then tapped it rapidly on the edge of the desk, making a dry, drumming sound. Finally he held it a long time against the hot glass of the lamp, so that the warmth soaked through the pithy wood and into the hollow center.

Now he was ready.

Carefully he took up his position between the edge of the table and the open door of the hut. Then he bent over Lansing, holding the butt of the tube in one hand, in the other its cap—pointing downwards, six inches from Lansing's face. With a sharp movement, he pulled off the cap and stepped backwards. There was a soft "plop" and a small dappled snake fell onto the desk.

Maddened by the noise and the movement and the heat, the snake struck and struck again at Lansing's cheek. Then it slithered off the table and disappeared in the shadows of the hut.

Anesthetized by the liquor, Lansing felt no pain and made no movement. Kumo stood a moment looking down at his victim and at the twin punctures just below his cheekbone. Then, as silently as the snake, he, too, went out into the darkness, and soon, over the beat of the drums, the villagers heard the thudding feet of the cassowary bird.

Chapter Seven

A RUNNER FROM LANSING'S VILLAGE brought the news to Patrol Officer Lee Curtis as he sat taking the census outside the Kiap house. He had come loping steadily over the mountain trails, and he arrived, sweating and breathless, to pour out, with oratorical flourish, the carefully rehearsed message from the luluai.

The white man was dead. The whole village grieved for the loss of their brother. Except that the Kiap disapproved, they would chop off their finger joints in the old fashion of mourning. The white man was dead, struck down by a snake while he slept thus over his table. The marks of the snake were here and here on his face. There was a girl who served him his food. She had discovered him when she came to his hut early in the morning. The white man had been drinking. There was water and a bottle of yellow spirit thus and thus on the table. The snake had come and gone and the white man had not stirred. If the Kiap wished, the villagers would smoke the body for him and send it over the mountain. Otherwise he should come and fetch it quickly; if not, it would stink very soon. The white man was dead and the luluai had given orders that none should touch him until word came from the Kiap. The door of his hut was closed and the white man was still as they found him, waiting for the Kiap to come.

There was more and more yet, as the courier, drunk with his own eloquence, embellished the tale for the Kiap and the police boys and the circle of awestruck villagers. Yet, stripped of its primitive rhetoric, it was a good story, well told. All the facts were there, the setting was sharply and accurately sketched. The pivotal incident—that of the striking snake—was more than feasible. Reptiles abound in the high valleys. They are as much at home in the

440

thatched villages as they are in the kunai grass. Most of them are deadly poisonous.

Yet Lee Curtis was not satisfied. Young as he was, he had been well trained, first in the School of Pacific Administration, then under the watchful eye and the rasping tongue of George Oliver, A.D.O., at Goroka. And the theme dinned and drummed into him every day and all day was: Mistrust the simple and the straightforward. The native mind deals in subtleties and inversions and complexities not always apparent to the white man.

This story was too simple, too bland and pat, too careful and too accurate to be the whole truth.

When the runner had finished his peroration, Curtis sat a long time in silence watching him. He asked no questions. The answers would have told him nothing. The man was a mouthpiece who would say what he had been told to say and after that would relapse into blank stupidity. Under the word-less scrutiny, the runner began to be uneasy. He glanced about him furtively to see only the stony stares of the coastal police boys and the gaping curiosity of the mountain folk. He hung his head and scuffed his toes in the dust.

Curtis stood up. He snapped an order to the sergeant to continue with the census and see that none of the villagers left the Kiap hut until he came back. He would have the boys ready to march within the hour.

The fuzzy-haired sergeant saluted smartly and took his place at the table, while Curtis walked slowly up the path in the direction of Sonderfeld's plantation.

On the face of it, his duty was simple. He would go out to the mountain village. He would confirm that Lansing had died of snakebite. He would bury him with simple ceremony. He would pack his notes and his belongings and send them with an inventory to the A.D.O. at Goroka. He would file a report of his findings and his procedures—and the case would be closed. No problems, no complications, no personal involvement for a young official with his way still to make in the world.

Even as he thought it, he knew that he could not do it. The talk of the night before, Lansing's blunt comment on the restlessness of the tribes, the under-current of tension between Sonderfeld and the missionary and Lansing him-self, still nagged at him like an aching tooth. Behind these three was Gerda, the woman he loved, the woman whose lover was dead. And behind these again, in the background of bright mountains and dark valleys, was the shadowy figure of Kumo the Sorcerer. Before he could close the case, he must know more of these people and their relationship one to another. He must investigate without appearing to do so. He must presume a crime where the evidence said there was no crime. He must have constantly in mind the un-easy position of the Trustee Administration responsible to the United Nations, sensitive to "incidents" that might make headlines in the world press.

Halfway up the path he stopped to light a cigarette. From this point he could command a view of the house and of the plantation itself. He saw that Sonderfeld and Nelson and Wee Georgie were half a mile away studying the

441

drainage problems of the new clearing. His first impulse was to go to them and tell them the news. Then he looked up at the bungalow. Gerda would be there—alone. She had a right to hear the news from someone who felt for her. Perhaps, in the first shock, she would give him something on which to ground his dangerous investigation.

Again he looked across at the plantation and saw Sonderfeld and his companions moving farther away from the house. He had twenty minutes at least. With a gesture of decision he tossed away the half-smoked cigarette and walked swiftly up to the bungalow.

Gerda was in the summerhouse among the orchid blooms. She wore sandals and a frock of flowered cotton and a wide straw hat caught under her chin with a bow of ribbon. She looked up when he entered, smiled with pleasure and surprise, pulled off her stained gloves and stretched out her hands in greeting.

"Dear Mr. Curtis! This is a nice surprise. You must have known I was lonely."

He took her hands and, moved by a sudden boyish impulse, raised them to his lips.

The gesture seemed to make her uneasy. When he released her, she stepped back a little and leant against one of the shelves that held the orchid pots. She was still smiling, but there was puzzlement in her eyes and a small flush crept upwards under her ivory skin.

For a long moment Curtis stood irresolute, eyes downcast, searching for the words to frame his message. Then he raised his head. His voice was unsteady.

"I—I'm afraid I've brought you bad news."

She stiffened. Her eyes widened, her lips parted. The words came in a faltering whisper.

"Bad news? I don't understand."

"Max Lansing died last night. Snakebite. A runner brought me the news ten minutes ago."

She did not cry out. She did not weep. But her whole body was rigid and her eyes were staring with blank horror. She held tightly to the rough wood of the shelf, arching her back against it.

Lee Curtis stood helpless, incapable of even a small gesture of comfort. Gerda shuddered and buried her face in her hands. He laid a tentative hand on her dark hair. She jerked away.

"No! No! Don't touch me."

He drew back and watched her recover herself, slowly and painfully. Then at last she faced him, dry-eyed, tight-lipped. The horror was gone from her eyes. Now they were blazing with hate. Her voice was tight, but steady and full of challenge.

"Mr. Curtis!"

"Yes?"

"Mr. Curtis, you are the representative of the Administration."

"That's right."

"You have police powers as well?"

"In this area—yes."

"Then—" She looked him full in the eyes. Her voice was as cold as stone. "Then I want to tell you that Max Lansing was murdered—by my husband."

The blunt accusation shocked him like a douche of cold water. He spoke carefully.

"Lansing died sometime last night in a village fifteen miles from here. Your husband did not leave the plantation."

"I know that. He did not need to. He arranged for Max to be killed by Kumo the Sorcerer."

"Can you prove that?"

"No. But I believe it to be true."

"Why?"

"Because of what was said last night. Max made it plain that he believed Kurt was implicated in the trouble among the tribes."

"There is no trouble yet—"

Her anger blazed out at him.

"No, but there will be—and why? Because you and your kind will not listen to the men who know—like Max and Père Louis. You come up here with your police boys and your guns and your little book. You make a great show and then you go away—and all the time Kurt and Kumo and the rest have been laughing at you, throwing dust in your eyes."

Breathless with anger, she stood facing him, battering on the light armour of his youthful self-control. Before he had time to answer her, she returned to the attack.

"And now a man is dead. A snake bit him. The verdict? Accident—act of God—death by misadventure! It is murder, I tell you. Murder! And the man who planned it is Kurt, my husband, who is so filled with his own pride that he imagines himself Lord of All, Master of Life and Death—like the Red Spirit."

Then, without warning, she wept. Her body was shaken with great sobs, and she buried her ravaged face in her white hands. This time he reached out and drew her to him and held her, unresisting, pressed against his breast, until the spasm passed and she was crying quietly.

She drew away from him at last and lifted her face again. Hands and lips and eyes were eloquent in the broken appeal.

"What do I have to do? What more do I have to say to make you believe me?"

"I believe you, Gerda," said Lee Curtis softly.

"You do?" There was wonderment and gratitude in her eyes.

He nodded.

"I believe you, because I love you."

"Oh, no!" It was a cry of pure anguish. She cringed away from him as if he had struck her. "Not you, too. Please leave me alone. I'm tired. I have my own life to live. I cannot bear the burden of yours as well."

Lee Curtis was hurt and troubled, but he had delicacy enough to apologize.

443

"I'm sorry. I shouldn't have said that. I—I promise not to bother you. Really I won't. I understand what you're telling me. I believe you may be right. But you must understand I can't move. I can't give even a hint of suspicion until I have evidence. Solid evidence. You see that, don't you?"

She nodded wearily.

"I do. I'll try to get it. I don't know how, but I'll try. Meantime, have you told my husband?"

"No. I thought it would be kinder to tell you first."

She reached up and patted his cheek with the same vague, tender gesture that had irritated Max Lansing.

"You're a good, kind young man. I'm sorry I made a scene."

Curtis stiffened. Mention of his youth brought back all his uneasiness and his sense of isolation. He spoke crisply, officially, to cover his embarrassment.

"If you can carry it off, I'd rather you didn't let your husband know I've seen you. He's in the plantation. I'm going to tell him now."

Gerda nodded.

"I can carry it off, as you say."

"Good. Find out whatever you can and let me know. But . . ." He hesitated, then the words came out with a rush. "For God's sake, be careful, Gerda. Be very, very careful."

"I'll be careful. I promise."

But he did not hear her. He was already gone, a shamefaced, troubled, scared young man striding through the dappled sunlight to see Kurt Sonderfeld.

Sonderfeld professed himself deeply shocked by the news. He swore softly in German and beat his forehead with his fist.

"The poor fellow! The poor, poor fellow! Gerda will be upset. I am myself. He was angry with me, I think. He left without saying good-bye. Now he is dead and we have no time to be friends again. He was drunk, you say?"

Curtis nodded.

"Sounds like it from the reports."

"Natural enough. He would be lonely when he got back. He would drink to put himself early to sleep. That is the curse of this life—the isolation, the black depression. I know. I have felt it myself."

Wee Georgie whistled softly. His beady, bloodshot eyes were bright with interest.

"Snakes, eh? Makes you think, don't it? Place is alive with the bloody things and yet a man walks about all day in bare feet, sleeps six inches from the floor. Strewth!"

Theodore Nelson clucked his sympathy. He had travelled too much and too comfortably to be moved by Lansing's untimely death. He was more interested in Lee Curtis. The boy knew more than he was telling. He was unhappy about something, scared, too, probably, but he was putting up a good front.

444

His hands were steady and his eyes were cold, and there was a reassuring firmness in the set of his downy chin.

"If there is anything I can do—?" said Sonderfeld tentatively.

"There is—yes." Curtis's voice was crisp with authority. "I'm going up to the village this afternoon. I'll have to inspect the body, arrange for the burial, collect Lansing's things, make a report. I'd like you to come with me."

Sonderfeld could not conceal his surprise.

"If you say so, of course. But I do not see what good I can do."

"You're a doctor," said Curtis bluntly. "I need a death certificate. I may need a postmortem. You're entitled to refuse, of course."

"My dear fellow!" The big man was bland and smiling. "I wouldn't dream of refusing. The Administration has been good to me. I am happy to serve the Administration. When do you want to leave?"

"In half an hour. Even at that we'll be walking in the dark."

Sonderfeld shrugged.

"I shall be ready. Now, if you'll excuse me, gentlemen, I should like a few minutes with my wife. She was very—attached to our friend, Lansing. Come, Georgie!"

He strode off over the soft, black earth with the fat man shuffling and wheezing at his heels like a decrepit spaniel. Nelson and Curtis were left alone in the clearing.

"Cigarette?" said Nelson gently.

"Thanks."

They lit up. Curtis was still staring across the plantation at the retreating figure of Sonderfeld.

"Trouble, Curtis?"

"Part of the job."

Nelson grinned at the cryptic reply. He was a hard man to snub.

"That doesn't answer my question."

Curtis slewed round to face him. His patience was wearing thin, and the older man's mockery was not calculated to improve it.

"Do I ask you about growing coffee?"

"No. But I'd be happy to tell you if you did."

"This is police business."

"What? Snakebite?"

"Yes."

"Look, Curtis—" He was serious now. His pale eyes were shrewd and penetrating. "One of the things you learn in a job like mine is to keep your mouth shut and your eyes open. If you say so, I'll do just that. I'm not a policeman. I don't belong to the Administration. You can blow this island off the map and I'll still have a job. On the other hand, I may be able to help you."

"How?"

"There's trouble blowing up. I have no more than an inkling of what it may be—but one thing I'm sure of, this Lansing business is part of it."

445

"How do you know that?"

The question was sharp with professional interest. Nelson shrugged.

"I don't *know* anything. I'm guessing. I'm guessing that you're taking Sonderfeld with you for a reason. I'm guessing that you're not satisfied with the report from the village and that you're going to make inquiries on your own account. I'm suggesting—only suggesting, mind you—that if you give me a little of the background, I may be able to pick up some information while you're away. I presume I'll dine at the house. Wee Georgie's a gossipy sort of soul. Mrs. Sonderfeld will probably react to a little sympathy. And sometimes the onlooker sees more of the game than the man on the field."

Curtis nodded slowly.

"That's fair enough. But why? What's your interest?"

Nelson chuckled and gave a comical shrug of defeat.

"Damned if I know. I'm breaking the habit of a lifetime. Perhaps I like you. Perhaps I don't like Sonderfeld. Perhaps . . . ." His eyes darkened. "Perhaps I'm scared of a place where a man can be killed in his cups and never know what struck him. Perhaps I need an ally as much as you do. Anyway, there it is. Take it or leave it."

Seconds passed while Lee Curtis stood, silent and abstracted, staring out across the valley. Then his tight features relaxed into a boyish grin. He held out his hand.

"All right. I'll take it! Walk with me down to the Kiap house. I'll talk to you as we go."

As he walked slowly across the plantation and up the gravelled path that led to the bungalow, Kurt Sonderfeld took stock of his situation. The first glance showed him a neat profit. His dominion over the sorcerer was established. The swift and sudden death of Lansing proved that. With Lansing gone, one major danger to his project was removed. His mouth was stopped; such evidence as he might have given was stifled forever. Unless . . .

A new fear halted him in his tracks—Lansing's notes.

The man was a scholar, a meticulous recorder. Was there any mention of Sonderfeld's activities in the notebooks which Curtis was bound to find when he came to collect the belongings of the dead man? He weighed the possibility, measured the risk. Then he was no longer afraid. There might be nothing. At most there would be the scrawled and cryptic jottings, the groundwork of a thesis that would never be written. They would harm him no more and probably a good deal less than Lansing's blunt challenge over the whisky.

He became aware that Wee Georgie was standing beside him, studying him with shrewd and furtive eyes. He turned abruptly and began giving him orders for the conduct of the plantation during his absence. Wee Georgie listened and nodded continuously like a mandarin figure. He knew it all by heart. He knew exactly how little he could do and still escape the wrath of his master. Then, without warning, Sonderfeld heeled to a new tack.

446

"Then, there is the girl."

"N'Daria, boss?"

"That's right."

Wee Georgie leered happily.

"I'll keep me eye on her, boss. Never fear. I'll see she doesn't go whorin' around with the—"

"Shut up!" said Sonderfeld harshly. "Shut up and listen to me."

"Yes, boss." Wee Georgie was fervently contrite.

"You will have nothing to do with the girl, nothing to say to her. Let her go where she wants, do what she will. But you will arrange that her every movement is watched by your women or by one of the work boys. When I come back, I shall want a complete account, hour by hour, day and night. Understand?"

"Yes, boss. Yes . . . leave it to me. Those girls of mine have got eyes in their backsides."

"Keep your own eyes open, Georgie—and your ears, too. Don't drink too much. There are things moving that you do not understand. I will not have them complicated by a babbling fool with a bellyful of liquor."

"You can trust me, boss. You know that."

"I know, Georgie." His thin lips were a smiling threat. "I know that I can trust you. Why else would I have kept you alive so long?"

With that, he left him, a flabby, quaking wreck, cold in the warm sunshine. Wee Georgie shivered and licked his dry lips. He thought he had never needed a drink so badly.

As Sonderfeld came closer to the bungalow, he realized with something of a shock that he did not know what to say to his wife. In a curious fashion he was, for the first time, afraid of her. When, in the past, he had meditated the death of Lansing, it had been part of his pleasure to anticipate her reaction when he told her, bluntly and brutally, that her lover was dead. He had framed little speeches of mockery, little tricks of surprise to recall the presence of her lover, even when she was prepared to forget him.

Now, with Curtis alert and Nelson a shrewd and prying presence, with his plans for the pig festival so near to fruition, he could not afford the luxury of cruelty. So he must be gentle with her, grave, considerate, even tender, as if regretful of the past and faintly hopeful for the future of their married life. If he could not deceive her, at least he might puzzle her long enough to lull her suspicions of himself.

Then, when Curtis was gone, and Nelson, when the valley was his, and his the dominion of all the mountains, he could abandon himself to the luxury of tormenting her with mockery of her lover's death.

At the foot of the steps he paused to compose his features in an expression of seemly grief. Then he walked into the house.

Gerda was in the living room arranging a great fan-shaped display of gladioli. She looked up when he entered and greeted him with the polite indifference that was habitual between them.

447

"Hullo, Kurt."

Across the polished table he faced her. His eyes were grave, his lips almost tender.

"I'm afraid I have bad news for you, Gerda."

"Bad news?"

She was only mildly surprised. He hesitated as if at a loss for words. He stumbled a little, stammered over the first awkward phrase. It was a magnificent performance.

"I— You may think I find a pleasure in this. Believe me, I am surprised that I do not. I feel grief for him—and grieve for you. Max Lansing is dead!"

"No!"

Her performance matched his own for depth and subtlety. She hid her face in her hands, as if trying to blot out a vision of monstrous horror. Her voice came to him in a muffled whisper.

"How? When did he die?"

"He was drunk last night. He was bitten by a snake and died in his sleep. At least that is the report we have had from the luluai. Curtis and I are going up to—to make an inspection and bury the poor fellow."

"You are going up?"

Her surprise was genuine now. This was a move she had not expected. Sonderfeld nodded.

"Yes. Curtis wants a death certificate, possibly a postmortem. Don't ask me why. I don't know. In any case, I am hardly in a position to refuse."

"When are you going?"

"As soon as I have changed my clothes and packed some instruments."

"I'll help you."

"There is no need."

"I should like to do it. You have been kind to me in this—kinder than I could have believed possible with you. I am grateful, Kurt. Please let me help."

Amused by her humble gratitude, elated by the success of his acting, he made no further protest but went with her to the bedroom. He stripped off his shorts and knee stockings and the white, short-sleeved shirt and put on a pair of denim slacks, greenhide jungle boots, webbing gaiters and a long-sleeved shirt of military pattern. It would be a long walk and the insects would be bad; it was wise to leave as little as possible of the body exposed.

While he was dressing, Gerda packed shaving gear and a box of cigars and a clean change in his canvas shoulder bag and laid out the small leather case of surgical instruments. She gathered up his discarded clothes and laid them in a heap on the bed for the houseboy to collect. She rubbed his hands and his face with repellent oil and went down on her knees to adjust the straps of his gaiters. Nothing more was said between them, but Sonderfeld watched her with cynical amusement, remembering the first days of her servitude to him.

He was so absorbed in this refinement of pleasure that he quite forgot the bamboo tube which he always carried in the pocket of his white shorts.

He was halfway over the mountains with Lee Curtis before he remembered it.

Long before it had reached Patrol Officer Lee Curtis, the news of Lansing's death was reported to Père Louis. His village was only a few miles from Lansing's, and the commerce between them was easy and constant. A man with a load of canes met an old woman leading a blind pig. They whispered a moment, furtively, fearfully, and then they parted.

The woman met a man and his son armed with bows and arrows out on the hunt for bird of paradise plumes. She hailed them and they came to her with reluctance, but when they had heard her low-spoken message, they turned back, running in the direction of the village.

The man and his son passed the taro patch where his wife was working. They told her the news in hurried undertones, then went back to the hunt. The woman told another woman and she told her husband's father.

The old man told the luluai and the luluai, who was a Christian, told the catechist, and so, like a coin passed from hand to hand, the news came finally to the old priest.

The white man who lived in the next village was dead of the snake sorcery, and the man who had killed him was Kumo, the cassowary man.

Père Louis sat for a long time in the cool darkness of his hut, weighing the whispered words of the catechist. The burden of his years lay heavy on his shoulders and the accumulated guilt of other men was an oppression to his tired spirit.

Death held no terrors for him, but he shared the terror of those who met it unprepared, without shriving or viaticum. To Lansing it had come in the days of his adultery, at a moment when he was farthest from the grace of repentance. It had come violently, as a vengeance, not gently, as a merciful release.

Père Louis bowed his face in his hands and prayed the last loving prayer of the Crucified.

"Father, forgive them, for they know not what they do."

Lansing was a lost and lonely man, but not an evil one. The evil was in those who had compassed his death and set him beyond the reach of mercy, when mercy was his greatest need.

There was Sonderfeld, cold, calculating, saturnine, a newcomer from the monstrous twilight of Europe. There was Kumo, the man from the old time, before the Decalogue, before the New Promise—Kumo who had been offered salvation but had rejected it, turning back to the groves of Baal and Dagon and the god who was a great pig. Between these two there was a bond, a dark brotherhood whose beginning was pride and whose end was death and eternal damnation.

The old priest asked himself what he should do. The dead were beyond his help. His business was with the living. Sonderfeld and Kumo were out of his reach—if not yet beyond the reach of God Almighty. Curtis was a man bound by an oath of service to a cause that was not his own. There remained Gerda,

449

the woman with the warm body and the cold heart, and N'Daria, the brown girl who had followed the drums and the flutes and was now lost in the wilderness of sin.

So the light came to him, clear and unmistakable. Let the dead bury their dead. Let Curtis and his police boys do what must be done for Lansing. He himself would go back to the bungalow.

He had his catechist beat the drum that called his Christians to prayer, and when they came huddling into the small chapel, he put on the black stole and the black chasuble and offered the Mass for the Dead. After the Communion he spoke to them, exhorting them to persevere in faith and prayer and to arm themselves with innocence against the powers of evil. Then he gave them the last blessing and the ritual dismissal and heard their voices raised with his in the invocation to Saint Michael, Prince of the Heavenly Spirits, for defense against Satan and the pillagers of souls.

When the last of his little congregation had filed out of the chapel, he took off his vestments and knelt a few moments in prayer before the altar.

Then he stood up, walked out into the bright sunshine and took the road to Sonderfeld's plantation.

Chapter Eight

"FINISHED YET?"

Curtis looked up from his reading of Lansing's notebooks to ask the question of Sonderfeld, who was still bending over the body, intent on the grim business of evisceration and dismemberment.

"Very soon now."

Sonderfeld's voice was cool and professional.

It was morning. They were in Lansing's hut, Curtis slightly in shadow at the table, Sonderfeld in the shaft of light from the doorway working under the curious stares of the villagers, who were held back by the line of police boys standing with rifles at the port, motionless as ebony statues.

They had come to the village late the previous night. They had made a cursory inspection of the scene, then posted a guard of police and retired to spend the night in the Kiap house. When morning came, Curtis had called the villagers together and questioned the luluai in their presence without shaking his story in the slightest particular. All the evidence confirmed its truth: the position of the body, the scars of the snakebite, the liquor and the shattered glass. No jury would have disputed a verdict of death by misadventure.

But Curtis was still not satisfied. He made a thorough search of the hut, collected all Lansing's belongings, listed them carefully and had the police boys parcel them in woven mats for transport back to the bungalow and later to Goroka. The notebooks he had kept apart to read while Sonderfeld did his postmortem.

The body was already puffy with poison and incipient decay. The ants had begun to crawl on it and the big bush rats had begun to gnaw at the ex-

451

tremities, but Sonderfeld went about his work with calm and precision. His strong hands were encased in rubber gloves, and a sweating police boy stood near him with a wooden bowl of steaming water, a clean towel and a cake of disinfectant soap.

When he had finished, he straightened up, stripped off the gloves, washed his hands carefully and gave directions in pidgin for the sterilizing of his gloves and instruments. Then he turned to Curtis.

"It is done."

"What's the verdict?"

Sonderfeld shrugged.

"As before. He must have been very drunk. His stomach was still full of unabsorbed spirit."

"The cause of death?"

"Paralysis of the motor centers, following the snakebite. One hour, two perhaps, after he had been bitten."

"Can you identify the poison?"

"No. I have not the knowledge for that. I doubt if anyone has yet."

Curtis closed the book with a snap and stood up. He pointed to the desk and the vacant chair.

"Mind writing me a report on it? Might as well get everything straight now."

Sonderfeld made a gesture of indifference, sat down at the rough table and wrote his report with Lansing's pencil on Lansing's notepaper. His hand was steady, his script was firm and businesslike. When he had finished, he scribbled a signature, folded the paper and handed it to Curtis, who slipped it into his notebook and buttoned it in his breast pocket.

"What now?"

"We bury him," said Curtis simply. "We bury him and then go home."

They buried him under the shade of the tangket trees on the outer fringe of the village. They buried him deep to keep him safe from the snuffling pigs, and Curtis recited the Lord's Prayer while Sonderfeld stood bareheaded and the villagers waited in theatrical grief and the police boys stood rigidly at attention. Then they fired a salute over the open grave, Curtis threw in the first handful of black earth and the natives filled the hole with their hands, chattering and laughing and stamping the earth down with their bare feet.

They marked the grave with a big square stone and left him there—lonely in death as he had been in life—loveless, barren of achievement, Max Lansing, crowned with dust, naked in the naked earth of the oldest island on the planet.

At the moment of Max Lansing's burial in the mountain village, Gerda Sonderfeld, Theodore Nelson and Père Louis sat together on the stoop of the bungalow.

Between them on the table lay the small tube of bamboo which N'Daria had given to Sonderfeld. Père Louis leant forward and lifted the tube between the thumb and forefinger of his right hand. Gerda and Nelson watched him, fascinated. His eyes were hard, his mouth was grim under the grey beard.

"Tell me—" He gestured with the shiny brown tube. "Tell me again how you came by this."

"I picked it up in the bedroom," said Gerda. "It fell from the pocket of Kurt's trousers when the houseboy came to take them to the wash."

"Do you know what it is?" asked Theodore Nelson.

"I do."

"Have you seen it before?" It was Gerda's question this time.

"I have seen others like it," said Père Louis gravely. He slipped the cap from the tube and showed them the noisome, clotted wad inside. "In the other cases there was a handful of moss, a fragment of bark cloth. But the meaning is the same."

He replaced the cap and laid the tube on the table.

"What is the meaning, Father?" Gerda's anxious eyes searched his face.

"Before I tell you that, madame, I should like to know"—he turned his grim old eyes on Theodore Nelson—"what is your part in this?"

It was Gerda who answered for him, eagerly, as for a trusted ally.

"Mr. Nelson has been asked by the patrol officer to look after me and to pick up whatever information he can during the absence of proper authority."

The answer seemed to satisfy the little priest. He nodded absently and spent a long time examining the wrinkled, mottled skin on the backs of his small hands. Then he spoke, slowly and carefully, like a man whose strength is running out and for whom even the effort of speech is a costly loss.

"What you saw in that tube was the life of a human being. The cotton wool is impregnated with the spittle and the blood and—I believe—the seed of a living man. Whoever holds this tube holds that man in bondage, because he holds his life and can compass his death."

"My husband!" The words were a long-drawn whisper of horror.

Père Louis nodded soberly.

"It would seem so."

"But—but—" Nelson stammered the words in his excitement. "To whom does that belong—that messy thing?"

Père Louis turned his grave, tired eyes on Gerda.

"Can you answer that, madame?"

Without hesitation she rose to the challenge.

"I believe so. I think it belongs to Kumo the Sorcerer. I think also that he is the man through whom my husband killed Max Lansing."

"God Almighty!"

Theodore Nelson swore softly and mopped his clammy forehead. Père Louis was staring down at his old and knotted hands. It was a long time before any of them spoke again. Nelson was the first to break the silence.

"Does—does this thing really work?"

Père Louis nodded somberly.

"It works, my friend; be in no doubt of that. It works, as fear and superstition always work to corruption and death and the destruction of man's immortal soul."

"How in God's name would he get such a thing?"

Père Louis spread his hands, palm upwards, on the table as if to emphasize the simplicity of the answer.

"He would get it through a woman, a woman whom he would send to seduce this man and fornicate with him. It is as blunt and as easy as that."

Nelson shot a sidelong glance at Gerda, then averted his eyes in shame and embarrassment. Père Louis began to light his pipe, puffing furiously and sending great clouds of foul smoke curling over the table. Gerda alone was calm and contained. She said flatly, "The woman, of course, is N'Daria. She works for my husband. She is passionately in love with him. She would do anything he asked."

Père Louis nodded agreement but said nothing. It was left to Theodore Nelson to lay down the final pieces in the pattern.

"So that's what Lansing meant about the cargo cult and the domination of the tribes. That's why he was killed, because he came too close to the truth. That's why—"

"That is why we must say nothing of this until I have had the chance to speak to Curtis and decide what we must do." The old priest picked up the bamboo tube and put it in his pocket. He pushed aside his chair and stood up. "Now, my friend, if you will excuse us, I should like a word in private with Madame. I suggest you walk in the garden awhile. The fresh air will do you good."

Still dabbing at his damp forehead, Theodore Nelson made an awkward, stumbling exit, and Gerda was left alone with Père Louis.

The old priest laid his hand on hers with a gentle, comforting gesture.

"Now, my child, we will talk of things that concern only the two of us. But first—" His lined face relaxed into a boyish grin. "But first I should like a drink—a strong one!"

She brought him whisky and a jug of ice water. She waited patiently while he sank the first drink at a gulp and sipped at the second with careful relish. His silence and his deliberation troubled her not at all. Of all the people who surrounded her in this time of shame and crisis Père Louis was the one she trusted most. There was in his stringy old body an enduring strength. His spirit was endowed with a patient, compassionate wisdom to which the others were strangers. He had the bluntness of the man who has faced the final consequences of his belief, the tenderness of the man who knows the burden that belief lays on the shoulders of weak men and women. His presence rested her, gave her time and courage to collect her scattered strength.

Père Louis finished his drink and set down the empty glass.

"Now," he said gently, "we will talk about you."

"About me, Father?" She took it calmly enough, but she was as wary as a cat.

"About you and your immortal soul."

She smiled bitterly.

"You are the first man I have met who was interested in my soul."

Père Louis did not smile. His eyes were grave and gentle.

"Max Lansing? Did you love him?"

"No."

"Do you love your husband?"

"I hate him."

"So . . . you are married to a man you hate. You have committed adultery with a man you do not love."

"With many men, Father."

"Did it make you happy, my child?"

She shrugged, still smiling the rueful, crooked smile.

"Long ago, Father, I learnt that I should not expect happiness. I have tried to make myself content with what is left to me."

"Do you believe in God, child?"

"No."

"And yet you are a Pole. You were born and baptized in the Church."

"Yes."

"What happened to you? What happened to you that you came to lose the one thing that might have made you happy?"

There was no reproach in the old voice, only an attentive earnestness, as if he were a doctor probing a deep and painful wound. She felt no resentment—she was content to follow the line of his questioning, answering simply and without evasion because she had nothing to hide.

"There was a time, Father, when I needed God and He was not there. There was a time when I called on Him and He did not answer. It is as simple as that."

"Tell me about it."

She told him. She told him of the war and of the rape of the eastern cities. She told him of the long horror that ended with her meeting with Reinach and the new horror that had grown out of the same meeting. She told him of her maiming and her servitude. She told him how Reinach became Sonderfeld and of the monstrous bargain she had made with him. She told of their life together and of their loves apart; and, when she had finished, it was as if a weight had been lifted from her shoulders and a tight hand had loosened its grip around her heart. Père Louis lowered his eyes to hide the pity and the tenderness and the old, foolish tears. He took her white, slack hand between his own rough palms and patted it gently.

"To say that I am sorry for you, child, is to say an empty and a barren thing. I am a priest, an unworthy shepherd of the flock of Christ. You belong to that flock and you belong to me, though you have wandered a long, hard way from

455

the fold. I say to you now, you do not need pity. You need strength and love and the grace to forgive others as God is ready to forgive you."

She made a little shrugging gesture of despair.

"I have strength, I think. Otherwise I should not have endured so much and so long. But love . . . ? Perhaps I am incapable of love, as I am incapable of bearing children?"

"No!" Père Louis' voice was suddenly strong in rejection. "You think you are incapable of love, because all these years you have made the act of love an act of self-torment, an act of revenge upon the man who has wronged you. To sin with love and passion is one thing. It is a sin according to nature, but a sin that carries the seed of its own salvation. To sin without love is a perversion, a monstrous contradiction that will debase you lower than the man you wish to hurt. Child . . ." The old man's voice was warm again and soft with compassion. "Child, I am an old man. Like Solomon with all his years upon him, I have seen evil under the sun. But I have seen good, too—much good—so much that I am daily humbled and grateful to the good God. Believe me, I do not sell you cheap words. I am no huckster of the Gospel. I am a tired, spent man; I have no traffic but with the truth. Bend to me, child, bend a little and see at your feet the love of God, bright and beautiful, like the flowers in your garden."

Gerda Sonderfeld buried her face in her hands and wept. The old man stood beside her and patted her dark hair like a father comforting a grieving child. Then, when all her tears were spent and she lifted her ravaged face, he fished in his pocket for a handkerchief and handed it to her with a wry grin.

"There now, already it begins to be better. Dry your eyes and we will see what can be done to mend this madness in the valleys."

Père Louis was in a double dilemma.

Possession of the bamboo tube set him in a position of some power against both Sonderfeld and Kumo. Yet his status as a missionary deprived him of the authority to use it. There was only one authority in the valley—Cadet Patrol Officer Lee Curtis. He, being young and unsure of himself, might well resent the intrusion of the Church into secular affairs. He might, with more reason, object to paying the penalty for the Church's mistakes—and mistakes were very possible when one was dealing with the abnormal psychologies of paranoiac modern and primitive man.

Père Louis found himself wishing, as he had wished many times in the last days, that George Oliver were on patrol again and not beating his head and bruising his heart against mountains of paper in the District Commissioner's office at Goroka.

George Oliver would have understood and approved what he wanted to do. He had made his reputation by gambles such as this one. But George Oliver was two days away behind the southern barrier.

There was another problem, too—a moral one. Gerda Sonderfeld hated her husband and was prepared to revenge herself upon him for the death of her lover. To invite her cooperation in Sonderfeld's downfall would be to lay on her and on himself a new burden of guilt. He was, first and foremost, a priest, and sin was to him a disorder worse than final chaos. Whatever he did, therefore, he must do without her knowledge.

He needed time, prayer, and a little solitude, to extricate himself from his dilemma. So, in spite of Gerda's curiosity and disappointment, he took himself off in the direction of the big clump of bamboos that screened the boy houses from the main bungalow and Gerda's garden.

There, sitting on a mossy log, he made a short prayer and smoked a long, soothing pipe before he made up his mind what to do.

First, he hailed one of the houseboys and traded him a plug of tobacco for a bamboo container similar in size and texture to Sonderfeld's. He had the boy bring him a wad of cotton wool and, with the aid of spittle, tobacco juice and blood pricked from his finger, he made a reasonable facsimile of the contents of Sonderfeld's tube.

Then he took the wad containing Kumo's vital juices and transferred it to his own container. In its place he put the tampon he himself had made, closed both tubes and held them side by side in his outstretched hand—the real and the false—while he pondered how he should use them.

The forgery he would return to Gerda, so that Sonderfeld would find it when he came home. The original he would keep against the time of final conflict.

He saw it clearly and in detail: the assembly of the tribes in the Lahgi Valley, the tossing plumes, the spilt blood, the bodies of the sacrificial pigs piled high outside the spirit houses. He saw Sonderfeld proclaimed by Kumo as the incarnation of the Red Spirit. He saw himself, small and alone, in the center of the compound, challenging Sonderfeld for a liar and Kumo for a dupe and holding up his own bamboo capsule in proof of the challenge. He saw the doubt and the uncertainty in Kumo's eyes—for even the great sorcerer could not pierce the bamboo walls to know which man was a liar and which held his life in the hollow of his hand.

The next moment he could not foresee, because this would be the moment of the final gamble, the moment when the shrewd primitive would weigh him against Sonderfeld for truth and credit and strength. This would be the moment in which he would have great need of the sheltering mercy of God, for if he were found wanting, he would be cut down by the stone axes and his blood would be spilt with the spilt blood of the pigs.

He shivered in spite of the warmth, thrust the tube into his pocket and, carrying the other in his clenched fist, walked slowly back to the bungalow.

In the rich darkness of the cool mountain night, Kurt Sonderfeld came home to his bungalow. His bones were weary from the long trek over the mountains, his body stank with fatigue and his stained clothes were stiff with mud and drying sweat. He was ill-tempered and troubled by the stiff reserve of Lee Curtis, who, in spite of his youth and inexperience, had conducted the investigation with punctilious caution. In spite of the fact that he had found nothing suspicious or at variance with the village story, he was reserved and wary and he made no secret of his displeasure at Sonderfeld's constant questioning.

When, at the first homeward halt, he had asked to see Lansing's manuscript, Curtis had handed it to him without demur. But, as he skimmed it, thumbing quickly through the close-written pages with their cryptic notes in professional jargon, he was conscious that Curtis was watching him closely, studying his face for any reaction of surprise or displeasure. The boy mistrusted him, but Sonderfeld was unable to put a finger on the cause of his distrust. So far as he could see in the first quick glance, there was nothing at all in the notes that could be construed as an accusation. Finally he shrugged off his fear, but the ill temper stayed with him the rest of the way home.

More than all, however, the loss of the bamboo tube fretted him. So much depended on his possession of that small sinister capsule; so much more depended on keeping his possession a secret. If Gerda found it, all would be well. She was indifferent to such things, accustomed to his having about him such trifles of native workmanship.

It was the houseboys who troubled him. If one of them had picked it up, he would be certain to open it—the Highland native is curious as a jackdaw. Then, when he saw what it contained, he would either fall into a gibbering panic or he would keep it for a trade with Kumo or another sorcerer. Either event could spell disaster for Sonderfeld.

But, when he came into the bedroom where Gerda was sleeping soundly, he saw on the bedside table a pile of freshly washed handkerchiefs and, on top of them, the bamboo tube. Gerda had found it then. She had done as wives do with a mislaid cuff link or a forgotten wristwatch—laid it where he would be sure to see it when he came home.

Sonderfeld smiled with satisfaction. His ill humour fell away from him like sloughed skin. He thrust the tube into his trouser pocket, then, remembering the mishap of the previous day, thought better of it and put it far back in the drawer of his cabinet and covered it with the handkerchiefs. It would be safe there until he needed it.

He stripped off his soiled clothes, threw a towel over his arm and walked down to the shower room to refresh himself for sleep. As he passed the half-open door of the guest room, he heard the sound of deep, regular breathing, punctuated by an occasional snore. He stopped, pushed the door open and peered into the room. Père Louis was sleeping the sleep of the just and godly. Sonderfeld withdrew, frowning.

The presence of the priest puzzled him. He remembered their last meeting and the old man's refusal to visit him again unless he were summoned. He wondered if Gerda had sent for him. Then he remembered that Père Louis' village was close to Lansing's. He would have heard the news before any of them. But why had he come here instead of making straight for Lansing's place?

He chewed on the proposition as he bathed and towelled himself; and, finally, because he could not brook any thought that challenged the perfection of his own planning, he decided that the priest had come to offer sympathy to the friends of the dead man—a natural enough gesture in the isolation of the mountains, where any excuse is good enough for a gathering. Perhaps, too, the old man wanted to make friends again. He would miss the whisky and the regular dinner among civilized people.

Sonderfeld smiled with sour triumph and walked back to the bedroom. He told himself he was a fool to trouble over trifles. Let them suspect what they would; let them hate him as much as they dared; they could not shake a single stone of the empire of Kurt Sonderfeld.

He threw himself on the bed, drew the covers about his shoulders and lapsed immediately into a dreamless sleep.

He did not hear the running feet of the cassowary bird pounding down the mountain, drumming past the village, thundering up the slope, towards the laboratory where N'Daria tossed uneasily in her lonely bed.

Père Louis heard them and sat bolt upright, instantly awake. The habit of years was strong in him; he had lived through times and in places where death walked the jungle paths, and more than one lonely missionary had fallen under the stone axes and the heavy clubs of the people he had come to save. He knew, too, that the cassowary bird does not stir abroad at night but sleeps like other birds during the hours of darkness.

The muffled crescendo could have only one meaning. Evil was abroad under the stars. The village slept and the kundus were silent, but the sorcerers were active about their dark business of perversion.

He listened intently. The running feet were closer. They were passing the village. They were turning up the slope towards the plantation. He threw off the covers, dressed himself hurriedly and crept out of the house.

The night was empty of all but stars and shadowy trees, but the air vibrated with the sound of drumming feet coming closer and closer yet. Père Louis crossed himself and invoked the protection of Christ and His Virgin Mother and walked slowly down the path to meet the oncoming footsteps.

N'Daria heard them, too, and trembled with terror in the darkness. She buried her head under the blankets, but she could not shut out the sound of their inexorable approach. She knew what they meant. Kumo was coming for her as she had known he must come, now that Sonderfeld had rejected her.

She had betrayed her lover and had been betrayed in her turn. Now her lover was coming to exact vengeance, the terrible, dark vengeance that only a sorcerer could exact.

Ever since that night she had lived in constant terror. She had not dared to go to the kunande. She had not set foot in the village. She had hidden herself even from the work boys and had kept herself in the laboratory hut, trying frantically to concentrate on the tasks that Sonderfeld had set her but that were now without meaning or potency. She was lost and she knew it. She had tried to live in two worlds, and in both her foothold had crumbled. She had rejected her own people. The white man had rejected her. The knowledge he had given her was no armour against the secret wisdom of the sorcerers.

Fearful, alone, full of guilt and remorse, she could do nothing but lie there, shivering and helpless, while the footbeats came closer and closer and finally stopped outside the window of the hut.

Chapter Nine

AT FIRST IT WAS A SMALL, INSISTENT SCRAPING, like the brushing of a windy branch against the windowpane. N'Daria lay rigid under blankets and pretended to be asleep. Then the scraping became a hammering of knuckles, rapid and rhythmic like the beat of a tiny drum. This, too, she tried to ignore, but the pulse never slackened and the noise seemed to multiply in the hollow pipes of the bamboo walls until it filled the whole room and vibrated in every nerve of her body.

She could bear it no longer. She threw back the covers and looked up. Kumo was staring at her through the window. His eyes were twin coals; his lips were drawn back in a snarling grin that showed his red-stained teeth; his face was distorted into a monstrous mask by pressure against the glass.

She fought down a scream and tried to turn away her eyes from the terrifying vision, but the eyes of Kumo held her petrified. She stared and stared until it seemed that the horror would stifle her. Kumo gestured to her to open the door. Mechanically, like one in a hypnotic trance, she walked through to the laboratory, unlocked the door and let him in.

The night was still and airless, but the impact of his entry was like the rushing of great wind that robbed her of breath and thrust her back and back, until she felt the hard wood of the bench press into her thighs, and her spine arched backwards in a last futile effort to escape him. He towered over her, tall and menacing, his painted face hideous, his plumes tossing, the skin of his breast shining with sweat and oil.

If he had touched her, she would have crumpled at his feet. Instead, he stood there, grinning like a tusked beast, his eyes commanding her so that she could not look away but must stare and stare until his face swelled and

461

swelled like a bladder, blotting out the room, blotting out the stars that shone through the open doorway, until there was nothing left but the pair of fiery eyes full of gloating accusation. Then, as if from a great distance, she heard his voice.

"This is N'Daria, who stole my life to give it to the white man."

She tried to answer him, but her throat was full of mossy vapour and no sound came. She tried to struggle, but her limbs refused their functions. Her breast and her belly were pressed down as if by a great stone.

"This is N'Daria, who thought the magic of the white man was greater than the magic of Kumo. The white man is sleeping, N'Daria. He is weary from his journey over the mountains. He will not come to you until the morning."

She heard him laugh and the sound was an enveloping thunder. His eyes held hers, immovable in the terror of it.

"The white man holds my life, but he cannot touch me while he sleeps. Now we shall make proof of the magic of Kumo. Feel it, N'Daria! There is an arrow in your belly! Feel it!

He made no movement. He did not touch her even with a fingertip; but she writhed and twisted in agony, clutching at her middle, her face distorted in a soundless scream.

Kumo watched her, grinning with pleasure. Then with the sound of his voice the pain left her and she was still again, stiff and motionless as a cataleptic. His fiery eyes were a mockery, his voice was a bubbling chuckle.

"There is more, N'Daria. There is more. Your mouth is full of thorns and your throat is choked with pebbles. Feel them!"

Her eyes bulged, her cheeks puffed out. The arteries of her throat swelled and her diaphragm was sucked in under the rib cage. She was in the final agony of suffocation before he released her again and watched her retching with relief, her face grey and streaming with sweat.

So, in the timeless seconds of the hypnotic syncope, he led her through one agony after another. He made her flesh crawl with stinging bull ants. He set a fire in her brain and a gnawing animal in her stomach. He made her joints crack as if distended on a rack. He made her feel the lash of canes and the mutilation of stone knives. And still he did not touch her.

The whole performance lasted only a few minutes, but before he released her she had run the gamut of torment, endured a lifetime of affliction. Then she stood before him, trembling and broken, the tears streaming down her cheeks, her mouth slobbering open, her nerves twitching uncontrollably.

Kumo licked his lips, savouring the salt tang of vengeance. Then he took from his armband the same bamboo capsule with which he had killed Max Lansing.

N'Daria gasped with the impact of this final terror, but she had no strength to withdraw from it.

"You know what this is, N'Daria?"

"Yes." It was a stifled whisper.

"You took my life, N'Daria. You took my life and gave it to the white man.

Now I shall take yours and give it to the spotted snake, and the white man will never know."

She could not move. She could not cry out. She could only stand and wait as he brought the tube closer and closer to her body, so that when the snake was released, it would erupt like a spring and fasten on the tight skin of her breast. Wide-eyed, she saw Kumo's fingers tighten on the cap. She smelt the foulness of his breath and felt his trembling eagerness in this moment of triumph.

Then, as sharp and sudden as a cracking stick, came the voice of Père Louis. "Drop it, Kumo. Drop it!"

The bamboo capsule fell, bounced once and rolled into the shadows against the wall. N'Daria crumpled to the floor in a dead faint. Kumo and the priest faced each other.

The sorcerer towered over the old man like a grotesque carven idol. His painted face was twisted with fury, and in his eyes was the naked evil of all the centuries. Père Louis' blood ran like ice in his veins; his old flesh crawled with horror. This was Satan made manifest. This was the true biblical phenomenon of diabolic possession, in the presence of which even prayer was stifled and faith rocked for one perilous moment on the razor-edge of despair.

But only for a moment.

Père Louis' hand closed over the rosary in his pocket. With a sharp commanding gesture he thrust the small wooden crucifix full in the face of the sorcerer. His voice was sharp as a sword blade in the old and terrible command:

"Retro me Sathanas! Get thee behind me, Satan!"

Kumo's body was wrenched with a sudden convulsive tremor. He yelped like an animal, and a small yellow foam spilled from the corners of his mouth. Then he turned and ran from the hut, and Père Louis stood rocking on his feet and listening to the thudding flight of the cassowary man under the dark drooping of the tangket trees.

Down in the Kiap house, Lee Curtis woke with a start to find Père Louis bending over him.

"Get up. Dress yourself. Light the lamp. I want to talk to you."

"What the devil!" Curtis rubbed his eyes and tried to orient himself. By rights the old priest should have been in his village, miles away. His presence on the plantation was the final straw in the day's burden of irritations and mysteries. "What's the trouble? What are you doing here?"

"Keep your voice down. Do as I say. I will talk to you when you are awake."

Stumbling and cursing softly, Lee Curtis dressed himself and lit the lamp, while Nelson, awakened by their voices, sat bolt upright on his bedroll and fumbled for his spectacles. Then, when they were settled in the small circle of light, Curtis said bluntly, "All right, Father, let's have it."

"First," said Père Louis, "I want to show you how Lansing was killed."

He held the bamboo tube up for their inspection.

"God Almighty!" stuttered Nelson. "Not another one."

Curtis leant forward to take the tube from his hand, but Père Louis drew it back sharply.

"Careful. This one is dangerous. Look!"

He tilted it under the lamp so they could see the small circle of air holes punched in the pithy cap.

"Now listen."

He shook the tube and held it first to Curtis's ear, then to Nelson's. They heard a tiny movement and friction against the walls of the barrel.

"What's that?" It was Nelson who put the question. Curtis was tight-lipped and thoughtful.

"Snake sorcery," said Père Louis simply. "Inside that tube is a small and deadly snake. The sorcerers catch them and imprison them in these tubes, sometimes with a fragment of the clothing of those they wish to murder. They irritate the snake with noise and movement and hunger, so that when it is released it will attack the first object on which it alights."

"Where did you get it?" Lee Curtis's voice was grim.

"From Kumo. Not ten minutes ago he tried to murder N'Daria in the laboratory up there. Fortunately I had heard him coming and was ready for him."

"He—he gave it to you?" Nelson was stammering with excitement and fear.

"Not exactly. I—I commanded him in the name of God. He fled from me and left the tube behind."

"Just like that," said Curtis softly.

"As you say, just like that."

"And the girl?"

"I left her in the hut. She is badly frightened but unharmed. But you see"—Père Louis leant forward and gestured emphatically—"we now have the picture complete. Nelson will have told you that Sonderfeld has in his possession the life juices of Kumo."

Curtis nodded.

"Through Kumo he murdered Lansing."

"And tried to murder the girl."

The old priest shook his head.

"No, that was a private matter—vengeance against the woman who had betrayed him. The rest is clear. Through Kumo, Sonderfeld can dominate the tribes. I am guessing at this, but I think that Sonderfeld will use the pig festival to have himself proclaimed by Kumo as the incarnation of the Red Spirit."

"Lansing thought the same thing. That's why he was killed."

"Of course."

Nelson burst in excitedly. "Then you've got all you want. Arrest Sonderfeld. Arrest Kumo. You've broken the trouble before it starts."

Curtis shook his head.

"It won't work, Nelson."

"Why not, for God's sake?"

"Evidence. I've got no evidence against Sonderfeld. I've got nothing against Kumo except attempted murder, and to make that one stick I've got to tip my hand to Sonderfeld."

"But you just can't sit here and—"

"Look, Nelson!" The boyish face was tired and lined with anxiety. "Look! When you're up here, you feel as though you're ten thousand years behind the times. You are, too, in a way. But just fifty miles over those hills is Goroka: civilization, the law, the twentieth century—and the United Nations. They've got a long reach; and whatever I think myself, whatever I'd like to do, I'm still amenable to them. Sonderfeld's the man I want. I can't get him until I stand him in a dock and produce evidence that a judge and jury will accept. At this moment I've got nothing—nothing at all."

"You've got Kumo."

"I want Sonderfeld."

Père Louis wagged his beard like a wise old goat and said gravely, "Curtis is right. Destroy Sonderfeld and there will be no more trouble in the valleys. But you cannot destroy him without evidence—and, I tell you, you will get no more than you have now."

"There's the girl. If she would talk . . . ?"

"After what she has endured tonight, she will not talk. I tell you that now. You could take her a hundred miles from here and she would not talk because she would still live in dread of the sorcerers."

"Time!" said Curtis suddenly. "Time is the problem. Whatever we do must be done before the pig festival. If not, we're going to have the biggest blowup for twenty years—punitive expeditions, the lot! Time, time, time!"

He beat his fist angrily into his palm in frustration and puzzlement.

"When is the pig festival?" asked Nelson.

"That's the trouble. We don't know. It's not a matter of dates, you see. The tribes are moving into the Lahgi Valley, the outer ones first, then the nearer. These folk down here could move tomorrow or the next day. Once they're all assembled, the elders and the sorcerers set the day for the big show—the rest is all preparation and buildup. After what's happened, I think Kumo and Sonderfeld will see that the big ceremony starts almost immediately. That's my problem, don't you see? I can't leave the place. I'd like to discuss it with my people at Goroka, but I can't."

"If I might make a suggestion?" said Père Louis mildly.

"Go ahead, Father. We're in a jam. I'll listen to anything that will help us out of it."

"Good!" The old man's voice was eager and sharp with authority. "This is what you will do. You will write a report now. I will help you do it to save time. Then you will send your best and most reliable runner over the mountains to Goroka. You will send him before dawn so that Sonderfeld will not know. It will take him—how long?"

"A day and a half—say forty hours. It's a long haul even for a good man."

"Very well. Who will deal with the matter at Goroka?"

"Oliver, I should think, George Oliver. He's the A.D.O. in charge of this territory. He was the man who opened it up."

"So! While you are waiting for Oliver, you will go about your duties in the normal fashion. You, Nelson, will concern yourself with the plantation and with nothing else. I shall return to my village and I shall say nothing about what has happened tonight. The girl will say nothing either. I have seen to that. Nothing will happen till the pig festival."

Curtis frowned in dissatisfaction.

"But that's the whole point. It's two days down and two days up—four days at the very best. What happens if Oliver doesn't get here in time?"

It was a long moment before Père Louis answered.

"Then, my friend, you will take your police boys and go up to the Lahgi Valley. To get there, you will have to pass through my village. I shall be waiting and I shall go up with you."

"And then?"

"Then," said Père Louis with a wry grin, "we shall trust in the power of God and a small stratagem of my own. I confess I am not happy about using it, but at the worst I shall do so."

"Do you mind telling me what it is?"

"I should prefer not to tell you . . . yet. But if your senior officer arrives in time, I shall tell him."

Curtis was irritated by this apparent reflection on his capacity. He challenged the little priest.

"Why tell Oliver and not me?"

"Because, my son," said Père Louis soberly, "you are a young man who is bearing with some courage a big responsibility. I do not wish to add to that responsibility the burden of a grave decision."

"What sort of decision?"

"The life or death of a man."

"But you'd let Oliver make it?" He was still fidgeting under the slight.

"Oh, yes," said Père Louis simply, "I would let Oliver make it. I know him, you see—he knows me. And both of us know the tribes. Now I suggest we write this report and send your messenger on his way."

Forty minutes later a fuzzy-headed police boy was trotting southward over the switchback trails that led to Goroka. He carried no rifle. His bayonet was strapped between his shoulders, and in his shining bandolier he carried the reports of Lee Curtis and Père Louis on the situation in the high valleys. His eyes rolled in his head and he licked his lips as he padded up the ridges and down into the black hollows of the defiles. He was a coastal boy from Madang. This country was strange and frightening to him. Its speech was strange to him and he had no talisman against its magic.

He was so scared that he did the fifty miles to Goroka in thirty-three hours.

Chapter Ten

GEORGE OLIVER was a disappointed man. He was forty-five years of age and he had reached the limit of his stretch—Assistant District Officer, third in the small pyramid of authority whose apex was the District Commissioner and whose base was the thin line of cadet patrol officers strung out over ten thousand square miles of half-controlled territory. He knew it and he knew why, but the knowledge was no salve to his pride.

More than twenty years of his life had been spent in the Territory and his record of service was unblemished. He had come as a cadet when the Highlands were a blank space on a green map, and he himself had opened up and brought under control more territory than any other single man in the service. His work during the Japanese occupation had earned him a D.S.O. and a Military Cross, and his knowledge of the tribes was intimate and encyclopedic. Yet promotion had passed him by. The higher honours of the service had been denied him. He knew now that they were beyond his reach.

The defect was in himself. He was no diplomat. He lacked the subtlety to sway with the eddies of politics, to profit from the influence of men whose experience and knowledge were less than his own, but who understood the devious shifts of the lobbies and the arts of patronage and preferment. His trenchant decisions were often unpalatable. His raw tongue had made him many enemies. So they left him, close at hand because they needed him, low in the scale of authority because they disliked and often feared him.

Yet there was much in him to love. He had charm and sympathy, rare justice and a cool courage, and he loved the rich, bursting island and its dark peoples with a deep, passionate attachment, unsoured even by his frustrated ambition. He was generous to his younger colleagues and he covered their mistakes even when he castigated their follies.

Now he sat in his small bare office at Goroka, a lean, compact man, with a tight face and a jutting jaw, and a firm, ironic mouth under the small cavalry moustache. He was a tidy fellow in his person as in his thought. His whites were starched and immaculate. His body, brown as a nut, had an air of disciplined cleanliness. His movements were few and carefully controlled. Absorbed as a student in his texts, he was reading the reports of Père Louis and Lee Curtis on the situation in Sonderfeld's valley.

The runner, sweating and exhausted, had been dismissed to his quarters, glowing with the curt approval of the Kiap, and George Oliver was alone. He was glad of the solitude. He needed it as other men need company, to refresh his spirit and clear his mind of trifles and distractions for concentration on the problem in hand.

The problem was far from simple. Lee Curtis's report, written in haste and anxiety, was not likely to appeal to the District Commissioner, a shrewd, subtle fellow, who liked his files kept dry and academic against the possibility of inquiry from Moresby or Canberra or an unscheduled mission from the United Nations. Père Louis' hasty addendum was no improvement. The District Commissioner had small sympathy with the Missions, and tribal magic was to him an anthropological oddity better ignored.

These, however, were minor things beside the problem of Sonderfeld himself. The big German stood well with the Administration. His services were a matter of record. The Administration had approved his tenancy. The Administration would be involved in any charges made against him and would be less than happy with the flimsy case presented by a half-trained youth and an eccentric French cleric.

Yet George Oliver knew that they were right. He had lived too long and too dangerously to be skeptical about tribal unrest and the fermenting influence of the sorcerers. As to Sonderfeld, there had been adventurers before him, and their bids for wealth and power were recorded in more than one bloody page of the history of the Territory.

He laid the reports on his desk, covered them carefully with a blotter and leant back in his chair, pondering.

First he must see the Commissioner and present the reports with his own summary of the situation. The Commissioner would accept it, because then the responsibility would be shifted to the shoulders of an unpopular subordinate—and because he knew that George Oliver was the best man to deal with an explosive situation like this one.

Then he would go up himself to the valley. He would take two police boys and a pair of cargo carriers. He might take twenty or fifty, but they would serve him no better than two against the massed violence of the assembled tribes. It was his job to forestall violence. He had done it before, he could do it again. It wasn't a question of strength but of courage and understanding and, above all, timing. His mouth relaxed into an ironic grin. They paid him few compliments; they gave him little thanks; but whenever they landed themselves in a mess—"Let George handle it!" He'd still be handling it when they pensioned him off with an O.B.E. to comfort his declining years. To hell with them! See the Commissioner and get it over. Get on the move again. There was nothing to hold him here but paper and red tape. He would feel better once he started slogging over the hills—brushing the dust off his heart, sweating the sourness out through the pores of his skin.

He was halfway to the door when he remembered Gerda Sonderfeld. He walked slowly back to his desk, fished in the drawer for a pack of cigarettes, lit one and sat on the edge of the table looking out his window at the trim lawn with its border of bright salvias.

Gerda Sonderfeld! She had dismissed him long ago with tender indifference, but she was still an ache in his heart and a slow fire in his blood. Of all the women he had ever met, this was the one with whom he had come nearest to love—the only one who had left him without clinging and without apparent regret.

It was an old, stale story that had begun during his brief tour of duty on relief in Lae and had ended when Sonderfeld returned from his first survey in the northern valleys. Yet it had touched him more deeply than he was prepared to admit, even to himself. The new Gazette had just been published and his name was not listed among the promotions. He was obsessed with a sense of futility and failure. He was lonelier than he had ever been in his life. He shunned the bar and the club and spent himself, without restraint, in the fierce hunger of a late romance. Gerda had given herself without question and without stint. Her passion charmed him, her rare, perceptive gentleness soothed him. Her uncalculating generosity was a constant surprise. When she dismissed him, his heart was wrenched and he felt empty and old and solitary.

Now he was going back—as her husband's executioner. He toyed with the sardonic thought but found no pleasure in it. Gerda had made no secret of her cold dislike of her husband; the secret lay in her refusal to leave him for any one of half a dozen men who would gladly have married her—George Oliver among them! He wondered how she would receive him now, how he would bear himself with her. If he indicted Sonderfeld, what then? Would she support her husband in loyalty or would she turn in love to George Oliver, the man who was sending him to criminal trial?

It was a fruitless question, but he worried it like a dog gnawing a dry bone. He told himself he should have more pride, but with the long, disappointing years ahead of him, he knew that pride was a threadbare coat with little warmth in it.

The cigarette burnt down till it scorched his fingers. A long tube of ash fell soundlessly on the desk. He brushed it carefully into the ashtray, stubbed out the butt and walked across the passage to see the District Commissioner.

The District Commissioner had the hard eyes of a politician and the soft voice of a bishop *in partibus infidelium*. He looked like a retired colonel, which he wasn't, and talked like a very canny businessman, which he was.

"These reports—" He tapped the stained, scrawled sheets which the runner had brought. "They're no earthly use to me. They say everything and nothing.

Curtis expects a revival of the cargo cult in the area under patrol. He believes Sonderfeld is in league with a man named Kumo to set it up. This belief is confirmed by unspecified evidence in the hands of the local missionary, Père—whatever his name is. Curtis expects serious trouble at the pig festival. He suggests we check Sonderfeld's background. What the hell does he mean by that? Sonderfeld was checked and double-checked before he was accepted as a migrant in Australia. If there's anything wrong with his background, that's the business of Immigration, not External Territories."

"Yes, sir," said George Oliver flatly.

There was a pit opening under his feet and one more thrust from the Commissioner would land him at the bottom of it. If Sonderfeld's background was shady, so would Gerda's be. If Sonderfeld were deported from the Territory and Australia, so would Gerda be. And he, George Oliver, would be the instrument of her ruin.

He was relieved when the Commissioner thrust the sketchy report back in his hand with a petulant command.

"Can't put that sort of stuff in the files. You keep 'em, Oliver. Give me, say, half a page of your own summary for the record—with your suggestions for appropriate action, then we'll deal with it. Yes?"

"No," said George Oliver.

"Oh? Why not?" He spread his palms and set his fingertips together in a gesture of clerical distaste.

"Because that leaves me holding the can, and I'm not paid to do that. You are."

The District Commissioner was nettled, but he knew better than to argue with this sardonic, grinning fellow who knew too many answers for his own good.

"I don't see that you have to be rude about it, Oliver."

"I'm not being rude. I'm stating a fact. I've been in the game too long. I'm tired of being bumped around. Those are the reports. What do you want to do about them?"

"It's your area, isn't it?"

"And yours."

"But you are in direct control. What do you suggest?"

"I'll go up there, take a look and report when I get back."

"What—er—force will you take?"

"Two police boys, two cargo carriers."

The District Commissioner looked relieved. Apparently Oliver didn't expect too much trouble.

"You don't think there's much to worry about then?"

"I didn't say that. Curtis already has his own detachment up there. Between the two of us we should be able to keep things in hand."

"I see. You know the area, of course."

The Commissioner pursed his lips and frowned over the small spire of his fingertips while he considered the next question. Oliver watched him with ironic amusement. The D.C. was worried. He had reason to be. And George Oliver had no reason to spare him the experience.

"Er—ah—with regard to Sonderfeld . . ."

"Yes?"

"These reports are a flat contradiction of our own knowledge of the man."

"How much do we know about him?"

"Well—ah—ah—the Immigration people must have checked his record before they accepted him. He did good service as a medical man in Lae. He's been very helpful over this malaria control business. It's not a great deal, of course, but—er—"

"No, it isn't."

"Dammit, man!" The Commissioner was suddenly and unreasonably angry. "What are you trying to do? Convict the man without evidence? I tell you there's a first-class scandal in this if ever—"

"I'm not trying to do anything," said George Oliver mildly. "I'm going up to investigate a situation that is reported to exist. Until I get there and look round, I can't tell you what I'm going to do or even whether there is a situation at all. If you want a memo to that effect, I'll give it to you before I go. Is there anything else?"

The Commissioner was beaten but couldn't afford to admit it.

He said curtly, "No, there's nothing else. You'll want to get away this evening, of course. But I warn you, Oliver, if you make a mistake on this one, I'll have your head."

"I'll give it to you—on a chafing dish."

George Oliver grinned sourly and went out. He had won a victory, but it was as tasteless as the dust of defeat.

One hour and twenty minutes later he was slogging over the first foothills northward to Sonderfeld's valley. He reckoned it would take him two days to get there. The runner had made the trip in thirty-three hours, but George Oliver had to think of his heart and his arteries.

He was forty-five years old. He was beginning to feel his age.

Kurt Sonderfeld was beginning to feel the strain. His plans had been laid a long time now, but as the day of their fulfillment approached, he was conscious of a mounting tension, a thrusting eagerness that battered against the barriers of his habitual control. His project had been framed in isolation and retirement; now he was hemmed in by people, familiar but unfriendly, polite but mistrustful, whom his courtesy could not charm or his cleverness wholly mystify.

Père Louis had stayed to breakfast and luncheon and dinner. He had slept a second night in the guest room and taken his departure at first light the following morning. He had paid careful respect to the memory of Max Lansing; he had shared, solicitously, the grief of his friends. For the rest, he had refused to involve himself in discussions with Sonderfeld and had interested himself in the small problems of Gerda's garden, the gossip of the plantation and the minor comedies of Curtis's census-taking.

Sonderfeld had tried, more than once, to reopen the question of the unrest in the valleys, but the old man refused to be drawn. There had been one rift between them. He did not care to risk another. Sonderfeld had the impression that the priest regretted his bluntness but dared not lose face by an open apology. His attitude towards Gerda was one of solicitude and paternal interest in her feminine affairs. He wondered vaguely if Père Louis were trying to convert her to the Church.

He was glad to see the last of the canny old cleric.

The attitude of Lee Curtis troubled him even more. The boy was terse and abrupt, refusing all invitations to drink or share a meal as if he wished to be spared the demands of courtesy to a host whom he disliked. The Kiap house and the village—these were his domain, and he kept to them religiously, as a monk to his cloisters.

Theodore Nelson was a different proposition. The round-faced Englishman was too seasoned a voyager to involve himself in the personal affairs of his company's clients. He made the rounds with Sonderfeld, talked volubly and accurately of pest control and double cropping and experimental strains and marketing problems; but he was blankly disinterested in any but professional subjects or the safe reminiscences of European exiles. His thick spectacles were a visor that hid his wary eyes and the fear that lurked behind them. He, too, was warmer in his attentions to Gerda, more gentle in his courtesy, more attentive to her quiet conversation. Sonderfeld asked himself if it were the beginning of a new attachment. He would have welcomed it as a useful diversion.

Gerda herself was as distant as the moon and just as cold. If she grieved for the death of Lansing, she gave no sign. If she suspected his own part in it, she made no show of resentment. She kept his house and tended her flowers and slept, unsmiling, the whole night through. She had walled herself round with indifference, and he was not yet ready to lay siege to her defense.

It seemed to Sonderfeld that Wee Georgie was the only one whose attitude towards him had not changed. The gross old reprobate shuffled and wheezed around him like a court jester, tattered and filthy in his motley, full of bawdy tales and sly obscenities, fawning at his frown, leering happily when Sonderfeld, for want of better company, bent to his shabby slave. But when he came to question him on his surveillance of N'Daria, Wee Georgie's face went suddenly blank.

"There was nothin', boss. Nothin' at all, I tell yer. Twice she went up to the bungalow to draw rations. That was all. The rest of the time she stayed in the laboratory. True as Gawd she did."

"But the nights. What did she do then?"

"Same thing, boss. Stayed in the hut. Never stirred a foot outside it."

Sonderfeld took hold of him by his shirtfront and shook him till his face was purple and his eyes were popping.

"You're lying to me, Georgie! Lying!"

"Why should I want to lie, boss?" Georgie choked and spluttered unhappily. "Why should I want to lie?"

"Because you were drunk! Because you don't know what she did."

"Even suppose I were—which I weren't—me girls were awake, weren't they? Think they'd let her get out without knowin'? They went to the carry-leg every night, whoring down the village the way they always do. But she wasn't there. They'd have seen her if she was, wouldn't they? Ask 'em yourself, if you don't believe me."

The logic of it was sound enough, but Sonderfeld refused to accept it.

"Did anyone talk to her? The priest perhaps? Or Curtis or Nelson? Or my wife?"

"How could they, boss? When she was in the hut the whole time. The missus might have had a few words with her when she went up to the house. But I doubt it. They haven't been speakin' for a while, have they? Anyway, why ask me when you can get it from the girl herself? So help me, if I'm lyin' you can cut me liquor ration! I can't say better than that, now can I?"

"No, Georgie, you can't." Sonderfeld's lips parted in a thin smile. 'And you know I'll do it, don't you? I'll have you screaming in torment in forty-eight hours. You know that, don't you?"

He turned on his heel and walked up the path towards the laboratory. Wee Georgie watched him go and licked his dry lips. Already he was regretting his offer to submit to trial by ordeal. His story was true as far as it went. The only part he hadn't told was the night when he and his two girls had huddled, cursing and scared, under the blanket listening to the footsteps of the cassowary bird and the low murmur of voices from the open door of the laboratory.

Halfway to the hut, Sonderfeld stopped to light a cigar. As he held the match, he noticed with surprise and irritation that his hand was trembling. He tossed away the match and stretched out his arm full length, his wrist rigid, splaying out his fingers like a fan. Still he could not control the tremor. He frowned and dropped his arm to his side.

He was disappointed in himself. Weakness like this was for other men, not for Kurt Sonderfeld. He was tired, of course. He had underestimated the pressures of the last few days. A small sedative and his nerves would be under control again. A sedative or—?

He smiled at the simplicity of the diagnosis. He had not had a woman in a long time. He was a potent man, but he had been so busy with affairs of importance that he had ignored the needs of his nature. Gerda's coldness had helped him to continence, and his desire for N'Daria had been tempered by his need to discipline her. Now she would serve him in a different fashion.

Slowly, and with infinite relish, he finished his cigar, standing in the warm sunshine, surrendering himself to the soft, crawling itch of desire. He had worked hard, he had planned meticulously, he had gambled against the folly and blindness of inferior men. He had only to wait a little longer and the winnings would tumble into his lap. He needed pleasure and relaxation—there was a woman waiting to give him both. He tossed away the stub of his cigar and went into the laboratory.

The first sight of N'Daria shocked him deeply. Her eyes were puffy. Her skin was grey and tired. Her movements were slack and listless. When he greeted her, she answered him mechanically, her voice empty of resentment or pleasure, and bent again to her notes. He remembered the urgent, pleading youth of her and was faintly disappointed.

But desire was still strong in him and he flattered himself with the thought that he could make such ravages on a woman and still repair them with a touch of his hand. Softly, restraining his eagerness, he began to coax her. She shivered at his touch and tried to draw away, but his grasp was too strong for her. She stiffened in revulsion, but he laughed softly and held her closer. Then slowly her body began to awaken and she was divided against herself.

Suddenly she clung to him, urging him, native fashion, by beating her body against his own. Then he lifted her in his arms and carried her into the sleeping room and made her teach him kunande and carry-leg, as if he were Kumo and she the bright and bird-like girl with the cane belt of courtship and the crown of green beetles and red feathers.

Spent at last, he lay beside her, wrapped in the soft, sad triumph of completion. . . .

After a long while he got up, dressed himself and walked out into the laboratory without a word or a backward glance. When he stretched out his hand again, it was as steady as a rock. He smiled and told himself that he was a sensible fellow who kept a wise balance between discipline and enjoyment.

He did not understand that Kurt Sonderfeld had already cracked under the strain.

Chapter Eleven

"ACHILLES . . ." Sonderfeld smiled tolerantly and pointed his cigar in the direction of the Kiap house. "Achilles is sulking in his tent. Unfortunately he is too young to make such gestures with any grace. He succeeds only in making himself ridiculous."

It was late in the afternoon—the afternoon of Oliver's departure from Goroka, the afternoon of his coupling with N'Daria. He was sitting on the stoop with Gerda and Nelson, relaxed, expansive, at ease with himself and his small world. Wee Georgie hovered in the background, shambling and solicitous.

The absence of Curtis was the only flaw in his pattern of contentment. It was a small loss, to be sure. The boy was callow, uninformed, gauche. It was not his absence but his refusal to attend that fretted Sonderfeld. It was an affront to his hospitality, a small reverse in the lengthening tally of victories.

Gerda and Nelson said nothing but watched him covertly over their drinks. Something had happened to the big man, but they could not put a name to it. His stringent control had slackened. His laugh was louder, his irritation more patent. His movements and his gestures were suddenly out of rhythm. The smooth-running machine was ever so little unbalanced, its beat was out of kilter, its bearings whined in protest.

Sonderfeld tossed off his drink and gestured to Wee Georgie to refill his glass. He turned to Nelson.

"Do you think, Nelson, it is because I have offended him?"

Nelson shrugged.

"Don't know. He hasn't said anything to me. He's very busy, of course."

"Busy! Busy!" His voice was harsh with anger and contempt. "A mission clerk could do in half a day what these fellows do with a dozen policemen and all the trappings of military authority. No, I will tell you what it is. It is one of the defects of the present system that sends these fellows—schoolboys most of them, half-trained, half-educated—into isolated areas and expects them to do a man's work. They are not prepared for it, mentally or physically. They are at an age when it is dangerous to live alone. They are armed with an authority beyond their strength. Small wonder that they become eccentric, cross-grained, a burden to themselves, a trial to those who are forced to have dealings with them."

Wee Georgie set a fresh drink at his elbow. Sonderfeld seized it and half emptied it at a gulp. Gerda watched him anxiously. She had never seen him like this before. She could deal with him sober, but drunk and out of control, there was no knowing how dangerous he might be. She shivered and looked inquiringly at Theodore Nelson. The small fluttering movement of his hand told her that he was helpless.

Then Wee Georgie caught her eye. He was standing behind Sonderfeld's chair and he jerked his thumb back and forth in the direction of the Kiap house. His meaning was plain. Gerda herself should go down and fetch Curtis.

Sonderfeld was frowning as he slipped the band off a new cigar and pierced the end with ritual care. His hands were trembling again and he fumbled uneasily with the small sharp instrument. Gerda stood up. She masked her uneasiness with a cool smile and addressed herself to Theodore Nelson.

"If Kurt is right—and I think he may be—we should be gentle with the young man. We are the older ones. It is our business to make the first approaches. I'll go down and talk to Mr. Curtis myself."

Sonderfeld looked up sharply. Then his tight mouth relaxed into a smile of tolerant approval.

"Good! Good! If he will come, I am prepared to forget his bad manners and welcome him back into the circle. My wife has many defects, Nelson, but she has all the talents of a diplomat. Go, my dear, and charm Achilles into the sunlight. Georgie—drinks for Mr. Nelson and myself."

Gerda smoothed her skirts and patted her hair into place and walked swiftly down the path to the Kiap house. A small icy finger of fear was probing at her heart.

Lee Curtis greeted her with surprise and pleasure and drew her into the cool half-light of the hut.

"Gerda! This is the nicest thing that's happened to me. What brings you here? Here, sit down. Make yourself comfortable."

The boyish warmth of his greeting touched her and she was filled with tenderness towards him, young, lost and afraid, but stiffening his courage to a man's work in a harsh and alien country. She seated herself in the canvas chair while he perched himself on an upturned box, eager and grateful for this small mark of her favour.

476

"I've been wanting to see you, Gerda. But I've had to keep away. I'm—I'm not very good at hiding my feelings and—well—it seemed safer."

"I know that. But now I want you to come."

"Why?"

"Because my husband is irritable, unsettled. Your absence annoys him. He's drinking more than he usually does."

"Oh!" His hurt was so obvious that it touched her to pity and she leant forward to lay a cool hand on his wrist.

"That isn't the only reason, believe me. I want you there, too. I'll be glad of your company. I won't be so afraid if you're there."

"Afraid of what?"

"I don't know. I wish I did. Kurt is changed. Always before he was so controlled, so much master of himself that nothing seemed to touch him. Now he is uneasy, restless. His whole manner is different. His voice is louder. He does not trouble to conceal his thoughts. I—"

"He's scared."

"Perhaps. But I am afraid, too. I know him so well, you see. I have seen the cruelty of which he is capable."

"Has he—been cruel to you?"

The young mouth tightened, the eyes were suddenly grim.

"No. But don't you see? It isn't that only. I am so isolated. When the pig festival comes, you will leave us and I shall be alone, completely alone. If Kurt succeeds in this crazy plan of his, what then?"

"I'll look after you, Gerda, I promise you."

Then he was at her side, his arms about her shoulders in a protective gesture, his eyes tender, his lips brushing her cheeks. There was so much simple love in him that she had not the heart to reject him. He drew her to her feet and held her to him and kissed her lips and cradled her head awkwardly on his shoulder. She was warm to him, but there was no passion in her response and she drew away as quickly as she could.

He pleaded with her.

"I love you, Gerda. You know that now, don't you? You understand that I won't let anything happen to you. We've got more than half a case against your husband now, and when George Oliver comes up—"

The words were out before he remembered that this was to be a secret between himself and Nelson and Père Louis. Gerda's face went grey; her mouth dropped open; her eyes stared blankly. Her voice was a frightened whisper.

"George Oliver?"

"That's right. He's the A.D.O. at Goroka. He's my boss. It was to be a secret, but I don't see that it matters if you know. Père Louis and I sent reports to him. He's probably on his way now. . . . I say, are you sick? You look awful."

"No, no! I'm all right. Just let me sit down and give me a drink of water."

He settled her solicitously in the chair and turned away to fill a mug from the canvas water bag hanging in the doorway. Gerda closed her eyes and tried vainly to marshal her scattered thoughts.

George Oliver! One love remembered from the many now forgotten. One warmth remembered out of all the cold and barren years. The one regret from all the loveless laughter. Now he was coming back—not for her, but for her husband. She remembered his brooding eyes and his hurt mouth and the droop of his tired shoulders when he turned away for the last time.

"Drink this. It'll make you feel better."

Lee Curtis was squatting beside the chair offering the pannikin of water like a lover's token. She sipped it slowly, veiling her eyes from him lest he should read his own rejection before she had time to prepare him for it.

"Thank you, my dear. I am better now."

He took the tin cup from her hands and moved away a pace or two to set it on the table. When he came back, she was standing up, smoothing her frock, patting her hair with the old familiar, intimate gesture. He watched her, puzzled and half afraid. Then she took his hands in hers and spoke softly and with compassion.

"Lee, you have paid me a very great compliment. I shall remember it all my life. But I am not for you. I am too old, for one thing. For another, I know that I could never make you happy. No, listen to me, please—" He opened his mouth to speak, but she closed it with the palm of her cool hand. "You are too young to bind your life to that of a woman who has lived as I have. I have loved many men. I am married to a man I hate. The burden of a past like that would crush you and you would come to hate me. I could not bear that. Besides . . ." Now she knew she must say it, as much for herself as for him. She might deny it later, she probably would, but here in the shadows of the Kiap house she must make affirmation of the last shred of faith left to her. "Besides, I am in love with George Oliver."

For a long time he stood there, head drooping, his body slack, his hands plucking helplessly at the seams of his trousers. When at last he straightened up, his mouth was twisted into a tremulous, youthful grin.

"Well, that's it. I daresay I can take it, given time. Now wait till I spruce up, and I'll drink myself silly on your husband's grog."

He washed his face and straightened his hair, changed his shirt and buckled on his belt, and then walked with her back to the bungalow. His heart was empty and his brain was tired; he felt like a man who had wakened suddenly from a nightmare and groped frantically for a handhold on reality. But his back was straight and his head was high, and he greeted Kurt Sonderfeld with a smile.

Cadet Patrol Officer Lee Curtis had entered into man's estate.

Once again they were dining together in the candlelit room with its vista of stars and dark mountains, while the kundus thundered up from the valley and the chant rose and fell into crests and hollows of melody. Once again there was the warmth of wine and the savour of fine food and the smell of flowers and the shifting play of flames on silver and crystal.

But there were ghosts at the banquet—the ghost of Max Lansing, querulous, demanding, disappointed, inescapable; the crackling echo of Père Louis' voice, interpreting the signs and the portents; the monstrous tossing shadow of Kumo the Sorcerer, symbol of all the dark evil of the valleys. There were ghosts at the banquet and their presence could not be ignored, their voices could not be stifled.

The talk eddied uneasily round the quartet at the table, lapsed and stirred again as Sonderfeld, flushed and emphatic, commanded their attention to a new subject or an old argument. He had been drinking deeply and steadily since the end of the afternoon and he was by turn truculent and goading, or given to fantastic condescensions and wild laughter. Gerda was shocked and helpless, afraid to provoke him, ashamed for herself and her guests. Theodore Nelson kept his eyes on his plate and tried vainly to escape the attention of his host. But Sonderfeld nagged at him with perverse amusement and soon reduced him to mumbling confusion.

Then he turned his attention to Lee Curtis. His big voice boomed in drunken mockery.

"Now, Curtis, you are among friends. You can afford to be frank. Tell me, have you never found yourself tempted to try the village women?"

"Kurt, please—"

"No, my dear, you must not be prudish. It does not become you. Mr. Curtis is a man of the world—even if a very young one. He lives much alone. He would be the first to admit his need of the satisfactions of the flesh. Well, my friend?"

Curtis flushed with anger, but he kept a tight hold on himself.

He said, coldly, "So far I haven't been interested."

"Yet some of them are beautiful, are they not? Scrape off the pig fat, take the lice out of their hair, wash them well with soap and water, don't you think they would grace your bed as well as—say, Gerda here?"

"I—I—I say, old man . . ." Nelson began to stammer a half-hearted protest.

Curtis cut him short with a gesture.

"If you'll leave your wife's name out of it, Sonderfeld, I'll answer your question."

"Forgive me!" Sonderfeld waved a regal hand. "I offend you. I mentioned Gerda simply for comparison. She is beautiful, is she not? I believe other men find her desirable. I did myself once. However, we will omit her from the proposition. You will admit that in certain circumstances dark flesh might be very desirable?"

"Possibly."

"To you?"

"I doubt it."

"And yet there are cases on record of—shall we call them lapses?—even among your own colleagues."

"Not within my experience."

"But then"—Sonderfeld's voice dropped to a low purring pitch of calculated insult—"you are so very young, Curtis. Your experience is so very limited. How can you say what the years may do to you? How can you promise that you will not sicken of hothouse fruit and turn to the wild vine and the apples of Sodom? What would you say if I told you that I, myself, have tasted them and found them sweet?"

"I would remind you," said Curtis bluntly, "that it's an offense against Territory law to cohabit with native women. I'd also remind you that you've had too much to drink. I suggest it's time you started to sleep it off."

"Gott im Himmel!" Sonderfeld crashed his fist on the tabletop, so that the glass shattered and the cutlery danced and rattled under the flickering candle flames. "In my own house, at my own table, I am reprimanded by a puppy!"

"I didn't ask to come," said Curtis quietly. "I didn't expect to be insulted."

"No, that's true."

As suddenly as it had come, his anger seemed to leave him. His features composed themselves into a mask of smiling approbation. Ignoring the wreckage on the table, he leant forward in the attitude of a great gentleman delivering a careful compliment.

"You know, Curtis, I like you. You have more brains than I gave you credit for. You have courage, too. Do you never feel that you are wasted in this pitiful routine—poking through the valleys, sitting in judgment on childish disputes, listening to childish lies, making little lists of folk who will be dead in two years, writing reports that no one ever reads?"

"No, I don't."

"But you are, you know. Look!" He slewed round, unsteadily, in his chair and flung his arm out in a forensic attitude towards the picture window that framed the stars and the black barrier of the mountains. "Out there is the last unknown country on the map of the world. Behind those mountains there is wealth undreamed of, gold and oil and manpower, to turn this wilderness into a paradise. There are a million men in the valleys waiting for a leader, ten thousand drums waiting to burst into the march of the conqueror. And you have—what? Ten thousand Europeans and a shabby charter from the United Nations. Look at it, man! Look and look again and tell me whose way is right—yours or mine?"

"What is your way, Sonderfeld?"

The question was soft and innocent, but it had the impact of a bullet. Sonderfeld's hieratic attitude was gone in an instant. His face twisted into a grin; his eyes were cunning and wary as an animal.

"Oh, no, Curtis! I am not so big a fool! Why should I peddle my visions to the blind and shout my message to the deaf? Go back to your hut! Suck your pencil stub and scribble your little notes and wait for the thunder and the lightning that will strike you dead!"

He heaved himself from his chair and lurched unsteadily to the door. Then he turned and looked at them. His face was distorted, his lips slobbered, his

480

eyes were sullen and bloodshot. His voice was hoarse with liquor and excitement.

"The cassowary men are abroad in the valleys. They run from village to village with the news of the great coming. There is a name spoken that is louder than the drums. There is a chief promised who will raise the tribute of the valleys, who will sweep from the Sepik to the Huon Gulf, and the name of the chief is—is—"

He broke off. He seemed suddenly to understand where he was and what he was saying. They saw him struggling for control, shaking his head to clear it of the liquor fumes, composing his flushed features into a travesty of smiling charm. He steadied himself against the doorjamb and surveyed them with something of the old mockery. Then he made them a little bow and left them. They heard him stumbling out onto the veranda, down the steps and onto the path that led to the laboratory.

Then they looked at each other with relief and with horror, and in the eyes of each was the same unspoken verdict.

Gerda buried her face in her hands and sobbed. Lee Curtis patted her shoulder awkwardly and made a sign to Nelson to wait for him on the veranda. He hesitated a moment, as if unwilling to be left alone, then he went out, polishing his glasses, peering anxiously into the shadows as if afraid that Sonderfeld might be waiting to leap upon him out of the darkness.

Slowly, painfully, Gerda recovered herself. She dried her eyes on Curtis's handkerchief and took the cigarette that he offered her. She smoked a few moments in silence until her hands stopped trembling and her tight nerves began to relax. Then she turned to him with a simple, pathetic question.

"What am I going to do, Lee? Tell me, please."

"Wait. That's all you can do. Wait till George Oliver gets here."

"But Kurt . . . ? You saw him. What . . . ?"

"He was drunk. He'll sober up before morning."

"He was mad. You know that as well as I do."

"There's no one here to certify him, Gerda."

"But what am I to do?" It was a cry of terror wrung from her by the sudden press of memories she had thought buried forever—memories of Rehmsdorf and the gas chambers and the protracted torment of the damned and the dispossessed.

"Nothing. Nelson and I will stay here tonight, in the guest room. You've only to raise your voice and we'll come running. Besides, he may not even come back. He may decide to sleep it off in the laboratory."

She saw him then with new eyes. She saw him tempered, as steel is tempered, violently and abruptly in fire and water, to a new strength and hardness. The soft lines of youth had disappeared. His mouth and his eyes were hard and the skin of his cheeks was tight as vellum on a drum. This was what must have happened to George Oliver—this and things like it—until youth was dead and there were no illusions left and the heart was empty of all but strength.

She came to him then and took his face in her hands and kissed him gently on the lips, and though he knew that she was kissing another man, he did not resent it. He took her arm and led her out onto the veranda where Theodore Nelson was waiting for them.

For all his huckster's shrewdness, for all the bright burnish that travel had given him, the round-faced, myopic fellow was of indifferent courage. He drove hard bargains for the men who stood behind him in business. He made profit for scant payment in the casual commerce of the bed. His mind was a card index of facts and figures and dossiers of people who might be useful to him. He was amusing when he cared to be, brusque and inconsiderate when his comfort or convenience were involved. He had travelled the world in pursuit of one star, apparently unaware that it was a gaudy pasteboard pinned to his own navel. Inside, he was as hollow as a coconut.

He had made his alliance with Lee Curtis because, despite his youth, the patrol officer represented the big battalions. Now, when the treaty seemed to demand service in return for protection, he wanted to dissolve it as soon as possible. Sitting alone in the darkness, listening to the beat of the drums, he had framed his proposition with some care. Now he laid it before Lee Curtis.

"Have you told Mrs. Sonderfeld about the—er—arrangements?"

"About Oliver coming up? Yes. There was no good reason why she shouldn't hear about it."

"Good. When do you expect Oliver to get here?"

"Late tomorrow, possibly. More than likely the following morning."

"Will he be bringing more police with him?"

"I should think so. Depends on what's available in the pool at Goroka. Why?"

"Well—er—I have a very tight schedule, as you know. Lots of places still to see in the Territory. Then I have to get back to Sydney to catch a ship for Colombo—"

"Yes?"

The monosyllable wasn't encouraging, but Theodore Nelson stuck to his script.

"Well, I'm not much use to you here. This sort of fandango isn't my choice of entertainment. So I thought—er—with Oliver on the way, you'd be able to give me a couple of police boys for escort back to Goroka. I could leave first thing in the morning."

"You could leave tonight."

"Well, there's not that much hurry. But, of course, if you thought . . ."

"You want to know what I think, Nelson?"

"What?"

Curtis's voice was a savage lash of anger and contempt.

"I think you're a yellow-livered bastard. So far as I'm concerned, you can get out any time you like—alone!"

"You have a duty to protect me. That's the understanding on which the company . . ."

"You're being protected. You're sitting on this veranda with your belly full of food and whisky. What more do you want?"

"There's trouble blowing up. If you can't guarantee my safety, then I demand to be sent back under escort."

"I can't spare an escort. Besides, the southern tracks are as safe as King's Cross—a damn sight safer, come to that. The trouble's up there, fifteen, twenty miles north. You'll be going the other way. I'll give you two days' rations and you can sleep in the Kiap houses. That's the best I can do. Make up your own mind."

Before Nelson had time to frame his reply, the drums stopped abruptly. The sudden silence was as commanding as a trumpet blast. Tense, expectant, they peered out across the valley. They saw no movement. Even the trees and the feathery bamboos hung still in the windless air. Then, distant but distinct, they heard the crescendo beat of the running cassowary.

"What's that?" Gerda whispered the question close to Curtis's ear.

"Cassowary," said Curtis flatly.

"Kumo?"

"Probably."

"What do you mean—Kumo?" Nelson's voice was a husky croak. "A man doesn't run like that. He couldn't."

"I know," said Curtis quietly.

"Then what the devil . . . ?"

Curtis was silent a moment, as if debating whether to answer. When he spoke, it was with a sort of calculated calm.

"I can't tell you very much because I don't know. It's common belief among the tribes that certain sorcerers have the power to change themselves into cassowaries and travel between the villages faster than a man could possibly run. I've heard accounts from reliable men, old hands, missionaries, that point to such things actually happening. I've never heard one who was prepared to deny it flatly. Two things I do know." He paused a moment, listening to the drumming crescendo. "The first is that that's a cassowary out there. And yet . . . the cassowary never travels at night."

"What does it mean?"

"I don't know. I've half a mind to go down and find out."

"No, please!" Gerda clung to him desperately.

"You can't leave us here. It's your duty to protect us."

"Oh, for God's sake, Nelson!"

For a few moments he sat, undecided whether to go or stay, then he decided with some relief that there would be little profit and possibly a great loss in an abortive effort to confront the sorcerer. Even if he succeeded, what could he say or do? Sonderfeld was the man he wanted, and already Sonderfeld had played halfway into his hands. He relaxed in his chair, lit two cigarettes, handed one to Gerda and listened to the steady chuff-chuff-chuff of the great earthbound bird that never travelled at night.

When they reached the village, the footbeats stopped, and for twenty minutes or more there was silence, broken only by the small crepitant noises of the night and the low murmur of their own desultory talk. Then, from down in the village, came a wild shout of triumph whose echoes rang startlingly across the sleeping valley. Then the drums broke out again, and the singing—a new rhythm and a new chant, savage, exultant, rolling like thunder round the ridges and the peaks.

"To hell with it!" said Lee Curtis. "Let's go to bed. We share the guest room, Nelson. Four-hour watches. If Gerda calls, wake me immediately."

"You can't give me orders like that!" Nelson's voice was high and petulant.

"I give 'em, you take 'em. If not, you spend the night in the Kiap house— alone. Come on, Gerda, you've had enough for tonight. It won't look half so bad in the morning."

Together they walked into the house with Theodore Nelson at their heels like a frightened puppy. At the door of her room she kissed him lightly and left him.

He went straight to the guest room and flung himself, fully dressed, in the armchair, leaving Theodore Nelson to sleep the first four hours of the night watch.

At two in the morning Sonderfeld had still not returned, so he woke Nelson and sat him, grumbling and ill-tempered, in the chair, while he himself stretched out on the bed for a few hours of uneasy slumber.

But Nelson was a man who needed his rest. He nodded and dozed fitfully and finally slept, forgetting even to awake Curtis to relieve him.

When morning came, they found that Sonderfeld was gone, taking N'Daria with him, and that the whole village was moving out to the pig festival.

Chapter Twelve

THEY POURED OUT OF THE VALLEY like an army on the march.

Plumed and painted, armed with stone axes and clubs and bows and arrows, the warriors strode out to the beat of the black kundus. Their marching song was a long repetitive ululation, counterpointed to the pattern of the snakeskin drums. The sound echoed and re-echoed till it hung like a moving haze of melody along the shoulders of the mountains.

Behind the warriors came the unmarried girls dressed in their finery, their blood pulsing in time with the kundus, their flesh fired by the sight of the sweating male bodies rippling and swaying in the stamping gait of the march. Between them were the pigs—some carried trussed on long poles, others leashed and led like dogs, while the laughing, screaming children prodded them with sticks to urge them to greater speed. They grunted and snuffled and squealed, and the sound was a new theme in the wild orchestration of the tribal triumph.

Then came the married women, old and young, their bodies bowed under the weight of suckling children and huge string baskets filled with taro and paw-paws and bananas. They, too, were decked in unaccustomed finery, with necklets of green snail shell and pubic skirts of fresh taro leaves. They giggled and gossiped and took up the refrain in short breathless bursts of song. For them the pig festival was a rare release from the domestic slavery into which they had lapsed when their kunande days were over and they shed the cane belt and the ornaments of courtship.

The procession wound through the defiles like a long, bright snake. It formed into a solid, shouting phalanx when they broke out of the jungle into broad patches of kunai grass, and drummed up the rises onto the high spine of

485

the ranges. They were the last to come to the assembly of the tribes. It was part of their pride to make an impressive entrance into the broad, green crater of the Lahgi Valley.

When they topped the final rise, they halted and reassembled and looked down into the broad, rich basin that was the cradle of their race. Here was the spreading village of the tribe paramount, grown now to double its normal size, with new huts and long kunande houses for the reception of the guests. Here were the broad taro plots, crisscrossed by the sluggish runnels of the irrigation ditches. There was the long formal avenue of the dancing place and, at the end of it, a great palisade pen of casuarina wood to hold the pigs that would be slaughtered at the festival.

The village was alive with plumed and painted figures, misty with the smoke of a hundred cooking fires, and murmurous with the gossip of a dozen valleys. A small knot of elders was moving towards the main entrance of the compound, ready to offer formal welcome to the last-comers and receive the pigs and the taro that were their tribute to the festival.

When the watchers on the hill caught sight of them, they set up a great shout that rang and echoed round the crater rim, to be answered by another cry that drifted up from the village like a wind. Then the luluai gave a sharp command. The drummers dressed their ranks; the warriors hefted their axes and their clubs. The women took a tight grip on their children and their baskets. The unmarried hoisted the pig poles on their shoulders and waited.

There was a moment of tense silence. Then the drums broke out, and the singing—a mighty roar that crashed like thunder over the valley as the plumed and painted army rolled down the green slope to the meeting of the tribes.

Lee Curtis stood on the veranda of Sonderfeld's bungalow and stared across the empty valley. Gerda was with him, and Nelson, and Wee Georgie. Below him, on the lawn, the police boys were drawn up waiting the order to march. It was three in the afternoon. The silence and the emptiness were strange to them—strange and frightening after the disciplined activity of the normal plantation days. There were no labourers among the coffee rows. The new clearing was deserted. There was no smoke from the village. No chattering garden boys clipped the lawns or raked the river gravel on the paths. Even the houseboys had left them, and the bungalow was a hollow, echoing shell.

Curtis finished his cigarette and flicked the stub over the bamboo rail. Then he gave them his final instructions.

"You'll stay around the house until Oliver arrives. He may come tonight. Personally, I don't expect him till tomorrow morning. I don't think you'll have any trouble—in fact, I'm sure you won't—but, just in case, I want you to stay together. Understand?"

The others nodded agreement but said nothing. On the face of it, what was there to say?

Curtis continued briskly.

"You'll sleep at the house, Nelson. Same with you, Georgie—and lay off the liquor or I'll run you in on a charge of sleeping with tribal women!"

Wee Georgie grinned and tugged his shaggy forelock.

"I'm leaving you one rifle and fifty rounds. That's all I can spare. Gerda, you'll look after that."

Nelson flushed at the snub but made no reply.

"When Oliver comes, tell him I've gone up to the Lahgi Valley. I'm picking up Père Louis on the way, and we'll camp tonight on the lip of the crater. I'll wait for him there, unless they turn on the big ceremony sooner than I expect. In that case I'll move into the village. Is that clear?"

"I'll tell him," said Gerda simply. "Is there anything else?"

"No. That's the lot. Take it easy and don't worry. Whatever happens will be twenty miles away. I count on having it under control before you hear a whisper back here."

"Er—care for a drink before you go, Mr. Curtis?" said Wee Georgie, licking his dry lips.

"No, thanks, Georgie. I'm on duty."

He grinned boyishly, hitched up his pistol belt and held out his hand to Gerda.

"Good luck, Gerda. Good luck with Oliver, too."

"Good luck, and thank you, Lee."

Ignoring Nelson's offered hand, and with a friendly pat on Wee Georgie's drooping shoulder, he left them and walked swiftly down the steps to the lawn.

The police boys snapped to attention. The fuzzy-wuzzy sergeant came to the salute. Curtis barked an order. They shouldered arms like guardsmen, and the next moment saw them striding down the path—a tiny army of black-skinned mercenaries, led by a stripling boy.

Gerda Sonderfeld stood watching them until they disappeared in the turning of the valley, then without a word she walked into the house and shut herself in the bedroom.

Wee Georgie stuck his thumbs in his string belt and puffed out his belly like a great, happy toad.

"What would you say to a drink—eh, Mr. Nelson?"

George Oliver was still plugging over the high saddles of the southward ranges. He was making good time. He expected to arrive in Sonderfeld's valley shortly before midnight. He grinned wryly as he remembered his constant lectures to the young patrol officers on the costly folly of forced marches. If they had to meet trouble, they should meet it fresh. Tired men make mistakes of judgment and timing. Weary bodies fall easy prey to the parasitic infections of the wild valleys.

His own body was bone tired. Weariness was lead in his marrow and a stink on his brown, sweating skin. His feet were swollen in his soft boots and his throat was parched like a lime pit. As he walked, he rinsed his mouth with water and spat the residue on the ground. That was another lesson in his syllabus. A tired man cannot march with liquid slopping around in his stomach.

He looked round at the police boys and the cargo carriers. They were dragging their feet with weariness, panting with effort to match his steady slogging pace. He was driving them as hard as he was driving himself—but they were loaded with packs and rifles while he had his shoulders free.

When they dropped down into the shadows of a narrow valley and came to the edge of a small creek, he halted them for a brief rest. They slipped off their packs, laid their rifles against a rock and threw themselves flat on their bellies, scooping up the water with their cupped hands.

George Oliver sat propped against the rock face and smoked a cigarette.

Times like these, he thought, were the happiest of his life. He was alone, master of himself and of the situation of the moment. He need not defer to the opinions of the uninformed, or bend to the pressures of the diplomats and the politicos. Success was sweeter because it was seasoned with his own sweat. Even failure was bearable when it came from the strength of the opposition and not from the folly of colleagues or the blindness of superiors.

But a man could not always be alone. The time would come when his strength would fail him and he would be forced to turn to the comfort of a community in which he had no firm place, the support of friendships, rare in his lonely life. It was easier when a man was married. There was love and companionship, sometimes a family. There was a pride of possession and a place of refuge. There was the small but decent kingship of his own household.

So, by inevitable conjunction, his thought came back to Gerda Sonderfeld.

He knew now that he still loved her. Else why was he driving himself on this crazy, breakneck march over the mountains? He had travelled slower to more urgent meetings than this with Père Louis and Lee Curtis. He could, if he chose, make camp for the night and still arrive in time for the critical performance of the pig festival. What else but love compelled him to the final trial of her heart and his own, to the abasement of the beggar and the imminent despair of the rejected?

He hoisted himself stiffly to his feet, shouted an order to the boys and stood over them while they loaded the packs and adjusted the webbing straps for the last, stiff haul. Then he grinned at them and jerked his thumb towards the farther hills.

"Come! We will show the mountain men how we can march."

Soon they were back into the plodding rhythm of the road, and the dusty paths were falling away beneath them while the shadows lengthened and the slow chill of the mountains crept into their bones.

When they came to the last great shoulder that stood like a black sentinel on the southern limit of Sonderfeld's domain, Oliver called another halt. The stars hung low in the velvet arch of the sky—so low and so bright it seemed he had only to reach up and pluck them like silver fruit. There was no moon. The air was keen as a knife blade, and he shivered as the chill struck him after the warm exertion of the trek.

The boys squatted on the ground, glad of the respite, chewing betel nuts and asking themselves whether the Kiap would let them rest in the valley or whether he would thrust them farther into the dark and tedious mountains. The Kiap was a hard man and an ill one to cross. Their eyes followed him as he walked to the edge of the plateau and stood looking down at the broad valley, locked between the black arms of the mountains.

He saw it first as a dark and brooding pool refusing even the reflection of the cold stars. He heard it first as a silence, for there were no drums and the singers were far away. He felt it as an emptiness, from which even the pungent smoke of the village fires was long since blown away and lost. Then he saw the light—a tiny yellow pinpoint, far away at the bottom of the shadowy lake. It was so small, so faint and pitiful, that it moved him almost to tears—as if it were a star at the bottom of a well or a last brave hope in the black desert of despair.

The tribes had left the valley. He had come later than he wished, to assert the authority of the Kiap law. There was a light in the bungalow. Gerda was there. He asked himself with sour irony whether he had come too late for love.

Then, because he was a tidy fellow, he put the thought away and set himself to consider the situation in the light of Curtis's report and his own knowledge. The villagers had moved out. They always moved at sunrise, so they had been gone at most two days—possibly only one. If the villagers were gone, Sonderfeld was gone also, since the success of his project depended on his presence at the festival.

Curtis would have moved out. Père Louis would be waiting in his own village. That left Wee Georgie, the coffee fellow—whatever his name was—and Gerda. Two men and a woman waiting for the curtain to rise on a primitive drama of ambition, sorcery and lust.

To hell with it! He was dramatizing the situation to make it fit his mood—a dangerous luxury which had brought more than one luckless fellow an arrow in the guts or a stone ax crashing into his skull.

He called the boys to their feet and together they walked down the long, winding path that led to the tiny yellow light in the center of the valley.

Wee Georgie was drunk and snoring on the veranda. Theodore Nelson tossed restlessly behind the locked door of the guest room. Gerda Sonderfeld sat alone in the lamplight and waited for George Oliver to arrive.

In spite of Lee Curtis's warning not to expect him before morning, the conviction was strong in her that he would come that same night. It was as if she were plotting the stages for him, willing him to be at this point or that in time to make the final landfall before midnight. It was folly and she knew it, just as it was folly to expect love to survive the shock of such humiliation as she had inflicted on George Oliver—not a boy, like Lee Curtis, but a lonely, tired man with a bitter strength and a perverse dignity. It was folly, too, to believe that, after so much profanation in the name of love, she herself could ever come to the enjoyment of the fruits of love. Love—so simple a reality to which others came, effortless, unknowing, but, for herself, a peak beyond attainment. Folly! Yet what was left to her but folly, with Kurt raving after his crazy crown, and Curtis gone, and Père Louis solicitous for the needs of his own flock so that he had little time for the lost, contrary lamb still bleating in the dark desert? What was left but folly and folly's dream to rest her heart on as she dozed over the tabletop and waited for George Oliver to come?

She woke to the sound of his footsteps on the veranda, and when she leapt up, in sudden fear, she saw him standing in the doorway.

"Hullo, Gerda!"

"George! Thank God!"

Her heart cried out to him, but she stood motionless as a statue. She saw him, rocking with weariness, his face lined and haggard, his eyes bloodshot, his clothes dusty and stained with sweat—and yet her feet would not carry her to him and her slack hands were empty of comfort.

For a long moment he stood looking at her, drooping and tired, then he straightened up and his voice was dry with dust and fatigue.

"When did the tribe move out?"

"This morning."

"Where's Curtis?"

"Left this afternoon. He's picking up Père Louis. They'll wait for you on the lip of the crater. He said—"

"Where's your husband?"

"Gone."

"When?"

"Early this morning. He's mad, George. We think he left with Kumo and—"

"That's all I need to know for the present."

He stood a moment, eyes closed, weighing the facts, then apparently satisfied, he relaxed once more. He lurched into the room, pulled out a chair and sat down heavily.

"Have you got a drink? I'm dog tired." He grinned wearily, brushing his grey face with the back of his hand. "Fifty miles in thirty-eight hours. Not bad for an old stager."

She came to him then—came with little running steps from the far side of the table. She wanted to throw her arms around him and kiss him on the lips and on his tired eyes, but she dared not. Instead she took off his slouch hat and unfastened the webbing pistol belt and knelt to loosen the boots from his swollen, blistered feet. He suffered the service with the thankless resignation of a man too tired to care. He was slumped across the table, head pillowed on his arms, his breath coming in long, sobbing gasps. She laid a tentative hand on his dusty greying hair, but if he felt it he gave no sign.

She brought him whisky and soda and watched while he drank two stiff

490

drinks in succession and sat silently till the slow, illusory strength flowed back into his body.

"Thanks," he said flatly. "Thanks, I needed that."

"Have you eaten, George?"

He nodded absently.

"On the road. I've told my fellows to camp in your boy houses, do you mind?"

"Of course not. You—you're staying then?"

She tried to conceal her eagerness, but her voice was shaky and she stammered over the question. He answered in the same flat, listless voice.

"Yes, I'll sleep the night here and push off in the morning. Nothing will happen till the day after tomorrow."

"Are you sure of that?"

"Yes. The big ceremony comes last of all. There's a ritual of preparation first."

"Lee Curtis seemed to think—"

"Lee Curtis is new. He doesn't know everything."

His voice was edged with irritation. Without waiting for an invitation, he splashed another drink into his glass and drank, more slowly this time. Then he set it down, half finished, and lifted his eyes, studying her feature by feature as if seeing her for the first time.

Now, she thought, it would come—the tired mockery, the knife pricking at the one tender spot in her heart, the pressure on the hilt, slow and calculated, the blade sliding in, the brief but final agony before love was slain and faith and hope died with it. Silent and rigid, she sat with downcast eyes, waiting. When he spoke, his voice seemed to come from a great distance.

"You'd better give me the whole story. The reports I got were pretty scrappy."

So the execution was to be deferred. George Oliver was a good official. He would postpone his private pleasures until the business of the state was dispatched. She felt no relief—only a chill calm. She raised her eyes and saw that he was lighting a cigarette and that his hands were unsteady. He pushed the pack across to her.

"Have one yourself."

"Thanks."

He did not offer her a light, so she reached across for the matchbox, lit up, pushed the box back across the shining tabletop and smoked for a few moments while she collected her thoughts.

Then she told him.

So that he would understand fully, so that there would be no doubt at all in his mind when he came to the moment of execution, she told him from the beginning—the far beginning when Sonderfeld was Reinach and Gerda was Gerda Rudenko and there was still hope in the world and love had not yet become a folly-fire beyond the stretch of her fingers.

As she talked, he smoked and drank, sitting slackly in the chair, his chin sunk on his chest, his eyes closed as if in sleep. But he was not sleeping. When she told him of N'Daria and Kumo and Lansing and Père Louis and Sonderfeld's final madness at the dinner table, he became alert, questioning her closely on detail after detail, while his eyes darkened and his tired mouth stiffened into a thin line. Then at last her story was finished.

"That's all, George. I have no secrets left."

That was what her voice said; but her heart was crying, "Now you know everything. There is no spice lacking to the enjoyment of the triumph. I am bound and blindfolded—at least let the execution be swift."

Now he was looking at her again, measuring her with brooding eyes, like a gambler calculating the odds on his final, fateful throw.

Then he spoke.

"I've got one more question."

"Yes?"

He waited a long moment, then, one by one, he laid the words down like chips on a green baize tabletop.

"I told you once I loved you. I still do. If—if you could be free of Sonderfeld, would you marry me?"

The next moment she was in his arms, crying, laughing, sobbing in a wild ecstasy of relief.

"Oh, God! Oh, God in heaven! Yes! Yes! Yes!"

Chapter Thirteen

GEORGE OLIVER groaned and mumbled and tossed uneasily in his sleep. Gerda sat up in bed and looked across at him in the half-light. He was lying on his back, one hand under his head, the other extended and plucking spasmodically at the covers. His lean face was still unrested, and his naked breast rose and fell in the gasping, unsteady rhythm of the nightmare.

Pity and love and desire welled up in her and she longed to go to him, settle him to calm again and lie beside him in the narrow bed until the first sunburst broke over the ridge and flowed down into the valley.

Yet she dared not touch him.

Once, in the old time together, she had awakened him out of such a nightmare and he had sat up instantly, eyes staring, his mouth full of wild curses, while his hands throttled the first scream of terror in her throat. Then he had warned her—tenderly, regretfully.

"Never do it, sweetheart! Never waken me like that. Just call me. If you must touch me, stand at the head of the cot out of reach of my hands."

"But why? In heaven's name, why?"

She was hurt and frightened and more than a little angry. He was gravely apologetic.

"Because, my dear, when you live the life I do, you sleep like Damocles under the hanging sword—only in my case it's a stone ax or a twelve-pound club. You wake at the slightest movement and your instinctive reaction is to defend yourself. It's a good reaction. It's saved my life more than once; but"—he grinned ironically—"I understand it's damned uncomfortable to live with."

She lay there now with the memory of that other night and watched him with love and loneliness.

She understood now what this country did to men like George Oliver. It gave them fungoid ulcers and infective tinea and swollen spleens and scrub typhus. It thinned their blood and honed the youth out of their bodies and gave them nightmares, peopled with plumed monsters, haunted with savage drums, nightmares whose end was death and a grave without an epitaph.

And yet they loved the Territory and its peoples—loved it with the shamefaced passion of a lover for a fickle mistress, of a husband for a thankless, contrary wife.

They had no part or possession in the land, as Kurt had, or the settlers along the Highland road, or the shrewd businessmen from the south, with their sawmills and their pulping factories and their holdings in gold and transport and the big earth-moving enterprises.

These were the rootless ones, the unrewarded and the unremembered, the first to come, the last to go, despised by the hucksters, resented by the exploiters, unthanked by the tribes whose women they kept clean, whose taro patch they held inviolate. These were the officials in exile, wards of the outer march, poorest yet proudest of all the proconsuls.

George Oliver stirred again, wrestling with his pillow, tugging the white sheet up around his shoulders. Then, quite suddenly, the nightmare left him and he relaxed, breathing as regularly as a sleeping child, while the corners of his mouth twitched upwards into a smile.

Her heart warmed to him and her body, too, and she smiled at him across the narrow gap that separated them. She remembered all the other nights—and asked herself whether this was not the sweetest of all, passionless and celibate though it was.

For the short, wild moments after the revelation they had clung to each other; then, when they drew apart, George Oliver had grinned at her boyishly.

"Time for bed, sweetheart. I'll take a shower and turn in."

"I'll get the bed ready."

"Oh—er—Gerda?"

"Darling?"

He tilted up her chin and kissed her lightly.

"I couldn't make love to the Queen of Sheba tonight. Besides, I'll be wearing your husband's pajamas."

She was instantly serious. She caught at his shirt and drew him to her and laid her head on his breast, so that he could not see the shame in her eyes or the fear that he might reject her in this final moment.

"George, let me say something."

"Make it short, my dear. I'm dead on my feet."

"It will be short. I love you, darling, I need you, desire you, but I don't want you until I can come to you as your wife, without concealment, without all the shame of the old years. From a woman like me, perhaps, that is too much a folly to be borne. But at this moment I feel it is what I wish."

"Good. I feel the same way. Now, please—" He disengaged himself gently. "Please, let's get some sleep."

She led him to the bedroom and helped him to undress and fussed about him with soap and towels and clean pajamas—and was happier than she had been in her whole life.

Now, in the dull darkness that comes before the false dawn, when life is at its lowest ebb and happiness is a small unsteady candle, she sat watching her sleeping lover and seeing, as if for the first time, all the things that must be done, all the wild miracles that must come to pass, before their joy was halfway complete.

First, the tribes must be brought to discipline, the unrest among them stifled before it broke into a bloody madness, spilling through the network of the high valleys. Easy to say, easy to record in the dry and dusty phrases of a patrol report. But there were ten thousand men in the Lahgi crater—ten thousand warriors, enacting in symbol the ancient battles of their race, coming hourly closer to the high pitch of dramatic passion that would be vented in the ritual slaughter of a thousand pigs, while the tribes ran wild, trampling the spilt entrails, smearing themselves with blood, screaming and shouting to the climactic fury of the drums.

Against the ten thousand were George Oliver, Père Louis, Lee Curtis and a small handful of Motu police boys. In other times, in other valleys, it might have been enough. George Oliver had told her more than once of tribal battles stopped and district rebellions crushed by one man's courage and dramatic timing. But now behind the ten thousand primitives was a twentieth-century man—mad, perhaps, with the explosion of his own pride, but cunning and ruthless, armed with the dark dominion of the sorcerers. A word from him and the chant would turn to a battle cry and the plumed and painted men would trample down George Oliver and his pitiful army as they trampled the steaming carcasses of the sacrificial swine.

She shivered at the chilling impact of the thought and lay back, drawing the covers about her shoulders. Now she understood the nightmares of George Oliver and her own helplessness against them.

Then another thought came to her. Even at the best, even if George Oliver suppressed the madness, holding it down as a man holds a spring with the flat of his hand and the weight of his bent body, there would still be no triumph in it.

There would still be Kurt. He was her husband in law—and though in law she might free herself from him, she would still be in reach of his malice. Her identity, her new charter of citizenship, was a forgery, at which she herself had connived. The authorities might choose to deport her, not only from the Territory, but from the Commonwealth itself. If they did that, there would be an end of love and of hope, and Kurt Sonderfeld would have the last and the sweetest revenge.

Now it was hers to toss and turn and mutter in her own nightmare, while

George Oliver slept peacefully until the dawn was a blaze in the valley and the lizards sunned themselves on the stones and the flaring birds chattered in the casuarina trees.

Theodore Nelson was in a filthy temper. He had drunk too much and slept too little. His vanity was raw from the repeated snubs of Lee Curtis. He resented the lean, sardonic fellow who sat serenely at the breakfast table after a night of love in another man's bed. While Gerda was in the kitchen, he broached his grievances.

"Oliver, I've got a complaint to make."

"You have?" Oliver's eyebrows went up in quizzical surprise.

"Yes. I asked Curtis for an escort back to Goroka. He refused it. I pointed out that I had obligations to my company and that the Administration was responsible to the company for my safety. Curtis was quite rude."

"Was he, indeed?"

"Yes. He called me a coward and a—"

"Well . . . aren't you?"

It was as if Oliver had thrown a glass of cold water in his chubby face. He flushed and spluttered and stammered, while Oliver watched him with cold amusement.

"You—you—I don't have to put up with insults from jacks-in-office. As soon as I get back, I shall make a written report to the company and to the Administration. I'll see that this business is opened up on—on a ministerial level."

"By all means do," said George Oliver blandly. "I'll make a report, too. I'll point out that when I came last night you were sleeping behind a locked door while Mrs. Sonderfeld was left alone. I'll point out that your company is one of three competing for the coffee crops in the Highlands and that your representation does little credit to you or to your directors. I'll allege obstruction and disobedience to local authority—and I'll take that one to ministerial level! We're not always one big happy family in the district services, Nelson, but by the living Harry, we close the ranks when a potbellied pipsqueak like you starts throwing his weight around! Now, for God's sake, eat your breakfast and stop making a bloody fool of yourself."

Theodore Nelson mumbled vacuously and buried his nose in his fruit. Wee Georgie made a shamefaced entrance at the top of the steps and stood grinning unhappily, just out of Oliver's reach.

"Hullo, boss! Got in late last night, eh? Sorry I wasn't fit to meet you."

George Oliver surveyed him with amused disgust.

"You're a drunken bum, Georgie!"

"I know, boss, I know." He tugged uneasily at his forelock and wished himself a mile away from Oliver's accusing presence.

"Georgie?"

Oliver's voice was poor medicine for a guilty hangover.

"Yes, boss?"

496

"I'll forgive you last night, because you're shrewd enough to know nothing would have happened anyway. But tonight and tomorrow night you'll stay with Mrs. Sonderfeld—and you'll stay sober! I'll tell her to cut your ration to half a bottle and keep the key of the cupboard. If you slip this time, I'll have the hide off your back. Understand?"

Wee Georgie nodded desperately. The A.D.O. was a bad man to cross. He had never been known to break a promise or to make an idle threat.

"I'll lay off it—strike me dead if I won't." He licked his lips fearfully. "You—er—you think there'll be trouble, boss?"

"I'm damned sure there will be. How big it'll come, I can't say. I'm leaving one police boy here, and I'm posting another at the top of the Lahgi ridge, when we go down into the valley. If anything happens to us, he'll come straight back here and take you and Nelson and Mrs. Sonderfeld south to Goroka."

"Gawdstrewth!" Wee Georgie swallowed dryly. "So it's like that, is it?"

"Like what, Georgie?"

Gerda stood in the doorway with the breakfast plates in her hand. Oliver made no attempt to reassure her.

He said crisply, "We could have trouble tonight or tomorrow. If a runner comes from me, you get out, fast. You take food and water and a blanket and walking shoes—and you make the best time you can to Goroka. Report to the Commissioner when you get there. Tell him the whole story. Is that clear?"

"Yes."

"That's the girl!" He grinned his approval and pointed to the vacant chair. "Now sit down and let's enjoy our breakfast. I've been a long time in the Territory and the worst things that have happened to me have been night-mares and hangovers."

She set the plates on the table and sat down. Wee Georgie squatted on the step and picked his teeth. Theodore Nelson kept his eyes on his plate and ate steadily through his breakfast.

Each for his own reasons was glad of the sardonic, reassuring strength of George Oliver.

The cargo boys were waiting on the lawn. Theodore Nelson sat unhappily on the veranda, smoking a tasteless cigarette. Wee Georgie was shuffling in and out, clearing away the breakfast dishes. Gerda Sonderfeld was in the bedroom with George Oliver.

He buckled on his pistol belt, slung the binocular case over his shoulder, put on his hat and cocked it at a jaunty angle over his shrewd eyes. Then he came to her, put his hands on her white shoulders and held her a little away from him. His voice was grave and quiet.

"There's something I want to say to you, Gerda."

"Say it, George."

"I've told you that I love you and I want to marry you. Nothing can change that."

497

Her eyes filled with tears, but she held them back. She waited while he pieced out his next deliberate words.

"I'm being blunt about it. Nothing would suit me better than to see your husband dead. It would make things easy for both oɪ ⅄.

"I know that."

"But it's my job to bring him back alive, to give him a fair trial and a chance to prove his innocence. I—I propose to do that, if I can."

She tried to move close to him to tell him with her body what her lips refused to say, but he held her firmly away from him and went on.

"I've had a long life in the Service. It hasn't paid me very well, but I've kept my hands clean. I want them clean at the end of this. You understand that?"

"Oh, my dear! Of course."

His eyes softened and his grim mouth relaxed, but still he held her at arm's length.

"It's possible—it's even probable—that I may not succeed. If I have to come back and tell you that your husband is dead, I want you to know, for truth, that I had no part in his death. If you thought otherwise, if you had even the faintest doubt, there would never be any hope for us. You know that."

"I know it," said Gerda softly.

He released her then and saw with a pang of regret that his hands had made red, bruised spots on the white skin of her shoulders. Then she was in his arms, clinging to him, kissing him passionately, and he knew in the instant of wry relief and triumph that she was afraid—not for her husband but for him.

Then he left her and walked out into the sunshine, and as she watched him striding down the path at the head of his tiny troop, she knew that she was seeing the first love and the last hope of all the locust years.

Heedless of Nelson and Wee Georgie and the goggling police boy, she buried her face in her hands and wept.

Chapter Fourteen

LATE IN THE AFTERNOON Oliver came to the high ridge of the crater where Curtis and Père Louis were waiting for him.

They were camped in a circle of towering rocks looking southward away from the valley in which the tribes were assembled. They ate dry rations and slept huddled together against the cold, lest the smoke of a cooking fire betray them to the people in the valley. All day long one or the other of them sat perched between two great tors with field glasses trained on the village, watching the ritual preparations for the great moment of the festival, and in the evening Père Louis' catechist would come up, furtively, to report on the doings among the sorcerers and the elders.

When Oliver arrived, he went immediately to the observation post with Curtis and Père Louis and sat a long time staring through the glasses at the green sweep of the valley and the sprawling grass huts between the checkerboard squares of the farm patches.

All round the village and along the valley paths white poles were set up to signify that the pig festival was near at hand. In the center of the compound two new huts had been built—one large and one small.

The larger hut belonged to the fertility spirit. Its uprights were cut from a sacred tree by a man who held the office by hereditary right. When the hut was built and thatched, four carvers began to ornament the twin poles with a crude geometric pattern in which the repeated motif was the long diamond, which represented the female cleft. They killed a pig to consecrate the house and hung its fat from the rooftrees as a propitiation to the spirit who gave increase to pigs and gardens and women.

The smaller hut was the dwelling place of the Red Spirit. It was circular in shape and its center pole was a long phallic projection which was kept from festival to festival, buried in a secret place. In front of this hut a large tree had been set up. Its branches had been stripped of leaves, and in their place were hung the plumed headdresses that the men would wear at the festival. It was like a tree full of birds of paradise, scarlet and gold and purple and green, fluttering and swaying outside the house of the greatest spirit of all.

The village itself was an eddy of movement and sound and colour.

There was a continual procession of women to and from the garden patches. They came, singing and shouting and gossiping, and they returned laden with taro and kau-kau and sugarcane and clusters of yellow bananas, which were piled in long rows in front of the spirit houses along with the offerings of the visiting tribes.

The unmarried girls were excused from this service. This was the meeting time, the wooing time, which a girl remembered all the years of her married life as the symbol of her lost youth and freedom. Bright with feathers and clattering shell ornaments, girls and youths moved about the village, preening themselves, playing the drums, making kunande in the huts, and love-play wherever there was privacy enough to enjoy the consummation of the erotic rituals.

In the sunlight the wigmakers were putting the final touches on their gaudy confections, while in the shadowy burial grounds the sorcerers and the elders held communion with the ancestor spirits on the secret details of the festival.

George Oliver sat a long time watching the threads of colour weave themselves into a primitive but complex harmony—novel to the white man, but older than the panoply that was Solomon's welcome to the dark queen of the south. The oppression of the centuries was heavy on his shoulders, and the fear of the centuries' dark secrets fluttered like a bird in his belly. He put down the glasses and set the fuzzy-wuzzy back on watch. Then he turned back to Père Louis and Curtis and jerked his thumb down the slope.

"Let's sit down somewhere. I want to talk to you."

They squatted in the open to catch the last warmth of the sun, for it was late and the shadows were lengthening. Oliver and Curtis lit cigarettes while Père Louis filled his pipe and nursed it carefully to life in the thin mountain air. Then the old man spoke.

"I take it you have been told all that has happened with Sonderfeld?"

Oliver nodded. "Most of it, I think. Where's Sonderfeld now?"

Curtis jerked his thumb vaguely towards the valley.

"Down there somewhere—we think. We haven't seen him and we don't think anybody else has."

"Would you know if they had?"

Père Louis waved his pipe in a Gallic gesture.

"You must understand that my people are down there also. My catechist came up to report to me last night. He will be here again soon after dark. He says Kumo has been seen conferring with the elders and the other sorcerers. But there is no sign of either Sonderfeld or N'Daria."

"Are you sure he hasn't been killed?"

"Oh, yes. There is still talk of the coming of the Red Spirit. And besides, these people have a sense of theater. Kumo will wish to stage-manage the entrance of the Red Spirit. I believe he will proclaim him at the moment of climax, which is at the great slaughter of pigs outside the house of the Red Spirit."

"So that's where he is!" Oliver snapped his fingers as if at a sudden revelation.

Père Louis shook his head slowly.

"No, my friend . . . no, I do not think so. Sonderfeld is too clever to sit in a cage like a bird waiting for the fowlers. He will be hiding somewhere on the slopes of the valley, in the caves perhaps, or in one of the smaller villages. When all the preparations are made, Kumo will bring him down under cover of darkness."

Curtis broke in, as if anxious to have his own part in the discussion.

"The important thing seems to me to be that Sonderfeld is still master of the situation. According to Père Louis' boy, lots of the ceremonies are being telescoped, while others are being left out altogether, to bring the big ceremony forward. That means Sonderfeld is directing operations and not Kumo."

"He'll continue to direct 'em so long as he holds Kumo's life in his hand."

"He holds it no longer," said Père Louis in smiling triumph.

"What?"

Oliver and Lee Curtis stared at him in gaping amazement. Grinning like a conjuror at a children's party, the old priest held under their noses a small bamboo tube.

"Mrs. Sonderfeld will have told you that she found the brother to this in her husband's pocket."

Oliver nodded. "That's right. She did. She also told me that you'd given her orders to replace it."

"But what she did not tell you, because she did not know, was that I had removed the contents and substituted another piece of cotton wool, soiled with spittle and blood and tobacco juice to resemble the one I have here."

"We've got him!" said George Oliver with sudden triumph. "We've got him!"

He threw back his head and laughed and laughed till the tears ran down his face. Then he looked up and saw the face of the old priest, and the laughter died in him like a match flame. Père Louis was smiling no longer. His eyes were grave and his old face was lined with fatigue and with sorrow for the follies of the world in which he had lived too long.

"As you say, my friend, we have got him. The power he holds now is an illusion, because we, in our turn, have come into possession of the vital essences of Kumo. It falls to us—you and me—to decide how we shall use it."

"So—so this is what you meant by your stratagem?"

It was Curtis who asked the question. George Oliver was chewing the cud of a new and unpleasant thought.

"That's right, my son. This is my stratagem."

"But—but you said—"

"I said that its use would involve the life or death of a man." He gestured with his pipe. "Ask your superior officer. He will tell you that it is so."

George Oliver looked up and nodded in weary assent.

"It's true enough."

"But I don't see—"

"You tell him, Father."

He heaved himself up from the ground and walked a little way down the slope, where he stood backed against the rock looking down into the green emptiness of the valley approach. Père Louis turned his old eyes on the puzzled youth squatting on the ground in front of him.

"To understand what is at stake in this, you must realize that we can do nothing until the great moment of the festival. You could go down now into the valley, you and Oliver and the police boys. You could demand that Sonderfeld and Kumo be handed over to you. You would be met with blank stares and hostile murmurs, but you would achieve nothing. They would be there. You could beat the valley and still you would not find them—and all the time the people would be laughing at you."

"I know. It's happened to me before in the villages. I've been looking for a man wanted for a tribal killing. I might as well have saved my boot leather."

"Exactly. So now . . ." Père Louis took another long draw at his pipe. "So now we are back to the big moment of the festival, the moment when Sonderfeld is revealed as the Red Spirit and proclaimed to the people by Kumo. It is a wild moment, remember. The people are drunk with the slaughter of the pigs, their skins are smeared with blood, the smell of blood is in their nostrils, their memory is full of the old bloody frenzy of the wars. We are there, too. We watch as spectators from the shadows. But we do nothing, because there is nothing to do—nothing at all until the moment of proclamation."

"And then?"

"Then George Oliver—or I, myself—steps forward with this tube and proclaims that Sonderfeld is not the Red Spirit but a liar and an impostor."

"It's one thing to proclaim it," said Curtis dubiously. "The point is, can you prove it to Kumo?"

"That's the least of our worries," said George Oliver bluntly. "The Kiap and the priest—two men who have never lied to the tribes! We'll convince him all right."

"So!" Père Louis took up his theme. "So, if Kumo is convinced as we hope, he is released from his bondage. No matter that he enters into a new one. He is released from Sonderfeld. What happens then?"

"Then," said Curtis slowly, "then, I think, somebody's going to get killed."

"Exactly," said Père Louis softly. "But who? Kumo or Kurt Sonderfeld?"

"God knows," said Curtis lightly. "I don't see that it matters so very . . ."

Then he saw George Oliver leaning against his rock in an attitude of dejection and utter weariness, and the truth hit him like a smack in the mouth.

"The poor bastard!" he whispered. "The poor, tired bastard."

"I know," said Père Louis softly. "Love is a terrible burden—and the burden of justice is more terrible still."

Shortly after dark Père Louis' catechist came up to join them on the ridge. He was sweating with fear and exhaustion and his eyes were rolling in his head. Oliver gave him a cigarette to soothe him, then he squatted in front of them and, in a mixture of pidgin and place-talk, embellished with many gestures, he told them:

Tonight, in the village, they were making the preparatory magic. Already the first pigs had been taken to the burial ground to be clubbed to death in sacrifice to the ancestor spirits. Their blood would be collected in bamboo tubes and smeared on the house poles and on the lintels of the spirit houses. Tonight the people would eat their meat and feed some of it to the living pigs to fatten them for the great sacrifice.

Then they would sit in silence round the cook fires while, inside the spirit huts, the sorcerers played the spirit flutes so that ancestor spirits would hear them and would know that they, too, were invited to the big festival. The women would huddle together and clasp their children close to stifle their crying, and if any of them asked what the flutes were, they would be told that they were the voice of a great bird whose name was Kat and whose wings they heard beating in the wind and in the storm.

When the flutes stopped playing, there would be a mock battle between the clans. They would shout and stamp and charge each other, stopping in the second before impact. They would rehearse old wrongs and cover each other with insults in memory of the time before the white man came, when there was enmity and killing between the clans.

Then they would sit down together and eat the pig meat and the taro and the kau-kau wrapped in banana leaves and cooked in the ashes of the fire pits. They would sing together and tell stories and the young ones would make kunande and carry-leg until, at the rising of the moon, the sorcerers would drive everybody into the huts to wait for the coming of the Red Spirit. The flutes would play all night, and on the morrow there would be the great slaughter of the pigs and the Red Spirit would show himself to the people.

When the catechist had finished, Oliver handed him another cigarette and the four of them sat smoking in silence, listening to the small creaking noises of the night and the shuffling murmurs of the police boys settling themselves to sleep. It was George Oliver who broke the silence.

"When will the great killing be made?"

The catechist swept up his arms in a double quadrant so that they met at the zenith.

"Tomorrow, when the sun is high."

503

"Daytime," Oliver grunted laconically. "That makes it awkward."

"There is a way."

Père Louis took the pipe out of his mouth and pointed eastward along the jagged rim of the crater.

"It means that we rise early and make a half-circuit of the ridge. There is a steep fall into the basin, but if we follow the creek that begins there, we can come down through the jungle and the kunai without being seen."

"How close can we get?"

"A hundred meters perhaps."

"Good enough. Curtis, warn the boys to be ready to move at first light. Then we'll all turn in. Tomorrow's going to be a very busy day."

Lee Curtis nodded and walked over to the police boys to give them their orders. Père Louis dismissed the catechist with a word and a pat of encouragement and watched him melt quietly back into the shadows. Then he turned to face George Oliver. Oliver held out his hand.

"If you don't mind, Father, I'll take possession of the evidence."

"It's more than evidence, my friend," said Père Louis soberly. "It is a man's life."

"You think I don't know that?"

"I am sure you do. I should like to be equally sure that you understand your responsibility in the matter."

For a moment it seemed as though Oliver would break into anger, then his mouth relaxed into a rueful grin.

"And what is my responsibility, Father?"

Père Louis shrugged.

"To keep peace among the tribes. To administer justice without fear and with favour to none—not even to yourself."

"Easy to say. But how can one be sure where justice lies?"

"One can never be sure. When in doubt, one is free to accept the most expedient course."

"That doesn't help much, either—afterwards."

"No. Therefore—" Père Louis seemed to hesitate. He bent down and knocked out the dottle of his pipe on the heel of his boot. Then he straightened up. "Therefore, if you wish, I am prepared to keep this—this thing in my possession to do what we both know must be done, and to accept the full responsibility for what comes out of it."

"That makes you the scapegoat for me."

Père Louis smiled a wise, tired old man's smile.

"I am a priest of God. My life is barren of love and my loins are without issue. Why else but to be a scapegoat for my brethren and my friends? It is a little thing, believe me. I am too old to fret and the mercy of God has long arms. Well, my friend?"

"No!" said George Oliver bluntly. "No! I'm grateful, but I can't do it." He held out his hand. "Give it to me, Father."

504

Without a word the little priest handed him the bamboo tube that held the life of a man. Oliver looked at it a moment, then thrust it into his pocket.

"Thanks, Father."

The old man's eyes were soft with compassion.

"You are a hard man, George Oliver. Hardest of all, I think, to yourself. I shall pray for you tonight."

"Pray for both of us, Father," said George Oliver simply. "Pray for both of us."

Chapter Fifteen

DURING THE NIGHT the sorcerers had been busy. To the sound of the flutes they had danced around the house of the Red Spirit and smeared its posts with pig fat and hung about it the clattering jawbones of the slain pigs, so that the people would say that the spirits had eaten of their sacrifice and were pleased with their offering.

Then, from a secret place, they had brought out little boards of casuarina wood, each pierced with a rhomboid hole and daubed with moss. Each of these boards was handed up to a man standing on the roof of the spirit house and slipped over the long, projecting center pole, in symbol of the act of union. The Red Spirit was the spirit of fertility. Through him the seed quickened and grew to life in the womb of the earth and of pigs and of women.

All through the ceremonies the sorcerers spoke in the whispered voices of spirit men and the flutes played and the tribes listened, fearful and withdrawn in the smoky darkness of the huts.

Then, when the flutes were silent and even the sorcerers had retired to rest their strength for the great killing, a shadowy figure emerged from a clump of bamboos at the edge of the compound. He wore no ornaments, his face was lowered against recognition and he peered about the deserted compound as if afraid some late-walking lovers might surprise him. But at the sound of the flutes even the lovers were afraid, and they had all gone into the huts to lie in one another's arms until the sunlight came and the evil haunters of the night were blown away with the leaves of the sacred plant which is called bombo.

Satisfied that there was no one watching, the stooping figure signalled with his hand, and two others stepped out from the cane clump. They, too, were bowed and naked of ornament, but they carried in their arms the ceremonial wigs and little gourds and coloured pigments and a small bundle of food against the long hours of waiting. They hurried across the compound in the wake of their guide and came to the house of the Red Spirit with its clacking bones and its crown of coital symbols.

The grass curtain was lifted and they climbed inside and drew it close behind them. Then their guide stole another furtive look at the circle of huts and, satisfied that no one had seen him, straightened up and walked swiftly back into the shadows.

Kumo the Sorcerer had accomplished his task. The ransom of his life was almost paid. Tomorrow the Red Spirit would reveal himself to his people.

In the stinking darkness of the spirit house Kurt Sonderfeld and N'Daria lay together in loveless union, and when the first light showed through the chinks of the bamboo wall, N'Daria began to daub her master's body with pig fat and paint his face for the moment of revelation to the tribes.

In the village they rose with the sun and purged themselves and began to dress themselves for the festival. Even the married women were absorbed in the unfamiliar rituals of adornment. Some wore coronets of feathers and bee-tle shards, but most wore headdresses of leaves from the sweet-potato vines. Their pubic belts were of fresh twigs and green leaves, and their necklets were of green snail shells and crescents of gold-lip trochus.

The bucks and the unmarried girls wore cane belts and bird of paradise plumes, while the chiefs and the sorcerers and the ceremonial dancers wore massive wigs of plaited hair, daubed with golden gum and glistening with green beetles and tossing plumes—scarlet and orange and purple and irides-cent green.

When they were dressed, the men took up their clubs, whose shafts are made from the wood of the sacred tree, and which are used only for the ritual killing at the pig festival. The women followed them out of the huts into the sunshine, each carrying the family store of taro and kau-kau and bananas, which they arranged in a small mound in front of the spirit house.

Then they squatted on the ground, jostling one another to come as close as possible to the dwelling of the Red Spirit, gasping with wonderment at the sight of the pig bones, nudging one another and pointing at the symbols of fertility that crowned the roof. The children hung about them, chattering, giggling, lost in the wonder of the carnival day, awed by the noise and the colour and the air of tension and expectation. They, too, wore pubic skirts of fresh leaves, and the little girls wore on their foreheads or round their necks the diamond of womanhood, so that their breasts would grow and they would mature quickly.

Now the men had withdrawn from the compound, hiding themselves in the bushes and the kunai grass while they donned the last of their finery and finished their face-painting and warmed up the drums for the dance of the Red Spirit, while the sorcerers gave the last instructions on the ritual of the ceremony.

They then formed up—the sorcerers and the chiefs with their great golden

507

wigs, the drummers with their black kundus and behind them the warriors with clubs and spears and stone axes.

Kumo stood in front of them, greatest of the sorcerers, chief paramount of the secret valleys by virtue of his alliance with the Red Spirit himself. His headdress was a triple tier of bird of paradise feathers, blue first, then orange and scarlet. His wig hung almost to the nipples of his breast, and two crescent shells hung down from its green fingers. His forehead was green, dappled with yellow, his cheeks were red, and his nose ornaments were a crescent pearl shell and a circle as large as a saucer. Round his neck were ornaments of shell and a stole of possum fur, and in his hand was a great club made of the sacred wood, with a circular head of dark obsidian.

He was a monstrous, challenging figure as he stood surveying the serried ranks of the tribes, holding his stone club high above his head, signalling them to attention, holding them rigid and expectant till his arm swung downwards and the drums burst out like thunder and the chant rang round and round the ridges of the valley.

He led them in a wild charge into the compound and through the dancing grove. He dropped to his knees and the whole army followed him. He rose again, shouting, and led them five paces, then dropped again to his knees—three paces, and another genuflection—two paces—one—and they were ranged in front of the spirit house, the drums thudding and the chant going on and on—"Ho-ho-ho-ho"—a surging, wave-like monotony in the still and sunlit air.

Halfway down the steep fall into the valley, George Oliver heard them and looked across at Père Louis.

The old priest waved his hand and shouted breathlessly, "No need to worry, my friend. There is more and more yet."

Oliver raised his hand in acknowledgment and plunged down the slope, stumbling through the thick undergrowth, tripping over trailing vines, stubbing his feet against rocks and fallen tree boles, until they broke out at last into the tall kunai that masked their last approach to the village.

Cramped and sweating in the half-dark of the spirit house, Kurt Sonderfeld abandoned himself to the mounting fervour of the ritual. The drums were a thunder in his brain and a pulsing fire in his blood. It was as if their energy were being stored up inside him, cramming him to bursting point for the explosive moment of the great revelation. When he peered out through the cracks in the walls, he saw the tossing plumes and the dusty dancing bodies and knew them for his subjects, spending themselves in his honour, preparing themselves by ritual frenzy for the great moment of immolation.

His body was naked, as theirs were. His wig was greater than Kumo's, its plumage richer, its colour a flaring ochre, spilling down over his daubed face and his glistening breast. His arms were bound with cane and golden fur; his anklets whipped like live tails as he walked, and his belt was sewn with alternate rows of gold-lip and cowrie shells. In his hand was the jawbone of a monstrous pig.

508

N'Daria, too, was dressed in her finery as became the bride of the Red Spirit. She squatted on the floor and watched Sonderfeld with doting eyes, all her hurts forgotten, all her fears submerged in the fierce wonder of the drums and the singing and the pounding rhythm of the dance.

Then, suddenly, the drums stopped. The dancers were still. The singers fell silent and there was no sound but the grunting and squealing of pigs, penned in the big palisade.

Kumo raised his club and pointed. Two hundred men went at a run towards the enclosure, leapt the low fence and seized, each one, a pig, looping a halter about its neck and hauling it towards the gate. The gate was opened and a great shout went up as the pigs were dragged out. Then the gate was thrust shut again and the pigs were pulled and pushed into the clear space facing the entrance to the spirit house.

Kumo raised his club again. A group of warriors stepped forward, fingering the shafts of their weapons, licking their lips, bracing themselves for the leap. The air was crackling with excitement. Kumo's club swept down in a great arc, cracking the skull of the nearest pig.

A wild cry broke out from the assembly and the warriors leapt in among the pigs, beating them with their clubs, crushing their skulls, breaking their backs, laughing, screaming with delight, splashing in the spilt blood, scooping it up in handfuls and tossing it over the yelling, stamping multitude that crowded around the killing place.

When all the pigs were dead, they were dragged in front of the spirit house and stacked in a wide semicircle, their heads pointing inward to the dwelling of the Red Spirit, their hindquarters splayed outward to the watching crowd.

Then a new batch was brought out and a new batch of warriors made the killings, and the sickening ceremony was repeated time and time again until nearly a thousand carcasses were piled in the compound and the air was full of the stench of blood and the ground was black with flies and the whole crowd was drunk with the smell and the spectacle and the orgiastic delight of cruelty.

Now the great moment was come!

A signal from Kumo and the whole assembly of the tribes were dumb with wonder and expectation. They saw the monstrous figure of the sorcerer mount to the top of the pile of pig bodies and stand there, arms outspread in hieratic exaltation. They heard his voice roll over them like a drumbeat.

"Behold, my people! Behold the Red Spirit! Lift up your eyes and see the bringer of riches and the source of all fruitfulness."

There was a moment's pause. Then the grass curtain parted and Kurt Sonderfeld stood, deified, on the raised platform of the spirit house, while N'Daria crouched at his feet in an attitude of adoration. For one suspended moment of glory and terror the crowd watched him, his pale body shining in the sun, his head a scarlet wonder, his hands full of promise, his smile a benediction, and a threat.

Then they buried their faces in their hands and moaned—a long, sobbing wail of fear and supplication.

George Oliver walked into the center of the compound. His voice cracked over them like a lash.

"Fools! Blind fools! Cheated by a liar! Seduced by a coward! They have crammed dust into your mouths and called it food! They have rubbed your faces in filth and called it riches! Lift up your eyes and see! The Red Spirit is a white man, like I am! Kumo the Sorcerer fears him because he holds his blood and seed and spittle in a little tube, like this!"

Slowly, fearfully, they raised their eyes and saw George Oliver standing alone and unarmed in their midst with the bamboo capsule in his hand, and behind him, a long way behind, Père Louis and Lee Curtis with the police boys, rigid and alert, at their backs.

They looked up at Kumo and saw that he was standing, mouth slack, arms dangling, staring as if at an apparition. Then they looked at Sonderfeld, and as their faces turned to him, the big man opened his mouth and screamed at them:

"Kill! Kill! They are liars, all of them! They want to cheat you of the wealth that is yours by right. They are few! You are many! Kill them now!"

But his reason had left him and he spoke in German, which they did not understand, and they turned their faces back to Kumo, begging him to interpret for them.

Slowly the sorcerer took possession of himself. He looked at Sonderfeld and remembered the power that lay in his hands. He looked at Oliver and saw that he was unarmed. He looked at his people and saw that they were many and at the police boys who were so pitifully few. He hefted his club and began to move slowly, cautiously, along the slippery platform of carcasses in the direction of George Oliver.

Oliver stood stock-still and watched him come. Then he raised his hand so that the people saw the bamboo tube, and his voice was like the crack of exploding wood.

"Wait!"

Kumo stopped. Oliver paused for two seconds to gather himself for the final attack.

"The white man lied to you, Kumo. He told you he held your life in his little tube. He did once, but not now. I have it. He left it unguarded and I took it into my hands. Look, Kumo—look!"

A long, gasping exhalation went up from the crowd as they saw Oliver stretch out his hand towards the sorcerer. They saw Kumo cringe away, then stiffen as Oliver lifted his voice again.

"I will give you your life, Kumo. I will give it to you now, if you will lay down your club and come to me."

Then Sonderfeld found his voice again. He gave a great shout and leapt towards the sorcerer.

"He lies, you fool! He lies! I hold your life! Look!"

All eyes were turned on him as he stood there, arms outflung, holding in one hand the bamboo tube and in the other the bleached jawbone of the great pig.

510

This was the moment of challenge—the moment of choice between the old gods and the new—between the small isolated authority of Oliver and his police boys and the ancient dominion of the sorcerers.

And the choice was in the hands of Kumo.

He had but to lift his hand in acknowledgment of Sonderfeld and the tribes would rise in fury, trampling down the white men and their alien mercenaries from the coast. Their few weapons would be powerless against ten thousand men, and they would be trodden like grass under the black, naked feet. But Kumo hesitated. He was paralyzed by doubt. Of the two men who challenged him, Sonderfeld and Oliver, one was a liar and the other had the power to destroy him utterly.

He looked from one to the other. He saw the wild fury of Sonderfeld and the stony calm of Oliver. He remembered that Sonderfeld had once betrayed him through N'Daria and that Oliver was a man who had never spoken a lie to the tribes or made an idle threat. But it was not enough. His life hung in the balance. He needed more proof. There was none to give it to him.

Then Père Louis stepped forward, small, withered and old, and raised his voice in the tingling silence.

"Look at me, Kumo!"

Kumo shifted his grip on the club and turned slowly to the little priest. Père Louis spoke again.

"Look at me, Kumo, and tell me! Have you ever heard a lie from my mouth? Have I ever taken what was not mine? Have I ever done injury to man, woman or child? Have I not tended your sick and cared for your old?"

He paused. Kumo made no answer. He was as tense as an animal at the moment of attack. The old man's voice rose again, vibrant and strong.

"You cannot name me a liar. Hear then when I tell you the truth. The man who holds your life is Kiap Oliver. I gave it myself into his hand. I took it from the house of the red-headed man, whom you call the Red Spirit, and who is a liar and a cheat."

There was a moment of dreadful silence. Kumo turned slowly back to face Sonderfeld. He cried out, desperately demanding an answer from the man whom he had made a god. Sonderfeld opened his mouth to speak, but the words were a frothing babble on his lips. He made wild, flailing gestures, but even his limbs would not obey him, and the bamboo tube and the bleached bone dropped from his twitching fingers on the bloody carcass at his feet.

N'Daria screamed, leapt from the platform and ran, stumbling and tripping, into the shelter of the bushes.

Then Kumo whirled on Sonderfeld and crashed his club into his skull and, when he fell, struck him again and again, while the tribes watched, fascinated, and George Oliver stood in helpless horror, unarmed, in the middle of the compound.

Then he heard Curtis's voice behind him and saw the police boys coming at a run to seize the sorcerer and wrench the bloodied club from his hands and hurl him to the bottom of the small mountain of pigs. They hauled him to his feet and twisted his arms up behind his back, and one of them tore off his plumes and his golden wig and trampled it in the dust, before they ran him, stooped and gasping, along the squatting ranks of the women and forced him to the ground at Oliver's feet.

For a long moment Oliver stood looking down at him, then he spat contemptuously in the dust and turned back to face the crowd. He flung out his arms in the attitude of the tribal orators and his voice rang out sharp as a sword blade.

"You see what happens to those who turn away from the white man's law to follow the lying voices of the sorcerers? You see that the white man is dead and Kumo, too, will die in his own time. Your festival is ruined and the voices of your ancestors will cry out in anger against you. Their spirits will haunt this valley, and there will come a blight on the crops and a barrenness on your women. And I, myself, will punish you. I will raise a double tax on your pigs and on your gardens. I will set you to build a new road without pay. I will strip the badges from your luluais and will set new ones to rule over you. And I will publish your folly to the Kiaps in Goroka and to the folk in the far valleys so that your names will be a laughter in the mouths of all men."

A moan of fear and penitence went up and they hid their faces from his anger. But they could not escape the relentless castigation of his voice.

"The festival is finished, do you hear? You will leave the valley and return to your own homes. When you are gone, my men will burn this village, because the luluai was a fool who listened to the lying voices. But he will not depart from it. He will stay here and rebuild it with his people, because now he is a luluai no longer. Go now, all of you! Lest you be burnt in the fire of my anger and die as the white man died—as Kumo, too, will die, because he killed one man with his club and another by the snake sorcery."

He turned away from them, but they could not move for the terror of his voice and the anger of the outraged spirits whose festival had been denied them and whose sacrificial pigs would rot in the sun.

Kumo was on his feet now, sullen and glowering, in the strong grasp of the police boys.

"Take him away," said George Oliver wearily.

"No," said Père Louis. "Not yet."

George Oliver whirled on him. The little priest stood his ground. He held out his hand.

"You owe me a debt, George Oliver. I want it paid."

They faced each other, eye to eye, toe to toe, like wrestlers, looking for an opening. George Oliver was the first to give ground. He fished in his pocket, brought out the bamboo tube and slapped it in the palm of the old man's hand.

"All right, Father, you've got it. Now what?"

The priest said nothing. He stood in front of Kumo, holding the tube in his outstretched palm. His voice was low and secret in the place-talk of the tribe.

"Kumo, you were once my son. You are not a fool but an intelligent man. Once you knelt at the altar and received the body of God into your body. Then you turned away to give your soul to the Devil. See, now, where he has brought you—to death, which you cannot escape, almost to damnation. See, I hold your life in my hands. I give it back to you in return for your soul. Turn back to God and I will plead for you with the Kiaps. Even if they will not listen, I will be with you when you die, and I will promise you, in the name of God, the salvation of your soul. Take it, Kumo! Stretch out your hands. Take your life and give me your soul!"

Kumo lifted his head. His eyes were blank. His lips framed the toneless words.

"How can I stretch out my hands when I am held like this?"

"Let him go," said Père Louis in Motu.

The police boys looked inquiringly at George Oliver. He nodded curtly. Kumo was released to stand towering over the little priest. He held out his hand.

"Give me my life."

Père Louis laid the tube in his outstretched palm. Kumo's fingers closed around the tiny cylinder. Then he threw back his head and laughed horribly.

"You offer me my life! You think to buy Kumo, the greatest sorcerer in the valleys! You want my soul? I tell you, you will never have it. Go home, missionary! Go home to your village and talk to the women!"

Once again the old priest's heart sank and his flesh crawled at the spectacle of primitive pride rejecting mercy, rejecting life itself in order to preserve face with the tribe.

He stood there facing the man who had been his son in Christ, wrestling with him for his life and for his soul, praying desperately that Kumo would bend his stubborn spirit to the last mercy. But Kumo was beyond even mercy. In the next instant he made the act of final rejection.

He raised his hand and sent the tube spinning through the air into one of the smoking fire pits. Then he laughed again and spat full in the face of the old priest.

Before the police boys could lay hands on him, he had whirled away from them and raced into the thickets. The boys were swift in pursuit, but above the soft padding of their feet, monstrous and horrible came the thudding beat of the taloned claws of the cassowary bird.

Père Louis wiped the spittle from his face and stood waiting while Oliver and Curtis and all the villagers watched him curiously.

He knew better than they the meaning of Kumo's defiant gesture. Locked in the bamboo tube was his life and his life principle—all that primitive man knows of soul. He had tossed away his life. When the fire consumed the bamboo shell, his life would be consumed as surely as if he had been cut down with a stone ax. The old belief was stronger than the new. Its roots plunged down, darkly, to the life spring itself.

513

Slow and inexorable, the seconds ticked away. Then, sudden and startling, the bamboo tube exploded in the fire pit. In the silence of the valley it rang like a gunshot, and before the echoes were dead, from far up the valley came the long, raucous, soul-wrenching scream of a dying cassowary.

The plumed multitude stood rigid in a long suspension of shock and terror. They rolled their eyes from side to side, looking for one to step forward and lead them out of the cursed valley, away from the vengeful presence of the spirit ancestors and the angry Kiaps, but no one moved.

They saw Père Louis turn away, bowed and shrunken, an old, defeated man, walking slowly out of the village and up the hillside. They saw his few frightened Christians break from the ranks and straggle after him, like sheep led homeward by a tired shepherd.

Later they would come to his chapel and confess themselves of adultery and fornication and lapses into the old idolatry, and he would shrive them and comfort them and read them stern lectures on the power of the Evil One and the fate of those who allied themselves with him.

But for Père Louis himself, there would be neither comfort nor shriving. The nearest brother priest was fifty miles away across the mountains. So he must bear alone the burden of his own presumption. He had tried to bribe a man with the gift of life—which, like the grace of repentance, God holds in His own gift. He had made himself party to an act of despair, a positive rejection of salvation. There was no recourse left to him but mercy, and he felt so old and spent and useless he wondered whether God would take the trouble to bestow it.

George Oliver stood and watched him go, while the assembly waited, breathless, for his next move. He did not see them. He saw only the figure of the old priest stumbling up his Calvary with the tiny crowd at his back, and his heart went out to him, because he, too, was tired and was beginning to be old.

He had brought peace to the tribes. He had yet to attain it for himself. To the end of his days he would never know whether he might have prevented the death of Sonderfeld and whether, with prevention in his power, he would have had the courage to avail himself of it. He had tumbled down the idols of the grove, but their shadows were still long across his path.

Then Curtis came and tapped him on the shoulder and said gently, "Go back, sir. Go home and tell her the news. I can handle the rest of it."

George Oliver looked at him a long time before he answered. Then he grinned and held out his hand.

"Good luck, youngster. It's all yours."

Then he, too, turned his face to the hills and began the long trudge back to where Gerda was waiting for him.

Curtis made a sign to one of the police boys who trotted quietly after Oliver. All the way to the plantation he would walk in his tracks—a faithful servant seeing his master home safely from a long and weary war.

Kumo the Sorcerer was dead on the upland path. N'Daria cowered, lost and trembling, in the bush at the fringe of the camp. Kurt Sonderfeld lay on the mountain of pigs, with the flies crawling over his bloody face.

And, silent among the silent, fearful people, Cadet Patrol Officer Lee Curtis was left alone—master of ten thousand men, fountain of the law, collector of the tribute, lord of life and death in the valley of the tribes.

He was twenty-four years old.